AN ILLUSTRATED COMPANION TO THE FIRST WORLD WAR

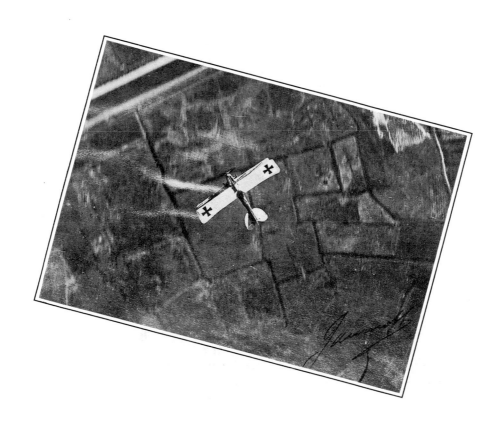

FINLAND

Helsinki

St. Petersburg

Revel

Riga

Moscow

RUSSIA

Vilna

Smolensk

Minsk

Pinsk

Brest-Litovsk

Kiev

Kharkov

Dnieper

Lemberg

Czernowitz

Rostov

Debrecen

Odessa

Sea of Azov

HUNGARY

Arad
Temesvar

Brasov

RUMANIA

Black Sea

Batum

Bucharest

Trebizond

Belgrade

Danube

SERBIA

Sofia

Constantinople

BULGARIA

GREECE

Angora

Smyrna

OTTOMAN

PERSIA

EMPIRE

Athens

Mosul

Rhodes

Aleppo

Euphrates

Tigris

Diyala

Crete

Cyprus
(British)

Beirut

Damascus

Baghdad

Sea

Jerusalem

Basra

Danube

Tisza

HUNGARY

Buda Pest

Jassy

Szegedin

Maros

Brasov

Zagreb

Sava

Sibiu

Rother-
Turm Pass

Galatz

SLAVONIA

Vulcan Pass

Targu Jiu

RUMANIA

Dobruja

Dniester

BOSNIA

Belgrade

Bucharest

Sarajevo

SERBIA

Danube

Turtucaia

Spalato

Rakhovo

Sistove

MONTE-
NEGRO

Sofia

Cetinje

ALBANIA

Skoplie

BULGARIA

Salonika

Constantinople

GREECE

Gallipoli

TURKEY

Athens

Smyrna

CRETE

Rhodes

0   100 miles

0   150 km

The BALKANS
~1914~

AN ILLUSTRATED COMPANION TO THE FIRST WORLD WAR

ANTHONY BRUCE

MICHAEL JOSEPH   LONDON

MICHAEL JOSEPH LTD

Published by the Penguin Group
27 Wrights Lane, London W8 5TZ, England
Viking Penguin Inc., 40 West 23rd Street, New York, New York 10010, USA
Penguin Books Australia Ltd, Ringwood, Victoria, Australia
Penguin Books Canada Ltd, 2801 John Street, Markham, Ontario, Canada L3R 1B4
Penguin Books (NZ) Ltd, 182–190 Wairau Road, Auckland 10, New Zealand

Penguin Books Ltd, Registered Offices: Harmondsworth, Middlesex, England

First published in 1989
Copyright © Anthony Bruce, 1989
Maps by Peter McClure

Typeset in 11/12pt Perpetua by
Wilmaset, Birkenhead, Wirral
Printed and bound in Great Britain by
Butler & Tanner Ltd, Frome, Somerset

A CIP catalogue record of this book is available from the British Library

ISBN 0–7181–2781–1

Captions to preceding pages:

page i: *An Albatros DV, the most widely used of the German Albatros fighters, flying over the Ypres battlefield*

page ii: *(reading from top to bottom): 1914 pattern Rolls Royce armoured cars*

Motorcycle despatch riders of the Royal Engineers

German soldier throwing a gas bomb on the Western Front. There was always the danger of gas blowing back on your own trenches

Horse ambulances and wounded outside an Advanced Dressing Station, Ypres, 1917

page v: Top: *Italian cavalry crossing the Piave river on pontoon bridge, November 1918*

Bottom: *Railway guns operated in support of heavy artillery at the front. This 14-inch gun was moved around rapidly to confuse the enemy and to support sectors under particularly heavy pressure*

CONTENTS

Top: *An ammunition column passing an Australian 9.2-inch Howitzer Battery, Battle of the Somme, 1916*

Bottom: *Under pressure from the Austrian and German armies to the west and east of Belgrade, the Serbian army was forced to withdraw, 1915*

INTRODUCTION

The First World War was the result of a decade of rivalry between two major alliances and was to involve, for the first time since the Napoleonic Wars, all the states of Europe. The character of the war was fundamentally different from earlier conflicts, in that it was based on mass-produced weapons and mechanised transport. It was, in fact, the first total war, in which the combatants were compelled to mobilise all their military, industrial and human resources in a conflict unprecedented in its scale and impact.

The most distinctive feature of the war was the prolonged siege warfare of the Western Front, which was as destructive as it had been unexpected. Most professional soldiers had predicted a short war of movement that would be over by Christmas 1914, but they had not correctly assessed the effects of the increased power of modern weapons, which gave significant advantages to the defence. The seemingly endless demands for more men, munitions and supplies for the trenches brought the war directly to the home front for the first time. The civilian population on both sides had originally greeted the war with patriotic fervour, but their enthusiasm was gradually eroded as the huge losses in the trenches quickly accumulated with no apparent gains. New propaganda techniques helped to counteract poor civilian morale, but nothing could prevent the war from acquiring the reputation of being the most terrible of all modern conflicts. In spite of all the destruction that has followed, the First World War has largely retained its original image.

Soldiers' experiences on the Western Front, recorded in a vast library of published memoirs and oral histories, provide a focus for the continuing popular interest in the First World War. Totally alien to normal civilian life, the conditions of trench warfare prompted a variety of responses from the rank and file – reluctant acquiescence, extraordinary acts of courage, even mutiny – that have engaged the imagination of later generations. Another strong area of interest is the changing technology of war, particularly in the new weapons designed to break the deadlock on the Western Front. The arrival of the tank and the use of chemical warfare are the main examples, although several other weapons, including, for example, the sub-machine-gun and the flamethrower, particularly associated with the Second World War, also made their first battlefield appearance between 1914 and 1918.

Siege warfare was also an important stimulant to the development of military aviation, which had been in the hands of a relatively small group of pioneers at the beginning of the war. Its role was orginally limited to reconnaissance in support of the land forces. By 1918, however, aerial combat had developed out of all recognition, with rapid progress in airframe design, the creation of specialist reconnaissance, fighter and bomber units, and the emergence of independent air forces. Naval warfare was also to be profoundly affected by air power but its impact during the war itself was limited. The major new influence on naval operations was in fact the submarine, which made the naval powers cautious about the operational use of their own battleships. It was also to have a devastating impact on merchant shipping until effective counter-measures, namely convoy, were introduced.

Popular and academic interest in the First World War have also been stimulated by the controversies surrounding the making of grand strategy. These have included the mainly British debate between 'Easterners' and 'Westerners' about the value of land operations outside Western Europe, which, according to the former, offered a cheaper and quicker way of defeating Germany than trench warfare. The conduct of the war of attrition in France is, of course, still fiercely debated, but few would give unqualified support to Douglas Haig's unimaginative tactics. Indeed, Ludendorff's statement that British troops were 'lions led by donkeys' would find wide support today. Argument still rages over the broader question of the merits of fighting the war, which has been seen by some as a necessary battle for freedom against the evils of German militarism.

The First World War resulted in a radical reshaping of the political map of Europe. Four ancient dynasties were destroyed and freedom for the subject peoples of the Austro-Hungarian and Turkish empires was secured. Belgium was freed and significant Allied territorial gains were made. The war also promoted internal social and economic change. In England, for example, it accelerated the introduction of a new social and political order that was 'less rigid, less paternalist and less deferential' than its Edwardian predecessor. On the other hand, the costs of over four years of war were enormous. It resulted in almost ten million battle deaths and produced severe short-term economic and social dislocation. The German question remained unsolved and indeed the harsh terms of the peace settlement helped to create the conditions in which Hitler could seize power. Soviet Russia, a creation of the war, remained outside the peace-making process. The Allies' abortive attempt to destroy her by military intervention led to the 'permanent estrangement of the Bolsheviks from the rest of the world'.

This *Illustrated Companion* provides, in encyclopaedic form, a complete account of the First World War. The war has not been presented in this reference format before, but its many different facets make it particularly suitable for such treatment. The book is extensively illustrated with contemporary photographs, drawn largely from the Imperial War Museum's fine collections, which help to re-create the reality of war more directly than the text alone could hope to do. It describes the plans and military forces of each of the combatants and outlines the strategies they employed. The political context of the war features prominently in the book and there are numerous concise biographies of political leaders as well as of all the major military figures. The social context of the conflict is not overlooked, with brief articles on, for example, conscription, propaganda and military mutinies. Considerable space has been devoted to the new weapon systems introduced during the war. Every major ship, aircraft, artillery piece, armoured vehicle and hand weapon are described in some detail. The origins of the war and its progress are charted by means of a general chronology. There are also separate chronologies for each of the main theatres, which provide readily accessible lists of the main battles. All these engagements are the subject of separate entries, where they are described in outline and are related to one another, in order to provide a coherent account of the sequence of events. Many of the accounts of individual battles give insights into the nature of combat during 1914–18, but there is also a separate description of the development of trench warfare. Finally, the *Companion* describes how the war was brought to an end and gives details of the peace settlement that followed. A system of cross-references has been used to indicate where fuller information on a particular topic may be found within the book.

It is unlikely that this book could have been completed without the support and forebearance of my wife and daughter, to whom this book is dedicated. In its initial stages the encouragement and advice of John Lawton, who was then on the staff at Curtis Brown, proved to be invaluable. I would also like to acknowledge the support and interest of my publisher in the project and in particular the contribution of Peter Robinson, commissioning editor at Michael Joseph, to the final product.

Anthony Bruce
March 1989

A7V STURMPANZERWAGEN

It was only in the final few months of the war that the German High Command fully acknowledged the potential military significance of the tank. By then it was too late to take corrective action and by the Armistice little more than twenty tanks had been produced. Their origins can be traced back to the autumn of 1916 when the appearance of the first British tank on the battlefield prompted the Germans into action. The approved model was designated the A7V – after the initials of the war department group responsible for its development – and the first production machine was delivered in October 1917.

Like its British and French counterparts, the A7V was based on a modified version of the Holt tractor chassis, on which was mounted a rectangular, armour-plated box. It was powered by two 4-cylinder Daimler Benz engines and had a relatively high maximum speed of 8m.p.h. The A7V was fitted with underhung tracks which, unlike its contemporaries, had sprung suspension – an innovation in tank design. Internally there was a single large compartment accommodating as many as eighteen men, of whom twelve operated six 7.92mm **Maxim machine-guns** – two on each side and two at the rear. The gunner fired the 57mm Sokol – a Russian weapon

captured by the Germans in some quantity – that was positioned at the front; other personnel included the commander and driver. The A7V chassis was also used as a basis for a supply carrier – the A7V Uberlandwagen – that was produced in limited numbers in the last year of the war.

The A7V was first used operationally at St Quentin on 21 March 1918 and was in combat again on 24 April at Villers-Bretonneux, notable as the first tank versus tank action. It was subsequently employed on a limited number of occasions, but made little contribution to the German war effort. Although the A7V had a few advantages over its contemporaries – the front mounted gun being the most important – it had poor cross-country performance and limited trench-crossing ability because of insufficient ground clearance and a high centre of gravity. To overcome these problems a modified version, the A7VU, with all-round tracks on the British pattern, rather than the underhung variety, was developed, but did not appear before the end of the war. The Germans themselves acknowledged the superiority of British tank design by using captured machines to equip five of the eight companies of the German tank arm.

ABDULLAH IBN HUSSEIN, 1882–1951

The second son of Sherif Hussein of Mecca and brother of **Feisal**, commander of the Arab forces in the Hejaz during the First World War, Abdullah was himself one of the leaders of the **Arab Revolt** (1916–18). He played a key role in the guerrilla operations in

the southern area of the Hejaz, attacking the Turkish garrison at Medina and raiding the railway, with the result that large numbers of enemy troops were tied down. After the war he became Emir of Transjordan and in 1949 was crowned the first King of Jordan.

ABOUKIR

An early wartime disaster for the Royal Navy was the destruction of three armoured **cruisers** – *Aboukir*, *Cressy* and *Hogue* – on 22 September 1914. They were

all Cressy class cruisers, built in 1901–03, with a displacement of 12,000 tons and a maximum speed of 21 knots. Patrolling off the Dutch coast, without destroyer protection, *Aboukir* was torpedoed by the German submarine U-9 some thirty miles west of Ymuiden. Suspecting a mine rather than a submarine, *Cressy* and *Hogue* came to the aid of survivors but they too were torpedoed by U-9 almost immediately and sank within minutes. As many as 1,459 men were killed, with just over 800 saved. The loss of three elderly ships had little military significance in itself, but the incident was damaging to British morale and increased German interest in the development of submarine warfare.

ABRUZZI, ADMIRAL LUIGI DE SAVOIA-AOSTA, DUCA DI, 1873–1933

This noted Arctic explorer was appointed commander-in-chief of the Italian navy in 1913, following a period of active service in the Italian–Turkish War. Criticised for his lack of initiative during the First World War, Abruzzi retired from the high command in 1917 after internal dissension. He was succeeded by Paolo Thaon di Revel.

A-CLASS SUBMARINE

The first British-designed submarines, the A-class boats, were based on the experimental Holland types that had been produced under licence by Vickers in 1901–03. Built in 1902–05, they had twin torpedo tubes in the bow (with seven torpedoes carried) and the first real conning tower. Power was provided by a 16-cylinder Wolseley petrol engine which gave a maximum speed of about 11.5 knots on the surface. Surviving units were still in Royal Navy use during the First World War, mainly in a training role.

AEG CIV

The AEG was one of the C-type (armed two-seater) machines selected by the German air force in 1916 following its decision to expand its aerial reconnaissance role. The CIV, a well-constructed two-bay biplane, was the main production model of the series and became one of the best-known German two-seaters of the war. It was still in service at the Armistice and some 400 CIV machines may have been built; the total for all AEG C-types was 658.

Based on the CII, the AEG CIV was immediately recognisable by its fuselage, which was very short in relation to the wing span. It had a large triangular fin and rudder and the airframe was, rather unusually, constructed of steel tube. The power output of the single 160hp Mercedes D III engine was no more than adequate for an aircraft of this size and the maximum speed was 98m.p.h. at sea level. As as result, the CIVa, a variant with the more powerful 180hp Argus engine, was produced, but only in small quantities. The CIV had side radiators and a large 'rhino horn' exhaust. Armament consisted of a synchronised forward firing Spandau machine-gun and a **Parabellum** gun on a Schneider ring mounting in the observer's cockpit; a bomb load of 200lb could also be carried.

The CIV was used widely on reconnaissance duties by the German air force on the Western Front, and in Italy and Macedonia. Bulgarian and Turkish forces also used it in a similar role. With good defensive armament, the CIV was sometimes employed as an escort to aircraft (including other CIVs) on reconnaissance missions.

AEG GIV

The GIV was a twin-engined two-bay biplane which first appeared in 1916. It was a slightly modified version of the earlier AEG G types – the GI, GII and GIII – which had been used by the German air service as both fighters and bombers. Total wartime production of the series amounted to 542 machines, but only the GIV was manufactured in quantity. Accommodating a crew of three or four, the GIV used the same 260hp Mercedes DIVa engine as the **Friedrichshafen** and **Gotha** bombers. With a maximum speed of 103m.p.h. and an endurance of up to five hours, it lacked the range and lifting power of other G-class aircraft. A relatively small load of 880lb was carried, with **Parabellum** guns in the front and rear cockpits.

As a result of its performance limitations, the GIV was mainly used in a tactical role. On the Western Front, for example, GIVs made short-range day and night attacks on Allied rear positions. With additional fuel tanks in place of a bomb load, the GIV was able to carry out long-range reconnaissance missions. It served in Macedonia, Italy and Rumania as well as on the Western Front. A much improved replacement design, the GV, with enlarged wings, increased bomb load and greater range, appeared too late for operational use in the war.

AEG JI & JII

The AEG J-types were armoured, two-seater biplanes, used by the German air service in 1917–18 for infantry contact patrol duties. They were allocated to the newly formed *Infanterieflieger* units until the arrival of sufficient aircraft specially designed for this role.

The JI was closely based on the **AEG CIV**, but was equipped with a larger 200hp Benz BZ IV engine, which gave a maximum speed of 94m.p.h. and a duration of $2\frac{1}{2}$ hours. The extra power was essential to propel an aircraft whose engine and cockpit were protected by a shell of armour plate. To improve control of this much heavier plane, double ailerons

connected by struts were fitted. Armament consisted of two Spandau machine-guns, fitted to the cockpit floor, which fired forwards and downwards at enemy troops and other ground targets. The observer was also equipped with a ring-mounted **Parabellum machine-gun** for defensive purposes. The JII, which appeared in 1918, had extended armour and redesigned control surfaces.

In total, AEG produced as many as 609 J-types for the German air service, although they were less highly rated than the **Junkers** and **Albatros J-type** aircraft.

AERIAL BOMBS

The largest aerial bomb produced during the war was the British 3,360lb S N device, which could only be carried by the Handley Page V/1500. Other large bombs (1,600, 1,650, 1,700 and 1,800lb) were also produced for the Handley Page bombers, but most aerial missiles of the First World War were relatively small. The first French missiles were in fact small steel darts (the flechette), no more than six inches long. Before they were able to develop a bomb of their own, the French dropped modified artillery shells from aircraft. These included the shell of the famous **75mm field gun** which proved to be so effective that the Aviation Militaire was still using them in 1918.

In Britain the Royal Naval Air Service, which pioneered aerial bombing, already had the 20lb Hale bomb and the 112lb naval bomb at its disposal in August 1914. The RFC was also soon to acquire Hale bombs (10, 20, 100lb), but had no missiles of its own when the war began. Larger bombs were developed for RFC use during 1915–16, with a maximum size of 585lb. Its standard medium bomb for much of the war was the 112lb missile produced by the Royal Laboratory; a 230lb bomb made by the Royal Aircraft Factory was also widely used by the RFC. The Cooper bomb, an excellent 20lb device, was employed from the spring of 1917 on low level bombing missions.

The pear-shaped Carbonit bomb, with a propeller activated fuse, was the standard German bomb of the first part of the war. It was made in 4.5, 10, 20, and 50kg sizes. In 1916 they were replaced by the torpedo-shaped P.u.W. bomb, which had improved aerodynamic qualities. Manufactured in sizes from 22lb to 2,200lb, P.u.W. missiles remainded in use until the Armistice.

AGINCOURT

This British-built dreadnought, which was originally ordered by Brazil, was acquired by Turkey before she was completed, but was taken over by the Royal Navy on the outbreak of war. She was the longest battleship in the world but not the best protected, her armour falling short of normal British standards. However, she had the largest number of main guns (fourteen 12-nch guns in twin turrets) and the heaviest secondary armament of any warship, and was capable of producing an impressive volume of fire. *Agincourt* had a maximum speed of over 22 knots and a displacement of 27,500 tons. She served with the **Grand Fleet** throughout the war and fought at **Jutland** without sustaining any damage.

AGO CI, CII & CIII

These two-seat pusher biplanes were used by the German air service for reconnaissance duties on the Western Front, where they were present in relatively small numbers. They had two fuselage booms supporting the tail unit and were armed with a **Parabellum machine-gun** in the nose, operated by the observer. The CI, which was normally powered by a 160hp Mercedes D III engine, entered service in the summer of 1915. By the end of the year it had been replaced on the Western Front by the AGO CII, a heavier aircraft which had a more powerful 220hp Benz BZ IV engine, giving a maximum speed of 86m.p.h., and minor improvements to the airframe. The CII was also constructed in floatplane form and was used by the German navy in a local defence role. The CIII was a smaller variant, of which only a few were built. The last examples of the series were withdrawn from the front in mid-1917.

AIR ACES

The word ace was first used by the French in the context of air fighting, and was applied to pilots who shot down five or more enemy aircraft. This standard was adopted by several other air forces in the early stages of the First World War and was widely retained even when, as a result of improvements in armament, the figure seemed much too low. The Germans recognised this and set the minimum number at ten, while the RFC never officially adopted the ace system, because of the personal difficulties it could cause. The procedures for confirming victories varied considerably between air forces, but in general regulations were stringent and tended to underestimate the number of victories. The British produced the highest number of aces, with 785 pilots scoring five or more victories. Comparable figures for Germany were 363 and for France 158.

The First World War's most successful pilots were as follows:

Britain and the Empire	*Hits*
Major Edward Mannock	73
Lt-Col William Bishop	72
Lt-Col Raymond Collishaw	60
Major James McCudden	57
Captain Anthony Beauchamp-Proctor	54
Major Donald MacLaren	54
Major W. G. Barker	52

Germany	
Rittmeister Manfred von Richthofen	80
Oberleutnant Ernst Udet	62
Oberleutnant Erich Loewenhardt	53
Leutnant Werner Voss	48
Hauptmann Bruno Loerzer	45
Leutnant Fritz Rumey	45
Hauptmann Rudolph Berthold	44

France	
Capitaine René Fonck	75
Capitaine Georges Guynemer	54
Lieutenant Charles Nungesser	45
Capitaine Georges Madon	41
Lieutenant Maurice Boyau	35

United States	
Captain Edward Rickenbacker	26
Captain William Lambert	22

United States contd.	
Captain August Iaccaci	18
2nd Lieutenant Frank Luke	18
Major Raoul Lufbery	17

Italy	
Maggiore Francesco Baracca	34
Tenente Silvio Scaroni	26
Tenete-Colonello Pier Ruggiero Piccio	24
Tenete Falvio Torello Baracchini	21

Austro-Hungary	
Hauptmann Godwin Brumowski	40
Offizierstellvertreter Julius Arigi	32
Oberleutnant Franke Linke-Crawford	30
Oberleutnant Benno Fiala, Ritter von Fernbrugg	29

Russia	
Major A. A. Kazakov	17
Captain P. V. d'Argueeff	15
Lt-Cdr A. P. de Seversky	13
Lieutenant I. W. Smirnoff	12

Belgium	
2nd Lieutenant Willy Coppens	37
Adjutant André de Meulemeester	11
2nd Lieutenant Edmond Thieffry	10
Capitaine Fernand Jacquet	7

AIRCO DH1 & DH1A

This two-seater pusher biplane saw limited service in the RFC from mid-1916 until 1918. Designed for fighter and reconnaissance duties, it provided the observer/gunner in the front cockpit with an unrestricted field of fire for his .303 **Lewis machine-gun**. The original 70hp Renault engine was soon replaced by the 120hp Beardmore and in this form (known as the DH1A) its performance, in terms of speed and manoeuvrability, was significantly better than the comparable **Royal Aircraft Factory FE2b**. The Factory machine was, however, already being manufactured in quantity and as a result production of the DH1/1A was on a small scale, a total of only 73 being delivered to the RFC. A few were actively employed as fighter escorts in Palestine; otherwise their use was confined to home defence and training duties.

AIRCO DH2

A scaled-down version of the **Airco DH1**, with a single seat, this fighting scout was a two-bay pusher biplane which served with the RFC in 1916–17. The typical nacelle and tailbooms arrangement was frail in appearance, but the airframe was well constructed and reliable in service. The DH2 was powered by the 100hp Monosoupape, a rotary engine that was dangerously unreliable as one of its 9 cylinders had a tendency to blow out. It was also slow, with a maximum speed of only 93m.p.h. at sea level. The pusher arrangement had been adopted in the absence of a synchronising mechanism, but there were initial problems with the forward firing .303 **Lewis machine-gun**. A movable mounting was adopted but it proved too insecure to be used effectively and eventually the gun was clamped in a fixed position. Pilots soon adopted the technique of aiming the whole machine at the target, with the result that the gun was also aligned with it.

The DH2 arrived in France early in 1916 and it equipped No 24 Squadron, the first single-seat fighter squadron ever formed. Within a few months, two other squadrons (Nos 29 and 32) also adopted the DH2 as their sole machine. Other units followed and in all 266 DH2s served on the Western Front.

Its arrival there was timely: it was the fighter primarily responsible for overcoming the threat of the **Fokker monoplanes** and establishing British air superiority by mid-1916. Its manoeuvrability and excellent rate of climb (6,000 feet in eleven minutes) were important factors in its success. The new fighter's first victory came on 2 April 1916, the first of 44 hits against enemy aircraft in 744 engagements. Amongst the most notable was the single-handed attack by Major Lionel Rees (commanding officer of No 32 Squadron) on ten German two-seaters. Two were destroyed and Rees was awarded the Victoria Cross.

The DH2's pusher design was, however, already dated and its slow speed made it vulnerable to the new **Albatros** and **Halberstadt** fighters. It was in fact an Albatros DII flown by **von Richthofen** that shot down **Major Lanoe Hawker** (commander of No 24 Squadron) in a DH2 on 23 November 1916, after a prolonged fight. Although losses mounted from late 1916, the DH2 was retained in service on the Western Front until June 1917 because of the absence of any suitable replacement. DH2s continued to serve in Palestine and Macedonia but most were returned to England where they were used as trainers until the end of the war.

AIRCO DH4

This two-seater, two-bay tractor biplane was one of the most successful designs of the war, and was the first British aircraft conceived specifically for high speed day bombing. Constructed of wood and covered in fabric in the normal way, the prototype flew in the summer of 1916 and was originally powered by a 160hp BHP engine. Early production models were fitted with the 250hp Rolls Royce engine, but several alternatives were also used because of the large number of aircraft produced. When powered by the 375hp Eagle VII engine it outclassed almost all contemporary fighters: it had a maximum speed of 143m.p.h., a ceiling of 21,000 feet, and an excellent rate of climb. The DH4 had a very wide speed range and was easy to fly. Armament consisted of a synchronised forward firing **Vickers machine-gun** and one or two **Lewis guns** on a Scarff ring mounting in the rear cockpit. A bomb load of up to 460lb could be carried, although naval versions were sometimes equipped with **depth charges** instead. The cockpits were separated by a large fuel tank, which was very vulnerable to enemy action and made communication between the pilot and observer very difficult. It did, however, locate the pilot's cockpit at a point which gave him the best possible downward view when aiming his bombs.

The DH4 first arrived in France in March 1917 and it served widely with the RFC and RNAS until the Armistice. Apart from regular tactical bombing oper-ations on the Western Front, DH4s were employed by the Independent Force, RAF, on long-range strikes against strategic targets in Germany. Capable of operating without an escort, they were also used for artillery spotting, photographic reconnaissance and coastal patrol duties. On 5 August 1918, for example, a naval DH4 operating from Great Yarmouth shot down Zeppelin L70. Not long afterwards, four DH4s based in Belgium sank the German submarine UB-12. DH4s also operated in the Aegean, the Adriatic, Macedonia, Mesopotamia, and Russia, and a total of 1,449 were built by seven companies.

The aircraft was in fact manufactured on a larger scale in the United States where nearly 5,000 were produced. Designated here the DH4A, it was fitted with a 400hp Liberty 12 engine and was armed with two forward firing **Browning** or **Marlin** guns. Two Lewis guns were available to the observer and a maximum bomb load of 382lb could be carried. Some 1,885 'Liberty planes' served in France from August 1918. They were operated by thirteen squadrons of the AEF and four squadrons of the US Naval Northern Bombing Group. In a modified form the aircraft remained in American service until 1932, but in England the original DH4 did not long survive the Armistice.

AIRCO DH5

The DH5 was a tractor biplane fighter of unconventional appearance, designed in 1916 as a replacement for the ageing **Airco DH2**. Its wings had a pronounced backward stagger in order to retain the excellent field of vision of the earlier pusher type, but combined with the improved performance of the tractor biplane. This arrangement of the power plant was made possible by the introduction of the Constantinesco synchronising mechanism which enabled a **Vickers machine-gun** to fire through the airscrew. The DH5 was powered by the 110hp Le Rhône rotary engine, which gave a maximum speed of 103m.p.h. at 10,000 feet.

It arrived in France in May 1917 and served with five squadrons of the RFC, proving within weeks to be deficient as a fighter. Its poor performance above 10,000 feet was a major reason, but many pilots had reservations about the safety of its unorthodox design. With its strong construction and good forward view, the DH5 was, however, more successfully employed on low level ground attack duties, when four 25lb Cooper bombs were carried. In this role it gave valuable service during 1917 in the **Battles of Ypres** and **Cambrai**. By January 1918 sufficient **Royal Aircraft Factory SE5s** were available to enable the withdrawal of DH5s to be completed, after only eight months' operational service. It was the least successful of De Havilland's wartime designs, although as many as 550 were built.

AIRCO DH6

The rapid expansion of the RFC in 1916–17 meant that many more pilots would be needed and the DH6 was a two-seater tractor biplane designed specifically for this training programme. It was easy and quick to produce, simple to maintain, and relatively safe in the air, after structural modifications had been made. These advantages had been obtained by sacrificing its appearance which was far from elegant: the wings and tailplane were square cut and the fuselage was flat topped. The standard power unit was the 90hp RAF Ia, but many DH6s had Curtiss OX-5 or 80hp Renault engines.

Well over 2,000 DH6s were manufactured and they were widely used in 1917 by training squadrons at home and overseas. During this period the DH6 acquired many nicknames, indicating that it was not always popular with those who learned to fly in it: 'the clutching hand', 'the dung hunter', 'the flying coffin', and 'the sky hook'. The DH6 was gradually withdrawn following the introduction of the **Avro 504K** as the standard British trainer towards the end of 1917.

Early in 1918, 300 surplus DH6s were transferred to the RNAS for use on anti-submarine patrols around British coastal waters. This interim arrangement in fact continued until the Armistice and 34 DH6 flights were created, five of them operated by the US Navy. With insufficient power to carry both an observer and 100lb of bombs, DH6s scored no notable successes, although their patrols may have helped to reduce shipping losses. Over 1,000 were still in RAF service at the end of the war.

AIRCO DH9 & DH9A

The DH9 was a modified version of the **Airco DH4** and was intended for long-range bombing duties. Following the first daylight raid by German aircraft on London on 13 June 1917, it was decided to increase the operational strength of the RFC, placing particular emphasis on its strategic bombing capability. The DH9 was one of the aircraft ordered in quantity to meet this need.

This two-seat, two-bay biplane was very similar to its predecessors, the main difference being the new 230hp Siddeley Puma engine, with cylinder heads and exhaust manifold visible above the rounded nose. Like the **DH6**, armament consisted of a synchronised forward firing **Vickers machine-gun** and one or two **Lewis machine-guns** on a Scarff ring in the rear cockpit. Two 230lb bombs or their equivalent could be carried internally and a camera or wireless was installed. The cockpit layout was greatly improved by closing the large gap between the pilot and observer that was the major disadvantage of the DH4. In other respects, however, it was clearly inferior to the aeroplane it was intended to replace, with the result that many DH4s were retained in service. Weaknesses had been detected in the DH9 well before operational use began in March 1918, but production was well underway and the order could not be cancelled. The Siddeley Puma engine proved to be extremely unreliable and did not provide sufficient power for an aircraft of this size. It had a maximum speed of 112m.p.h. at 10,000 feet and a poor rate of climb; it could barely reach 13,000 feet with a full load.

The DH9 equipped nine squadrons on the Western Front and remained in use until the Armistice. Serving with the Independent Force, RAF, DH9s made many raids on strategic targets, although they were vulnerable to enemy attack and losses were often heavy. In Britain they were used, in conjunction with DH4s, on coastal defence and anti-Zeppelin duties. DH9s were present in almost every theatre of the war and a total of 3,204 machines were built by sixteen companies. Steps were taken at an early date, in response to criticisms from **Trenchard** and others, to provide the aircraft with a more powerful and reliable engine. The American 400hp Liberty 12 engine was selected and the plane was modified because of its greater weight. Designated the DH9A, it saw only limited operational use with four units, although 885 examples had been completed by December 1918. In this modified form it was an outstanding strategic bomber and production continued after the war.

AIRCRAFT CARRIERS

It was not long after the first powered flights were made that aircraft were operated from the decks of warships. The first take-off from a British ship was made from the *Hibernia* early in 1912; in the following Many a take-off was made from a ship underway. These early experiments encouraged the Admiralty to convert *Hermes*, an old cruiser, to carry three seaplanes. A launching platform was added, but the aircraft were normally lowered over the side. In December 1914, she was followed by *Ark Royal*, often described as an aircraft carrier, but in fact the first purpose-built seaplane carrier. She could accommodate ten aircraft in her hold and they were raised and lowered by cranes into the sea. Several fast cross-Channel ferries, including the *Empress*, *Engadine* and *Riviera*, were taken over during the period 1914–17 and converted as seaplane carriers. These vessels were used extensively during the **Dardanelles operation**, when the first effective air torpedo attack was by a seaplane operating from the carrier *Ben-my-Chree*.

The Admiralty gradually realised the potential of ship-based aircraft and in 1915 the *Campania*, a converted seaplane carrier, was fitted with a taking-off deck. It was from this ship, in August 1915, that the first take-off by an aircraft with wheeled floats occurred. A month later a land plane took off from *Vindex*, another conversion, but like the seaplane it landed in the sea, supported by flotation bags rather than floats. The need for aircraft to return to their ships without them stopping soon became obvious. As a result, the first flush-decked aircraft carrier, the *Argus*, was commissioned in 1916, but it was not to be ready until the final weeks of the war.

To provide landing facilities, the Royal Navy was, therefore, compelled to rely on conversions, which included the *Furious*, a light battlecruiser. Landings remained difficult because of the air disturbances caused by the funnels. One of *Furious*'s notable successes was the raid on the Zeppelin sheds at Tondern in July 1918, when the seven aircraft involved flew from the ship. By 1918, the results of wartime experimentation were evident as the first ship to be designed as an aircraft carrier – *Hermes* – began construction, although it was not to be completed until 1923. Aircraft also operated from many British warships, taking off from platforms mounted on gun turrets.

AIR RAIDS

Although reconnaissance in support of ground forces was viewed as the principal role of air power in 1914–15, it was soon apparent that strategic bombing – an attack on the sources, industrial and human, of an enemy's military power – would be an important feature of military aviation during the First World War. Indeed as early as October 1914 the RNAS launched a strike against German airship sheds at Düsseldorf.

Such attacks did not prevent the Germans starting **Zeppelin** raids against England early in 1915 – the first being a bombing mission by three naval airships on East Anglia on 19 January 1915. Attacks by small single-engine aircraft on the English coastal towns had begun slightly earlier, on 24 December 1914, although no German aircraft attacked London until 28 November 1916. Airships first bombed the capital on 31 May 1915, following the lifting of the Kaiser's restrictions on aerial attacks on London. Tyneside, the Humber and the Midlands were among the other major areas that were attacked by Zeppelins in 51 raids during the period 1915–18. As a result, 557 people were killed and 1,358 were injured. With improvements in aircraft performance the airship became increasingly vulnerable and from 1916 the number of raids on Britian diminished sharply.

London was not the only large city to be attacked by the Germans: Paris was bombed 30 times by airships and aircraft, the first occasion being on 29 August 1914.

The use of aircraft for strategic bombing had been pioneered by the RNAS, whose early raids against airship sheds were followed up by a campaign against industrial targets during 1916–17. Mounted by No 3 Wing from a base at Luxeuil, operations came to an end when doubts were expressed about their value.

The German air force did not, however, share these reservations and in May 1917 an 'England Squadron', equipped with the new **Gotha GIV** heavy bomber, began operations. The **Zeppelin Staaken RVI** was also used, and in fact one of these machines (R39) delivered more bombs (26,000kg in 20 raids) than any other aircraft during the war. Eight daylight raids were made against England in May–August 1917; 73,000lb of bombs were dropped and 1,364 people were killed or injured.

GERMAN AIR RAIDS ON THE UK, 1914–18

Type	Number of Raids	Bombs Dropped	Casualties	
			Killed	Injured
Airship	51	5,806	557	1,358
Aircraft	52	2,772	857	2,058
Total	103	8,576	1,414	3,416

The German U-boat shelter at Zeebrugge after a successful British air raid

British and French Air Raids on Germany, 1915–18

Year	Number of Raids	Bombs Dropped
1915	51	940
1916	96	917
1917	175	5,234
1918	353	7,117
Total	675	14,208

At first the British had little success in shooting down these large bombers, but improvements in home defence organisation were quickly made during the summer of 1917, forcing the Germans to switch to night raids, which continued until May 1918. The desire to retaliate and to destroy military targets in Germany led to the formation of 41 Wing, RFC, in October 1917. Following the creation of the RAF, a larger Independent Force was established to undertake strategic bombing, mainly using the **Handley Page 0/400**. The scale of its operations never matched expectations and only 543 tons of bombs had been dropped by the end of the war. The effect of strategic bombing during the First World War was very limited: there was no significant loss of war production and no evidence of any real effect on civilian morale in Britain or Germany.

AISNE RIVER, FIRST BATTLE OF THE, 15–18 September 1914

As the **Battle of the Marne** ended, the German armies withdrew quickly northwards until they had crossed the River Aisne, a tributary of the Oise. On 13 September, they halted on the crest of high ground above the river, which formed a great natural barrier in the north of France. From the Aisne the Germans were deployed eastwards as follows: the First Army (**von Kluck**), the Seventh (von Heeringen) and the Second (**von Bülow**). The longstanding gap between the First and Second Armies had been filled by an improvised Seventh Army just in time to meet a major attack. The Allies, who had not perhaps pursued the enemy from the Marne with sufficient vigour, sought to envelop the German right wing in a frontal assault by their left wing – made up of the French Sixth Army (**Maunoury**), the British Expeditionary Force (**French**) and the French Fifth Army (**Franchet d'Espérey**). Further to the east, where trenches were already beginning to appear, were positioned the French Ninth, Fourth, Third, Second and First Armies.

The Allies began to cross the Aisne under heavy fire. They mainly used pontoon bridges, as only one of the permanent crossings remained intact; a bridgehead was established on the north of the river and was soon enlarged. On the following day, 14 September, they made further small gains in an assault on the enemy line, which was located on the plateau above them. However, within hours German counter-attacks, with strong artillery support, had pushed back the French Sixth Army almost to its starting position. The Allies were unable to make any real progress against the Germans' well-prepared positions and, with the French also coming under pressure at Reims, this largely stationary battle was abandoned on 18 September.

It was already becoming clear that a frontal assault by infantry alone, without heavy artillery support, was unlikely to be successful. As the Aisne offensive drew to a close **Joffre** moved his forces north-west in an attempt to attack the exposed German right flank at Noyon; the enemy responded by moving reserves to the area with the aim of outflanking the Allies themselves. Both manoeuvres were unsuccessful but the opposing armies made several further attempts to outflank each other during the so-called 'Race to the Sea', which continued until the Allies reached Nieuport early in October. The Battle of the Aisne and its sequel marked the closing stages of the war of movement and the beginnings of trench warfare.

AISNE RIVER, SECOND BATTLE OF THE, 16 April–9 May 1917

Nivelle's offensive on the Aisne River, between Soissons and Reims, followed a week after the British diversionary attacks at **Arras**. The new French commander-in-chief had promised a breakthrough and final victory but he underestimated the capacity of the opposition and the results were to fall far short of his exaggerated expectations. Although his plans were largely unaffected by the German withdrawal to the Hindenburg Line, the enemy had learned of his intentions from captured documents. His army group commander, **General Micheler**, was opposed to the offensive, as was **Pétain**, commander of the secondary front towards Arras. The French attack, which began on 16 April along a 50-mile front, involved two armies, under the overall direction of General Micheler. To the left in the Soissons sector was the Sixth Army (**Mangin**) and to its right was the Fifth Army (Mazel). A subsidiary attack was made by the Fourth Army (**Anthoine**) to the east of Reims.

As the bombardment by heavy artillery came to an end the French began their advance towards Laon, but heavy opposition was soon encountered, particularly from enemy gunners in fortified positions on the northern slopes of the Aisne. The German Seventh Army (von Boehm) checked the French advance – in the Chemin des Dames area – as did the First Army (**Fritz von Below**) to the east. In spite of losing as many as 150 tanks, Nivelle renewed the attack on the second day, but little progress was made. The promised breakthrough could not be achieved, but by 20 April there had been some modest gains: the Fort Malmaison salient had been abandoned; the Aisne valley had been cleared; the Reims–Soissons railway freed; and 20,000 German prisoners taken. Reinforced by the Tenth Army, which moved in between the Sixth and Fifth Armies, Nivelle's forces now amounted to 1,200,000 men and 7,000 guns. Partial attacks continued until the end of the month and some further progress was made, the capture of $2\frac{1}{2}$ miles of the Hindenburg Line on the Chemin des Dames ridge being the most notable success. A final, more general, attack was launched on 5 May, but little had been gained by the time it ended four days later.

French casualties amounted to 187,000 men, compared with 163,000 on the German side. Widespread mutiny in the demoralised French army followed Nivelle's costly failure to break the German lines. The commander-in-chief himself was soon replaced by Pétain, who brought the situation under control and restored the morale and fighting effectiveness of the French army.

AISNE RIVER, THIRD BATTLE OF THE, 27 May–2 June 1918

The third German offensive of 1918 was to be a diversionary attack on the Chemin des Dames sector of the Aisne. **Ludendorff** aimed to damage the French in order to prevent them coming to the aid of the British in Flanders when he turned to attack them again.

The attack was to be led by the First Army (**Fritz von Below**) and the Seventh Army (von Boehm), which now had a combined strength of 41 divisions. The sector was only lightly defended by units of the French Sixth Army (Dûchene): at the front were four French divisions and three battle-weary British divisions. To the rear were a further nine divisions. The defending troops were badly positioned and there was no defence in depth.

The attack, which began on 27 May, opened with a massive artillery bombardment, in which 4,600 guns were used. Seventeen divisions moved forward on a nine-mile front, storming the Chemin des Dames ridge and destroying the Allied centre almost immediately. The Germans advanced to the River Aisne where they captured the bridges intact. On the Allied left the French were forced back towards Soissons but were able to contain the German right to some extent. The British divisions put up strong resistance, preventing the German front from widening too much. By the end of the first day the Germans had advanced ten miles to the Vesle, the biggest movement on the front since trench warfare began in 1914.

Although the Germans' limited objectives had already been achieved they decided to push on towards Paris, only 80 miles away. They advanced another five miles on the second day and by 30 May were on the Marne once more, at Château-Thierry. In response to this rapid German progress, two American divisions were rushed to the area. Bolstered by the American victory at **Cantigny** (28 May), the

Third Division went into action to hold the Marne crossings at Château-Thierry and on 6 June the Second Division launched an attack on **Belleau Wood**.

By this time, however, the offensive was effectively already over, and Ludendorff had been unable to widen the salient sufficiently: it was 35 miles deep but little more than 20 wide. Allied casualties amounted to 127,337, of which 28,703 were accounted for by the British. German losses matched the combined Allied total. As the Aisne operation came to an end, the Germans launched another diversionary attack – this time on **Noyon-Montdidier** – on 9 June, their fourth offensive of the year.

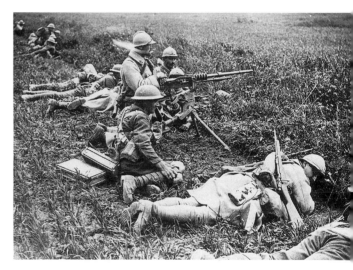

British and French troops, unprotected by trenches, prepare for an expected German attack during the Aisne offensive, May 1918

AITKEN, MAX, LORD BEAVERBROOK, 1879–1964

Newspaper proprietor and politician, Max Aitken amassed a fortune in Canada before emigrating to England in 1910. Within a few months he had become a Conservative MP and a close associate of **Bonar Law**, the party leader. In 1915–16, he was the Canadian government's representative on the Western Front, based at the British general headquarters at St Omer. On his return to England, he

helped to bring **Lloyd George** to power in December 1916. He was rewarded with his appointment as Chancellor of the Duchy of Lancaster and a peerage. In February 1918, be became Minister of Information, a post he held until the end of the war, when he left to concentrate on building up a newspaper empire.

ALBATROS B-TYPES

This series of unarmed two-seater biplanes made an important contribution to German air reconnaissance in the first part of the war. The BI, which served with Field Reconnaissance Units from August 1914, appeared in single- and two-bay forms and was powered by either the 100hp Mercedes D I or 120hp D II engines. As was common at the time, the pilot sat in the rear cockpit and the observer, often armed with a rifle, was positioned at the front. A smaller version, the BII, with three alternative power plants, also appeared in 1914.

It was used widely on the Western and Eastern Fronts for well over a year and was popular with those who flew it. The BIII, with a large 120hp Mercedes D II engine and redesigned tail surfaces, was produced in smaller quantities. Nicknamed the 'Blue Mouse', it saw active service in 1915. Unable to respond effectively to attacks by the new Allied scouts, the Albatros B-types were withdrawn from active service towards the end of 1915 and were replaced by armed C-type two-seaters. The excellent flying qualities of this series ensured that it continued in use as a trainer until the end of the war.

ALBATROS CI

An enlarged version of the unarmed **Albatros BII**, the CI was one of the first of the new C-types (armed two-seaters) to enter service in the spring of 1915. This soundly constructed, two-bay biplane had a more powerful engine than its predecessor – either the 160hp Mercedes DIII or the 180hp Argus As III was normally used. Crew positions were reversed, with the observer, who was armed with a ring-mounted **Parabellum** machine-gun, now being located in the rear cockpit. The CI was immediately recognisable by the large radiators that were positioned on either side of the forward cockpit.

It was used in very large numbers by the *Feldflieger Abteilungen* on the Western and Eastern Fronts in 1915–17, its principal duties being reconnaissance and artillery observation. It also carried a small quantity of bombs stored between the front and rear cockpits. CI pilots, including the future ace **Oswald Boelcke**, demonstrated that it was possible for a two-seater armed with a machine-gun to take effective action against enemy aircraft. The leading ace of the war – **Manfred von Richthofen** – also flew an Albatros CI as an observer on the Eastern Front. Like the Albatros B-types, this aircraft was also used as a trainer, with a dual control version appearing in 1917.

ALBATROS CIII

The CIII, which was derived from the **Albatros BIII**, was produced in larger numbers than any other Albatros C-type. It had an expanded fuselage and revised tail surfaces which enhanced its flying qualities. Most CIIIs were powered by the reliable 160hp Mercedes D III engine, which gave a maximum speed of 88m.p.h. and a flight time of four hours. Initially it had the same armament as the **CI**, but after a few months in service a forward firing Spandau machine-gun was fitted. The additional weight had no significant effect on performance although the interrupter gear proved to be unreliable and sometimes the Spandau destroyed the aircraft's own propeller.

In use on the Western Front in 1916–17, the CIII

served widely on reconnaissance and artillery observation duties and also as a light bomber, carrying a bomb load of 200lb. Its rugged, wood-covered fuselage could sustain a considerable amount of damage from Allied scouts and still remain airborne. It was also used on the Russian Front and in Macedonia. Following its withdrawal from the front line early in 1917, the CIII was used as a trainer until the Armistice.

ALBATROS CV

Unlike previous Albatros C-types, which were based on the earlier **B series**, the CV was a completely new design. A successor to the **CIII**, it was planned around a powerful new Mercedes engine – the 8-cylinder 220hp D IV – which appeared in 1916 and produced a maximum speed of 106m.p.h. The CV was a two-bay, two-seat tractor biplane of wood and fabric construction, which had a torpedo-shaped fuselage and a rounded tailplane. The engine was almost completely enclosed and the airscrew had a large spinner. Armament consisted of a synchronised forward firing Spandau machine-gun and a **Parabellum** gun on a ring mounting.

Known as the CV/16, it entered service in 1916 with reconnaissance units on the Western Front, where the weaknesses of the design soon became apparent: it was heavy on the controls, difficult to fly, and the engine was unreliable. A modified version, the CV/17, appeared in 1917, and its handling was much improved. Production of the troublesome Mercedes engine was, however, stopped before the end of the year and as a result no more CVs were built. A total of 424 machines were made but as few as 65 were in operational service at any one time.

ALBATROS CVII

The CVII appeared in 1916 as an early replacement for the **Albatros CV**, whose Mercedes D IV engine had proved to be very unreliable. This two-bay, two-seat tractor biplane adopted CV/16 and CV/17 components wherever possible, although there were obvious differences. The cylinder block protruded well over the cowling and the fuselage was substantially modified because of the smaller 200hp Benz Bz IV engine that was now used. It has a maximum speed of 106m.p.h. and an endurance of three hours.

Armament consisted of a fixed, forward firing Spandau machine-gun for the pilot and a ring-mounted **Parabellum** for the observer. A light bomb load could also be carried.

The CVII was widely used on the Western Front in 1916–17 on long range reconnaissance and artillery observation patrols. Popular with crews, it was easy to fly and was manufactured in large numbers by three companies. At the peak of its operational use early in 1917, as many as 350 were in service.

ALBATROS CX & CXII

The two-seat Albatros CX followed the general pattern of its predecessors but was designed on a larger scale, with an increased wingspan, to accommodate the more powerful and reliable 260hp Mercedes D IVa engine. It had a maximum speed of 110m.p.h., an endurance of 3 hours 25 minutes, and a ceiling of 16,400 feet, which necessitated oxygen being carried. Armament was the same as the CVII and like earlier C-types it could carry a light bomb load. The CX was used by reconnaissance and artillery co-operation units from mid-1917 for just over a year; about 300 were in service in the autumn of 1917, built by four manufacturers.

Its more elegant successor, the Albatros CXII, was also widely employed by reconnaissance units on the Western Front and was in operational use in the last year of the war. The main changes were a streamlined oval section fuselage, a redesigned tailpane with a small underfin, and a modified undercarriage. The new version, which had strong similarities to the **Albatros D-types**, retained the 260hp Mercedes D IVa engine, with no significant improvement in performance. Like the CX, it was armed with two machine-guns and could carry a light bomb load.

ALBATROS DI & DII

The Albatros DI single-seat biplane was introduced in the autumn of 1916 in a successful attempt to regain the supremacy which the **Fokker** monoplanes had lost to the **Airco DH2**s and the **Nieuport 11**s of the RFC. The DI was elegant in appearance with the clean lines of its fuselage, curved tail surfaces and large airscrew spinner marred only by the radiators mounted on the sides between the wings. Powered by either the 150hp Benz Bz III or the 160hp Mercedes D III, it had a maximum speed of 109m.p.h. and a good rate of climb. It was in fact the most powerful single-seater used by the German air service at this time. Armament consisted of two fixed 7.92mm Spandau machine-guns, which for the first time were carried by an aircraft without any significant loss of performance.

In the autumn of 1916, it went into service on the Western Front with the new *Jagdstaffeln* and was first used operationally by *Jasta 2* (commanded by **Oswald Boelcke**) on 17 September. It was found to be less manoeuvrable than the Fokker monoplanes and its main weakness was the restricted forward and upward view. This was corrected by repositioning the upper wing and the modified aircraft, designated DII, entered service in October 1916. By the beginning of 1917 over 200 examples of the later model were in service on the Western Front. The DI and DII proved to be superior to their opponents and before long Allied losses were mounting. In fact, within a matter of weeks their speed and armament had restored Germany's ascendancy in the air. The DII was superseded by an improved version, the DIII, in January 1917.

ALBATROS DIII

The most successful of the series of Albatros fighters that served during the First World War, the DIII single-seat biplane preserved German air superiority on the Western Front in the spring of 1917. It was closely based on the earlier DI and DII, retaining the latter's basic fuselage, but had a high compression 160hp Mercedes D IIIa engine. As a result it had an improved ceiling (18,000 feet) and endurance (two hours), although its maximum speed (just under 109m.p.h.) was marginally less than its predecessor. The Albatros designers also sought inspiration from

the French **Nieuport** scouts, which had fought with such success, and as a result the wing cellule was completely redesigned. Supported by V-struts, the lower wings were of much narrower chord than the upper pair, helping to improve its rate of climb; pilot visibility was also significantly better. Armament consisted of two fixed, forward firing 7.92mm Spandau machine-guns.

The DIII or 'vee-strutter', as it was named by Allied pilots, appeared on the Western Front early in 1917. **Richthofen's** *Jasta* was one of the first to receive the new fighter, but by the spring all front line units had been equipped with them. Production figures are not available, but in November 1917 – the peak month – there were 446 DIIIs at the front. It was the principal cause of the RFC's heavy losses during 'Bloody April'. The **BE2c** reconnaissance machine was no match for its faster, heavily armed opponent. Richthofen himself flew an all-red D III during this period. As new Allied fighters – including the **Sopwith Camel** and the **SE5** – appeared later in 1917 the D III's superiority was quickly brought to an end.

Von Richthofen's 'circus' was one of the first Jastas *on the Western Front in 1917 to receive the Albatros DIII, the most successfull of the Albatros fighters*

ALBATROS DV & DVa

By mid-1917 the highly successful **Albatros DIII** and its predecessors had been outclassed by a new generation of Allied planes, including the **Sopwith Pup**, the **Sopwith Triplane** and the **SE5**. Its successor, the Albatros DV, turned out to be little improved and unlikely to restore German air superiority on the Western Front. The new machine retained the wings, interplane struts and tail of the DIII, but it had an oval section fuselage (rather than its flat sided predecessor) and a bigger spinner. The slightly uprated 180hp Mercedes D IIIa, which gave a maximum speed of 116m.p.h. at 3,280 feet and a ceiling of 20,500 feet, was the standard power unit. Armament consisted of twin synchronised 7.92mm Spandau machine-guns. The DVa was virtually identical to the DV except for the arrangement of its aileron control wires.

Operational use, which followed the first deliveries in May 1917, soon revealed serious weaknesses in the wing structure, which required modifications to be made. In spite of its performance limitations it was the most widely used of all the Albatros fighters and a total of 1,512 DV/DVas were supplied; it was flown by many of Germany's leading aces, including **Goering**, Hippel and **von Richthofen**. Such success as it achieved on the Western Front has been attributed to the sheer weight of numbers rather than to the quality of its design. Production ended in February 1918 as priority was given to the **Fokker DVII**, although many DV/DVas remained in service until the end of the war.

ALBATROS JI

The JI and JII were armoured contact patrol biplanes, introduced in 1917 to supplement the AEG and Junkers J-types that were already serving with the *Infanterieflieger* units on the Western Front. The

Albatros JI was closely based on earlier Albatros designs and its two-bay wings were in fact identical to those of the **Albatros CXII**. Armour plate protected the two-seater cockpit but not the underpowered

200hp Benz Bz IV engine, which gave a maximum speed of no more than 87m.p.h.

Although this heavy plane had a poor rate of climb, its close support role was carried out at low altitudes, often to great effect. Allied troops were attacked in the trenches with twin Spandau machine-guns, which were fixed to fire downwards through the cockpit floor. The observer, who occupied the rear cockpit, was also armed with a movable **Parabellum** machine-gun for defensive purposes. The lack of armour around the engine proved to be the aircraft's main weakness in service and was rectified when the slightly reduced JII appeared in 1918.

ALBATROS W4

This single-seater seaplane appeared in 1916 in response to an order from the German Admiralty for a fighting scout to defend its air stations on the Belgian coast. Based on the **Albatros DI** landplane, it had many components in common, although there were many important differences. It was significantly larger than the DI, the tail section was modified, and there was an increased gap between the upper and lower wings. Several different float designs were tested before an acceptable streamlined version was adopted. The W4 was powered by a 160hp Mercedes D III engine, which gave a maximum speed of 100m.p.h., and could climb to 1,000m in five minutes. Armament normally consisted of two fixed forward-firing Spandau machine-guns on top of the fuselage.

The W4 was used in small numbers by the German navy, serving from September 1916 in Belgium and the Aegean, where it was used to defend coastal air stations. Its speed, manoeuvrability and armament enabled it to deal effectively with most enemy seaplanes, although the later British flying boats proved to be more difficult opponents. By 1918, the W4 had been replaced by the faster and better armed **Brandenburg W12** two-seater seaplane. No more than 118 W4s were built in total.

ALBERT I, KING OF THE BELGIANS, 1875–1934

As the German invasion of Belgium began on 4 August 1914, King Albert assumed command of the country's small army, determined to offer real resistance. However, the fortress at Liège, which had been expected to hold out for weeks, was taken within days. Albert quickly withdrew his army behind the fortifications of Antwerp, where it carried out several attacks on the enemy's flank. After the city's fall, Albert moved south-west along the coast and the Belgians made a successful defensive stand at the Battle of the Yser (18–30 October).

Albert, who only retained control of a small coastal strip, distanced himself from Britain and France to some extent as the war progressed: 'he wished to preserve Belgium's status as an innocent country, forced into the war and fighting merely to retain its territorial integrity'. Differences in war aims meant

King Albert, Belgian army commander, viewing the British front near Arras, May 1917

that for much of the war Albert was unwilling to participate in Allied offensive operations. He always hoped to negotiate a compromise peace, in spite of political opposition from within the Belgian government. By the autumn of 1918, however, his position had modified and the Belgian army joined in the final Allied offensives. At the same time, Albert himself was appointed commander of the Flanders Army Group by **Marshal Foch** and led his troops to final victory.

ALBRECHT, DUKE OF WÜRTTEMBERG, 1865–1939

When Belgium and Luxembourg were invaded in August 1914, Albrecht, Duke of Württemberg commanded the German Fourth Army. Albrecht, whose career progress had been facilitated by his royal connections, had pushed forward to the **Marne** by 5 September. Reconstituted after the battle, the Fourth Army remained under Albrecht's command during the 'Race to the Sea' and as trench warfare was established. On 22 April 1915, he launched a major attack at **Ypres**, notable for the first use of poisonous gas on the Western Front. Promoted field marshal in August 1916, Albrecht concluded his wartime service as commander of an army group on the relatively quiet southern wing of the Western Front.

ALEKSEEV, GENERAL MIKHAIL, 1857–1918

The son of a Russian officer who had been promoted from the ranks, Alekseev became a general in 1904. On the outbreak of war he was appointed chief of staff of the South-Western Army Group under **Ivanov**. He planned the initial operations in Galicia which drove back the Austrian Army but failed to destroy it. In March 1915, he was promoted to the command of the North-Western Front, where he displayed a reluctance to co-operate with his former colleagues to the south when the Germans broke through the Russian defences at **Gorlice** in May 1915. However, his reputation suffered less than most as the Germans advanced further during the summer and, in September, when the Tsar became commander-in-chief, he was appointed chief of staff.

In these circumstances, Alekseev was a far from ideal choice. 'He was not a powerful personality. Many complaints were made about his indecision and prolixity on paper.' Alekseev did, however, play a more active role in coordinating the three army groups than had previously been customary, even though he operated a basically defensive strategy. He gave reluctant support to the **Brusilov Offensive** and had no enthusiasm for shoring up the Rumanian army after its failures in the field. During the winter of 1916–17, Alekseev was absent from his post recovering from a serious illness, but returned in time to arrange the Tsar's abdication during the March Revolution.

He was appointed commander-in-chief by the new Provisional Government, but was dismissed in May because of his lack of real enthusiasm for an early offensive. After the Bolshevik revolution he helped to develop the White forces, but he died before the civil war had really begun.

ALEXANDER, PRINCE REGENT OF SERBIA, 1888–1934

Appointed Prince Regent of Serbia in July 1914, Alexander was nominally commander-in-chief of the Serbian army throughout the First World War. Although substantive responsibility for the direction of the country's military effort rested with **Field Marshal Radomir Putnik**, Alexander helped to preserve the army's morale during the retreat through Albania in 1915. As the Serbian forces returned in 1918, advancing from Salonika to Belgrade, Alexander's plans for a South Slav state came to fruition. On 1 December 1918, Yugoslavia was born and in 1921, on the death of his father, Alexander became king.

ALLENBY, FIELD MARSHAL EDMUND, 1st VISCOUNT, 1861–1936

Allenby's early wartime career in the British army was as undistinguished as his peacetime military service had been. As commander of the BEF cavalry in France he did not perform particularly well and in the operations around Mons, for example, it was said that 'his brigades lacked proper direction'. With a reputation for being 'an obedient agent of GHQ', he was appointed as the head of the Third Army in October 1915. It was a promotion owing more to the influence of **Sir John French**, the commander-in-chief, than to merit. Known as 'The Bull', because of his violent temper and great size, Allenby commanded a sector that remained relatively quiet until the **Battle of Arras**, which began on 9 April 1917. The opening stages of the battle were relatively successful, but it soon ran into serious difficulties. With little concern for the realities of the situation or the mounting casualties, Allenby continued to commit new troops once the opportunity for a breakthrough had passed, and it was **Haig** who was forced to suspend operations.

Field Marshal Allenby, the able conqueror of Palestine, enters Aleppo shortly after the end of the war

Soon afterwards, he was moved to Egypt as commander-in-chief, with instructions to reopen the offensive against Turkey. False rumours suggested that Haig, with whom Allenby was on poor terms, had arranged his removal from the Western Front, but **Lloyd George** had expressed his full confidence in him. The prime minister's judgement was soon to be vindicated. With orders to capture 'Jerusalem as a Christmas present for the British nation', he revitalised the Allied forces after their defeats at **Gaza** in March–April 1917, and a subsequent period of inaction. The capture of Beersheba (31 October 1917) marked the beginning of his first campaign, which secured Gaza before he advanced northwards to Jaffa and to the Holy City, which fell on 8 December. This much-needed Allied victory, which was Allenby's most important and difficult achievement, may be attributed in part to his 'singlemindedness and the wholehearted response of his troops'.

The German attacks on the Western Front in March 1918, which resulted in the transfer of many of Allenby's troops back to Europe, delayed his plans to press on towards **Damascus** and beyond, with the aim of destroying the remains of the Turkish army. The final offensive did not in fact begin until 19 September, when he broke through the Turkish lines at the **Battle of Megiddo**, the last mass cavalry action in military history. Advancing rapidly, with support on the eastern flank from Arab forces under T. E. Lawrence, he entered Damascus on 1 October. Before the end of the month, Aleppo, 400 miles to the north of Jerusalem, had been taken.

Allenby was hailed as one of the 'great captains of all ages' and was rewarded with a peerage and other honours. Although the praise of contemporaries was exaggerated, Allenby had established himself as an outstanding commander in Palestine. Freed from the constraints of the Western Front, he had developed almost beyond recognition in his first truly independent command.

AMERICAN EXPEDITIONARY FORCE

When the United States entered the war in April 1917 it was ill-prepared for a major military intervention in Europe. Its small, poorly equipped peacetime army was to be transformed under the direction of

'Doughboys' march from Meaux to the front, July 1918, as the American Expeditionary Force intervenes in strength on the Western Front for the first time

[handwritten note: → FAILED TO FIND PANCHO VILLA IN MEXICO!]

General Pershing, who had been appointed to command the American land forces in France. He arrived there in June and estimated that as many as three million men would need to be sent across the Atlantic, with a million arriving in less than a year. By the Armistice some two million 'doughboys' had in fact been brought to France, where they were trained and equipped; there were over 300,000 American casualties.

The American build-up in France was slow and Pershing was unwilling to commit his troops to the front until they were available in sufficiently large numbers to intervene decisively. He had also insisted on United States forces operating independently, but as the German onslaught of 1918 began he immediately placed his forces at the disposal of the Allies. (This change had the effect of delaying the creation of the American First Army until July 1918.) The AEF was concentrated in Eastern France to the east of Verdun, with general headquarters being located at Chaumont.

It was not until May 1918 that the AEF engaged in offensive action, when **Cantigny** was captured. This was followed by victories at Château-Thierry and **Belleau Wood**. Some 275,000 American troops were engaged in the **Second Battle of the Marne**, but only in September, when the **St Mihiel** salient was removed, did the AEF launch a major offensive within its own independently controlled sector. This preceded the final **Meuse-Argonne** offensive, where American progress was slow at first. During the second phase, following the reorganisation of the AEF into two armies, a faster advance was achieved. It was 'proof that the American army could produce leadership and staff work worthy of the gallant sacrifice of the fighting troops – the American nation in arms.'

AMIENS OFFENSIVE, 8 August – 4 September 1918

Following the removal of the Aisne salient (5 August) **Foch** turned his attention to Amiens, where the next major Allied blow was to fall. The need to free the Paris–Amiens railway, which was subject to frequent enemy artillery attack, as was Amiens itself, was one of the major aims of the operation. The Germans, who had been expecting an attack to the north in Flanders, were taken by surprise by the Amiens offensive. The well-planned attack, which began in foggy weather on 8 August, was

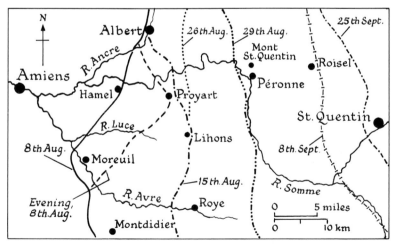

made by the British Fourth Army (**Rawlinson**) along a 14-mile front. The main blow was to be struck by the Canadians in the centre.

A brief artillery bombardment and an attack by 435 tanks preceded the assault by 11 British divisions and the left wing of the French First Army (Debeney) to the south. Opposing them were the German Second Army (**von der Marwitz**) and the right of the German Eighteenth Army (**von Hutier**), a total of 14 divisions with 9 in reserve. The enemy was forced back along the whole line and by the end of the first day the Allies had advanced by up to ten miles, with the Canadians being the most successful. Some progress was made by the French First Army to the right of Rawlinson.

During the 'Black day of the German army', battle-weary enemy troops had, at some points, fled from the front, and for the first time entire units disintegrated. As many as 6,000 prisoners had been taken and 100 guns seized. However, tank losses had been heavy and the RAF had suffered badly. On the next day, 24,000 German prisoners were taken and 200 guns captured, although the British advance slowed as the Germans re-established themselves.

On 10 August, the French Third Army (Humbert) joined the offensive, attacking the southern face of the salient, but by this time the enemy was already withdrawing. They recaptured Montdidier, enabling the Allies to use the Paris–Amiens railway once more. On 12 August, as progress came to a halt, the first phase of this offensive was ended. German losses amounted to about 40,000 killed and wounded and 33,000 taken prisoner. British losses were 22,000 and the French 24,000.

On 21 August, the British Third Army (**Byng**) to the north of Rawlinson and the First Army (Horne), even further north, joined in as the attack was renewed. The French Tenth and Third Armies also attacked again. In response to a significant advance by the British First Army, **Ludendorff** ordered a general withdrawal along the 55-mile front. He came under further pressure as the **Anzacs** advanced across the Somme on 30–31 August, taking Péronne and Mont St Quentin. Near Quéant, on the northern flank, the Canadian corps broke through on 2 September.

In these unfavourable circumstances the Germans, who had suffered heavy losses, were forced, on 3 September, to retire to the Hindenberg Line, their starting point in the March offensive, bringing the whole operation to a close. By 10 September, the Allies had closed up to the new line. The Amiens salient had been eliminated in a major Allied victory that finally convinced Ludendorff of the need to end the war. **Haig**, who had used all his available reserves, was unable to exploit the British victory further.

ANATRA D & DS

This two-seater tractor biplane, which first appeared early in 1916, was produced by the Anatra Company of Odessa for reconnaissance work with the Russian air service. Anatra drew heavily on contemporary German designs in developing the aircraft, which was also known as the Anade.

Armament consisted of one or two defensive machine-guns and it was powered by a 100hp Gnome Monosoupape rotary engine, which enabled it to climb to 2,000m in 15 minutes. Some machines were fitted with 130hp Clergets because of supply difficulties with the original engine. The manufacturers ran into difficulties with this later design. The engine often lost power because of cooling problems and the aircraft was nose heavy. More seriously, it suffered from wing failure caused by improvised construction methods, which resulted in several fatal crashes. Production was therefore ended after only 205 Ds had been delivered.

They were replaced by the Anatra DS, which appeared in the summer of 1917. Powered by a 150hp Salmson-built Canton-Unné engine, it was widely known as the Anasal (Anatra-Salmson) and was similar in appearance to its predecessor. It was armed with a synchronised **Vickers machine-gun** and a ring-mounted **Lewis gun** in the rear cockpit. Useful reconnaissance work was carried out by the DS, which was capable of matching the opposing Albatros fighters. Production was ended by the November Revolution, after about 100 had been produced.

ANDREA DORIA

An improved version of the Cavour-class battleship, *Caio Duilio* and *Andrea Doria* had the same main armament as their predecessors but larger 6-inch secondary guns. The central 12-inch triple turret was lowered by one deck level in order to maintain stability with these heavier medium weapons. Entering Italian naval service in 1915–16, these dread-nought battleships had an uneventful operational career during the remainder of the war.

ANSALDO A-1 BALILLA

The A-1 was the first Italian-designed single-seat fighter to enter service. A prototype of the small, single-bay biplane, with equal span wings constructed of wood and fabric, appeared late in 1917. Twin synchronised .303 **Vickers machine-guns** were mounted on each side of the fuselage top. The A-1 was equipped with the powerful 220hp SPA 6A engine which gave a high top speed of 137m.p.h. at 6,500 feet and a good rate of climb (10,000 feet in eight minutes). These characteristics were not matched by its manoeuvrability, which was poor in comparison with the French aircraft then in Italian service.

Modifications were made before it went into production, but the Balilla (or Hunter), as it was now named, was regarded as inferior to the **Hanriot HD-1**, the standard Italian fighter, and only 150 were manufactured. It was used by the Italian air force in 1918 for home defence duties, where its high speed was often used to good effect, and as a bomber escort.

ANSALDO SVA SERIES

The SVA (Savoia-Verduzio-Ansaldo) multi-purpose tractor biplanes, which first appeared in the autumn of 1917, represented an important stage in the development of the Italian aviation industry. Designed by Savoia and Verduzio and produced by Ansaldo, it had originally been conceived as a single-seat fighter, but was soon found to lack the required manoeuvrability. Speed and endurance were, however, excellent and it was adopted as a long-range reconnaissance and bomber aircraft.

The SVA 4 was the first production model, entering service in February 1918; it differed little from the main single-seat version, the SVA 5. Distinctive features of the SVA types were their diagonal interwing struts, the very limited use of wire bracing, and flared upper wings. The triangular section fuselage was tapered from cockpit to tail. The entire series, except for the SVA 10, was powered by the 220hp SPA 6A engine, which gave a maximum speed of 143m.p.h. at sea level and an endurance of four hours. Armament normally consisted of two synchronised **Vickers machine-guns**.

Equipped with one or two cameras, the SVA 4 and SVA 5 were widely used on photo-reconnaissance missions beyond the Alps and along the Adriatic; they also carried out a series of notable bombing raids against Germany and Austria, including attacks on Innsbrück and Bolzano in October 1918. SVAs were used intensively in the final campaigns of the war attacking enemy troops and installations and providing valuable photographic information. Their international reputation was established by the famous leaflet raid on Vienna in August 1918. Seven SVA 5s escorted a modified SVA 9 two-seater (normally used for training purposes) on the successful seven-hour journey.

The main two-seater variant was the SVA 10, which entered service in the summer of 1918; it was similar in appearance to the single-seaters, except for fuselage modifications. It was powered by a 250hp Isotta-Fraschini V6 engine and had a flexibly mounted **Lewis gun** in the rear cockpit. The SVA was the second most widely built Italian aircraft of the war; about 1,250 of all types (including a seaplane version) were produced. The basic soundness of the design was also confirmed by the fact that it remained in service with the Italian air force until 1935.

ANTHOINE, GENERAL FRANÇOIS, 1860–1944

Anthoine was chief of staff to General **Pétain**, commander-in-chief of the French army during the difficult period from November 1917 to July 1918, when the final German offensives were launched.

Although he spent most of the war as a staff officer, he commanded in the field during 1917. At the **third Battle of Ypres** in July his force served on the British left wing, where it 'acquitted itself excellently'.

ANTWERP, SIEGE OF, 28 September–9 October 1914

As the Germans advanced towards Brussels after the fall of **Liège**, the Belgian army (65,000 men), under **King Albert**, withdrew to the port of Antwerp, a huge fortress with a perimeter of 60 miles. It had a garrison of 80,000 second-line troops. Based here the field army would always be a potential threat to German communications, a fact demonstrated as early as 24 August when an attack was launched against the rear of the enemy's right wing. Of more significance was its sortie on 9 September – the critical day of the **Battle of the Marne** – which reminded the Germans of the urgent need to reduce Antwerp and seize the Channel ports. General Hans von Beseler, who was placed in command of the operation, had 173 heavy guns but only five divisions when the bombardment began on 28 September. The outlying forts were destroyed one by one by the Germans' powerful artillery as they advanced steadily towards the centre of the city.

Allied concern about the vulnerability of the Channel ports eventually led to British action; **Winston Churchill**, First Lord of the Admiralty, who had strongly urged intervention for some time, was authorised to send three naval brigades. These inadequate and ill-equipped reinforcements delayed the end but could not prevent it.

In the face of civil disorder, King Albert was forced to begin the evacuation of the city on the night of 6 October. The Belgian army's escape south-west down the Flanders coast was covered by a British force, under the command of **General Sir Henry Rawlinson**, which had originally been sent to relieve them but arrived too late. All the Belgian and British troops managed to leave, with the exception of one of the naval brigades which was interned in Holland. The city finally surrendered on 9 October.

Although its loss was a severe blow to the Allies, the delay in capitulating slowed the German advance to the coast. The British had time to move up from the Aisne and the Belgians could establish themselves on the extreme left of the line between Dixmunde and the sea; it may have made all the difference between defeat and victory in the imminent battles on the Yser and in front of Ypres.

ANZAC

The Australian and New Zealand Army Corps (ANZAC) was formed in Egypt, where its constituent forces had begun to arrive for training from November 1914 onwards. Under the command of General Birdwood, it consisted of two New Zealand brigades and 20,000 Australian troops. It was first employed at Gallipoli, where it landed on 25 April 1915, remaining there under continuous pressure from the Turks until it was evacuated from the peninsula eight months later.

ANZAC troops (four infantry divisions) were first sent to France in 1916, serving in the **First Battle of the Somme** and at **Arras**, **Messines** and **Ypres** in the following year. During the costly war of attrition on the Western Front in 1917, ANZAC suffered as many as 50,000 casualties. It made an important

CHURCHILL FIASCO LED
TO ANZAC SLAUGHTER!

contribution to halting the first German offensive of 1918 and was prominent in the Allied action at **Amiens** (August 1918); it also captured St Quentin and, in September, breached the Hindenburg Line with other Allied forces. ANZAC mounted troops were employed during the advance from Egypt into Palestine in 1916–18.

General Birdwood, the cheerful and stout-hearted ANZAC commander, who added to this reputation during the disasters at Gallipoli

ARAB REVOLT, 5 June 1916–31 October 1918

British wartime fortunes in the Middle East improved considerably in mid-1916 when the Sherif of Mecca raised a revolt in the Hejaz against Turkish rule. The Sherif had already done the British a service by refusing a Turkish request to declare a Holy War (Jihad) against them. The Arabs captured Jeddah on 12 June and Taif on 21 September, but they were unable to take Medina, the southernmost Turkish garrison, where resistance was particularly strong. These initial successes in Arabia encouraged the British to advance across Sinai to El Arish, which they reached by December 1916.

The arrival late in 1916 of **T. E. Lawrence**, who became chief of staff to **Feisal**, the commander of the Arab force, revived operations in the Hejaz, which were beginning to lose their momentum. Lawrence secured Arab agreement to a flanking move up the coast to Wejh, which would leave Medina in Turkish hands. From their new base they launched regular guerrilla attacks on the southern end of the Hejaz railway, forcing the Turks to abandon their plans to recapture Mecca and devote growing resources to defending their principal lifeline. To allow the Arabs to operate freely further north on the left flank of the Turkish forces opposing the British, it was first necessary to expel the enemy from the port of Aqaba on the Red Sea. Its capture by Lawrence in a surprise attack early in July 1917 meant that any danger to British communications in Sinai was removed and it enabled Feisal's forces, which had been moved round by the Royal Navy, to establish their base there. As Arab operations expanded during 1917–18, more Turkish forces were needed to guard the Hejaz railway and the territory to the south of it than were employed fighting the British in Palestine. An indication of the task facing the Turks was the fact that a 600-mile stretch of the line, from Medina to Amman, was subject to frequent raids.

Following the change in the British command in Palestine in June 1917, when **General Sir Edmund Allenby** succeeded **General Murray**, material support for the Arab revolt increased substantially. The armoured cars, machine-guns and other weapons they were provided with enabled the force of 6,000 Arabs to protect the British flank as they advanced through Palestine. It also put an end to German propaganda in south-west Arabia and removed any danger of a German submarine base on the Red Sea.

Lawrence and the Arabs provided more direct assistance to the British in the closing stages of the war in Palestine. During the **Battle of Megiddo** (16–17 September 1918), they blew up the railway north, south and west of Deraa, stopping the flow of Turkish supplies. The Arabs marched on **Damascus** capturing the remnants of the Turkish Fourth Army as it retreated from the battle, and arrived in the

Turkish prisoners captured in one of the minor engagements that preceded the Battle of Megiddo, September 1918

capital on 1 October shortly before Allenby's forces. Relations between the two forces soon became strained when it transpired that one of the political rewards – Syria – expected by the Arabs had already been allocated to the French by the terms of a secret agreement with the British.

ARISAKA RIFLE

The standard infantry weapon of the Japanese army during the First World War, the Arisaka rifle was adopted in 1895 as the Meiji 30, replacing the obsolete Murata gun. It was a five-round magazine rifle in 6.5mm calibre and had been produced by a group headed by Colonel Arisaka. The influence of Western ideas in the design was particularly strong,

with **Mauser** and **Mannlicher** features being clearly in evidence.

A quantity of the weapons did in fact end up in Europe during the early stages of the war when Britain ordered them for training purposes. Its rapidly growing army used the improved 1905 rifle and carbine as well as the original pattern.

ARMED MERCHANT CRUISER

During the First World War merchant ships were commandered in large numbers as naval auxiliaries, with many of the faster vessels being used as armed merchant cruisers (AMCs). Passenger liners and merchant ships were both converted for this purpose,

being equipped with medium size naval guns. They relieved regular cruisers in carrying out patrol duties and the German navy, in particular, used them to attack merchant ships and troop convoys.

Actions between AMCs were relatively rare, but

one notable example occurred at the beginning of the war, in September 1914, when HMS *Carmania* sank the German *Cap Trafalgar* after a hard-fought battle in the South Atlantic. AMCs did, however, suffer from a number of weaknesses, including the absence of armour protection and relatively poor armament. In the latter stages of the war, as submarine operations intensified, they were reassigned to other work. The Germans turned to decoy vessels as an alternative to the increasingly vulnerable AMCs.

The armed merchant cruiser Carmania, *formerly a Cunard transatlantic liner, was taken over by the Royal Navy at the start of the war*

ARMISTICE

Terms for the suspension of fighting between the Allies and Germany were signed at **Marshal Foch's** headquarters, a railway carriage in the Forest of Compiègne, on 11 November 1918 ('the eleventh hour of the eleventh day of the eleventh month').

Germany and Austro-Hungary had first proposed an armistice to **President Woodrow Wilson** on 4 October, but the terms of his reply were less favourable than they had expected: acceptance of his **Fourteen Points** and their withdrawal from foreign territory were among the main preconditions. However, the deteriorating military situation and the outbreak of mutiny and revolution forced Germany's hand and she was compelled to accept the Allied terms.

These included the immediate evacuation of all occupied territory, including Alsace-Lorraine, and the occupation of Germany west of the Rhine. All U-boats were to be surrendered and the **High Seas Fleet** was to be disarmed and interned. Large quantities of arms, equipment and transport were to be surrendered. The treaties of **Brest-Litovsk** with Russia and of Bucharest with Rumania, which had been dictated by the Germans, were set aside.

Hostilities in other theatres of the war were brought to an end by separate armistice agreements which the Allies signed with: Bulgaria, on 29 September 1918 at Salonika; Turkey, on 30 October 1918 on Mudros; Austro-Hungary, on 3 November 1918 at Padua.

Earlier in the war, the Central Powers had them-selves signed armistice agreements with Russia (at Brest-Litovsk, on 15 December 1917) and with Rumania (9 December 1917).

The railway carriage – Marshal Foch's headquarters – in which the Armistice agreement was signed on 11 November 1918 arriving at Compiègne station

ARMOURED CAR

A variety of experimental armoured cars had appeared in the years before the First World War, but in August 1914 the principal combatants had very few examples at their disposal. As the German army advanced through Belgium, the small defending army used fast touring cars on hit-and-run raids. The Royal Naval Air Service also used standard cars on recon-naissance duties, to protect their bases and to rescue crashed airmen. During these missions both the Belgians and British came into contact with the enemy and it soon became clear that these unmodified vehicles were too vulnerable for operational use.

Armour was soon being fitted locally to provide greater protection, but these improvised vehicles were quickly superseded by specially designed ones.

A typical vehicle consisted of an armoured box, possibly incorporating a turret, which was built on a strengthened car chassis; armament was normally a single machine-gun. There were few further inno-vations in armoured car design during the war apart from four-wheel drive and half-tracks. Heavier armoured vehicles, based on commercial vehicle chassis, were also built by Britain and France; a 47mm quick firing gun was normally fitted. The latter were retained on the Western Front as mobile artillery long after the standard armoured car had virtually disappeared. The static conditions in France meant that from the end of 1914 there was no longer any real place for these vehicles on the main battle front.

This did not, however, apply on the Eastern Front and both the British and Belgians sent armoured car forces there. The Russians themselves had always been in the forefront of armoured car development and had a supply of vehicles available from the beginning of the war. The **Rolls Royce** and **Lanchester** armoured cars that formed the backbone of the RNAS division in Europe were also employed in Palestine, **South-West Africa**, and **East Africa**, where the greater fluidity of the military situation was much more favourable to their use. They returned to the Western Front in small numbers in the changed circumstances of 1918; at **Amiens**, for example, a group of armoured cars successfully attacked behind the enemy's lines, demonstrating their unrealised potential.

ARMSTRONG WHITWORTH FK3

The FK3 was a two-seater tractor biplane which served with the RFC and RNAS from September 1916 until the end of the war. Designed for bombing and reconnaissance duties, it was known as 'Little Ack' to distinguish it readily from the larger **Armstrong Whitworth FK8**. Most FK3s were powered by the 90hp RAF 1a engine, which gave a maximum speed of 87m.p.h. at sea level, but a few had the 120hp Beardmore. The observer, who occupied the rear cockpit, was armed with a .303 **Lewis machine-gun**. It could also carry a bomb load in excess of 220lb.

Although the FK3's performance was generally superior to that of the **Royal Aircraft Factory BE2c**, which it was intended to supplement, its only operational use was in Macedonia, where it was employed on bombing, reconnaissance and artillery spotting duties. The RFC used most of the 499 FK3s produced as trainers, a role for which they were admirably suited.

ARMSTRONG WHITWORTH FK8

The Armstrong Whitworth FK8 was a two-seater tractor biplane designed for reconnaissance and bombing duties, which served with the RFC from late in 1916. Known as 'Big Ack', it was an expanded version of the Armstrong Whitworth FK3 ('Little Ack'), and was powered by a 160hp Beardmore engine, which produced a maximum speed of 98m.p.h. at sea level. It included a fixed, forward firing .303 **Vickers machine-gun** mounted in the fuselage and a .303 **Lewis gun** on a Scarff ring for the observer in the rear seat. External racks held a bomb load of up to 200lb.

The 'Big Ack' was well constructed, reliable and capable of being used effectively in several different roles – reconnaissance, day and night bombing, contact patrol, and ground attack. It was comparable in function and superior in performance to the **Royal Aircraft Factory RE8**, but never achieved the same prominence. In fact, only five squadrons on the Western Front were equipped with it during the battles of 1917 and 1918. Although the FK8 proved itself in combat and featured in two Victoria Cross actions, large numbers remained in storage. It was also used in Macedonia and Palestine and on home defence duties.

ARNAULD DE LA PERIÈRE, LOTHAR VON, 1886–1941

The most successful submarine commander of the First World War, Arnauld de la Perière sank as many as 189 Allied merchant ships, mainly by gunfire, while serving in U-35, from November 1915 to March 1918. Awarded the Pour le Mérite for his achieve-ments, this ace of aces commanded U-139, a cruiser submarine, during the last six months of the war. He also served in the German navy during the Second World War, rising to the rank of vice-admiral before being killed in an air crash early in 1941.

ARRAS, BATTLE OF, 9 April–16 May 1917

The main Allied offensive of 1917, planned by **General Nivelle**, the French commander-in-chief, was to be launched on the **Aisne** on 16 April. A week earlier, the British army launched a diversionary attack at Arras, with the aim of diverting large numbers of German reserves to the north. The Germans now occupied a heavily fortified defensive position – the Hindenburg Line or *Siegfried Stellung* – to which they had withdrawn during the period from 23 February to 5 April 1917.

Following a massive five-day artillery bombard-ment, using 2,800 guns, **Haig**'s offensive began on 9 April on a 14-mile front. Six divisions of the German Sixth Army (Falkenhausen) faced the 14 divisions of the British First Army (Horne) and the Third Army (**Allenby**). The Germans also had fewer aircraft than the RFC although they were superior machines. North of Arras, to the left, the Canadian Corps (**Byng**), part of the First Army, seized a section of Vimy Ridge after three hours' heavy fighting. In the centre near Arras, the Third Army advanced $3\frac{1}{2}$ miles into German-held territory, the biggest gain since trench warfare had begun in 1914. To the south of the River Scarpe very little progress was made. The gains in the north were extended on 12 April, but in the centre resistance was stronger than had been expected and the front there was almost stationary.

Haig's plans for an immediate further attack were put off with the arrival of German reserves. However, the British held their ground and maintained pressure on the Germans as the Nivelle offensive was launched. The second phase of the battle began on 23/24 April,

when, during fierce fighting, a mile was added to the British gains all along the front. To the right of the Third Army, **Gough**'s Fifth Army had attacked the German Second Army from 11 April, but made no progress in breaching the Hindenburg Line at Bulle-court; subsequent attempts in May also failed.

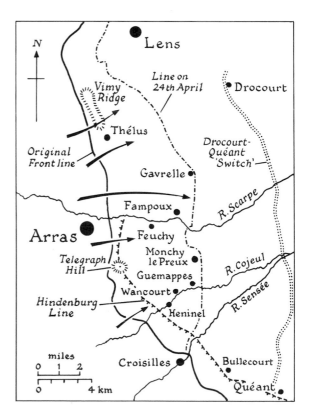

In order to encourage the French to continue fighting on the Aisne and to divert attention from British preparations for an offensive at **Ypres**, Haig renewed the action once more on 3 May. It was a failure: there was only one small gain – Fresnoy – but fighting continued on a reduced scale until the end of May. By the time it had finally died out, the British had lost 150,000 men and the Germans well over 100,000. The northern six miles of the Hindenburg Line had been seized, along with a large number of prisoners, in this costly battle of attrition.

British infantry moves up in formation on the first day of the Battle of Arras

ARTILLERY

The First World War was an artillery war in which medium and heavy guns played a key role. In the opening stages of the conflict, the German army successfully attacked the **Liège** fortress and other Belgian fortifications with massive 42cm howitzers. The first tactical surprise of the war, '**Big Bertha**', was larger than any previous gun used by a field army, having been transported in five separate loads and assembled on site.

The Allies had given priority to field artillery, of which the **French 75** was the most notable example, but in the static conditions of trench warfare medium and heavy artillery, particularly howitzers, firing high explosive shells, came into their own. Typical of the huge, immobile weapons in use at the front was the British 12-inch siege howitzer, which fired a 750lb shell over 14,300 yards. Each side shelled the other's trenches regularly, but the huge artillery bombardments associated with the war on the Western Front were normally a prelude to major offensives designed to achieve a breakthrough. The **Third Battle of Ypres** (July–November 1917), for example, began with a 19-day bombardment, using as many as 4,300,000 shells – a year's output for 55,000 munitions workers, which was carried to the front in 321 trains.

As the war progressed there were major advances in the use of artillery, in terms of command and control, the location of targets, and accuracy of fire. An example of the former was the creeping barrage, introduced at the Somme in 1916, which allowed the artillery and infantry to co-operate more closely in an attack. A 'tremendous curtain of fire' moved slowly ahead of the ground troops at an agreed rate, allowing them to advance with much greater protection.

In spite of these innovations, massive artillery attacks often achieved relatively little. Important in

British 9.2-inch gun in action during the Battle of the Somme, July 1916

the first part of the war was the fact that British artillery shells were in short supply and were of often of very poor quality. They churned up the ground and when combined with rain adversely affected the progress of advancing forces. The prime aim of such attacks – the destruction of the enemy's barbed wire – was not always achieved and his fortifications often survived intact. German defence in-depth tactics involved pulling back their front line troops when a bombardment began, and sending them forward again as soon as the shell fire had lifted and the Allies began to advance. Perhaps the most successful use of artillery occurred during the German offensives of 1918 when the brief 'hurricane bombardment' featured as a part of German shock tactics, causing the maximum disruption to Allied defences.

Railway guns supported heavy artillery at the front. Varying in size from 8–12-inch they were moved around rapidly to confuse the enemy and to support sectors under particularly heavy pressure; some were long-range guns developed to attack rear areas. The most famous long-range artillery piece was the Paris gun; too large to be railway mounted, it operated up to 68 miles from the French capital and fired 367 shells at the city between March–August 1918.

Another artillery weapon which first made an impact during the war, although it was developed shortly before it, was the anti-aircraft gun. They were often mounted on truck chassis so that slow-moving airships and balloons could be pursued. There were, however, considerable practical problems in operating these mobile guns successfully on the Western Front. Hitting aerial targets proved to be difficult until sights were improved, but German AA guns shot down as many as 1,600 aircraft during the war.

The most numerous type of artillery, the field gun, was of limited value on the Western Front once trench warfare had begun, its firepower being unable to destroy the heavily protected trenches. However, in other theatres – the Eastern Front and in the Middle East, for example – field artillery could still play its proper role in supporting other arms.

A 75mm anti-aircraft gun, which exacted a heavy toll of German machines, on a camouflaged lorry mounting

ARTOIS, BATTLE OF, 9–15 May 1915

While the **Second Battle of Ypres** was in progress, **Joffre** made preparations for another major offensive in Artois, which began on 9 May. A massive artillery bombardment preceded the attack by nine divisions of the French Tenth Army (General D'Urbal) on a six-mile front between Lens and Arras. The main assault in the centre, which was made by a corps commanded by **General Pétain**, broke through by a depth of up to three miles within 90 minutes, almost reaching the crest of Vimy Ridge. Elsewhere, however, the attack had been quickly checked. Without sufficient reserves immediately available, the French were unable to exploit their partial victory and as the Germans brought up reinforcements they were forced back some distance. A costly battle of attrition, with neither side making any real progress, lasted until 15 May, and was resumed on 15 June for four days. By the time it had been called off, the French had lost just over 100,000 men, while German casualties (75,000) were significantly less.

Fifteen miles to the north, the much smaller British share of the operation began at the same time as the French, but because of a shortage of shells their opening bombardment was completely inadequate, and lasted only 40 minutes compared with their ally's five days. The British First Army (**Haig**) attacked north and south of Neuve Chapelle towards the Aubers ridge. It made little progress because of the strength of the German defences and the lack of artillery support; fortunately, the British recognised that their situation was very unfavourable and the attack was broken off on the first day, with 11,000 casualties.

However, mindful of the need to co-operate fully with the French and under pressure from Joffre, the British had no immediate plans to abandon this offensive altogether. It was in fact renewed on 15 May along a three-mile front near Festubert, south of Neuve Chapelle. Sufficient ammunition had been found for a four-day bombardment and the opening night's attack made some progress. By the time the British operation had ended on 27 May some $\frac{3}{4}$ mile had been gained from the Germans at a cost of 16,000 casualties.

Major Allied action was suspended over the summer to give the British and French armies an opportunity to reorganise and replenish their supplies; there were no large-scale offensives until September, when attacks in **Artois** and **Champagne** were launched.

ARTOIS-LOOS, BATTLE OF, 25 September – 4 November 1915

Joffre's major autumn offensive in **Champagne** was to be accompanied by coordinated Angle-French attacks on German positions in Artois, which also began on 25 September 1915. The French Tenth Army (**Dubail**) attacked positions held by the German Sixth Army (**Crown Prince Rupprecht**) and one division managed to reach the crest of Vimy Ridge; overall, however, little progress was made and once the strength of the defence was discovered the French called off the action, with the loss of 48,000 men. The French took over part of the British front to the north, but did not renew the offensive because of the need to move troops to the Balkans.

Douglas Haig, who had expressed major objections to the British part in the offensive because of the shell shortage and the unsuitability of the terrain, launched an assault with six divisions at the same time as the French. The British used poison gas for the first time, with mixed results, as in places it drifted back and affected their own troops.

On the right the village of Loos was overrun and the suburbs of Lens were reached; the First Army also had some success in the centre, but on the right, on either side of the La Bassée canal, there was complete failure. With a seven-to-one superiority, they had in places reached the German rear lines by the end of the first day but were brought to a halt because no reserves were immediately available. For reasons of 'personal jealousy', **Sir John French**, the BEF commander, had kept them under his own control 16 miles to the rear and they could not be employed until the next day, after a long and arduous night march.

Without effective artillery support, an unsuccessful assault was launched against the German second lines which had been reinforced overnight, and the British were forced back. The action was renewed on 13 October but 'brought nothing but useless slaughter of infantry'. The onset of winter weather fortunately prevented any further action, the British having already lost over 50,000 men. German losses amounted to no more than 20,000, a reflection of their better organisation, more plentiful supplies of ammunition and superior machine-gun tactics. The failure at Loos led to the downfall of Sir John French later in the year. His relationship with Haig, the man who was to replace him, was undermined by his delay in releasing reserves during the battle. In his official account of the battle, French compounded the error by misrepresenting the time at which he had actually handed them over to Haig.

ARZ von STRAUSSENBURG, GENERAL ARTHUR, BARON, 1857–1935

Chief of Staff of the Austro-Hungarian army from March 1917 until the end of the war, Arz was 'more pliable and pleasant mannered' than his predecessor, **Conrad von Hotzendorff**. During his earlier war service, in 1914–15, Arz had led VI Army Corps against the Russians and had commanded the First Army during the invasion of Rumania in 1916. As chief of staff, with the situation in the East stabilised, he planned the successful attack on the Italian front at **Caporetto** in October 1917. Further offensive operations at the **Piave River** in the following June were unsuccessful, and during his final months in office he presided over the disintegration of the Austrian army.

ASIAGO, BATTLE OF, 15 May–25 June 1916

Major action on the Italian front before the end of 1917 was, with one significant exception, concentrated on the **Isonzo River**: **Conrad**'s offensive in the Trentino, which began on 15 May 1916. Fifteen Austrian divisions were concentrated there early in 1916 for a major attack which had, as its immediate objective, the occupation of the northern Italian plain and the city of Padua. It would then be possible to cut off the Italian army on the Isonzo River and elsewhere on the front, bringing closer Italy's defeat and withdrawal from the war.

Under **Archduke Eugen**, Army Group Commander, the Austrian Eleventh Army (**Dankl**) and the Third Army (**Kövess**) initially made good progress, advancing on a 40-mile front, with up to five miles being gained by the fifth day. Although aware of a build-up of enemy troops, the attack took the Italian First Army completely by surprise; commanded by General Roberto Brusati, it fell back under the weight of the Austrian attack, which was supported by a considerable superiority in heavy artillery. By 31 May, Asiago, the gateway at the foot of the Dolomite Alps, had fallen, with Arsiero to the south-west being taken on the same day.

In the face of impending disaster, **Cadorna**, the Italian chief of staff, responded effectively. Making full use of the excellent rail network, he quickly concentrated all his available troops in order to meet the Austrian threat. As a result of Italian efforts and the difficult terrain, the pace of the advance began to lessen and by 3 June it had been checked. A week later, the immediate need to move Austrian troops to the Eastern Front to stem the **Brusilov Offensive** brought the campaign to an end; Eugen was forced to withdraw his troops to new defensive positions not far from their original starting point.

A final assault on the new front line was mounted by the Italian Eighth Army on 25 June, but the Austrians could not be dislodged. The cost of halting the Austrians was high – with Italian losses of 147,000 men – and shocked public opinion, leading directly to the fall of the Prime Minister, **Salandra**. Cadorna did, however, seize the opportunity to strike back at the Austrians, launching an offensive against their weakened lines on the Isonzo on 6 August 1915. The value of any limited Austrian gains in the Trentino was further reduced by the fact that their position on the Russian Front had been considerably weakened.

ASQUITH, HERBERT, 1st EARL OF OXFORD, 1852–1928

British Prime Minister from April 1908, Asquith was faced with a variety of complex problems – including Ireland, the suffragettes and industrial strife – that threatened to overwhelm his government before they were swept to one side on the outbreak of the First World War. At first, Asquith's management of the war effort was uncontroversial, but as it became clear that a long war of attrition was in prospect, difficulties began to emerge.

Lack of preparation for a conflict of this character produced severe supply problems: the notorious shell shortage in France was one of the main reasons for the demise of the Liberal government in May 1915. The failure of the naval phase of the **Dardanelles** expedition was the other major factor that forced Asquith to include several Conservatives and one Labour minister in his reconstituted government.

However, the new coalition proved to be little more successful in its wartime role than its predecessor. There were major political divisions within the Cabinet about war strategy, with Asquith himself firmly committed to the view that victory could only be achieved by defeating the enemy on the Western Front. The issue of **conscription** and Irish Home Rule also caused bitter conflicts.

Asquith's reputation declined steadily as the slaughter of British troops in France increased during 1916, with a campaign against him, led by **Lloyd George**, gathering momentum as the costly **Somme offensive** failed. Asquith also lost the support of leading Conservatives who sought his replacement by a more effective and dynamic war leader. He finally resigned in December 1916, after a secret proposal to put control of the war effort under a council chaired by Lloyd George had been urged on him and then publicised. As leader of the opposition for the remainder of the war period, Asquith's criticisms of the government's conduct were relatively muted, although his feud with Lloyd George was to have disastrous longterm implications for the future of the Liberal party.

Asquith, leader of the coalition government, on a tour of inspection in France a few months before his downfall

ATLANTIC, BATTLE OF THE, 1915–17

The main surface fleets of Britain and Germany were used cautiously during the First World War, acting mainly as blockading forces: they met in battle only at **Jutland** and on four other occasions. The German navy turned to the **submarine** to increase economic pressure on Britain, waging a three-year war against Allied merchant ships in the Atlantic Ocean and elsewhere.

The U-boat blockade of Britain began on 18 February 1915; from that date Allied shipping of all kinds which entered the 'war zone' – defined loosely as all the approaches to the British Isles – was to be torpedoed without warning. Among the victims of this first campaign were an American tanker and a number of American citizens, passengers on two British liners, the *Lusitania* and the *Arabic*, that were sunk by the Germans. These incidents outraged American opinion and brought her intervention in the war closer.

Following the destruction of the second passenger ship on 19 August, the Germans were in fact compelled, on 1 September 1915, to announce the ending of unrestricted submarine warfare. In future, no liners would be attacked without warning and the safety of non-combatants would be assured, as long as no resistance was offered. The destruction of Allied merchant vessels, which were unaffected by these changes, continued to rise and a million tons of shipping were lost in 1915–16. Following the sinking of the *Sussex*, a cross-Channel steamer, in the spring of 1916, **President Wilson** secured a promise from Germany that it would not attack any more merchantmen without warning and would do its 'utmost to confine the operations of war for the rest of its duration to the fighting forces of the belligerents'.

However, pressure from the navy to reintroduce unrestricted submarine warfare grew during 1916 as it became clear that Germany could not hope to win the war by the efforts of its army alone.

After considerable internal debate, its resumption was authorised from 1 February 1917, on the assumption that Britain would be starved out within six months, well before the American intervention could become effective. Allied shipping losses did in fact begin to rise at an alarming rate: 259 in February, 325 in March and 423 in April, when losses reached a peak. This was well in excess of the rate of replacement and Britain was in danger of being cut off. Counter-measures, which included the use of improved **mines**, hydrophones and **depth charges**, were not sufficient in themselves to provide the protection required.

The Royal Navy had been long opposed to the introduction of the **convoy system** but it proved to be the only way of winning the battle against the U-boat in the Atlantic. Following the intervention of the Prime Minister, **Lloyd George**, convoys were introduced on 10 May 1917 and shipping losses gradually diminished during the year as the system was extended, covering eventually neutral as well as Allied ships. By the last quarter of 1917 the destruction of Allied shipping tonnage was running at little more than half that of six months earlier. Helped by the laying of new minefields, to which the Americans made a large contribution, losses continued to fall in the following year and by May 1918 the Allies were building more shipping than were being destroyed by U-boats. The Battle of the Atlantic had been won and the threat to Britain's lifeline was virtually over.

AUFFENBERG VON KOMARÓW, FIELD MARSHAL MORITZ, BARON, 1852–1928

The Austro-Hungarian army's defeat at Rava Russka during the Lemburg campaign in September 1914

ended Field Marshal Auffenberg's brief wartime career. The Russians had advanced between him and the forces of **General Dankl**, resulting in the withdrawal of the Austrians to the Carpathian mountains. He was removed from his command soon afterwards. Auffenberg's main military achievement was his contribution to the modernisation of the Austrian army during his short term as war minister in 1911–12.

AUGAGNEUR, JEAN, 1855–1931

French Minister of Marine from the early days of the war, Jean Augagneur had been first appointed to the Cabinet in 1911. Like **Churchill**, Augagneur's reputation suffered as a result of his role in planning and approving his country's involvement in the **Dardanelles operation**. His position was further weakened by the absence of an effective French naval response to the growing activities of German submarines throughout the Mediterranean. As a result, when the government of **René Viviani** fell in October 1915, Augagneur went with it; he was replaced by **Admiral Lacaze**. Jean Augagneur never returned to government but retained his seat in the Chamber of Deputies until 1919.

AUSTIN ARMOURED CAR

Soon after the outbreak of war the Austin Motor Company produced a prototype armoured car at the request of the Russian government. A series of production orders followed, the first examples appearing in October 1914; deliveries ceased after the November Revolution. Built on the Austin 30hp 'Colonial' chassis, the armoured car's most distinctive feature was its twin cylindrical turrets, each fitted with a **Vickers machine-gun**; the driver's cab had sloping sides and at the rear the hull was square. It was operated by a crew of five. A second version had a shortened cab and other changes to the hull.

Some of these vehicles were subsequently modified by the Russians, who rebuilt them with thicker armour plate and repositioned the turrets to improve the field of fire. In this form they were known as the Austin-Putilov, after the armament works which made the changes. This factory was also responsible for converting some of the original Austin and Austin-Putilov vehicles to half-tracks. These were the first half-tracked armoured cars to have appeared anywhere and they proved to be highly mobile at the front.

Austin vehicles on order at the time of the Revolution were deployed elsewhere: some went to Persia but early in 1918 a number equipped the 17th Battalion Tank Corps in the absence of any available tanks. The latter were equipped with **Hotchkiss machine-guns** in place of the Vickers and first saw action in France on 11 June. Used to great effect in operations behind enemy lines during the summer of 1918, their success was underlined when the vehicles led the British army across the frontier into Germany after the Armistice. The Austin, which was produced in larger numbers than any other British armoured car, continued in service after the war and was soon in action again in Ireland.

AUSTRO-HUNGARIAN AIR SERVICE

Small, under-funded and dependent on German support in 1914, the Austro-Hungarian *Luftfahrtruppen* (Aviation troops), under the command of Emil Uzelac, were ill-equipped to fight a major war. The air service and manufacturing base were expanded during the First World War, but Austria always remained in a position of relative weakness, her difficulties increasing when Italy entered the war in 1915.

There had been delays in forming independent fighter groups and by 1917, for example, the *Luftfahrtruppen* had no more than seven such *Jagdkompagnien*, equipped with 16–20 single-seaters each. Even though this was ultimately increased to 14 companies, Austria was unable to challenge Italy's dominance of the skies during 1918. Reconnaissance companies (*Aufklarungskompagnien*), to which priority was given, along with their fighter escorts, and the bomber companies (*Fliegerkompagnien G*) were the other major components of the Austrian service. The latter were responsible for the daylight and night raids on Milan and other cities and towns in northern Italy made throughout the war.

The separate naval air arm established five naval air stations during the war, including the central base near Pola, from where it launched reconnaissance and bombing missions against Italy. The service, which had 173 operational machines at the end of the war, made extensive use of seaplanes produced by **Lohner**, the Austrian aircraft manufacturer.

AUSTRO-HUNGARIAN ARMY

An essential prop of the Habsburg monarchy, the Austro-Hungarian army of 1914 was a conscript force of 49 infantry and 11 cavalry divisions. Unlike the German military machine, on which it was modelled, it lacked national cohesion and reflected the racial diversity of Austro-Hungary itself: Germans, Magyars, Czechs, Poles and several other nationalities were represented. These racial groups spanned the borders of Austro-Hungary and it was often necessary to redeploy troops to avoid a situation where they might refuse to fight their own kinsmen. German was the official language, but only a minority was fluent in it. However, it was not until the last year of the war that the army's operations were to be significantly affected by its racial mixture.

A more immediate problem confronting the army's chief of staff, **Conrad**, was the length of Austria's borders and how they might best be defended. It was decided that both enemies – Russian and Serbia – should be engaged simultaneously and Austria's six armies were deployed accordingly. The three stronger were positioned in **Galicia**, while the others were used against Serbia, on the assumption that Austria's smaller neighbour would soon be disposed of. In fact, she proved to be a worthy adversary and the Austrian army was unable to conquer the country in 1914. Russian strength was even more formidable and the Austrian army was quickly forced to abandon Galicia and retreat into the Carpathians.

True to its 'tradition of defeat rather than of victory', very severe losses were sustained in the first few months of the war. The professional core of the army was seriously weakened. From this low point, it underwent, with German support, a programme of reconstruction and expansion. By the end of 1916, five million men had been mobilised and 20 new divisions created; the provision of artillery and other equipment had been greatly improved.

With Italy's entry into the war in May 1915, a third front opened, creating serious difficulties in balancing the manpower needs of the three theatres. As a result, during the counter-offensive against the Russians in 1915, the Austrians were less successful than the Germans in pushing them back. Serbia finally fell in October 1915, but not without German and Bulgarian assistance. In 1916, Austrian defensive positions required German support during the **Brusilov offensive** and, as a result, the latter's requests for a unified command on the Eastern Front now had to be agreed to. As the war in the east ended in 1917, the Austrian army turned its attention to the Italian front, where it achieved a notable breakthrough at **Caporetto** after the long war of attrition on the **Isonzo**.

By the beginning of 1918, the army still appeared to be in a relatively strong position after four years of war; successes had been achieved on all fronts even though the human cost had been high. However, revolutionary and nationalistic stirrings on the home front and in the army were followed by the failure of the June offensive on the **Piave** to extend earlier

Austrian gains. Morale at the front declined rapidly as the supply system broke down in the face of internal unrest and impending political collapse. By the time the Allies launched their final offensive towards **Vittorio Veneto** in October 1918, some of the national contingents had already decided to abandon a war of which they wanted no further part. Within days, the Austro-Hungarian army had ceased to exist and the formal Armistice provision of an organised demobilisation did not accord with reality.

AUSTRO-HUNGARIAN NAVY

Although the main function of the small Austro-Hungarian navy had always been defensive – to protect the coast against a possible Italian attack – there were influential officers before the First World War who argued that it should have a more active role. Expansion plans – including the construction of dreadnoughts – were approved in 1911, but had to be abandoned on the outbreak of war. Wartime operations were restricted because of the fact that Austria's naval forces in the Adriatic were soon bottled up by the Allies, who held the Otranto Straits. In fact, apart from the three separate operations on which they were employed, Austria's capital ships were inactive at Pola, the principal base, throughout the war. It did mean, however, that several Allied battleships were needed at Taranto and Brindisi for over three years.

At the beginning of the war, the Austrian fleet left to go south with the intention of escorting the German Mediterranean Squadron back to Pola. However, **Souchon**, the German commander, decided to go on to Constantinople. The second operation – a major shore bombardment – was mounted when Italy declared war on Austro-Hungary on 23 May 1915. Finally, a raid was launched on the Otranto barrage in June 1918, but was abandoned following the sinking of a battleship.

The routine wartime work of the Austrian navy consisted of regular destroyer and torpedo boat patrols, which sought to deny the Allies access to the area. Their efforts were supplemented by the navy's air arm, which was relatively well developed and successful. At the end of the war, the Austrian fleet formed the nucleus of the navy of the new Yugoslav state, but following Allied objections many of the ships were re-allocated to Italy and France.

AVERESCU, LIEUTENANT-GENERAL ALEXANDRU, 1859–1938

Rumania's greatest soldier of the First World War, Averescu had been chief of staff during the Balkan Wars and previously minister of war. On Rumania's declaration of war in August 1916, he became commander of the Fourth Army and led it into Transylvania. During a lull in the fighting there he conceived and executed a bold plan to attack **Mackensen**'s army in the south, but was unsuccessful. He returned to the north to head the defensive operations against the Germans.

Early in December 1916 Averescu covered **Prezan**'s bold attack on the enemy near Bucharest before being forced to retire to the north-east, where

Military defeat late in 1916 left Averescu with no more than a fragment of Rumania to defend

his Second Army successfully held on to a small fraction of the country adjoining the Russian border. He added to his reputation during the offensive of July 1917, particularly in his planning of the successful defensive actions at Marasesti and Marasti. In February 1918, he succeeded **Bratianu** as prime minister in the hope that he might be able to secure more favourable peace terms, but was quickly ousted when it became clear that he was unable to do so.

AVIATIK BI & BII

This two-seat, unarmed reconnaissance aircraft was a pre-war design that was used widely on the Western and Eastern Fronts during the first few months of the war. Built by the German Aviatik company and a subcontractor, it had a 100hp Mercedes D I tractor engine, two- or three-bay swept back wings and a triangular fin. The BII, which first appeared at the end of 1914, was powered by a 160hp Mercedes D II engine and had an improved airframe.

Closely related to this model was the two-seater B-type series designed and manufactured by Aviatik's Austro-Hungarian subsidiary. Produced in BII and BIII forms from 1915, these long-range reconnaissance aircraft gave useful service, particularly on the Russian front. The BIII was the first of either the German or Austrian series to be equipped with a machine-gun – a ring-mounted **Schwarzlose** – and it also carried three 22lb bombs. They were withdrawn from active service in 1917, but some were retained by the Austro-Hungarian air service for training purposes.

AVIATIK CI & CIII

This German-built, armed two-seater biplane, which appeared early in 1915, was the first Aviatik aircraft to be produced in substantial numbers. Related to the earlier German **Aviatik B-types**, it was powered by the 160hp Mercedes D III engine, which gave a maximum speed of 89m.p.h. and a ceiling of 11,480 feet. It had unequal span, two bay wings, a kidney shape tailplane, and a vee-type undercarriage. Crew positions were the reverse of what was by now standard, with the observer being positioned at the front. He was equipped with a **Parabellum** machine-gun which could be moved between two separate rails on each side of his cockpit.

A CII version with a 200hp Benz Bz IV engine appeared in 1916, but the CIII was the next model to be produced in quantity. Entering service in 1916, the new design was powered by the same 160hp Mercedes engine as the CI, but its cleaner lines increased maximum speed by 11m.p.h. The CI's outmoded seating arrangement was adopted at first, but was later reversed; the observer now had two machine-guns, one on each rail. The Aviatik C-types served with German reconnaissance units on the Western Front until 1917 and were often used as escorts to unarmed two-seaters.

AVIATIK DI

The DI fighter was a single-seater biplane, the first to be designed and built in Austria, which entered service in the autumn of 1917. The product of Aviatik's chief designer, Julius von Berg, it was sometimes known as the Berg Scout. It had square-cut wings, a deep, narrow fuselage and a large cockpit with a good view. It was powered by a variety of Austro-Daimler engines (185, 200, 210, or 225hp), which gave a maximum speed of up to 115m.p.h. at sea level and a good rate of climb, although they had a tendency to overheat. Early production aircraft also had structural weaknesses in the wings that were rectified on later examples. Armament consisted of twin synchronised **Schwarzlose** machine-guns, although some early models were fitted with a single gun that fired above the airscrew.

DIs were used widely by the Austro-Hungarian air service until the Armistice, particularly as escorts to two-seaters, and about 700 were produced by Aviatik and five sub-contractors. The Austrian Aviatik company also made a very similar two-seater reconnaissance model, the CI, which appeared at about the same time as the DI. Although it was fast and well armed, the CI was unpopular with pilots who preferred the stronger and more durable **Brandenburg CI**.

AVRO 504

The standard British training aircraft for much of the First World War and for many years afterwards, the 504 dated back to June 1913, when the first prototype was tested. A lightly constructed two-seater biplane, it had equal span, two-bay wings with a rectangular section box girder fuselage. The pilot sat in the rear seat where visibility was relatively good; the observer was badly positioned amongst the wing

structure. Power was provided by the 80hp Gnome rotary engine, which gave a maximum speed of 80m.p.h. Armament, when carried, consisted of a **Lewis gun** and four small bombs.

An early variant (the 504A) of the Avro multi-purpose trainer, produced in vast quantities by Britain and her allies throughout the war

The RFC's operational use of the aircraft was very limited, although it was employed on reconnaissance duties in France during the first part of the war. An RFC Avro 504 was in fact the first British aircraft to be shot down by the Germans, on 22 August 1914. The RNAS used Avro 504s much more extensively both for reconnaissance and bombing duties. Their most notable achievement was the attack on 21 November 1914 when three 504s bombed the Zeppelin sheds at Friedrichshafen on Lake Constance; it was the first organised bombing raid of the war. They were also employed by the RNAS as anti-Zeppelin fighters, and a variant, the 504C, was developed specially for these patrols. It was a single-seater which had an auxiliary petrol tank in place of the front cockpit, extending its endurance to eight hours. An RFC equivalent, the 504D, also appeared, but it was produced in very small numbers and was used only for training purposes.

Once the 504 had been outclassed as a combat aircraft, in 1915–16, it was selected as a trainer by the RFC because of its excellent flying qualities. By 1918 it had become the sole training type (with a standard training programme to accompany it) and replaced other trainers. The 504J, a variant designed specifically for training, appeared in the autumn of 1916. Initially it was powered by the 100hp Monosoupape, although other power plants were subsequently fitted, partly because of supply problems. Another training variant, the 504K, had a universal engine mounting that could be adapted to any of the available engines: it superseded the 504J as the standard trainer. Early in 1918 the 504 was revived for combat use, when the K-type, powered by the 110hp Le Rhône rotary engine, equipped some of the Home Defence Squadrons in the London area and elsewhere. Converted to a single-seater, with a ceiling of 18,000 feet, it was armed with a Lewis gun mounted above the top wing. A total of 8,340 Avro 504s of all types were produced during the war.

BACHMANN, ADMIRAL GUSTAV, 1860–1943

Head of the Baltic naval station, Kiel, at the beginning of the war, Admiral Bachmann was a short-lived chief of the Admiralty staff, February–September 1915. He was a strong advocate of the submarine and held office while the first unrestricted U-boat campaign was underway. Following the sinking of two passenger liners, American protests forced the Germans to revert, in September 1915, to submarine warfare according to prize rules. Bachmann, did not long survive the collapse of the first U-boat war, and was replaced by **Admiral von Holtzendorff** in September. He returned to the command at Kiel, remaining there until his retirement in October 1918.

BACON, ADMIRAL SIR REGINALD, 1863–1947

Commander of the Dover Patrol from April 1915 to January 1918, Sir Reginald Bacon was responsible for the security of military transport crossing the English Channel and for the shipping passing through it. He had been brought out of retirement early in 1915 to command the Royal Marine Siege Brigade in France and had been moved at **Churchill**'s request. An experienced ordnance officer, he had been closely involved in **Lord Fisher**'s naval reforms.

During 1917, concern was expressed about the effectiveness of the Dover Patrol's response to the unrestricted warfare being waged by German U-boats and Bacon was eventually relieved of his command. He made way for **Sir Roger Keyes**, who was to implement a plan for the blocking of **Zeebrugge** and Ostend. Bacon's skills were, however, too valuable to lose and for the rest of the war he served as naval controller of munitions and inventions.

BAGHDAD, CAPTURE OF, 17 February–11 March 1917

After the fall of **Kut** in April 1916, British forces went on the defensive and the Turks caused no further difficulties for the remainder of the year. Under the new British commander, **Sir Frederick Stanley Maude**, preparations were made for a new offensive, while the Cabinet debated whether it should go ahead. There was a gradual build-up of British forces and significant improvements in transport were made.

Authorisation for an advance on Baghdad was eventually received from London and, on 13 December 1916, Maude moved forwards from Basra on both banks of the Tigris. Some 50,000 men, organised in two corps, were involved in the operation. It took as long as two months to clear the west bank below Kut. Progress was slow because of rain and the need to keep casualties to a minimum.

On 17 February, the British crossed the Tigris at the Shumran bend to the right of the Turks and attacked them on both flanks. With only 12,000 men, under the command of General Kara Bekr Bey, they were heavily outnumbered and fled from the Kut area on 24 February, under the weight of the British attacks. They were pursued with great skill by a flotilla of naval gunboats, although too little was done by the cavalry to follow up the success at Kut.

On 5 March, the advance continued, with troops moving along the east bank of the Tigris. Some resistance was encountered at the Diyala River, ten miles south of Baghdad, where the Turkish Sixth Army, under Halil Pasha, had positioned itself. As a result some of the Maude's troops crossed to the west bank by a pontoon bridge, with the aim of making an outflanking move direct on Baghdad. Faced with a major converging advance, the Turks decided to evacuate their forward positions, enabling the British to enter the city without further difficulty on 11 March. Some 9,000 prisoners were taken. The capture of Baghdad was an 'event which impressed the imagination of the whole world', partly because 'it symbolised the first streaks of dawn coming to illuminate the darkness which had lain like a pall over the Allied cause throughout 1916'. Some further gains were made beyond Baghdad during the next few weeks before operations were suspended until the autumn.

BAKER, NEWTON, 1871–1937

As American Secretary for War, 1916–21, Newton Baker, who was a close and trusted associate of **President Wilson**, prepared the US Army for intervention in Europe. His considerable organising abilities provided the basis for expanding, within 18 months, a small, totally inadequate peacetime force of 95,000 men into a conscript army of four million men. Over half of them were sent to France and many were equipped with the Enfield Rifle, a British design adopted by Baker in a bid to save time. He also reorganised and expanded the General Staff and secured the removal of generals who could not meet the requirements of modern warfare.

Secretary Baker, who prepared the American army for war, on a morale boosting visit to the front with General Pershing

BALFOUR, ARTHUR, 1848–1930

A former Conservative Prime Minister, 1902–05, Balfour returned to power in May 1915 as First Lord of the Admiralty in **Asquith**'s coalition government. Here his lethargic style contrasted with that of his more dynamic predecessor, **Winston Churchill**, although he had a deep knowledge of naval matters. The negative side of his term of office included his opposition to the final withdrawal of Allied forces from **Gallipoli**, his failure to present the results of the **Battle of Jutland** correctly and his lack of effectiveness in responding to the U-boat threat.

When he came to power in December 1916, **Lloyd George**, who voiced doubts about Balfour's performance, moved him to the Foreign Office,

where he remained until October 1919. Although his influence on war policy was to be limited, he played a key role in ensuring that Britain received maximum cooperation and assistance from the United States, once she had entered the war. In April 1917, he headed an important diplomatic mission to America for this purpose. The most famous legacy of his term at the Foreign Office was, of course, the Balfour Declaration (2 November 1917), which promised British support for the establishment of a Jewish national home in Palestine. Balfour attended the **Paris Peace Conference** where he played a prominent role in shaping the map of post-war Europe.

A DISASTER!

Balfour exchanges the Admiralty for the Western Front, August 1916. A 9.2-inch howitzer is ready for action

BALKAN FRONT, CHRONOLOGICAL LIST OF EVENTS

Jadar River, Battle of, 1914
Kolubra River, Battle of, 1914
Dardanelles Operation, 1915
Gallipoli, Expedition to, 1915–16
Serbia, Invasion of, 1915
Salonika Front, 1915–18
Rumania, Invasion of, 1916–17

The Balkans in 1916: the monotony and discomfort of the trenches were not confined to the Western Front

BALL, ALBERT, 1896–1917

Albert Ball was one of Britain's early fighter aces and the first to become a popular hero, both at home and among his colleagues in the RFC.

Qualifying as a pilot early in 1916, his flying career was compressed into little more than a year. His early service in France was in two-seaters, initially with No 13 Squadron, although as soon as the opportunity arose, in May 1916, he transferred to a fighter squadron (No 11). There he began flying **Bristol Scouts** and the **Nieuport 17**, the single-seater he liked best. His first two victories were achieved on 22 May, but only one of them was in fact confirmed. He was awarded the Military Cross at the end of July, after an intensive period of combat. During the autumn he added the Distinguished Service Order to his growing list of achievements and by the time he returned to England in October 1916 he had gained nine victories.

Ball's combat style probably contributed more to his emergence as a public figure than his growing list of hits. An individualist who chose to fight alone wherever possible, he was notable for his aggressive tactics and total disregard for his own personal safety. His favourite method of attack was to dive under the tail of his opponent's machine and rake the underside of the fuselage with his **Lewis gun**. Ball was an excellent marksman who had the sense of timing necessary to effect this difficult manoeuvre successfully.

He returned to active service in April 1917, flying an **SE5** or Nieuport with the newly formed No 56 Squadron. Arriving at a particularly difficult moment for the RFC, Ball's score steadily mounted during 'Bloody April'. By 6 May, he had achieved his final victory, bringing the score to at least 44 German aircraft. The next day Ball, still only twenty, was killed in a dog fight with his old opponents in **von Richthofen**'s *Jagdgeschwader I*, in circumstances that have never been adequately explained. Further official recognition of Ball's outstanding contribution came with the award of a posthumous Victoria Cross.

PERHAPS KILLED BY A SNIPER FROM A CHURCH STEEPLE.

BANFIELD, GOTTFRIED, 1890–1986

The Austrian navy's leading air ace, Gottfried Banfield, had achieved 18 victories by the end of the war, of which four were against balloons. Joining the service before the war, he gained his first key appointment in 1916 as commander of a naval air station at Trieste. Here he organised the navy's air defences in the face of the growing strength of Italian naval aviation in the Adriatic. Some of his victories arose from the successful interception of Italian aircraft attacking Trieste, but his reputation rests on his leadership of a series of offensive raids on military targets in northern Italy, often flying a **Lohner L** or **Brandenburg CC**. On one of these operations in 1916 he engaged the Italian ace **Francesco Baracca** over the **Isonzo**, but neither was able to secure the decisive advantage. In August 1917 he became Freiherr von Banfield in recognition of his outstanding war services.

BARACCA, FRANCESCO, 1888–1918

Italy's leading air ace, Francesco Baracca, scored 34 hits before his death in the final months of the war. When Italy entered the war in May 1915, Baracca, already an experienced pilot, was confined to flying **Nieuport** two-seaters and had to wait until the end of the year for his opportunity. He was then allocated a Nieuport 11 single-seater and over the next 12 months, flying with 70a Squadriglia, he destroyed five enemy aircraft. It was at this time that Baracca adopted his famous prancing horse insignia, a reminder of a brief period of cavalry service in his youth. This personal symbol appeared on his Nieuport 11 and has been retained ever since as the emblem of an Italian air force unit.

In May 1917 he transferred to the new élite 91a Squadriglia, flying the far superior **Spad VII**. He was soon appointed squadron commander and his score steadily mounted. The air war intensified after Italy's defeat at **Caporetto**, and Baracca, who was now flying a **Spad XIII**, had achieved a total of 30 hits by the end of the year. After a brief interlude advising **Ansaldo** on the design of a new fighter aircraft, Baracca was back at the front with his squadron in May 1918. During this period he added four more hits to his total, the last being on the first day of the **Battle of the Piave** (June 1918). Four days later he was dead, shot down by troops while on ground attack duties.

BARKER, WILLIAM, 1894–1930

With a final score of 52 victories, Wing Commander William Barker, a Canadian, was one of the leading Allied aces of the war. Transferring to the RFC from the Canadian Mounted Rifles late in 1915, he first served as an observer/gunner in a **Royal Aircraft Factory BE2d** on reconnaissance duties, and scored his first hit the following July. He qualified as a pilot early in 1917, having completed his training in the shortest possible time, and at first was allocated to a two-seater squadron. A fighter unit was, however, more to his taste and he managed to secure a transfer to No 28 Squadron in the autumn of 1917. It was soon evident that Barker was an exceptional airman and his score steadily grew during a long period of service on the Italian front from November 1917. During this period Barker was given command of No 66 Squadron and was decorated twice by the Italian government, to add to his other awards which included the Military Cross.

Barker returned to England briefly in September 1918 as an instructor, but anxious to resume active service he obtained a temporary attachment to No 201 Squadron in France. His wartime service ended on 27 October, the day he was due back in England. While attacking a lone two-seater Barker ran into a formation of 60 **Fokker DVII**s: he was injured by enemy gunfire more than once and his **Sopwith Snipe** was hit some 300 times in a remarkable battle that lasted 40 minutes. Although the outcome of this single-handed fight was never in doubt, Barker managed even in these circumstances to add three more hits to his total before being sent spinning towards the ground. Severely injured and only half-conscious he controlled the aircraft well enough to survive a crash landing. Barker's final engagement was a fitting end to a distinguished career, his heroism being recognised by the award of a Victoria Cross. Barker recovered from his wounds and served in the Royal Canadian Air Force for a time after the war.

BARRAGE BALLOONS

Balloon barrages were among the new defensive measures against aerial attack developed during the First World War, although they appeared rather late in the conflict. Barrages were established around a number of European cities in 1917–18 and they were also used to protect industrial sites in Germany. The barrage protecting London, which was 51 miles long, was one of the most elaborate. Established in 1918, it consisted of groups of three balloons, set at an altitude which made it difficult for enemy planes to fly above them. They were interconnected by means of steel cables; from these an number of lighter cables hung vertically, providing a formidable barrier for German bombers to negotiate. The barrage balloon was reintroduced, virtually unchanged, at the beginning of the Second World War.

BATTLECRUISER

Largely the personal creation of **Admiral Fisher**, First Sea Lord, 1904–10, the battlecruiser, which first appeared in 1908, was closely related to the **Dreadnought** battleship. It was to be more powerful and better armed than an armoured cruiser and able, if necessary, to engage a battleship. Main armament was to be of the same calibre as the Dreadnought, but the battlecruiser would have a higher maximum speed of 25 knots; improved performance would be achieved by reducing armour protection. Battlecruisers would have the traditional cruiser roles of protecting trade routes and reconnaissance, acting in the latter case as the advanced scouts of the battle fleet. They were also expected to attack the enemy's scouting cruisers and deal with stragglers. The British Invincible class, the first to appear, had eight 12-inch guns, a displacement of over 17,000 tons and a maximum speed of 25.5 knots.

In practice, during the First World War, their role was extended well beyond the designers' original conception. As a result of their armament and size, the battlecruiser was considered fit to fight in the line of battle, even though its armour was weak. This new role had already been indicated when its name was officially changed from fast armoured cruiser to battlecruiser in 1912. As the spearhead of the **Grand Fleet**, these warships were engaged in much of the heavy fighting of the war. They proved to be ideal in situations such as the **Battle of the Falkland Islands** where their superior speed and long-range guns allowed them to bring the enemy's ships to battle with little risk to themselves. In the earlier **Battle of Heligoland Bight**, for example, British battlecruisers had sunk two German cruisers.

Their limitations had first been evident at the **Dogger Bank**, but their extreme vulnerability to heavy gunfire was particularly obvious at **Jutland**, when three British battlecruisers were sunk. The German equivalents were better protected while losing little in terms of speed. *Derfflinger* and *Lützow*, for example, each had eight 12-inch guns, a maximum speed of 28 knots and 12-inch armour. The best British battlecruiser of the war was *Tiger*, which had a displacement of over 28,000 tons and was armed with eight 13.5-inch guns; it was capable of 29 knots. In the inter-war period the development of aerial reconnaissance meant that battlecruisers were no longer relevant to the needs of naval warfare.

BATTLESHIP

At the beginning of the First World War, the battleship was the most important component of the world's navies and a major expression of national power. Its design had been revolutionised eight years earlier when **HMS Dreadnought**, the first 'all big gun' ship, had been launched. Rendering every existing battleship obsolete, it intensified the naval race between Britain and Germany, because the former's enormous lead in capital ships effectively disappeared. With the advantage of an earlier start, Britain had 20 dreadnoughts in service by August 1914, compared with Germany's 15; both navies had a further two nearing completion. In the Royal Navy they constituted three of the five battle squadrons of the **Grand Fleet**; there were also two squadrons of pre-dreadnoughts, but the majority of these older capital ships was based in the English Channel. Dreadnoughts equipped two squadrons of the German **High Seas Fleet**; pre-dreadnoughts comprised a third squadron, while others operated separately in the Baltic.

The Royal Navy's wartime deployment of dreadnoughts was largely determined by its strategy of a distant blockade, which avoided the risks of operating too near to the German coast. Germany's policy was to try to reduce the strength of the Grand Fleet by destroying individual squadrons before fighting the main fleet. The result of **battlecruiser** engagements at **Heligoland** and the **Dogger Bank** increased German caution about risking its modern warships, and it was not until 1916 that the High Seas Fleet, under **Scheer**'s command, adopted a more aggressive strategy. As a result, British capital ships were lured out and engaged the enemy at the **Battle of Jutland**, the only occasion in which dreadnoughts fought each other, although even here they were deployed cautiously. Unwilling to risk these ships again, the German navy kept them in port for the remainder of the war apart from a couple of pointless forays, and turned to the **submarine** as its principal weapon in 1916–18. On the other hand, British battleships continued to be used to maintain the blockade which helped to undermine the German economy in 1917–18.

Pre-dreadnoughts were employed more adventurously, most notably in the **Dardanelles** where the Allies attempted, unsuccessfully, to force a passage through to Constantinople early in 1915. The operation revealed their vulnerability to mines and torpedoes and they were withdrawn from the area after three capital ships had been lost. The First World War provided considerable evidence that the era of the battleship was gradually drawing to a close, to be replaced by that of the submarine and the aircraft carrier. Thirty-six capital ships were lost during the war.

BAYERN

The last German battleships to be laid down before the beginning of the war, *Bayern* and *Baden* attempted to match the firepower of contemporary British warships with the adoption of eight 15-inch Krupp guns as the main armament. They were located in superfiring pairs of turrets mounted fore and aft. The hull, which was a larger version of the *König*'s, had excellent protection against underwater damage; maximum speed was 22.25 knots and the ship had a displacement of 28,000 tons. Both ships served with the **High Seas Fleet**. *Bayern* was commissioned in 1916 and *Baden* early in the following year. Interned by the British at Scapa Flow, *Bayern* was scuttled and *Baden* was beached before sinking on 21 June 1919.

B-CLASS SUBMARINE

Generally similar to the **A-Class**, the British B-type boats were larger, had a proper deck and an improved reserve of buoyancy. The 16-cylinder Wolseley petrol engine provided a range of 1,000 nautical miles at 8.75 knots and they were armed with two 18-inch torpedoes in the bow. Although these boats were designed for coastal patrols, six went to the Mediterranean, B11 penetrating the Dardanelles minefields and sinking the Turkish warship *Messudieh*. Unused after the autumn of 1915 because of a shortage of spares, the B-types were rebuilt by the Italian navy as surface patrol vessels.

BEARDMORE W.B.III

The Beardmore W.B.III, a derivative of the **Sopwith Pup**, was produced for carrier-based operations. Designed to conserve storage space, it differed from the Pup primarily in featuring folding wings and an undercarriage which could be folded into the fuselage. It was, in fact, widely known as the 'Folding Pup'. In some later versions the undercarriage was fixed, but it could be jettisoned in the event of the aircraft being ditched in the sea. A **Lewis machine-gun** (instead of the Pup's **Vickers**) was mounted above the centre section, firing over the airscrew.

By the end of October 1918, 55 examples of this single-seater scout were in service, of which 18 were with the **Grand Fleet**. They operated from the aircraft carriers *Furious*, *Nairana* and *Pegasus*.

BEATTY, ADMIRAL DAVID, 1st EARL, 1872–1936

Commander of the British **Grand Fleet**, 1916–18, Admiral Beatty's leadership, energy and courage had marked him out for early promotion. He was appointed rear-admiral at the age of 39, in 1910, the youngest British officer to achieve that rank in over 100 years. In 1912 **Winston Churchill** selected him as his naval secretary and two years later he was appointed, over the heads of many of his colleagues, to the command of the Battle Cruiser Squadron, raising his flag in *HMS Lion*. He commanded the Battle Cruiser Force with 'dash and elan' during the war, taking the opportunity for offensive action whenever it arose. His intervention in the **Heligoland Bight** on 28 August 1914 resulted in a decisive British victory and the loss of three German light cruisers. At the **Battle of the Dogger Bank** (24 January 1915) he destroyed the *Blücher* and seriously damaged the battlecruiser *Seydlitz*, but signalling errors enabled the rest of **Admiral Hipper**'s squadron to escape.

At **Jutland** his decisive contribution was to draw the **High Seas Fleet** towards the approaching Grand Fleet, manoeuvring successfully to prevent the Germans from sighting it. It was, however, achieved at the cost of three battlecruisers, and Beatty has been criticised for acting prematurely without the support of his associated squadron of four super-dreadnoughts. He was also ultimately responsible for several important signalling and reporting failures evident in the operation of his force at Jutland. In spite of these weaknesses, the drawn battle did no damage to his reputation. In fact, there was speculation that if Beatty rather than **Jellicoe** had been in overall command of British forces the outcome would have been very different.

Beatty did in fact succeed Jellicoe as commander of the Grand Fleet in December 1916 when the latter was appointed First Sea Lord. He was responsible for refitting the fleet after Jutland, rectifying the weaknesses in ship and shell design that the battle had revealed. Until this work had been completed, Beatty followed the same cautious strategy as his predecessor and maintained the distant blockade of Germany.

The Germans were even more unwilling to risk their main battle fleet and the opportunity for a decisive encounter never materialised. Beatty did, however, have the pleasure of accepting the surrender of the High Seas Fleet on 21 November 1918, giving the famous signal: 'the German flag will be hauled down at sunset, and will not be hoisted again without permission'. Beatty was appointed First Sea Lord in 1921 and remained at the Admiralty until June 1927.

Force of circumstance constrained Beatty's naturally offensive spirit during his term as commander of the Grand Fleet, 1916–18

BEHOLLA AUTOMATIC PISTOL

Adopted as a substitute standard weapon by the German army, this 7.65mm automatic pistol appeared shortly before the outbreak of war. As supplies of the Luger PO8 could not meet wartime demand, the Beholla was allocated to officers who did not require the superior combat performance of the standard gun.

This blowback pistol had a magazine of seven rounds, a weight of 0.64kg and an overall length of 140mm. A simple, rugged design, it was easily produced in quantity throughout the war by Becker and Hollander and a number of sub-contractors.

BELGIAN AIR SERVICE

On the outbreak of war the Belgian *Compagnie des Aviateurs* consisted of no more than four squadrons, each supporting one of the four divisions of the Belgian army. The number of experienced pilots, civil or military, available at that time was very small and the force fared badly during the initial German invasion.

Reorganised and gradually expanded, in 1915 it was renamed the *Aviation Militaire*. Its five squadrons were largely equipped with modern French aircraft and it made a useful, if modest, contribution to the air war on the Western Front. Fighter units were first created in 1917 and in the following year a fighter group, with three squadrons, was formed. In the closing months of the war the *Aviation Militaire* consisted of eleven squadrons (of which one was a bomber unit), with less than 140 aircraft of all types.

BELLEAU WOOD, BATTLE OF, 6 June–1 July 1918

By the end of May 1918, the third German offensive of the year (the **Aisne Offensive**) had reached as far as Vaux and Belleau Wood, west of Château-Thierry. The American Second Division (General Bundy) replaced a French corps on this sector and quickly checked the German advance; on 4 June, **Ludendorff** was forced to abandon the whole offensive. Two days later the Americans counter-attacked, with the Marine Brigade and the Third Infantry Brigade leading. Six successive assaults were launched against superior German forces (four divisions) that held the wood, which was about a mile square. After three weeks' heavy fighting, Belleau Wood was cleared and Vaux was retaken. The Americans had lost over 1,800 men and about 7,000 wounded in their first major battle with the Germans.

BELLEROPHON

Almost identical to *HMS Dreadnought*, the Bellerophon-class battleships, which were completed in 1909, shared the same strengths and weaknesses as the original design. Some improvements were, however, adopted: armoured protection was increased with the installation of anti-torpedo bulkheads, secondary armament was enhanced by the fitting of sixteen 4-inch guns, and the layout of the masts was modified. *Bellerophon*, like her sister ships *Superb* and *Temeraire*, served successfully throughout the war with the **Grand Fleet** and all three saw action at the **Battle of Jutland**. As flagship of Vice-Admiral Gough Calthorpe, *Superb* led the Allied fleet through the Dardanelles after the Turkish surrender in 1918.

BELOW, GENERAL OTTO VON, 1857–1944

Below's military reputation was established on the Eastern Front in the first few months of the war, but his varied service in the German army included periods in Macedonia, on the Italian Front and in France. As commander of I Reserve Corps he helped to defeat the Russians at **Gumbinnen** and at the **First Battle of the Masurian Lakes**. Late in 1914, he became head of the Eighth Army and soon afterwards contributed to the defeat of the Russian Second Army at the **Second Battle of the Masurian Lakes** (February 1915).

He remained on the Eastern Front until he was sent to Macedonia in October, 1916. His operations there stabilised the front near Monastir and denied the Allies a decisive victory. Below was next sent to the Italian Front, where he commanded a German-Austrian army of 12 divisions during the **Battle of** **Caporetto** (October–November 1917), where it played a decisive role. He concluded his wartime career on the Western Front as commander of the Seventeenth Army, although shortly before the end of the war he was involved in preparations for a possible final battle on German territory.

Victory at Caporetto consolidated Below's reputation, gained on the Eastern and Balkan Fronts

BENSON, ADMIRAL WILLIAM, 1855–1932

Chief of naval operations (1915–18) of the US Navy, Admiral Benson's primary concern was the defence of American waters rather than the principal areas of naval activity during the First World War. However, under pressure from Admiral Sims, who worked with the Royal Navy in a liaison capacity, he moved more American ships to Europe to help in the anti-submarine effort. He also helped to establish an inter-allied Naval Council and was present at the **Paris Peace Conference** in 1919, where he contributed to the naval provisions of the treaty.

BERCHTOLD, LEOPOLD, COUNT VON, 1863–1942

As Foreign Minister of Austro-Hungary in 1914, Berchtold responded to the assassination of **Franz** **Ferdinand** at Sarajevo by pressing for immediate action against Serbia. He was, however, restrained by

Count Tisza, Hungarian Prime Minister, who argued that German backing was necessary before any move could be made. Once a positive response had been obtained, Berchtold drafted an ultimatum to Serbia. All but two of the clauses were accepted, providing Austro-Hungary with the justification to declare war. 'Silly Berchtold, who had started the whole thing' resigned early in 1915 over disagreements about whether Austria should offer any concessions to neutral Italy.

BERETTA PISTOL

The first Beretta pistol was produced in 1915 for wartime use by the Italian army. A 7.65mm blowback automatic, it had an overall length of almost six inches and a muzzle velocity of 875 feet per second. The detachable box magazine held seven rounds. A second version of this pistol was chambered for the 9mm Glisenti cartridge. Based on an out-of-date design, the 1915 Model was not produced to the same standard as subsequent Beretta pistols.

BERETTA SUB-MACHINE-GUN

A modified version of the original **Villar Perosa sub-machine-gun**, the 9mm Parabellum Beretta had a single barrel and was a more compact and practical weapon. The new model, which appeared in 1918, retained the basic Villar Perosa mechanism, barrel and 25-round magazine. New features included the trigger, a one-piece stock and a folding rod bayonet. It had a cyclic rate of fire of 900 rounds per minute, slightly slower than the original model but higher than other contemporary weapons. It was available in two forms with a choice of automatic and semi-automatic fire or with semi-automatic fire only. This highly successful conversion was employed by the Italian army in the closing stages of the war and was still in use at the beginning of the Second World War.

BERGMANN MACHINE-GUN

A water-cooled German machine-gun, the 7.92mm Bergmann MG15 was used during the war but could not compete with the highly successful **Maschinengewehr 08**. A lightened version, the MG15 nA, was air-cooled and had a slotted barrel casing. It had a curved metal ammunition box which held a 200-round belt; the cyclic rate of fire was 500 rounds per minute. Equipped with a bipod and a pistol grip, it weighed 28lb and was used in aircraft (fitted on a flexible mounting) as well as by the infantry.

BERGMANN MASCHINENPISTOLE 18/I

The world's first blowback sub-machine-gun appeared in prototype form early in 1918 after an extended period of development by Hugo Schmeisser,

Forerunner of the modern sub-machine-gun

GREAT GUN IN WW II !

a leading small arms designer. It was produced in response to the need for superior short-range fire-power when using the new shock tactics developed by **von Hutier**. Following some modifications the weapon entered mass production and from the summer of 1918 it was issued to German troops on the Western Front and elsewhere. The design was strong, relatively simple and trouble free, except for the 'snail type' magazine – a small drum, containing 32 rounds – which had to be used with an adaptor to prevent it fouling the bolt. It fired 9mm Parabellum cartridges at a cyclic rate of 500 rounds per minute.

Air cooling was facilitated by the numerous holes which had been cut in the tube that enclosed the barrel.

Although the MP 18/I appeared too late to make much of an impact during the war, it established a standard pattern for the sub-machine-gun and had a continuing influence on its design during the inter-war years, both in Germany and elsewhere. It proved to be sufficiently important and influential for the Allies to have banned it from the post-war German army, although it was employed in limited numbers by the police of the Weimar Republic.

BERTHELOT, GENERAL HENRI, 1863–1931

One of **Joffre**'s closest advisers, Henri Berthelot was assistant chief of staff when war was declared. He contributed much to the survival of French military power after the failure of **Plan XVII**, the offensive strategy to which he had contributed, and the German invasion. On Joffre's removal from office in

1916, he went to Rumania where he reorganized the army after its defeats in the field. In 1918 he returned to the Western Front as commander of the French Fifth Army, which he led during the Allied counter-offensive in the summer.

BERTHIER RIFLE

Produced by a committee chaired by André Berthier, a leading French small arms designer, the Berthier rifle first appeared as a cavalry carbine in 1890. The new weapon was developed because of weaknesses in the **Lebel**, the standard French rifle, and the adoption of superior weapons by the Germans and the Austrians. The Berthier bolt action was in fact based on that used in the Lebel rifle M86, but the box magazine was derived from the **Mannlicher**. However, with a three-round clip the new weapon, which fired 8mm cartridges, was at a disadvantage to its main rivals.

The carbine was followed in 1902 and 1907 by Berthier rifles, which were of the same 8mm calibre

as the carbines and similar to them except in dimensions. They were issued in small numbers to French colonial troops.

During the First World War the limitations of the Lebel design became ever more apparent and in 1915 it was decided that the 1907 Berthier rifle should enter mass production as a partial substitute, being known as the Fusil Modèle 07/15. The design was modified in 1916 in order that a five-round box, which would be more suitable for use in the trenches, could be fitted. Manufactured on a large scale for the French during the war, the Modèle 07/15 was widely used by a number of foreign armies during the inter-war years.

BETHMANN HOLLWEG, THEOBOLD von, 1856–1921

The fifth Chancellor of the German Reich, Bethmann

Hollweg, a career civil servant, succeeded Bernhard

von Bülow in 1909. Domestic problems dominated the political scene at that time, but foreign policy, of which Bethmann Hollweg had no experience, was soon to be come pre-eminent. One of the new Chancellor's major objectives was to weaken the alliance of Entente Powers opposing Germany and her allies, but all his bilateral overtures were rejected. His special attempt to reach agreement with England on naval construction and other matters also failed, partly because of pressure from German military and naval leaders. By 1914 he regarded a localised war, with Britain remaining neutral, as imminent and likely to be beneficial to German interests. In the general European war that developed, he did not believe that Germany could ever achieve a decisive victory. Sooner or later, a compromise peace would need to be negotiated, but he did not reveal his view of Germany's wartime prospects until he judged the moment to be right.

His wartime achievements include bringing Turkey and Bulgaria into the war on the German side and delaying the reintroduction of unrestricted submarine warfare, proposed in 1916, because it would force America to abandon her neutrality. **Hindenburg** and **Ludendorff** supported the navy's demand as the only way to win the war and Bethmann Hollweg was forced to agree in January 1917. In the hope of arranging discussions about peace before a U-boat campaign started, he had already sent a note to the Entente Powers. The correspondence came to nothing because the Allies' peace terms were incompatible with Germany's.

In July 1917, Bethmann Hollweg was forced to resign and Ludendorff's dominant position was consolidated. The immediate cause of the departure was uncertainty about his attitude to a radical peace resolution passed by the Reichstag, which called for an end to the war with no annexations. Its 'only effect was to break Bethmann Hollweg, the unhappy rope in the tug-of-war between the military and the political parties'.

'BIG BERTHA'

The two massive Krupp 42cm howitzers used to attack the fortifications of **Liège** at the beginning of the war were nicknamed 'Big Bertha'. It was a designation derived from Baroness Bertha Krupp, daughter of Alfred Krupp, the arms manufacturer. Dismantled while in transit, the guns weighed over 43 tons when operational; they could fire a shell of 1,786lb over 10,000 yards. These formidable weapons, larger than any mobile gun ever used in the field before, destroyed the defences of Liège and Namur with unexpected speed and were then transferred to the Eastern Front, where they were also used successfully. They were eventually withdrawn late in 1917, having become vulnerable to Allied counter-attack. In addition, their accuracy diminished considerably over time as barrel wear developed.

BISHOP, WILLIAM AVERY, 1894–1956

Billy Bishop, like so many successful RFC pilots, was a Canadian who became the second highest scoring British pilot and ranked second only to **Fonck** of the aces who survived the war. His achievement was even more remarkable because his period of operational flying lasted for no more than about six months. He qualified as a pilot early in 1917, after a frustrating few months as an observer with No 21 Squadron, when he saw no action of any kind. Bishop was posted to No 60 Squadron in March 1917, and within a few weeks his outstanding qualities as a fighter pilot became evident. His first victim – an **Albatros DIII** – was shot down on 25 March and his score steadily increased during the spring and early summer.

An individualist who was determined to become a high scorer, Bishop's tactics were aggressive and reckless, showing little concern for his own safety. A dramatic example of Bishop's approach was his single-handed attack on a German airfield on 2 June 1917. He destroyed three of the Albatros IIIs that came up to intercept him, showing his skill as a marksman and airman as well as his extraordinary personal courage. He evaded at least five other German pursuers and returned home to receive the Victoria Cross, having already been awarded the Military Cross for his achievements during 'Bloody April'. By August 1917 Bishop's score had risen to 47 and he returned to Canada on leave with the rank of major. Bishop had no further combat opportunities until his appointment to the command of No 85 Squadron in March 1918.

During a further brief period in France, Bishop fought with the same skill and aggression, adding another 25 victories to his total. His last victim was destroyed on 19 June, before his recall to London and the end of his operational flying career. Final recognition of his service was given with the award of the

Bishop checking an upward firing Lewis machine-gun before taking off on patrol

new Distinguished Flying Cross. Bishop also served in the Second World War, holding a senior staff appointment in the Royal Canadian Air Force and ending his career as an air marshal.

BLACKBURN KANGAROO

The Kangaroo was a twin-engined bomber which was operated by the RAF in very small numbers from April 1918. Based on earlier Blackburn seaplanes, the Kangaroo was a land plane powered by two 250hp Rolls Royce Falcons, giving a maximum speed of 100m.p.h. at sea level. The crew of two or three had available front and rear .303 **Lewis machine-guns**

mounted on Scarff rings and four 230lb bombs accommodated in the long, narrow fuselage. A further four bombs could be held in external racks. As maritime patrol bombers, operated by only one squadron, Kangaroos contributed to the sinking of one U-boat and damaged several others. The RAF disposed of its Kangaroos at the end of the war.

BLÉRIOT XI

Closely resembling the aircraft that Louis Blériot flew across the English Channel in July 1909, the military Blériot XI was adopted by the French and Italians in the same year and by the RFC two years later. By the beginning of the First World War it had a proven record as a reconnaissance aircraft with excellent flying qualities, having been used in French Morocco, the Balkan Wars and the Italo-Turkish confrontation of 1911–12.

This shoulder-wing tractor monoplane was unarmed and had a box girder fuselage only partly covered in fabric. The XI was produced in five versions: as one-, or two- or three-seaters using the 50, 70 and 140hp Gnome engines respectively, and with other more minor airframe variations between them. A further model with parasol wings was also used by the French and British air services and a floatplane version was produced.

Blériot XI: a slightly modified Channel type

The Blériot XI was widely used during the first year of the war on observation duties and as a nuisance bomber, carrying a bomb load of about 55lb. It equipped six squadrons of the RFC and it was in fact a Blériot of No 3 Squadron that made the first British reconnaissance flight of the war on 19 August 1914. It also served with eight *escadrilles* of the French Aviation Militaire and with six *squadriglie* of the Italian air force. Other users of the aircraft included the RNAS and a number of more minor air services. The Blériot's performance limitations (which, for example, precluded the installation of fixed armament) and its rather frail construction meant that it was phased out during 1915 in favour of more modern designs. However, a number of air services subsequently used the aircraft extensively for training purposes.

BLISS, GENERAL TASKER, 1853–1930

Appointed chief of staff of the US Army in May 1917, shortly after America's entry into the war, Bliss worked effectively with his civilian counterpart, **Newton Baker**, Secretary of War, in overseeing the rapid expansion of the service. He also maintained good relations with **General Pershing**, the American field commander in France. Bliss was in fact a skilled diplomat who served as his country's representative on the Supreme War Council and was present at the **Paris Peace Conference**. He was opposed to punitive peace terms and was strongly committed to the creation of the League of Nations.

BLÜCHER

This German armoured cruiser was sunk by the British during the **Battle of the Dogger Bank** in January 1915, after being hit by some 50 shells and two torpedoes. A development of the Scharnhorst class, *Blücher*, which was completed in 1911, had a displacement of 15,500 tons and a maximum speed of about 24 knots; armament consisted of twelve 8.2-inch and eight 5.9-inch guns.

British preoccupation with Blücher *at the Dogger Bank allowed other German ships to escape*

BODEO REVOLVER

The Bodeo Model 1889 was adopted in 1891 as the standard Italian service revolver. Superseded by the **Glisenti pistol** in 1910, this six-shot, double action weapon of .41 in calibre remained in service throughout the war and was still used by some Italian units in 1939–45. Simple and well-constructed it was produced in two models: with an octagonal barrel, a folding trigger and no trigger guard; and a round barrel version with a guard. Both types were produced in quantity by several manufacturers during the First World War.

MOVIE: THE BLUE MAX!

BOELCKE, OSWALD, 1891–1916

One of the leading German aces of the Great War, Boelcke was a critical figure in the development of air fighting. Qualifying as a pilot as war was declared, he joined *Feldflieger Abteilungen 13* and flew an **Albatros BII** with his brother as the observer. He gained the Iron Cross before moving on to *Fl Abt 62* in April 1915, where he flew an armed aircraft – the **Albatros CI** – for the first time. He scored his first hit in this aircraft in July, but all his other victories were achieved in single-seaters.

Boelcke was in fact involved in the testing of the early **Fokker** monoplanes and during the autumn he flew an **EII**, armed with a synchronised machine-gun, often in company with his rival **Max Immelmann**, another member of the same unit. He soon freed himself from the defensive tactics of the German air service, searching out victims across enemy lines and gradually increasing his score as more and more Allied aircraft fell victim to the Fokker scourge. By the beginning of 1916 he had scored eight hits and had been awarded the Pour Le Mérite. Further success followed at Verdun, and Boelcke, who had become a national hero, was sent on a tour of German air units, with the aim of raising morale.

Boelcke's real opportunity came in July 1916 when he was asked to command *Jasta 2*, one of the new fighter units, whose formation he had long advocated. His ideas on the tactics of air fighting, summarised in the ten-point Dicta Boelcke, provided the basis for the instruction of members of his new unit. It was an élite group hand-picked by Boelcke, with some of the most promising pilots in the German air service, including the future ace of aces, **Manfred von Richthofen**.

'The father of air fighting', Boelcke was a noted tactician as well as a famous fighter ace

Under Boelcke's active leadership, the development of team fighting, rather than individual combat was encouraged. Using the new D-class aircraft, it was a highly successful strategy, reflected in the 76 hits achieved by his group by the end of 1916 and the re-establishment of German dominance in its sector of the battlefield.

Boelcke himself was not so fortunate: on 15 October, on his sixth mission of the day, one of his colleagues collided with him; his plane fell to the ground out of control and he was killed. Had he survived longer there is every chance that the score of the 'father of air fighting' would have equalled that of von Richthofen's. At the time of his death he had accumulated a total of 40 victories.

BÖHM-ERMOLLI, FIELD MARSHAL EDUARD, BARON von, 1856–1941

Austro-Hungarian field marshal who commanded the Second Army when war was declared in 1914. His forces were hastily transferred from the Serbian front to Galicia in August 1914 in an unsuccessful attempt to halt the Russian advance. It was not until June 1915 that he reoccupied Lemburg as the enemy retreated. As commander of Army Group Böhm-Ermolli, his greatest test was in opposing the **Brusilov Offensive** in June 1916; his war ended in the Ukraine, serving with the occupying forces.

BOROEVIC von BOJNA, FIELD MARSHAL SVETOZAR, 1856–1920

Austrian general who spent most of the war on the Italian front with the Fifth Army, Boroevic was first appointed to the Third Army in 1914. He commanded it during the Battle of the Carpathians (January–March 1915) and the **Gorlice-Tarnow breakthrough** (May–June 1915), when he rescued Przemysl from its siege. Soon after Italy entered the war Boroevic went to the **Isonzo Front**, where he fought eleven costly battles, preventing a real advance eastwards. At **Caporetto**, his army, on the left flank, supported the main thrust towards the Piave. Appointed field marshal early in 1918, Boroevic now commanded the entire Piave front. He opposed **Conrad**'s plans for an attack from the Trentino in favour of a concentration of forces on his own front. As a compromise, simultaneous attacks were launched in both sectors but with the Austrians divided the offensive (15–22 June 1918) was unsuccessful.

BOSELLI, PAOLO, 1838–1932

During the First World War, Paolo Boselli, a veteran Liberal politician, was appointed prime minister of Italy as a result of one military crisis and dismissed during another. A national government, with Boselli at its head, had come to power in the summer of 1916 after a series of setbacks, including the Austrian Trentino offensive. The **Sixth Battle of the Isonzo**, which produced the first Italian gains of the war, was followed by a declaration of war against Germany. It also contributed to the new government's initial popularity. However, support for Boselli soon waned as the effectiveness of his direction of the war effort was called into question. Critics on the left and right joined forces after the disaster at **Caporetto** (October 1917) to remove the weak and ineffectual prime minister from office.

BOTHA, GENERAL LOUIS, 1862–1919

An outstanding guerrilla leader during the South African War, Botha was the first prime minister of the Union, holding office from 1910 until his early death. He had established good relations with his former enemies and was active in his support for Britain from the beginning of the First World War.

For example, South Africa assumed full responsibility for its own defence, allowing the imperial garrison to be withdrawn to Europe. More important, he agreed to act against German South-West Africa, although he was first forced to deal with De Wet's pro-German rebellion against the South African government in 1914. The colony finally surrendered in July 1915 after a well-conducted campaign, with Botha himself in command. In the final stages of his career he attended the **Paris Peace Conference** where he argued for relatively lenient terms to be imposed on the vanquished.

BOTHMER, GENERAL FELIX GRAF von, 1852–1937

Commander of the Austro-German South Army in Galicia from July 1915, Count Felix von Bothmer led his forces during the **Brusilov Offensive** of 1916, when he was forced back to the Carpathians. When Brusilov renewed his attack on the southern front, in July 1917, Bothmer was better prepared, forcing the Russians back in a successful counter-offensive. After the armistice was agreed in the east, General von Bothmer moved to the Western Front as head of the Nineteenth Army in Lorraine.

BOUÉ DE LAPEYRÈRE, AUGUSTE, 1852–1924

A former French Minister of Marine (1909–11), Lapeyrère was commander of French naval forces in the Mediterranean, 1911–15. Failure to intercept the German cruisers *Goeben* and *Breslau* was followed by his inability to take offensive action against the Austrian fleet, his principal task at the beginning of the war. His opponents remained in port and would not fight. Lapeyrère's declining reputation was reflected in his exclusion from the planning of the **Dardanelles Operation**. His inability to respond effectively to the new problems of submarine warfare led to his resignation from the Mediterranean command in the autumn of 1916.

A succession of failures forced Lapeyrère (left) to resign his Mediterranean command

BOUVET

Named after Admiral Bouvet, this French battleship participated in the Allied attack on the Dardanelles and was one of three pre-dreadnoughts lost during the bombardment of Turkish forts on the Gallipoli peninsula on 18 March 1915. *Bouvet* hit a Turkish mine and sank within two minutes, with the loss of 660 men. Launched in 1896, *Bouvet* was a successful design which had a displacement of 12,007 tons with two 12-inch and two 10.8-inch guns. The last variant of the Charles Martel class, she had triple screws and could operate at up to 17 knots.

BRANDENBURG CI

This two-seat armed biplane was a highly successful German design widely used by the Austrian air service from 1916. Produced in large numbers by two Austrian manufacturers, in a total of eighteen series, it was nicknamed 'Big Brandenburg'. ('Little Brandenburg' was the BI training aircraft.)

Many different engines were fitted to the CI, ranging from the 160hp Mercedes D III to the 230hp Hiero. The 160hp Austro-Daimler, for example, gave a maximum speed of 87m.p.h. at sea level and a ceiling of 19,000 feet. Other features were more standardised, including the single communal cockpit and the observer's free-firing **Schwarzlose machine-gun**; in later models a forward mounted gun of the same type was also fitted. A distinctive feature of this elegant aircraft was its inward sloping interplane struts; it was also one of the first aircraft to be fitted with dual controls.

The Austrian reconnaissance units equipped with the CI valued its stability and reliability and the fact that it could take off and land in a relatively small area. The CI was also used for artillery observation and light bombing, making its first raid in May 1916. In late 1917 Austrian dependence on the CI was reduced with the arrival of two improved designs – the **Phönix CI** and the **Ufag CI** – but it continued in service until the end of the war.

Inward-slopping wing struts were a distinctive feature of the Austrian Brandenburg CI reconnaissance biplane

BRANDENBURG CC

This small single-seat fighter flying boat was designed by Ernst Heinkel and first appeared in 1916. It had a streamlined wooden hull and star-strut interplane bracing similar to that used in the **Brandenburg DI**. Power was provided by a 150hp Benz Bz III pusher engine mounted just under the top wing. Armament initially consisted of a single Spandau machine-gun, with twin guns sometimes fitted to later examples. The German navy received 36 of these aircraft in the year from May 1916, but little is known of their operational service in the North Sea or Baltic.

The CC was in fact much more extensively used by the Austrian navy, which fully recognised the potential military value of flying boats. Designated the

A-Class, the Brandenburg CC was manufactured under licence by the **Phönix** company and 135 examples were produced. It was very similar to the German original, although different engines were used and the **Schwarzlose machine-gun** was adopted instead of the Spandau.

The main function of the CC was to defend the ports and naval bases of the Adriatic and Aegean against the **Nieuport 11** and other aircraft in Italian service. It was often flown by **Gottfried Banfield**, the Austrian navy's leading air ace, and on one occasion he made contact with **Francesco Baracca** over the **Isonzo** in January 1917. With a maximum speed of 109m.p.h. it proved to be effective in its defensive role until the last few months of the war. By that time it had been overwhelmed by the scale and frequency of Italian air attacks.

BRANDENBURG DI

The Brandenburg DI was a single-seat fighter biplane used exclusively by the Austro-Hungarian service as a standard type in 1916–17. Like the **Brandenburg CI** it was designed by Ernst Heinkel in Germany but produced exclusively in Austria. A distinctive feature was its novel interplane bracing, consisting of eight struts that met half-way between each pair of wings. Not surprisingly, it was given the nicknames 'Star-strutter' and 'Spider'. The DI's short fuselage, deep nose, and the position of the radiator above the top wing, all contributed to its unattractive appearance. The power plant varied according to the manufacturer, with **Ufag**-constructed aircraft having the 185hp Austro Daimler engine and **Phönix**-built machines the less powerful 160hp version. The smaller engine gave a maximum speed of 116m.p.h. at sea level, with a good rate of climb.

Armament consisted of an unsynchronised 8mm **Schwarzlose machine-gun** enclosed in a casing and mounted above the upper wing. Problems were caused because the gun mechanism was inaccessible to the pilot in flight and the casing caused drag. Other difficulties emerged after the DI entered service in the autumn of 1916: visibility was restricted and it had poor lateral control, resulting in a number of fatal accidents until modifications were made. The DI was phased out from mid-1917 when other more suitable aircraft became available.

BRANDENBURG FB

This three-seat patrol flying boat served in small numbers with the navies of Germany and Austro-Hungary from early in 1916. Powered by either a 150hp Benz engine or a 160hp Daimler, this pusher biplane had an excellent range, enabling it to patrol the seas for hours at a time. A single **Parabellum** machine-gun, operated by the gunner, was mounted in the nose; the pilot and observer occupied a separate communal compartment behind. This soundly constructed design remained in Austrian service until the Armistice.

BRANDENBURG KDW

The KDW was a nautical version of the **Brandenburg DI**, which had been designed by Ernst Heinkel in Germany and was used exclusively by Austria. Heinkel was also responsible for developing this single-seat floatplane fighter whose airframe was very similar to the DI, apart from its increased wingspan and a small fixed fin below the fuselage; the distinctive star-type interplane bracing was retained. The KDW also shared most of the DI's drawbacks, including the reputation of being difficult to fly. Three different engines were fitted during the KDW's long production run (September 1916–February 1918): the 150hp Benz Bz III, 160hp Mercedes D III and 160hp Maybach Mb III. Armament consisted of a single synchronised **Spandau machine-gun**, except for a final batch which was equipped with two.

This interim design, produced to meet the German navy's urgent need for fighters to defend its seaplane bases, actually remained in service until the Armistice, operating from stations on the Flanders coast and on the Adriatic. The KDW's impact was limited by the fact that only 58 were produced. By 1918 it was obsolete, having been superseded by more advanced types, including the **Brandenburg W12**.

BRANDENBURG W12

The W12 was designed by Ernst Heinkel in response to the German navy's need for a seaplane capable of defending itself from an attack from the rear. This two-seat, single-bay biplane, which appeared early in 1917, was equipped with a **Parabellum machine-gun** in the rear cockpit, mounted on an elevated ring to give a good field of fire; it also carried one or two forward firing Spandau machine-guns. The W12 had a deep fuselage, with a tailplane mounted on top of it, and a comma-type rudder. Powered by either the 160hp Mercedes D III or the 150hp Benz Bz III tractor engine, it had a maximum speed of 100m.p.h. and excellent manoeuvrability for an aircraft of this size. Radio equipment was carried when the W12 was used for reconnaissance purposes.

In service with the air stations at Zeebrugge and Ostend, the new floatplane soon established itself as an efficient weapon against the opposing Allied

seaplanes operating from Dunkirk. By the time production ended in March 1918, 145 W12s had been made; they remained in service until the Armistice.

The German Brandenburg W12 seaplane fighter launched many attacks against Allied ships and planes in the North Sea and Channel

BRANDENBURG W29

A monoplane version of the **Brandenburg W12** floatplane, but otherwise little changed, the W29 two-seater entered the German navy in April 1918 and was one of the most successful aircraft of its type. With less drag than the biplane version, it was introduced as a quick solution to the problem of maintaining German air superiority in the North Sea. Most were powered by a single 150hp Benz Bz III

engine, which gave a maximum speed of 110m.p.h. and an endurance of about four hours. It had one or two forward firing Spandau machine-guns and a further gun in the rear; some were equipped with radios and some carried bombs.

With excellent speed, manoeuvrability and vision, the W29 proved to be a valuable addition to the W12s and W19s operating from bases in Flanders and

Northern Germany. During its short operational life it was used to escort U-boats and minesweepers and to attack small Allied naval vessels, as well as for local defence duties. It proved to be a worthy opponent of the best British seaplanes and flying boats and achieved some notable successes. In July 1918, for example, W29s attacked and crippled a British submarine and the following month they sunk three coastal motor boats. The aircraft's main weakness – its limited range – was overcome by the use of other machines scouting ahead, and calling on the W29 by radio when circumstances demanded it.

BRATIANU, ION, 1864–1927

Wartime prime minister of Rumania who delayed the country's entry into the war on the side of the Allies until August 1916. He first secured from the Entente powers the pledge of territorial gains that were central to Rumania's war aims, joining the war after the initial successes of the **Brusilov Offensive**. In spite of the army's long period of preparation the result of Rumania's intervention was military defeat within a few months, and only a small fraction of her territory remained unoccupied.

With the **Russian Revolution** and the collapse of her military power, Bratianu was compelled to agree a separate armistice with the Germans (December 1917). Bratianu had resigned in the hope that **General Averescu** would be able to negotiate more favourable terms, but he was to be disappointed. Returning to power in December 1918, he had been influential in the decision to re-enter the war two days before the Armistice, thus securing a place with the peace-makers. Bratianu used all his considerable political skills in representing Rumania's interests at the **Paris Peace Conference** and eventually most of her territorial demands were met.

BREGUET 4 & 5

The Breguet 4 and 5 were two-seater pusher biplanes developed from a prototype bomber which appeared early in 1915. The first production version was the Breguet 2, a large three-bay biplane powered by a 200hp Canton-Unné pusher engine, and manufactured by the Michelin brothers. An improved model, the Breguet 4, appeared in response to a French government specification for a new bomber. It had wings of unequal span and was powered by a 200hp Renault engine, giving a maximum speed of 84m.p.h. at sea level. Armament consisted of a single movable **Hotchkiss** or **Lewis machine-gun** in the front cockpit and forty 16lb bombs carried in the Michelin automatic bomb rack. A further variant, the Breguet 5, was designed to act as an escort to the 4. Similar in appearance, the new model was armed with a 37mm cannon in the front cockpit.

The 4 and 5 served with several *Escadrilles de Bombardement* of the French Aviation Militaire, from 1916 until the beginning of 1918, and with the RNAS in France and the Aegean. A large number of successful bombing raids were made but the aircraft were found to be too slow for daylight operations and difficult to take off and land.

BREGUET 14

The Breguet 14 was a large, sturdy two-seater biplane which first entered French service in the summer of 1917, replacing ageing **Caudron** and **Farman** machines. It was an advanced design, with duralumin alloy being used extensively in the airframe. Powered by a 300hp Renault engine, with a large frontal radiator, the A2 reconnaissance version had a maximum speed of 115m.p.h., while the heavier B2 bomber variant could do no more than 98m.p.h. The bomber also differed from the A2 in having transparent side panels, a longer, lower wingspan, and an external bomb rack that could hold thirty-two 8kg bombs. Both types normally had fitted as standard a single forward firing **Vickers machine-gun** and twin ring mounted **Lewis guns** for the observer.

Breguet 14s served with 71 *escadrilles* of the French Aviation Militaire on the Western Front, and were used in Serbia, Greece, and Macedonia. They were also employed by the Belgian and American air services. B2s were widely used by the French for day bombing in the last year of the war and they dropped nearly 1,900 tonnes of bombs on the Germans. During this period of intensive activity their front cockpits were partially protected by armour and downward firing machine-guns were fitted. A2s were extensively employed by the Corps d'Armée units on reconnaissance missions until the Armistice. The Breguet 14 was the most successful French bomber to appear during the war and production continued until 1926, with as many as 8,000 machines being built in total.

BREST-LITOVSK, TREATY OF, 3 March 1918

The peace treaty between Bolshevik Russia and the Central Powers, which ended the war on the Eastern Front and allowed the Germans to concentrate all their military strength in the west. An armistice had been signed by Russia and Germany on 3 December 1917 and a conference to negotiate an end to Russia's participation in the war began immediately at Brest-Litovsk in eastern Poland. In the vain hope that workers' strikes in Germany and Austro-Hungary marked the beginnings of socialist revolution in those countries, **Trotsky**, the head of the Russian delegation, employed delaying tactics at the conference. Refusing to sign the dictated treaty, he adopted the policy of 'neither peace nor war'.

However, on 18 February 1918 the Germans responded by renewing their advance eastwards; it progressed rapidly, and Petrograd was threatened. Powerless to respond effectively, the Russians were forced to accept the imposed German terms, which compelled them to relinquish the Ukraine, Finland, the Baltic provinces, the Caucasus, White Russia and Poland. As a result, at one stroke, 'Russia lost all the conquests which the tsars had made during the last two hundred years.' Although the German armistice on the Western Front in November 1918 rendered the Treaty null and void, the frontiers determined at Brest-Litovsk, except for the Ukraine, were maintained by the Allies. It was not until the Second World War that Russia was able to recover much of the ground lost.

BRETAGNE

These French dreadnought battleships were similar to the Courbet class, having exactly the same hull and dimensions as their predecessors. Significant improvements included the removal of the wing turrets with all main armament being located on the centre line. Mounted in twin turrets were ten larger (13.4-inch) guns, although their maximum range (14,500m) was inadequate. *Bretagne*, *Lorraine* and *Provence* entered service with the French navy in 1916 and were employed in the Mediterranean until the end of the war.

BRIAND, ARISTIDE, 1862–1932

French wartime Prime Minister for 18 months from October 1915 to March 1917, Briand was a former socialist who had moved towards the centre. He held the office of premier eleven times altogether. A premier's ability to shape policy during the war was restricted by the role of the President, divisions within the Cabinet, and the influence of **Joffre**, the commander-in-chief. As a result, Briand 'survived events; he never dominated them.' A prominent 'Easterner', he preserved the Balkan Front in the face of British opposition at the end of 1915, and, in 1916, he survived the attack on **Verdun**, which he had ordered to be held at all costs.

When a succession of military failures, notably the **Somme Offensive**, began to threaten Briand's government he eased Joffre out and replaced him with **Nivelle**. It was, however, a dispute with the Chamber of Deputies about its right of access to military information, rather than military defeat, that was the immediate cause of his own downfall in March 1917. He remained outside government for the rest of the war but in mid-1917 he was the object of an unsuccessful approach by the Germans about the possibility of a compromise peace.

BRISTOL F2A & F2B

Designed as a replacement for the **Royal Aircraft Factory BE2c**, the F2A or Bristol Fighter was a large two-seater fighter-reconnaissance biplane that proved to be an outstanding success in RFC/RAF service. It was, perhaps, the best aircraft of its type in France in the last year of the war. A two-bay, equal-span wing arrangement was adopted, with power being provided by a 190hp Rolls Royce Mk I Falcon engine. It had a maximum speed of 110m.p.h. at sea level and a ceiling of 16,000 feet. The crew, who were accommodated close together to facilitate communication, enjoyed excellent all-round visibility. The pilot was armed with a forward firing .303-inch **Vickers machine-gun**, while the observer operated a .303-inch **Lewis machine-gun** mounted on a Scarff ring.

The first F2As appeared in December 1916 although they were not used at the front until the Battle of Arras, April–May 1917

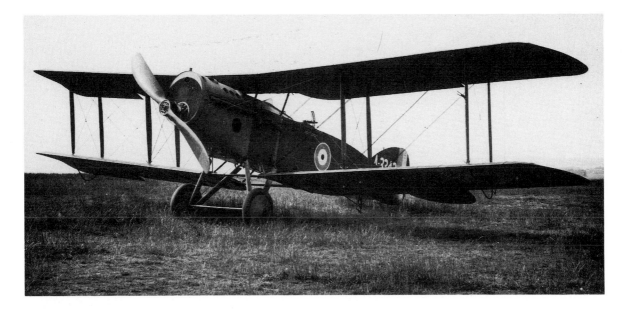

The first production F2As, or 'Brisfits', as they were nicknamed, appeared in December 1916, but, in order to achieve maximum surprise, they were not used at the front until the **Battle of Arras**. However, their operational debut, on 5 April 1917, was a disaster: four Bristols were lost to **von Richthofen**'s 'circus' as their crews clung to standard two-seater tactics. The observer's gun was regarded as the primary weapon and the pilot manoeuvred to give his colleague the best position. There were further heavy losses over the next few days, but soon F2A crews adjusted their tactics and it was flown as if it were a single-seat fighter. The Vickers was the principal offensive weapon, with the observer's rear gun being used defensively. When employed in this way, the aircraft, which was strong and manoeuvrable, was a great success and was soon ordered in large numbers.

In July 1917 it was decided to re-equip all fighter reconnaissance and corps reconnaissance squadrons with the Bristol and a total of 3,101 machines were delivered to the RAF before the Armistice. They served in Italy, Palestine and the United Kingdom, as well as in France. Almost all of these were delivered in modified F2B form, with a revised tailplane, an even better cockpit view and a succession of different engines, including the 220hp Rolls Royce Falcon Mk II and the 275hp Falcon Mk III. A further indication of the quality of this Bristol design is the fact that it was retained by the RAF as a standard type until 1932.

The popular 'Brisfit' F2B fighter reconnaissance biplane, a modified version of the F2A

BRISTOL M.1C

The potential of the excellent Bristol M.1C monoplane fighter was never properly exploited because of official reservations about this class of aircraft, which dated back to before the war. Bearing some resemblance to the **Morane Saulnier Type N**, this Bristol monoplane, which first emerged from the production line in September 1917, had a circular cross-section fuselage and a large fin braced to the tailplane by two wires. It was powered by a 110hp Le Rhône rotary engine with a large rounded spinner, giving a maximum speed of 112m.p.h. and a good rate of climb. (In prototype form in July 1916 this manoeuvrable aircraft had reached the very high speed of 132m.p.h.)

The pilot, who sat directly over the wings, had excellent visibility and was armed with a single .303 **Vickers machine-gun**.

Unwilling to allocate the Bristol M.1C to the Western Front, ostensibly because of its high landing speed, the RFC ordered no more than 125 production machines. A small number served with three squadrons in Mesopotamia and Macedonia, but most were used for training purposes in Britain and Egypt. There is little doubt that the Bristol monoplane would have made a considerable impact if it had been used in quantity on the Western Front.

BRISTOL SCOUT

Originating as a pre-war racing design, the single-seat Bristol Scout served with the RFC and RNAS from the outbreak of war. The two existing Scout Bs were sent to France in August 1914, but series production did not begin until later in the year, with the first Scout Cs emerging off the production line in April 1915. Powered by the 80hp Gnome, Le Rhône or Clerget engines or the 110hp Clerget, this single-bay biplane had a good maximum speed of 93m.p.h. and excellent flying qualities. An improved version, the Scout D, which appeared in December 1915, had minor airframe modifications and alternative power units.

A total of 161 C-types and 210 Ds were produced. Most examples were unarmed except for a rifle or pistol carried by the pilot, although some were subsequently fitted with a **Lewis gun** that fired over top wing. Production ceased before more than a few could be fitted with a synchronised machine-gun and as a result the Scout was unable to realise fully its undoubted potential as a fighter.

The aircraft served with most RFC squadrons on the Western Front, being allocated in small numbers to individual two-seater units for escort duties. Although its lack of effective armament was a serious limitation, the Scout did score some notable combat successes, of which **Lanoe Hawker**'s achievement in shooting down three two-seaters is the most memorable.

The Scout was also used extensively by the RNAS on anti-Zeppelin patrols, operating from coastal air stations and from carriers; it was armed with 48 Ranken darts for this purpose. Relatively unsuccessful in this role, its main achievement as a naval aircraft was to become, on 3 November 1915, the first landplane with a wheeled undercarriage to take off from the deck of an aircraft carrier. Operational use of the Bristol Scout on the Western Front had largely ended by mid-1916, although it continued in service for some time in Palestine, Macedonia and Mesopotamia, and was also employed as a trainer.

With no suitable armament available in 1914–15, the Bristol Scout's considerable potential as a fighter was never realised

BRITISH ARMY

Unlike its continental counterparts, the British army of 1914 was a small, professional force which relied on voluntary recruitment. Its size reflected the government's belief that the Royal Navy would make the major British contribution to a war in Europe. Its participation in the land war was to be confined to the British Expeditionary Force, a highly trained professional army of 150,000 men (six infantry and one cavalry divisions), commanded by **Sir John French**.

The force, which was positioned on the left of the French line, played a more prominent role in the initial fighting than its small size might have suggested. It fought delaying actions at Mons and **Le Cateau** before making a key manoeuvre during the **Battle of the Marne** which threatened the flank of the German First Army. Casualty rates were high, with 86,237 men being killed or injured in 1914. One of its major strengths was its standard of rifle shooting, which was 'unique amongst the world's armies'. In fact, during the Battle of Mons, the enemy believed that it was facing machine-guns rather than the rapid rifle fire of British troops. However, its technical skills were not matched by realistic tactical doctrines: it failed to acknowledge the power of fire defence or the fact that the cavalry was largely redundant in modern warfare.

As trench warfare began late in 1914 it quickly became clear that the war would not be over by Christmas as most British soldiers had originally expected. France could not defend a front of 400 miles alone and Britain was now faced with the need for a massive expansion of its army – from the original 200,000 men to 2 million – to cover the sector between Ypres and Givenchy. Under **Lord Kitchener**'s direction, a mass volunteer army was created, 1,186,350 recruits having joined up by the end of 1914. The effectiveness of Kitchener's 'New Armies' was undermined by poor training facilities – many experienced professionals having been lost in the first few months of the war – and acute shortages of artillery ammunition and other equipment required in trench warfare.

The British were unable to convert their industry to the production of munitions quickly enough and for a time were forced to rely on American imports, often of poor quality. The build-up in British strength in the Flanders trenches was therefore slow and the army's contribution in 1915 was relatively small. BEF launched two offensives – **Neuve Chapelle** and **Artois-Loos** – during the year, and the failure of the latter brought French's period in command to an end. He was replaced by **Sir Douglas Haig** who remained in command until the end of the war.

Haig's name is, of course, closely associated with the costly war of attrition on the Western Front, of which the **First Battle of the Somme** was the first major example during his command. It was described as the 'glory and the graveyard of Kitchener's army'. Rising casualty figures and insufficient volunteers had already led to the introduction of conscription in Britain in January 1916. At that time there were 987,000 British troops in France, along with strong contingents from Canada, Australia, New Zealand and other parts of the Empire. Total wartime enlistment from all sources in Great Britain came to nearly 5 million, representing nearly 25 per cent of the male population.

Conscription provided the manpower for the costly battles of 1917 – **Messines**, **Third Ypres** and **Cambrai** – when Britain played the leading role in offensive action after the virtual collapse of the French army. These all ended in disappointment but marked the arrival of the tank as a major weapon. **Lloyd George**'s disenchantment with the strategy of attrition led to the dismissal of the Chief of Staff, **Sir William Robertson**, and restrictions on the supply of men to the Western Front. At the same time the British share of the front had been extended and, by the beginning of 1918, 60 British divisions faced nearly 100 German.

The British line held during **Ludendorff**'s first offensive of 1918 although it was pushed back to within 30 miles of the sea. Now under a unified Allied command and heavily reinforced, the British army, equipped with over 450 tanks, won the famous victory at **Amiens** ('the black day of the German army') on 8 August 1918. During the concluding operations of the war the British army played a major role, breaking the Hindenburg Line and recovering all the territory lost by the British in 1914. Victory on the Western Front had been secured at a cost of nearly 350,000 British casualties.

British troops, with major support from imperial forces, were also involved in campaigns against Turkey in **Gallipoli**, Palestine and Mesopotamia. With the possible exception of the Gallipoli expedition, none of these campaigns had any prospect of directly affecting the outcome of the war in Europe, but involved the diversion of resources from the main front. Gallipoli was badly managed, costly in human life and duplicated the siege conditions of the Western Front. Imperial troops also captured the German colonial possessions in Africa, with the exception of **German East Africa**, where operations continued until the end of the war.

British and French troops, now under a unified command, on the move during the Aisne offensive, May 1918

BRITISH 18-POUNDER FIELD GUN

The standard field gun of the British army during the First World War, the 18-pdr (calibre 3.3 inches) was a sound and reliable design that first appeared in 1904. It was mounted on a pole trail carriage and was equipped with a standard protective shield. The barrel was wire wound and there was a single-action breech; its maximum range was 6,525 yards and it weighed 2,821lb. Design modifications, including a new recoil system, were made during the war, but a more fundamental revision, which became known as the Mark IV, was only just entering mass production as the war ended. The 18-pdr was also used extensively by the American Expeditionary Force in 1917–18 and by some Commonwealth forces.

An 18-pounder field gun – the standard British artillery piece of the First World War – in operation at the Battle of Arras, 1917

BROKE

In a notable action in the Straits of Dover on the night of 20/21 April 1917, ships of the Dover Patrol sank two German destroyers. *Broke* and *Swift* were on regular patrol in the area of the net barrage that ran from the South Goodwins when they intercepted an enemy flotilla. Twelve German destroyers in total (two flotillas) had left their base at Zeebrugge with the aim of attacking the trawlers that regularly patrolled the barrage. The action began in the early hours of 21 April when *Swift* torpedoed one German warship and gave chase to another; *Broke* also hit a boat with a torpedo and then rammed another.

Commander Evans of the *Broke* graphically described how they carried the German destroyer 'bodily along on our ram, pouring a deadly fire into her terrorised crew. Many clambered on to our forecastle, only to meet with instant death from our well-armed seamen and stokers. When we eventually broke clear, we left G42 a sinking, blazing wreck.' *Broke*, which was by now badly damaged and had 57 casualties, tried unsuccessfully to ram another enemy ship before returning to base. As a result of this engagement there were no further German raids into the Straits of Dover until 1918.

BROWNING AUTOMATIC RIFLE

This weapon was designed by John Browning in 1917 in response to an American requirement for an assault rifle for use on the Western Front. Troops advancing from the trenches were particularly vulnerable without the rapid covering fire that could be produced by a portable automatic rifle. Operated by one man, the .30 calibre Browning had a gas operated mechanism that could fire 550 rounds per minute and a muzzle velocity of 2,650 feet per second. With a box magazine that held only 20 rounds, the Browning could be used as a single-shot weapon and there was a selector switch for this purpose. It was well made and could be stripped down easily for repair or maintenance. Manufactured by Colt and two sub-contractors, some 52,000 examples appeared before the Armistice.

The rifle entered service on the Western Front in September 1918, too late to make any real impact on the course of events. Well received by American troops, it remained in use with the US army until after the Second World War. It did not, however, become the assault rifle it was intended to be: it was too heavy (16lb) and large (overall length 47 inches) and could not be fired from the shoulder or hip with any accuracy. Yet, as an automatic weapon its main limitations were its relative lightness and the small capacity of its magazine. Adapted as a result of wartime experience, the Browning Automatic Rifle was fitted with a bipod and was used as a light machine-gun in support of infantry rather than as an assault weapon.

BROWNING MACHINE-GUN

John Browning's design for a machine-gun with a short recoil operating system was tested in prototype form in about 1910, but it was not until America's entry into the war was imminent that the military authorities demonstrated any interest in it.

With only very limited reserves of obsolete machine-guns available, the Browning Model 1917

was quickly ordered into production and three manufacturers had made some 57,000 examples by the end of the war. Generally similar in external appearance to the **Vickers**, apart from the pistol grip at the rear of the breech, the water-cooled Browning was chambered for the American .30 cartridge. With a 250-round belt magazine, it had a cyclic rate of fire of 450–600 rounds per minute and a muzzle velocity of 2,800 feet per second.

The gun made little impact on the course of the war as it was not used in action until 26 September 1918 and by the Armistice only a proportion of the total production had reached Europe. Normally reliable, even with intensive use, it remained in US service (in a slightly modified form) as a standard heavy machine-gun throughout the Second World War and beyond.

BRUMOWSKI, GODWIN, 1889–1936

The leading ace of the Austrian air service, Brumowski's 40 victories were all achieved on the Italian Front, where he served for most of the war. He successfully adopted German ideas about the organisation and tactics of *Luftfahrtruppen* in unfavourable circumstances in 1916–17. Like many of his German colleagues, Brumowski also devised an individual emblem – a white skull on a black background – for *Fliegerkompanie* 41, the unit he commanded. Many of Brumowski's victories were achieved in the last few months of 1917 when the Central Powers had gained air superiority on the front. He survived the last difficult period of the war when the Italians were increasingly dominant and remained in the air force of the new Austrian Republic.

BRUSILOV, GENERAL ALEXEI, 1853–1926

A Russian cavalry general of 'supreme energy and self-confidence', Brusilov was the architect of his country's only successful offensive during the First World War. At the beginning of the war, he was commander of the Eighth Army and fought against the Austrians in Galicia. In the spring of 1915, his army was pushed back 300 miles from the foothills of the Carpathians during **Hindenburg**'s major offensive. Brusilov's forces were active in bringing the attack to an end in the autumn, launching a counter-offensive against the Austrians at Luck.

In March 1916, Brusilov was promoted to the command of the South-Western Front, replacing **General Ivanov**. When Italy asked the Russians to launch an offensive to relieve Austrian pressure in the Trentino, Brusilov responded quickly and effectively. Abandoning the traditional tactics of attrition in a narrow sector, he launched a bold offensive with his four field armies attacking along a 300-mile front. These surprise attacks were followed up with the help of reserve forces and the Austrian line was breached in two places; Brusilov advanced to capture the Bukovina and most of Galicia before the momentum was lost. The appearance of additional German troops

Russia's most successful First World War general studying the progress of the war on the Eastern Front

was the main reason for his failure to achieve a decisive victory and was a major cause of the heavy losses he sustained during the third assault (2 August–20 September 1916), which was continued for too long. Although Brusilov's operation had many positive political effects, the large casualties 'undermined morally, even more than materially, the fighting power of Russia.'

One of the leading generals who supported the Tsar's abdication, Brusilov replaced **Alekseev** as commander-in-chief soon after the March revolution. Brusilov's new offensive, launched in July 1917, gained some initial successes, but the demoralised Russian army soon gave way as the Germans counter-attacked: they were quickly driven from Austro-Hungary and Brusilov was replaced by **Kornilov**. He remained in Russia under Bolshevik rule and joined the Red Army in 1920.

BRUSILOV OFFENSIVE, 4 June–20 September 1916

Continued German pressure on **Verdun** and Austrian attacks in Italy, led the Russians to launch a major new offensive on the Eastern Front in support of their Allies in June 1916. **General Brusilov**, commander of the South-Western Front, was the only Russian military leader ready and willing to attack. His four armies – the Eighth, Eleventh, Seventh and Ninth – were positioned along a line extending 300 miles from the Pripet Marshes in the north to the Rumanian border in the south. Opposing him from north to south were five numerically weaker German and Austrian armies: the Austrian Fourth, and Austrian First, the Austrian Second, Austro-German South and the Austrian Seventh.

The offensive began on 4 June, following a massive artillery bombardment, and was launched in two main sectors: opposite Luck on Brusilov's right and in the valleys of the Dniester and Prut to his left. The Austrians had not been aware of the precise location of the attacks and quickly fell back in disarray. In the north, as the Fourth Army retreated, Luck was taken on 6 June and Kovel, a communications centre 50 miles further west, fell four days later. In the south the Austrian Seventh Army offered little effective resistance and Czernowitz, in the Bukovina, had fallen by 17 June. On the front between the two attacks, the South Army and the Austrian First and Second Armies also retreated, even though they had come under little pressure.

By the middle of the month the initial advance was brought to an end as Brusilov ran into serious transport and supply problems. In addition, a pro-mised supporting attack by **General Evert** to the north did not materialise. A maximum advance of 50 miles had been achieved in the north and prisoners were taken in large numbers, with nearly 90,000 men in Russian hands by 9 June.

The Germans reacted quickly to the deteriorating situation. Fifteen German and eight Austrian divisions were transferred from other sectors to support their weakened defences. The Germans counter-attacked in the northern sector on 16 June, but little progress (8–9 miles) was made during the eight-day battle. The Russians also reinforced but at a slower rate because their railway network was less efficient.

On 28 July, they attacked again but the operation was soon halted because of a shortage of ammunition. Brusilov's offensive was reopened once more on 7 August and despite the arrival in the south of more German troops, the Russians reached the foothills of the Carpathians and took the whole of the Bukovina. By this time the Germans, under the command of **Hindenburg**, who now controlled the whole front, had been able to stabilise their positions and Brusilov was forced to abandon the attack once more. It was briefly renewed in September when Rumania began her offensive, but after the 20th there was no further movement. Russia had exhausted her supplies of manpower and other resources. Casualties were massive, with each side losing a million men, half of whom were prisoners of war.

This was the last great campaign on the Eastern Front and 'the most competent Russian operation of the First World War'. However, Brusilov failed to receive the real support from his fellow army group commanders or from the high command that might have produced further successes. The offensive also further weakened Russia and increased internal ten-

sions. The Germans had succeeded in halting the Russian 'steamroller', but Austria, which suffered severe losses, became increasingly dependent upon its principal ally, Germany.

B-TYPE MOTOR BUS

At the beginning of the war the British army, like its European counterparts, still depended heavily on horse-drawn transport, having no more than 1,200 motor vehicles in service. These were all fully committed when British naval forces were sent to protect the Channel ports in September 1914 and the Admiralty requisitioned 70 Daimler buses, which were operated by a subsidiary of the London General Omnibus Company (LGOC). Used for general transport and patrol work in the coastal areas of Belgium, they proved to be particularly useful in moving troops to **Antwerp** in October to help with its defence.

These early experiences convinced the army that buses could help meet the large gap in its transport needs and in October it received an allocation of 300 B-type buses from the LGOC. Some of these were converted to lorries, ambulances, mobile workshops, anti-aircraft platforms and other service vehicles. The B-type chassis, produced by the Associated Equipment Company (AEC), had in fact provided the basis for a variety of purpose-built army lorries since 1913. The remaining buses, staffed by volunteer crews, were sent to France and Belgium with very little modification at first. Later they were painted khaki and their

lower windows were boarded up. Powered by a 25 or 30hp four-cylinder engine, with a maximum speed of 20m.p.h., they could carry up to 25 troops.

As the war progressed arrangements for the movement of troops at the front became more efficient and better organised. Auxiliary Omnibus Companies, each with 50 or more buses, were established in the autumn of 1916. However, to facilitate troop movements along the whole front more centralised arrangements were established – the seven companies being grouped together as the Auxiliary Omnibus Park and controlled by General Headquarters.

The B-type remained in service until the Armistice, with over 900 vehicles – a third of LGOC's strength – being used. They returned to the streets of London after the war and one of them, subsequently named 'Ole Bill', after Bruce Bairnsfather's First World War cartoon character, has been preserved in the Imperial War Museum, London. The French army also acquired buses in large numbers and the Schneider PB2 Omnibus from Paris was a familiar sight at the front throughout the war.

BULLARD, GENERAL ROBERT LEE, 1861–1947

Appointed commander of the American Second Army, which was created in October 1918 and located between the Moselle and the Meuse, Bullard had little further opportunity to use his professional skills before the Armistice. He had already established

an excellent reputation in France, particularly as a result of the capture of **Cantigny** in May 1918 and his role in the **Second Battle of the Marne**, July–August 1918.

BÜLOW, FIELD MARSHAL KARL VON, 1846–1921

German field marshal who commanded the Second Army during the invasion of Belgium and France in 1914. Positioned to the left of **Kluck**'s First Army, Bülow passed through the Liège corridor and across the Meuse, defeating the French at the Battle of the Sambre (22–23 August). Advancing through France early in September, he fell well behind Kluck. The gap widened as the latter turned westwards to meet the attack from the French Sixth Army (**Maunoury**). As the **Battle of the Marne** developed, the British moved forwards into the gap and the right flank of the Second Army became vulnerable. Bülow, who now feared defeat, considered a German withdrawal inevitable; he was ordered to do so on 9 September.

In order to coordinate the German retreat more effectively, Bülow was placed in overall command of the First and Second Armies during the **Battle of the Aisne** and the 'Race to the Sea'. He remained as commander of the Second Army until March 1915 when, because of ill health, he was replaced by **von der Marwitz**. Although he had been promoted field marshal earlier in the year, Bülow was later unable to secure another army command, his role in the Battle of the Marne having damaged his reputation.

BYNG, FIELD MARSHAL JULIAN, 1ST VISCOUNT, 1862–1935

British field marshal who established his reputation during the South African War, commanding a regiment of light horse that he had raised himself. On the outbreak of war he was recalled from his command in Egypt to head the Third Cavalry Division and subsequently the Cavalry Corps. In August 1915 he was sent to **Gallipoli** as commander of IX Corps, but by then the fate of the expedition had been sealed. He was a firm advocate of the early evacuation of the peninsula and prepared the plan on which it was eventually based. His next major appointment, in May 1916, was to the command of the Canadian Army Corps, where he established himself as a popular and effective commander. The Corps' greatest achievement under his leadership was, of course, the capture of Vimy Ridge in April 1917.

In the following June, Byng succeeded **Allenby** as head of the Third Army, a post he held until the end of the war. He planned and carried out the **Cambrai offensive** in November 1917, the first mass attack by tanks operating independently. Byng was over-optimistic about the course and outcome of the operation, which failed partly because of insufficient reserves. More successful was the Third Army's response to the German offensive in March 1918, when it conceded only limited gains. During the Allied counter-offensive in the autumn, Byng's forces made a substantial contribution to driving the enemy back to the Hindenburg Line and beyond. In recognition of his wartime services he was raised to the peerage as Baron Byng of Vimy in 1919.

CADORNA, FIELD MARSHAL LUIGI, COUNT, 1850–1928

The **Caporetto** disaster effectively ended the military career of General Luigi Cadorna, who was appointed chief of staff of the Italian army less than a year before Italy's entry into the First World War.

Charged with modernising this antiquated force, he started but could not complete the process of improving its equipment, overhauling mobilisation arrangements and strengthening border defences. As war was declared, Cadorna assumed command in the field and in May 1915 launched the first major offensive against the Austro-Hungarian army, on the **Isonzo Front** towards Gorizia and Trieste.

With the Italian army in less than a full state of readiness, the advance soon ground to a halt and, as on the Western Front, trench warfare appeared in its place. On the completion of mobilisation Cadorna launched a fresh attack (23 June 1915), the first of four Battles of the Isonzo fought in 1915. Facing a determined enemy without adequate artillery, Cadorna's attacks resulted in disproportionate Italian losses (250,000 men) and produced no gains.

An Austrian advance from the Trentino in May 1916 temporarily halted Cadorna's plans for a further assault and in fact his own personal position was in jeopardy until the situation had been stabilised. He recovered his reputation during the Sixth Battle of the Isonzo (August 1916), when the Italians advanced several miles. However, three more offensives in the autumn of 1916 made no further impact and it was not until his army had been reinforced that he tried again. The Eleventh Battle (August-September 1917) also achieved nothing, but it produced alarm in Austria, which successfully sought German military assistance.

In October 1917, German and Austrian troops attacked the Caporetto sector, a lightly defended part of the Isonzo and the whole front soon collapsed. Cadorna, who was not expecting an attack until 1918, was unprepared; after hesitating for two days he ordered a general retreat. The line stabilised 70 miles further back at the River Piave, with the Italians suffering heavy losses and French and British reinforcements being brought in.

Cadorna was removed from his command and replaced by **General Diaz**; after a brief term on the new Supreme War Council – a product of the defeat and of the **Rapallo conference** that followed it – he retired. His main weakness was 'his lack of touch with and understanding of the fighting troops', which led him to ignore the negative effect of more than two years of trench warfare on their operational effectiveness.

Inadequate preparation before Caporetto cost Cadorna (centre) his job as chief of staff almost as soon as disaster had struck

CAILLAUX, JOSEPH, 1863–1944

Arrested for treason during the war, Caillaux had briefly been premier of France in 1911–12 and held the office of Minister of Finance under seven different administrations. Noted for his pro-German sympathies, he advocated a policy of appeasement towards her before 1914. During the war he was associated with a group of defeatists who favoured reconciliation with France's principal enemy. Their campaign helped to undermine morale on the home front in 1916–17 and was a contributory cause of the French army mutinies of 1917.

Caillaux had been considered for the premiership when the wartime coalition broke down in the autumn of 1917 but President **Painlevé** ruled out a negotiated peace and appointed **Clemenceau** instead. Not long afterwards Caillaux, along with some of his associates, was arrested and charged with correspondence with the enemy. Although he was not convicted until after the war, the charges succeeded in their principal purpose – stirring 'patriotic emotions into enthusiasm for Clemenceau'. His three-year prison sentence was commuted and in the changed climate of the 1920s he was able to resume his political career.

CAMBRAI, BATTLE OF, 20 November–7 December 1917

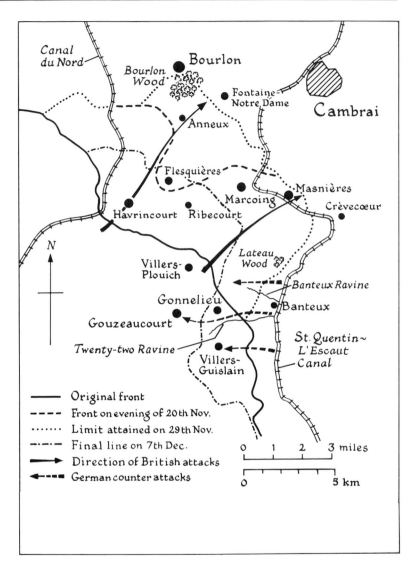

The first massed tank attack in history began on 20 November 1917, when the British Third Army (**General Byng**) moved against the Hindenburg Line in the rolling downland to the south-west of Cambrai. Byng had 19 divisions on the whole Cambrai front as opposed to six German, two of which were in the area to be attacked. Eight British divisions and 324 tanks were involved in the main attack, but only five cavalry divisions were available for use.

It began in the early morning mist on 20 November, without the normal preliminary bombardment. The German Second Army (**von der Marwitz**) was taken completely by surprise and within a few hours the formidable Hindenburg Line had been overrun. By the late afternoon, the British had advanced by up to four miles on a six-mile front, but progress was soon halted by tank losses and failures (179 in total), inadequate reinforcements and strong German resistance. To the right, the advance had reached the St Quentin canal, but the village of Flesquières remained in enemy hands and no attack had yet been made on Bourlon Ridge; its capture was necessary for the advance north-east and **Haig** gave it priority. On 23 November, after heavy fighting, it was taken.

The limit of the British advance had now been reached. An area five miles deep and seven miles wide, which extended a little beyond the Canal du Nord to the west, had been won, but the front was still three miles from Cambrai, the initial objective of the whole offensive. On 27 November, Bourlon Wood was recaptured by the Germans in local operations as **Ludendorff** planned a major counter-offensive against both sides of the rectangular salient.

Twenty divisions were assembled before the massive attack began on 30 November and the British Third Army, now outnumbered, was ill-prepared to meet it. On the south flank of the salient the Germans penetrated up to three miles and pushed back the British right wing from the St Quentin canal. To the north, stronger defensive positions held back the Germans and on the third day (2 December) the offensive was brought to an end.

Haig was now compelled to shorten the salient by withdrawing three miles in the centre and left during

4–7 December. Britain retained much of the ground seized on the first day but had lost a strip nearly as large to the south. The British sustained 44,000 casualties and 6,000 prisoners, the Germans slightly more: 50,000 killed or wounded and 11,000 prisoners. The causes of the British failure included the lack of close supporting infantry, weaknesses of command and inexperienced troops. The Battle of Cambrai was, however, the 'type of battle of the future and its influence on the Second World War was as great as that on the remainder of the First.'

Horses, not tanks, predominated as the British advanced during the Battle of Cambrai

CAMBRAI–ST QUENTIN OFFENSIVE, 27 September–11 November 1918

The final Allied offensive against Germany on the Western Front, which began on 26 September 1918, aimed to disrupt vital German rail links and supply centres. If it were successful it would help to undermine the whole basis of Germany's position. Two massive converging attacks, as well as a subsidiary operation in Flanders, were planned, with the Franco-American element (the **Meuse–Argonne offensive**) starting first. Two hundred miles to the west, the British, supported by the French left, were preparing to attack towards Cambrai and St Quentin. In total, 41 Allied divisions, under **Haig**'s command, were to advance on a comparable number of Germans, making it larger than the main Meuse–Argonne operation.

The British First (Horne) and Third (**Byng**) Armies, positioned on the north of this line, which ran for 18 miles, attacked on 27 September. After a few hours they had crossed the Canal du Nord and were within three miles of Cambrai. The Third Army entered the western suburbs of the town on 30 September, while Canadian forces were threatening to outflank it from the north. Although Cambrai itself did not fall until 9 October, **Ludendorff** was immediately alarmed by the Allies' rapid progress, even though no breakthrough had been achieved and their progress on the other two fronts had been temporarily halted. The military situation was now so difficult that Germany should, he suggested, request an armistice. It was the beginning of the process that ended with the cessation of hostilities on 11 November.

On the south of the line, in the St Quentin sector, the British Fourth Army (**Rawlinson**) joined in the action on 29 September, after a massive artillery bombardment. It was supported by a number of American divisions and the French First Army (Debeney). Under heavy pressure from Rawlinson, the Germans, under Max von Boehn, were unable to hold the Hindenburg Line, which was finally abandoned on 4 October. They then withdrew on a broad front, not just opposite Rawlinson's position but also facing the British Third, First and Fifth (Birdwood) Armies. The Germans stopped at the River Selle, about nine miles from their original positions, but were soon forced to resume their retreat as the Allies moved forward in strength.

The Selle line was seized during an attack which began on 17 October; 20,000 prisoners were taken in a significant British victory. The Third Army forced a crossing lower down on 20 October. By the end of the month the German armies in the north had been pushed back behind the Scheldt on a 20-mile front.

Haig's forces were now joined on their left by 'the Group of Armies of Flanders' – Belgian, French and British troops – under **King Albert**'s command. It had launched its converging Flanders offensive on 28 September, quickly taking the Ypres ridge and moving along the coast. Progress had slowed in the swampy conditions of Flanders but began to move again at the end of October. On the right, the French Fifth and Tenth Armies prevented the movement of reserves to the main battle zone.

Haig's offensive resumed on 1 November, with his forces advancing along a 30-mile front. The Germans were now in a critical state with the army suffering severe manpower and equipment shortages. The line of the Scheldt was crossed on 8 November, with Ghent and Mons being freed by the time of the Armistice. The French/American offensive further south had ultimately made more dramatic progress, but it was the combined impact of these two thrusts that finally brought the war to an end.

CAMEROONS

The Allies had no clear plan for the conquest of the Cameroons, a German colony that was larger than Germany itself, and underestimated the difficulties involved. Although it was garrisoned by no more than 1,460 Germans and 6,550 African troops, roads were very poor and disease was rife, particularly in the coastal areas. British, French and Belgian troops invaded the Cameroons in August 1914 from their adjoining colonies, with the force from French Equitorial Africa making particularly good progress in the eastern part of the country. The British advance went less well but an Anglo-French amphibious expedition captured the capital, Duala, on 27 November.

The planned concentric advance on Yuande, in the hilly interior where the enemy was now concentrated, was delayed for many months because of unfavourable conditions and was not resumed until October 1915. By the time the Allies arrived there, few Germans remained, the commander and his troops having fled to Spanish Guinea, where they were interned. Isolated German outposts further inland held out until February 1916, when all resistance ended. As many as 24,000 Allied troops had participated in this protracted and costly minor campaign.

CANADA

Originally ordered by Chile, this British-built battleship was purchased for the Royal Navy on the outbreak of war and was completed in September 1915. She served with the **Grand Fleet** for the remainder of the war and fought at **Jutland**. A longer version of the Iron Duke class, *Canada* had a displacement of 28,600 tons and a good maximum speed of nearly 23 knots. Armour protection did not compare favourably with the navy's other capital ships, but she was well armed, having ten 14-inch guns in twin turrets and good secondary armament. Work on *Canada*'s sister ship was stopped in August 1914 but she was also acquired by Britain and completed in 1920 as the aircraft carrier *Eagle*.

CANOPUS

Based on the Majestics, this class of 13,000-ton British battleships, built for service in the Far East, was completed in 1900–02. They were smaller and lighter than their predecessors and used stronger but thinner

Krupp armour for the first time. Main armament consisted of four 12-inch guns mounted in fore and aft pairs; there were also twelve 6-inch guns and four 18-inch torpedo tubes. The first battleships to be fitted with the more efficient water tube boilers, the Canopus class had a maximum speed of just over 18 knots.

Canopus and her sisters – Albion, Glory, Goliath, Ocean and Vengeance – were used extensively during the war. Canopus herself was part of **Rear Admiral** **Cradock**'s force in the South Atlantic but she did not participate in the **Battle of Coronel**. She did, however, fire the opening shots in the **Battle of the Falkland Islands** as guardship at Port Stanley, although she was unable to join in the pursuit. All but Glory were present in the **Dardanelles** in 1915 and formed a significant part of the battleship force there. Ocean and Goliath were lost, but the others survived and remained in service until the Armistice.

CANTIGNY, BATTLE OF, 28 May 1918

On the second day of the German offensive on the **Aisne River**, the first American attack of the war took place at Cantigny, a village near Montdidier. To the east of the Somme River sector, which was occupied by the American First Division (**Bullard**), it was held by the German Eighteenth Army (**von Hutier**). Cantigny was captured on the first day (28 May 1918) and 200 prisoners were taken. The Americans withstood a series of strong counter-attacks which died out during the second day. The victors suffered 1,603 casualties, of which 199 were killed. Although Cantigny was a local action and had little strategic significance, its psychological impact was more important. Allied morale was boosted when American troops, in their first engagement, defeated a veteran German formation. A few days later the American Second and Third Divisions were in action on the **Marne** River.

CAPELLE, EDUARD von, 1855–1931

Appointed as **Tirpitz**'s successor as Secretary of State of the Ministry of Marine in March 1916, Admiral von Capelle had worked in the Navy Office for most of his career, where he was an expert on financial matters. He co-operated with the Chancellor, **Bethmann Hollweg**, in opposing the reintroduction of unrestricted submarine warfare, but early in 1917 this policy was reversed in the face of pressure from naval and military leaders. It was, however, Capelle's failure to respond adequately to the issues raised by the sailors' revolt in August 1917 that significantly weakened his position, although he was retained in office for a further year.

CAPELLO, GENERAL LUIGI, 1859–1941

Appointed commander of the Italian Second Army on the **Isonzo Front** in the spring of 1917, Capello was generally considered to be one of the most able generals in the Italian service. During the Sixth Battle of the Isonzo in August 1916, Capello's corps played a major role in achieving Italy's first major advance of the war. Capello's period in command of the Second Army was, however, overshadowed by ill-health and ended with the **Caporetto** disaster in October 1917, for which he, as well as **Cadorna**, received some of the blame. He was criticised for not preparing his defences effectively in response to warnings of an impending Austrian attack and for being too concerned with offensive action. The destruction of the Second Army and the withdrawal to the Piave ended his career in the field. Although his health was eventually restored, he was never offered another command during the First World War.

Capello: another victim of Caporetto whose solid record on the Isonzo Front was overshadowed by the disaster

CAPORETTO, BATTLE OF, 24 October – 12 November 1917

In mid-September 1917, the Italian High Command brought the Eleventh Battle of the **Isonzo** to a close and put its forces on the defensive because of fears that the Germans might be about to intervene. The Austrians had in fact already called on their principal ally for urgent assistance because the regular Italian offensives had started to undermine their defensive capability even if they had not produced significant territorial gains. A joint attack on Italy was necessary 'in order to prevent the collapse of Austro-Hungary'.

Ludendorff was unable to contribute more than six German divisions to the planned offensive, which

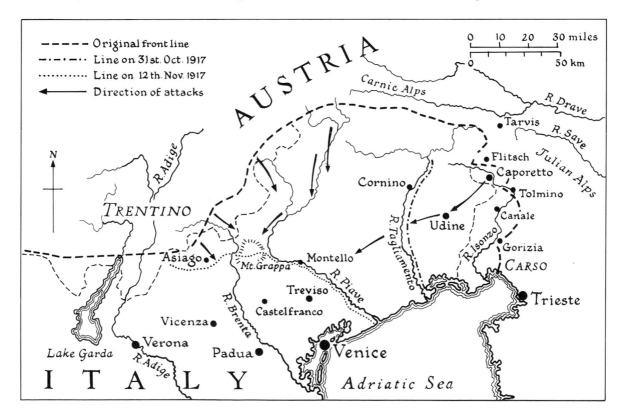

was to be launched in the Caporetto sector, a relatively lightly defended area on the north of the Isonzo lines. They were combined with nine Austrian divisions to form the German Fourteenth Army, under the command of **General Otto von Below**; **General Krafft von Delmensingen** was chief of staff. Defending the Italian line at this point was the Second Army under **General Luigi Capello**; he had received general information about an impending attack but had been unwilling to strengthen his defences at their most vulnerable points. On the right of the Fourteenth Army was the Austrian Tenth Army and to its left was the Austrian Fifth. They faced the Italian Fourth and Third Armies respectively. In numerical terms the Italians retained their superiority on this front, with 41 divisions available to the Austrians' 35.

The surprise attack was launched at Tolmino, a small bridgehead on the west bank of the Isonzo, early in the morning of 24 October, with an artillery and gas bombardment that lasted for five hours. Moving forward in the mountain fog, the centre group of the Fourteenth Army broke through the Italian lines almost immediately. Unprepared and demoralised, the Second Army quickly disintegrated and the troops surrendered or retreated in vast numbers as the Germans advanced up to 14 miles on the first day. To the north in the mountains, the Tenth Army was also able to make good progress, the Italian Fourth Army being forced to withdraw as its flank collapsed. To the south the Austrians made less rapid progress, with the Italian Third Army retreating in good order as the situation in the north deteriorated.

The next day **Cadorna** decided on the inevitable – a general withdrawal to the Tagliamento River, where he planned to make a stand. However, Below's advance guard had crossed the river to the north as early as 2 November, well before the Italian Third Army had reached the area and Cadorna was forced to order a further retreat to the River Piave. Seventy miles from the Isonzo front, it was a torrent rather than a river, much shorter in length and an excellent natural barrier to any further enemy advance. By the time the remnants of the Italian army had arrived there on 10 November, Cadorna had been replaced by **General Diaz**, who was organising the defences of the new line as the enemy moved towards it. The Italian army was also bolstered by the rapid arrival of six French and five British divisions. Attacks on the Italians continued, with assaults on the rear from the Trentino and in the sector between the Piave and the Brenta. By the end of the year, however, the new position had been stabilised and the work of reconstructing the army could begin.

Italian losses were enormous: 275,000 prisoners had been taken and 2,500 guns had been captured; 10,000 had been killed and 20,000 wounded. Although Caporetto had 'almost knocked Italy out of the war', it produced a new determination to fight and achieve victory. The defeat also led to the conference at **Rapallo** and the creation of a Supreme War Council, with the aim of improving Allied military co-operation and developing a unified strategy.

CAPRONI Ca2 & Ca3

Caproni's giant multi-engined aircraft was used by the Italian army air service from 1915 to 1917, and formed the basis of its first strategic bomber force.

Based on pioneering work dating back to 1913, this three-bay biplane had equal-span wings, a central cabin and twin fuselage booms, with a tail assembly which included three rudders. It was powered by three 100hp Fiat A10 engines: two tractor units at the end of each fuselage and a pusher in the nacelle. Delivered to the air service in 1915–16, they carried

out the first Italian bombing raid on Austro-Hungary in August 1915 and they were also the first Italian aircraft to undertake night bombing. A total of 164 Ca2s were produced before being superseded by the Ca3 in 1917.

Generally similar to its predecessor, the new model was equipped with more powerful engines – three 150hp Isotta Fraschini V4Bs – and was known as the 450hp Caproni. They improved the performance of this large machine, which had a wingspan of 23m and a weight of 3,890kg, giving a maximum speed of 88m.p.h. and an endurance of $3\frac{1}{2}$ hours. The aircraft was operated by a crew of four – pilot, co-pilot, and two gunners; in the front there was a single **Fiat-Revelli machine-gun** or cannon and in the rear, on an exposed platform, up to four Revellis. The aircraft could also carry up to 1,000lb of bombs.

The Ca3 served in Italy until the Armistice. It was used intensively in bombing raids on enemy territory and also operated with the Italian navy as a torpedo bomber. It was noted for its reliability and good flying qualities as well as its ability to sustain combat damage. Some 269 examples were built in total. The Ca3 was also produced under licence in France, where it served with the Aviation Militaire.

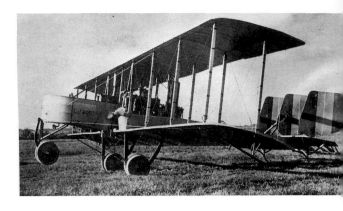

The multi-engined Caproni Ca3 provided the basis of the Italian strategic bomber force

CAPRONI Ca4 & Ca5

The Ca4 bomber retained the same basic layout as its predecessor (the **Caproni Ca3**) although it was a triplane constructed on an even larger scale.

First appearing late in 1917, four main variants were produced under the Ca4 designation, with differences in power plants, seating arrangments and defensive armament. A floatplane model was also made for use by the Italian navy as a torpedo bomber. The major production version, of which 41 were produced, was powered by three 270hp engines and could carry a bomb load of over 3,000lb. It had a crew of four, including two gunners who operated the four **Fiat-Revelli machine-guns**. All the Ca4 aircraft were strong and reliable, but because of their great size they were slow and vulnerable to enemy attack. Their operational service was, therefore, largely confined to night bombing.

With the Ca5, Caproni reverted to the biplane configuration of the Ca3 in order to correct the weaknesses of the Ca4. Produced in a number of different versions, it was smaller than the Ca4, had a reduced bomb-carrying capacity and was equipped with only two machine-guns. This three-engined machine was powered by a variety of units in the 200–300hp range and its performance was excellent. A total of 255 machines was delivered to the Italian air service from early in 1918 and they were used for day and night bombing in France and on the Italian front in the last few months of the war. Others were produced under licence by French and American companies. The Ca5 was undoubtedly the best of the long series of Caproni heavy bombers that had given Italy and her allies reliable service throughout the war.

CARDEN, ADMIRAL SIR SACKVILLE, 1857–1930

Following the escape of the *Goeben* in August 1914 and the departure of **Admiral Milne**, Carden was chosen to command the British battle squadron that operated with the French in the Mediterranean. It was largely on Carden's advice that the British War Council decided to mount an operation to try to force the **Dardanelles** by ships alone. The Anglo-French naval bombardment of the Turkish forts began on 19

February 1915, but it soon became clear that the defences and minefields were much more formidable obstacles than had been envisaged. The prospect of failure brought Carden, whose recent sea experience was limited, to the verge of a nervous breakdown and on 16 March 1915 he resigned. He was replaced in the Dardanelles by **Admiral de Robeck**.

CARMANIA

A British **armed merchant cruiser**, the *Carmania* was a Cunard transatlantic liner (19,600 tons) that had been taken over by the Royal Navy on the declaration of war. It operated in the South Atlantic and on 14 September 1914 it found the *Cap Trafalgar*, a German armed merchant cruiser, coaling off an island near the Brazilian coast. After a spirited action, which lasted 90 minutes, the German ship was sunk. The victorious *Carmania* sustained some damage.

CAROL I, KING OF RUMANIA, 1839–1914

The last few months of King Carol's 48 years as monarch of Rumania were among the most unhappy of his whole life. Popular support for the acquisition of Transylvania, which formed part of Austro-Hungary, made it politically impossible for Rumania to fulfil her treaty obligations to the Central Powers on the outbreak of war. Humiliated by the decision to remain neutral, all the pro-German monarch could do in the short time remaining to him was to frustrate plans for the occupation of Transylvania and fight demands for an alliance with the Allies.

CARSON, EDWARD, BARON, 1854–1935

Leader of the Ulster Unionists and implacable opponent of Irish home rule, Carson was briefly (May–October 1916) Attorney-General in **Asquith**'s coalition government, but resigned over the prime minister's conduct of the war. When **Lloyd George** became premier in December 1916, Carson was appointed First Lord of the Admiralty, although he knew little of naval matters. He lacked the energy to make a real impact on the service and was reluctant to introduce the **convoy system** in the face of opposition from his professional colleagues. He was replaced by **Sir Eric Geddes** in July 1917.

CASEMENT, SIR ROGER, 1864–1916

Senior British consular official who, on his retirement, became an active Irish nationalist. Convinced that external military assistance was necessary to secure Ireland's independence from Britain, he went to Berlin in November 1914, where he remained for 18 months. Casement was unable to secure active German support and returned to Ireland in a U-Boat in April 1916, to advise against the planned **Easter uprising**. However, he was arrested soon after his arrival and taken to London; he was found guilty of high treason and executed on 3 August 1916.

CASTELNAU, GENERAL NOEL DE, 1851–1944

As deputy chief of staff to **Joffre**, Castelnau had, in the immediate pre-war period, made an important contribution to the preparation of **Plan XVII**. When the war began, Castelnau commanded the Second Army, advancing into German Lorraine in accordance with his own war plan. Defeated at the Battle of Morhange on 20 August 1914, he was forced to retreat, but managed to hold the line at Le Grand Couronné; Nancy was saved and the front stabilised on the French–German border. As a result, he helped to make possible the positive outcome of the **Battle of the Marne**.

In June 1915, Castelnau became commander of the centre group of armies and he directed the major **Champagne offensive** in the Autumn. At the end of the year Castelnau's direct working relationship with the commander-in-chief was resumed on his appointment as Joffre's chief of staff. When **Verdun** was attacked in February 1916, Castelnau was sent there with full executive powers: he made 'the crucial decision to hold Verdun and to place **Pétain** in charge of the overall defence'. Castelnau left office with Joffre, but in the last year of the war was appointed to the Eastern Army Group and directed the final offensive in Lorraine.

CASUALTIES

The total cost of the war, in terms of military dead and wounded, can only be estimated very imprecisely because of omissions and inaccuracies in the official records of some of the belligerents. Up to 13 million combatants may have been killed on the battlefield or died from disease, but some authorities give a significantly lower figure.

The losses of individual countries between 1914–18 were as follows:

	Manpower mobilised	Military deaths	Military wounded
British Empire	9,496,170	947,023	2,121,906
France	8,410,000	1,385,300	4,266,000
Italy	5,615,000	462,391	953,886
Russia	12,000,000	1,700,000	4,950,000
United States	4,355,000	115,660	205,690
Germany	11,000,000	1,808,545	4,247,143
Austro-Hungary	7,800,000	1,200,000	3,620,000
Turkey	2,850,000	325,000	400,000

CAUCASUS FRONT, CHRONOLOGICAL LIST OF EVENTS

Sarakamish, Battle of, 1914–15	Erzincan, Battle of, 1916

CAUDRON GIII

This unarmed two-seat reconnaissance aircraft, which first appeared in May 1914, was widely used during the first two years of the war. Based on the GII, an earlier single-seater design that also saw wartime service, the GIII was a small tractor biplane with the nacelle and tailbooms layout normally associated with pusher aircraft of the period. It had unequal span wings and twin fins and rudders. A variety of power units was fitted, with the 80hp Gnome rotary engine being common in early machines and the 100hp Anzani radial in later ones. With the larger motor its maximum speed at sea level was no more than 68m.p.h., but it had a good rate of climb and an endurance of four hours.

Built in large quantities by Caudron and foreign sub-contractors, the GIII saw service on the Western Front with French, British and Belgian forces, and was used extensively on reconnaissance and artillery target-spotting duties. It was also employed by the Italian and Russian air services. Although it was slow and without defensive armament (except for hand held weapons) the Caudron GIII remained in operational use until well into 1917, when it was redeployed as a trainer. In 1918, the United States air service acquired almost 200 surplus GIIIs specifically for training purposes.

Caudron GIII: an early reconnaissance aircraft that was also used for training and bombing operations

CAUDRON GIV

An enlarged version of the **GIII**, the Caudron GIV was a two-seat, long-range bomber and reconnaissance aircraft which first appeared early in 1915. Powered by two 80hp Le Rhône or two 100hp Anzani engines, it had a maximum speed of 82m.p.h., a ceiling of 14,000 feet and a duration of four hours. It could carry a bomb load of up to 220lb in external racks and, unlike its predecessor, was armed with one or two machine-guns. These were operated by the observer who sat in the front and had a relatively poor view to the rear.

The GIV served with the French Aviation Militaire from November 1915 for about a year, when it was withdrawn because of mounting losses that were attributable to its growing vulnerability to enemy attack. The Italian air service, which valued its reliability in long-range missions over the Alps, also used it. It was, however, the RNAS that first fully exploited the potential of the GIV as a bomber; during 1916, 55 machines were used by Nos 4 and 5 Wings, based in Belgium, in sorties against German submarine, seaplane, and Zeppelin bases. The RNAS phased out its GIVs during the spring of 1917 as the **Handley Page 0/100**s arrived. Like the GIII, the Caudron GIV was retained in service for a while as a training aircraft.

CAUDRON R4 & R11

The R4 three-seat, three-bay biplane, which first appeared in June 1915, was designed as a bomber, but was in fact used by the French almost exclusively for reconnaissance purposes. It had a pointed nose, oval section fuselage and triangular fin. Armament consisted of one or two ring-mounted **Lewis machine-guns** in both the front and rear cockpits; the pilot was positioned in the middle. It was intended that the R4 would carry a bomb load of up to 220lb, but even this modest weight proved too much for the twin 130hp Renault engines, mounted midway between the wings. As a result the R4 was successfully adapted for use as a photo-reconnaissance aircraft, serving with the French Aviation Militaire from the spring of 1916 for about a year. It was replaced during 1917 by the more powerful Letord Type I.

A substitute for the R4 as a bomber appeared early in 1918. Designated the R11, this more compact two-bay biplane was lighter than its predecessor, but was equipped with more powerful engines – two 180hp or 220hp Hispano-Suizas – giving a maximum speed of 114m.p.h. at 6,560 feet. At first it was used by the Aviation Militaire as a night bomber, although its effectiveness was severely limited by the fact that it could carry no more than 265lb of bombs. It was in fact much more effective as a fighter escort, using its five Lewis machine-guns (two in both the front and rear cockpits, as well as a downward firing weapon) to repel enemy attacks.

Equipping eight *escadrilles*, the Caudron R11 was used extensively in the closing months of the war to protect the **Breguet 14** and other day bombers on their raids over enemy territory. There is little doubt that their activities helped significantly to reduce casualties.

CAVELL, EDITH, 1865–1915

An English nurse working in Brussels since 1907, Edith Cavell remained there after the Germans occupied the city. She soon attracted the attention of the authorities and in August 1915 was arrested on a charge of assisting some 200 Allied soldiers to reach the Dutch border. Her fate was sealed by a signed confession of her activities and by confirmation at the trial that neutral Holland had repatriated some of the escapees to England. Cavell's execution by firing squad on 12 October 1915 aroused popular anger in Britain and other Allied countries and helped to fuel anti-German propaganda. The military authorities in Brussels had created a martyr, a major political blunder committed without the prior knowledge of the German High Command.

CAVOUR

Completed in 1914–15, the Cavours were Italian dreadnoughts with improved armament compared with their predecessor, *Dante Alighieri*. However, their guns were of a smaller calibre than those carried by many other modern warships: thirteen 12-inch weapons were mounted in five centre line turrets, of which three were triples and two twins. Armour protection was also relatively poor, although the Cavours had a good maximum speed of 22 knots. *Leonardo da Vinci* was sunk by the Austrians in August 1916, but *Conte di Cavour* and *Giulio Cesare* survived the war.

C-CLASS SUBMARINE

The first British submarine to be produced in quantity – 38 were built between 1906–10 – the C-type was similar to its predecessors in appearance and performance. It gave useful service during the war in spite of its limitations as a small coastal vessel. Four were transported by ship and rail via Archangel to the Gulf of Finland to attack German shipping but were subsequently scuttled in April 1918 to avoid capture. The C-type was often used in conjunction with a trawler acting as a decoy for patrolling U-boats.

CENTRAL POWERS

At the beginning of the First World War the term Central Powers was used to describe the alliance of Germany and Austro-Hungary, which opposed the Allied or Entente Powers. Turkey entered the war on the side of the Central Powers in October 1914 and Bulgaria followed a year later. The term had been used before 1914 to describe the alliance of Germany, Austro-Hungary and Italy, of which Bismarck was the author in 1882. Italy did not join her former allies in 1914, but remained neutral until she declared war on Austro-Hungary in May 1915.

The initial mobilisation figures and manpower totals are as follows:

	Mobilisation on outbreak of war	Total manpower mobilised
Austro-Hungary	3,000,000	7,800,000
Bulgaria	280,000	1,200,000
Germany	4,500,000	11,000,000
Turkey	210,000	2,850,000

CHAMPAGNE, FIRST BATTLE OF, 20 December 1914 – 17 March 1915

The consolidation of the trench barrier on the Western Front after the **First Battle of Ypres** (October–November 1914) did nothing to deter **Joffre** from seeking an early victory against the Germans and expelling them from French soil. The renewed Allied action in December 1914 was based on a strategy that was to guide French action for the rest of the war: Artois and Champagne, the two sides of the German salient in France, which had its apex west of St Quentin, would be the primary targets. Once the Germans began to weaken, a third offensive would be launched from Verdun, to cut the enemy's lines of communication south of the Ardennes.

Joffre's general winter offensive began in Artois, where it made little progress, and extended along the whole line from Nieuport to Verdun. The main effort was concentrated in Champagne, beginning on 20 December and continuing into the new year; it was eventually suspended in the face of strong German counter-attacks, but renewed again a month later, in March. The French Fourth Army made a few gains on the slopes of the hills of Eastern Champagne, but the smaller German Third Army demonstrated the advantages bestowed by the machine-gun and the trench on the defence. Although the fierce and bloody fighting was finally halted on 17 March, with the French (like the Germans) having lost some 90,000 men, Joffre was determined to launch another attack as soon as practicable.

CHAMPAGNE, SECOND BATTLE OF, 25 September – 6 October 1915

Joffre's lack of success in the **Battle of Artois-Loos** did not deter him from renewing the offensive on a grand scale later in the year. With the growth of British and French forces during the summer and the large number of German troops absent in Russia, he planned a simultaneous advance on both sides of the

German salient – the major thrust being in Champagne, with a subsidiary attack in Artois. As a result 'a great door was to be opened to the Meuse and Belgium', with a breakthrough signalling a general attack along the whole front.

In Champagne 900 heavy guns and 1,600 field guns were used in an intensive bombardment that lasted for three days before the French Second Army (**Pétain**) and the Fourth Army (**Langle de Cary**) began moving westwards on a 15-mile front towards the Argonne Forest on 25 September. Thirty-five divisions (500,000 men) heavily outnumbered the German Third and Fifth Armies (12 divisions), but the Germans had the advantage of higher ground and an advance warning of an attack. The Germans were pushed back by as much as 3,000 yards in places but their reinforced second line of defence generally held. Some of these gains were lost in the German counter-attack which began on 30 October, and those that the French retained had no strategic significance; they did, however, take 25,000 prisoners and 150 guns. By the time the main action was called off on 28 September, the French had lost 145,000 men, with the Germans losing as many relative to their strength.

Although the attack was briefly renewed on 6 October and the whole plan not formally abandoned until 6 November, it had already clearly failed.

CHARLEMAGNE

The three Charlemagne class battleships, which entered French naval service in 1899–1900, were in active use during the First World War and all participated in the **Dardanelles operation**. *Gaulois* was sunk by the German submarine UB-47 on 27 December 1915, but *Charlemagne* and *Saint Louis* survived the war. These well-protected warships had a displacement of 11,200 tons, a maximum speed of 18 knots, and were equipped with four 12-inch guns in twin turrets.

CHARLES I, EMPEROR 1887–1922

Last Emperor of Austria and King of Hungary, Charles succeeded his great uncle, Franz Josef, in November 1916. His overriding aim was to preserve the territorial integrity of Austro-Hungary by securing a separate peace before the empire disintegrated under the impact of military defeat. Secret preliminary discussions were held with the Allies in 1917 but they came to an abrupt end when Germany learnt about them. As a result Charles was forced to accept greater German control over the direction of Austria's war effort. His efforts at constitutional reform, announced in the last month of the war, were similarly unsuccessful. The changes came too late to save the empire, which collapsed in November 1918. Charles himself refused to abdicate but was forced to flee to Switzerland early in 1919.

CHARRON ARMOURED CAR

Used by French, Russian and Turkish forces, the French-produced Charron appeared in its original form in 1904. Two years earlier the company had in fact produced the world's first armoured vehicle, a private car partly protected by armoured plate. The later model also used the Charron touring car chassis, but it had a substantial hull that was completely armoured. A distinctive feature was its large side windows, which could be covered in combat conditions. Armament consisted of a single 8mm **Hotchkiss machine-gun** which was enclosed in a revolving turret and positioned towards the rear.

Early models were excessively heavy and underpowered, but later examples, which were fitted with a 35hp engine, had better performance.

CHAUCHAT MACHINE-GUN

A cheaply produced French automatic weapon, the Chauchat had a poor reputation for reliability

One of the least successful weapons of the war, the CSRG or Chauchat light machine-gun was named after the chairman of the French commission that had accepted it in 1914. Formally designated the Fusil Mitrailleur Modèle 1915, it used a long recoil-operated system, a fairly complicated mechanism whose pronounced internal movement made accurate aiming difficult. The detachable magazine was of an unusual semi-circular shape because the French 8mm cartridge was tapered with a large base; it could hold 20 rounds. The Chauchat weighed 20lb and had a relatively slow cyclic rate of fire of 250 rounds per minute. It was cheaply produced by a variety of French manufacturers to low standards using sub-grade materials.

In the field it quickly gained a universal reputation for unreliability amongst French troops, although it continued in use until the end of the war. In spite of its weaknesses, when the United States entered the war the American army was persuaded to accept 16,000 Chauchats. There was a further delivery of 19,000 examples of a modified version – the M1918 – which would accept the American .30 round. The main visible difference between the two versions was in the shape of the magazine. The American cartridge was more powerful than the French and put the gun's inferior components under even more stress. It has in fact been estimated that as many as 50 per cent of all Chauchats delivered to the Americans were discarded as unserviceable.

CHURCHILL, SIR WINSTON, 1874–1965

British war leader who served as First Lord of the Admiralty from 1911 to 1915. From social reform and the Home Office, Churchill turned with equal enthusiasm and energy to the navy, which he expanded and modernised in preparation for war. He introduced a naval staff system, encouraged the development of naval aviation and improved conditions in the lower deck. His pre-war achievements at the Admiralty were later acknowledged by **Lord Kitchener**, who said to Churchill: 'There is one thing at least they can never take away from you. When the war began you had the fleet ready.'

However, his popularity soon began to decline as the war progressed. His personal involvement in the defence of **Antwerp** in October 1914 led to accusations that he was neglecting his duties at the Admiralty. Other setbacks, including the **Battle of Coronel**, followed.

He responded to the stalemate on the Western Front with the idea of an expedition to the **Dardanelles**, which would begin with a naval attack, giving the Royal Navy a much needed opportunity to come into the front line. The naval operation failed and was followed by landings on the Gallipoli peninsular.

Although his plan was sound in principle, it was badly executed and the invading troops were not able to make any progress following their arrival in April 1915. **Lord Fisher**, the First Sea Lord, who had never supported the expedition, resigned in May after a disagreement with Churchill over the supply of ships to the area. Churchill himself was the scapegoat for the failure of Gallipoli and was removed from the Admiralty during the same month.

He became Chancellor of the Duchy of Lancaster, a post of 'well-paid inactivity', but was retained as a member of the War Council, which was renamed the Dardanelles Committee. When it was later reconstituted Churchill was dropped from it and he returned to the army. He served on the Western Front from November 1915 to May 1916 as commander of the 6th Royal Fusiliers. On his return Churchill was regularly consulted by **Lloyd George** and he was brought into the government as soon as it was politically possible. Once an official enquiry had cleared him of having disregarded professional advice about the feasibility of the Dardanelles expedition he was appointed, in June 1917, Minister of Munitions.

He retained the post until after the end of the war and established a reputation as an able departmental minister.

CLEMENCEAU, GEORGES, 1841–1929

French Radical Prime Minister during the last year of the war, whose leadership and determination made a substantial contribution to the defeat of Germany. Out of office for the first three years of the war, Clemenceau, known as 'The Tiger', was a vociferous critic of the French political and military leadership.

When the last of the divided and indecisive wartime coalitions fell in November 1917, Clemenceau was invited to form a government, which proved to be very different in character from its predecessors. He ruled out a negotiated peace: his aim was total victory and he established a wartime dictatorship in order to wage war more effectively. A Cabinet of loyal acolytes was appointed and defeatists such as **Caillaux** were arrested. He secured greater political control of the military and good working relations were established with **Foch** and **Pétain**. Operational effectiveness was further improved when, in April 1918, the British accepted his proposal to establish a unified Allied command under Foch. By this time

Clemenceau, 'The Tiger', led France to victory in 1918. He raised morale after the setbacks of 1917, enabling the country to withstand the final German onslaught

C MARK THIS A DISASTER!

Clemenceau had become 'a symbol of France's commitment to fight the war to a successful conclusion', and his leadership helped the army to withstand the German onslaughts of 1918.

After the war, Clemenceau presided at the **Paris Peace Conference** where he had less success; he was unable to secure France's territorial objectives in relation to the border with Germany and was later criticised for being too lenient towards its former enemy.

COASTAL CLASS AIRSHIP

An improved and enlarged version of the original **Sea Scout airship**, the new 'Blimp' was delivered to the RNAS from mid-1916. These non-rigid airships had a normal endurance of five hours and were powered by twin 150hp Sunbeam engines, although later examples were fitted with alternative power plants. They were armed with two .303 **Lewis machine-guns** and a bomb load of up to 400lb, although a modified version had an increased capacity of 660lb. Produced in very small numbers, Coastal Class airships were used until the end of the war on patrol and convoy protection duties.

COASTAL MOTOR BOAT

A small, fast surface warship used by the Royal Navy during the First World War, the coastal motor boat (CMB) was designed and mainly produced by Thornycroft. They first appeared in the summer of 1916 and were produced in three sizes: 40-foot, 55-foot, 70-foot. All three designs had hydroplane hulls constructed of wood, and were powered by petrol engines of varying types. The 55-foot version, for example, had twin power plants and a maximum speed of 42 knots. They were normally armed with torpedoes, which were launched tail-first over the stern. Some carried mines instead and several 70-foot boats were built as minelayers only. The CMBs also carried depth charges when they were used in an anti-submarine role.

COLLISHAW, RAYMOND, 1893–1976

Raymond Collishaw's total of 60 confirmed victories made him the highest scoring RNAS pilot of the war and the third ranking British ace overall. As a Canadian airman he was second only to **William Bishop**. His first victory was gained in October 1916 while serving in France with No 3 Wing, the strategic bombing unit, but his most successful period was as leader of B Flight, No 10 (Naval) Squadron – the famous 'Black Flight', based at Furnes in Belgium.

The Royal Navy's most successful pilot, Collishaw, a Canadian, led the formidable Black Flight, which was equipped with Sopwith Triplanes

Equipped with the highly manoeuvrable **Sopwith Triplane**, partly painted black, Collishaw and a group of fellow Canadians proved to be formidable opponents. In total, B Flight hit as many as 87 German aircraft between May and July 1917, while Collis-haw's personal score rose to 37. A second period of concentrated success followed in 1918 as commander of No 203 Squadron: flying a **Sopwith Camel** he scored a further 20 hits in the four months from June.

COLOSSUS

The only battleship of the **Grand Fleet** to be hit at **Jutland**, *Colossus* was one of eight capital ships to be constructed as part of the Admiralty's 1909 building programme. Originally only four new ships had been planned, but the number was doubled in response to fears that Germany was secretly building dread-noughts. *Colossus* and her sister ship *Hercules* were generally similar to *Neptune*, which had been laid down a few months earlier, but there were a number of minor differences: the arrangement of the secondary armament was improved, side armour was increased, and 21-inch torpedo tubes replaced the 18-inch.

Colossus served with the Grand Fleet throughout the war and was Flagship, 1st Battle Squadron, from August 1914. After the damage sustained at Jutland had been repaired she served the remainder of the war with the 4th Battle Squadron. *Hercules* was also part of the Grand Fleet in the First World War and after the Armistice transported the Allied Naval Commission to Kiel, where it had the task of ensuring that the Armistice terms were implemented.

COLT AUTOMATIC PISTOL

The standard pistol of the United States army and navy, the Colt Model 1911 was one of the best weapons of its kind ever to appear, being used in both world wars and beyond. Based on an earlier design by John Browning, this self-loading weapon was of the locked breech type and was accepted for military use in 1911 after a contest with several alternative designs. It was a sturdy and powerful weapon which fired a .45-inch bullet at 860 feet per second; the magazine held seven rounds and was carried in the grip. Although the weapon was produced by several sub-contractors as well as by Colt, output was not sufficient to meet American wartime demand. It was necessary, therefore, to supplement this fine pistol with **Smith and Wesson** and **Colt revolvers**. The Model 1911 was also made in British .455 calibre for the Royal Navy and Royal Flying Corps.

COLT-BROWNING MACHINE-GUN

John Browning's first machine-gun, the .30 calibre Colt-Browning Model 1895 was a gas-operated weapon that was still in use during the First World War. It was known as the 'potato digger' from the movement of an external gas-operated lever that activated the gun mechanism. The weapon had a cyclic rate of fire of 400–500 rounds per minute and ammunition was loaded from a 300-round belt. It was air cooled and had a tendency to overheat after prolonged use.

In 1895, it was adopted by the US Marines but rejected by the army; it was not in fact until 1917, when Colt produced a further 1,500 examples, that the latter adopted this outdated weapon. A small number went to France with the AEF for front line use, but most were employed in training. Belgium and Russia had also been supplied with earlier batches of the weapon and their forces used them throughout the war. The Colt-Browning was, however, much more in evidence during the First World War in its modified form as the **Marlin machine-gun** than in the orginal version.

COLT REVOLVER

Like the **Smith and Wesson** Model 1917 revolver, the Colt New Service revolver was acquired in large numbers when the United States entered the war, supplementing inadequate supplies of the Colt automatic pistol. Advantage was taken of the wide availability of the .45-inch pistol cartridge, by modifying the six-round cylinder of the Colt revolver to take it. Over 150,000 examples were produced for the United States army during the war; in a slightly different form they were also supplied to the British army during 1915–16.

COMMERCE RAIDERS

After the failure of converted passenger liners as commerce raiders, the German navy turned in 1915 to ordinary merchant ships as an alternative. These were the equivalent of the Royal Navy's **Q-ships** – disguised **armed merchant cruisers** – with added torpedoes, acting as decoy vessels. Unlike their British counterparts, merchant ships rather than submarines were their target and they also had minelaying duties – indeed, the German navy insisted that their mines were laid before raiding activities started. Operations began when the *Moewe*, the most successful of the German armed commerce raiders, left on the first of her sorties late in 1915. She was followed by a number of others, including *Greif*, *Wolf*, *Leopard* and *Seeadler*. The latter was a fully rigged sailing ship rather than the normal tramp steamer. Apart from their immediate toll of Allied ships, the commerce raiders caused considerable disruption to shipping and troop movements during their widely scattered operations in 1915–17.

CONRAD von HOTZENDORF, FRANZ, COUNT, 1852–1925

Austrian Chief of the General Staff for much of the First World War, Conrad was an experienced staff officer who had contributed to the much needed modernisation of the army on his first appointment to the post in 1906. Conrad's enthusiasm for war in 1914 was not matched by his ability to manage the twin demands made on his forces in its early stages: the defence of Galicia and the invasion of Serbia. Although the territory lost to the Russians was regained in 1915 during the bold **Gorlice-Tarnow offensive** and Serbia was eventually occupied, Conrad was forced to accept severe limitations on his powers in these German-dominated operations. His attempt to deliver a decisive blow against the Italians in the Trentino offensive (May–June 1916) was unsuccessful, further undermining his position.

One of Conrad's major weaknesses was his inability to execute his often imaginative strategic ideas, as he lacked the determination and usually the forces to do so. An important defensive role has, however, been attributed to him, the suggestion being that he 'saved his country from much devastation by his skilful thrusts against the enemy'.

By September 1916, the Germans had compelled their main ally to accept a unified command, with **Hindenburg** assuming ultimate responsibility for the overall direction of their forces on all fronts. Conrad survived these arrangements by only a few months, being relieved of his post in March 1917. He returned to the field as commander of the Trentino Front, where he remained until his dismissal in July 1918. The failure of the Austrian offensive against Italy in June had brought his military career to an end.

CONSCRIPTION

Compulsory enlistment for military service was introduced by most continental armies during the 19th century, but Britain and the major Commonwealth countries had always relied on voluntary recruitment. In 1914, Britain had expected a short conflict in which her limited contribution to the land war in Europe could be sustained without conscription. During 1915–16, BEF's casualty figures rose rapidly but the army still had more recruits than it was able to equip and train. However, there were signs that voluntary recruiting was beginning to dry up and there was widespread popular concern about the large numbers who were said to be evading the call to arms.

To avoid the need for conscription, which was anathema to Liberalism, two new measures were adopted. In August 1915, every adult was registered and the names of those aged from 18 to 41 were forwarded to recruiting offices so that they could be encouraged to enlist. The Derby scheme, which was introduced in the autumn of 1915, resulted in two and a half million men attesting their willingness to serve if called, but it did not produce enough recruits for immediate service. Insufficient single men had offered their services and the government could not contemplate calling up married men before the other group had been taken.

The second phase of conscription in Britain: the calling up of the married men, May 1916

In January 1916, therefore, the Military Service Act, which replaced voluntary enlistment with compulsory military service, was passed. As a result, all unmarried men between the ages of 18 and 41 were enlisted. In May 1916, compulsion was extended to married men as well, when it became clear that the original legislation had failed significantly to increase the supply of recruits.

One of the effects of conscription had in fact been to produce a large number of valid claims to exemption from those working in reserved occupations. Another ground for exemption was conscientious objection, some 16,000 men registering under this category. Local tribunals were established to assess these cases and there was also a mechanism for hearing appeals. Even so, many genuine applicants were in fact conscripted. During the German offensive in the spring of 1918, the government was compelled to raise the upper age limit to fifty and to end its previous undertaking not to send troops abroad until they were 19. Compulsory enlistment was in principle extended to Ireland, but never put into action.

In Canada and New Zealand conscription was introduced during the war, but in both countries the decision was even more controversial than it had been in Britain; Australia, on the other hand, rejected conscription altogether. Selective service, a limited form of conscription, was introduced in the United States in May 1917, with exemptions and a ballot reducing numbers to a manageable figure of under three million men. Like Britain, America abandoned conscription soon after the end of the war.

CONSTANTINE I, KING OF GREECE, 1868–1923

Constantine succeeded to the Greek throne in 1910 on the assassination of his father, George I. He was a professional soldier, trained in Germany, whose career had been marred by his failure in the war against Turkey in 1897, although it had later been redeemed by his successful leadership during the First Balkan War.

Greece remained neutral on the outbreak of war as the King's pro-German outlook conflicted with the strong bias which **Venizelos**, the prime minister, always displayed towards the Allies. Constantine thwarted his plans to provide military aid to the British and French in the **Dardanelles**, prompting Venizelos' resignation in March 1915. Later that year the King opposed Venizelos, who had returned to power, in permitting an Anglo-French force to land in Macedonia in support of **Serbia**. The King dismissed his premier but was unable to dislodge the Allies, even though he sought German assistance.

Their conflict came to a head in 1916 when the failure of the Greek army to resist a Bulgarian offensive led to a revolt by Venizelos' supporters. A pro-Allied government was formed in Crete but elsewhere Constantine's troops put down the uprising and in December 1916 Allied intervention, in the form of Franco-British landing parties at Athens, was necessary to secure the rear of the **Salonika** force. In June 1917, the Allies forced King Constantine to abdicate and go into exile; Venizelos was immediately restored to power and Greece entered the war on the Allied side.

CONSTANTINOPLE AGREEMENTS, March–April 1915

Inspired by a fear that Russia might conclude a separate peace as Allied operations in the **Dardanelles** began, Britain and France gave secret assurances early in 1915 about her territorial gains after the war. Russia would receive Constantinople and the Bosphorus on condition that the Allies secured their war aims in the Middle East. The agreements were repudiated after the **Russian Revolution** and, much to the embarrassment of Britain and France, the Bolsheviks published the texts.

CONVOY SYSTEM

It was not until May 1917 that Britain introduced the convoy system in response to the increasingly serious threat posed by the U-boat. Enemy activity at sea had intensified during 1916–17 and Allied shipping losses had reached unacceptable levels. The Admiralty continuously monitored the problem of protecting the main trade routes and at first its response was to increase patrols by warships and **Q-ships**. Even though these measures made little impact, the navy maintained its opposition to the convoy system, reflecting the view that 'defence was an unacceptable principle, offense correct. . . . To protect merchant-men, to scurry about them like a sheepdog, was defensive.' Its negative view was even more surprising in view of the fact that convoys had already been used successfully during the war – on some cross-Channel trade, during the **Dardanelles** expedition and for long distance troop transports.

The credit for introducing convoys in mid-1917 was later claimed by the Prime Minister, **Lloyd George**, but the intervention of the Cabinet Secretary, **Maurice Hankey**, was of critical importance. As soon as merchant ships were provided with warship protection, the rate of loss was reduced, although the new arrangements were not fully implemented until the end of the year because of a shortage of escort ships. Without the contribution of the American navy, the full protection of Allied and neutral ships would not have been possible. Of the 88,000 ships escorted across the oceans in 1917–18, only 436 were torpedoed. Without ocean convoy, the outcome of the war might have been very different.

COPPENS, WILLY, 1892–1987

The leading Belgian air ace of the war, Coppens did not score his first hit (against a German fighter) until 25 April 1918, at the age of 25, although his flying career had begun late in 1916. Coppens subsequently made his reputation as a 'balloon buster' and is credited with destroying as many as 28 German observation balloons, developing special tactics for attacking them at close range with incendiary ammunition. His wartime career came to an end in October 1918, when his aircraft was brought down by German anti-aircraft fire and he sustained severe injuries. Coppens had a final score of 37 victories (including balloons); his nearest Belgian rival could manage no more than 11.

CORFU, PACT OF, 20 July 1917

An important step towards the creation of Yugoslavia at the end of the war, the Pact declared that Croats, Montenegrins, Serbs and Slovenes should form a single democratic state. Local autonomy would be guaranteed but all would be united under the Serbian monarchy. It was signed by **Pašić**, the Serbian Prime Minister, and Ante Trumbić, president of the Yugoslav Committee (an émigré organisation based in London), on 20 July 1917 on Corfu, the Greek island seized by the Allies in 1915 as a base for the exiled Serbian government.

CORONEL, BATTLE OF, 1 November 1914

When Japan entered the war on the Allied side in August 1914, **Vice-Admiral von Spee** decided to move his East Asiatic Squadron away from Far Eastern waters. He crossed the Pacific to the west coast of

South America, where he could operate his two armoured cruisers (*Scharnhorst* and *Gneisenau*) and three light cruisers (*Dresden*, *Leipzig* and *Nürnberg*) against British shipping. He was at Valparaiso in Chile when on 31 October he heard that a British warship (*Glasgow*) was at Coronel, a port 200 miles to the south.

The Royal Navy had in fact been alerted to von Spee's journey across the Pacific and **Rear Admiral Cradock**, in command of the South American station and based in the Falklands, was ordered to respond. His squadron, which consisted of an armoured cruiser (*Good Hope* – flagship), a cruiser (*Monmouth*), a light cruiser (*Glasgow*), and an armed merchant cruiser (*Otranto*), was greatly inferior to von Spee's. A pre-dreadnought battleship, *Canopus* had been dispatched from England as a reinforcement, but Cradock had left the Falklands on 23 October, before she arrived.

Von Spee moved south from Valparaiso to attack the *Glasgow* as the British squadron travelled north; the two forces met 50 miles off Coronel, just before 5.00 p.m. on 1 November 1914. Cradock was outnumbered and outgunned, but he decided to engage the enemy even though he could have escaped southwards. The memory of the escape of the *Goeben* and of **Troubridge**'s failure to engage the enemy was fresh in his mind. Von Spee's ships used their superior speed to their own advantage. He had the British ships silhouetted against the setting sun and attacked them at long range with more powerful guns.

Rough seas prevented the British ships from using their secondary guns. *Good Hope*, which was hit many times, blew up and sank at about 8.00 p.m. Soon after, *Monmouth* went down, but *Glasgow* and *Otranto* managed to escape. There were no survivors from either British ship and 1,600 men, including Cradock, were lost. The Germans suffered no casualties or damage.

This major British defeat must largely be attributed to Cradock's failure to act in concert with *Canopus*, in disregard of explicit orders to the contrary issued by the Admiralty. However, Coronel was redeemed only five weeks later at the **Battle of the Falkland Islands**, when von Spee's squadron was destroyed.

COURAGEOUS

No proper wartime role could be found for *Courageous* and *Glorious*, British light battlecruisers that had originally been intended for use in a possible amphibious operation against Germany. They were in fact correctly described as enlarged cruisers, with a displacement of 19,230 tons, a high maximum speed (32 knots) and very limited armour protection. Very heavily armed, they had four 15-inch and eighteen 4-inch guns.

Both ships served with the **Grand Fleet** after their completion early in 1917, even though their thin armour rendered them unsuitable for such operational use. They were allocated to the 3rd Light Cruiser Squadron (later to the 1st Cruiser Squadron), engaging (with *Repulse*) German cruisers in Heligoland Bight on 17 November 1917. *Courageous* and *Glorious* were converted to aircraft carriers in the 1920s; a third light battlecruiser (*Furious*) was modified during construction and entered service as a carrier in March 1918.

COURBET

The French navy's first dreadnought-type battleships were not completed until as late as 1913–14, having already been superseded by more advanced British and American designs. Main armament consisted of twelve 12-inch guns rather than the larger calibre weapons that were common elsewhere; powerful secondary guns were mounted in wing turrets that were not well positioned. Although armour protection was improved in comparison with previous French battleships, it was thinner than that provided in contemporary Allied warships. *Courbet* and her three sister ships – *France*, *Jean Bart*, *Paris* – served in the Mediterranean throughout the war. *Courbet* was flagship of the French Mediterranean fleet in 1914–15, as was *France* in 1916.

CRADOCK, REAR ADMIRAL SIR CHRISTOPHER, 1862–1914

Commander of the North America and West Indies Station since 1913, Rear Admiral Sir Christopher Cradock's principal responsibility on the outbreak of war was the protection of the main British trade routes in the region. In August 1914, he forced the German cruisers *Dresden* and *Karlsruhe* into the South Atlantic, having only just failed to destroy the latter. Cradock himself was then ordered south, with instructions to search for **von Spee**'s East Asiatic Squadron, which was expected to appear off the west coast of South America. Despite the Admiralty's failure to provide reinforcements, apart from the old battleship *Canopus*, which had not yet arrived, Cradock decided to engage Spee's greatly superior forces. He was impetuous by nature and was determined to avoid repeating **Troubridge**'s misktakes in the Mediterranean when two German cruisers had escaped to Turkey because of inaction. The battle began off **Coronel** in the afternoon of 1 November and within an hour two British cruisers, including *Good Hope*, Cradock's flagship, were sunk. The British commander, who was lost with his ship, received the public blame for the disaster, which was attributed to his recklessness.

CRUISER

A cruiser was originally defined as any warship detached from the fleet with the task of cruising independently on patrol and scouting duties. Fast and manoeuvrable, they were to report back to the fleet when the enemy had been sighted. During the pre-dreadnought era two principal types of cruiser were developed. The big armoured cruiser, which was designed to form part of the battle fleet, had a displacement of up to 15,000 tons. Rendered obsolete by the development of the battlecruiser (itself originally described as a fast armoured cruiser) in 1907, some were still in service during the First World War. Their ability to escort and assist battleships was limited by their relatively slow speed, small guns and inadequate armour protection. Three British cruisers of this type were lost at **Jutland**.

The second type, protected cruisers, had improved performance as a result of their reduced armour, which was confined to the steel decks covering the vital lower levels. At the beginning of the war, these elderly ships were used to escort troopships and guard the world's trade routes. Supported by **armed merchant cruisers**, their role declined as the activities of the German raiders lessened. Some were, however, employed on the North Atlantic convoys in the latter stages of the war.

The British battlecruiser, HMS Furious

The appearance of the battlecruiser did not, contrary to some contemporary opinion, mean that there was no further place for a standard cruiser. The new ships were far too costly to be produced in sufficient numbers to protect merchant shipping, while destroyers were too small for scouting duties. New classes of light cruisers were in fact already under construction by the principal naval powers. For example, the British Town class (1904–12), which consisted of 21 ships of up to 5,500 tons, was able to scout with the fleet in all conditions. It could attack enemy destroyers and operate at long distances. The lightly built Scout class (1909–15) acted as the leaders of destroyer flotillas. As destroyer speeds increased, larger and better armed cruisers appeared, of which the Arethusa class is an early example.

In the opening stages of the war, the German navy used the detached light cruiser as a commerce raider, the well publicised exploits of the *Emden* in the Indian Ocean being the most notable. However, their primary employment was in the war of attrition in the North Sea: at Heligoland they played a critical role,

while at **Jutland** and the **Dogger Bank** light cruisers made the initial contact between the opposing forces. Cruisers were also an important factor in the other two major naval engagements – **Coronel** and the **Falklands** – of the war.

One of the British Birmingham class light cruisers, Lowestoft *had an active war; she was present at the Dogger Bank action and served in the Mediterranean, 1916–19*

CTESIPHON, BATTLE OF, 22–25 November 1915

After seizing Kut on 28 September 1915, **Major-General Townshend** was ordered by **General Nixon** to advance on Baghdad without waiting for the reinforcements that the War Office had promised to send. Although Baghdad's strategic significance was limited, the British government needed a major success to restore its prestige, which had been badly damaged by the evident failure of the **Gallipoli Expedition**. With a force of 14,000 men, Townshend moved up the Tigris from Aziziya, meeting General Nur-ud-Din's Turkish army at Ctesiphon, where they occupied heavily fortified positions on the east bank of the river, sixteen miles from Baghdad.

Although he was heavily outnumbered – the Turks were being reinforced and would have 30,000 men –

Townshend unwisely ordered an advance on the Turkish left. At first the British were successful, moving through the enemy's forward lines, but as the Turks brought up more troops they were forced to withdraw. After four days' heavy fighting, Townshend, who had suffered as many as 4,500 casualties, decided to withdraw. The sick and wounded were sent back to **Kut al Imara** before the rest of the British left on 25 November. Retreating without difficulty, except when he was forced to fight a rearguard action at Umm-at-Tubal, Townshend reached Kut on 3 December, determined to hold the place that was the cornerstone of the British presence in Mesopotamia.

CURTISS H4

The H4 was a twin-engined reconnaissance flying boat which served with the RNAS in small numbers

from November 1914 until the end of the war. Constructed of wood and fabric, it was the first of a series of biplane flying boats acquired either direct from Curtiss in the United States or from British manufacturers producing them under licence. The H4 was fitted with a variety of engines, including the 90hp Curtiss OX-5 and the 100hp Anzani, but none proved entirely adequate. Accommodating a crew of four, it carried a light bomb load beneath the wings and a flexibly mounted machine-gun in the bows. This model was designated 'Small America' when the **Curtiss H12** ('Large America') appeared.

Apart from insufficient power, the H4's hull was not very seaworthy and its usefulness for coastal patrol work was limited. As a result, the majority of these aircraft were used by the RNAS in a training role. Of greater long-term significance was the fact that John Porte, the flying boat designer, used the H4 for experimental purposes and the results were incorporated into the design of later Curtiss models and the **Felixstowe flying boats**.

CURTISS H12

The H12 was a twin-engined patrol flying boat which served with the US Navy and with the RNAS. It was known as 'Large America' to avoid confusion with the **Curtiss H4** ('Small America') from which it was developed. Like the H4, it was constructed from wood and fabric and carried a crew of four. It was, however, much more heavily armed, with up to four **Lewis machine-guns** (operated by front and rear gunners) and over 400lb of bombs on board. Performance remained a problem until the original 275hp Rolls Royce Eagle I engines were replaced by 375hp Eagle units. To overcome continuing weaknesses in hull design, some aircraft were substantially modified and these were known as 'Converted Large Americas'.

The H12 was in service with the RNAS from the spring of 1917 until the end of the war and had a distinguished record in its anti-submarine and anti-Zeppelin roles, destroying a small number of each. Its achievements include the first victory by an American-built machine against a German aircraft and the first Zeppelin shot down by a flying boat. H12s were also the first aircraft to operate the famous 'spider's web' system of maritime patrols over the North Sea.

'Large America': the Curtiss H12 was a well-armed and seaworthy flying boat

CURTISS H16

The H16 'Large America' anti-submarine patrol flying boat served with the RNAS and with the US Navy in the closing months of the war. It was a development of the more widely known **Curtiss H12**, incorporat-

ing an improved hull design, comparable to those of the **Felixstowe** seaplanes of John Porte, and larger span wings. The RNAS version was powered by twin 320hp Rolls Royce Eagle engines, while the US Navy boat had twin 330hp Liberty motors. It had a maximum speed of 98m.p.h. at 2,000 feet and an endurance of six hours. A crew of four was retained, but armament was further increased compared to the H12: it had two additional machine-guns which fired through each side of the hull. Over 900lb of bombs could be carried, mounted on racks beneath the wings. About 20 H16s were operated by the RNAS at the end of the war; these were supplemented by the 50 H16s flown by the US Navy on patrols around the British coast.

CURTISS JN SERIES

The JN series of two-seater tractor biplanes, universally known as the 'Jenny', provided the US army with its major training aircraft of the war. The first important version was the JN-3, powered by the 90hp Curtiss OX-5 engine and fitted with wheel type flying controls. In 1915–16 it served in small numbers with the RFC and RNAS, which at that time urgently required a basic trainer, as well as in the United States. An improved version, with ailerons on all wings and a modified tail, was designated JN-4A, but large-scale production, following America's entry into the war, concentrated on the JN-4D. This variant, which featured a stick control and had large cut-outs in the wings at the fuselage, retained the original Curtiss engine.

The important contribution of the OX-powered JN4s to the training of American pilots is indicated by the fact that over 5,500 examples were produced during the war. Specialist instruction in observation, gunnery and bombing techniques was provided in the JN-4H, an advanced trainer powered by a 150hp or 180hp Hispano-Suiza engine. Jennies with this more powerful motor survived in US army service until 1927, but the OX-engined JN4s were declared obsolete at the end of the war.

CURTISS N-9

The N-9, a seaplane variant of the famous **Curtiss Jenny**, was a standard basic trainer of the US Navy from 1917. Based on the JN-4B, which in turn was a large wingspan version of the JN-4A, it was equipped with the 100hp OX-6 engine, a more powerful version of the Jenny's OX-5. The navy found, however, that the aircraft was still underpowered and the 150hp Hispano-Suiza engine, which could handle the extra weight of the float undercarriage, was used instead. The N-9 remained in US Navy service until 1927.

DAMASCUS, SEIZURE OF, 1 October 1918

After the **Battle of Megiddo**, **Allenby** exploited his decisive victory by advancing towards Beirut and Damascus. The Allies fought two minor engagements as they advanced on Damascus, but **Liman von Sanders**, the German commander, was unable to gain sufficient time to prepare the city's defences. They reached Damascus on 1 October, shortly after the Arabs under **Feisal** and **Lawrence**. The Third Australian Light Horse was the first unit of Allenby's army to enter the city; there was no more than token resistance and the garrison of almost 20,000 men was taken prisoner.

The British commander handed over the administration of the city to the Arabs but, by the terms of the

Sykes-Picot agreement, Syria was to become a French mandate after the defeat of Turkey.

Beyond Damascus, Beirut was seized on 2 October and Aleppo, 200 miles further north, had been reached by 25 October. The armistice with Turkey brought hostilities to an end on 30 October. The protracted, but successful, reconquest of Palestine under Allenby had cost the British 50,000 casualties, although the great majority of these were because of disease rather than combat.

The fall of Damascus marked the end of Turkish dominance in the Middle East, although it was the British and French not the Arabs who were to be the beneficiaries

DANIELS, JOSEPHUS, 1862–1948

Woodrow Wilson's Secretary to the Navy (1912–21), Daniels prepared the service for war with a major programme of reform, which included changes in promotion procedures and the creation of a Chief of Naval Operations. When America joined the war in April 1917, Daniels presided over the rapid expansion of the navy, authorising, for example, the construction of 200 destroyers as a contribution to the Allied anti-submarine effort. Daniels, who knew little about naval strategy, relied heavily on the advice of **Admiral Benson**, his Chief of Naval Operations. He was opposed to the President's decision to abandon the principle of the freedom of the seas – one of the **Fourteen Points** – in the face of British opposition but remained in office until 1921.

DANILOV, LIEUTENANT-GENERAL YURY, 1866–1937

Deputy chief of staff of the Russian army during the first year of the war, Danilov had been involved in the preparation of Russia's war plans. In the absence of a capable superior, Danilov directed the country's wartime strategy, which involved simultaneous offensives against Germany and Austria as soon as hostilities began. An 'able but orthodox' soldier, Danilov was unable to implement his plans effectively or coordinate the separate operations successfully because 'the means were lacking and the instrument defective'. Along with his senior colleagues, he was removed from office in August 1915 as the prolonged Russian retreat through Galicia and Poland came to a halt. By 1917, Danilov had retrieved something of his career, commanding the Fifth Army for a while before leaving the service for good.

DANKL VON KRASNIK, GENERAL VIKTOR, COUNT, 1854–1941

'The most resolute' of the Austro-Hungarian generals of the First World War, Dankl commanded the First

Army during the advance into Russian Poland from Galicia in August 1914. Dankl's victory was, however, shortlived as Russian forces drove back the Austrians on a broad front towards Lemburg. When Italy declared war on Austria, Dankl was moved to that front, commanding the Eleventh Army in the Tren- tino offensive of May 1916. Initially successful, the advance ran into difficulties partly because of the need to move troops to the east to halt the **Brusilov Offensive**. The suspension of operations on the Italian front marked the end of Dankl's active military career.

DANTE ALIGHIERI

Completed in 1913, Italy's first dreadnought battle- ship was claimed to be the fastest vessel of its type, with a maximum speed of 22/23 knots. It was also the world's first ship to carry its heavy armament in triple turrets, with twelve 12-inch guns being mounted in four turrets on the centre line. Also novel was the positioning of some of the 4.7-inch medium calibre guns in turrets rather than side batteries. *Dante Alighieri*'s wartime service in the Mediterranean was uneventful, her only action being the bombardment of Durazzo shortly before the Armistice.

DANTON

This class of pre-dreadnought battleships, which had a displacement of over 18,000 tons each, was well armed and had improved armour protection. *Danton* and her five sister ships – *Condorcet*, *Diderot*, *Voltaire*, *Mirabeau*, *Vergniaud* – entered French naval service in 1911 and all served in the Mediterranean between 1914–18. *Danton* was sunk by a German submarine (UB-64) off Sardinia in 1917, but all the others survived the war unscathed.

DARDANELLES OPERATION, 19 February–18 March 1915

The ill-fated **Gallipoli expedition** was preceded by an Allied operation that was to attempt to force a passage through the Dardanelles by naval forces alone. Constantinople could then be attacked and seized, forcing Turkey out of the war and allowing a secure supply route to Russia to be established. An Allied fleet, consisting of 14 pre-dreadnoughts, four old French battleships, a battlecruiser, and a super- dreadnought, under the command of **Vice-Admiral Carden**, was made ready at Mudros Bay on Lemnos, 50 miles west of the Dardanelles.

The attack began on 19 February 1915, initially with a long-range bombardment of the outer forts of Cape Helles and Kum Kale, which were eventually put out of action on 25 February. Marines landed almost immediately to destroy whatever remained intact. Five battleships and a battlecruiser had taken part in the operation, but the 15-inch guns of the super-dreadnought *Queen Elizabeth* had made the decisive impact.

The next stage, which was much more difficult, involved the silencing of the intermediate Turkish defences, which could only be attacked from inside the Narrows, where the danger from mines was always present. The effectiveness of the preliminary shelling and minesweeping activities, which extended over a period of days, was severely restricted by continuous heavy fire from Turkish shore positions. The ineffective Carden, whose health had broken under the strain of command in the Dardanelles, was replaced by **Admiral De Robeck**, a more able commander, just before an all-out attack was launched against the enemy's positions on 18 March. Sixteen battleships and many other smaller vessels were involved in the massive bombardment which extended to a point six miles up the straits. Even so the Turkish batteries could not be silenced and disaster soon occurred, with the French battleship *Bouvet* running into an undetected minefield and sinking. The first victim was soon followed by *Irresistible* and *Ocean*, which were also sunk; three other British and French capital ships were seriously damaged by mines or gunfire.

At this point De Robeck cancelled the operation. Although some British officers believed that the enemy was close to collapse after their attack, the British commander was unwilling to take any further risks. **Churchill**, who had sent replacement ships to the Dardanelles, also wanted the attack to be renewed, but found no support within the Admiralty. The Turkish guns and minefields were in fact still largely intact and, as a result, the purely naval phase of the operation ended and an amphibious landing was made a month later.

DARTIGE du FOURNET, ADMIRAL LOUIS, 1856–1940

Commander of French naval forces in the Mediterranean from October 1915, Admiral Dartige du Fournet was **Boué de Lapeyrère**'s short-lived replacement. His main preoccupation was the German U-boat threat and his counter-measures included the provision of escorts for merchant ships. Even more problematic was the use of naval power to try to ensure the continued neutrality of the Greek government. The landing in Athens of a British and French force under his command in December 1916 ran into armed opposition, in spite of the assurances of **King Constantine** to the contrary. Fournet's threats of further military action proved to be counter-productive; he was removed from command before he could alienate the country further and was never employed again.

D-CLASS SUBMARINE

The first British submarine capable of patrolling the oceans, it was much larger than its **B- and C-class** predecessors, with a surface displacement of just under 500 tons and a crew of 25. Power was provided by two diesel-driven screws which gave it a range of 2,500 nautical miles at 10 knots. There were three 18-inch torpedo tubes (two bow, one stern), and one unit of this class (D4) was the first submarine to carry a gun – a 12-pounder. Eight D-class boats were built in 1908–11 and three were lost during the war, including one sunk in error by a French airship. The successful development of these boats led directly to the British **E-class**, the most important Allied submarines of the First World War.

DECLASSÉ, THÉOPHILE, 1857–1923

Appointed Foreign Minister for the second time in August 1914, Declassé's conduct of French foreign policy during the war achieved less than it had done in peace. Generally viewed as being too pro-Russian, he failed to win over Bulgaria to the Allies, although he helped to bring Italy into the war. Declassé's ministerial career ended in October 1915 when he resigned because of his opposition to the dispatch of French forces to **Salonika**.

DELAWARE

Much larger successors of the South Carolina class, *Delaware* and *North Dakota* were completed in 1910 and were the first American battleships with a displacement of more than 20,000 tons. Major changes included an additional twin 12-inch turret on the centre line and an increased maximum speed of 21 knots. For the first time, therefore, the US navy possessed ships that were comparable in standard to the British dreadnoughts. However, unlike their counterparts in the Royal Navy they had a heavy secondary battery of fourteen 5-inch guns. Along with *New York*, *Wyoming* and *Florida*, *Delaware* served with the 6th Battle Squadron of the British **Grand Fleet**, employed on convoy and support duties until July 1918.

DEPTH CHARGE

A creation of the First World War – it first appeared in 1916 – the depth charge was an explosive weapon that was used to attack submerged submarines. It consisted of a canister containing explosive, which was detonated at a pre-selected depth by means of a hydrostatic valve operated by water pressure. They could be launched from the ship's stern or fired from either beam using a depth charge thrower as it passed over the target. They were widely employed by the Royal Navy during its struggle with the U-boat in 1916–18.

DERFFLINGER

The last German battlecruisers produced before the war, the Derfflingers were highly successful capital ships that were superior to contemporary British designs, with the ability to absorb considerable damage. *Derfflinger* herself suffered light damage at the **Battle of the Dogger Bank** but was much more severely attacked at **Jutland**, being hit by 21 shells. She survived fires and 3,350 tons of flood water to be repaired and resume operational service. Even more badly affected at Jutland, *Lützow* was sunk on the orders of **Admiral Hipper**; she was the only German battlecruiser lost between 1914 and 1918.

Hindenburg, which was not completed until late in 1917, had a less eventful war, but like *Derfflinger* she was interned at Scapa Flow and scuttled there on 21 June 1919.

This class differed considerably from its predecessor, *Seydlitz*; it had, for example, a flush deck and the twin 12-inch turrets were arranged in superfiring pairs fore and aft. Heavy secondary armament – twelve 5.9-inch guns – was located in an upper deck battery. These ships had excellent firepower and at Jutland *Derfflinger* accounted for *Queen Mary* and *Lützow* for at least one other capital ship.

DE ROBECK, ADMIRAL SIR JOHN, 1862–1928

Appointed second-in-command of the naval forces at the **Dardanelles**, under **Vice-Admiral Carden**, in January 1915, De Robeck was an experienced naval officer who had served in a variety of posts at home and sea. He participated in the successful bombard- ment of the outer forts at the end of February and in the failed attempt to negotiate the minefields across the Narrows early in March. Carden's health was damaged by the strain of these difficult operations and he was succeeded by De Robeck on 17 March

1915. On the very next day he commanded the disastrous Anglo-French assault that resulted in the destruction of three battleships and other serious losses.

Now convinced that the Dardanelles could not be taken by naval force alone, De Robeck suspended all offensive action while the combined assault on **Gallipoli** was being prepared. De Robeck was in command of the naval side of the Gallipoli operations and both his handling of the initial landings on 25 April and the eventual withdrawal of Allied troops early in 1916 won high praise. De Robeck spent the remainder of the war in home waters in command of the Third Battle Squadron (subsequently the Second) of the **Grand Fleet**.

DESTROYER

First developed by Britain in the last decade of the nineteenth century, the destroyer was originally designed as a 'torpedo boat catcher'. Speed was the key to the success of this light, fast warship and the introduction of the turbine engine helped to produce the required margin over the torpedo boat. Armed with guns and torpedo tubes, the typical British destroyer of the First World War had a displacement of more than 1,000 tons, a crew in excess of 70, and a maximum speed of around 30 knots.

As the destroyer's size and performance increased, it was no longer confined to a defensive role and in both the British and German navies its primary wartime task was to attack the enemy's main battle fleet. They were first deployed in this way at the **Battle of Jutland** when a large force of over 60 British destroyers was ranged against the battleships and battlecruisers of the **High Seas Fleet**. More than once they were able to turn these capital ships away and they repelled several attacks successfully. However, the price was high, with eight British destroyers sunk and almost all of the remainder damaged to some degree. Jutland demonstrated the need to reduce their vulnerability and increase the power of their armament, and proved to be an important influence on future destroyer design.

The destroyer's main defensive function during the war was to protect the fleet against the submarine rather than the torpedo boat and they were used by all the principal navies for this purpose. Standard equipment for anti-submarine warfare included hydrophones and **depth charges**. Some destroyers were converted for minelaying, while others were widely used on convoy duties in the latter part of the war.

DEUTSCHLAND

Deutschland and her four sister ships were Germany's last pre-dreadnought battleships. Launched in 1904–05, they had a displacement of 13,993 tons and main armament consisting of four 11-inch guns. With weaknesses in armour protection and armament, the Deutschlands were obsolete in the age of the 'all big gun' battleship. During the First World War, they formed the 2nd Squadron of the **High Seas Fleet** and were present at **Jutland**, where *Pommern* was torpedoed. Unable to contribute much to the strength of the German battle fleet, the surviving ships of the class were withdrawn towards the end of 1916.

DFW BI & BII

This three-bay, two-seater biplane was used by the German air service on reconnaissance duties during the first year of the war. The most unusual feature of this basically conventional design was its sweptback wings, which earned it the nickname 'flying banana'. It had a 100hp Mercedes D I engine, with a downward pointing exhaust pipe and side radiators on the fuselage. The observer, who sat in the front cockpit, normally carried a rifle as no fixed weapons

were available. The BI, and the similar BII, were present in small numbers on the Western and Eastern Fronts until the appearance of the armed two-seater **C-types** in 1915. The B series continued in service for some time as training aircraft.

DFW CI & CII

The CI armed two-seater appeared in 1915 as a replacement for the unarmed **DFW B-types**. A strengthened version of its predecessor, the CI was equipped with a more powerful 150hp Benz Bz III engine, giving a maximum speed of 78m.p.h. at sea level. The observer, who remained in the front cockpit, was now armed with a ring-mounted **Para-**

bellum machine-gun, raised above the top wing, which gave a good field of fire. The CI was employed by German reconnaissance units on the Western and Eastern Fronts, with about 130 examples being produced. A modified version, the CII, had stability problems and was soon withdrawn from service.

DFW CV

This armed two-seater was one of the most successful German aircraft of its type to appear during the war. Based on the DFW CIV, this two-bay biplane had the same airframe as its predecessor, but used the 220hp Benz Bz IV engine in place of the smaller 150hp power unit. Its maximum speed was 97m.p.h. and it had a duration of $3\frac{1}{2}$ hours. Distinctive features included an enclosed engine and a heart-shaped tailplane. The observer was armed with a ring-mounted **Parabellum machine-gun** in the rear cockpit and there was a forward-firing Spandau machine-gun for the pilot.

The CV appeared in the summer of 1916 and was used for a wide range of duties – reconnaissance (visual and photographic), artillery observation, and infantry contact patrol. Valued by its crews for its excellent flying qualities, particularly its manoeuvrability and defensive capability, it remained in service on the Western Front until the end of the war. It was also used by Germany and her allies in Italy, Macedonia and Palestine. The CV was produced in large numbers by DFW and three sub-contractors, and some 600 were still operational in November 1918.

DIAZ, FIELD MARSHAL ARMANDO, 1861–1928

Replacing **Cadorna** in November 1917, after the **Caporetto** disaster, General Diaz's first task was to secure the new line on the Piave. With the help of British and French troops, Diaz, an experienced and competent field commander, prevented the Austrian and German armies from making any further progress. His main preoccupation during the winter was to rebuild the shattered Italian army, a task for

which he was well equipped: his 'supreme value was that he understood the minds of soldiers and knew how to reinvigorate their morale', although he was not a great leader or strategist. He was much more cautious than his predecessor and secured political support for a defensive strategy, resisting regular demands from the Allies for a large-scale offensive.

The next major action on the front came in fact

when the Austro-Hungarian army launched a final, desperate assault in June 1918. The revitalised Italian forces successfully repulsed the attack but the outcome did not prompt any change of heart by General Diaz. It was not until 23 October, when the collapse of the Austro-Hungarian empire was a certainty and there was no chance of German assistance, that Diaz moved. With a major contribution being made by British forces, he crossed the Piave and separated the enemy's armies as he pushed forward to **Vittorio Veneto**. They had advanced 60 miles by the time the Austrians capitulated on 4 November. In recognition of his wartime services Diaz was created Duke of Vittorio Veneto in 1920.

DJEMAL PASHA, AHMED, 1872–1922

Turkish general and one of the leaders of the Young Turks, Djemal was an influential member of the government from 1913, and served briefly as navy minister. Following Turkey's entry into the war, he went to Damascus as governor of Syria. Early in 1915, he led 20,000 men across the Sinai desert and launched an attack on the Suez Canal which failed completely. He was more successful in suppressing threats to his own authority in Syria, which he did with great brutality. Djemal returned to Constantinople following the **Fall of Jerusalem** in December 1917 and was forced to flee abroad when the Young Turk government collapsed in October 1918.

DOGGER BANK, BATTLE OF THE, 24 January 1915

During the night of 23 January 1915, the German First Scouting Group (**Rear Admiral von Hipper**) left Wilhelmshaven for the Dogger Bank, a shoal in the North Sea about 60 miles east of the Northumberland Coast. Hipper's force of four battlecruisers – *Seydlitz* (flagship), *Moltke*, *Derfflinger* and *Blücher* – and accompanying light cruisers and torpedo boats were to attack British patrols and fishing boats near the Bank on the following day.

The element of surprise had been lost because the German plan was already known to British naval intelligence and the Battlecruiser Force (**Admiral Beatty**) had left its base at Rosyth to intercept the enemy. Beatty's squadron, which consisted of *Lion* (flagship), *Tiger*, *Princess Royal*, *New Zealand* and *Indomitable*, was to rendezvous with the Harwich force (**Admiral Tyrwhitt**) north-east of the Dogger Bank, at dawn on 24 January.

Not long afterwards, the Germans were sighted heading westwards and as soon as he saw the larger British force in pursuit Hipper changed course and headed for home. As the faster British ships closed the distance between them, *Lion*, at the head of the British line, opened fire at extreme range (more than 20,000 yards).

In a running battle *Lion* hit the slow-moving *Blücher* at a range of about 10 miles; *Tiger* attacked *Seydlitz* and *Princess Royal* hit *Derfflinger*. *Seydlitz* and *Derfflinger* were both badly damaged, while *Blücher* was crippled. *Tiger* was then hit by a shell and Beatty's flagship was forced to retire. Admiral Moore on *New Zealand* temporarily took over the command, but misinterpreted Beatty's instructions: instead of pursuing the enemy fleet he abandoned the chase to concentrate on sinking *Blücher*, a task that had previously been allocated to *Indomitable*.

By the time an angry Admiral Beatty was able to resume the pursuit it was too late, as all the surviving German ships had escaped. The loss of *Blücher* accounted for most of the 954 German fatalities; British casualties amounted to no more than 15 killed and 80 wounded. Although the battle was technically a British victory, the opportunity to destroy three German warships had been missed. The unfortunate

Admiral Moore was quickly removed from command.

One of the most important outcomes of the battle was the German discovery of the vulnerability of the ammunition chamber to the flash of bursting shells.

They lost no time in fitting anti-flash devices to them; the British lost five ships at **Jutland** through unprotected magazines.

DREADNOUGHT

The first 'all big gun' ship, HMS Dreadnought *revolutionised battleship design but saw little action herself during the war*

Launched at Portsmouth in 1906, *Dreadnought* was the first 'all big gun' battleship and marked a turning point in the design of capital ships. Based on ideas developed by **Admiral Fisher**, her powerful primary armament consisted of ten 12-inch guns which were intended to be fired together over long distances. (Secondary armament was confined to anti-torpedo guns only.) Her speed (21 knots) was also unmatched by any other contemporary warship, although it had been necessary to reduce armour protection to achieve the required performance figures. *Dreadnought*, which had a displacement of just over 18,000 tons, was also the first capital ship to have an all-turbine power plant. She was also notable for the remarkable speed with which she had been built (366 days), a record that was never to be beaten for a ship of this size.

The appearance of the *Dreadnought* rendered all existing battleships obsolete and she gave her name to a type of capital ship that followed her. *Dreadnought* had a relatively uneventful war, serving with the Third Battle Squadron, Home Fleet, for much of the war. She rammed and sank U-29 in the North Sea on 18 March 1915, but otherwise saw no action.

DREYSE MACHINE-GUN

Used by the German army in reasonable numbers during the First World War, the 7.92mm Dreyse machine-gun Model MG10 was overshadowed by the much more successful **Maschinengewehr 08**. Water-cooled and short-recoil-operated, it was tripod-mounted and had a higher than average cyclic rate of fire. A modified version, the MG15, was introduced in 1915 in order to meet the need for a light machine-gun in Palestine and Turkey.

DUBAIL, GENERAL AUGUSTE, 1851–1934

Commander of the First Army in August 1914, General Dubail led his troops during the French offensive in Lorraine. After retreating in the face of superior German forces, he established a strong defensive position behind the Meurthe River, holding it during the **Battle of the Marne**. As the front stabilised, Dubail was allocated the largest sector, which ran from Belfort to Verdun. It was a relatively quiet area and **Joffre** drew on it regularly for reinforcements. Dubail himself was not directly involved in the defence of **Verdun** in 1916, although many of his troops were. Like Joffre, Dubail had failed to appreciate its vulnerability to enemy attack, but in his case the penalty was rapid removal from command. Dubail spent much of the rest of the war as military governor of Paris.

DUNCAN

This class of six pre-dreadnought battleships, commissioned in 1903-04, was a development of the Formidables, but with improved speed (19 knots) and firepower (four 12-inch and twelve 6-inch guns). The ships were also longer and had a displacement of 13,270 tons. With the exception of *Montagu*, which was lost in 1906, all the Duncans served during the war, their operational use being concentrated in the English Channel and the Dardanelles. *Russell* and *Cornwallis* were sunk off Malta at different times, but *Exmouth*, *Duncan* and *Albemarle* survived to go into the reserve in 1917.

EASTER RISING, 24–29 April 1916

A nationalist uprising against the British in Dublin, led by Patrick Pearse of the Irish Republican Brotherhood and James Connolly of Sinn Fein. Their aim was to secure the immediate independence of Ireland from British rule. Five days' street fighting, involving 1,000 insurgents, was concentrated on the Dublin General Post Office. It came to an end on 29 April, when their leaders surrendered in the face of overwhelming British military power and heavy casualties. Originally there had been hopes of direct German military aid, but these were not realised, despite the efforts of **Sir Roger Casement** during his mission to Berlin. Only a single arms shipment was sent by the Germans, but it was intercepted by the British off the Irish coast.

EASTERN FRONT, CHRONOLOGICAL LIST OF EVENTS

Gumbinnen, Battle of, 1914
Galicia, Operations in, 1914–15
Tannenberg, Battle of, 1914
Masurian Lakes, First Battle of, 1914
Warsaw Offensive, 1914
Lodz, Battle of, 1914

Masurian Lakes, Second Battle of, 1915
Gorlice-Tarnow Offensive, 1915
Naroch Lake, Battle of, 1916
Brusilov Offensive, 1916
Kerensky Offensive, 1917
Riga Offensive, 1917

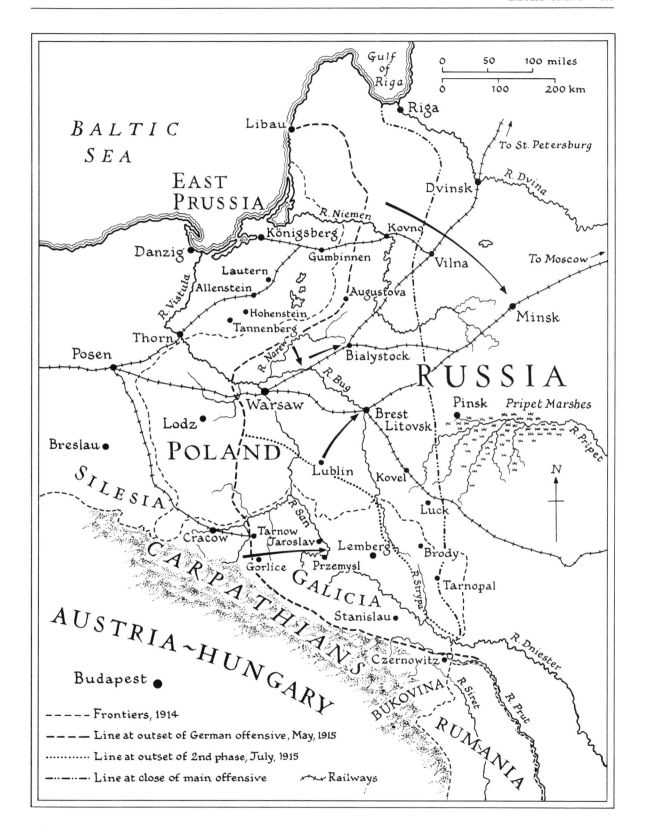

BALTIC SEA

Gulf of Riga

0   50   100 miles
0   100   200 km

Riga

EAST PRUSSIA

Libau

To St. Petersburg

R. Dvina

Dvinsk

R. Niemen

Königsberg

Kovno

Gumbinnen

Vilna

To Moscow

Danzig

Augustova

R. Vistula

Lautern

Allenstein

Hohenstein

Minsk

Tannenberg

Thorn

R. Narew

Bialystock

RUSSIA

R. Bug

Posen

Warsaw

Pinsk   *Pripet Marshes*

Lodz

Brest Litovsk

R. Pripet

Breslau

POLAND

N

SILESIA

Lublin

Kovel

R. San

Luck

Cracow

Tarnow

Jaroslav

Lemberg

Brody

Gorlice

Przemysl

Tarnopal

GALICIA

R. Strypa

CARPATHIANS

Stanislau

AUSTRIA~HUNGARY

Czernowitz

R. Dniester

Budapest

BUKOVINA

R. Siret

R. Prut

RUMANIA

- - - -   Frontiers, 1914
— - — -   Line at outset of German offensive, May, 1915
....   Line at outset of 2nd phase, July, 1915
—-—-—   Line at close of main offensive   ⌇⌇⌇ Railways

EBERHARDT, ADMIRAL ANDREI, 1856–1919

Commander of Russia's Black Sea Fleet from 1911, Admiral Eberhardt, an officer with wide command and staff experience, pursued the war against Turkey with some vigour. With the Black Sea ports protected by mines and the *Goeben* neutralised, Eberhardt's forces interrupted Turkish shipping, supported the Allied operations in the **Dardanelles** and countered the German U-boat threat. However, these missions were only partially successful and in response to a demand for a younger and more dynamic commander, Eberhardt was replaced by **Admiral Kolchak** in July 1916.

E-CLASS SUBMARINE

The most advanced submarine in British service at the beginning of the war, the E-class, of which 56 were built between 1912–16, incorporated some important design modifications.

It had a large and strong hull with two watertight bulkheads, and there was a pair of beam torpedo tubes as well as one at the bow and stern. Submarine E9 and subsequent units were slightly increased in length to permit a second torpedo tube in the bow; they also had a third watertight bulkhead. A 12-pounder gun was fitted as standard following the successful trials with D4. Twin 800hp diesels were now used and they produced a range of 3,000 nautical miles at 10 knots; underwater it could travel for about 120 miles at low speed before the electric power failed. Six E-class boats were modified as minelayers, the first of their kind, and could hold 20 mines each. E22 became the world's first aircraft-carrying submarine when, early in 1916, it was fitted with a launching ramp.

The E-class boats were at the forefront of the Allied submarine offensive during the First World War and they achieved some notable successes in the Baltic and the Sea of Mamora. E9 was, in fact, the first British submarine to score a victory, sinking the German cruiser *Hela* on 13 September 1914. Their record in the Sea of Mamora was dominated by the exploits of E11, commanded by Lt-Cdr Martin Nasmith: during the course of his two missions against the Turks (amounting to a total of 96 days in the area), he destroyed 101 enemy ships. The cost of such operations was, however, very high and almost 50 per cent of these submarines had been lost by the end of the war.

EGYPT AND PALESTINE, CHRONOLOGICAL LIST OF EVENTS

Suez Canal, Defence of, 1914–16
Arab Revolt, 1916–18
Romani, Battle of, 1916
Rafa, Battle of, 1917
Gaza, First and Second Battles of, 1917

Gaza, Third Battle of, 1917
Jerusalem, Fall of, 1917
Megiddo, Battle of, 1918
Damascus, Seizure of, 1918

EICHHORN, FIELD MARSHAL HERMANN VON, 1848–1918

Commander of the German Tenth Army on the Eastern Front from 1915, Eichhorn led his troops during the winter battle of the **Masurian Lakes** and in the capture of Kovno, a heavy blow to the Russians. In July 1916 Army Group Eichhorn was formed and in the following year he was promoted field marshal.

After the **Treaty of Brest-Litovsk** was signed, Eichhorn was appointed to the army group that occupied the Ukraine and the Crimea. In July 1918, he was assassinated by a member of the Social Revolutionary Party who objected to any form of co-operation between the Germans and the Bolsheviks.

EINEM, GENERAL KARL VON, 1853–1934

Commander of the German Third Army on the Western Front from 12 September 1914, Einem held the post until the end of the war. He was an experienced staff officer and had, as Prussian war minister, been involved in the modernisation of the

army in the 1900s. The Third Army held its line in **Champagne** during successive French offensives and it was not until the autumn of 1918 that it gave significant ground in the face of a strong Allied advance.

EMDEN

The best known and most successful of the German surface raiders of the First World War, the *Emden* was a light cruiser of 3,544 tons. She left **Admiral von Spee**'s squadron at the beginning of the war and headed for the Indian Ocean. She bombarded Madras on 22 September, but her main preoccupation was enemy merchant ships. She captured or sank 23 of them (101,182 tons) in the period up to 9 November. She also sank a Russian cruiser and a French

destroyer, as well as generally disrupting shipping movements across a wide area.

The Allies had difficulty in tracking the *Emden* and even when she was forced to undertake emergency repairs in the British Maldive Islands she eluded capture: the local population had no direct links with the rest of the world and they had not yet heard that Britian and Germany were at war. Her final action was to sabotage the cable station at Cocos Keeling

Island, when her work was interrupted by the arrival of the *Sydney*, an Australian light cruiser, on 9 November: she was easily destroyed and 142 Germans lost their lives. Much of the success of *Emden*'s remarkable hit-and-run campaign must be attributed to the skill and courage of her captain, Karl von Miller, who must be regarded as one of the outstanding seamen of the period.

ENTENTE POWERS

Widely used during the First World War as an alternative general name for the Allies, before 1914 it was originally applied only to Britain, France and Russia, who were linked by military alliance. At the beginning of the war these three major powers were joined by Belgium, Japan, Montenegro and Serbia. In May 1915, Italy entered the war on the side of the Entente Powers, to be followed by Rumania and Portugal in 1916 and by Greece and the United States in 1917.

The initial mobilisation figures and manpower total are given below:

	Mobilisation on outbreak of war	Total manpower mobilised
Belgium	117,000	267,000
British Empire	975,000	9,496,170
France	4,017,000	8,410,000
Greece	230,000	230,000
Italy	1,251,000	5,615,000
Japan	————	800,000
Montenegro	50,000	50,000
Portugal	————	100,000
Rumania	290,000	750,000
Russia	5,971,000	12,000,000
Serbia	200,000	707,343
United States	————	4,355,000

ENVER PASHA, 1881–1922

Turkish general and one of the leaders of the Young Turks, Enver had been in command of the Turkish army during the Balkan Wars. Early in 1914 he entered the Cabinet as Minister of War and was soon an influential member of the government. Strongly pro-German, he helped to bring Turkey into the war on the side of the Central Powers, having negotiated a defensive alliance with them. He was the principal

Enver Pasha (left) *in Damascus with Djemal Pasha, the Governor of Syria*

architect of Turkey's wartime military policy, which was strongly influenced by his personal aim of imperial expansion in the Caucasus.

He assumed command of the first campaign against the Russians, but badly planned and timed, it was launched during the middle of winter. It led to the disaster of **Sarakamish** (29 December 1914), and was followed by major defeats in 1916 at the hands of General **Yudenich**, the able Russian commander.

Enver's interest in the Caucasus intensified after the **Russian Revolution** and it was given priority at the expense of operations in Palestine. Turkish troops advanced into Russian Armenia early in 1918, but massacres there severely damaged his reputation. With the fall of the Young Turk government in October 1918, Enver was forced to flee the country.

ERIN

Originally ordered for the Turkish navy as the *Reshadieh*, *Erin*, as she was renamed, was seized by the Admiralty on the outbreak of war. This powerful dreadnought battleship served with the 2nd Battle Squadron, **Grand Fleet** and was present at the **Battle of Jutland**, where she was undamaged. The design drew heavily on the **King George V class**, but with differences in dimensions, a shallower armour belt and reduced coal-carrying capacity. She was, however, well armed, with a better arrangment of armament than other British warships of the period.

ERZINCAN, BATTLE OF, 25 July 1916

The Turkish defeat at **Sarakamish** on the Caucasian front early in 1915 was followed by intermittent fighting which had died out by the autumn. Both the Russians and the Turks then prepared for a major offensive to be launched on the Lake Van–Black Sea line early in 1916. The Russians, commanded by **General Yudenich**, acted first: they advanced from Kars and launched a surprise attack before the enemy's forces were in place. The Turkish Third Army, under the command of Abdul Kerim, was in the process of being reinforced with troops from **Gallipoli** after the withdrawal of the Allied expeditionary force.

Moving west, the Russians captured Koprukoy on 17 January 1916, but failed to envelop the Turks who quickly retreated, having lost 25,000 men. By 16 February the Russians had captured the fortress of Erzerum, 40 miles farther west, after a three-day battle. During the same period a Russian column pressed northwards to take Trabzon (Trebizond), a Black Sea port, on 17 April. The victory, achieved with the help of the Russian navy, opened up a valuable new supply route.

The main Russian offensive proceeded without difficulty beyond Erzerum, even though Turkish reinforcements continued to arrive at the front. Yudenich pierced the Turkish lines at Bayburt, 60 miles to the north-west, on 2 July and, turning south-west, took Erzincan, 96 miles west of Erzerum, on 25 July. It was a major victory for Yudenich, whose opponents were routed with 34,000 casualties.

On the Russians' eastern flank progress was less rapid. An eastward advance by **Kemal Ataturk**, the able Turkish commander and hero of Gallipoli, was one of the few positive aspects of their campaign; his corps (part of the Second Army) took Mus, 45 miles from Lake Van, and Bitlis (15 August), 30 miles from the lake. Even these modest gains were, however, lost on 24 August in a final Russian counter-offensive which brought the year's campaign to a close.

The whole front remained quiet during 1917, but after the November Revolution the Russian army quickly drifted away. When the peace negotiations at **Brest-Litovsk** broke down in February 1918 the Central Powers' offensive on the Eastern Front was renewed and the Turks advanced into the Caucasus, regaining all the territory lost in 1916. There followed a race between Turkey and Germany for the Baku oilfields which the Turks won (14 September). A British expedition under Major General Dunsterville had reached Baku on 4 August but had been forced to withdraw. By the terms of the Armistice, Turkey was required to withdraw from the Caucasus back to her pre-war frontiers and on 17 November the British reoccupied Baku.

ESSEN, ADMIRAL NIKOLAI von, 1860–1915

Commander of Russia's Baltic Fleet from 1909 until his death in May 1915, Admiral Essen had established his reputation as one of the country's leading naval officers during the war against Japan. Essen was constrained by the superiority of German naval forces and his main wartime task was to maintain Russia's Baltic defences, giving first priority to the protection of Petrograd. A further barrier to offensive action, which was limited to the mining of German ports, was the fact that the Baltic Fleet was subject to the overall control of the commander of the Russian Sixth Army.

ETRICH TAUBE

The Taube was an unarmed tractor monoplane that was used by the air forces of Germany, Austro-Hungary and Italy for reconnaissance duties in the first year of the war.

Designed by Igo Etrich, an Austrian engineer, in 1910, this standard military type was named the Taube or 'Dove' because of the bird-like appearance of its swept-back wing tips (warped to provide lateral control). The complex wing design gave the machine great stability, a characteristic much valued by aircraft designers at this time. Originally a single type, the Taube became the name for a whole class of aircraft, produced by a variety of manufacturers. Two versions in Austrian service were made by **Lohner**: the AI was powered by an 85hp Austro Daimler engine with twin radiators over the observer's cockpit; the AII was equipped with a 120hp engine of the same type, with a radiator at the front. Taubes were used by the Austrian air service in action on the Italian front and for training purposes.

Its wider military use had already been encouraged when it became the first aircraft from which a bomb was dropped, during the Libyan campaign, 1911–12. Large scale production was started in Germany and in total some 500 Taubes were built for the German air service. Several different single- and two-seat variants appeared, including a steel framed version, although most Taubes had a strong wooden airframe covered with fabric. A wide variety of engines was used, the most common being the Argus, Benz and Mercedes units with outputs ranging from 80 to 100hp.

The Taube gained some notable credits during the early months of the war. In its reconnaissance role it gave the Germans early warning of an unsuspected Russian advance during the **Battle of Tannenberg** in August 1914. During the same month it carried out the first air raid on Paris, dropping five small bombs. A single Taube was active during the siege of **Tsingtao** (September to November 1914) when it carried out reconnaissance missions and unsuccessfully attacked a Japanese ship.

By 1915, however, the age of the Taube design was becoming increasingly evident and it was withdrawn from front line duty in the spring, being replaced by more manoeuvrable and faster B-type biplanes. For a limited period, it continued to play a useful role as a training aircraft.

EUGEN, FIELD MARSHAL, ARCHDUKE OF AUSTRIA, 1863–1954

With the help of royal influence, Archduke Eugen's military career advanced rapidly in pre-war Austro-Hungary. In December 1914 he was appointed commander of the empire's armies in the Balkans, but he moved to the Italian front after war between the two countries was declared in May 1915. He remained formally in command there until his retirement in January 1918, leading the Trentino offensive in May 1916 and the attack at **Caporetto** in October 1917. In practice, however, **Conrad**, the chief of staff, and other senior officers played a critical role in the planning and conduct of both these operations.

EVERT, GENERAL ALEKSEI, 1857–1918

An elderly Russian infantry general, Evert was recalled from a command in Siberia in August 1914 to lead the Fourth Army in the Galicia campaign. The successful German spring offensive of 1915 did not seem to damage Evert's military reputation because he soon received promotion to the command of the large Western front, part of the old North-Western Front, which ran from Lake Naroch to the Pinsk area.

Evert's severe limitations as a general did, however, become much more evident in 1916 when he failed to co-operate effectively in support of the **Brusilov Offensive** to the south. His front remained relatively inactive and he was unable to supply the reserves required by **Brusilov**. In July, Evert was in fact allocated the northern part of Brusilov's front, with specific responsibility for the offensive against enemy positions before Kovel. Evert was opposed to Brusilov's new tactics and his ineffectual response helped to bring the whole offensive to a halt.

No action was taken against him and it was not until after the March Revolution that he was dismissed, mainly because of his extreme right wing views.

FAIREY CAMPANIA

The Campania was the first aircraft specifically designed to operate from an aircraft carrier. It was a two-seat, two-bay biplane with folding wings, and was powered by either a single 275hp Sunbeam Maori II or a 345hp Rolls Royce Eagle VIII engine. The Eagle gave a maximum speed of 80m.p.h. at 2,000 feet, with an endurance of three hours. Armament consisted of a .303 **Lewis gun** on a ring mounting and a rack below the fuselage for two 100lb bombs.

This reconnaissance seaplane served the RNAS from late in 1917 until after the end of the war and 62 were produced in total. It was named after HMS *Campania*, a former passenger liner converted to a carrier, to which the first examples of the new aircraft were allocated. Fitted with twin landing floats, it could take off from the ship with the aid of trolley gear that was jettisoned as it became airborne. Its routine ship-spotting role was also carried out from two other carriers, *Nairana* and *Pegasus*, and from several coastal air stations.

FALKENHAYN, GENERAL ERICH von, 1861–1922

The conventional career of a Prussian officer of Junker stock seemed in prospect for Erich von Falkenhayn until he was noticed by the Kaiser. Some perceptive reports from China during the Boxer Rising had first brought him to prominence and he subsequently established his reputation as a successful chief of staff to **General von Prittwitz**. Rapid promotion followed, including his remarkable move from the line to the command of a Guards regiment. In 1913, he was appointed Minister of War; he did the job efficiently and made an important contribution to the effective working of the German army as it entered the war in 1914.

Falkenhayn, German chief of staff, 1914–16

When **Moltke** failed as chief of staff in September 1914, Falkenhayn replaced him. For six months he combined this post with his old one and thus had far greater executive powers than any other wartime military leader. The 'Race to the Sea' did not redeem Germany's position after the setbacks on the **Marne** but he successfully reorganised her military machine during this period. He also increased the supply of raw materials and munitions and developed the network of military railways.

Noted for his caution and indecisiveness as well as his aloofness, Falkenhayn did not launch a major attack on either the Eastern or Western Fronts in the autumn of 1914, but decided on the more prudent policy of assuring security on all fronts by means of several limited offensives with specific objectives. Although Falkenhayn was a committed 'Westerner', he was compelled to weigh the competing needs of his three separate fronts. Early in 1915, he gave priority to operations on the Eastern Front, which resulted in the breakthrough at **Gorlice-Tarnow** (May) and the capture of Poland. It meant that Russia would never again be a serious threat to Germany itself.

Although Falkenhayn had been unwilling to risk an all-out offensive in 1915 he recognised the need for a decisive victory in 1916. He aimed to 'bleed France white' at **Verdun**, but failure there cost him his job in August.

He was then given his first operational command – head of the Ninth Army in Rumania – and served there with distinction. After the fall of Rumania in December 1916, he was sent to Turkey to reorganise the army and to recapture **Baghdad**. The latter proved to be an impossible objective and, in July 1917, he turned his attention to Palestine, where **Allenby** was moving towards **Jerusalem**. Falkenhayn was outmanoeuvred at Beersheba and when the decisive British blow fell on 6 November he had not the reserves to meet it. Jerusalem then fell and after an ill-conceived attempt to re-capture it, he was replaced by **Liman von Sanders** early in 1918. He ended his wartime career in relative obscurity in an unimportant garrison post in Lithuania.

FALKLAND ISLANDS, BATTLE OF THE, 8 December 1914

Following his overwhelming victory against **Cradock**'s squadron at **Coronel** on 1 November 1914, **Admiral von Spee** returned briefly to Valparaiso before proceeding south towards Cape Horn en route for home. His progress was slow because of poor weather and a shortage of coal, but early in December he decided to attack Port Stanley in the Falkland Islands. This British communications centre and coaling station was, he thought, undefended, and he would take the opportunity to destroy the wireless station there. The Royal Navy's response to the Coronel disaster had been to reinforce the available British warships in the South Atlantic with two battlecruisers (*Invincible* and *Inflexible*) from the **Grand Fleet**. They had left England on 11 November. The whole force was placed under the command of **Admiral Sturdee** and concentrated in the Falklands, where it arrived on 7 December.

Von Spee reached there during the early hours of the following day. *Gneisenau* and *Nürnberg* – an advance guard of the squadron – were sent to reconnoitre and, to their surprise, discovered the much more powerful British force at anchor in Port Stanley harbour. Spee headed south-east at full speed, with the British fleet following as soon as its coaling operations had been completed. The long pursuit began at 11.00 a.m. in excellent weather conditions. As the British came in range of *Leipzig*, the slowest German ship, at about 1.00 p.m., von Spee ordered his light cruisers to break away and a number of separate actions developed.

The battlecruisers dealt with the enemy's principal ships. *Scharnhorst* was sunk at 4.15 p.m. and *Gneisenau* almost two hours later. *Leipzig* was pursued and sunk by *Glasgow* and *Cornwall*, while *Nürnberg* was destroyed by *Kent*. *Dresden* was the only German warship to escape, but was scuttled three months later after a brief engagement with *Kent* and *Glasgow* in the South Pacific. The Germans, who fought with great bravery and determination, lost almost 2,000 men, while the British suffered virtually no casualties. As a result of this engagement 'the high seas were again in the sovereign grasp of the British navy'.

Survivors from Gneisenau *being picked up by the battlecruiser* Inflexible *off the Falkland Islands*

FARMAN F40 SERIES

This two-seat pusher biplane was produced jointly by Henry and Maurice Farman, incorporating the positive features of the brothers' earlier designs which had been produced separately. The collaborative nature of this series was emphasised by the nickname – 'Horace' Farman – that the British bestowed on it. Similar in structure to the Farman HF20, the F40 had unequal span, three-bay wings, a streamlined nacelle, and wooden, wire-braced tail booms. Appearing late in 1915, it was powered by a 160hp Renault engine, which gave a maximum speed of 84m.p.h. at 6,560 feet. Armament normally consisted of a **Lewis machine-gun** in the front cockpit and a small bomb

load, but a few were equipped with Le Prieur rockets when used for 'balloon busting'.

A number of variants followed the initial model, the principal differences relating to the size of the engines and the wing span, but only the F41, 56, 60 and 61, as well as the F40 itself, were produced in quantity for operational use. Together these models equipped almost 50 French *escadrilles* and were also used in much more limited numbers by the Belgian Aviation Militaire and the RNAS.

Employed on reconnaissance and bombing duties, this pusher aircraft was outdated even before it entered service, although the Belgians managed to retain it in operational use until the end of the war. However, with no possible defence against attacks from the rear, the French had recognised its limitations and acted on them much earlier. The Aviation Militaire ceased using the machines for reconnaissance purposes early in 1917, although it was forced to retain them for a while for night bombing duties. They remained in use for some time with the AEF and other forces for training purposes.

FARMAN F50

This twin-engined, two-seater tractor biplane, which first appeared in 1918, was unrelated to the extensive **Farman F40** series. A heavy bomber, powered by 265hp Lorraine Dietrich engines, it was built in relatively small numbers and equipped two French *Escadrilles de Bombardement*. Development of the heavy bomber was slower in France than in Britain or Germany and the F50 was the only French aircraft capable of lifting a bomb load comparable to that of a **Gotha** or **Handley Page**. It could in fact carry up to eight 165lb bombs and was equipped with one or two defensive machine-guns. The F50 was, however, unable to achieve any notable operational successes and it was not retained in French service for long after the war.

FARMAN HF20 SERIES

This series of two-seat pusher biplanes was already in service when war was declared in August 1914. Designated the HF20, 21 and 22, they were generally similar in appearance, although there were variations in their dimensions and in the power plants fitted. None of their standard engines – the 70 or 80hp Gnome or 80hp Le Rhône – produced sufficient power to lift a good bomb load or carry defensive armament without an unacceptable loss of performance. They were used by the RFC and RNAS as well as by the air forces of France, Belgium, Russia and Rumania. In RNAS service a floatplane version was used. They were quickly recognised as being unsuitable for operational use on the Western Front and were relegated to training duties in 1915, after a brief period of use on reconnaissance operations.

Only one model in the series – the HF27 – proved to have any real military value. Larger than its predecessors, it had, unusually, an all-steel airframe, making it much more suitable for use in hot climates than aircraft constructed of wood. It also had three bay wings, a four-wheel undercarriage and a 140 or 160hp Canton-Unné engine. Armed with a .303 **Lewis machine-gun**, it could carry a substantial bomb load. In fact, in December 1915, an HF27, flown by Wing Commander Samson from Imbros, attacked a Turkish barracks with a 500lb bomb, the largest then available. Operated by the RFC and RNAS, the HF27 was also employed on the Western Front, Mesopotamia (during the siege of **Kut**), and in East and South-West Africa. Outside the main theatres of war in Europe it was retained in use until well into 1918.

FARMAN MF7

The MF7 was an unarmed two-seat biplane which entered service in Britain and France well over a year before the beginning of the war. The British nicknamed it the 'Longhorn', because of the long upswept extension to the undercarriage skids which carried the forward elevator. Apart from this strange feature, the MF7 followed the standard pusher arrangement of the time. The nacelle was positioned on the lower wings, it had parallel tail booms, and a biplane tail unit. The Longhorn was normally powered by a 70hp Renault, although other engines were also used.

The performance of all types was relatively poor, although the aircraft was widely used on reconnaissance duties in the first few months of the war by the French (seven *escadrilles*), British and Italians. With the appearance of the **Farman MF11**, its career on the Western Front ended quickly, but it subsequently gained a notable reputation as a primary trainer. In this role it was used extensively by Britain for much of the rest of the war, being manufactured there by three sub-contractors. The Longhorn was also employed for various experimental purposes, including the testing of machine-guns, and made a useful contribution to the development of military aviation.

FARMAN MF11

Replacing the **Farman MF7 Longhorn** on the Western Front in 1915, the MF11 variant was very similar in appearance, except for its short landing skids, which gave rise to the nickname 'Shorthorn'. Other differences included the position of the nacelle (now midway between the wings) and a single horizontal tail surface, with twin rudders, in place of the biplane tail unit. A variety of power units was used, from the 80hp Renault upwards. The observer, who sat in the rear cockpit, was armed with a single **Lewis** or **Hotchkiss** machine-gun and up to 288lb of bombs.

Produced in much larger quantities than the Longhorn, the MF11 served with the French Aviation Militaire, the RFC and the RNAS. Employed on the Western Front and in Italy, Russia and Mesopotamia, it was used frequently as a bomber as well as for reconnaissance duties. In fact, an MF11 in RNAS service made the first night bombing raid of the war, attacking German gun emplacements near Ostend in December 1914. Towards the end of 1915, the Shorthorn started to be replaced at the front line, although it served until 1918 as a primary trainer, establishing an excellent reputation.

FAYOLLE, GENERAL MARIE, 1852–1928

French artilleryman who had retired early in 1914 as a brigadier-general, but was recalled to active service when the war began. Appointed to the command of an infantry division in August 1914, Fayolle gained much more rapid promotion than he had in peacetime and was given the Sixth Army in February 1916. During the **First Battle of the Somme**, his army fought on the southern flank of the British army without notable success. In fact, after the failure of the attacks on 25 September 1916, Fayolle asked to be relieved of his command. His request was refused but he was transferred to the First Army early in 1917, an appointment that lasted only a few months. When **Pétain** became commander-in-chief, Fayolle, with whom he was closely associated, succeeded him as the head of the Centre Army Group.

Such were his reputation and prestige that he was sent to Italy after the **Caporetto** disaster to help stabilise the front during the winter of 1917–18. He returned to France in March 1918 and was given the command of the Reserve Army Group, 40 divisions strong, which he led successfully until the end of the war. Positioned where the French and British armies met, it opposed the German offensives in March and May 1918 and, in a significantly expanded form, made an important contribution to the final Allied counter-offensive in the autumn. Fayolle's wartime services were rewarded, in 1922, with his appointment as a Marshal of France.

FEGYVERGYAR PISTOL

The standard automatic pistol of the Honved, the Hungarian element of the Austrian army, during the First World War, the Fegyvergyar Model 'Stop' used the long recoil system of operation. Manufactured in Budapest, it was chambered for the standard 7.65mm ACP cartridge and was noted for its reliability. Production continued after the war and for many years it was the official service pistol of the independent Hungarian army.

FEISAL I, 1885–1933

The third son of Sherif Hussein of Mecca, Feisal was one of the military leaders of the **Arab Revolt** against Turkey, which his father had launched on 5 June 1916. He was commander-in-chief of the Arab forces in the Hejaz, working closely with **T. E. Lawrence**, who was formally British military representative at his headquarters. In practice, of course, Lawrence of Arabia led the revolt and determined the course of strategy, reducing Feisal's military role. After the capture of Aqaba (April 1917), Feisal and Lawrence moved northwards, protecting the flank of the advancing British forces under **Allenby**.

Feisal's troops reached Damascus in advance of the British army and captured it on 1 October 1918. In taking rapid possession of the Syrian capital he was aware that Britain had agreed that France should have a mandate over the country (the secret **Sykes-Picot agreement**) but was determined to circumvent it. He argued the Arab case at the **Paris Peace Conference**, but was unable to prevent the French deposing him from the throne of Syria in 1920. As a result of British intervention, a new throne was created for him in Iraq (Mesopotamia).

King Feisal with T. E. Lawrence in Paris, January 1919. At the Peace Conference both men argued the Arab case with little success

FELIXSTOWE F2A & F3

The Felixstowe F2A flying boat, which was used for long-distance patrols in the North Sea, established its reputation as one of the war's great aircraft during the last year of the conflict.

Like the F1 it was based on the **Curtiss flying boat** – in this case the **H12 Large America** – and used its wings and tail. The hull was redesigned by John Porte, the flying-boat pioneer, and a much more efficient and seaworthy version resulted. Powered by two 345hp Rolls Royce Eagle VIII engines, this heavy aircraft (10,978lb) had a maximum speed of 95m.p.h. and a normal endurance of six hours. Its formidable armament consisted of between four and seven **Lewis machine-guns** on flexible mountings and two 230lb bombs. There were two pilots (one of whom also acted as front gunner) among the crew of four, as well as an engineer-gunner (who monitored engine performance) and a rigger-gunner. Production of the F2A began late in 1917 and by the end of the war 100 had been produced although more had been ordered.

The F3 was an enlarged version with double the bomb-carrying capacity, but otherwise little changed. Produced in similar numbers, it was less manoeuvrable and less seaworthy than its predecessor.

The F2A/F3 operated from several flying-boat stations around the coast of Britain, including Dundee, Felixstowe, Great Yarmouth and Scapa Flow. They were employed on long-range anti-submarine and anti-Zeppelin patrols over the North Sea, using the famous 'spider's web' patrol method, as well as on general reconnaissance duties.

Dog fights with enemy seaplane fighters were common and on 4 June 1918, off the German coast, they were in fact involved in one of the great air battles of the First World War. Five British flying boats (four of which were F2As) engaged a force of 14 enemy seaplanes and shot down six of them. Many other successes, including the destruction of Zeppelin L62 in May 1918, were achieved by the F2A before the war ended.

FERDINAND, KING OF BULGARIA, 1861–1948

Ruler of Bulgaria from 1887, the 'evil and cunning' Ferdinand maintained the country's neutrality in 1914 in the hope of furthering his expansionist foreign policy. After securing territorial concessions from the Central Powers, particularly about Macedonia, Bulgaria entered the war in September 1915. **Serbia** was successfully invaded, but a stalemate developed on the **Salonika front**. Ferdinand's position was weakened by the unpopularity of the country's involvement in the war and by the fact that it had become a 'satellite kingdom', stripped of its food reserves for the benefit of Germany. Ferdinand did not survive the collapse of Bulgarian military power as **Franchet d'Espérey**'s forces pressed forward on the Salonika front. As the war ended, he left for exile in Germany, at the Allies' insistence.

FERDINAND, KING OF RUMANIA, 1865–1927

Succeeding his uncle **Carol** as King of Rumania in October 1914, Ferdinand shared his pro-German outlook and had close connections with the Austro-Hungarian court. In practice, however, he supported the policy of Rumanian neutrality which continued until her entry into the war on the Allied side in August 1916. The subsequent German invasion was a disaster which left Ferdinand with no more than a small part of the country still in Rumanian hands. He maintained popular support and kept his forces intact but in December 1917, with the collapse of Russian military power, Rumania was forced to end hostilities with the Central Powers. Shortly before the Armistice, to safeguard her future, Rumania again declared war on Germany, and at the **Paris Peace Conference**, where Ferdinand was present, she secured substantial territorial gains.

FIAT-REVELLI MACHINE-GUN

The first mass-produced Italian machine-gun was designed by Bethel Revelli in 1908 and officially adopted in 1914. Externally it was similar to the **Maxim**, but its operating mechanism – the delayed blowback system – was very different. Weighing almost 38lb, it was water cooled and had a cyclic rate of 400 rounds per minute. The weapon's feed system was unusual and highly complex: instead of the normal fabric belt there was a magazine containing ten compartments, each of which held five 6.5mm rounds. As the first five rounds were used up the whole magazine moved towards the gun, presenting the next five cartridges for firing.

Although this mechanism was liable to jam, the Revelli was produced in large numbers by the Fiat Company and was used by the Italian army throughout the war. A lightened aircraft version, dating from 1915, was also made by Fiat for the Italian air service. Air cooled, with a higher rate of fire, it was the standard observer's weapon until early in 1918, when it was replaced by the more effective **Lewis** and **Vickers machine-guns**.

FISHER, JOHN, 1ST BARON, 1841–1920

Outstanding naval administrator whose major reforms and improvements in efficiency gave Britain supremacy at sea at the beginning of the First World War. As First Sea Lord, 1904–10, Fisher introduced the world's first 'all big gun' battleship, *HMS Dreadnought*, as well as the new battlecruiser; ships with limited fighting power were scrapped. He concentrated the fleet in home waters, where the main threat was likely to materialise, rather than in the Mediterranean. Entry to the officer corps was widened and its training improved to reflect fundamental changes in warfare and technology.

Fisher returned to the Admiralty as First Sea Lord on 29 October 1914. He soon had evidence that his own earlier work to improve the war readiness of the British fleet had been successful. Following the **Battle of Coronel**, he detached two battlecruisers from the **Grand Fleet** and sent them to the South Atlantic to engage **Admiral von Spee**'s squadron, which was destroyed at the **Falklands** on 8 December 1914. He was also responsible for the creation of a vast naval construction programme that paid substantial returns later in the war and he promoted the development of semi-rigid airships ('Blimps'), which were used effectively against U-boats.

Fisher's relations with **Winston Churchill**, First Lord of the Admiralty, were good at first but soon deteriorated: his intervention in purely professional matters was an irritant, as were their volatile temperaments, but the **Dardanelles operation** was the major cause of conflict between them. Fisher's original lukewarm support turned to opposition when

The architect of the wartime Royal Navy, Fisher clashed with the political head of the Admiralty, Winston Churchill, about strategy

it proved to be a significant drain on naval resources in the North Sea. He resigned on 15 May 1915 in response to Churchill's demand for substantial new reinforcements for the Mediterranean and never held high office again.

Churchill himself later acknowledged the value of Fisher's work in sustaining 'the power of the Royal Navy at the most critical period in its history'.

FLAMETHROWER

One of the new assault weapons of the First World War, the flamethrower was first used by the Germans in 1914. Available in portable or static versions (which needed up to three men to operate), the *Flammenwerfer* used gas to force a supply of petrol through a small projector nozzle where it was ignited. Flame technology was at an initial stage of development during the war and the impact of these early models was limited by their inadequate range (25–40 yards) and low destructive power. However, liquid fire was used extensively by the Germans as another tactical accessory, at **Verdun** in 1916 and in many subsequent operations. It was not until the Second World War that the flamethrower was to be fully developed and produced on a large scale.

FLORIDA

Like *Delaware*, of which she was a repeat design, *Florida* was an American dreadnought which served with the 6th Battle Squadron of the British **Grand Fleet** in 1917–18. Completed in 1911, the layout of the funnels and mast was changed and some armour protection was provided for the secondary battery, although the main armament was identical. She was turbine powered and had a maximum speed of 21 knots. *Florida*'s sister ship, *Utah*, was flagship of the American Atlantic fleet and from September 1918 was based at Bantry Bay, Ireland, and employed on convoy duties.

FN BROWNING PISTOL

Starting from Browning's 1897 patents, the Belgian arms manufacturer Fabrique National produced a long series of automatic pistols, and many were employed during the First World War. The Model 1900, which was used by the Belgian army, was a 7.65mm blowback, with a four-inch barrel and a seven-shot magazine. Apart from its military role, it is notable as the weapon used by **Gavrilo Princip** to assassinate **Archduke Ferdinand** at Sarajevo. The Model 1903, which was chambered for the 9mm long cartridge, was one of the subsequent designs also officially adopted by the Belgian army.

FOCH, MARSHAL FERDINAND, 1851–1929

Marshal of France and generalissimo of the Allied armies in 1918, Foch was one of the outstanding soldiers of the First World War. His pre-war reputation was based on his contribution as a teacher and military thinker; his ideas, which were a major influence on the development of French tactics, stressed the importance of the offensive.

He entered the war as head of the élite XX Corps, which formed part of the Fifth Army, and during the **Battle of the Frontiers** in August 1914 attacked towards Morhange. He was forced to withdraw quickly but in a successful counter-attack was largely responsible for saving Nancy. Having established his reputation as a military leader as well as a thinker, Foch was selected by **Joffre** to take command of a new Ninth Army, which played a key role in the

Allied achievement at the **Battle of the Marne**, 4–9 September. Foch was notable for his optimism and determination even when under extreme pressure and for the frequent counter-attacks he ordered. In a notable signal sent during the battle he reported: 'I am hard pressed on my right; my centre is giving way; situation excellent; I am attacking.'

Recognition of his success at the Marne came on 4 October 1914 when he was appointed deputy commander-in-chief and given the task of coordinating the operations of the northern wing of armies during the 'Race to the Sea'. His main task was to organise the movement of men and equipment and ensure that they arrived at the crucial areas in time. It involved working very closely with and influencing the British and Belgians, a role he carried out successfully: by 15 November the enemy had been held and a defensive victory secured.

From January 1915 to December 1916, Foch commanded the Northern Army Group, directing the unsuccessful offensives at **Arras** in May and September 1915. It was, however, the enormous Allied losses during the **First Battle of the Somme** that damaged his reputation, largely because of his close association with Joffre; Foch himself had been sceptical about the value of the offensive.

When the commander-in-chief was dismissed in December 1916, Foch was transferred to an unimportant advisory post and it was not until May 1917, with his appointment as chief of staff under **Pétain**, that he returned to favour. In this post he advised the Italians after the **Caporetto** disaster (October 1917) and was appointed to the military committee of the Supreme War Council, but it was not until the spring of 1918 that his real opportunity materialised.

In response to **Ludendorff**'s major Somme offensive, the British proposed that Foch should be appointed to command (initially 'to coordinate') the operations of the Allied armies, at first on the Western Front, but later in other theatres as well. As generalissimo he coordinated the Allied forces that halted the German offensives, by controlling their reserves and moving them quickly by road and rail wherever they were required. When Foch launched an offensive in July he did not repeat the mistakes that Ludendorff had made: he avoided too prolonged or too deep an advance so as not to expend resources in an exploitation that he knew would be impossible; his successive attacks were coordinated so that one reacted on the other.

Foch: supreme Allied commander who repelled the German offensives of 1918 and led the Allies to victory

Foch's successful push led to the recovery of almost all of occupied France and a part of Belgium before the Armistice. His achievements were widely acknowledged by the Allied governments as well as by his own country; he was in fact the only French commander to have been made an honorary field marshal in the British army. Before leaving public life he played an important part at the **Paris Peace Conference**, but failed to persuade **Clemenceau** to impose more severe terms on Germany.

FOKKER DI TO DV

As the Fokker monoplane lost its supremacy on the Western Front, work started on a replacement series of biplanes which appeared during 1916. The DI, which was actually produced after the DII, had equal span two-bay wings and a flat-sided fuselage. Wing warping was used for lateral control. It was powered by a 120hp Mercedes engine, which gave a maximum speed of 94m.p.h., and was equipped with a single forward firing Spandau machine-gun. The DII was very similar, but the engine – a 100hp Oberursel rotary in a horseshoe cowling – was superior. Performance of both types was disappointing, their manoeuvrability and rate of climb being inferior to their Allied opponents.

The DI soon disappeared from the Western Front but the slightly more powerful DII was used for a time on escort and protection duties. The DIII had a strengthened fuselage to take the 160hp Oberursel U III engine, a more powerful but unreliable unit. A total of 291 DIIs and DIIIs were manufactured. The latter was used by several German aces, including **Boelcke**, **von Richthofen** and **Udet**, during its brief operational career, but was replaced by the new fighter aircraft – the **Albatros** and **Halberstadt D-types** – which arrived at the front during the summer of 1916. They were subsequently used at training schools along with the DIV (a re-engined version of the DI) and DV, which were also outclassed by the new machines.

FOKKER DVI

This single-seat German fighter, which first appeared in prototype form late in 1917, was overshadowed by the famous **DVII**, even though it was very manoeuvrable and had a higher top speed at lower altitudes. Its fuselage and tail surfaces derived from the **Fokker DrI** triplane, while its wings were a smaller version of the DVII's. Armed with twin Spandau machine-guns, most examples were powered by the 110hp Oberursel U II engine. Between April and August 1918, 59 DVIs were produced and some saw limited service with front line fighter units.

FOKKER DVII

Perhaps the best German fighter of the First World War, the DVII was a strongly constructed single-seat biplane, with wooden cantilever wings and a welded steel fuselage. It was easy to fly, visibility from the cockpit was excellent and it had outstanding high altitude performance. Early models were powered by the 160hp Mercedes D III engine, but there were further significant performance gains when the DVII was fitted with the 185hp BMW engine from the later summer of 1918. With this more powerful unit, the DVII could climb to 5,000m in only 16 minutes and had an endurance of 90 minutes. Armament consisted of two fixed 7.92mm Spandau machine-guns that were synchronised to fire forward through the airscrew.

The first production DVIIs reached the Western Front in April 1918 and were allocated to **von Richthofen**'s *Jagdgeschwader 1*. By the end of the war some 760 examples had been delivered to 48 *Jastas*. (As many as 2,000 had originally been ordered.)

The DVII was operated with great success during the summer and autumn of 1918 and was acknowledged by Allied pilots as a formidable opponent. One of its outstanding features was its ability to hang on its propeller at angles of up to 45 degrees: while other aircraft would have stalled into a spin, the DVII remained a stable gun platform. Its reputation was such that it was singled out for a specific mention in the article of the Armistice agreement dealing with items that were to be handed over to the Allies.

FOKKER DVIII

Designed as a replacement for the **Fokker DVII**, the DVIII parasol monoplane first appeared in prototype form in May 1918. The German High Command was impressed with its performance and manoeuvrability, placing an immediate order for 400 examples of this single-seat fighting scout. Normally powered by a

110hp Oberursel UR II engine, enclosed in a circular aluminium cowling, it had a one-piece cantilever wing and the fuselage was a welded steel tube box girder. It had a maximum speed of over 127m.p.h. at sea level and an endurance of 90 minutes. Armament consisted of twin Spandau machine-guns mounted immediately in front of the cockpit.

The first production models, which appeared in August 1918, were given the designation EV. Follow- ing three crashes they were withdrawn from service for modifications to the wing units and the design reappeared as the DVIII. No more than 85 examples had reached the front by the end of the war, although some of the entire order of 400 had been built. The DVIII was known as the 'Flying Razor Blade' by the British, even though there had been no real oppor- tunity for it to prove itself in combat.

FOKKER DrI

Notable as the fighter in which **von Richthofen** was shot down, the Fokker DrI *Dreidecker* was Germany's response to the **Sopwith Triplane**. Fokker himself had seen the Sopwith in action on the Western Front in April 1917 and three prototypes were produced in record time. By the summer 318 had been ordered and production began. This small, compact aircraft had three sets of cantilever wings, supported by two hollow struts. It was normally powered by a 110hp Le Rhône rotary engine, built by Thulin under licence in Sweden, which gave a maximum speed of only 103m.p.h. at 13,000 feet. Armament consisted of twin synchronised 7.92mm Spandau machine-guns, which could be fired independently. The DrI was noted for its outstanding manoeuvrability, although its relati- vely low top speed at combat height was a major limitation.

Its fighting potential was soon established when **Werner Voss** of *Jasta 10*, flying one of the proto- types, scored 10 victories during September 1917. The first production models reached von Richtho- fen's *Jasta 1* in mid-October, but the aircraft were soon grounded after a series of fatal crashes. Faulty wing construction was found to be the cause, and

The highly manoeuvrable Fokker triplane fighter in which von Richthofen met his death

although the DrI was back in service again at the end of November, its reputation never fully recovered. As a result it was not supplied to many *Jagdstaffeln*, although *Jasta 1* used it extensively, demonstrating that it was a dangerous weapon in the right hands.

Von Richthofen himself flew it to the exclusion of almost all other fighters in the months before he was killed in April 1918. During the summer of 1918 the DrI, now outclassed by newer designs, was withdrawn from the front line.

FOKKER E-TYPES

Based on a pre-war design, which was heavily influenced by the French Morane-Saulnier Type H monoplane, the Fokker E-Type represented an important step in the development of the fighter aircraft. It was in fact the first single-seater to be fitted with a synchronised machine-gun that worked effectively.

The capture of **Roland Garros' Morane-Saulnier L** in April 1915 with its crude interrupter gear had prompted Fokker's engineers to develop an efficient synchronisation device. Operated with a 7.92mm Spandau machine-gun, it was installed in the Fokker M.5K, formerly an unarmed reconnaissance machine, which now became the EI. It was powered by the 80hp Oberursel UO rotary engine, which gave a maximum speed of 81m.p.h., and was constructed of steel and wood; it had a comma rudder.

Produced in small numbers, the first EIs appeared in mid-1915. A strengthened version, the EII, which had a smaller wing area, arrived at the front in the autumn of 1915; it was also manufactured in small numbers. The EIII, with larger wings and a 100hp Oberursel UI engine, was the most successful version, with some 150 being produced.

The E-types served on the Western Front from mid-1915 until the summer of 1916. Once they were used offensively rather than in defence of their own two-seaters, the manoeuvrable and well-armed Fokkers took a heavy toll of their much less effectively equipped opponents. Their principal victims were the

Fokker EIII: one of the series of armed monoplanes that revolutionised aerial warfare in 1915

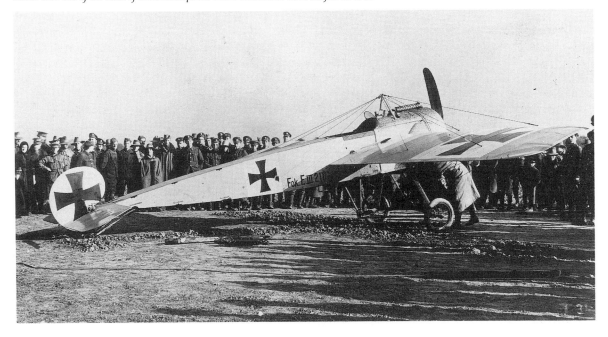

Royal Aircraft Factory BE2cs, which were soon to be described as 'Fokker Fodder'; in total, some 300 E-types shot down more than 1,000 Allied machines.

New fighter tactics were soon developed as the machines were used in combat and they were particularly associated with the creation of the 'Immelmann turn', a manoeuvre created by the ace Max Immelmann for attacking enemy aircraft. The E-Type's dominance of the air lasted for a relatively short period as new and greatly improved Allied machines reached the front during 1916. An attempt to prolong the effective life of the type was made in the form of the EIV. Armed with two machine-guns and powered by an unreliable 160hp engine, it proved to be less manoeuvrable than its lighter predecessors and was soon withdrawn from combat duties.

FONCK, RENÉ, 1894–1953

With a score of 75 confirmed hits, René Fonck was the Allied as well as the French ace of aces. Second only to von Richthofen, Fonck claimed that his actual score was 127, far exceeding that of the German ace of aces. It was, however, not until April 1917 that Fonck joined France's élite fighter unit, Groupe de Chasse No 12 – Les Cigognes, serving in Escadrille SPA 103. Since qualifying as a pilot early in 1915 he had been allocated to a reconnaissance unit flying two-seaters, and his application for a transfer was not acted upon until he had achieved two confirmed victories. Fonck destroyed four German aircraft during the first month in his new unit, demonstrating that his talents were far more productively engaged as a fighter pilot.

Like von Richthofen, he was aloof and arrogant and a superb shot. Cautious and meticulous in his approach, he left as little as possible to chance and never enjoyed the popularity of his more reckless French rivals. He personally supervised the maintenance of his Spad's machine-guns and checked the ammunition individually to reduce the possibility of jamming. Much of his spare time was spent in firearms practice and in studying the tactics and machines of his opponents in order to identify weaknesses that he might exploit. He normally attacked the enemy from above, taking advantage of speed and height to surprise them, hardly ever using more than a single burst to shoot them from the sky. He was in fact notorious for the small quantity of ammunition he invariably used.

Notable moments in his long career with Les Cigognes were the two occasions (in May and September 1918) when he shot down six German aircraft in a single day, a record unmatched by any other Allied or German pilot. His consistently good performance meant that he would often be able to destroy two or three German aircraft in one day. His last victim was a two-seater hit on 1 November while it was dropping propaganda leaflets over the French trenches. Fonck survived the war unscathed and was decorated by Britain, Belgium and Serbia as well as by his native country.

FORD MODEL-T LIGHT PATROL CAR

One of the most widely used vehicles of the First World War, the famous Model-T Ford served with both the British and American armies. It had a 20hp engine, a two-speed gearbox and weighed 7 cwt; both the saloon and open tourer versions were acquired. Apart from staff and ambulance work, the Model-T was used primarily as a light patrol car, armed with a machine-gun. They were used successfully in the North African desert in the operations against the German-backed Senussi, 1915–17. Weighing considerably less than the armoured cars that accompanied them, they were much easier to operate in the sand. They were also employed in Allenby's campaign in Palestine and in Mesopotamia, where motorised infantry was used extensively for the first time; some 300 Model-Ts provided the transport for two half-battalions of infantry.

FORMIDABLE

Enlarged versions of *Canopus*, the Formidables, which were completed in 1901–02, had a displacement of 14,500 tons and additional Krupp armour protection. The main 12-inch guns were greater in length and could be used at all angles of elevation, but were otherwise unchanged. *Formidable* was sunk in January 1915 and *Irresistible*, which was serving in the **Dardanelles**, struck a mine and suffered the same fate almost three months later. Like several other British pre-dreadnoughts, *Implacable* operated in support of the Italian navy in the Adriatic during 1915, after a brief period in the Dardanelles.

FOURTEEN POINTS

CLEMENCEAU COMMENTED: 'GOD ONLY NEEDED TEN!"

Outlined by **President Wilson** in an address to the American Congress on 8 January 1918, his Fourteen Point Peace Programme was designed to prevent another destructive war. Its guiding principles were self-determination and collective security, with the creation of a League of Nations being a novel feature of his programme.

Although the Allies, who had not been consulted in advance, had general reservations about the principles underlying the programme, they accepted it with two caveats: the idea of the freedom of the seas (clause 2) was unacceptable to them and they insisted on the need for reparations. The Fourteen Points provided the basis on which German and Austro-Hungary sought armistices late in 1918 and formed the agenda for the **Paris Peace Conference**.

1 Open convenants of peace; no secret agreements.
2 Freedom of the seas, except when curtailed by international action.
3 The removal, wherever possible, of all economic barriers.
4 Guarantees for the reduction in armaments.
5 Impartial adjustment of all colonial claims, with the interests of the subject populations being equal with the claims of governments.
6 Evacuation of all Russian territory.
7 Restoration of Belgian sovereignty.
8 Occupied French territory to be restored and Alsace-Lorraine to be returned to France.
9 Readjustment of Italian frontiers 'along clearly recognised lines of nationality'.
10 Opportunity of autonomous development for the people of Austro-Hungary.
11 Evacuation by occupying forces of Rumania, Serbia and Montenegro; Serbia to have free access to the sea. Relations of Balkan states to be settled on lines of allegiance and nationality.
12 Opportunity of autonomous development for non-Turkish peoples within the Ottoman empire. The Dardanelles to be free for all shipping.
13 Creation of an independent Poland with access to the sea.
14 Formation of a general assembly of nations with the aim of 'affording mutual guarantees of political independence and territorial integrity to great and small states'.

FRANCHET D'ESPÉREY, GENERAL LOUIS, 1856–1942

Commander of I Corps (French Fifth Army) at the beginning of the war, 'Desperate Frankie', as he was known to his British colleagues, was an experienced veteran of France's colonial wars. He won the tactical victory at Guise (29 August 1914) and succeeded **Lanrezac** as commander of the Fifth Army just before the **Battle of the Marne**. His reputation was enhanced at the Marne by the energy and skill with which he engaged the German Second Army along the Petit Morin. A few days later he recaptured Reims before trench warfare was established. In 1915, he was promoted to the command of the eastern group of armies and, in 1917, to that of the north.

In 1918, Franchet D'Espérey's high standing seemed to have been permanently damaged by the third successful German offensive of the year (the **Second Battle of the Aisne**, 27 May–6 June), which pushed his army group back over 20 miles. The high command quickly concluded that he could 'now no longer be left at the head of a group of armies' and

sent him to command the Salonika front in place of **General Guillaumat**. Here he fully redeemed his reputation, persuading the Allies to launch a major autumn offensive, which began on 15 September. In a highly successful campaign, the Bulgarians were forced to seek an Armistice and the Allied forces crossed the Danube, ready for a further advance if the war had not ended. In 1922, Franchet D'Espérey was promoted to Marshal of France in recognition of his wartime services.

Franchet d'Esperey, whose reputation seemed to have been permanently damaged by the successful German offensives of 1918, redeemed himself with a successful campaign in the Balkans

FRANCO-BRITISH AVIATION TYPE-H

The Type-H anti-submarine and coastal patrol flying boat was the major production model of a series made by Franco-British Aviation, a company which, despite its name, was entirely French. It was probably produced on a larger scale than any other flying boat in operational use during the war and had an excellent reputation for reliable service.

Initially, this three-seat, two-bay machine was powered by a 150hp Hispano-Suiza pusher engine,

but later a 160hp Lorraine Dietrich or higher output Hispano-Suiza power plants were used. Depending on the engine used, the Type-H could reach a maximum speed of 90m.p.h. at sea level and had a range of just over 370 miles. It had a raised strut-mounted tailplane and an oval rudder. There was a single defensive machine-gun in the front cockpit and a small bomb load could be carried.

In a modified form, the Type-H was enthusiastically received by the Italian *Squadriglie della Marina*; it was built under licence in Italy by six sub-contractors, with as many as 982 being produced. It had a 160hp Isotta-Fraschini V-4B engine, a **Fiat-Revelli machine-gun**, and was fitted with a fin. The Type-H served in the Russian and Belgian navies as well as those of France and Italy. Four Italian Type-Hs were transferred to the RNAS at Otranto in 1917, but the machine was not otherwise used by the British service. The aircraft continued in use until the Armistice, although the Franco-British Aviation Type-S, a development of the earlier model, was also in service in the final year of the war. With a larger engine and an increased bomb load, it was widely used by the French navy.

FRANZ FERDINAND, ARCHDUKE, 1863–1914

On the death of his son in 1889, **Emperor Franz Joseph**'s nephew, Franz Ferdinand, became heir to the Hapsburg monarchy. An unpopular and unenlightened soldier of long experience, by 1914 he was a field marshal and Inspector General of the Austro-Hungarian army. In June 1914, he visited Bosnia in his professional capacity, to inspect the army units there. With much Slav resentment at the country's incorporation in the Austro-Hungarian empire, plans were made by the Black Hand, a Serbian terrorist group, to strike back at one of the principal representatives of the crown. As Franz Ferdinand and his wife rode through the streets of Sarajevo, the capital, on 28 June, they were assassinated by two shots from the gun of **Gavrilo Princip**. This open challenge to the authority of Austro-Hungary set in motion the sequence of events that led to the outbreak of the First World War.

Franz Ferdinand and his wife begin their final journey in Sarajevo on 28 July 1914

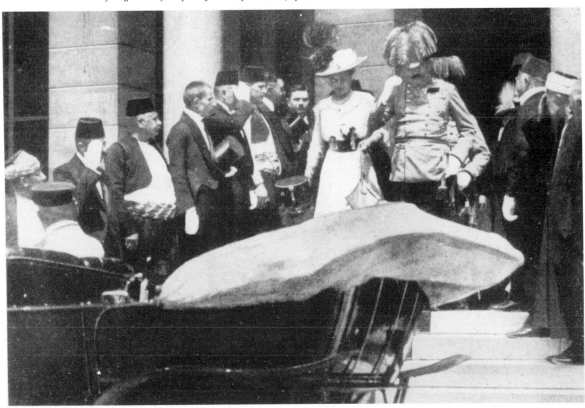

FRANZ JOSEPH I, EMPEROR 1830–1916

The 68-year reign of Franz Joseph, Emperor of Austro-Hungary, had been marked by regular political crises and personal tragedy, but none matched the monarch's experiences during the First World War. Franz Joseph had concurred, without enthusiasm, in the belligerent reaction of Austria's political and military leaders to the assassination of **Franz Ferdinand** at Sarajevo in June 1914. Setback after setback followed the initial Austro-Hungarian military action against Serbia and although the strategic position had subsequently improved, it was clear, by 1916, that the country, now dependent on German military power, had little chance of winning the war. By 1916, Franz Joseph himself was well aware that his life's work – preserving the integrity of the empire – was in jeopardy. As he lay dying he said: 'I took over the throne under the most difficult conditions and I am leaving it under even worse ones.' **Charles I**, the last Austro-Hungarian emperor, succeeded his great uncle.

FRENCH ARMY

French troops manning a forward trench in Lorraine in 1915. With limited British manpower then available, the French army had prime responsibility on the Western Front

In August 1914, the French army was mobilised with great efficiency, some two million men being quickly moved to the front by 4,278 trains. Sixty-two infantry divisions (14 reserve) and 10 cavalry divisions were readily available, but the army's ability to expand further was restricted because France's total population was declining at this point. In fact, she possessed no more than 60 per cent of the potential manpower of Germany. During the long years of peace in Europe, the army had been weakened by political and social divisions – exemplified in the Dreyfus episode – although some officers had received useful combat experience in the colonies.

A more serious problem was the army's strategic doctrine, which was based on a total dedication to offensive action. Defensive tactics were absent from the agenda, the success of the defence in recent wars having been almost completely ignored by the General Staff. This attitude was reflected in the fact that the French were content to rely on the famous **75mm field gun**, having very few medium or heavy artillery pieces compared to the Germans. This fine gun was, of course, more suited to an attack across open country than to the needs of trench warfare.

The French approach found expression in **Plan XVII**, its strategic plan in the event of war, which involved a concentration of four of its armies along the eastern frontier for an immediate two-pronged attack through Alsace-Lorraine. Two additional French armies were to be prepared to shift westwards if the Germans violated Belgian neutrality, but the High Command failed to uncover the enemy's real intentions until it was too late. As the Germans swept through Belgium and France in accordance with the **Schlieffen Plan**, the French army suffered heavy losses, sustaining 300,000 casualties during the **Battle of the Frontiers**.

However, **Joffre**, as Chief of Staff, kept the army intact as it retreated southwards and brought the German advance to an end at the **Battle of the Marne**. His power was further enhanced by the fact that the political leaders, shaken by these early defeats, effectively abdicated responsibility to the army. Political control of the army was only properly restored towards the end of the war when **Clemenceau** became premier.

In the first year of trench warfare the main burden was shouldered by the French army, which carried out several costly attacks against both sides of the German salient in France with no real gains. The heavy losses seemed to have no adverse effect on Joffre's position; in fact his power was enhanced when the **Salonika Front** was placed under his direct control.

In the summer of 1916, the French Army planned a major push on the **Somme** in conjunction with the British, but **Verdun** intervened first. The fortress was defended heroically, but **Falkenhayn** nearly succeeded in his aim of 'bleeding the French army white'. This disastrous battle led eventually to the departure of Joffre and the promotion of **Nivelle**, a general with a strong belief in the value of offensive action.

The new commander-in-chief promised to shorten the war by achieving a breakthrough during his **Aisne offensive** in the spring of 1917, but this ended in failure and the virtual disintegration of the French army. These heavy losses, following so soon after the enormous casualties at Verdun, contributed to the outbreak of a serious mutiny in the army (29 April–9 June). There were well over 100 separate mutinous acts but the enemy did not discover until it was too late how precarious the situation actually was.

Pétain was now brought in to try to restore order and raise morale. Improvements in the conditions of the rank and file were combined with an almost total stoppage of offensive action on the French front; the British assumed the principal defensive role for the rest of 1917. Gradually the army was restored as an effective defensive weapon and it was able to play a major role in **Foch**'s operations during the summer and autumn of 1918 which led to final victory. However, 'the offensive spirit in France had gone for many years, perhaps for ever' as a result of the events of 1917. The French army also paid a high price in human terms for its wartime achievements as it had the highest mortality rate of all the combatant nations of the First World War.

FRENCH, FIELD MARSHAL SIR JOHN, 1st EARL OF YPRES, 1852–1925

First commander of the British Expeditionary Force in France, August 1914 to December 1915, Sir John French had served as a cavalry officer in the Sudan, India and during the South African War. He contributed to Haldane's army reforms and had been Inspector-General before his appointment as Chief of the Imperial General Staff in 1912. He was forced to resign in the aftermath of the Curragh Mutiny in 1914, but was sent to France on the outbreak of war, as had long been planned.

Positioned on the extreme left of the French line, the BEF was engaged by the German First Army near Mons on 23 August. With II Corps facing envelop-

ment, French was forced to retreat, but he did so with unjustified haste. In the process he allowed his two corps to separate as they passed through the forest of Mormal. **Smith-Dorrien** decided to stand and fight at **Le Cateau**, securing French's agreement even though it contradicted his original orders. Exaggerating II Corps' losses, French became extremely pessimistic about his situation. On poor terms with **General Lanrezac**, commander of the French Fifth Army to his right, French's only concern became the preservation of his own force. He announced his intention to retreat to St Nazaire for a period of recuperation, but before he could do so **Kitchener** arrived in France (1 September). Persuaded to remain in line, he retreated with the French beyond the Marne. He was criticised for his slow response as he advanced between the German First and Second Armies during the **Battle of the Marne**.

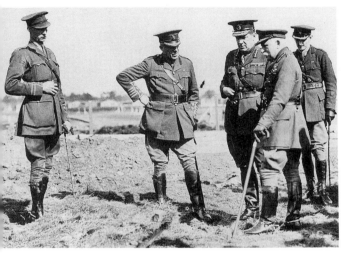

First commander of the British Expeditionary Force, French was removed from his post in December 1915 after a series of command failures

During the 'Race to the Sea', when BEF was transferred to Flanders, French became much more optimistic: in October, he even claimed that 'the enemy was playing their last card'. He remained convinced of the possibility of an Allied breakthrough during the **First Battle of Ypres** and in the minor attacks early in 1915; however, bitter experience subsequently convinced him otherwise.

Although his period in France is scattered with examples of his poor judgement and unjustified actions (for example, Smith-Dorrien's removal in May 1915), it was not until the **Battle of Artois-Loos** that serious doubts were widely raised about his fitness for high command. He agreed only reluctantly to participate in the battle and his conduct during it was inexplicable: he remained isolated in his head-quarters; he had no direct link with **Douglas Haig**, his principal commander; he failed to deploy his reserves properly; and he prolonged the battle long after it had ceased to serve any useful purpose. A decent interval having elapsed, in December 1915, he was replaced by Haig. He then became commander-in-chief of home forces, where he remained until early in 1918, when he was appointed Lord Lieutenant of Ireland.

FRENCH 75mm FIELD GUN

Designed in 1897, the Canon de 75 was one of the finest artillery pieces of the First World War. It incorporated several novel features and was in fact a model for the future field guns of all armies. It was quickly adopted by the French army, which had almost 4,000 in service in August 1914; by the end of the war more than 17,000 had been produced in France. The US army also used it extensively when it joined the war in 1917. The gun had a revolutionary hydro-pneumatic recoil system which helped to ensure that it remained stable when fired; wheel brakes and a trail spade also had the same effect.

The French 75 was able to fire well over 20 rounds per minute because of its rapid acting breech mechan-ism. It could propel a shrapnel shell, weighing 16lb,

over a range of more than four miles. Another valuable feature was the shield that protected the gun's operatives from small arms fire. Several improvements were subsequently made, including better ammunition, but the basic design remained unchanged.

Even though this highly mobile and accurate gun was more suited to offensive action than trench warfare – its shell was too light to make much of an impact – it remained the standard field piece of the French army throughout the war. They were also used as anti-aircraft guns, coast defence weapons and tank armament.

FRENCH AIR SERVICE

On the outbreak of war in August 1914 the French Aviation Militaire was able to mobilise 21 *escadrilles* (or squadrons) of two-seaters, each with six aircraft. An *escadrille* was normally equipped with aircraft of a single type to facilitate maintenance and to allow pilots to fly any of the unit's machines. There were also two single-seat squadrons, both equipped with three **Blériot monoplanes**, which were to liaise with the cavalry. Each *escadrille* was a self-contained unit, identifiable by a letter and number designation: for example, *Escadrille MF2* was the Second Squadron, which was equipped with Maurice **Farmans**. The main function of these units was reconnaissance, both strategic and tactical, and their value in providing essential information was soon demonstrated during the **Battle of the Marne** in September 1914.

As a result a major expansion programme was authorised, increasing the number of *escadrilles* to 65 and establishing specialist units. The plans included 16 fighter squadrons (*escadrilles de chasse*); 30 corps squadrons (*escadrilles de corps*), which would undertake reconnaissance and artillery spotting duties; 16 bomber squadrons (*escadrilles de bombardement*); and three *escadrilles de cavalrie*. A further expansion to 119 *escadrilles*, with up to 10 aircraft a squadron, was agreed in 1915. By 1917 there were 2,263 front line aircraft available and steady growth continued for the remainder of the war, with 3,222 operational machines in service at the time of the Armistice.

This rate of expansion meant that even the well-developed French aircraft industry could not always meet production levels or design requirements. The **Sopwith 1-Strutter** was, for example, acquired in quantity, as was the famous Hispano-Suiza engine. **Vickers** and **Lewis machine-guns** were used almost exclusively as aircraft armament.

Growth and changes in air warfare produced further organisational development: the group, consisting of three or more *escadrilles*, was adopted early in 1915; in the final months of the war, groups were brought together under *escadres* (wings), which were in turn allocated to *groupements*, major formations of up to 20 squadrons under a single command.

The French air service was responsible for reconnaissance, combat and bombing duties on the Western Front and for home defence, as well as supporting the Allied armies in the Balkans and helping in the defence of Italy. The French gave some priority to the bombing of strategic targets and its mass attacks with the **Breguet 14** were often highly successful. It was, however, the activities of its fighter squadrons that made the most immediate impact and France produced some notable aces, many of whom served with the *Les Cigognes* (the Storks), the élite fighter unit. Another notable French fighter squadron was the *Escadrille Lafayette*, originally known as *Escadrille Américaine*. Manned exclusively by American volunteers, it was responsible for 38 hits during the war.

FRENCH NAVY

After years of decline France was no more than a second-class naval power at the beginning of the 20th century. However, following the appointment of **Admiral Boué de Lapeyrère**, Minister of Marine from 1909, a new building programme was begun and the armeé navale, a powerful striking force, was formed in the Mediterranean.

French naval efforts during the First World War were in fact concentrated in this area; the English Channel, Atlantic and North Sea were left primarily to the Royal Navy. The French navy's first priority was to control France's vital communications with her North African colonies, with the aim of escorting the frequent troop transports safely to the mainland. At the same time the main French fleet went to the Adriatic where it successfully blockaded the Austrian navy, its involvement continuing, at a lower level, after Italy entered the war. French ships participated, with the Royal Navy, in the **Dardanelles operation** and its losses included a battleship (*Bouvet*) and four submarines.

Following the Central Powers' invasion of **Serbia** in the autumn of 1915, the French navy evacuated 270,000 Serbian soldiers and their equipment from Albania to Corfu without a single loss. Its escort duties increased as the **Salonika front** expanded and, not surprisingly, a number of transport ships were lost to German U-boats. The landing of French sailors in Athens in December 1916 to increase pressure on the Greek government to join the Allies was a less successful operation.

The French navy also contributed to Allied anti-submarine warfare operations and developed a substantial naval air service, with over 1,200 aircraft in service by the end of the war. Losses sustained in France's unspectacular naval war included four battleships, 23 destroyers and torpedo boats and 14 submarines; few surrendered ships were transferred to her at the end of the war.

FREYBURG, GENERAL BERNARD, 1st BARON, 1889–1963

The future commander of the New Zealand Expeditionary Force during the Second World War, Freyburg served with distinction and courage during the Great War. Arriving in England from New Zealand in August 1914, he joined the Royal Naval Division and served with it during the expedition to **Antwerp**. At **Gallipoli** he won the first of his DSOs, swimming long distances to lay diversionary flares on the beaches. Returning to the Western Front, he was wounded four times and awarded the Victoria Cross during the **Battle of the Somme** in 1916. In April 1917, he was promoted brigadier-general, serving first with the 58th Division and then with the 29th. Before the end of the war he had won two bars to his DSO.

FRIEDRICHSHAFEN FF33

Manufactured in larger numbers than any other German seaplane, the FF33 appeared in reconnaissance and fighter forms, with a large number of variants. Dating back to the first example, which appeared late in 1914, the reconnaissance versions (the FF33, 33b, 33e, 33j and 33s) were two-seat, three-bay biplanes, with twin float landing gear. A small bomb load was normally carried, but not all were armed. Several different engines were fitted, but the standard type was the 150hp Benz Bz III, which gave a maximum speed of 75m.p.h. and an endurance of 5–6 hours. The main production model, the FF33e, of which 188 examples were built, was powered by this unit. It was also the first version to be fitted with a radio, although the later 33j had improved equipment and instruments; the 33s was fitted with dual controls for training purposes.

The two-seat fighter variants, which first appeared in October 1915, had two-bay wings and were smaller and more manoeuvrable. The FF33f and FF33h were succeeded by the main fighter version, the FF33l, of which 135 were built. It also used the 150hp Benz engine and was equipped with a forward firing Spandau machine-gun and a second gun in the rear. This series of aircraft was widely used by the German navy on patrol, reconnaissance and escort duties over the North Sea and English Channel. An FF33e carried by the merchant raider *Wolf* operated in much more distant locations – the Indian Ocean and the Pacific – searching out enemy ships. Nicknamed *Wölfchen* (Little Wolf), this famous aircraft assisted in the destruction of 28 Allied vessels in 1916–18. A total of 491 FF33s of all types were produced and they continued in service until the end of the war.

FRIEDRICHSHAFEN FF49

The FF49 two-seat patrol seaplane appeared in German service May 1917 as a replacement for the **Friedrichshafen FF33j** reconnaissance aircraft. Designated the FF49c in its production form, it resembled its predecessor quite closely, although it was larger and had balanced control surfaces, which resulted in an improvement in flying qualities. The airframe was strengthened and performance was improved by fitting the more powerful 200hp Benz Bz IV engine, which gave a range of 430 miles. The new machine was the first FF reconnaissance type to be fitted with a rear firing **Parabellum machine-gun** for the observer. Some later examples were also fitted with a forward firing Spandau machine-gun for the pilot.

The FF49 soon gained a reputation for reliability and was well suited to the often unfavourable conditions of the North Sea, where it was used until the Armistice. A total of 218 FF49s were built by Friedrichshafen and two sub-contractors. An unarmed bomber variant, with the positions of the crew reversed, appeared in the autumn of 1917. Designated the FF49b, only 25 examples were built and it made little impact.

FRIEDRICHSHAFEN GII & GIII

Known primarily as a seaplane manufacturer, Flugzeugbau Friedrichshafen also produced a series of twin-engined bombers. The first production model, the GII, entered service on the Western Front late in 1916. A two-bay design, with a single tail, it was powered by two 220hp Benz Bz IV pusher engines. Well armed with **Parabellum machine-guns** in the nose and behind the wings, it could only carry a small bomb load of no more than 150kg. As a result its usefulness was limited and it was only produced in small numbers.

The main production model of the series, the GIII, was a much larger three-bay aircraft, with a wingspan of almost 78 feet and a gross weight of 6,934lb. It had a much increased maximum bomb load of over 3,000lb. Twin 260hp Mercedes D IVa engines produced the necessary power, giving a maximum speed of 84m.p.h. and a duration of five hours. It operated with a crew of two or three (pilot, gunner, bomb aimer/gunner) and they were armed with one or two Parabellum machine-guns in the front and rear cockpits. A variant known as the GIIIa had a biplane tail unit but was otherwise similar.

The GIII served on the Western Front from early in 1917 until the end of the war and was an essential component of the German *Bombengeschwader* force. Together with the **Gotha GV**, which it closely resembled, the GIIIs were used for long distance night raids on France and Belgium and may also have been used in similar strikes against England. The GIII/GIIIa were built in quantity by Friedrichshafen and two sub-contractors. Further development of the series was undertaken in 1918, but these later examples – the GIVa, GIVb, and GV – had relatively little military impact.

FRONTIERS, BATTLE OF THE, 14–25 August 1914

In accordance with the **Schlieffen Plan**, the German army wheeled through Belgium during the first three weeks of the First World War. By 14 August, the seven German armies had made contact with the French, who were advancing northwards in accordance with **Plan XVII**, their own guidelines for offensive action in the event of war. The latter involved an immediate attack through Alsace-Lorraine, which had been held by the Germans since 1870. The Allied forces – which consisted of five

French armies and one British – were numerically inferior, particularly in the west. The opposing armies were engaged in four separate, but related battles along the frontiers of France, extending from the Swiss border to Mons in Belgium.

In the Battle of Lorraine, on the eastern end of the front, the French First (**Dubail**) and Second Armies (**Castelnau**) crossed the frontier into Germany on 14 August; they advanced towards Sarrebourg and Morhange. The defending German armies – the Sixth, (**Crown Prince Rupprecht**) and Seventh (**von Heeringen**) – a total of 25 divisions, delayed counter-attacking until the enemy had advanced further. The Germans wanted to make it difficult for the French to extricate themselves quickly and go to the assistance of their forces further north. When there were indications that the French did in fact intend to withdraw, the Germans mounted a converging counter-attack, on 20 August, defeating their opponents at Morhange. **Foch**'s XX Corps performed with distinction during the battle, which cost the French 20,000 men and 150 guns. As they fell back to the border a new line was established along the Moselle, with the Germans failing to take Nancy.

To the west of Metz, the French Third (Ruffey) and Fourth Armies (**Langle de Cary**) advanced northwards on 21 August, a day after the German counter-offensive in Lorraine had begun. The aim was to attack the German centre in the flank as it passed through the thickly wooded hills of the Ardennes. In thick fog, they engaged two German armies – the Fifth Army (**Crown Prince Frederick William**) and the Fourth (**Albrecht, Duke of Württemberg**) – which were the pivot of the Schlieffen Plan. For a while the Germans were in a critical situation, but the outnumbered French eventually withdrew after a series of strongly contested actions spread over four days.

During the heavy fighting the French had suffered particularly from German superiority in field and heavy weapons. The Third Army moved back across the Meuse to Verdun, where its commander, Ruffey, was removed. His replacement, **Maurice Sarrail**, was able to hold on to Verdun. The French Fourth Army withdrew to Stenay and Sedan, where, on 26–28 August, it engaged and temporarily halted the pursuing Germans.

On the same day as the French had attacked in the Ardennes, the German Second Army (**Bülow**), further to the west, had forced two crossings of the River Sambre between Namur and Charleroi. Some troops were left behind to besiege the fortress of Namur, which fell on 25 August. To Bülow's left was the German Third Army (Max von Hausen), which had taken Dinant on 15 August. It soon threatened the right flank of the French Fifth Army (**Lanrezac**), which had moved forward into the Sambre-Meuse area to meet an enemy thrust that was much further west than pre-war French planners had expected. Lanrezac's position weakened as the French Fourth Army on his right fell back. His forces, which constituted the French left wing, defended Charleroi strongly, but they were attacked on the front and the right. The latter received a blow from the German Third Army, which had crossed the Meuse and was now striking westwards. With the northern frontier open, Lanrezac was forced to retreat rapidly on 24 August, suffering heavy losses. He counter-attacked towards Guise on 29 August, briefly checking Bülow's advance along the Oise River.

Lanrezac's retreat quickly forced the hand of the newly arrived British Expeditionary Force (**Sir John French**) on the extreme left of the Allied line. The four divisions (70,000 men) had been moving into position behind the canal at Mons when the German First Army (**Kluck**) attacked on 23 August. More than double the size of the British force, it was delayed for nine hours by the rapid, accurate fire of professional soldiers. There were relatively few casualties on the British side. Plans to withdraw to a new, more defensible position $2\frac{1}{2}$ miles south of the town were abandoned when the British learnt of the French withdrawal from Charleroi. Rapidly pursued by the Germans, I Corps, BEF, was forced to fight a rearguard action at **Le Cateau**.

Both sides suffered heavy losses in this massive battle which was an overwhelming German success. The French army's offensive action had failed and 300,000 casualties, a quarter of its combatants, had been sustained. The Germans lost a similar number. The frontier was breached at every point and the Germans moved southwards in accordance with the Schlieffen Plan, ensuring that the decisive battles of the war would be fought on French territory.

Yet the situation for the Allies was far from hopeless. The French army had not collasped and morale remained high. While the First and Second

Armies held the eastern pivot of the line, from Nancy to Verdun, the Third, Fourth and Fifth Armies withdrew southwards in good order, giving **Joffre** time to regroup his forces and plan the counter-attack that was to be mounted at the **Marne**. Partly because of poor communications, the German High Command had over-estimated the extent of its success and had reduced the strength of the critical right wing prematurely as it marched through France, moving some units to the Eastern Front.

FULLER, MAJOR-GENERAL JOHN, 1878–1964

A noted British military writer and thinker between the wars, Fuller played a key part in the development of tank tactics during the First World War. After a succession of staff appointments, he was appointed GSO 2 (later GSO 1) in the headquarters of the Tank Corps (originally Heavy Branch, Machine-Gun Corps), late in 1916. Under the command of Sir Hugh Elles, Fuller, who was nicknamed 'Boney' because of his resemblance to Napoleon, had considerable scope for innovation in building up the new arm and in deciding how it should be used in battle.

He was responsible for the plan for the **Battle of Cambrai** (November 1917), the first great tank engagement in history, which represented the successful outcome of his year's work with the new weapon. As a direct result, a tank branch of the General Staff was established in July 1918, and Fuller was appointed as its head. By this time he had prepared 'Plan 1919', an ambitious proposal for a mass tank army that was shelved with the ending of the war.

FUSIL D'INFANTERIE MODÈLE 1889

The standard Belgian rifle of the First World War, the 7.65mm Model 1889 was a modified German **Mauser** design. It was built under licence by Fabrique National, the arms manufacturer created specifically for this purpose. The main Belgian change to the basic design was the encasing of the barrel in a metal tube to prevent it from coming into contact with the woodwork, which was liable to warp. The appearance and internal arrangement of the five-round magazine was also slightly different to other Mauser weapons. A carbine variant also appeared in 1889 and like the standard rifle could be fitted with a long-bladed sword bayonet. With German forces occupying most of the country, wartime manufacture of the weapon was transferred to the United States thus ensuring that supplies continued to reach the Belgian army. The Belgian Mausers gave long and reliable service throughout the war and well beyond.

GALICIA, OPERATIONS IN, 1914–15

As soon as its troop deployments were completed, some two weeks after the outbreak of war, Austria launched simultaneous offensives on two fronts. In accordance with plans prepared by **Conrad**, the chief of staff, Serbia was the secondary target, the main attack being launched against Poland from Galicia, Austria's most easterly province. Conrad hoped to cut off the Russian army in the Polish salient, but it later became clear that the enemy had concentrated its forces elsewhere on the front. At first, however, neither side had much information about the location or intentions of the other.

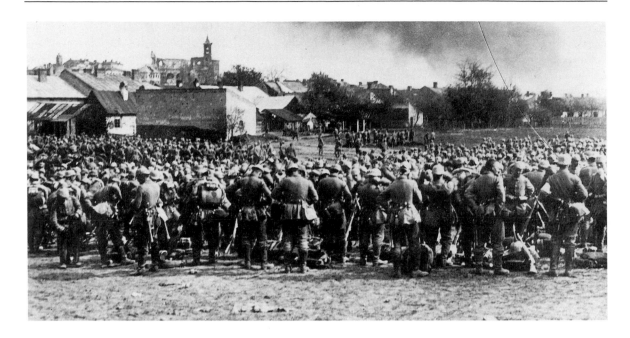

German troops massing in preparation for the Gorlice–Tarnow offensive, which finally cleared Galicia of Russian troops in the spring of 1915

Three Austrian armies, from left to right, the First (**Dankl**), Fourth (**Auffenberg**) and Third (Bruder-mann), moved north and east from Lemberg into Poland on a 200-mile front. On this route they passed straight across the Russian front, which was held by **General Ivanov**'s South-Western Army Group. Consisting of four armies – from north to south the Fourth (**Evert**), Fifth (**Plehve**), Third (**Ruzski**) and Eighth (**Brusilov**) – its main attack was to be in the general direction of Lemberg. To the north of the front, Dankl crossed the border into Poland first, meeting the smaller Russian Fourth Army at Krasnik on 23 August. Heavy fighting lasted for three days before the Russians were pushed back northwards to Lublin. Fighting spread along the front as the Austrian Fourth Army fought with the Russian Fifth at Komarów, in a battle that lasted a week (26 August–1 September). For a second time the Austrians gained the upper hand, but Auffenberg's forces were called to the assistance of the Third Army, which had suffered a heavy defeat, before victory was assured.

To the south of the front, the main Russian invasion had begun: the Third Army crossed the Austrian frontier near Brody, while the Eighth moved forward from Odessa on a convergent path. Mean-while, the much smaller Austrian Third Army, sup-ported by elements of the Second which had arrived from Serbia, had advanced to the Gnila Lipa River. On 26 August, they met the Russians at Zlotchow and were defeated. As a result, Conrad quickly ordered the withdrawal of the Second and Third Armies to Lemberg.

On 30 August, Brusilov forced the line of the Second Army south-east of Lemberg and during the main battle in front of the city, on 1 September, a Russian breakthrough to the north threatened to outflank Austrian positions. Conrad was compelled to abandon Lemberg on 2 September, ordering a retreat of the Second and Third Armies to the Wereszyca. He continued to plan offensive action but his forces were soon to be overwhelmed by the Russian 'steamroller'. Heavy fighting continued on the Austrian right as the Russians tried to envelop it, while Plehve and Auffenberg fought an inconclusive battle at Rava Russka (6–7 September), 32 miles north-west of Lemberg. Both sides launched new offensives on 8 September, but without much result.

The Russians now planned their final blow, order-ing Plehve to move through the gap in the enemy lines north of Lemberg and behind the Austrian Second and Third Armies. At the same time Brusilov and Ruzski on the left would keep them occupied. Aware from intercepted radio messages of Russian intentions, Conrad decided, on 11 September, to pull back all his troops to the San, over 60 miles away. However, Conrad soon discovered that Evert from the north had appeared on his flank and he did not stop until he had reached the Dunajec on 3 October, 140 miles west of Lemberg.

As they withdrew, a garrison was left in the key fortress of Przemysl, which was soon besieged. By the end of September the Austrians had surrendered almost all of Galicia to superior Russian forces and had sustained very heavy casualties, more than 250,000 being killed or wounded and 100,000 taken prisoner. Fighting came to a temporary halt as the Russians made no immediate attempt to cross the Carpathian Mountains into Hungary.

A combined German/Austrian operation to drive the Germans from the Carpathians began on 23 January 1915. It was part of the **Hindenburg**'s dual offensive on the Eastern Front, the other half of the operation being mounted in East Prussia. From left to right, the Third Army (**Boroevic**), the Austro-German South Army (**Linsingen**) and the Seventh Army (**Pflanzer-Baltin**) advanced in terrible winter conditions. Progress was generally very limited, except on the right where Pflanzer-Baltin advanced some 60 miles before being pushed back into the mountains. The Russians had been reinforced by troops released once Przemsyl had fallen into their hands (22 March 1915) after a siege of 194 days. A Russian counter-offensive followed but their advance through the Carpathians was checked by the South Army. Galicia was finally cleared of Russian troops during the **Gorlice-Tarnow offensive** in the spring of 1915.

GALLIÉNI, GENERAL JOSEPH, 1849–1916

A distinguished French general who had made his reputation in the colonies, Galliéni was recalled from retirement at the beginning of the First World War. He was appointed deputy commander-in-chief under **Joffre**, his former subordinate, and military governor of Paris, where he soon made his decisive contribution to the war.

As the German army moved east of Paris, Galliéni was the first to perceive the opportunity it presented for a flanking attack, and with considerable difficulty secured Joffre's agreement to his plan. On 5 September, Galliéni ordered **Maunoury**'s Sixth Army eastwards towards the Orcq River where it attacked the flank of the German First Army (**Kluck**). The French were forced on to the defensive after the Germans brought up reinforcements and two days of heavy fighting followed (7–9 September). With the First Army tied down and reports of a British advance, the enemy's progress southwards was brought to an end. If, however, Galliéni had received all the reinforcements he had requested, the outcome of the **Battle of the Marne** might have been very different: 'German forces south of the Marne might have been cut off and the battle been as decisive tactically as it was strategically.' On 11 September, Joffre resumed direct control of the Sixth Army, abandoning any further flank attacks in favour of advancing from the front.

Galliéni, military governor of Paris, planned the flanking attack that led to the strategic victory at the Marne

Poor relations with Joffre ended any hope Galliéni might have entertained of a field command, but, in October 1915, he became War Minister in **Briand**'s government. Concerned by the fact that the Western Front dominated Joffre's strategic thinking, Galliéni sought to constrain the commander-in-chief by the appointment of subordinates with a wider vision. The **Verdun** disaster increased Galliéni's determination to reassert political control over the direction of the war, but his Cabinet colleagues were unwilling to bring the issue to a head. In poor health, he resigned in March 1916 and died soon afterwards. Galliéni's outstanding services at the beginning of the war were recognised when he was posthumously created Marshal of France in 1921.

GALLIPOLI, EXPEDITION TO, 25 April 1915–9 January 1916

After the failure of the Anglo-French naval operation against the Dardanelles in March 1915, a land force was despatched to the Gallipoli peninsula with the aim of securing the decisively important waterway. The ultimate objective was the capture of Constantinople, which would open up the first effective route for supplies to Russia and might lead to the collapse of the Turkish empire. There was also the more remote possibility of creating a new front against the Germans and of breaking the stalemate on the Western Front.

Difficulties were soon encountered in the execution of this imaginative plan, of which **Winston Churchill** was one of the main architects. The commander of the expeditionary force, **General Sir Ian Hamilton**, left England without a staff or any up-to-date information about Turkish defences; there were also long delays in despatching the required troops. As the first elements arrived on the island of Lemnos, the rear base for the invasion, the whole expedition was diverted to Alexandria, Egypt, to enable men and equipment to be rearranged in their transports. In order to correct

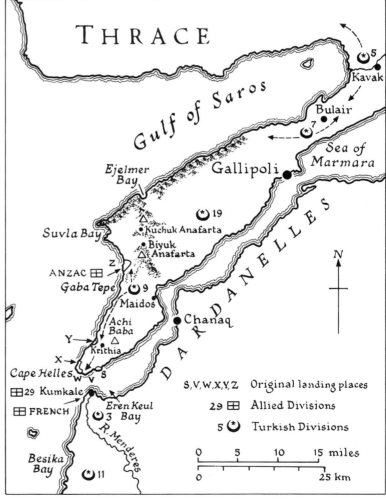

the evident chaos, the operation had to be delayed by over a month, giving the Turks, who were soon aware of the Allies' intentions, ample time to prepare their defences.

Six Turkish divisions (84,000 men), under **General Liman von Sanders**, were moved to the area and were concentrated at the expected landing places. The smaller Allied force of five divisions (75,000 men) seemed less than adequate for the difficult amphibious landing that it was about to undertake. Yet the Allies still retained the advantage of surprise in deciding when and where to attack.

The landings were made at two points on the southern tip of the Gallipoli peninsula on 25 April 1915. The main force of 35,000 men, under the command of Sir Aylmer Hunter-Weston, came ashore at five points at Cape Helles. Further up the coast, the much smaller Australian and New Zealand Corps (**Anzacs**) of 17,000 men, commanded by General Sir William Birdwood, disembarked at Ari Burnu, a mile north of Gaba Tepe, its intended landing point. The French division made a diversionary landing at Kum Kale on the Asiatic shore, while the remainder of the British force steamed north, with the aim of giving the enemy the false impression that there was a further invasion point.

The widely dispersed action momentarily confused the Turks. It took von Sanders two days to concentrate his forces and in the meantime there was only one Turkish division defending the area under direct attack. The invading forces, however, failed to exploit this initial opportunity, which was soon lost to them for good. Landings at two of the beaches at Cape Helles, where British troops were pinned down by constant machine-gun fire, quickly ran into difficulties, but elsewhere little or no opposition was encountered. However, once the beaches had been secured, the whole British force remained inert instead of moving forward to cut off the Turkish defenders, a disastrous failure of leadership and of tactical coordination. The landing by the Anzacs north of Gaba Tepe was almost unopposed and here, at least, the Allies quickly pressed inland, up the slopes towards Chunuk Bair, a height dominating the whole peninsula. The advance was soon checked by a determined counter-attack launched by Colonel Mustafa Kemal (**Kemal Ataturk**), who drove the Anzacs back to the beaches by the end of the first day.

'W' Beach, Gallipoli: here, as elsewhere, Allied troops were soon pinned down by the Turkish army and made little progress beyond their original landing points

Evacuation day, 'W' Beach, Gallipoli, 8 January 1916. Turkish shell fire did not disrupt this operation which was completed successfully without loss of life

Thus, at every point the Allies were confined to their small beachheads, and every effort to dislodge the Turkish forces that ringed them and held the commanding heights ended in failure. The Allies were handicapped by a shortage of ammunition, which meant that their artillery could not be used to full effect. The Turks, in spite of a ready supply of reserves, could not expel their opponents who were firmly entrenched by the shore. A stalemate similar to that on the Western Front developed and the cost of trying to gain the upper hand was similarly high. In two weeks of bitter fighting following the landings, Hamilton had lost almost a third of his force.

Two months were to elapse before the British government decided to increase the force to a total of twelve divisions, by which time Turkish strength had also risen. A major cause of this fatal hesitation was the resistance of British and French commanders on the Western Front who were strongly opposed to the diversion of manpower from what they regarded as the critical theatre of the war.

In August 1915, Hamilton made his second attempt to gain control of the peninsula. It was to involve a double strike against the Turks. The Anzacs, based at Ari Burnu (now renamed Anzac Cove), were to make the main effort, with a night attack towards their primary objective – the heights of Chunuk Bair. Although they came close to success, a series of errors and the exhaustion of the troops determined otherwise. At the same time a new landing was made at Suvla Bay, a few miles to the north, but this also ended in failure.

About 25,000 men landed without serious opposition in a good position to outflank the main Turkish contingent at Anzac Cove. However, the force consolidated its position at the landing point rather than pressing forward when the opportunity presented itself. This inaction has been attributed largely to the lack of energy of the commander, Sir Frederick Stopford, who preferred to remain on board his ship during this critical period. By the time they were

ready to move inland on 9 August it was too late –
Turkish reserves had already been brought up.

Once again the Allies were in a precarious position,
with the added problems of disease and approaching
winter. It was clear by now that the operation had
failed, although the British government hesitated
before ordering a withdrawal. National prestige was
an important consideration and there was the fear of
possibly heavy casualties from the difficult evacuation. Hamilton, who was in favour of mounting a
further offensive with more troops, was out of tune
with official thinking and on 22 October he was
replaced by **General Sir Charles Monro**, who was
also directing the **Salonika** campaign. After a brief
visit to the front the new supreme commander
recommended complete evacuation: 'He came, he
saw, he capitulated', in Churchill's memorable phrase.
The Cabinet eventually accepted Monro's advice as
the only realistic option.

The withdrawal of troops from Suvla Bay and
Anzac Cove was completed on 18 December and
from Cape Helles on 9 January 1916. This was the
single most successful phase of the entire campaign
during which not one life was lost. Overall the cost
was very high: British, French and colonial casualties
totalled about 250,000 and those of Turkey were
probably about the same. As many as 410,000 British
and 70,000 French troops had been landed on the
peninsula.

The failure of this ill-planned and executed operation meant that the straits of the Black Sea remained
closed and that Russia remained cut off from her
Allies. Failure further strengthened the hand of those
who believed that the Western Front was the decisive
battleground and that all the Allies' energies should be
concentrated there. Finally, one of the main propo-
nents of the expedition, Winston Churchill, left the
government with a much tarnished reputation which
he never recovered during the war.

GALLWITZ, GENERAL MAX von, 1852–1937

A German artillery officer of long experience, Gallwitz was already serving on the Eastern Front when
early in 1915 he was appointed to the command of an
army group in south-eastern Poland. He participated
in **Mackensen**'s campaign in Galicia before being
appointed to the Eleventh Army, which helped to
conquer Serbia in the autumn of 1915. Germany's
'best general utility man', Gallwitz was moved to the
Western Front in March 1916, where he remained for
the rest of the war. He served on the **Somme**, at
Verdun and, in the final days of the war, as
commander of Army Group Gallwitz, opposite American forces on the Meuse–Moselle front.

GANGUT

Completed in 1914, the Ganguts were the first
Russian-produced dreadnoughts. With a maximum
speed of 23 knots, they were relatively powerful, but
at the price of thinner than normal armour protection. Armament consisted of twelve 12-inch Obukhov
guns, mounted in four triple turrets on the centre
line. These weapons were highly accurate and gave a
significantly greater weight of broadside than the best
contemporary battleships. *Gangut* and her sister ships
– *Poltava*, *Sevastopol* and *Petropavlovsk* – formed the
First Battleship Brigade of the Baltic Fleet, based at
Helsingfors (Helsinki). However, the Russian High
Command was unwilling to risk the dreadnoughts
unnecessarily and they were confined to uneventful
patrols in the Gulf of Finland. *Petropavlovsk* was active
during the Civil War and was torpedoed by the
British at Kronstadt in August 1919.

GARROS, ROLAND, 1882–1918

A pioneer pre-war racing pilot, Roland Garros served with *Escadrille MS 23* of the French Aviation Militaire and became the first ace in aviation history. After trials with Raymond Saulnier's deflector plates, Garros's **Morane Saulnier Type L** was fitted with the device, enabling him to fire his **Hotchkiss machine-gun** through the airscrew for the first time, and his first victory, on 1 April 1915, was an important step in the history of military aviation. Four further hits followed quickly, but on 19 April he was shot down. He was unable to destroy his machine before the Germans arrived and their discovery of Saulnier's device resulted in Anthony Fokker's invention of a proper interrupter gear, which he fitted to a **Fokker EI**. Garros eventually escaped from imprisonment and rejoined the Aviation Militaire; he was killed in action a month before the end of the war.

GAS WARFARE

The French were the first combatants to use chemical weapons, firing tear gas grenades as early as August 1914. At Neuve Chapelle, in October 1914, the Germans fired shrapnel shells treated with a chemical irritant and during the following January they used tear gas shells on the Eastern Front. However, poisonous gas was not used on a significant scale until 22 April 1915, when the Germans used chlorine against British and French positions on the **Ypres** salient. More than 500 cylinders were opened and their contents – 168 tons of pressurised chlorine gas – were forced by wind on to the Allied line. Chlorine results in death if inhaled for more than a minute or two and this first operation cost the lives of 5,000 troops, with another 10,000 injured. The attack produced a break in the line but the Germans, without sufficient reserves, were unable to exploit their success; the opportunity for a decisive result did not reoccur because an antidote was soon to be available.

The first chlorine attack led almost immediately to the development of fairly primitive protective measures: within days handkerchiefs soaked in bicarbonate of soda were in use. A more elaborate device – the small box respirator – did not appear until August 1916; it was subject to continuous improvement and in its final form incorporated chemical solutions and charcoal filters to neutralise the weapon.

Following the first British use of chlorine gas – at **Artois-Loos**, on 25 September 1915 – it was employed frequently by both sides. One of its major disadvantages was the fact that it could be blown back on to the positions of those making the attack, as indeed happened at Loos. This difficulty was overcome when the Germans started, in July 1915, enclosing chlorine in an artillery shell; mortar and projector shells were also used by both sides for this purpose.

Gas masks, worn here by American troops, quickly provided an effective counter to most types of gas

There was also a need to respond to improvements in respirator design by introducing new types of gas. Phosgene, which first appeared in December 1915, is, like chlorine, a choking gas, but is more deadly. Mustard gas, first introduced to the battlefield by the Germans in July 1917, was the most widely used toxic substance of the war. Odourless and virtually colourless, it causes severe burning to the skin and respiratory system; it evaporates slowly and effective protection is difficult.

Gas was regarded by the combatants as a useful 'tactical accessory', rather than as a weapon that might itself have ended the deadlock of **trench warfare** on the Western Front. Germany's reputation was damaged by her first use of gas, although 'both experience and statistics proved it be the least inhumane of modern weapons'. Gas attacks caused at least a million casualties during the war.

GAUCHET, VICE-ADMIRAL DOMINIQUE, 1853–1931

Commander-in-chief of the French fleet in the Mediterranean from December 1916 until the end of the war, Gauchet succeeded **Admiral Dartige du Fournet**, who had been dismissed after his unfortunate landing at Athens. Although Gauchet was formally in command of all Allied naval operations in the Mediterranean, in practice he 'proved to be little more than a passive observer of events', who 'saw himself above all as a squadron commander'.

GAZA, FIRST AND SECOND BATTLES OF, 26–27 March & 17–19 April 1917

Under pressure from the War Office to make the 'maximum possible effort', **Sir Archibald Murray** decided to continue his march eastwards towards Palestine. With the fall of **Rafa** in January 1917, the route to Gaza, the coastal gateway to southern Palestine, was clear.

Although the permanent Turkish garrison of 4,000 troops was small, Gaza was likely to be a difficult objective: a surprise attack was impossible and the town's defences were strong. The operation, which began on 26 March 1917, was entrusted to Sir Charles Dobell, Murray's immediate subordinate. He ordered two cavalry divisions to move to the east and north of the town with the aim of preventing the arrival of reinforcements; to the south, the 53rd Infantry Division launched the main assault on the ridge of Ali Muntar, which overlooked Gaza. Although victory was in sight towards the end of the first day, Sir Philip Chetwode withdrew his cavalry forces prematurely from the field, believing incorrectly that the main infantry attack had failed. When the attack resumed the next day, the commander of the Turkish forces, Baron Kress von Kressenstein, had reinforced the garrison and the British were eventually driven back. Their losses amounted to 4,000 men compared with Turkish casualties of 2,400.

A report on the battle sent to the War Office by Murray soon afterwards gave the misleading impression that the battle had been a British success and in reply he was given new orders: to continue the advance and occupy Jerusalem. As a result Murray felt impelled to launch a further assault on Gaza at an early date, even though circumstances soon became less favourable as the Turks had extended their lines south-east along the road to Beersheba.

A courageous frontal assault on this well-defended position was launched by three British infantry divisions on 17 April, but they were unable to make anything more than minor gains. The fighting was called off on the third day; the British had lost over 6,000 men and the smaller Turkish force 2,000. Dobell was soon relieved of his command, but it was Murray himself who was responsible for the highly questionable decision to launch the second battle. On 28 June 1917, he was recalled by the War Office, and replaced by **Allenby** in the hope that more effective offensive action could be taken.

GAZA, THIRD BATTLE OF, 31 October–7 November 1917

On his arrival in Egypt as **Murray**'s successor, **Allenby** worked hard to restore the morale of British troops which had been undermined by the two defeats at **Gaza** in March and April 1917. Unlike his predecessor he was able to secure large reinforcements and by the autumn an effective fighting force of seven divisions (88,000 men) was in place. It seemed strong enough to achieve the objective that the War Cabinet had set for Allenby of capturing Jerusalem as 'a Christmas present to the British nation'. Allenby's immediate task was to break through the well-defended Turkish line, held by 35,000 troops, that ran from Gaza south-east to Beersheba, a distance of 25 miles. The Turks were commanded by **General von Falkenhayn**.

On 31 October, the British assault began unexpectedly with an assault on the Turkish left flank at Beersheba, the Turks having been fed the false information that Allenby intended to strike at Gaza. The Turkish forces at Beersheba were heavily outnumbered by their opponents; their single division was opposed by five British divisions (supported by eight tanks). Advancing from both east and west, the town was occupied on the first day, after a final charge by Australian cavalry had overrun the defences and captured the vital water wells intact. The Turkish Seventh Army was forced to retire to Sheria and their heavily fortified line quickly came under pressure from a flanking movement from the east. Gaza also suffered a more intensive attack, including a naval bombardment.

On 6 November, Allenby launched the decisive strike at Sheria, outflanking the town from the east, routing the Seventh Army and pushing towards the coast behind the Eighth Army. The garrison at Gaza was now in danger of being cut off and the town was evacuated by the Turks on 6–7 November.

Allenby pursued the Turks aggressively northwards up the coastal plain and they fell back to Junction Station. It was taken on 14 November and two days later Jaffa fell. Allenby was now in sight of his principal objective, Jerusalem, 35 miles to the north-west, although with Falkenhayn now concentrating his reinforcements some of the most difficult fighting of the entire campaign still lay ahead.

GEDDES, SIR ERIC, 1875–1937

Best remembered for his chairmanship of a committee that advised on reductions in public expenditure in 1921 ('the Geddes axe'), Sir Eric Geddes was First Lord of the Admiralty from July 1917 until the general election of 1918. An experienced businessman, who had worked for the North Eastern Railway, he held senior appointments in the field of army transport and supply for much of the war. In May 1917, his wartime career changed direction when he became Controller of the Navy; he moved on within a matter of weeks, following his election to Parliament and appointment as First Lord of the Admiralty.

Geddes proved to be an able administrator who overcame the navy's initial suspicions of him, although he came into conflict with **Jellicoe** and eventually dismissed him. A major achievement was the expansion of the **convoy system**, of which he was a leading advocate, and there were demands from within the navy for his retention after the war. **Lloyd George** had, however, already decided to move him elsewhere.

GEORGE V, KING, 1865–1936

King of England, 1910–36, whose devotion to duty during the First World War won him great popularity. He made several morale-boosting visits to the Western Front and to the **Grand Fleet**, as well as regular tours of military hospitals at home. The war years, however, provided few of the opportunities for the monarch's involvement in political and constitutional matters that existed in the troubled period before the European conflict began. In 1917, George V adopted the surname Windsor because it was decided that the former dynastic name, Saxe-Coburg, with its obvious German connections, was inappropriate during the war.

George V, who had an important propaganda role, visits the Western Front, with King Albert in 1916

GERMAN 77mm FIELD GUN

The standard German field gun during the first part of the war, the Feldkanone 96 n/A was a reliable and well-constructed piece built by Krupp. One of its major limitations was the fact that it could only fire a light projectile over a maximum range of 7,655 yards, and during 1916 a revised model was produced. Better suited to conditions on the Western Front, the Feldkanone 16 (FK 16) could fire a variety of different shells – high explosive, shrapnel or gas – over an extended range of 11,264 yards. The FK 16 had a longer barrel (106 inches) than its predecessor, but shared a sliding breech block, which had become a standard feature of German field artillery design.

GERMAN AIR SERVICE

Although German interest in airships had delayed their development of military aviation, by the beginning of the war they had more planes available (240) for front line duty than either the British or the French. They were organised in 33 field flight sections (*Feldflieger Abteilungen*) of six planes each and eight fortress flight sections (*Festungsflieger Abteilungen*) of four planes each. The former, whose main duty was reconnaissance, were closely integrated with the army, a unit being allocated to each army headquarters and army corps. The *Festungsflieger* were created in order to help protect fortress towns along the German frontier.

To these groups was soon added a bomber unit, based at Ostend, universally known by its cover name, the Ostend Carrier Pigeon Unit. It was the forerunner of the units that carried out bombing raids on both European fronts and against civilian targets in England. To control these diverse activities, a Chief of Field Aviation, responsible to the German High Command and the War Ministry, was appointed early in 1915.

The German air service's early aircraft included the Taube, parasol wing monoplanes and B-type biplanes. The appearance of a French **Morane-Saulnier Type L**, armed with a forward firing machine-gun

operated by a crude synchronising device, prompted Fokker to produce a proper firing mechanism of its own. Fitted to the Fokker *Eindecker*, its introduction marked the beginnings of real air combat over the Western Front.

The first German single-seater fighter units (*Kampfeinsitzer Abteilungen*) were formed late in 1915 and expanded rapidly, soon establishing air superiority over the Allies. Five battle wings (*Kagohl*), under the direction of the Army High Command, were also formed, in 1915–16, and were moved around by train to whichever formation needed their support. The Field Flight Sections and bomber units were also expanded during this period.

Another area of growth, as trench warfare established itself, was artillery observation, and it became necessary to establish special *Artillerie Flieger Abteilungen*. The changes did not affect the basic structure of the German air service, which still consisted of a number of support bodies allocated to higher army formations; there seemed to be no practical possibility of forming an integrated air force at this stage.

The Halberstadt CLII which originally entered service in 1917 as a fighter escort. Its most important military function, however, was as a ground attack aircraft

German fighter units suffered heavy losses during the major battles of 1916 – **Verdun** and the **Somme** – as improved Allied fighters arrived at the front in larger numbers. However, the appearance of new D-type fighters and a series of organisational changes enabled the Germans to regain air superiority early in 1917.

The first general commanding the air service (Ernst von Hoeppner) had been appointed in October 1916. The service was reorganised and centralised and new operational units were created to replace the old. *Flieger Abteilungen* were to undertake long-range reconnaissance on behalf of army headquaters, while *Flieger Abteilungen (A)* were to carry out artillery spotting duties. They were to be protected by escort squadrons – *Schustas* – which were later used for ground attack duties. These battle flights (or *Schlacht-staffeln*) played an important offensive role in 1917–18, particularly during the **Battle of Cambrai** and in the following spring.

The *Kagohls*, redesignated as bomber units, were to attack enemy rear areas. The original fighter units became *Jagdstaffeln* or *Jastas* and were charged with eliminating enemy fighters. Expansion plans in 1917 were concentrated on the *Jastas*, and 40 new units were created. As the nature of aerial combat changed, the need for larger fighter formations became apparent; *Jagdgeschwader*, consisting of four *Jastas*, were permanent groupings of some 50 aircraft.

As **Ludendorff**'s offensive began in the spring of 1918, the air force had 81 *Jastas*, 153 *Flieger Abteilungen*, 38 *Schlachtstaffeln* and 7 *Bombengeschwadern*. However, by this time overall superiority had been lost, never to be regained, as new Allied fighters appeared in large numbers. Germany no longer had the manpower nor the material to match her enemies' scale of production and her air force could do nothing to influence the final outcome of the war. At the time of the Armistice the air service had some 15,000 aircraft and about 80,000 personnel; it had lost 6,840 men killed and 7,350 injured during the war.

GERMAN ARMY

The German army was the most efficient and best trained of the forces mobilised on the outbreak of war in 1914. It was based on **conscription**, which meant that most Germans became liable for service from the age of 17; they spent two or three years in the regular army before moving into the reserve. The latter, which was intended to bring the army up to war establishment at the time of mobilisation, enabled the German army to put 87 divisions into the field in 1914.

Short service conscripts were managed by long service officers and NCOs who provided the tactical leadership. Unlike the colonial armies of Britain and France, it was a peace trained army, as almost none of the regular troops had any war experience. Apart from its large reserve of trained manpower, it possessed other advantages, including the quality of its general staff and its superior equipment. It had considerable initial advantages in the weapons – for example, howitzers, mortars, machine-guns and **gre-nades** – that were to be essential in the static warfare of the Western Front. Industry was better geared to meet the needs of the army and it never suffered the initial problems of ammunition shortages that faced the Allied armies. In these circumstances, it is perhaps not surprising that the General Staff welcomed the opportunity provided by the assassination at Sarajevo to launch its long planned preventative war.

Like the French, the German army was firmly committed to offensive action. It would knock out France first on the basis of a plan produced by Count Schlieffen and modified by the younger **Moltke**. Rapid mobilisation and deployment – totalling 84,000 officers and 2,314,000 men – gave the Germans the initiative at first. Violating Belgian territory the army wheeled through northern France with the aim of ending the war on the Western Front within six weeks. In the meantime, the German army stood on the defensive against Russia and only one of its eight armies was allocated to the Eastern Front, the Austrians bearing the brunt of the initial fighting.

Among the failures of the German plan were its inaccurate assessment of the quality of the opposing armies and the fact that it had insufficient forces to achieve its objectives on two fronts. On the Western Front, the German right wing was not strong enough and its movement east of Paris exposed its flanks. The French army held the Germans at the **Marne** and forced them to take up defensive positions on this front. **Falkenhayn**, who replaced Moltke as chief of staff in September, attempted to outflank the French during the 'Race to the sea.' His failure to achieve a breakthrough during the **First Battle of Ypres** marked the beginnings of trench warfare, with the German army defending a line from the Channel to the Swiss border and quickly demonstrating a mastery of defensive tactics.

In the east, the army, under **Ludendorff** and **Hindenburg**, had saved East Prussia in 1914, but their victory at **Tannenberg** did not settle the campaign.

Divisions soon appeared in the army about where Germany should concentrate her main efforts, with Hindenburg and Ludendorff arguing for a major offensive on the Eastern Front that would lead to Russia's defeat. Falkenhayn believed that priority should be given to the battle against France, but military pressure on Austro-Hungary forced the chief of staff to launch an attack on the Russians in 1915. The result was substantial German gains but it did not bring Russia to the negotiating table. The army had also participated in the occupation of Serbia and had withstood major Allied offensives on the Western Front.

However, the German army could not, in the long run, hope to win a defensive war of attrition on the Western Front and in 1916 Falkenhayn sought to break the deadlock. The attempt to 'bleed France white' at **Verdun** ended in failure, with Germany losing more men than its opponents. As a result, it was unable to exploit French weaknesses elsewhere along the line. The army also suffered heavily during the **Battle of the Somme**, with the quality of replacement troops deteriorating from this point. The war effort received a new impetus from the Hindenburg/Ludendorff team that replaced Falkenhayn in August 1916, but a lack of reserves – because of the situation on the Western Front and the campaign in Rumania – prevented a new offensive in the east. At this stage there were 2,850,000 troops on the Western Front and 1,730,000 in the east.

The army's defensive position on the Western Front was strengthened by the construction of the Hindenburg Line, a system of flexible defence in depth. The High Command had hoped to break the impasse during 1917 by unrestricted submarine warfare but failed to bring Britain to its knees. It was not in fact until the Bolshevik Revolution brought Russia's involvement in the war to an end that further offensive action on the Western Front could be contemplated.

German shock troops, widely used during the 1918 offensives, ready to go over the top

Forty-four divisions were transferred from the Eastern Front and five great offensives were launched. Using new shock tactics the army pushed back the front line but a breakthrough eluded them because of logistical failures and the enemy's numerous reserves. The Allied counter-attack at **Amiens** on 8 August 1918, 'the black day of the German army', marked the 'limits of its endurance'. During the final two months of the war the German army retreated in the face of superior Allied numbers (boosted by American intervention) and mechanised warfare. Army discipline began to break down in response to military failure and social and political unrest on the home front.

Outside Europe the German army's operations, with the exception of **Lettow-Vorbeck**'s remarkable campaign in East Africa, were short lived. German officers also provided much command and staff support to the Turkish army throughout the war.

GERMAN EAST AFRICA, OPERATIONS IN, 1914–18

The long and costly British campaign against German East Africa began in 1914 with a humiliating defeat. An expeditionary force, under the command of Major-General Aitken, had been despatched from India and assembled in British East Africa. In response to German raids on the Mombasa–Kisumu railway, the British abandoned their defensive strategy and launched an attack on the small port of Tanga. For reasons best known to itself, the Royal Navy gave the enemy warning of the attack and after three days the Indian army was compelled to re-embark. The invasion force of 8,000 had suffered 800 casualties, with the much smaller German contingent losing very few. Aitken was replaced by Major-General Wapshire and the War Office assumed direct control of operations.

At the beginning of the war, the entire German colony, which was about the same size as France, had a garrison of only 260 Europeans and some 2,500 Askaris (African soldiers); it was later expanded to a maximum of 3,000 Germans and 11,000 Askaris. They were commanded by **Colonel** (later General) **Paul von Lettow-Vorbeck**, who sought to occupy as many Allied troops as possible in a campaign that was to last until the end of the war. Vorbeck, who proved to be an outstanding guerrilla fighter, responded to the assault on Tanga with a series of successful raids across a wide area, and the adjoining territories of the Belgian Congo and Rhodesia as well as British East Africa came under attack early in 1915.

Britain was in fact able to achieve more at sea than she did on land during 1915. The German light cruiser *Königsberg*, which had been stationed at Dar-es-Salaam at the beginning of the war, was sunk by two British monitors in the Rufiji river delta in July 1915. (Vorbeck did, however, manage to remove the ship's 4.1-inch guns, giving him his only artillery pieces of the campaign.) The Germans' Lake Tanganyika fleet, which consisted of three river boats, was also destroyed by the British, in October 1915; their boats on Lake Victoria and Lake Nyasa had already suffered the same fate.

It was not until 1916 that the prospect of Allied offensive action against German East Africa materialised: additional forces arrived from South Africa and **General Jan Smuts**, who had a distinguished combat record in the South African war, was placed

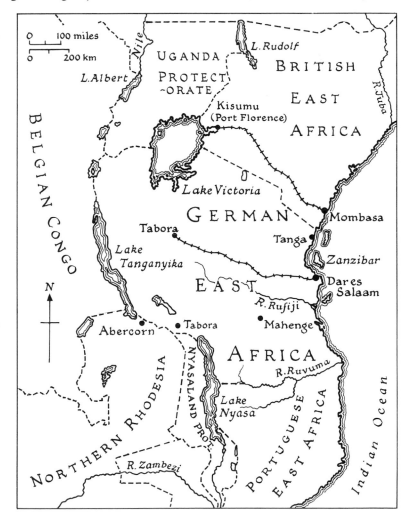

in command. At their peak, British forces amounted to 350,000 men, of whom about 200,000 were porters. In the spring of 1916, the main force, under Smuts, advanced due south through the bush, while the Belgians, who had agreed to co-operate fully in the action, marched south-east from the Congo on Tabora. From Nyasaland a small colonial force moved north-east, eventually meeting the main army from the north. Driving forward in several columns Smuts tried to surround his opponents, but Vorbeck and his troops were highly mobile and were always able to slip away. Vorbeck was, however, unable to prevent the steady British advance and by September 1916 Dar-es-Salaam and the whole of the north of the country had been taken.

East Africa, 1917: Indian troops leaving Dar-es-Salaam for the front by boat

Early in 1917 Smuts departed, but once the rainy season was over the advance continued under his successors. The South Africans were not acclimatised to the harsh environment of East Africa and were badly affected by the climate and disease, with thousands dying during the protracted campaign. By this time most of the white South African troops had been replaced by African troops who were better able to survive there. As a result greater progress was made and at Mahenge late in November Major-General van Deventer, the new South African commander, captured the main German force of 5,000 men under Tafel, the second-in-command. The two other German forces, including Vorbeck's, managed to escape south, crossing the border into Portuguese East Africa on 25 November 1917, where they were pursued by local troops.

Moving about the colony, they lived off the land and carried out guerrilla raids, remaining there until 28 September 1918. Vorbeck then travelled north again, moving round the head of Lake Nyasa into Northern Rhodesia, with the eventual aim of crossing Africa to reach Portuguese Angola. However, he surrendered at Abercorn on 23 November when he received delayed news about the Armistice.

The undefeated expert in bush warfare, Vorbeck's skill and determination had forced the Allies to devote enormous resources to an arduous and unprofitable campaign. Some 80,000 British and African soldiers and auxiliary troops were killed and much of the military strength of South Africa had been committed there.

GERMAN NAVY

In August 1914, the German navy was the world's second largest, with 17 capital ships to Britain's 27. During the previous 20 years it had been transformed from a minor coastal defence force under the direction of **Admiral von Tirpitz**, 'the father of the German navy', into a powerful opponent of the Royal Navy. His aim of breaking Britain's 'Two Power standard' became more realistic with the appearance of the *Dreadnought* in 1906 which rendered all

existing battleships obsolete and forced all naval powers, including Britain, to start from scratch.

German battleship design in the pre-war period proved to be superior to the British in many respects, particularly in terms of protection, gunnery and machinery. Weight of numbers meant, however, that the German navy's surface operations outside the waters of northern Europe were quickly brought to an end during the first few months of the war. With the notable exception of the dramatic escape of the *Goeben* and *Breslau* across the Mediterranean to Turkey, where they played a major role in bringing her into the war, almost all her cruisers and **commerce raiders** were efficiently intercepted by the Royal Navy.

British policy throughout the war was to confine the German navy's principal fleet – the **High Seas Fleet** – to the North Sea by means of a distant blockade. Organised in three battle squadrons, with a separate battlecruiser squadron, the German navy had 15 dreadnoughts, four battlecruisers, 32 pre-dreadnoughts, nine armoured cruisers, 10 light cruisers, and 88 destroyer/torpedo boats. German policy on the use of this fleet was extremely cautious: the **Kaiser**, who took a special interest in naval matters, had decided that it should not be risked unnecessarily. He expected the land war in Europe to be over quickly and he wanted to use the intact fleet as a lever in peace negotiations with the Allies.

Although this expectation soon proved to be unrealistic, restrictions on the use of the fleet continued indefinitely. Limited operations in the North Sea were, however, authorised after the Battle of Heligoland Bight (28 August 1914), in an effort to reduce the **Grand Fleet**'s superiority. The High Seas Fleet would try to engage individual squadrons and only when parity between the two fleets had been achieved would a final engagement between opposing battleships be contemplated. Several towns on the east coast of Britian were bombarded in November/ December 1914, but all operations were suspended after the narrow German escape at the **Battle of the Dogger Bank** (24 January 1915). Dreadnoughts were also used on occasion against the Russian navy in the Baltic, where German operations were sometimes affected by British submarine patrols.

With **Scheer**'s appointment as commander of the High Seas Fleet in January 1916, a more aggressive policy was pursued, leading to the **Battle of Jutland** (May 1916) when the main fleets of Britain and Germany clashed. Jutland confirmed British dominance of the North Sea and as a result the High Seas Fleet only ventured into the North Sea on three further occasions before the end of the war. Its efficiency was undermined by the transfer of personnel to the expanding U-boat fleet and by mutiny. Unrest in 1917 was followed by open mutiny in October 1918, in response to Scheer's plans for a 'death ride' into the North Sea, where a final battle with the Grand Fleet would take place. The sailors' action marked the demise of the High Seas Fleet as a fighting force.

After Jutland the German navy turned increasingly to the submarine as the means of defeating England by cutting off her supplies. The first U-boat campaign in 1915 had been ended for political reasons – primarily the fear of American intervention – and the reintroduction of unrestricted submarine warfare in February 1917 was preceded by a long struggle between **Bethmann Hollweg**, the Chancellor, and the German Admiralty. The U-boat war, which resulted in heavy Allied shipping losses, might have succeeded had it not been for the Royal Navy's belated adoption of the **convoy system**, which had reduced losses to manageable levels by the end of the year.

At the end of the war all 160 German submarines were surrendered and transferred to Britain. The Armistice also provided for the surrender of the High Seas Fleet to the Royal Navy on 21 November 1918 and its internment at Scapa Flow. It was scuttled there on 21 June 1919, the final act of the wartime German navy.

GLISENTI PISTOL

Adopted by the Italian army in 1910, this automatic pistol was a standard type used throughout the First World War. With some external similarities to the **Luger Pistol**, the Glisenti was a locked breech type which fired 9mm cartridges. A detachable magazine contained seven rounds of ammunition. Although the design proved to be reliable in service, it never enjoyed great popularity: it was not very strong and the cartridge was less powerful than its Parabellum equivalent.

GOEBEN

Few warships can have had as much impact on the course of modern history as the German battlecruiser *Goeben*, which was the instrument that brought Turkey into the First World War. An enlarged version of the *Von Der Tann*, with a displacement of 23,000 tons, *Goeben* and her sister ship *Moltke* had ten 11-inch guns, protection approaching battleship standards and a crew of just over 1,000. *Goeben* was completed in 1912 and at the outbreak of war was stationed in the Mediterranean, under the command of **Admiral Souchon**. Her first wartime task, with the light cruiser *Breslau*, was to disrupt the flow of troops to France by shelling the Algerian ports of Bône and Philippeville on 4 August 1914.

Goeben's reputation of being the fastest warship in the Mediterranean was confirmed soon afterwards when she eluded the British battlecruisers *Indomitable* and *Indefatigable* which had given chase. After coaling at Messina in neutral Italy, *Goeben* headed for Constantinople, hoping that Turkey, which also enjoyed the same non-combatant status, would co-operate and make good her escape from the powerful British naval presence. The Royal Navy failed to intercept the ships as they steamed eastwards. **Rear Admiral Troubridge**, commanding a squadron of four cruisers, was in a position to bring *Goeben* and *Breslau* to action off the western coast of Greece but did not do so. Unhelpful Admiralty orders required him to avoid being drawn into battle with a force of superior strength and he was subsequently forced to defend his rigid adherence to them at a famous court-martial.

On their arrival at Constantinople on 11 August, the two ships were nominally transferred to Turkey, although they retained their German crews and commander. As Turkey was still neutral, *Goeben*, renamed *Yavuz Sultan Selim*, lay idle for some time, but on 29 October Admiral Souchon carried out a surprise raid on the Russian fleet at Sebastopol. From the German point of view the action produced a handsome reward as Turkey was forced to declare war on the Allied powers.

Goeben was based at Constantinople for the remainder of the war and was used from time to time against the Russian Black Sea Fleet and in the Mediterranean. On the way to a sortie against the

The dramatic escape of the German battlecruiser Goeben *to Constantinople greatly embarrassed the Royal Navy and helped to bring Turkey into the war*

British at Mudros in January 1918, both ships were hit by mines and *Goeben* ran aground at Nagara Point. During the week she was stranded there, British aircraft dropped 500 bombs, the heaviest bombing suffered by any ship during the war. However, only two hits were scored and it was possible for her to be towed away. Completely repaired and overhauled, she remained in the Turkish navy until she was decommissioned in 1960.

GOERING, HERMANN, 1893–1946

The creator of the Luftwaffe and Nazi leader was an air ace of the Great War, scoring a total of 22 victories. Goering succeeded **von Richthofen** as commander of his famous fighter squadron in July 1918 and was awarded the Pour le Mérite and several other decorations for his distinguished service.

GOLTZ, COLMAR, BARON VON DER, 1843–1916

German field marshal and prolific military writer who was ordered to Constantinople as military adviser to the Sultan, in November 1914. He was an advocate of an 'Oriental solution' to the war, which would involve a German thrust against the British in India, although his own operational experiences were confined to Mesopotamia. Appointed to the command of the Turkish Sixth Army, he laid siege to British forces under **Sir Charles Townshend** at **Kut**, in December 1915. Goltz died in Baghdad, possibly of cholera, some 10 days before the surrender of the British garrison on 29 April 1916.

GOLTZ, GENERAL RUDIGER, COUNT VON DER, 1865–1946

Commander of a German expeditionary force that landed at Hango in Finland in April 1918, Goltz and his 12,000 men captured Helsinki a few days later along with some 20,000 Russian troops. Goltz had secured both his objectives: acquiring extra territory and increasing pressure on the new Russian government. He remained in Finland until the Germans evacuated it at the end of the war.

GORLICE-TARNOW OFFENSIVE, 1 May–19 September 1915

In an attempt to strike a decisive blow against the Russians, **Falkenhayn**, German Chief of Staff, made plans for a massive assault on the Gorlice-Tarnow sector, south-east of Cracow. If successful it would finally dislodge the Russians from the Carpathians and save Austria. **Hindenburg**, Eastern Front commander, had proposed a more ambitious alternative plan for a breakthrough from East Prussia, but it had been rejected by the **Kaiser** on Falkenhayn's advice.

Preparations began in April 1915, when a new

German Eleventh Army (**Mackensen**), composed of eight divisions, was transferred there from the Western Front; to its left was the Austrian Fourth Army (**Archduke Joseph-Ferdinand**) which, under higher German command, was also to play a major role in the operation. This sector was thinly defended by the Russian Third Army (Dimitriev), which had about 56,000 men.

German troops help to liberate Russian occupied Galicia during the Gorlice–Tarnow offensive, which resulted in large territorial gains for the Central powers

The offensive, under Mackensen's overall command, began on 1 May with a massive four-hour artillery bombardment. Some 950 German guns fired 700,000 shells at the Russian lines in an attack which took the enemy by surprise. Their defences were shattered and there was hardly any response from the Russian artillery. Mackensen moved forward on a 28-mile front and by the end of the second day the enemy line had collapsed. Some 140,000 Russian prisoners were taken and the Russian Third Army was almost destroyed as an effective fighting force.

In order to keep their remaining forces intact and to avoid encirclement the Russians maintained an orderly withdrawal eastwards. The Germans advanced 95 miles in two weeks, continually expanding their front. Towards the end of May, the Russians fought delaying actions on the San and on the Dniester, inflicting serious casualties on the advancing German forces. However, they lacked sufficient heavy artillery and other resources to be able to stop them for long. Przemysl was evacuated on 3 June and Lemberg, the capital of Galicia, fell on the 22nd; the Dniester was crossed on 23–27 June.

The Germans, who now received substantial reinforcements, changed direction at this point, turning north towards Brest-Litovsk, some 120 miles east of Warsaw; it was taken on 25 August. As the Russians continued to retreat, the Polish capital became increasingly isolated. The German Twelfth Army (**Gallwitz**), which was positioned behind the southern frontiers of East Prussia, seized the opportunity to attack towards the south-east. Warsaw fell on 4–5 August but again the Russians avoided encirclement. Their retreat speeded up as they tried to establish a new, defensible front line that ran from north to south. In an attempt to slow down the German advance a large garrison was retained in the huge fortress of Nova-Georgievsk, but it fell within three weeks.

During September, fighting intensified on the two wings. The Austrians secured little beyond the capture of Lutsk, but far to the north Hindenburg made more progress. Kovno and then Vilna (19 September) were seized, but a decisive victory eluded the Germans.

The whole operation now finally came to an end as the onset of bad weather helped the Russian army to halt the German advance. A new front line was established some 180 miles east of Warsaw; it now ran for 600 miles from Lithuania on the Baltic, east of the Pripet Marshes, down to the Rumanian border. The Russians had lost Galicia and Poland – a valuable political pawn – as well as a million men killed and another million taken prisoner. Vast areas of valuable agricultural land were now in enemy hands. However, many more had managed to escape the German trap as the Russian army had retreated in good order and avoided envelopment. On 8 September, in the wake of this disaster, **Nicholas II** removed **Grand Duke Nicholas** and took personal command of the Russian army.

GOTHA GIV & GV

The Gotha GIV and GV were standard German bombers that gained notoriety as the principal instruments of the bombing raids on the United Kingdom in 1917–18. Their impact was such that the British applied the name Gotha indiscriminately to any large German aircraft. The GIV, which entered service in 1917, was the first major production model, a development of the GII, which had appeared the year before. The earlier machine, which was a three-bay biplane with twin 220hp Benz units and two machine-guns, was quickly withdrawn from service (on the Balkan Front) after engine problems. Its replacement, the GIII, which was only produced in small quantities, had structural improvements as well as new 260hp Mercedes D IVa engines and an additional machine-gun.

The Gotha GIV, a giant three-bay biplane with a wingspan of nearly 78 feet, retained the same engines as its predecessor, giving it a maximum speed of 88m.p.h. and a range of just over 300 miles. Although it did not greatly differ from the GIII, there was an important change in its defensive capabilities: a tunnel was incorporated in the bottom of the fuselage, enabling the rear gunner to cover the bomber's blind spots by firing downwards and to the rear. Operated by a crew of three, the GIV was normally armed with three machine-guns and could accommodate a bomb load of between 300 and 500kg on external racks; six 50kg bombs were usually carried on the daylight raids on England.

The GV, which arrived in August 1917, had a number of relatively minor improvements, including the repositioning of the fuel tanks, and, in a slightly later variant, a biplane tail assembly. The last major Gotha G-type was produced in relatively small numbers, but 230 examples of the GIV were manufactured.

First appearing at at time when the **Zeppelin**'s useful life as a raider had ended, the GIV provided the means to continue bombing attacks on England. By May 1917, 30 GIVs had been allocated to *Bombengeschwader* 3, based at St Denis Westrem and Gontrode.

Gotha GV: Germany's principal instrument in the strategic bombing campaign against England, 1917–18

Day bombing of southern England then began. The first Gotha raid on London occurred on 13 June 1917. Initially the aircraft were relatively secure from attack and the British government was forced to withdraw several fighter squadrons from France in order to meet public concern about the raids, although relatively little serious damage had in fact been done. It was not, however, until an effective warning system was devised and faster climbing aircraft such as the **SE5A** were available that the crews of the well-defended Gothas had much to worry about. In response to better air defences the bombers were confined to night operations from September and by May 1918, when losses reached unacceptable levels, they were abandoned altogether. During this period *Bombengeschwader* 3 had carried out 22 raids and dropped nearly 85,000kg of bombs; some 61 Gothas had been lost, of which as many as 37 were due to accidents. (The Gotha's structure was relatively fragile and it had a tendency to nose over on landing.) More of the 24 Allied hits were attributable to anti-aircraft fire than to aerial combat. After operations against Britain ended, the Gothas were concentrated against French targets for the remainder of the war.

GOTHA WD14

The WD14 was a twin-engined torpedo attack aircraft which entered service with the German navy in 1917, operating primarily from North Sea bases. It was one of a series of twin-float seaplanes produced by Gotha, whose reputation was based on its twin-engined bombers. Most of its seaplane models were produced in prototype form, the WD14 being the only one manufactured in quantity: a total of 69 examples were built during 1917–18. Powered by two 200hp Benz Bz IV engines, the WD14 had three-bay wings, a rectangular fuselage and a tailplane with twin fins and horn balanced rudders. It had a maximum speed of 84m.p.h. and a duration of eight hours. A single torpedo was carried underneath the fuselage; it was released from the observer's front cockpit, where a **Parabellum machine-gun** was installed. The pilot was positioned under the wings and to the rear was a gunner's cockpit with a second Parabellum.

The WD14, which was underpowered when carrying its torpedo, achieved little in its intended role: successful launches proved to be very difficult to execute and depended in part on long and expensive training for the crew. When preparing to attack engine speed was reduced and the WD14 was normally a relatively easy target for a ship's guns. As the Allies' defensive tactics were perfected losses mounted and by 1918 torpedo attacks had been abandoned altogether by the Germans. Some WD14s were also used unsuccessfully as minelayers, but most remaining examples were converted for long-range reconnaissance work.

GOUGH, GENERAL SIR HUBERT, 1870–1963

A leading participant in the Curragh mutiny of 1914, Gough was a divisional commander in France in 1914–15. Early in 1916, he was appointed to the command of I Army Corps. He fought the **First Battle of the Somme** as the head of the new Fifth Army, and at 44 was easily the youngest army commander in the British army. Already widely unpopular in the army because of his arrogant manner, he also gained a reputation for being 'inexact in detail and slipshod in method'. His disregard for the lives of the soldiers under his command was also notorious, although his forces made the biggest gains at the Somme.

He was chosen by **Haig** to lead the attack at the **Third Battle of Ypres** in July 1917, because his impetuousity and 'cavalry spirit' were the qualities that seemed to be needed. However, in August, after his first two attacks had produced nothing except large casualties, **Plumer**'s Second Army was ordered to take over the main thrust. Some of the blame for the initial failures was attributed to poor staff work and to Gough's carelessness.

The final chapter in Gough's unhappy wartime career came on 21 March 1918, when **Ludendorff**'s offensive broke his Fifth Army on the Somme sector and he was forced to retreat. Although his army had been seriously depleted in the months before the attack, Gough received all the official blame for the defeat and he was removed from his command.

Gough visits the front with King Albert, shortly before Third Ypres, July 1917, exposed his limitations as a commander

GOURAUD, GENERAL HENRI, 1867–1946

Promoted general just before the war, Gouraud commanded a division in the Argonne before he was sent to **Gallipoli** as head of the French contingent. He was one of the heroes of the expedition and was badly wounded by a shell. In December 1915, he was appointed to the command of the Fourth Army in Champagne, but was transferred to take **Marshal Lyautey**'s place in Morocco when the latter became Minister of War. In 1918, Gouraud returned to the Fourth Army and played an important role in the **Second Battle of the Marne**, halting the German offensive east of Reims (15 July 1918). He successfully implemented **Foch**'s new manoeuvre of defence in depth, although it had apparently taken seven days to persuade him to adopt it. Gouraud was the 'most chivalrous of French generals, who felt any retreat like a personal stain'.

GRAND FLEET

The principal British fleet of the First World War.
See the **Royal Navy**.

GREIF

This German **commerce raider**, the former merchant vessel *Guben*, with a displacement of 4,963 tons, had a very limited operational life. On 29 February 1916, less than a month after she had been commissioned, she was intercepted by the British **armed merchant cruiser** *Alcantara* while operating in the North Sea. The two ships exchanged fire at short range and both began to sink. *Greif*'s fate was sealed by three vessels which had been summoned by *Alcantara*.

GRENADES

Relatively little used during the 19th century, the grenade was revived during the Russo-Japanese War, but came into its own in the trenches of the First World War. Production difficulties in 1914–15 meant that front line troops in France, who quickly recognised the value of grenades, had to produce their own crude models. Improvised missiles, using jam or tobacco tins, were widespread; sometimes they were wired to a wooden handle for greater stability. Soon, however, there was no shortage of officially approved

A German soldier practises throwing a stick grenade

designs: mass production began in 1915, and millions of grenades were produced every week.

Each army adopted several variants. The standard British anti-personnel grenade was the Mills bomb, which appeared in five versions and remained in use throughout the war. The British army also used the stick grenade, but it was the Germans who adopted it as their standard design.

The *Steilhandgranate* consisted of a steel canister filled with explosive, which was attached to the top of a short handle. A friction igniter, operated by a length of string, activated a delay fuse. More unusual was the French 'bracelet' grenade, which had a hand-held leather leash connected to the primer. As the grenade was thrown, the leash pulled out a friction wire, thereby igniting the time fuse.

Rifle grenades as well as hand-thrown designs were also extensively used: Hale's grenade was in fact employed by both the British and German armies until it was superseded by improved designs late in 1917. Apart from facilitating much development work on anti-personnel grenades, the First World War also produced completely new types. The first anti-tank grenades appeared during the war, as did new gas, smoke and illuminating versions.

GREY, EDWARD, VISCOUNT, 1862–1933

British Foreign Secretary from 1905 to 1916, Grey retained the office longer than anyone else. During that period he built on the Triple Entente with France and Russia in response to the growing threat from Germany and her allies. His attempts to prevent war in 1914 were unsuccessful, with his proposal for a European Conference following the assassination at **Sarajevo** being rejected. Once all hope of a peaceful solution had gone, Grey was an important influence in a divided Cabinet, arguing strongly for British military intervention in support of Belgium.

Grey's wartime record is mixed: he gave priority to preserving good relations with the United States, but his diplomatic interventions in the Balkans and his negotiations over the **Treaty of London**, which gave generous concessions to Italy, were less successful. His support for an American plan to convene a European conference in 1916 in a bid to end the war found little backing among his Cabinet colleagues, who sought the military defeat of Britain's enemies. In December 1916, on **Lloyd George**'s accession to power, he left the government and retired from political life. He did, however, go to Washington in 1919–20 in an attempt to resolve the American political dispute over the **Treaty of Versailles**.

GRIGOROVICH, ADMIRAL IVAN, 1853–1930

Russia's Minister of the Navy during the First World War, Admiral Grigorovich, who served with distinction during the Russo-Japanese War, held office from 1911 until the March Revolution. It was a period of service unequalled by any of his ministerial colleagues and a tribute to his political and administrative skills. Before 1914, he gave priority to the development of the Baltic Fleet and secured approval for a major shipbuilding programme. During the war he was an effective advocate of naval interests within the government, although his role was complicated by the navy's operational subordination to the army High Command.

GROENER, GENERAL WILHELM, 1867–1939

An experienced German staff officer, Groener headed the railway section of the General Staff when the army was mobilised for war in August 1914. He retained this responsibility until mid-1916, when he was briefly involved in arrangements for the wartime supply of food. More important, he established, in co-operation with the trade unions, a body which organised civilian manpower for the war effort. Brief periods of command on both main fronts preceded his appointment, in March 1918, as chief of staff of Army Group Eichhorn at Kiev.

General Groener succeeded **Ludendorff** as deputy chief of the General Staff at the end of October 1918, when a general collapse of the Central Powers seemed imminent. By 6 November, he was urging the government to seek an immediate armistice and it was Groener who informed the **Kaiser** that the outbreak of revolution in Germany could not be suppressed by the army. Told that the army no longer supported him, the Kaiser decided to abdicate.

Groener concluded an agreement with the new chancellor, Ebert, which provided the basis for the army's support for the new republic. He concluded his wartime work by managing the demobilisation of the German army.

Succeeding Ludendorff in October 1918, General Groener was a distinguished staff officer who helped to bring the war to an end

GUILLAUMAT, GENERAL MARIE, 1863–1940

With wide experience in French colonial wars, Guillaumat rose rapidly during the war from the command of a division to head of the Second Army at the end of 1916. He established his reputation as a leading French general at **Verdun**, recapturing Hill 304 and Morte Homme in August 1916, the first of **Pétain**'s offensives during the battle. In December 1917, he replaced **Sarrail** as commander-in-chief of the Allied army at **Salonika** and made preparations for a new offensive on the Balkan front. Relations with the Allies had been undermined by his predecessor

and Guillaumat was successful in improving them.

Recalled to France in June 1918, when the Germans threatened Paris, he was appointed military governor of the capital. He was regarded as a possible successor to Pétain if the latter were forced to resign over the crisis. When the danger had passed, Guillaumat joined the Supreme War Council, where he was successful in securing Allied agreement to a major new offensive in the Balkans. He returned to the Western Front in October 1918, commanding the Fifth Army as it advanced through the Ardennes.

GUMBINNEN, BATTLE OF, 20 August 1914

The war on the Eastern Front began on 17 August 1914 when the Russians invaded East Prussia with their First Army – 200,000 men under the command

of **General von Rennenkampf**. Opposing them were 150,000 men of the German Eighth Army, under **General von Prittwitz**, who covered the front from the Baltic coast to Frankenau and were based at Königsberg (Kaliningrad). Their role, according to the modified **Schlieffen Plan**, was one of defence and delay. As the Russians advanced on a 35-mile front, the two armies met on the first day at Stallupönen, a village five miles inside the frontier. The Prussian I Corps (General Hermann von François) launched a strong spoiling attack against Rennenkampf's centre and forced the invading army back to the border, with the loss of 3,000 men. General von François himself then withdrew to Gumbinnen (Gusev), 10 miles to the west.

Here Prittwitz planned a counter-attack against Rennenkampf, whose forces had soon started moving slowly forward again. François, on the German left, launched the attack in front of Gumbinnen at dawn on 20 August, pushing back the Russian right wing, which suffered heavy losses, for about five miles. However, in the centre, where the attack began four hours later, at 8.00 a.m., **General Mackensen**'s XVII Corps found progress much more difficult to achieve. The Russians had, of course, already been alerted by the earlier attack to the north and launched a heavy artillery bombardment, quickly checking the German advance in the centre. The corps commanded by Mackensen, 'one of the most over-advertised generals of the war', was driven back over 15 miles in a disorderly retreat.

On the southern flank, **General Otto von Below** now had little option but to withdraw, even though the fighting in this sector had only just begun. With the German centre and right in retreat, the position of the more successful von François was also dangerously exposed and he too was forced to abandon his gains before the end of the day.

The victorious Russians, who had taken 6,000 prisoners, did not pursue their enemy, but Prittwitz, in a state of panic after hearing of the German disaster, decided to pull back behind the Vistula River, abandoning East Prussia to the enemy. His alarm was reinforced by the advance of the Russian Second Army (**General Samsonov**) which, after a delayed start, was moving towards him from the south on a 50-mile front. Prittwitz's plans were completely unacceptable to the High Command, which wished to preserve the East Prussian front at all costs, and he was dismissed. He was replaced by the formidable combination of **Hindenburg**, who was brought out of retirement to command the Eighth Army, and **Ludendorff**, who became chief of staff. Their joint skills soon produced a dramatic reversal of German fortunes.

GUN CARRIER, MARK I

The difficulty of moving medium artillery across the shelled ground of the Western Front prompted the development of a gun-carrying tank. Mechanically it was based on the British Mark I tank, although it was very different in appearance: a 60-pdr gun or 6-inch howitzer, which was winched up a ramp, was mounted at the front, with a small armoured cab on each side. These housed the driver and brakesman, while a third box at the rear accommodated the engine and the rest of the crew. The gun carrier also differed from the Mark I tank in not being fitted with overall tracks. No more than 48 of these machines were produced and they entered service in 1917. Although they were used effectively in surprise night attacks from unexpected locations, their main function on the Western Front was to transport ammunition and supplies, carrying a load that would otherwise have required the services of 300 men.

GURKO, GENERAL VASILY, 1864–1937

Russian cavalry general who commanded the VI Army Corps in the Carpathians from January 1915, Gurko's wartime career progressed rapidly. In the summer of 1916, he was given the task of restoring the Guard

Army, the élite force that had suffered heavy losses near Kovel. Soon afterwards he was appointed chief of staff, temporarily replacing **General Alekseev**, who was ill. After the March Revolution Gurko was appointed to the command of the Western Front (part of the old North-Western Front) but disagreements with the Provisional Government led to his departure from the army in June 1917.

GUYNEMER, GEORGES, 1894–1917

At the time of his death in September 1917, at the age of 22, Guynemer was the highest scoring French ace. With 54 hits to his credit, he was noted for his aggression and lack of concern for his own safety. He also had great determination, refusing several opportunities to retire even when physically and mentally exhausted. He enjoyed great personal popularity amongst the French public and was 'a symbol of France's suffering during the 'Grand Guerre'. Guynemer, a frail and sickly youth, joined the Aviation Militaire as a mechanic in 1914 and qualified as a pilot during the following year. He was posted to the *Cigognes* group (*Escadrille MS3*), and at first flew **Morane Saulnier** scouts from Vauciennes.

His first confirmed victory was on 19 July 1915 and he rapidly added to his total during 666 flying hours, using **Nieuport 11**s and later the **Spad VII**, in which he achieved most of his successes. His total included one hat-trick and six doubles. Like the British ace **Albert Ball** he favoured the frontal attack, striking at the aircraft's most vulnerable areas. It was obviously much more dangerous than more conventional air fighting tactics and Guynemer was shot down seven times. The end came on 11 September 1917 when he failed to return from a flight over Poelcapelle; neither his body nor his aircraft was found and it was never established whether he had in fact been shot down, as the Germans subsequently claimed.

Guynemer's aggressive tactics helped to bring his distinguished career as a fighter ace to a premature end

HAIG, FIELD MARSHAL SIR DOUGLAS, 1ST EARL, 1861–1928

Commander-in-chief of the British Expeditionary Force in France, 1915–18, Field Marshal Earl Haig's tactics on the Western Front have always been the subject of controversy. Service in the Sudan, 1897, and in the South African War helped to establish his professional reputation, although his rapid promotion was also assisted by patronage. In 1906, he was recalled from India, where he had been Inspector General of Cavalry, to advise Richard Haldane, the new Liberal Secretary for War, on his programme of army reform. After a further period in India, Haig returned to England in 1912 on his appointment to the command of the army corps at Aldershot that would, if war was declared, become I Corps in the expeditionary force.

The next two years were spent preparing for war and, in August 1914, Haig, a lieutenant-general, led his highly trained troops to France. His approach was,

Commander of the British Expeditionary Force, 1915–18, Haig will always be associated with the costly war of attrition that has permanently tarnished his reputation

however, orthodox and unimaginative and he was slow to adapt to the changing nature of war. In 1914, for example, he viewed the machine-gun as a 'much overrated weapon'.

Haig himself had serious reservations about the competence of the British commander-in-chief, **Sir John French**, and was highly critical of the French operational plan to which they were required to adhere.

During the first phase of the war, Haig was little more than a 'competent corps commander', and 'no particular distinction came his way'. I Corps took the lead as the Allies advanced north from the Marne, but it was at the **First Battle of Ypres** (20 October–22 November 1914) that Haig and his troops first disginguished themselves. The British played the leading role in the battle, and Haig organised the defence with great skill against an enemy far superior in numbers. He maintained the morale of I Corps in these unpromising circumstances and deployed his limited reserves to great effect, stabilising the line by 11 November.

He was soon promoted to full general and on the reorganisation of BEF as two armies, he was appointed to the command of the First Army. British offensive operations in 1915 – **Neuve Chapelle**, Aubers Ridge, Festubert and **Artois-Loos** – were concentrated in the sector held by Haig. Sir John French's conduct of these operations was widely criticised and Haig may have contributed to his downfall in December 1915: a correspondent with King George V about the war in France, he regularly raised doubts about French's competence.

Haig succeeded French as commander-in-chief in December 1915 and retained the post until the end of the war. It was always his view that the war could only be won by the military defeat of Germany on the Western Front, the secondary operations elsewhere being no more than wasteful sideshows. Political considerations, including the need to support France, and his belief in the possibility of an early victory produced an offensive strategy that offered the prospect of a breakthrough. However, these hopes were destroyed at three major engagements – **the Somme**, **Arras** and **Third Ypres** – which developed into the prolonged battles of attrition that will always be associated with Haig's name. Third Ypres was, of course, notorious for the enormous loss of life and the marginal gains in territory associated with it.

His willingness to pursue these offensives, even at the cost of destroying his own forces more quickly than those of the enemy, convinced **Lloyd George** that Haig ought to be removed. However, this did not prove to be politically possible and the prime minister was forced to constrain him by reducing the size of the BEF early in 1918 and by agreeing to the appointment of **Foch** as generalissimo. Haig himself had in fact recognised the need for the coordination of the Allied armies on the Western Front after **Ludendorff**'s March offensive and had suggested Foch for the task.

Working closely with the new supreme commander, Haig spent the months May–June 1918 successfully rebuilding the British army. After Foch's counter-stroke at the **Second Battle of the Marne**, the Allies seized the initiative and Haig's forces led the attack. The **Battle of Amiens** was the first and most remarkable of his nine victories in the period leading to the Armistice. It was the most successful period of Haig's whole career, but it could never erase the memory of the costly offensives of 1917–18 that seemed to achieve so little.

HALBERSTADT CV

This two-seat German biplane was used for long distance photographic reconnaissance work at high altitudes from the summer of 1918 until the Armistice. A development of the Halberstadt CIII of 1917, its two-bay, heavily staggered wings were of very wide span and it had a disproportionately short fuselage, which resembled that used in the **Halberstadt CLIV**. The CV was powered by the 220 hp Benz Bz IV, a high compression engine which produced a maximum speed of 103m.p.h. and excellent performance at high altitude. Standard C-type armament was fitted: a ring-mounted **Parabellum gun** in the rear cockpit (the CLIV's rather uncommon communal accommodation was not retained) and a synchronised Spandau machine-gun at the front. Cameras were used through a gap in the floor and radio equipment was also often carried.

Operating with the **Rumpler CVII**, the Halberstadt CV made a valuable contribution to the collection of photographic intelligence on the advancing Allied armies in the difficult circumstances of the last few months of the war, when there was increasing pressure from their fighters. The aircraft was produced in large numbers by the Halberstadter Flugzeug-Werke and by at least three subcontractors.

HALBERSTADT CLII & CLIV

The first CL-type aircraft to be produced in Germany was the Halberstadt CLII, a compact two-seat, single-bay biplane of neat appearance. Strongly constructed, it had staggered wings and a sharply tapered fuselage. The crew shared a single long cockpit, with the observer's **Parabellum machine-gun** on an elevated ring mounting at the rear. Forward armament consisted of one or two synchronised Spandau machine-guns. Stick grenades or mortars were carried on external racks when the aircraft was used for ground attack. It was powered by the 160hp Mercedes D III engine which gave a maximum speed of 103m.p.h. at 5,000m and the ability to climb to that altitude in about 39 minutes.

The CLII entered service in the summer of 1917, equipping the *Schützstaffeln* (Protection Flights) as two-seater fighter escorts. It was, however, as a ground attack aircraft that the CLII made its most important military contribution. Amongst its first successful operations was the attack on British troops crossing the Somme bridges on 6 September 1917, when maximum disruption was created at the most vulnerable point. The CLII also made a considerable contribution to the succssful German counter-offensive during the **Battle of Cambrai** on 30 November 1917. British forces were unable to respond effectively to these low-flying aircraft which poured machine-gun fire and grenades into the trenches. As a result the CLII's activities had a very damaging effect on enemy morale and appeared in growing numbers on the Western Front. As the ground attack role developed, the *Schlachtstaffeln* (Battle Flights) – the

redesignated Protection Flights – were expanded in preparation for the offensive of March 1918.

To supplement the CLII at this critical point, a new version, the CLIV, was introduced. Powered by the same Mercedes engine, its manoeuvrability was improved as a result of several modifications to the airframe, including a shortened fuselage, revised tail surfaces and repositioning of the wings. After the failure of the German offensive, the Halberstadts were largely confined to a defensive role, supporting their own troops rather than attacking the enemy. They were also used to intercept British bombers and to make night attacks on enemy airfields, as well as acting as escorts.

Halberstadt CLIV fighter escort/attack aircraft

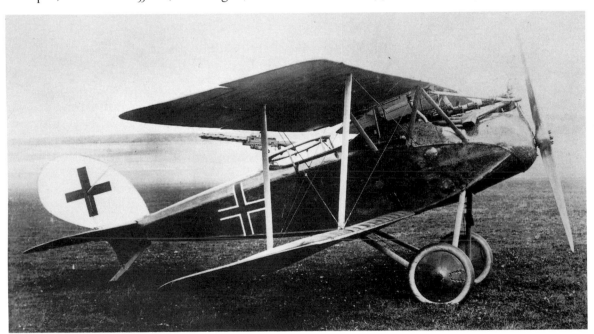

HALBERSTADT D-TYPES

This series of fighting biplanes first appeared on the Western Front early in 1916. Despite appearances to the contrary, this aircraft was of strong construction, with two-bay staggered wings and a triangular profile rudder. It was powered by a 100hp Mercedes D I engine, which gave a maximum speed of 90m.p.h. at

sea level, although some machines, designated DIa, had the 120hp Argus As II engine and a number of minor changes. The pilot had a good view from the cockpit, but a single, synchronised 7.92mm Spandau machine-gun was his only armament. The DII, which entered service in the summer of 1916, was equipped with the 120hp Mercedes D II engine but was otherwise very similar to the DIa. It was followed by the largely unchanged DIII, which reverted to the Argus As II engine and had a neater exhaust manifold. The DII and DIII were the main production models although it is unlikely that many more than 100 were manufactured. The DIV, which had a 150hp Benz Bz engine, and the DV, which was a more streamlined design, were built in very small quantities.

Initially, the Halberstadt fighters were used on the Western Front as escorts and were attached to reconnaissance units. From the autumn of 1916 they were allocated to several of the new *Jagdstaffeln*, where they served alongside the **Fokker DIII** and **DIV** and the superior **Albatros DIII** and **DIV**. Respected by their opponents, the manoeuvrable Halberstadt D-types helped in the struggle to regain air superiority from the Allies, but by the end of 1917, after a short operational life, they were obsolete. They were gradually withdrawn in favour of the new Albatros types, which were faster and better armed. The Halberstadts were retained for a few months longer on the quieter fronts of Macedonia and Palestine.

HALE'S GRENADES

On the outbreak of war, the British army quickly adopted Hale's rifle grenade, a design it had previously ignored. A 4oz charge of explosive was carried in a brass tube that was enclosed in a cast-iron ring; the external casing fragmented when the grenade detonated. A thin steel rod at the base, which was inserted into the barrel of a rifle, acted as a stabilising device, ensuring that the grenade landed nose first and that the fuse was activated. This system did, however, have a major weakness: the firing of grenades distorted the rifle barrel and, as a result, it could not be used for normal shooting. Hale's grenades, which were also used by the German army on the Western Front, remained in service until late in 1917, when improved designs – using the clip-on cup discharger – appeared.

HALL, SIR WILLIAM, 1870–1943

Director of British Naval Intelligence from November 1914 until the end of the war, Hall was an outstanding success, who 'not only exploited to the full every field of intelligence but made the best use of everything that came to hand'. A gunnery expert and former battlecruiser commander, he was generally known as 'Blinker' Hall because of a pronounced facial twitch.

At the centre of his division was the group responsible for deciphering intercepted signals, the main source of information during the war about the German fleet, including the U-boats. Known as Room 40 O.B., it was brought within Hall's control early on in the war and he expanded it considerably, with over 100 specialist staff eventually being employed.

Hall also gave priority to the interception of transatlantic diplomatic signals and had a number of notable successes, including the exposure of the famous **Zimmermann telegram**, which helped to bring the United States into the war, and information about the activities of **Sir Roger Casement**. He also established a network of agents and, in co-operation with the Metropolitan Police, was involved in counter-espionage activities in England. Hall's development of naval intelligence made a significant contribution to the ultimate Allied victory, and he was knighted for his wartime services.

HAMILTON, GENERAL SIR IAN, 1853–1947

General Hamilton's military reputation, established during the South African War and other colonial wars, was destroyed on the beaches of Gallipoli

By 1914, Sir Ian Hamilton's distinguished army career seemed to be drawing to a close. An aide-de-camp to **King George V**, he had been chief of staff to **Lord Kitchener** during the South African War and had served in several earlier colonial wars. He was also a military intellectual who had written on tactics and on the Russo-Japanese War. On the outbreak of the Great War, his services were required as commander of the Central Force, which had responsibility for home defence.

In March 1915, Kitchener ordered him to the **Dardanelles** in command of an Anglo-French military force that was to support the British fleet. It soon became clear to him that 'the Straits are not likely to be forced by battleships' and a full-scale assault by the army was eventually authorised. Hamilton's plans for the **Gallipoli** landings proved to be over-ambitious

and did not take into account the inexperience of his troops or the logistical difficulties involved. There were also serious problems with the organisation of the expeditionary force and a complete lack of security about its intentions. On 25 April, as the operation began, secure positions were established at the two principal landing areas and later slightly enlarged. However, trench warfare soon began and it became clear that there would be no quick victory. Hamilton, who was based on the island of Imbros, was physically separated from his forces: it 'detached him from the kind of overall command he should have exercised but never did'.

Eventually reinforced from England, Hamilton developed a plan for a further landing on Gallipoli, which began at Suvla on 6 August, and an assault by the **Anzacs**. The British commander, Sir Frederick Stopford, failed to exploit his successful landing until it was too late. The main attack by the Anzacs had already been halted and no further progress could be made. For a second time Hamilton was associated with a disastrously unsuccessful operation, poorly conceived and badly executed by inadequate subordinates. While he still remained optimistic and ruled out an evacuation, the British government had lost confidence in him and relieved him of his command on 14 October.

He was replaced by **Sir Charles Monro**, who recommended an immediate withdrawal from the peninsula. Hamilton's reputation was permanently damaged by the costly failure of the Gallipoli expedition and he received no further command during the war. It had become clear to all that he was 'lacking the iron will and dominating personality of a truly great commander'.

HAMPSHIRE

This British armoured cruiser struck a mine and sank off the Orkneys on 5 June 1916 while carrying **Lord Kitchener** and his staff on a mission to Russia. Kitchener was not among the 12 survivors and his body was never recovered. *Hampshire*, which had a

displacement of 10,850 tons and a maximum speed of 22.5 knots, had joined the 2nd Cruiser Squadron, **Grand Fleet**, earlier in the year, and had been present at the **Battle of Jutland**.

HANDLEY PAGE 0/100

Britain's first successful night bomber, designed in response to an Admiralty request for a 'bloody paralyser', appeared in prototype form late in 1915. A large twin-bay biplane, with a wingspan of 100 feet, it was powered by two 266hp Rolls Royce Eagle engines and had a maximum speed of 85m.p.h. and a range of about 700 miles. It was operated by a crew of four, armed with up to five machine-guns; its maximum bomb capacity of just under 2,000lb (in various combinations) was far in excess of other contemporary machines.

The 0/100 entered operational service with the Fifth Naval Wing at Dunkirk on November 1916 and later served with several other RNAS units on the Western Front. Although elaborate security precautions had been taken during its development, the Germans soon acquired a complete picture of the new machine: the third example to be produced landed undamaged at a German airfield because of navigational problems.

Employed on daylight patrols of the Belgian coast until losses were sustained, the 0/100s were then used exclusively for night bombing, concentrating on U-boat bases, airfields, and German industrial targets. Operational use was confined to the Western Front except for two machines that were employed in **Allenby**'s campaign against the Turks in Palestine. Only 46 were built before they were superseded by the **0/400**, but they continued in use until the end of the war, with some partially equipping squadrons of the RAF's Independent Force.

HANDLEY PAGE 0/400

A development of the **0/100**, the new machine was produced in much larger numbers than its predecessor, with about 550 being manufactured in Britain. Externally the 0/400 was almost identical, the main difference being extensive modifications to the fuel system, which included moving the tanks from the nacelle to the fuselage. More powerful engines, including 375hp Rolls Royce Eagle VIIIs or 275hp Sunbeams, were fitted, giving an increased maximum speed of 98m.p.h., but its range remained the same.

There was a slight improvement in the aircraft's bomb-carrying capacity although its defensive armament – up to five .303 **Lewis machine-guns** – was unchanged. A small initial order for the aircraft was increased after **Gotha bombers** started their attacks on southern England.

The 0/400s normally attacked in strength, with 30–40 aircraft in formation, bombing industrial and military targets. It often carried the 1,650lb bomb, the largest in general use by the Allies during the war. Losses were, however, heavy due to accidents and to the effectiveness of German anti-aircraft fire.

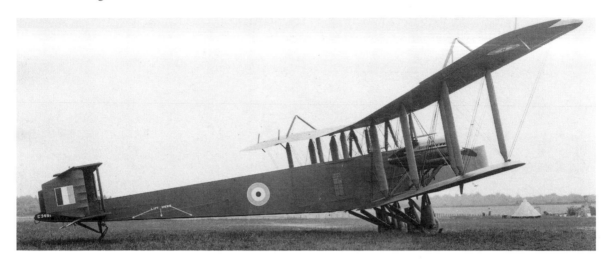

Appearing in significant numbers in the spring of 1918, it became the standard machine of the RAF's Independent Force, equipping seven bomber squadrons in the strategic air offensive against Germany.

The 0/400 was also built under licence in the United States, but only 107 machines had appeared by the Armistice. The aircraft continued in service after the war and some were adapted for civil use.

HANDLEY PAGE V/1500

Appearing in prototype form in May 1918, the V/1500 was the first British four-engined bomber and the largest British aircraft to be produced during the war. It was designed to meet an official specification for a machine capable of reaching Berlin and other long-range targets on German territory. With two tandem pairs of 375hp Rolls Royce Eagle VIII engines, it had a maximum speed of 91m.p.h. and an endur-

ance of 14 hours; up to twenty 250lb bombs could be carried. The first three production machines (from an order for 250) were delivered to No 166 Squadron only days before the Armistice and they had no operational use. If the war had continued the V/1500s would have been used to carry out a more intensive strategic bombing campaign against Germany.

HANKEY, MAURICE, 1st BARON, 1877–1963

An outstanding administrator and public servant, Maurice Hankey helped to reorganise the machinery of British government during the war. Before joining

the secretariat of the Committee of Imperial Defence in 1908, he had served in naval intelligence. He became secretary of the Committee in 1912, a post he held until retirement in 1938. During the war his duties expanded and he assumed responsibility for a number of *ad hoc* bodies, including the Dardanelles Committee. He enjoyed close relations with ministers and often advised them on strategic issues, his views being valued because they were untainted by sectional military interests. In 1917, for example, he pressed successfully, in the face of opposition from the navy, for the adoption of the **convoy system** in the fight against the U-boat.

His most valuable achievement was the creation of the Cabinet Secretariat in 1916. As a result, Cabinet meetings were organised on a business-like basis and a central coordinating and monitoring function was developed. With Hankey as its first head, it made a considerable impact on the efficiency of government and as a result 'the dangers and negligence' inherent in the old system were largely avoided. **Balfour** even went so far as to suggest that 'without Hankey we should have lost the war'. He continued to enjoy the confidence of successive post-war prime ministers and was raised to the peerage at the conclusion of his career.

HANNOVER CL TYPES

The CLII was the first original design produced by the Hannoverische Waggonfabrik AG, a railway rolling stock manufacturer which had been producing aircraft under licence since 1915. This compact two-seater biplane appeared in 1917 in response to an official German specification for new CL-type aircraft, which were to act as fighter escorts and as ground attack aircraft. They were to be lighter than C-type reconnaissance machines and powered by 160–180hp engines. The Hannover CLII was in fact equipped with a 180hp Argus As III unit, enclosed in a metal cowling, which gave a maximum speed of 103m.p.h. at sea level and an excellent ceiling of 24,600 feet. It was the only single-engined German aircraft of the war to have a biplane tail unit, enabling the tailplane span to be reduced. This provided the observer with a much wider field of fire than he would otherwise have had. The pilot, who also had a good view from his cockpit, was armed with a forward-firing Spandau machine-gun. Stick grenades, stored in external racks, were carried when the aircraft was being used for ground attack.

Variants of the original CLII model followed in 1918. The slightly modified CLIII, which was powered by the 160hp Mercedes D III engine and had overhung ailerons, was withdrawn after only 80 examples had been produced, because the power unit was in demand for fighter aircraft.

The CLIIIa, which was manufactured in the largest quantities, reverted to the original Argus engine. Over

Hannover CLV: a light, two-seat fighter escort that proved to be a formidable adversary

1,000 of these Hannover CL-types were produced and they rendered valuable service in the closing stages of the war. Their ply-covered fuselage was very strong and they were capable of absorbing considerable punishment. Their manoeuvrability at low altitudes was also a considerable asset in their ground attack role. Also capable of operating efficiently at very high altitudes, they were also effective as escort fighters. Known as Hannoveranas by the British, they proved to be formidable opponents: their compact design meant that they were often mistaken for single-seaters, and many unsuspecting RAF pilots came under surprise attack from the rear cockpit.

HANRIOT HD-1

This French-designed single-seat biplane fighter, which appeared in mid-1916, was little used in its country of origin, but was widely employed by the Italian and Belgian air forces. Elegant in appearance, it was strongly influenced by **Sopwith** designs and shared the same excellent flying qualities. Strong, manoeuvrable and easy to handle, it was powered by a single 110hp Le Rhône rotary engine, which gave a maximum speed of 114m.p.h. at sea level. Later models were often fitted with larger capacity engines of up to 170hp. Firepower – a single synchronised .303 **Vickers machine-gun** – was rather limited compared with other fighters appearing in the last two years of the war, although some later HD-Is were fitted with twin guns. However, the extra weight badly affected performance unless the fuel carried was substantially reduced.

Operational use of the aircraft in France was confined to the Aviation Maritime, which acquired a few machines for both ship- and land-based use in 1918; the French Aviation Militaire preferred the **Spad VII**. It was, however, adopted by the Italians as their standard fighter, replacing the **Nieuport Scouts** that were then being phased out. They acquired 831 examples, many of which were manufactured under licence, and by November 1918 sixteen of Italy's eighteen fighter squadrons were equipped with them. Tenete Scaroni, the highest scoring Italian ace to survive the war, flew a Hanriot HD-I. The Belgian air service, which acquired 125 HD-Is, operated them on the Western Front, where the aircraft was used by **Willy Coppens**, the country's leading ace. A twin float version, the HD-2, appeared in 1918 and was produced in small numbers.

HARMSWORTH, ALFRED, LORD NORTHCLIFFE, 1865–1922

British newspaper magnate who created the *Daily Mail* and owned other national papers. During the First World War, Northcliffe campaigned regularly with the aim of ensuring that the British war effort was as effective as possible. He drew attention, for example, to the delivery of obsolete shells and to the need for more news from the front. In 1917, he was sent to the United States as head of the British war mission and on his return he was created a viscount in recognition of his work as a diplomat. From February 1918 until the end of the war, he took charge of the direction of propaganda in enemy countries and was active, for example, in encouraging the growth of nationalism among the subject peoples of Central Europe.

HAUS, GRAND ADMIRAL ANTON, BARON von, 1851–1917

Haus was commander-in-chief of the Austro-Hungarian navy from early in 1913 until his death in February 1917. He ordered the bombardment of the Italian coast in May 1915, but operationally his wartime command was relatively uneventful, with Austria's modern capital ships being confined to Pola harbour for the next two years. His distinguished naval service was recognised in 1916 when he became Grand Admiral, a rank never held by any other officer of the Austro-Hungarian navy.

HAWKER, LANOE, 1890–1916

The RFC's first fighter ace, with nine confirmed victories, Lanoe Hawker was an outstanding pilot and a fine shot, who used a hunting rifle on reconnaissance and bombing missions during his early days in France. Early recognition of his talents came after a successful raid on a Zeppelin shed near Ghent in April 1915, when he received the Distinguished Service Order. With a machine-gun now mounted on his top plane, Hawker's score mounted and in August he was awarded the Victoria Cross for shooting down three enemy aircraft in a single day.

In September 1915, he was appointed commander of the first single-seat squadron (No 24), which was equipped with **DH2**s. Successful in opposing the **Fokker** scourge, by the autumn of 1916 the squadron's ageing pusher machines had been outclassed by the next generation of German planes. It was in fact the technical superiority of **von Richthofen**'s **Albatros** that eventually enabled him to shoot down Hawker on 16 November 1916, after almost half an hour's combat. The British ace had survived two previous crashes but this time he was killed.

H-CLASS SUBMARINE

Similar to the US Navy's H-class, these submarines were ordered by the Admiralty from an American company. Twelve units were delivered to the Royal Navy in 1915, but a further eight were not sent until after America entered the war in April 1917. These small, well-constructed submarines, which were

equipped with four 18-inch torpedo tubes, gave useful service in the Baltic and the Mediterranean. A further order for an improved H-class boat with 21-inch tubes was placed in 1917, and by the end of the war 22 had been delivered.

HELGOLAND

The Helgoland dreadnoughts, which were completed for the German navy in 1911–12, represented a significant advance on their predecessors – the **Nassau** class battleships. The 12-inch gun was adopted as their main armament, with the same arrangement of the six twin turrets as in *Nassau*. These weapons could fire a projectile of 893lb over 21,000 yards and their performance was comparable to the contemporary 13.5-inch British naval gun. The Hel-

golands had a maximum speed of 20 knots. With a displacement of 22,800 tons they had more space than the Nassaus and improved armour protection; they were immediately recognisable by their three short funnels positioned closely together. *Helgoland, Oldenburg, Ostfriesland* and *Thüringen* served with Battle Squadron I of the **High Seas Fleet** throughout the war and all were present at **Jutland**. They were transferred to the Allies after the Armistice.

HELIGOLAND BIGHT, BATTLE OF, 28 August 1914

The first naval battle of the First World War originated in a British plan to attack German patrols in the Heligoland Bight, off the north-west coast of

Germany. The raid was to be undertaken by the Harwich Force, under the command of **Commander Tyrwhitt**, which consisted of the light cruisers

One of several German ships damaged during the first naval battle of the war, Frauenlob, *a light cruiser, was later sunk at Jutland*

Arethusa and *Fearless* and two flotillas of destroyers. The latter were the 1st and 3rd Flotillas, consisting of 31 boats. They were to be covered by the First Battle Cruiser Squadron, under the command of **Vice-Admiral Beatty**, which had moved from **Scapa Flow** just before the operation. Tyrwhitt entered the Bight in the early hours of 28 August 1914 and the action began at 7.00 a.m. when two German torpedo boats were sunk. The Germans, who had been aware of the possibility of a British attack, quickly moved in the *Frauenlob* and *Stettin* to support the stricken boats. They were later joined by four other light cruisers, including *Köln*, the flagship of Rear Admiral Maas.

During the morning's running battle four of Tyrwhitt's ships were hit repeatedly and the whole force was by now outgunned. At 11.25 a.m. Tyrwhitt, who was now forced to withdraw, called for urgent assistance from Beatty's battlecruisers, which were then some 40 miles to the north. Travelling at top speed, they arrived in the Bight just in time; at 12.40 p.m. *Mainz*, *Köln* and *Ariadne* were sunk and three other German cruisers were damaged. The remnants of the German force quickly withdrew under cover of mist, having lost over 1,200 men.

The British, who had suffered only 35 fatalities as well as two damaged ships, then made for home. Their success was overshadowed by the fact that the operation had revealed serious weaknesses in terms of planning, communications and coordination, including several examples of confusion as to where – friend or enemy – the fire was coming from.

HENRY, PRINCE OF PRUSSIA, 1862–1929

The second son of Kaiser Frederick III, Grand Admiral Prince Henry was appointed commander-in-chief of German naval forces in the Baltic just before the war. He retained the post until February 1918, naval operations against the Russians having ceased after the Bolshevik Revolution. Prince Henry had originally been commander of the **High Seas Fleet**, but was posted to this secondary theatre in 1909 following disagreements with **von Tirpitz** over naval strategy.

HENTSCH, COLONEL RICHARD, 1869–1918

German staff officer whose action, on 9 September 1914, in ordering a general retreat of German forces during the **Battle of the Marne** has been the subject of considerable controversy. **Moltke**, Chief of the General Staff, had effectively lost touch with his field commanders in France and he sent Hentsch on a tour of the front. Hentsch was soon forced to use the wide powers given to him by Moltke, when he found that the Allies were in the process of exploiting a wide gap between the First and Second Armies and endangering their flanks. Their position had become untenable and the charge made that Hentsch's action had deprived the German army of the opportunity of victory at the Marne does not stand up. The whole front had been lost largely because the **Schlieffen Plan** had not been implemented in accordance with its author's original intentions. Hentsch himself held various staff appointments before his death in Rumania early in 1918.

HIGH SEAS FLEET

The principal fleet of the **German Navy** during the First World War. See the German Navy.

HINDENBURG, FIELD MARSHAL PAUL VON, 1847–1934

Popular hero during the First World War and subsequently President of the Weimar Republic, 1925–34, Lieutenant-General Hindenburg had retired from the German army in 1911, after an unremarkable career. He was recalled to active service on 22 August 1914, during a period of crisis, when East Prussia had been invaded by two Russian armies. With orders to stop the Russian 'steamroller', he was appointed to the command of the Eighth Army, with **Ludendorff** as his chief of staff. The new team developed plans already in existence to win a decisive victory over the Russian Second Army at **Tannenberg**, before turning north to deal with the First Army under **Rennenkampf**. These victories established Hindenburg's military reputation, although Ludendorff's leadership and Rennenkampf's incompetence were perhaps the more important determinants of the outcome.

In Novemeber 1914, Hindenburg was promoted to the command of the entire Eastern Front with the rank of field marshal; Ludendorff became his chief of staff. Together they won a series of tactical victories against the Russians in 1914–15, preventing them from further endangering German territory. However, a decisive blow that would knock the Russians out of the war eluded him. His ambitious offensive plans foundered because of insufficient reserves and problems of mobility.

As Eastern Front commander, Hindenburg (centre) failed to knock Russia out of the war; as chief of staff, 1916–18, he was dominated by his deputy, Ludendorff

In August 1916, **Falkenhayn**, who had refused to draw the required reserves from the Western Front, fell from office and was replaced by Hindenburg; Ludendorff returned with him from the Eastern Front as First Quartermaster-General. Hindenburg's formal position was chief of staff under the Kaiser's command, but in practice the control of military policy lay elsewhere. It has been suggested that Hindenburg was, in 1916–18, no more than a figurehead and was 'really the codename for a committee, one dominated during the First World War by Ludendorff'.

In the west, Hindenburg's policy was to strengthen German positions, and the defensive line that bears his name was constructed. However, on the Eastern Front the Germans went on the offensive, starting a process that ended in the **Treaty of Brest-Litovsk**, in which Hindenburg and Ludendorff imposed harsh terms on the Russians.

In the political domain, Hindenburg forced the resignation of the chancellor, **Bethmann Hollweg**, with whom he had disagreed over the reintroduction of unrestricted submarine warfare and electoral reform. With the appointment of Michaelis, his weak successor, in June 1917, the influence of the chief of staff and his deputy on the German government increased greatly; it has been described as a military dictatorship. Their gamble for victory in 1918 failed as the successive German offensives were halted. With the Allied advance on the Western Front from August and the collapse of the other fronts, Hindenburg, unlike Ludendorff, remained at his post. He was obliged to sue for peace and to advise Kaiser Wilhelm II to abdicate, but remained in command of the German army until July 1919.

HIPPER, ADMIRAL FRANZ von, 1863–1932

On the outbreak of war, Admiral Hipper commanded the scouting forces of the German **High Seas Fleet**, a post he held until August 1918. He deployed his forces with initiative and skill within the narrow limits set by the German Admiralty, leading two raids on the English coast in 1914. On 2–3 November, he shelled Yarmouth and Lowestoft and on 15–16 December Hartlepool, Scarborough and Whitby received similar treatment. Early in 1915, a further sortie, this time to the **Dogger Bank**, was intercepted by the stronger British Battlecruiser Force (**Beatty**). Hipper quickly withdrew but the battlecruiser *Seydlitz*, his flagship, was severely damaged and the armoured cruiser *Blücher* was lost.

He supported the idea of a decisive encounter with the British **Grand Fleet**, but it was not until May 1916 – the **Battle of Jutland** – that combat materialised. In the first phase of the battle he revealed his considerable tactical skill, out-manoeuvring Beatty and destroying two British battlecruisers without sustaining any losses himself. As events turned against the Germans, **Scheer** ordered Hipper to attack the enemy in order to facilitate the withdrawal of the main battle fleet. Hipper threw his

forces against the entire Grand Fleet and in an attack lasting only four minutes before orders were changed,

Briefly commander of the High Seas Fleet in 1918, Hipper had demonstrated his tactical brilliance at Jutland

his flagship *Lützow* was lost. *Moltke* was in fact the only German battlecruiser still functioning and it served as Hipper's flagship. Jutland enhanced Hipper's reputation considerably and he was awarded the Pour le Mérite.

On Scheer's promotion in August 1918, Hipper succeeded him as the last commander of the High Seas Fleet. He was unable to handle effectively the fleet mutinies of October–November, prompted in part by his own plan for a final attack on the Grand Fleet. He retired after having witnessed the surrender of his fleet to the British.

HOFFMANN, GENERAL MAX, 1869–1927

One of the outstanding German staff officers of his generation, Hoffmann made his mark on the Eastern Front in the first weeks of the war. As chief operations officer of the Eighth Army (**Prittwitz**), he opposed his commander's decision, on 20 August 1914, to withdraw behind the Vistula River after the **Battle of Gumbinnen**. His plans for the defence of East Prussia, which were based on his observation of the enemy during the Russo-Japanese War (1904–05), were, in large part, adopted by **Hindenburg** and **Ludendorff** when they arrived to replace Prittwitz. They led to the twin German victories of **Tannenberg** and the **Masurian Lakes**. Hoffmann did not, however, receive the full credit due to him and these early successes were publicly attributed to the Hindenburg–Ludendorff partnership.

As Ludendorff's deputy, Hoffmann succeeded him as chief of staff in the east when he left in September 1916. **Prince Leopold of Bavaria** replaced Hindenburg in overall command, but it was Hoffmann who was now in real control on the Eastern Front. His brilliant grasp of strategy completed the destruction of the Russian army and, in December 1917, he negotiated an armistice with the Bolsheviks. At the **Brest-Litovsk** peace talks he was the representative of Hindenburg and Ludendorff and he organised the German attack in response to **Trotsky**'s 'no war, no peace' resolution. Hoffmann remained on the Eastern Front until November 1918.

HOLTZENDORFF, GRAND ADMIRAL HENNING VON, 1853–1919

Chief of the German Admiralty Staff, from the autumn of 1915 until August 1918, von Holtzendorff, who had been a pre-war commander-in-chief of the **High Seas Fleet**, was forced into retirement in 1913 because of disagreements over naval policy. He never expressed a consistent view on the question of unrestricted submarine warfare, but was a significant factor in its reintroduction in 1917. The U-boat campaign would, in his optimistic view, bring the British to the conference table within a few months, before the Americans could have made a decisive impact. Promoted to the rank of Grand Admiral in July 1918, he was succeeded almost at once by **Admiral Scheer**, who was to run a new centralised naval headquarters.

HORTHY, VICE-ADMIRAL MIKLÓS, 1868–1957

Ruler of Hungary from 1920, Admiral Miklós Horthy served in the Austro-Hungarian navy during the First World War. He first came to public attention in May 1915 when he commanded a squadron that attacked and sank 14 Italian merchant ships off Albania. There were other notable operational achievements before his appointment as fleet commander early in 1918. At the end of the war he was responsible for the transfer of the Austrian navy's ships to the new state of Yugoslavia.

HOTCHKISS LIGHT MACHINE-GUN

One of the first of its type, the 8mm Hotchkiss light machine-gun appeared in 1909 in response to the French army's need for an infantry assault weapon. Using basically the same relatively uncomplicated gas-operated mechanism as the large Hotchkiss gun, the light machine-gun also employed its unsatisfactory strip feed magazine. However, the strip was now reversed with the cartridges mounted on the under-side, making the problem even worse. Weighing over 25lb, it had a cyclic rate of fire of 500 rounds per minute and a muzzle velocity of 2,420 feet per second.

The Fusil Mitrailleur Hotchkiss Modèle 1909 was never used for its intended purpose, partly because of the onset of trench warfare. Its weight, size and problems with the ammunition feed would in any case have restricted its potential as a mobile weapon. It was, however, widely and successfully employed as an aircraft and tank gun by France and her allies.

The weapon was also produced in Britain, where it was known as the .303 Hotchkiss Machine-Gun, Mark I; it was in fact still in use there during the Second World War for home defence purposes. It was also employed by the American army which knew it as the Benét-Mercié Machine Rifle.

Widely used in the air, this land-based Hotchkiss is seen on an aircraft mounting

HOTCHKISS MACHINE-GUN MODEL 1914

The standard heavy machine-gun of the French army during the First World War, the 8mm Model 1914 dated back to 1893 when an Austrian inventor sold a prototype of his novel gas-operated machine-gun to the Hotchkiss company. An improved production version was officially adopted in 1897, the design being subject to further minor revisions in 1900 and 1914.

A distinctive feature of the weapon was the brass or steel rings added to the air-cooled barrel, with the aim of reducing its marked tendency to overheat. Less successful was the unusual method of ammunition feed – metallic strips holding no more than 24 or 30 rounds; later models were, however, provided with a metallic strip belt (accommodating up to 249 cartridges) that was more appropriate for a machine-gun of this kind. A large, heavy weapon, weighing 52lb, it was normally issued with a tripod mounting, of which various designs were used. The Hotchkiss had a good cyclic rate of fire of 600 rounds per minute and a muzzle velocity of 2,380 feet per second. Well made and with a reputation for reliability, it was used during the war by the AEF, Greece and other Balkan states, as well as by France.

HOUSE, EDWARD, 1858–1938

A close adviser to **Woodrow Wilson** since his campaign for the presidency, House served as an unofficial diplomat during the First World War. Holding no formal office, he was responsible only to the president and had a great influence on the development of his foreign policy. House represented the president in negotiations with the Allies on many occasions during the war. In 1916, for example, he went to Europe on a secret mission with the aim of bringing the war to an end by the armed mediation of America. Perhaps his greatest achievement was to secure the Allies' agreement in October 1918 to an Armistice based upon the **Fourteen Points**.

HUTIER, GENERAL OSKAR von, 1857–1934

German general who commanded the Eighth Army on the Eastern Front for much of the war, Hutier was noted for his major tactical innovations. 'Hutier tactics' were first applied during the capture of **Riga** (1 September 1917), when the usual long preliminary bombardment was abandoned in favour of surprise. A short burst of artillery fire was followed immediately by infantry assaults, with fast-moving 'shock' troops concentrating on the area behind the front line. Enemy strong points, which were masked by gas and smoke shells, were mopped up by succeeding waves of infantry. The success of these tactics at Riga ensured their use at **Caporetto** and in the German offensives of 1918. Hutier himself was posted to the Western Front in the last few months of the war as commander of the Eighteenth Army, participating in the **Somme offensive** (March 1918) and in the **Noyon-Montdidier offensive** (June).

IMMELMANN, MAX, 1890–1916

Known as the 'Eagle of Lille', Max Immelmann was one of the great fighter aces of the first two years of the war, scoring a total of 15 victories. His first posting was to *Fl Abt 10* of the German air service, an artillery-spotting unit, in April 1915. Only a few weeks later his prospects improved when he transferred to *Fl Abt 62*, where he served with **Oswald Boelcke**, his partner and rival, who proved to be the other outstanding German pilot of the period. The dull routine of reconnaissance patrols ended with the arrival of the **Fokker EI** and, on 1 August 1915, Immelmann achieved the first victory by a pilot flying an aircraft that had been specifically designed as a fighter. He was awarded the Iron Cross First Class in recognition of this special achievement.

His score gradually increased over the next few months and by the end of 1915 he had hit seven enemy aircraft. Immelmann also reviewed how the new fighter aircraft with forward-firing armament might best be used and made an important contribution to tactical thinking. He is, of course, particularly remembered for the manoeuvre known as the Immelmann turn. This half loop, with a roll in the process, enabled the pilot to position himself above an opponent who had attacked him from behind. He was then able either to fly off in the opposite direction or dive down on his attacker.

Immelmann was awarded the Pour le Mérite in January 1916 and like Oswald Boelcke became a national hero. Spurred on to greater efforts he had shot down another seven enemy aircraft by April. The day of the Fokker Eindecker was, however, drawing to a close as Allied superiority in the air was established. Immelmann himself fell victim to the

RFC on 18 June 1916, in a dog fight with seven **FE2bs** of No 25 Squadron. It is not clear, however, whether Immelmann's death was caused by one of his opponents or by structural failure in his machine.

A pioneering fighter ace, Immelmann made a lasting contribution to the tactics of aerial warfare

IMPERATOR PAVEL

This pre-dreadnought battleship and her sister *Andrei Pervoswanni* were the principal units of Russia's Baltic Fleet on the outbreak of war. Completed in 1910, they had a displacement of 17,400 tons and a maximum speed of 17.5 knots; main armament consisted of four 12-inch guns and their hulls were completely armoured. Neither ship saw any action during the First World War, although they were both employed during the civil war, with *Andrei Pervoswanni* being torpedoed by the British in August 1919.

IMPERATRITSA MARIYA

Based on the **Ganguts**, the Imperatritsa Mariya class dreadnought battleships were destined for the Russian Black Sea fleet to counter Turkish naval strength, in particular the new warships she had on order in 1911. Armour and armament were improved, although 12-inch main guns were retained because larger calibre weapons were still under development in Russia. After little more than a year operating against the Turks and Bulgarians *Imperatritsa Mariya* was lost in October 1916: she capsized at Sevastopol following an internal explosion. Her sister ship *Ekaterina II* (named *Svobodnaya Rossiya* after the March Revolution) was sunk by the Bolsheviks in June 1918 to prevent her falling into German hands. This was in fact the fate of the third ship of this class – *Imperator Alexander III* (renamed *Volya*) which was seized in 1918 and commissioned in the German navy.

INDEFATIGABLE

The second trio of British battlecruisers, the Indefatigables, which were completed in 1911–13, were the cheapest capital ships produced in recent times. They were based on the **Invincibles** and because of the pressures of time and money shared most of their serious faults. The main change was a lengthened hull which enabled both midships turrets to fire on either beam. Main armament consisted of eight 50-calibre 12-inch guns (rather than the 45-calibre weapons in the Invincibles). They had a displacement of 18,800 tons and a maximum speed of 25 knots.

Like their predecessors their main weakness was poor armour protection and the vulnerability of their magazines, a fact that was graphically demonstrated at the **Battle of Jutland**: during the first phase of the battlecruiser action *Indefatigable* herself sunk following a magazine explosion caused by 11-inch shell fire from *Von der Tann*. The British had, ironically, once claimed (quite incorrectly) that this German battlecruiser had inferior armour to the Indefatigables.

Her sister ship *Australia*, which had been flagship of the Royal Australian Navy at the beginning of the war, served with the 2nd Battlecruiser Squadron, **Grand Fleet** from early in 1915. *New Zealand* – the third ship of this class – was built at the expense of the New Zealand Government, but had been presented to the Royal Navy, also serving with the Grand Fleet throughout the war. She was in action at **Dogger Bank** and at **Jutland**, where she sustained some damage.

INVINCIBLE

The armoured cruiser equivalent of the *Dreadnought*, the Invincible class also reflected **Admiral Fisher**'s concern with speed and firepower rather than armour. With the performance of a cruiser (maximum speed of 28 knots) and the heavy armament of a battleship (eight 12-inch guns), the Invincibles were prototype battlecruisers, representing a considerable improvement over their predecessors. *Invincible* and her sister ships – *Indomitable* and *Inflexible* – were completed in 1908; the former had a displacement of 17,250 tons, a complement of 784, and was powered by four steam turbines. She had a maximum range of 3,100 nautical miles.

As battlecruisers working with the fleet they had a serious weakness: their armour had been sacrificed in the interests of speed and was too thin – at six inches – to provide the protection they needed when operating as dreadnoughts. This became clear at the **Battle of Jutland** when *Invincible* was lost. She was hit in Q-turret, causing an enormous explosion which

Invincible: *one of three British battlecruisers lost at the Battle of Jutland*

blew her in half; she sank immediately and only three of her crew survived. *Invincible* had earlier taken part in the **Heligoland Bight** action and the **Battle of the Falkland Islands**, where she was Sturdee's flagship. *Indomitable*, which had participated in the hunt for the *Goeben* and *Breslau*, joined the Battle Cruiser Force of the **Grand Fleet** early in 1915. She was also present at Jutland. *Inflexible* was severely damaged in the Mediterranean by a mine in March 1915, but subsequently served with the Grand Fleet for the rest of the war. The armour of both surviving ships was improved after Jutland.

IOANN ZLATOUST

Based on their predecessor *Potemkin*, but modified in the light of experience in the Russo–Japanese war, *Ioann Zlatoust* and *Evstafi* were launched in 1906. These relatively powerful pre-dreadnought battle-ships, which had a displacement of 12,840 tons, were equipped with improved deck armour and more powerful armament: four 12-inch, four 8-inch and twelve 6-inch guns. Both ships served with the Russian Black Sea fleet, first with the flying squadron and later with the 3rd Manoeuvring Group, and were used intensively throughout the war. They frequently carried out shore bombardments against Turkish installations and during one engagement *Evstafi* hit the former German battlecruiser *Goeben*. At the end of the war the ships fell into British hands and their machinery was damaged in order to prevent the Bolsheviks from using them.

IRON DUKE

Based on the **King George V**s, four super-dreadnoughts, all of which were completed in 1914, constituted the Iron Duke class (named after the first Duke of Wellington). With a displacement of over 30,000 tons, they were heavier and longer than their predecessors and had improved secondary armament, the 6-inch guns replacing the inadequate 4-inch variety. They were also the first ships to be equipped with anti-aircraft guns as a defence against airships. *Iron Duke* herself was flagship of the commander-in-chief of the **Grand Fleet (Jellicoe)** until November 1916, and subsequently served with the 2nd Battle Squadron. Like her sister ships *Benbow* and *Emperor of India* she served at **Jutland** without sustaining any damage. *Marlborough* – the other ship in this class – was not so fortunate, being the only British dreadnought to be torpedoed during the war. The damage was sustained at Jutland and after major repairs she was able to resume her wartime career.

ISONZO, BATTLES OF THE, 1915–1917

With the signing of the secret **Treaty of London** on 26 April 1915, Italy agreed to declare war on her former allies, Germany and Austro-Hungary, in return for the promise of substantial territorial gains. She declared war against Austria on 23 May 1915 and had little time to prepare her forces before launching an attack on 23 June. The only suitable area for an offensive was in the east along the Isonzo River, because elsewhere the border largely followed the line of the Alps. The immediate objective in this sector was Gorizia but the army aimed to advance to Trieste and beyond.

Assembled on this 60-mile front were the Italian Second and Third Armies (with a strength of 35 divisions) under the command of General Cadorna, the chief of staff; the Austrians, who initially had only 14 divisions, were commanded by **Boroevic von Bojna**. In spite of their numerical superiority, the Italians, who were to fight eleven costly battles over the next 27 months, were unable to make the decisive breakthrough.

First Battle – 23 June–7 July 1915: After failing to make progress in his first offensive, Cadorna halted operations while his heavy artillery was reinforced. The Austrians also increased their forces by two divisions.

Second Battle – 18 July–3 August 1915: More intensive fighting left the front line unchanged and produced heavy casualties: 45,000 Austrian and 60,000 Italian.

Third Battle – 18 October–3 November 1915: During the autumn Cadorna brought forward replacement troops and further increased his heavy artillery to 1,200 guns.

Fourth Battle – 10 November–2 December 1915: The Third and Fourth engagements were in fact two elements of the same battle and by the time it had ended 117,000 Italian and 72,000 Austrian casualties had been sustained. The courageous assaults of the Italian infantry had produced no more than marginal changes to the front line. The strategic effects of the first four offensives were also very limited: 12 Austrian divisions had been transferred to the Isonzo from the Eastern Front and the Balkans but the reductions had no appreciable effect on the course of events in these two theatres.

Fifth Battle – 9–17 March 1916: Launched in accordance with agreements made at the Chantilly conference, this new offensive was a half-hearted gesture of co-operation with the Allies which soon died out in unfavourable weather conditions.

Sixth Battle – 6–17 August 1916: After blocking **Conrad**'s offensive in the Trentino in June 1916, Cadorna quickly moved back the troops that he had withdrawn from the Isonzo. Twenty-two Italian divisions were available, while the Austrians, who were unable to move their forces so rapidly from one front to another, had only nine. Three days after the assault was launched the Italians had crossed the river and had captured Gorizia but caution on the part of Cadorna and the arrival of Austrian reinforcements quickly brought the action to a close. A major breakthrough had not been achieved but the Italians had advanced three miles on a front of fifteen. Italy's first significant military success increased morale on the home front even though it cost 50,000 casualties (Austrian losses were 40,000).

Seventh Battle – 14–17 September 1916; Eighth Battle – 10–12 October 1916; Ninth Battle – 1–4 November 1916: Designed to enlarge the Gorizia bridgehead, these three actions in the autumn of 1916 were all one and the same battle. Italian tactics were modified with the all-out offensive being abandoned in favour of several sudden stabs at the Austrian line. The attacks stretched the resources of the Austrians but achieved nothing.

Tenth Battle – 12 May–8 June 1917: Cadorna had agreed to take part in the Allied offensive planned for the spring and had reinforced his troops during the winter. Thirty-eight Italian divisions faced 14 Aus-

trian and at first small gains were registered. However, these were soon lost in the Austrian counter-attack on 6–8 June and the Italians sustained very heavy losses (157,000 casualties compared to 75,000 Austrian).

Eleventh Battle – 19 August–12 September 1917: Further reinforced, the Italians, now 51 divisions strong, launched the last and greatest of all their offensives on the Isonzo River. The Second Army under **Capello** advanced five miles, the first significant Italian gain since the Sixth Battle in August 1916; however, the offensive was soon abandoned because Cadorna believed that the Germans were about to intervene on the Italian Front and he decided to concentrate all his efforts on defence. The expected Austro-German offensive materialised a month later as the Twelfth Battle of Isonzo, better known as the **Battle of Caporetto**.

Italian troops hauling a 149mm gun on the inhospitable Upper Isonzo Front

ITALIAN AIR SERVICE

Italy's first operational use of its military aircraft was as early as the autumn of 1911, during its war with Turkey for possession of Libya. However, the air service remained small and when Italy entered the First World War in May 1915, the *Corpo Aeronautico Militaire* (Military Aeronautical Corps) consisted of no more than 15 squadrons (86 aircraft). The naval air service was even smaller, with a total of 28 machines at its disposal. A major expansion programme was quickly instituted which increased the number of squadrons to 35 in 1916, 65 in 1917, and 68 at the time of the Armistice.

Total strength in November 1918 was 1,758 aircraft, many of which were foreign-designed machines built under licence. Good indigenous products – in particular the **Caproni**, **Macchi** and **SVA** – were also increasingly in evidence. Initally, priority was given to reconnaissance duties, as well as long range and tactical bombing missions, with fighter units being introduced more slowly. Special efforts were made in 1917 to integrate the air service as closely as possible with ground forces to improve co-operation and effectiveness. The *Corpo Aeronautico Militaire* shot down a total of 763 enemy aircraft during the First World War and was able to dominate the battle zone with Austro-Hungary in the closing stages of the conflict.

ITALIAN ARMY

Still recovering from the war against Turkey in Libya in 1912, the Italian army had declined to less than 300,000 effective troops as the First World War began. On Italy's entry into the war in May 1915, mobilisation increased this number rapidly and soon some 875,000 men were available. Organised in 36

Retreat from the Isonzo, October 1917. The disastrous defeat at Caporetto almost knocked Italy out of the war

infantry divisions, four cavalry divisions and two Alpine groups, the army was deployed according to the requirements of the offensive plan prepared by **General Cadorna**, the chief of staff, during Italy's period of neutrality.

Taking into account Austria's commanding position along much of its mountainous frontier with Italy, the army would remain on the defensive on the Trentino sector and concentrate offensive action on the **Isonzo front** towards Gorizia and Trieste. As the war began, the Second and Third Armies were based there, with the First and Fourth Armies on the Trentino; the two Alpine groups were positioned between the two main fronts.

Apart from its strategic disadvantages, the Italian army suffered from acute shortages of equipment. Ammunition, artillery and hand grenades were all in short supply; the importance of the machine-gun had been under-estimated and there were only just over 600 in the whole country. The Allies were forced to lend heavy artillery and other material to Italy throughout the war.

Under Cadorna's direction, the Italian army gradually expanded in spite of heavy losses during the war of attrition on the Isonzo front: at the end of 1916 there were 48 divisions, increasing to 65 by October 1917. At this point, the disastrous **Battle of Caporetto** destroyed much of this work (and the associated improvements in morale), with the result that only 33 divisions remained effective.

Italy was forced to rely on direct military support – 11 British and French divisions – as the new commander-in-chief, **General Diaz**, reorganised the army and restored its fighting effectiveness during the winter months.

The long-delayed final offensive began on 4 October 1918, after months of preparation. Fifty-seven Italian divisions, equipped with nearly 8,000 guns, pushed back the Austro-Hungarian army, which collapsed in the final days of the war. During 1915–18, Italy had mobilised 5,615,000 men, of whom 462,391 were killed and 953,886 were injured.

ITALIAN FRONT, CHRONOLOGICAL LIST OF EVENTS

Isonzo River, Battles of 1915–17
Asiago, Battle of, 1916
Caporetto Battle of, 1917

Piave River, Battle of, 1918
Vittorio Veneto, Battle of, 1918

ITALIAN MODEL 1891 RIFLE

The standard Italian service rifle of the First World War, the Fucile Modello 91 was designed at Turin arsenal and was officially adopted in 1892. The Mannlicher-Carcano, as the type was known, was an amalgam of features drawn from different weapons: a **Mauser** bolt action, adapted from the 1889 Belgian pattern, was used, and the clip-loaded magazine, which held six rounds of 6.5mm ammunition, was taken from a **Mannlicher** design. A bolt-sleeve safety mechanism was, however, an Italian contribu-

tion, designed by Salvatore Carcano, an employee of the arsenal. The weapon also appeared in short-barrelled carbine form, with a folding bayonet (some of which were spiked), for use by the cavalry.

Operational use of the weapon in Europe during the war was confined to the Italian army, as Japan was the only foreign power to have acquired any. The Modello 91, which had a muzzle velocity of 630m per second, performed well enough in the campaigns against the Austro-Hungarian army, although the

6.5mm cartridge was found to be relatively under-powered. A further weakness was the fact that the mechanism was more complicated than most of its contemporaries and required more routine maintenance; the straight-pull bolt action could jam if it were dirty.

ITALIAN NAVY

A period of pre-war expansion had provided the Italian navy with a relatively modern fleet of six dreadnoughts and eight pre-dreadnoughts in 1915; four super-dreadnoughts under construction were abandoned at an early stage of the war.

Its principal wartime role was to contain or neutralise the numerically inferior Austrian fleet in the Adriatic and, with the support of four British battleships, it was successful. Except for three limited sorties, Austria's capital ships remained in port throughout the war. As a result, Italy's battleships were relatively inactive apart from shore bombardments and some patrol duties. Both sides concentrated on hit-and-run raids, with the Italians making heavy use of the high speed Mas motor torpedo-boat, of which almost 300 were built. It was widely employed against German U-boats in the Mediterranean as well as in the Adriatic.

The Italian navy also had to devote considerable resources to the defence of its bases at Brindisi and Venice, which were subject to regular air attack, and to the Otranto barrage, a minefield across the Otranto Straits that was also subject to Austrian raids. Italian wartime losses included three battleships, two armoured cruisers and two small cruisers; in compensation, much of the former Austrian fleet was transferred to it at the end of the war.

IVANOV, GENERAL NIKOLAI, 1851–1919

Commander of the Russian South-Western Front facing Austro-Hungary, Ivanov's hesitancy and other weaknesses were soon revealed in the opening stages of the **Galician campaign** (August–September 1914), in spite of its relatively successful outcome. Notable examples include his delay in advancing on Lemburg at the end of August and the failure to pursue vigorously the retreating Austrian army as it fell back to the Carpathians in September. The resumption of the Russian advance in March 1915 produced a successful German counter-offensive: Ivanov had not accepted reports of an impending attack and was badly placed to respond to it. By September 1915, his forces had been pushed back as much as 300 miles and he was soon to be replaced by **Brusilov**. Ivanov then went to Stavka as a military adviser to the Tsar. He intervened in support of the monarch during the March Revolution and was commander of a White army during the Civil War.

IZZET PASHA, AHMED, 1864–1937

Former chief of staff of the Turkish army and Minister of War, Izzet emerged from retirement early in 1916 to command the Second Army on the Caucasus front. He led an offensive against the Russians in June 1916, but it was badly planned and executed, and by the time it had ended in August nothing had been achieved. Izzet's active military career was over, but he headed the short-lived government that agreed the Armistice with the Allies on 30 October 1918.

JACKSON, ADMIRAL SIR HENRY, 1855–1929

Appointed First Sea Lord on the resignation of **Lord Fisher** in May 1915, Jackson was a surprising choice as a wartime leader of the Royal Navy. He was noted for his scientific interests and achievements – in particular the introduction of radio telegraphy in the navy – rather than his command experience or leadership qualities. In fact, with **Arthur Balfour** installed as First Lord of the Admiralty in succession to **Churchill**, a much less dynamic style was soon evident at the heart of British naval administration. Jackson was unable to establish close relations with politicians and seemed incapable of delegating effectively. Mounting public concern late in 1916 about the growing Allied shipping losses caused by U-boats brought his unhappy tenure at the Admiralty to a close. He resigned in December 1916 and was replaced by **Admiral Jellicoe**.

JADAR RIVER, BATTLE OF, 12–21 August 1914

The first Austro-Hungarian invasion of Serbia was launched on 12 August 1914, to make Serbia 'realise that an archduke's murder had to be paid for'. Other motives included the wish to stamp out the only Allied power in the Balkans, which would in turn allow the Berlin–Baghdad railway to open. Some 200,000 Austrian troops, under the overall command of **Major-General Potiorek**, had been assembled on both sides of the Serbian salient. The main attack began when the Fifth Army and part of the Sixth Army moved across the River Drina to the west. The Second Army (**General von Böhm Ermolli**), which struck from the north, crossing the Save River on 14 August, was half its normal strength because of transfers to **Galicia**.

The main threat to the Serbians, whose slightly smaller forces were commanded by **Field Marshal Putnik**, came from the Austrian Fifth Army, and their Second and Third Armies were moved up to oppose it. On 16 August, the armies engaged along a 30-mile front on the Jadar River and the Austrians came under attack at the pivot between their VIII and XIII Corps. After five days' intense fighting the Austrians withdrew back across the Drina. The Austrian Second Army had also been forced to retreat from Serbian territory having made two futile attempts to assist the Fifth Army. The invading army suffered as many as 40,000 casualties, although this did not deter Potiorek from launching a further attack as soon as 7 September. Serbian losses in this first battle were relatively light.

JAPANESE NAVY

Dating back to 1868, the modern Japanese navy expanded rapidly and had soon defeated its two main adversaries in the Far East: China in 1894–95 and Russia in 1904–05. Japan, which had signed a defence treaty with Britain in 1902, entered the First World War on the Allied side, on 23 August 1914. With British forces concentrated in home waters, Japan was the only Allied power with a strong naval presence in the Pacific. At the beginning of the war, she occupied the German Pacific Islands in order to prevent **Vice-Admiral Reichsgraf von Spee**'s East Asiatic Squadron using them.

The German colony of **Tsingtao** on the Chinese mainland, which had been von Spee's base, fell to Japanese and British troops on 7 November 1914. It was a major amphibious operation with nearly 25,000 men being landed by the Japanese Second Fleet. The rest of the war was much less eventful for the Japanese navy: its principal tasks included escorting **ANZAC** troops to the Middle East and hunting down German **commerce raiders**. Japanese capital ships did not serve outside the Pacific during the war but, at the request of the British, several destroyers were assigned to the Mediterranean in 1917–18.

JAURÉGUIBERRY

Although she was in relatively poor structural condition, *Jauréguiberry* was intensively used by the French navy throughout the war. Launched in 1893, this elderly pre-dreadnought, which was similar to the battleship *Charles Martel*, had a displacement of 11,637 tons and a maximum speed of just under 18 knots. A turret-mounted 12-inch gun was positioned fore and aft, with two 10.8-inch guns amidships in a lozenge shape layout; secondary armament consisted of eight 5-inch guns and there were six 18-inch torpedo tubes. *Jauréguiberry* was used on convoy duties in the Mediterranean for much of the war, although in 1915 she served in the **Dardanelles** and was in action against Turkish shore positions.

JELLICOE, ADMIRAL JOHN, EARL, 1859–1935

Commander of the British **Grand Fleet**, 1914–16, Admiral Jellicoe had been **Fisher's** choice some years before the war as leader of the fleet in a future conflict with Germany. Appointed Controller and Third Sea Lord in 1908, he worked closely with Lord Fisher, particularly in organising the dreadnought construction programme. Command of the Atlantic Fleet and then of the Second Division, Home Fleet, followed, enabling him to develop his knowledge of strategy and tactics, his earlier career having been concentrated on the gunnery branch. A further period at the Admiralty, as Second Sea Lord, ended as war was declared.

He was appointed to the command of the Grand Fleet and flew his flag in *Iron Duke*, a super-dreadnought. The major sea battle with the German **High Seas Fleet** expected by Jellicoe and much of the navy did not materialise, the Germans preferring to keep their fleet in harbour until a favourable moment arrived. The Grand Fleet operated a distant blockade and apart from the isolated operations of the battlecruiser force, 20 months of inaction followed.

Jellicoe was a popular leader, who maintained morale and established a high standard of training, even though he was too preoccupied with details and was unwilling to delegate. He had always been noted for his caution and would avoid any risk that might reduce or destroy the superiority in numbers that was the main asset of the British fleet.

Admiral Jellicoe, the commander of the Grand Fleet, on board his flagship, the super-dreadnought Iron Duke

It was not until the **Battle of Jutland** (May 1916) that he was able to engage the High Seas Fleet. The result was a British strategic victory, but tactically Jellicoe could claim no more than a draw. British losses were heavier and there was great disappointment that Jellicoe had not been able to mount a decisive strike against the Germans. Although he had placed his fleet between the enemy and its base with considerable skill, there were a number of failures during the battle. Jellicoe's fear of torpedo and submarine attacks had led him to turn away rather than follow the enemy at two critical points, with the result that contact was lost. His unwillingness to risk the main battle fleet was, however, justified on the grounds that, as **Churchill** suggested, 'he could have lost the war in an afternoon.' There were also reservations about his use of the single line ahead battle formation, which did not offer sufficient flexibility in an engagement of this kind. He also suffered from serious signalling problems, in particu-lar the Admiralty's failure to inform him of the Germans' course of retreat.

In December 1916, he was moved to the Admiralty as First Sea Lord, being replaced by **Admiral Beatty** as commander of the Grand Fleet. Jellicoe's principal task was to deal with the German U-boat threat which had replaced the High Seas Fleet as the main danger. Although he was a strong opponent of the **convoy system**, he was responsible for its successful introduction from May 1917 after the Prime Minister's intervention had secured a change of policy. His relations with **Lloyd George** were always tense, the latter having little patience with a 'tired, over-conscientious man who could not delegate business, constantly overworked and always saw the black side of things too clearly'. It was no surprise when, in December 1917, Jellicoe was abruptly dismissed by the new First Lord of the Admiralty, **Sir Eric Geddes**, and his wartime career was brought to an end.

JERUSALEM, FALL OF, 8–9 December 1917

Allenby arrives in Jerusalem, having achieved the only notable British victory of 1916

Immediately following the Battle of Junction Station on 13–14 November 1917, **General Allenby**'s right wheeled eastwards into the Judaea Hills towards Jerusalem. His left maintained a defensive front at Jaffa, which had just fallen into British hands. The enemy's forces had been split in two. However, with the arrival of **General von Falkenhayn** to assume command, a new Turkish front was established from Jerusalem to the sea. From strong defensive positions the Turkish Seventh Army launched powerful attacks and as a result British progress was slowed down. It soon became clear that Allenby would not be able to seize the Holy City with the forces available to him and on 24 November he suspended further offensive action, enabling him to reorganise and reinforce his front line troops.

The task of capturing Jerusalem was allocated to 20 Corps under the command of Sir Philip Chetwode and the attack began on 8 December. The main thrust came from Nebi-Samweil, the commanding heights six miles to the west, with a secondary one from the south at Bethlehem. The morale of the Turkish defenders was low following weeks of abortive attacks and the city fell to the British after only a day's battle,

although some fighting continued in the hills prior to Allenby's arrival in the city on 11 December. A Turkish counter-attack on 26 December failed with heavy losses, the British having firmly established their position from Jerusalem to the sea.

Their ability to advance further was, however, dependent on re-establishing lines of communication and maintaining a force of sufficient strength. The fall of Jerusalem was an important moral victory even if its strategic significance was less obvious. In total Allenby's entire campaign had cost 18,000 Allied casualties against enemy losses of some 25,000 men.

JOFFRE, MARSHAL JOSEPH, 1852–1931

Joffre (left), removed as commander-in-chief of the French army in 1916, with (from left to right) Poincaré, George V, Foch and Haig, towards the end of the war

Marshal of France who established his reputation during colonial wars in Indo-China and Africa, where he served from 1885. Following his return to France,

Joffre was appointed Director of Engineers in 1905, and became Chief of the General Staff in 1911. One of his major responsibilities was the preparation of a new operational plan describing French strategy in the event of a European war breaking out. The result was **Plan XVII**, which provided for a French offensive into Alsace-Lorraine, with two French armies being prepared to shift westwards if the Germans violated Belgian neutrality.

When war was declared in August 1914, Joffre assumed command of France's forces in the field. The troop dispositions required by Plan XVII were soon found to be faulty as the Germans wheeled through Belgium west of the Meuse and as the French offensive in Lorraine ran into heavy resistance. Following the French defeat in the **Battle of the Frontiers**, Joffre disengaged his forces in good order. He held them together as they withdrew south-west and created two new armies from reserves and units on his right hand flank.

He originally planned to launch a counter-offensive on the Somme–Verdun line, but German pressure forced him to retreat further. By the beginning of September, Joffre regarded the moment as imminent, although the precise timing was determined by **Galliéni**'s plan to attack eastwards from Paris. His counter-attack orders were issued on 4 September and the **Battle of the Marne**, which began two days later, was Joffre's greatest success, even if some errors were made. A strong, able commander who never lost his nerve, Joffre became a national hero who had saved France from German domination.

After the enemy withdrew to the Aisne and began digging in, Joffre responded by manoeuvring to outflank their fortified front from the west. The 'Race to the Sea' marked the failure of his initial outflanking action and the beginning of trench warfare, although it did establish a strong defensive line across northern France. Joffre lacked the imagination to respond effectively to the new problems of trench warfare: attrition was his only method. There were costly failures in **Artois** (May 1915) and **Champagne** (September 1915), followed, in 1916, by **Verdun**, where serious weaknesses in the defence were revealed when the Germans attacked in February. The failure to achieve a breakthrough at the **Somme** (July–November 1916) and his apparent indifference to the heavy French losses weakened his position beyond redemption.

His resistance to legitimate political control also damaged him and at the end of 1916, **Briand**, the prime minister, replaced him by **General Nivelle**. Joffre had not been dismissed earlier because 'he alone had the prestige and influence to dominate France's Allies, particularly to keep the British faithful to the Western Front'. Promoted Marshal of France, he served as president of the Supreme War Council in 1917, but took no further active part in the direction of the war.

JOSEPH, GENERAL, ARCHDUKE, 1872–1962

Service in Galicia and on the Italian Front (the **Isonzo battles**) preceded Joseph's appointment as commander of Austrian forces on the Rumanian border. Known for his personal bravery and for his close contact with his troops, the successful invasion of Rumania in 1917 added to his reputation. He ended his wartime career on the Tyrolean front. After the war he became active in Hungarian politics and was briefly Regent of Hungary in 1919.

JOSEPH-FERDINAND, GENERAL, ARCHDUKE, 1872–1942

Commander of the Austro-Hungarian Fourth Army on the Eastern Front, Joseph-Ferdinand's was one of five armies covering Luck in 1916. He was a mediocre and uninspiring commander whose headquarters were 'the scene of incessant revelries relieved only by shooting expeditions'. The result of his frivolity was the rout of the Fourth Army at Luck in June 1916, as **Brusilov**'s surprise offensive began. Joseph-Ferdinand was relieved of his command and saw no further service in the army.

JUNKERS CLI

This two-seat German ground attack and escort monoplane, which first appeared in May 1918, was not produced in sufficient numbers before the end of the war to make any impact. Derived from the **Junkers DI** fighter, it was an advanced all-metal design of considerable strength, with cantilever wings covered in ribbed aluminium sheeting. The observer, who was armed with a **Parabellum machine-gun**, had a raised cockpit which provided a good field of fire; there was also a pair of forward-firing 7.92mm Spandau guns for the pilot. A limited number of anti-personnel weapons could also be carried on ground attack duties.

Powered by the 160hp Mercedes D IIIa engine, it had a maximum speed of 105m.p.h. and a good rate of climb, as well as excellent manoeuvrability. It was in fact the finest CL-type to appear during the war and would probably have been produced on a large scale if hostilities had continued into 1919.

JUNKERS DI

Developed from a long series of prototypes dating back to 1915, the Junkers DI was the world's first operational all-metal warplane. This single-seat monoplane fighter appeared for the first time in March 1918, but only 41 examples had been produced by the Armistice, probably because of the complexity of its construction. Distinctive corrugated metal sheeting covered the cantilever wings and the square section fuselage, which were of modern appearance. The DI was powered by either the 160hp Mercedes D III or the 185hp BMW IIIa and was armed with twin forward firing Spandau machine-guns.

The aircraft was manoeuvrable and fast, the 185hp engine giving a maximum speed of 116m.p.h. at sea level and the ability to climb to 5,000m in 22 minutes. There is little doubt that the DI would have made a considerable impact had it been available in large numbers before hostilities ended.

JUNKERS JI

The JI was a metal biplane designed by Hugo Junkers for infantry contact patrol duties, which it performed very effectively. Planned as a replacement for the interim **AEG** and **Albatros J-types**, the JI was delivered to German *Infanterieflieger* units late in 1917. It was powered by a 200hp Benz Bz IV six-cylinder engine, giving a maximum speed of 97m.p.h. at sea level and an endurance of two hours. The power plant was enclosed, along with the crew compartment, in an armoured nose section made from 5mm sheet steel; the only non-metal parts were the rear half of the fuselage, which was fabric covered, and the ash tail skid. A large upper wing and the much smaller lower wing gave the aircraft a distinctive appearance.

Armament consisted of two fixed, forward-firing Spandau machine-guns and a single ring-mounted **Parabellum gun** in the rear cockpit. The armoured shell offered crews excellent protection when they were operating at low altitudes, reporting on troop concentrations and movements (by means of a radio link), supplying their own forward units, and attacking the enemy. It was difficult for the JI to take off and land on rough ground and its heavy and cumbersome appearance gave rise to the nickname 'Furniture Van'. A total of 277 JIs had been produced by the end of the war.

JUTLAND, BATTLE OF, 31 May–1 June 1916

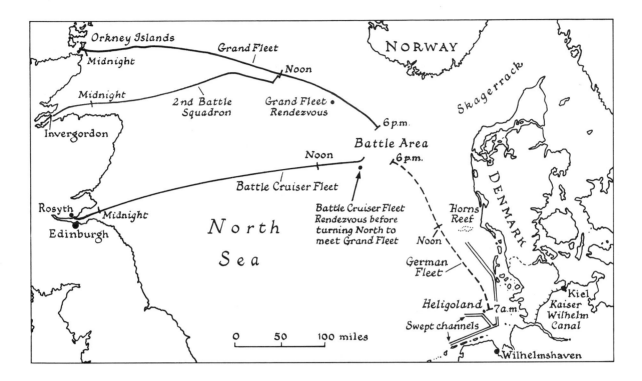

The greatest naval battle of the First World War, Jutland was the only full-scale encounter of the British and German battle fleets. It originated in a plan by **Admiral Scheer**, commander of the **High Seas Fleet** since January 1916, to lure the British **Grand Fleet** from its bases with the intention of bringing part of it to battle.

Early on 31 May 1916, the High Seas Fleet left the Jade Estuary and moved into the North Sea, parallel to the west coast of Denmark. **Hipper**, commander of the German scouting forces, led the way towards the Skaggerak with five battlecruisers and 35 other fast ships at his disposal. A long way behind was the main fleet consisting of 59 vessels, including 22 battleships (of which 16 were dreadnoughts). Radio messages intercepted by the Admiralty had given warning of the German sortie and the Grand Fleet was ordered to sail immediately.

The main fleet, under **Admiral Jellicoe**, left **Scapa Flow** on 30 May; it comprised 99 ships, of which 24 were dreadnoughts. Sixty miles ahead of Jellicoe was **Beatty**'s scouting force, which had left the Firth of Forth on the same day; it consisted of 52 ships, including six battlecruisers and an associated squadron of four super-dreadnoughts.

As the two fleets moved across the North Sea neither side had any clear information about the size of the opposing forces or their whereabouts. Contact was made during the afternoon of 31 May, when the British light cruiser *Galatea* sighted Hipper's force. Without waiting for his super-dreadnoughts, Beatty proceeded south at maximum speed on a parallel course to the German squadron, which was now moving in the same direction. Hipper had reversed course after having sighted Beatty, in the hope that he would be able to draw him towards the main German fleet.

The two scouting forces were soon in action, opening fire at 16,500 yards. More accurate German fire and faulty British ship design caused the loss of two of Beatty's battlecruisers – *Indefatigable* and *Queen Mary*. With four battlecruisers left to oppose

Hipper, Beatty ordered his ships to 'engage the enemy closer'. However, almost immediately, Beatty, who had been informed that the main High Seas Fleet was still in harbour, found it steaming towards him. He immediately changed course, moving north to join Jellicoe in the hope of luring the enemy into the hands of the Grand Fleet. The Germans, who were still unaware of its presence in the area, chased Beatty northwards for two hours, with both sides inflicting heavy damage.

As Beatty sighted Jellicoe's six divisions approaching from the north-west, he turned eastwards in front of the Germans to position himself correctly. Jellicoe deployed his fleet into the line of battle on the port wing column, placing the Grand Fleet across Scheer's line of retreat to his bases in Germany.

At about 6.30 p.m. the first British shells were fired and as all the ships of both fleets came into range there was a heavy general engagement during which the British fleet in line crossed the German 'T'. Realising that he faced imminent destruction, Scheer suddenly reversed course in a simultaneous 180-degree turn under cover of smoke and destroyer attacks. He headed west and soon his ships were out of range, as Jellicoe continued southwards. Just before 7.00 p.m. Scheer turned back again towards the British, apparently because he believed, incorrectly, that Jellicoe had divided his fleet. The Germans again came under heavy attack from the Grand Fleet and once more Scheer turned away, with the four remaining battlecruisers being ordered against the British line to cover the withdrawal. Fearing torpedo attacks Jellicoe decided to turn away at 7.20 p.m., allowing the enemy to escape to the south-west.

He positioned himself across one of the enemy's possible lines of escape in the hope of bringing Scheer to battle the following morning. However, the wrong route was chosen and Scheer was able to pass south-east through the rear of the British fleet during the night; there were several small actions but none affected the outcome of the battle. As soon as Jellicoe realised that the Germans had escaped he made arrangements to return home.

The last great naval battle fought solely with surface ships, Jutland (or the Skagerrak as it was called by the Germans) was a strategic victory for the British: the High Seas Fleet never again challenged British dominance in the North Sea and in future the German naval effort was concentrated on unrestricted submarine warfare. Tactically it was a drawn battle, there being considerable British disappointment at the failure to bring the enemy to a decisive action. British losses were heavier than the German and for this reason the battle was claimed to be the

The British dreadnought battleships Royal Oak *and* Hercules *at Jutland*

latter's victory. The British had suffered 6,784 casualties, and lost three battlecruisers, three cruisers and eight destroyers; the Germans lost one old battleship, one battlecruiser, four light cruisers and five destroyers, as well as 3,099 casualties.

KAISER

Like the **Helgolands**, the Kaiser-class dreadnoughts had 12-inch guns, but their turret arrangement was improved. There was one forward, two diagonally offset wing turrets and two superfiring aft, and as a result all five twin turrets could be fired to either side producing an increased weight of broadside. These arrangements were facilitated by the adoption of turbine propulsion, the first time it had been used in a German battleship. The Kaisers had a displacement of 24,333 tons, a maximum speed of 21 knots and further improvements in armour protection.

The class was completed in 1912–13 and *Kaiser*, *Kaiserin*, *Prinzregent Luitpold* and *König Albert* formed Battle Squadron III of the **High Seas Fleet**; *Friedrich der Grosse* was the flagship of the commander-in-chief. All except *König Albert* were present at **Jutland** and none sustained any serious damage during the war. The five ships surrendered and were interned at **Scapa Flow**, where they were scuttled on 21 June 1919.

KAMIO, GENERAL MITSOUMI, 1856–1927

A veteran Japanese soldier with extensive experience of China, General Kamio led a force of 25,000 men (including a British contingent) against the German possession of **Tsingtao** in September 1914. Overwhelming strength and superiority in heavy artillery ensured the eventual surrender of the garrison (on 7 November) and helped to minimise Japanese casualties in a well-managed campaign. Kamio remained in China as governor of the former German territory until his return to Japan in 1915, when he was appointed commander of the Tokyo garrison.

KÁROLYI, COUNT MIHÁLY, 1875–1955

Hungarian politician and leader of the pro-Entente Independent Party during the First World War. On 30 October 1918, he was appointed prime minister by King Charles and quickly sought an armistice. Károlyiwas, however, unsuccessful in his attempt to secure the more favourable peace terms that a newly independent Hungary might have expected. He became President of the Republic on 16 November 1918.

KAZAKOV, ALEXANDER, 1891–1919

The leading Russian fighter ace of the First World War, Staff Captain Kazakov is generally credited with 17 hits, although his actual score is likely to have been substantially higher. His first victim was an **Albatros** two-seater brought down in March 1915. In 1917 Kazakov commanded No 1 Fighter Group of the Imperial Russian Air Service and after the Revolution served with the British forces involved in the civil war. He was killed in a flying accident before the end of the conflict.

K-CLASS SUBMARINE

Like the earlier J-class, the Ks represented another British attempt to produce a submarine that was capable of operating with the main fleet – travelling with it on the surface and submerging when the enemy was engaged. Developed in 1915, the K-class was the biggest submarine then produced, being 330 feet in length, with a displacement of 1,980 tons (when surfaced) and a distinctive swan-shaped bow.

with ten 18-inch torpedo tubes, including a revolving twin tube in the superstructure; it was also equipped with two 4-inch and one 3-inch high-angle guns.

The K-class submarines, of which 17 were produced, had a disastrous operational record during the First World War, and only once was the enemy engaged. They were, however, involved in a large number of accidents, the most serious being a

The British steam submarine K6

The main power plant was based on the experience of *Swordfish*, Britain's first steam-driven submarine: the K's oil-fired steam turbines were then the only means of reaching the target speed of 24 knots. Batteries powered the boat underwater, while a third source – an 800hp diesel engine – was used while steam was being built up after surfacing or while in harbour. Although the Ks were technically advanced, they were relatively slow in diving because of the need to seal the funnels first. They were heavily armed

notorious incident in January 1918. A flotilla of submarines and other ships were involved in a series of collisions, which resulted in two Ks being sunk and four others being damaged. A jammed helm was the immediate cause but it raised questions about the suitability of operating submarines, with their limited bridge facilities, as part of the battle fleet.

KEMAL ATATÜRK, MUSTAFA, 1881–1938

Turkish statesman and general, Kemal was the first president of the Turkish Republic (1924–38). He had played a minor role in the revolution of 1908, but had later fallen out with its leaders and concentrated on his military career. Kemal strongly opposed Turkey's entry into the First World War on the German side, but was willing to do his professional duty once war was declared in October 1914.

Kemal Atatürk: hero of Gallipoli and first president of the Republic of Turkey

It was not until early in the following year that he was given a command – of the 19th Division in the **Gallipoli** peninsula. Unlike the German in overall command, **Liman von Sanders**, and many of his fellow Turkish officers, Kemal correctly predicted the landing points of the Anglo-French invasion force on 25 April 1915.

Under Kemal's inspired leadership his troops responded effectively to the enemy threat and held the key Sari Bair ridge, which commanded the whole peninsula. In August he again salvaged the situation, correctly identifying the place where a further wave of Allied troops would land. Immediately promoted to corps commander, he was now in operational control of the entire Gallipoli front. After a closely fought battle, the Allies were again unable to secure the commanding ridges, and Kemal's great tactical skills were an important factor in the successful outcome: 'with his swift intuitive convictions as to how an enemy would act and how best to act against him, he was a commander of outstanding vision.'

As the Gallipoli campaign ended, Kemal was rewarded with a transfer to the Caucasus, rather than promotion, in order to assist in retrieving the situation there. However, he soon became a general and commanded an army in the Turkish counter-offensive during the summer of 1916. It was unsuccessful although Kemal was the only Turkish commander who emerged from it with any credit. After the collapse of the Caucasus front following the **Russian Revolution**, Kemal was moved to Syria as commander of the Seventh Army. In August 1918, he opposed **Allenby**'s final offensive but was unable to hold the Turkish front line. He avoided defeat by a major retreat to the Turkish border beyond Aleppo and defended his position there until the Armistice was signed. He was the only senior Turkish commander who never suffered a defeat during the war.

KERENSKY, ALEKSANDR, 1881–1970

Russian Socialist-Revolutionary who emerged as the leading figure in the Provisional Government that was formed after the Revolution in March 1917. Initially appointed Minister of Justice, this energetic democrat became Minister of War in May and was appointed prime minister in July. He sought to continue the war in order to prevent a general German victory and launched a major new offensive in July. It collapsed quickly as the rank and file gave further indications of their unwillingness to fight, and the disintegration of the Russian army accelerated. With no prospect of the separate peace that might have saved his regime, Kerensky struggled to suppress his enemies on the right and left. In September, **General Kornilov**, the new commander-in-chief, was ordered to crush the Bolsheviks in Petrograd, but

fears grew about his political reliability. Kerensky was compelled to ask his revolutionary opponents to disarm the force as it moved on the city. As a result the Bolsheviks continued to grow in influence and when their insurrection was launched in November 1917 Kerensky could muster few troops in his support. Out of office he soon left the country, remaining in exile for the rest of his life.

KERENSKY OFFENSIVE, 1–19 July 1917

Under heavy Allied pressure, **Kerensky** and the Provisional Government agreed to launch a major new offensive on the Eastern Front, even though the Russian army was rapidly disintegrating. Using the most reliable units at its disposal, **General Brusilov** planned an attack at two key points, although there were also to be several minor associated operations. The main assault was launched against the Austro-German South Army (**General von Bothmer**), near Brody on 1 July 1917. The Russian Eleventh and Seventh Armies (31 divisions) made good progress on the first day, moving towards Lemberg on a 40-mile front.

However, low Russian morale and a good supply of German reserves ensured that the offensive soon ground to a halt. To the left of the South Army, the Austrian Seventh Army was also able to hold off the enemy. Further to the south, the situation was initially much more favourable to the Russians. The Eighth Army (**Kornilov**) advanced from Stanislau in an attack that surprised the defending Austrian Third Army. General Kornilov moved forward more than 20 miles on a 60-mile front and was soon in sight of the Drohobicz oil fields. Again, low Russian morale and the availability of German reserves eventually brought the advance to a halt.

With reinforcements quickly transferred from the Western Front, the Germans concentrated west of Brody, and launched a counter-attack on 19 July. A massive seven-hour artillery bombardment was followed by an infantry assault which broke through the Russian lines and then turned south-east, advancing 10 miles on the first day. They rolled up the front with little resistance as thousands of war-weary Russian troops threw down their weapons and fled the battlefield.

A two-week retreat began, with all the gains of the Kerensky offensive being lost and the Central Powers moving beyond the enemy's starting line. The final action took place in Rumania when, on 22 July, the Russians and the Rumanians attacked between Foscani and the Carpathians on a 60-mile front. They had some initial successes, but on 6 August **Mackensen** counter-attacked and drove the enemy back. He did not, however, have sufficient troops to achieve a decisive victory. As trench warfare returned on this part of the front, the final Russian offensive of the First World War was brought to an inglorious end.

KEYES, VICE-ADMIRAL SIR ROGER, 1st BARON, 1872–1945

The youngest captain in the Royal Navy on his appointment in 1904, Keyes quickly made his mark and became head of the submarine service in 1910. During the first six months of the war, based at

Harwich, he was responsible for submarine operations in the North Sea. He planned and took part in the **Heligoland Bight** operation in August 1914, which resulted in the loss of three German cruisers and a destroyer. Early in 1915 he became chief of staff to **Admiral Carden**, who was in command of the **Dardanelles operation**, and also served with his successor, **Admiral De Robeck**. Keyes had a more optimistic view of the value of the navy in this theatre than his chief and he even pressed for a further assault after a complete withdrawal had been decided upon.

In October 1917, after a period with the **Grand Fleet**, he became director of plans at the Admiralty and developed an imaginative proposal for a naval attack on the German U-boat bases of **Zeebrugge** and Ostend. He was soon appointed to the command of the Dover Patrol with the aim of implementing this plan. The action on 22 April 1918 failed in its military objective of blocking the entrance to the harbours, although it had a considerable psychological impact.

Keyes, who was knighted after the attack, remained in his command until the end of the war. He had always shown himself to be a 'fearless and inspired leader who had never missed an opportunity of striking at the enemy'.

During the Second World War, Keyes was recalled from retirement and appointed Director of Combined Operations in July 1940, a post he held until October 1941. In January 1943, he was created Baron Keyes of Zeebrugge and Dover.

Keyes with George V and King Albert at Zeebrugge, the port he failed to close during the war

KEYNES, JOHN MAYNARD, BARON, 1883–1946

British economist who served in the Treasury during the war and was its main representative at the **Paris Peace Conference**. He was strongly critical of the proposed financial settlement that emerged, believing that the German economy could not sustain the level of reparations demanded. Keynes recorded his negative views in a notable book, *The Economic Consequences of the Peace* (1919), and resigned as a civil servant.

KIGGELL, GENERAL SIR LAUNCELOT, 1862–1954

After a succession of staff appointments at the War Office, Kiggell became chief of staff to **Sir Douglas Haig** in December 1915. Without direct experience of modern warfare, he was subservient to the commander-in-chief and his views were 'exceedingly orthodox and plodding'. His judgement was also suspect: for example, he remained optimistic well into 1917 about the chances of removing the Germans from the Belgian coast and in October of the same year he was in favour of continuing the push on **Passchendaele** even though the exhaustion of the troops and other factors were clearly against it. Pressure was put on Haig to part with Kiggell, who in fact left for England early in 1918, suffering from 'nervous exhaustion'.

KING EDWARD VII

Completed in 1905–07, these British pre-dreadnoughts were an improvement on their predecessors, the **Londons** and the **Duncans**: secondary armament was enhanced by the introduction of four 9.2-inch guns and armour protection was increased. Maximum speed was a creditable 19 knots and their displacement was 15,630 tons. During the First World War the eight warships of the King Edward VII class formed the 3rd Battle Squadron of the **Grand Fleet**, where they were known as the 'Wobbly Eight'. Two ships were lost during the war: *King Edward VII* herself hit a mine and sank in January 1916 and *Britannia* was torpedoed two days before the end of the war. The remainder (*Commonwealth, Zealandia, Dominion, Hindustan, Africa, Hibernia*) were broken up soon afterwards.

KING GEORGE V

The King George V-class battleship was a modified version of the **Orions**, with a slight increase in dimensions, the repositioning of the mast before the two large funnels, and changes to the armour. A major weakness was the relatively poor secondary armament, the 4-inch guns being inadequate to meet effectively the increasing threat from destroyers and torpedo boats. *King George V, Centurion* and *Ajax* served with the 2nd Battle Squadron, **Grand Fleet**, throughout the war and all were present at the **Battle of Jutland**. *Audacious* – the other ship of this class – also joined the same unit in August 1914, but on 24 October she sank after hitting a mine off the Irish coast, one of only two dreadnought battleships to be lost by the Royal Navy during the war.

KITCHENER, FIELD MARSHAL HORATIO HERBERT, 1ST EARL, 1850–1916

Distinguished British soldier and former commander-in-chief in India, Kitchener was Secretary of State for War in **Asquith**'s cabinet from 5 August 1914 until his death in mid-1916. The first serving officer to hold the post, he recognised that the war would not be over within a few months. One of his first actions was to go to Paris to order **Sir John French** to remain in line after the retreat from Mons. He presided over the expansion of Britain's armed forces, with the aim of creating 'New Armies' of 70 divisions, and campaigned actively for new recruits. The slogan 'Your Country needs YOU' will always be associated with his successful wartime recruitment drive.

In other respects, however, his tenure at the War Office achieved less. He lacked the necessary political skills to work effectively with his Cabinet colleagues, he could not delegate and his relationships with some of the British commanders in France were strained. More serious were the attacks on him during the shell crisis of May 1915, which was resolved by the creation of a separate Ministry of Munitions under **Lloyd George**. His active support for the **Gallipoli expedition** and his opposition to the evacuation of British troops late in 1915 also proved to be damaging. It led to an offer of resignation which Asquith refused, but the effect of these setbacks was to undermine his power and prestige. He lost his role as the Cabinet's principal adviser on strategy, a function allocated to **Sir William Robertson**, the new Chief of the Imperial General Staff.

In mid-1916, he was sent on a mission to Russia in an attempt to boost the Russian army's efforts against the Germans. On 5 June, he was drowned when the cruiser *Hampshire*, which was taking him to Russia, struck a mine and sank. A popular symbol of Britain's determination to defeat Germany, he was the 'only outstanding military figure on either side who came to a violent end'.

Kitchener exploited voluntary recruitment to its limit in order to fill the British trenches in Flanders

KLUCK, GENERAL ALEXANDER von, 1846–1934

German general, a veteran of the campaigns of 1866 and 1870, who commanded the First Army during the first few months of the war. Kluck was positioned on the right wing of the invasion force as it wheeled through Belgium and France in August 1914. At first everything went according to the plan developed by von Schlieffen, with Kluck's army passing through Brussels and defeating the British army at Mons and again at **Le Cateau**. As he advanced with great speed across France, he changed direction to pass east of Paris (rather than west as stipulated in the **Schlieffen Plan**), in order to roll up the French Fifth Army as it retreated southwards.

Kluck: lack of resolve at the Battle of the Marne ended his career

In the process Kluck exposed his right flank to the Paris garrison and was forced to move westwards to deal with the French flanking attack (7–9 September). As a result, Kluck increased the gap between the First and Second Armies, and the BEF, which he had discounted, moved into the gap. The flanks of both armies were now threatened and **Moltke**'s staff ordered a general withdrawal, bringing the **Battle of the Marne** to an end. Kluck, who remained convinced that he had been deprived of ultimate victory by this premature action, left active service after being injured at the front in March 1915.

KOLCHAK, VICE-ADMIRAL ALEKSANDR, 1874–1920

One of Russia's finest naval leaders of the First World War, Kolchak acquired his reputation as an energetic and resourceful sea captain during wartime service with the Baltic Fleet. Supporting the aggressive strategy of the fleet commander, **Admiral von Essen**, against the German navy, he secured rapid promotion in a succession of staff and line appointments. In July 1916, he became commander of the Black Sea fleet, with the rank of vice-admiral, and led many successful operations against Turkish and German naval forces. In the aftermath of the March Revolution he was forced to leave his command and when the Bolsheviks seized power in November 1917, Kolchak assumed the leadership of the White forces in Siberia. As the civil war drew to a close, he was captured by the Bolsheviks and executed by firing squad.

KOLUBRA RIVER, BATTLE OF, 3–9 December 1914

The failure of the first Austrian invasion of Serbia in August 1914 did not deter **General Potiorek** from trying again little more than two weeks later, on 7 September. Attacking from both sides of the Serbian salient, the Austrian Fifth Army advanced from the north and the Sixth from the west. As a result the Serbians were forced to withdraw from Austrian Bosnia, which they had invaded only the day before. They launched a heavy attack on Potiorek's bridgeheads but after 10 days' heavy fighting along the River Drina, **Putnik**, the Serbian commander, was forced to withdraw to more defensible positions further east. At the same time (17 September), the Austrian commander halted his offensive to reorganise and reinforce his armies. The attack was renewed on 5 November and the Serbs were slowly driven back as the Austrians advanced with relative ease; Valjevo fell on 15 November and Belgrade, the Serbian capital, on 2 December.

To the south the Austrians held a position beyond the Kolubra River, some 50 miles east of the Drina, and had become over-extended in the mountainous terrain. On 3 December, the Serbians launched a major counter-offensive and after five days Potiorek ordered a withdrawal. Belgrade was re-captured on 15 December as the enemy finally left Serbian soil, their retreat having been covered by monitors on the Danube and Drina rivers. Putnik's forces were in no condition to pursue them across the frontier and the fighting ended. The casualties on both sides of this bitterly fought campaign, with both sides practising 'horrible brutalities', were high: the Austrians lost 227,000 men compared with a Serb total of 170,000. Potiorek was removed from his command, being replaced by **Archduke Eugen**. The front remained quiet until October 1915, when a new invasion, in which the Germans and Bulgarians participated, was launched.

KÖNIG

The last German battleships to be completed before the outbreak of war, the Königs were similar in many respects to the **Kaiser**-class. A major change was the location of all the turrets on the centre line – superfiring pairs fore and aft with the fifth between the funnels. The Königs, which had excellent armour protection and a maximum speed of 21 knots, were the last German warships to be equipped with 12-inch guns.

König, *Grosser Kürfurst*, *Markgraf* and *Kronprinz* served with Battle Squadron III of the **High Seas Fleet** throughout the war. All were present at **Jutland** and only *Kronprinz* escaped undamaged. *Grosser Kürfurst* was in fact subsequently torpedoed by a British submarine, in collision with *Kronprinz*, and damaged by a mine. All surrendered to the **Grand Fleet** in November 1918 and were scuttled at **Scapa Flow** on 21 June 1919.

KORNILOV, GENERAL LAVRENTI, 1870–1918

Kornilov's distinguished wartime service in the Russian Eighth Army (**Brusilov**) was temporarily ended with his capture during the Austro-German offensive at **Gorlice** in May 1915. Noted for his bravery, he escaped from the enemy just over a year later – the first Russian general to do so – and became a national hero. He was given command of the Eighth Army in recognition of his services. After the March Revolution, Kornilov's career progressed rapidly and, in August 1917, **Kerensky** appointed him commander-in-chief, with the task of restoring discipline to the demoralised troops. Kornilov soon came into conflict with Kerensky over the country's future political structure and in September led an unsuccessful counter-revolutionary march on the capital. Kornilov escaped from captivity soon after the November Revolution but was killed in April 1918, in a battle with Bolshevik forces.

KÖVESS von KÖVESSHÁZA, FIELD MARSHAL HERMANN, BARON, 1854–1924

As commander of the Austro-Hungarian Third Army, Kövess participated successfully in the invasion of **Serbia** in October 1915, in company with Germany and Bulgaria. The capture of Montenegro and parts of Albania was subsequently added to his list of achievements. His involvement in the abortive Trentino offensive was a less happy experience, but after driving back the Russians in the summer of 1917 he was promoted field marshal. Kövess was subsequently given command of an army group on the Eastern Front until peace was concluded in March 1918.

KRAFFT VON DELMENSINGEN, GENERAL KONRAD, 1862–1953

An expert on mountain warfare, Krafft was first appointed to the command of the German Alpine Corps early in 1915, after a period on the Western Front as a staff officer. He developed his specialist skills during the occupation of **Serbia** in October 1915 and in the invasion of **Rumania** late in 1916, where his troops played an important part in breaking through the Transylvanian mountains. In August 1917, **Ludendorff** sent him to the Italian front to assess the feasibility of a breakthrough at a weak spot in the enemy lines near Tolmino in the Julian Alps. His recommendations provided the basis for the German offensive plan that led to the victory of **Caporetto** in October 1917. Krafft returned to the Western Front for much of the rest of the war.

KROBATIN, ALEXANDER, BARON VON, 1849–1933

Austro-Hungarian War Minister for most of the war period, Krobatin played an important role in modernising the Austrian army. He ensured that it was equipped with up-to-date weapons, particularly artillery pieces, in sufficient numbers. Krobatin left the War Ministry at his own request in April 1917 and went to the Italian front as commander of the Tenth Army, serving there until the end of the war. The **Battle of Caporetto** was the high point of Krobatin's professional career and he was promoted field marshal for his contribution to the victory.

KUROPATKIN, GENERAL ALEKSEI, 1848–1925

Commander of all Russian field forces in the Far East during the Russo-Japanese War, General Kuropatkin had been demoted after his defeat at the Battle of Mukden. In 1915, the exigencies of war provided Kuropatkin with the opportunity of a further combat command and early in 1916 the ageing general was placed in charge of the whole Northern Front. However, his inaction during the **Brusilov offensive** confirmed his unsuitability for high command and he resigned in July 1916.

KUT AL IMARA, CAPTURE OF, 28 September 1915

The battle against Turkey on the Mesopotamian front began in October 1914 with the invasion of the coastal area by a British force which had been sent from India. The oil installations on Abadan Island were seized and Basra, 20 miles inland, was occupied on 22 November 1914. Qurna, at the junction of the Tigris and Euphrates rivers, was occupied in the last action of the year.

The first offensive operations of 1915 drove the Turks from Ahwaz, to the east, and brought the oilfields under permanent British control. In March, the main force of two infantry divisions and a cavalry brigade, under the overall command of **General Nixon**, moved northwards up the Tigris and Euphrates towards Kut al Imara. The immediate aim was to secure the British position by extending their control over the whole of Lower Mesopotamia, although Baghdad was seen as the ultimate prize. Imara, 100 miles to the north, was taken by the 11,000 troops under the command of **General Townshend** on 31 May. They had arrived there in a flotilla of native boats known as 'Townshend's Regatta', as the river was the only suitable route through the region. Similar progress was made on the Euphrates, where a smaller force under Major-General Gorringe protected Townshend's flank. After a month's hard struggle in the summer heat,

Nasiriya was captured in July 1915 with few British casualties.

As Turkish opposition had been relatively slight Nixon decided to continue the advance; Townshend, with his 6th Indian Division and a cavalry brigade, met the Turks again at Kut. Here a similar force of 10,500 men, under the command of General Nur-ud-Din, was well entrenched on both banks of the Tigris. Crossing the river he attacked from the north on 28 September, routing the Turks, who lost 5,300 men and all of their artillery. However, a fall in the water level delayed Townshend's advance and he was unable to prevent the escape of the Turkish survivors to **Ctesiphon**, where defensive positions had already been prepared. Without waiting for reinforcements, Townshend was ordered to move forwards from Aziziya on 11 November, with the aim of capturing **Baghdad**.

KUT AL IMARA, SIEGE OF, 3 December 1915–29 April 1916

After the failure of his assault on **Ctesiphon** late in November 1915, **Townshend**'s Anglo-Indian force was forced to retreat, reaching Kut on 3 December. With his exhausted infantry unable to travel further, Townshend decided to try to hold Kut, a key point in the territory held by the British in Mesopotamia. Defences were prepared around the village, which was situated in a loop of the Tigris, before the Turks besieged it on 7 September. Townshend soon became securly 'bottled with the cork in'. The operation involved two Turkish divisions (10,500 men) under the command of General Nur-ad-Din and **General von der Goltz**, who had been sent to Mesopotamia with orders to expel the British from the whole region. Three successive assaults failed to penetrate the fortifications and the Turks began a blockade, using most of their troops to prevent a relief expedition from reaching Kut.

The first attempt was made in January 1916 when

two Indian divisions, newly arrived from France, were sent out from Basra, under the command of Sir Fenton Aylmer. They were repulsed on 21 January and again early in March, with heavy losses. In April a further expedition, under Sir George Gorringe, met Goltz's Turkish Sixth Army; it broke through their lines 20 miles south of Kut but was unable to make any further progress. Without hope of relief, the Kut garrison surrendered on 29 April 1916, after a siege of almost five months; the defenders' limited food supply had run out and they were faced with imminent starvation. Some 8,000 men were taken prisoner, with a large proportion dying in captivity, although Townshend himself was relatively well treated. Goltz, who had died of cholera in March, did not live to see the final capitulation. Months of preparation were to be needed before **General Maude**, the new British commander, could launch another British offensive.

LACAZE, ADMIRAL MARIE, 1860–1955

French Minister of Marine from October 1915 until August 1917, Lacaze was an experienced staff officer who had also commanded a squadron of battleships in the Mediterranean during the first year of the war. One of his main concerns as Minister was the French response to the U-boat threat and, although he was a leading proponent of the **convoy system**, criticism of his handling of the problem led to his departure from the Cabinet.

LANCHESTER ARMOURED CAR

Apart from the **Rolls Royce** there were more Lanchester armoured cars in British service than any other design. Several standard Lanchester touring cars were used by **Commander Samson**'s force at Dunkirk, but by the beginning of 1915 the Lanchester armoured car – built on the 38hp chassis – was in production. The turret and fighting compartment were very similar to the Rolls Royce's, although the sloping frontal armour, which the Lanchester's mechanical layout made possible, was different and more effective. Operated by a crew of three or four, the vehicle was armed with a turret-mounted .303 **Vickers machine-gun** and weighed about five tons. It was powered by a six-cylinder 4.8-litre engine and had a maximum speed of 50m.p.h.

The Lanchester equipped three squadrons of the RNAS armoured car division, which were sent to France in May 1915. Some Lanchesters were also delivered to the Russians during the same year. With the prospect of trench warfare continuing indefinitely, the naval units were disbanded later in the year and most Lanchesters were quickly phased out of British service. One exception was the force of 36 Lanchester cars that was sent to assist the Russians in 1916–17. Their continuous service in the Caucasus, North Persia, Rumania and Galicia, often in very poor conditions, was testimony to the reliability and strength of the Lanchester design.

LANCIA IZ ARMOURED CAR

The standard Italian armoured car of the First World War, the Lancia was a substantial vehicle which used the IZ 25/35hp light truck chassis and was powered by a 5,000cc four-cylinder engine.

It was constructed of heavy armour and offered good protection to the crew. Hull design followed standard lines, except for an unusual turret arrangement: a small turret, accommodating a single **St-Etienne machine-gun** rested on a much larger one that was equipped with two further guns of the same type. (In later examples the smaller turret was removed and the surplus machine-gun was mounted at the rear.) Apart from the three gunners, the vehicle housed a commander, a driver and a mechanic, as well as 25,000 rounds of ammunition. The two wire-cutting rails at the front of the car were another useful feature.

The Lancia IZ was used throughout the war against Austrian and German forces and was retained in Italian service long afterwards. The same chassis was also used as a mounting for a 75/30 anti-aircraft gun and this self-propelled weapon was also in service from 1915 until the Armistice.

LANGLE DE CARY, GENERAL FERDINAND DE, 1849–1927

A distinguished veteran of the Franco-Prussian War, Langle de Cary was recalled from retirement at the beginning of the war, only weeks after he had left the service. As commander of the Fourth Army he was positioned to the east of **General Lanrezac**'s Fifth Army and fought the German Fourth Army in the Ardennes. After his defeat there, the Fourth Army retreated south-east in good order and during the **Battle of the Marne** held the line successfully between the Third Army (**Sarrail**) and the Ninth (**Foch**). As Langle de Cary advanced after the battle, on 11 September, he soon came into contact with the German army and in this sector the long period of trench warfare quickly began.

In December 1915, he was promoted to the command of the Centre Army Group, which included responsibility for **Verdun**. Following the major German assault in February 1916, Langle de Cary received much unjustified criticism for the neglected state of the fortress. Operational control of the forces defending the area passed to **General Pétain** and in March he was relieved. Although advanced age was given as the apparent reason, Langle de Cary was in fact sacrificed in an attempt to meet public disquiet about the Verdun disaster.

LANREZAC, GENERAL CHARLES, 1852–1925

Appointed commander of the French Fifth Army on the outbreak of war, Lanrezac was alarmed about its exposed position on the north of the French line facing the Ardennes. It risked envelopment by a major German thrust through Belgium, a possibility that had been discounted in pre-war French military planning. Agreement was secured to move the Fifth Army to the north-west on the line of the Sambre, where it could protect the French left. It was also to link up with the BEF, but one of Lanrezac's major failings was his inability to co-operate effectively with the British.

On 24 August, after the Battle of the Sambre, he withdrew southwards, far too rapidly in **Joffre**'s view. Ordered to counter-attack, Lanrezac won a tactical victory against the German First Army at Guise on 29 August. In spite of this small success, Lanrezac was battle-weary and pessimistic about the outcome of the campaign. On 3 September, he was removed from his command as the weakened Fifth Army retreated to the **Marne**, and was not employed again during the war.

LANSING, ROBERT, 1864–1928

American Secretary of State, 1915–20, Lansing was a strong advocate of US entry into the war. His role was, however, constrained by **Woodrow Wilson**'s special interest in foreign policy and by the activities of **Edward House**, the president's special envoy. Lansing accompanied President Wilson to the **Paris Peace Conference**, where the two men disagreed about the importance of the League of Nations and whether it had a place in the peace treaty. In spite of his reservations on this specific issue, Lansing advocated the ratification of the **Treaty of Versailles** by the US Senate. He was forced to resign in 1920 after further disagreements with the president.

LAW, ANDREW BONAR, 1858–1923

British Conservative Party leader since 1911 and future post-war prime minister, Bonar Law joined **Asquith**'s coalition government as Colonial Secretary in May 1915. Unable to form a government on Asquith's resignation, in December 1916, he buried his differences with **Lloyd George** and served under him as Chancellor of the Exchequer. He remained at the Treasury until the end of the war, his most notable achievement being to put Britain's war finances on a firmer footing. One important innovation was the promotion of national war bonds, which provided the state with a continuous flow of money until the end of the war. He worked in close partnership with Lloyd George and was consulted by him on all the important wartime decisions.

LAWRENCE, T. E., 1888–1935

British archaeologist and army officer who, as 'Lawrence of Arabia', was one of the leaders of the Arab Revolt against Turkey during the First World War. He spent the first two years of the war as an intelligence officer in Egypt, but in October 1916 he was sent on a mission to Jedda, where his deep knowledge of the Arabs and his sympathy for their aspirations were put to good use. He met and established cordial relations with Hussein, Sherif of Mecca, and his son **Feisal**. Subsequently appointed liaison officer and adviser to Feisal, Lawrence encouraged him to continue the guerrilla attacks against the Turkish-held towns of the Hejaz that had started on a small scale six months earlier. The Medina–Damascus railway, the lifeline of the Turkish garrisons, was the main target of Lawrence's raids. In May 1917 he went north as far as Syria with the aim of stirring revolt and raising new Arab forces.

On his return he defeated the enemy near Ma'an and opened a route to the port of Aqaba, which he captured in August 1917. The whole of the Hejaz south of Aqaba, except for Medina, was now in Arab hands, and Lawrence turned his attention northwards. With more British support secured, Lawrence was active during the winter of 1917–18 and beyond as a mobile flank on the right of **Allenby**'s forces in Palestine. Towards the end of 1917 Lawrence was briefly held by the Turks, but they did not recognise him even though a substantial reward had been offered for his capture. In the summer of 1918 Lawrence persuaded Feisal to advance on Damascus in support of Allenby's right flank. The Arabs defeated the Turkish Forth Army as it retreated after the **Battle of Megiddo** and arrived in **Damascus** early in October, shortly before Allenby.

Lawrence of Arabia, a leader of the Arab revolt, operated against the Turks on the right flank of Allenby's army. He adopted Arab clothing and customs when campaigning in the desert

Lawrence continued to advocate the cause of Arab nationalism as a delegate to the **Paris Peace Conference**, but he had no effect. In particular, he viewed the transfer of Syria to a French mandate as a betrayal of the goals for which he had fought. He subsequently retired from public life and lived in relative obscurity in the ranks of the RAF. He recorded his wartime experiences in several volumes, of which the *Seven Pillars of Wisdom* was the most notable. Although doubts have been raised about the value and effectiveness of his military role, no other wartime figure 'carried so mysterious a glamour of romance, enhanced as much by his aloofness and wilfulness, as by the superb prose in which he has recounted his story'.

L-CLASS SUBMARINE

Designed as replacements for the British **E-class**, the Ls incorporated several improvements suggested by wartime experience. This saddle tank version was longer than its predecessor, with improved crew accommodation and a greater range of 3,800 nautical miles at 10 knots. The first batch had six 18-inch torpedo tubes (four bow and two beam) but L9 onwards had four 21-inch tubes in the bow while retaining the same number of beam tubes; all L-class boats were also armed with a 4-inch gun at the front of the conning tower. Five units were completed as minelayers which could carry up to 16 mines. Only 12 examples of this excellent submarine had been completed by the Armistice.

LEBEL REVOLVER

Designed and produced by the French state arsenal, the Lebel revolver was adopted by the French army in 1892 and remained in service throughout both world wars. The chamber of this double action weapon, which took six 8mm cartridges, swung out to the right for loading. Although the cartridge was not very powerful, the Lebel had the advantage of being uncomplicated and relatively easy to maintain.

LEBEL RIFLE

The standard French rifle at the beginning of the First World War, the 8mm Lebel dated back to 1886. Named after a member of the French small arms committee, the Lebel or Fusil Modèle 1886 was the first service rifle to fire smokeless propellent cartridges, although it did not retain this lead for long. In other respects the weapon was not so advanced, retaining the straight action bolt system of the Gras rifle of 1874. The tubular magazine, in which eight rounds were loaded nose to tail, was located under the barrel; it derived from the earlier Austrian Kropatschek rifle. A bayonet could be fitted underneath the muzzle.

The weapon was modified in 1893 and 1898, but it had already been overtaken by superior German and Austrian designs. Its major weakness was the outdated tubular magazine: slow to load, there was always the danger of an explosion if the nose of one round hit the primer of the one in front. For this reason the clip-loaded **Berthier rifle** eventually found favour, entering mass production in the second year of the war.

LE CATEAU, BATTLE OF, 26 August 1914

After the British withdrawal from Mons on 23 August 1914, in the **Battle of the Frontiers**, **Sir John French**, commander of BEF, on the French left, retreated south-west. The German right advanced into France on a front of about 70 miles, with the British being closely pursued by the First Army (**Kluck**). The Germans had almost caught up with II Corps (**Smith-Dorrien**) on the British left flank by the time it reached Le Cateau, 35 miles from Mons and 18 north of St Quentin. Separated from I Corps (**Haig**) by the Forest of Mormal, a distance of 12 miles, Smith-Dorrien decided to stand and fight a rearguard action, despite contrary instructions from Sir John French. His decision, which showed 'wonderful courage', was based on a belief that his exhausted troops would be unable to escape from the Germans without fighting first.

On 26 August 1914, three and a half British divisions engaged the full strength of the First Army, which was double its size and had an even greater superiority in artillery. The British army's biggest battle since Waterloo lasted 11 hours as it fought a double envelopment. When night fell Smith-Dorrien disengaged successfully and continued to retreat towards St Quentin. British casualties amounted to 8,000 men (out of a total of 40,000) with the loss of 38 guns; the enemy had also suffered heavy losses during the battle and there was no real pursuit. The action had enabled the BEF to escape, but to strengthen the Allied left it was was necessary to move a new French Sixth Army, previously the Army of Lorraine (**Maunoury**), to Amiens.

LEE-ENFIELD RIFLE

The standard rifle of the British army during the First World War, the Short Magazine Lee-Enfield (SMLE) Mark III appeared in 1907. Dating back in its original form to 1903, a considerable number of SMLE variants were produced and it remained in British service until 1957.

It used the magazine system and bolt action that was developed by James Lee, an American designer, and first employed in the Lee-Metford Rifle of 1888. The rest of the design, including the rifling and barrel, was the responsibility of the Royal Small Arms Factory at Enfield Lock. A short (25-inch) barrel was adopted with the aim of producing a single weapon that could be used by both infantry and cavalry, and thereby avoiding the complexities of producing a separate carbine version. Lee's turnbolt action was reliable, fast and easy to operate. An experienced soldier was able to fire as many as 30 rounds a minute at a muzzle velocity of 634m per second. The magazine, which could be quickly loaded, held 10 rounds (instead of the usual five) of .303 ammunition. A magazine cut-off enabled single shots to be loaded while the rounds in the magazine itself were held in reserve until they were needed in an emergency.

On entering service the new short-barrel weapon was not at first well received and development of a possible alternative – the Rifle Pattern 1914 – was authorised. However, the weapon's operational performance was difficult to fault and the SMLE established itself as one of the best standard service rifles of the war. Its main weakness was its relative complexity, making it difficult and expensive to manufacture in the vast quantities needed. As a result wartime production concentrated on the SMLE Mark III, which had no magazine cut-out and no long range sights. To meet wartime demand from the British army and colonial forces, the SMLE was produced in India and Australia as well as at Enfield Lock.

LEMAN, GENERAL GERARD, 1851–1920

On the outbreak of war, General Leman was in command of the Belgian Third Division, which defended **Liège** against the German assault. Heavily outnumbered, he held on to the forts ringing the city until enemy artillery forced him to surrender on 16 August 1914, after 11 days' bombardment. Leman was captured unconscious after having blown up the fort he himself was occupying as a final act of opposition. His gallant defence of Liège gave the Allies time to deploy their forces before the main German advance resumed.

LENIN, VLADIMIR ILYICH, 1870–1924

Russian revolutionary leader who led the Bolsheviks to power in the November Revolution and was the principal architect of the new Soviet state. He had been in exile at the time of the March Revolution, but returned to Petrograd soon afterwards in the famous 'sealed train' provided by the German General Staff. His efforts to undermine the Provisional Government at first came to nothing and after an abortive Soviet coup in July 1917 he was forced to flee the country again. He returned in October and following the seizure of power became head of government – Chairman of the Soviet of Peoples' Commissars.

Although the First World War had created the circumstances in which a revolution could succeed, Lenin was well aware of the urgent need to end Russia's involvement in it before the new regime was endangered. The likelihood of successful workers' revolutions in Germany and Austria coming to the Bolsheviks' aid seemed increasingly remote and calls for a general armistice and a peace conference of all the belligerent powers produced a negative response from the Allies. As a result, Lenin agreed to a separate armistice with the Central Powers in December 1917, and **Trotsky** started negotiations with their representatives at **Brest-Litovsk**. Delaying tactics produced a renewed German offensive and Lenin recognised that an imposed peace settlement would have to be accepted. As the First World War drew to a close, Lenin acknowledged that any future threats to the new regime were likely to come from the Allies rather than the Central Powers.

Lenin celebrates the first anniversary of the Bolshevik Revolution, which ended Russia's involvement in the war

LEOPOLD, FIELD MARSHAL PRINCE, 1846–1930

Brought out of retirement in 1915, Prince Leopold, a field marshal since 1905, served as an army group commander on the Eastern Front. On 29 August 1916, he succeeded **Hindenburg** as *Oberbefehlshaber Ost* (Supreme Leader East), retaining this post until

peace was finally agreed in March 1918. Leopold's own chief of staff, the influential Colonel (later **General**) **Max Hoffman**, acknowledged his considerable intelligence, but said he was 'scarcely a star performer'.

LETTOW-VORBECK, COLONEL PAUL von, 1870–1946

An experienced colonial soldier who had served in China and South-West Africa, Colonel von Lettow-Vorbeck was appointed military commander of **German East Africa** early in 1914. His skilful and courageous defence of the colony made him a popular hero in his own country and established him as one of the 'greatest masters of the art of bush warfare'. An early indication of his abilities was provided in November 1914 when he inflicted a humiliating defeat on the British when they tried to capture the port of Tanga. During the following year he carried out a series of raids on the Belgian Congo and Rhodesia as well as on British East Africa.

When the British adopted an offensive strategy early in 1916, Vorbeck's knowledge of the bush and his greater mobility denied the enemy the opportunity to bring him to battle. Their fortunes changed

with the capture of the main German force in November 1917, although the remaining troops, including those commanded by Vorbeck, crossed into Portuguese East Africa. He remained there until September 1918, living off the land and carrying out guerrilla raids. He then moved northwards around the head of Lake Nyasa into Northern Rhodesia, where he surrendered on 23 November.

Although he never had any hope of saving the colony for Germany, he had succeeded in his main objective: for over four years a force of 14,000 German and African troops under his leadership had occupied the energies of an Allied army that was, at its peak, almost 10 times its size.

An outstanding military leader and bush fighter, Colonel von Lettow-Vorbeck (second from right) *prolonged the campaign in East Africa until the war in Europe had ended*

LEVETZOW, COMMODORE MAGNUS, von, 1871–1939

Spending much of the war with the **High Seas Fleet**, in August 1918 Levetzow was appointed chief of staff of the new Supreme Command of the German navy under **Admiral Scheer**. He was directly involved in developing the abortive Operations Plan No 19, a suicide attack on the **Grand Fleet** which was due to have been executed on 30 October 1918. Levetzow continued his naval career after the war and was an active participant in right-wing politics.

LEWIS MACHINE-GUN

A versatile, American-designed light machine-gun, the Lewis was used on the ground (as an assault weapon) and in the air (as an observer's gun)

The Lewis was one of the world's first light machine-guns and among the most successful, playing a prominent role on land and in the air during the First World War. Appearing in 1911, it was wholly American in origin, being invented by Samuel Maclean, the noted weapons designer, and developed further by Colonel Isaac Lewis. The American military authorities were unimpressed by the weapon and production began in Europe, first in Belgium, and then in Britain, where the Birmingham Small Arms Company obtained the manufacturing rights.

A distinctive feature of this gas-operated gun, which could fire 450–500 rounds per minute, was its flat pan-shape magazine. Mounted above the barrel, it held either 47 or 97 rounds of .303-inch ammunition, arranged like the spokes of a wheel. The Lewis could also be recognised immediately by its large steel air-cooling jacket, which enclosed the barrel; air was forced in through a rear opening and along a finned aluminium radiator. A bipod supported the barrel, which was just over 26 inches long. Its main weaknesses were the complicated operating system and the fact that it was relatively heavy (26lb) for a portable weapon. However, compared with the **Vickers machine-gun**, it was easy and quick to manufacture and was the first light automatic weapon to be used on a large scale.

The Belgian army used it in action before anyone else, but the British-made version, the Mark 1, soon became a common sight on the Western Front following its introduction in 1915. At that time, four Lewis guns were issued to each infantry battalion, replacing the Vickers guns that were then assigned to the Machine-Gun Corps. By the end of the war this number had been increased to 36. It was popular with troops and effective as a front line assault weapon, particularly when used in support of infantry, advancing across no man's land. It was also used on armoured cars, motorcycle units and tanks, although being unarmoured it was vulnerable to attack.

The Lewis was equally well known as an aircraft gun and became the standard observer's weapon in the RFC; it could not be used as a forward-firing weapon because it was not suitable for synchronisation. This lightened version, which had the cooling mechanism removed, appeared in 1915 as the Mark 2. Spade grips were provided instead of the butt and the 97-round magazine was standard. Lewis guns were often used in tandem on a Scarff ring mounting and, with an increased rate of fire available later in the war, they were powerful and effective weapons. Even the Americans eventually recognised its value and on their entry into the war, a locally produced version, chambered for the .30 American service cartridge, was ordered. Although the Lewis was withdrawn from front line service during the inter-war years, it was still widely employed in the Second World War.

LFG ROLAND CII

This armed two-seater reconnaissance and escort biplane, whose compact design was well ahead of its contemporaries, first appeared late in 1915. Its most distinctive feature was its deep, streamlined fuselage, which completely filled the gap between the two staggered single-bay wings. The upper plane was attached to the fuselage giving the pilot and observer a completely unrestricted upward view. A 160hp Mercedes D III engine was enclosed in the pointed nose and an airscrew spinner was fitted. It had a maximum speed of 103m.p.h. and an endurance of up to five hours. The observer operated a **Parabellum machine-gun** in the rear cockpit and in later models a forward-firing synchronised Spandau gun was also fitted.

Nicknamed 'the Whale', the CII entered service with German field reconnaissance units on the Western Front at the beginning of 1916. It was also widely used on escort duties, being no slower than the leading Allied fighters, although its rate of climb and manoeuvrability were less good. Its main weakness, however, proved to be its wings, which could distort in use, adversely affecting its rate of climb. As a result a modified version, the CIIa, with reinforced wing tips, was introduced in August 1916. The view forward and downward was also found to be less than satisfactory and was the cause of several accidents.

The CII remained on active service until the autumn of 1917 and up to 300 examples may have been built in total. The aircraft was more notable for its influence on the design of future C- and CL-types than for any spectacular achievements of its own in the field.

LFG ROLAND DI to DIII

The DI single-seat fighter was a streamlined and slimmer version of the **LFG CII**, a fact reflected in its widely used nickname – 'the Shark' (the two-seater was known as 'the Whale'). Its single-bay wings were unstaggered, but like the CII the deep fuselage completely filled the gap between them. Powered by the 160hp Mercedes D III engine, it entered German service late in 1916, but was soon superseded because of the crew's poor forward and downward view. A modified version, the DII, with the top wing carried on a narrow pylon and other improvements, came into service early in 1917. It quickly became clear that the visibility problem had not been solved and that, like the DI, it was heavy on the controls and difficult to land. Using the same Mercedes engine, it had a maximum speed of 105m.p.h. at sea level and an endurance of two hours. Armament consisted of twin forward-firing Spandau machine-guns. A DIIa variant, with an 180hp Argus As III engine and a slightly modified airframe, was also produced.

These early D-types compared unfavourably with the **Albatros** single-seaters that gained prominence in 1917, and no more than 300 were built. They served in the less critical areas of the Western Front, Russia, and Mesopotamia, and only one unit was completely equipped with them. Further modifications were made in 1917, and the new version, which was also powered by the 180hp Argus As III engine, was designated the DIII. It had struts rather than a pylon supporting the upper wing and a longer fin. The DIII was flight tested by **Manfred von Richthofen**, who was unenthusiastic, and no more than 25 examples reached the front.

LFG ROLAND DVIa & DVIb

Descended from the early **LFG D-types**, the German DVI single-seat fighter biplane was the first aircraft to appear with a clinker-built fuselage. Unlike its predecessors, it had a good view from the cockpit, was easy to fly and highly manoeuvrable. Production versions were designated DVIa, with the 160hp Mercedes D III engine, and DVIb, with the 200hp Benz Bz II and minor changes to the airframe. When equipped with the more powerful engine, which had a tendency to overheat, it had a maximum speed of 114m.p.h. at 6,500 feet and could climb to that altitude in 6.5 minutes. Armament consisted of two fixed forward-firing 7.92mm Spandau machine-guns.

At fighter trials held in January 1918, the DVI performed less well than the **Fokker DVIII**, which received the main order. The DVIa and DVIb did, however, enter production on a small scale to guard against any disruption to the supply of the winning machine. Large scale manufacture was probably ruled out in any case because of difficulties in producing the complex fuselage structure. With the Fokker being delivered in the required numbers, the DVIa and DVIb had only limited operational use with *Jasta 23* on the Western Front. They were also employed by the German navy for the defence of its seaplane bases.

LIÈGE, BATTLE OF, 5–16 August 1914

The first land operation of the First World War began on 4 August as the German Second Army crossed the frontier into neutral Belgium, with the aim of attacking France from the north. Specially organised for the purpose, the invasion force of 320,000 men was to seize the city of Liège, the gateway to Belgium, which blocked the narrow gap between the 'Limburg appendix' and the Ardennes. One of the strongest fortresses in Europe, it was protected by a ring of heavily defended forts, six on each side of the Meuse.

Under the command of **General Leman**, the Belgians, who numbered 70,000 in total, resisted the first German attack on the night of 5 August. It made no progress and heavy losses were sustained, with morale being an early casualty of the unexpectedly tough Belgian opposition. At this point **Major-General Ludendorff**, then on the staff of the Second Army, intervened; on his own initiative he led a brigade between the forts and entered the town, inducing the garrison to surrender on 7 August.

The main German advance through Belgium was, however, unable to proceed until the forts themselves had been neutralised – an operation requiring the use of 17-inch siege howitzers, an Austrian-built weapon whose existence was a complete surprise to the Allies. Resistance ended on 16 August – after 11 days' bombardment – and General Leman, whose leadership had inspired the determined Belgian resistance, was carried unconscious from one of the forts.

On 17 August, the Germans began to implement the next stage of the **Schlieffen Plan**, with the First, Second and Third Armies moving in a wide turning movement through Belgium. The Belgian army was forced back to Antwerp to avoid being cut off and Brussels was occupied without resistance by **General von Kluck**'s First Army on 20 August.

LIGGETT, GENERAL HUNTER, 1857–1935

Appointed commander of the American First Army on 16 October 1918, Liggett had established a reputation as an able tactician and the 'soundest reasoner and strongest realist in the American army'. In response to **Pershing**'s well-known aversion to overweight commanders, he said that 'fat doesn't matter if it does not extend above the neck'. During the final **Meuse–Argonne** offensive Liggett's forces broke through the Hindenburg Line and forced the

Germans to retreat behind the Meuse, reaching near to Sedan on 6 November 1918. Previously Liggett had been commander of I Army Corps, a post he had held since the beginning of 1918. In this capacity he had played a major part in the reduction of the St Mihiel salient (12–16 September 1918), the Americans' first victory in Europe and their largest operation since the Civil War.

LIMAN von SANDERS, GENERAL OTTO, 1855–1929

Liman von Sanders: one of the many German officers who served in the Turkish army

German general who spent the entire war in the Turkish service, Liman had first been sent to Constantinople late in 1913 as head of a military mission. He was soon appointed inspector general of the Turkish army and was heavily involved in its reorganisation. As the European war began he became commander of the Turkish First Army and worked actively to secure Turkey's entry into the conflict.

It was not until April 1915 that he was given an operational role as commander of the Fifth Army, which was responsible for the Gallipoli peninsula. Liman's reputation was considerably enhanced by his successful defence of the area against the Anglo-French invasion, although the victory was in large measure attributable to **Kemal Atatürk**'s leadership. Less impressive was his failure to intervene in the successful Allied evacuation of the Gallipoli beaches.

Liman returned to prominence early in 1918 as the head of an army group which was responsible for preventing **Allenby**'s advance through Palestine and Syria. In the absence of sufficient supplies and reinforcements he was unable to prevent the collapse of the front and was himself nearly captured at Nazareth in September 1918. Liman was able to do no more than hold the line near the Turkish border until the Armistice was signed at the end of October.

LINSINGEN, GENERAL ALEXANDER VON, 1850–1935

German army commander on the Eastern Front from November 1914, Linsingen's greatest challenge appeared in June 1916 when **Brusilov** launched his major offensive. Army Group Linsingen suffered the loss of the Austrian Fourth Army and its headquarters at Luck, but after regrouping a counter-offensive checked the Russian army's advance near Kovel. General Linsingen remained on this front until peace terms had been agreed with the Bolsheviks in March 1918.

LION

The battlecruiser counterparts of the **Orion** class of super-dreadnoughts, the *Lion* and *Princess Royal*, her sister ship, were known as the 'splendid cats' because of their speed and appearance. (*Queen Mary*, a 'half-sister', was often listed as a Lion.) They were equipped with the same 13.5-inch guns on the centreline as the Orions, but were required to operate at a speed of 27 knots (6 knots faster than their counterparts). To carry the very powerful machinery required, the Lions were substantially larger and had a greater displacement than the Orions. The eight 13.5-inch guns were located in four twin turrets and secondary armament consisted of sixteen 4-inch guns located in casement positions. The arrangement of the main turrets was not as efficient as it might have been, but the principal weakness was the inadequacy of the armour. Partial protection was provided, but the ends and upper decks of the ships were vulnerable. Other design faults required substantial modification, but even though changes were made the Lions have been described as 'the least satisfactory ships built for the Royal Navy in recent times'.

Completed in 1912, *Lion* joined the First Battle Cruiser Squadron as **Admiral Beatty**'s flagship early in 1913. On the outbreak of war she formed part of the **Grand Fleet** and was soon in action at **Heligoland Bight**. She was damaged at the **Dogger Bank**, and at **Jutland** she nearly sank: a shell penetrated one of her turrets and burst inside, and it was only the quick action of one of the crew that prevented the magazine from blowing up. In November 1916, she became the flagship of Rear Admiral Pakenham, Beatty's successor as commander of the Battle Cruiser Force. *Princess Royal* also served with the First Battle Cruiser Squadron and fought in the Heligoland and Dogger Bank actions; she was not damaged until Jutland, but after repairs remained in service until the end of the war.

LLOYD C-TYPES

This series of two-seat biplanes was in service with the Austrian air service throughout the war on reconnaissance and training duties.

The first major production model, the CII, appeared in 1915 and had swept-back wings which, unusually, were wood framed and plywood covered. Powered by the 145hp Hiero engine, it had a good rate of climb and excellent high altitude performance. No armament was fitted at first, but a **Schwarzlose machine-gun** for the observer was added later at the rear of the single cockpit. The CIII, which was produced in 1916, had a larger 160hp Austro Daimler engine and associated modifications. The final production version, the CV, had a substantially revised airframe and was of smaller dimensions; performance was enhanced by the use of an 185hp or 220hp engine.

With their excellent flying qualities, the C-types were widely used on the Italian Front and to a lesser extent in Rumania. As new C-type designs appeared in 1917–18, the Lloyd series was gradually relegated to training duties.

LLOYD GEORGE, DAVID, 1st EARL LLOYD-GEORGE, 1863–1945

British wartime prime minister (1916–22) and pre-war Radical, Lloyd George had served as Chancellor of the Exchequer in **Asquith**'s Liberal government since 1908. Initially he was an opponent of Britain's entry into the war, but he soon changed his mind. He called for the more vigorous prosecution of the war and claimed that Asquith 'does not recognise that the nation is fighting for its life'. He also opposed British strategy, advocating an attack against the Central Powers' southern flank in preference to the senseless war of attrition in France.

His first opportunity to contribute more directly to the war effort came in July 1915, when he was appointed to the new post of Minister of Munitions in Asquith's coalition government. He planned a massive expansion in the production of ammunition and weapons, refusing to accept conservative military estimates, which were based on peacetime levels of demand. Manufacturers were cajoled or bribed into producing more and for the first time women were employed in the war industries on a large scale.

Lloyd George succeeded **Kitchener** as Secretary of State for War in June 1916, but was affected by the same basic constraint: it was **Robertson**, Chief of the Imperial General Staff, rather than the War Office, who controlled military strategy. He remained critical of its preoccupation with the Western Front and demanded a 'knockout blow' against Germany. Asquith was not a sufficiently energetic war leader and, in December 1916, with the help of leading Conservatives Lloyd George replaced him as prime minister.

Now everything was to be subordinated to wartime needs. New ministries were created and there was more government control of essential industries. A war cabinet of five members was established, and the prime minister was supported by a group of close advisers, known as the 'garden suburb'.

Lloyd George acted decisively early in 1917 when the Admiralty refused to introduce **convoys**, even though British shipping losses were running at dangerously high levels. He overruled the navy and the action has been described as his 'greatest stroke'. Disagreements with **Haig** and Robertson, of whom he had a low opinion, were more fundamental and he struggled for two years to restore full political control over strategy.

In 1917, having failed to secure Allied support for a new offensive in Italy, he was converted to **Nivelle**'s plan for a further attack in France. Its main attraction was the fact that Haig would temporarily be under the French general's command. Otherwise, he had no sympathy for Haig's plans for further massive offensives, although he was not always able to veto them.

The creation of a Supreme War Council, at Lloyd George's suggestion, was a further blow to Haig's position. In February 1918, Robertson was dismissed and the more pliant **Sir Henry Wilson** succeeded him. It took the German offensive of March 1918 to change Haig's attitude to the appointment of a supreme allied commander, an innovation that the prime minister had always regarded as an essential

requirement for eventual victory. Lloyd George's coalition won the post-war 'coupon election' and he played a leading role at the **Paris Peace Conference**. He opposed a hard line approach towards Germany and had little enthusiasm for the League of Nations.

The prime minister, Lloyd George, with the Imperial War Cabinet; the major decisions were normally taken elsewhere

LODZ, BATTLE OF, 11 November–6 December 1914

Following the collapse of the German offensive on **Warsaw**, the Russians intended to resume their advance on Silesia as soon as communications had been restored. To block this, plans for a new German offensive in Northern Poland were made by **Hindenburg**, who was appointed to the command of German forces on the Eastern Front on 1 November 1914. Using more than 800 trains, the German Ninth Army (now under **Mackensen**) was moved northwards to the Posen-Thorn area.

The operation began on 11 November as the Ninth

Army attacked south-east towards Warsaw, with its left on the Vistula. It advanced quickly in unfavourable conditions, covering 50 miles in only four days. It moved between the Russian First and Second Armies, which protected the northern (right) flank of the Fifth Army's westward offensive against Silesia, which had begun on 14 November. The only corps of **Rennenkampf**'s First Army to be positioned south of the Vistula was crushed and the two Russian armies lost touch. The Second was attacked as it retreated towards Lodz and suffered heavy losses. Pushed back on the city itself, it was threatened with encirclement: only to the south was it not under immediate German pressure.

Saving the Second Army was **Grand Duke Nicholas**'s first priority, and on 16 November the Russian Fifth Army (**Plehve**) was ordered to abandon its offensive against Silesia and march northwards to relieve it. The Fifth Army covered 70 miles in 48 hours and when the action began on 18 November it was supported by an improvised group from the northern force. The battle, which was fought in terrible winter conditions, lasted until 25 November. Mackensen's right flank was checked but the Russians missed the opportunity to inflict a major defeat on their enemy. The German advance, spearheaded by the XXV Reserve Corps (General von Scheffer-Boyadel), was halted and then almost completely surrounded by a surprise Russian counter-attack. However, the northern exit had not been completely closed and Scheffer's 50,000 troops fought their way out on 24–26 November, taking 16,000 prisoners and 64 guns with them. It was a notable feat of arms.

German pressure continued for another month as a steady supply of reinforcements arrived. The Russians, short of munitions, withdrew from Lodz on 6 December, straightening their line to protect Warsaw. Hindenburg was unable to make any further progress in two further weeks of fighting and the capital was to remain in Russian hands until July 1915. The main purpose of Hindenburg's plan had, however, been achieved and the German homeland was never again threatened by the Russian army.

LOHNER B-TYPES & CI

This series of two-seat reconnaissance biplanes served with the Austrian air service from 1914 to 1917. The first example, the BI, was a prewar design that had swept-back, two-bay wings, a communal cockpit, a long narrow fuselage, and a tailplane with a rounded leading edge. Powered by a 100hp Austro Daimler engine, it was unarmed and was used for observation duties during the first few months of the war.

The BII, which served as a trainer, had a smaller 85hp Hiero engine and an extended fuselage. The third production B-type, the BIV, was the first to be armed, with a **Schwarzlose machine-gun** for the observer. Several other changes were made, including further lengthening of the fuselage, and it was now powered by a 100hp Mercedes D I engine. The same armament was retained in the BVII, which was in service in 1915. Equipped with the more powerful 160hp Austro Daimler, it was sometimes used as a bomber as well as for reconnaissance duties. The BVI, which in fact entered service after the BVII, had a modified airframe with reduced sweep and a shorter fuselage. It was powered by a 145hp Rapp engine.

Very similar was the Lohner CI, which reverted to the 160hp Austro Daimler engine, and was in service during 1916–17. None of these machines was built in any quantity and, partly because of their poor performance above 2,000 metres, they made very little impact on the course of the war.

LOHNER L

The Austrian navy's most widely used flying boat, the Lohner L served from 1915 until the Armistice. Succeeding the Lohner E, which was operational at the beginning of the war, the type L was a two-seat reconnaissance and patrol biplane and bomber.

Elegant in appearance and very seaworthy, it had swept-back wings of unequal length, with a complex arrangement of wing struts and bracing wires. The crew sat side by side and were protected by a windscreen; the observer was armed with a **Schwarzlose machine-gun** on a movable mounting. Bombs or **depth charges** up to a maximum of 440lb could be carried on external racks. A reconnaissance variant, with cameras in place of a bomb load, was designated type R. The Lohner L was normally powered by a 140hp Austro Daimler pusher engine, although other power units, including the 140hp Hiero, were often used. The 160hp Austro Daimler, for example, gave a maximum speed of 65m.p.h. at sea level and an endurance of four hours.

The aircraft was widely used against Allied shipping in the Adriatic and targets on the eastern coast of Italy. Night bombing raids, involving several Lohner aircraft, were a common method of attack. In fact **Gottfried Banfield**, the leading Austrian air ace, shot down his first victim at night – an Italian bomber – on 1 June 1916, flying a Lohner L-type, the first of a series of victories he gained with this machine. Another notable achievement was the sinking of the French submarine *Foucault* by two Lohner Ls on 15 September 1916. By the end of the war many hits had been scored against the Italian air service for the loss of only thirty L-types. The Italians themselves acknowledged the quality of the design when a captured Lohner L provided the basis for the successful series of **Macchi** flying boats. About 170 Ls were produced, as well as 36 examples of the type R reconnaissance variant.

LONDON

Very similar to the **Formidable** class, except for improvements to the armour, the London pre-dreadnoughts were completed in 1902–04. They had four 12-inch and twelve 6-inch guns, a displacement of 15,000 tons and a speed of 18 knots. *Bulwark*, which carried out patrols in the Channel at the beginning of the war, was destroyed while loading ammunition at Sheerness in November 1914, with heavy loss of life. All the other ships of the class – *London*, *Venerable*, *Queen*, and *Prince of Wales* – served throughout the war. They all joined the Dardanelles force in 1915, with *Venerable*, *Queen* and *Prince of Wales* subsequently participating in the blockade of the Austro-Hungarian navy in the Adriatic.

LONDON, TREATY OF, 26 April 1915

By the terms of this secret treaty with Britain, France and Russia, Italy agreed on 26 April 1915 to join the Entente powers and declare war on her former allies, Germany and Austro-Hungary, within a month. In return she would receive a variety of territorial concessions at the end of the war, including the Trentino, Trieste, the Dodecanese Islands and an area of Albania around Valona.

These generous terms were judged to be the minimum necessary to bring Italy into the war and reflected the Allies' exaggerated belief in the military contribution that she could be expected to make. She declared war on Austro-Hungary on 23 May but a stalemate soon developed on the **Isonzo front**. In spite of her treaty obligations she did not declare war on Germany until over a year later – on 27 August 1916. In the peace settlement Italy never received anything like the full gains promised by the treaty: there were strong objections from the United States as well as from two of the other signatories to the agreement – Britain and France.

LORD NELSON

Completed a year after *Dreadnought*, *Lord Nelson* and *Agamemnon* were in fact the last pre-dreadnoughts to enter British service. However, some of the new ideas about battleship design were incorporated in them with the result that, for example, small-calibre secondary weapons were not fitted. In their place were ten 9.2-inch guns (in one single and two twin turrets on each beam), as well as four 12-inch guns. With good armour protection, these ships had a displacement of 15,925 tons and a maximum speed of 18 knots. *Lord Nelson* and *Agamemnon* both served in the English Channel after the outbreak of war and went together to the **Dardanelles** in February 1915, operating in the Eastern Mediterranean for the rest of the war. The Armistice with Turkey was signed aboard *Agamemnon* in October 1918.

LOSSBERG, GENERAL FRITZ von, 1868–1943

A distinguished German staff officer, Lossberg made his name as a tactician who developed a new method of defence. Early in 1915 he was appointed deputy head of the General Staff operations section, although his talents were more profitably employed in his temporary attachments to front line forces during difficult periods: he was, for example, appointed chief of staff to the Fourth Army during the **Third Battle of Ypres**. As a military thinker he sought to replace defensive tactics based on a single line with defence in depth; behind these positions would be counter-attack forces, held in reserve until they were needed to support front line units under pressure. Lossberg's principles were embodied in the Hindenburg Line in 1917–18, and in that respect he made a major contribution to the failure of Allied attacks during that period.

LUDENDORFF, GENERAL ERICH von, 1865–1937

The 'silent dictator' of wartime Germany, 1916–18, Ludendorff was deputy chief of staff of the Second Army in August 1914. Noted for his great energy and intelligence, he had since 1895 served in a variety of staff posts, heading the important mobilisation and deployment section of the General Staff, 1908–13. A temporary setback occurred in 1913, when he was transferred to a minor regimental command because he had promoted his plans for army expansion too energetically. However, he rose to prominence almost as soon as the war began, helping to seize **Liège** by intervening directly with only a brigade available to him.

On 22 August, he was appointed chief of staff of the Eighth Army in East Prussia, where two Russian armies had invaded. As he travelled east he was joined by **Hindenburg**, the new head of the Eighth Army, beginning a partnership that was to last until October 1918. Adapting existing plans, Ludendorff and Hindenburg left no more than a cavalry division in front of **Rennenkampf**, while concentrating almost all their forces against the Russian Second Army (**Sam**-sonov) to the south. After their decisive victory at **Tannenberg**, Ludendorff and Hindenburg turned against Rennenkampf, defeating him at the **First Battle of the Masurian Lakes**.

In November 1914 Ludendorff was appointed chief of staff of a new supreme command in the east under Hindenburg and was promoted lieutenant-general. The Ludendorff–Hindenburg team won a series of important victories in the east in 1914–15, but the opportunity to strike a knockout blow never materialised. There were disagreements with **Falkenhayn**, chief of staff, over strategy and the availability of reserves, producing a more restrictive approach than that favoured by Ludendorff.

In August 1916 Hindenburg replaced Falkenhayn, with Ludendorff, who was promoted full general, becoming first quartermaster-general. During this period Ludendorff emerged as the dominant figure, first in the military sphere, and then in the civilian, Hindenburg now being little more than a figurehead. His political role was greatly enhanced after the departure of **Chancellor Bethmann Hollweg**, which Ludendorff himself had largely engineered; the main underlying reason for his resignation was the argument over the reintroduction of unrestricted submarine warfare.

His military strategy on the Western Front was to strengthen the German army's defensive position by constructing the Hindenburg Line prior to the expected Allied offensives of 1917. In the east his first

priority was to stabilise the front after the **Brusilov offensive**, but he returned to the attack during 1917 when conditions seemed favourable.

In the expectation that it would shorten the war, Ludendorff had already assisted the process of revolution by helping **Lenin** return to Russia in April. After the Bolshevik seizure of power, **Trotsky** sought peace at **Brest-Litovsk**, where Ludendorff imposed harsh terms which extended German control over much of European Russia.

With troops released from the East, Ludendorff gambled on victory on the Western Front before America could make a decisive military contribution. His ill-conceived Spring offensives on the **Somme**, with follow-up operations on the **Lys** and **Aisne**, forced the Allies back at three main points, but he was unable to exploit his initial successes effectively. His final offensive on the **Marne** in July met with an Allied counter-attack that marked the failure of his bid to bring the war to a successful conclusion.

On 8 August, the Allies pushed forward at **Amiens**, described by Ludendorff himself as the 'black day of the German army'. Now facing the prospect of defeat, Ludendorff lost his nerve and by the end of September was arguing for the immediate cessation of hostilities. He did not, however, follow a consistent line and on other occasions argued for the more vigorous pursuit of the war. On 26 October he was forced by the government to resign and fled in disguise to Sweden, leaving Hindenburg to bring the war to a conclusion. He was active in post-war German politics as a member of the Nazi movement.

LUFBERY, RAOUL, 1885–1918

The third highest scoring American fighter ace of the war, Lufbery was born in France but had emigrated to the United States at an early age. Returning to his native country at the time war was declared, Lufbery enlisted in the French air service although it was not until 1916 that he became a fighter pilot. Lufbery served with the *Escadrille Lafayette* and his score quickly mounted; he was decorated by the British as well as the French, being the first American to be awarded the Military Cross.

When the United States entered the war he was transferred to the USAAS, at first on ground duties. It was not in fact until 19 March 1918 that he saw operational service again, leading the first American air patrol over enemy lines. His command of the 94th Aero Squadron, effective from 8 April, lasted only a few weeks. On 19 May, flying a **Nieuport 28** he engaged a German two-seater; Lufbery's machine caught fire and he fell to his death. His final score was 17 hits.

LUGER PISTOL

Development by George Luger from an earlier pistol designed by Hugo Burchardt, the Parabellum-Pistole Modell 1908 or PO8, was the standard handgun of the German army during the First World War. One of the best-known weapons of the period, this self-loading pistol was intended to replace a variety of earlier revolvers used by the Germans. The earliest Luger design appeared in 1900 and was adopted by the Swiss army, but it was not until 1904 that the Parabellum – in long-barrelled form – was first adopted in Germany, when the Imperial Navy acquired the Marine Modell 1904.

The principal Luger-designed military pistol was first adopted by the German army in 1908 and was not superseded until the late 1930s, after a long production life; it was still in service during the Second World War.

Recoil operated, with a toggle-joint breech lock, it fired 9mm cartridges, was 8.75 inches in length and weighed 30 oz. The magazine, which held seven rounds, was inserted in the butt and held there by a spring catch. The PO8 was well balanced and easy to use and maintain; it was popular with German troops and as many as 1.6 million may have been produced by the end of the war. It was originally made solely by Deutsche Waffen und Munitions-fabriken, but in 1914 the government arsenal at Erfurt also started manufacturing Lugers to meet wartime demand.

A long-barrelled derivative of the PO8 – known as the Parabellum M17 or Artillery Model – was produced in 1917 to meet the need for a light semi-automatic machine carbine. It had a curved 'snail' drum magazine, containing 30 rounds, a detachable stock and long-range sights, but was otherwise very similar to the PO8. The magazine had a tendency to jam until the conical cartridge was replaced in 1918 by a round-nosed one. The M17 was widely used by artillery observers, shock troops and machine-gun detachments in the last year of the war.

LUKE, FRANK, 1897–1918

The second ranking fighter ace of the United States Army Air Service in the Great War, Luke specialised in the destruction of enemy **observation balloons** during his short operational career. In no more than two months, from 4 August 1918, he destroyed 14 balloons and four aircraft, flying a **Spad XIII** with 27th Aero Squadron. At the end of September Luke was brought down behind enemy lines after a dog fight with **Fokker DVII**s; he refused to surrender and was killed by German troops in the ensuing gun battle. Luke was posthumously awarded the Congressional Medal of Honour for his outstanding record.

LUSITANIA

British transatlantic liner sunk by the Germans off the coast of southern Ireland on 7 May 1915. Earlier German warnings that she would be attacked were disregarded and the *Lusitania* took no special precautions on her return journey from New York at the beginning of May. After being struck without warning by two torpedoes from the submarine U20 she sank very rapidly – in 20 minutes – and 1,198 passengers and crew were lost. Subsequent German claims that *Lusitania* was an **armed merchant cruiser** and therefore a legitimate wartime target are untenable: she carried no troops or guns; in fact nothing more suspect than a small cargo of ammunition. The action was vigorously denounced by the Americans, who lost 124 citizens when the *Lusitania* went down, and it may have contributed to their decision to enter the war in 1917.

The destruction of the British transatlantic liner Lusitania *brought American intervention in the war closer*

LVG BI, BII & BIII

The LVG BI was one of the unarmed two-seaters that was available to the German air service on the outbreak of war. A two-bay tractor biplane of conventional design, it was powered by either the 100hp Mercedes D I or the 110hp Benz engine. After a few months' active service on the Western Front on reconnaissance duties, it was withdrawn and used as a trainer.

The main production model, the BII, which appeared in 1915, was smaller than its predecessor but was otherwise little changed; it was powered by the 120hp Mercedes engine. With excellent flying qualities it proved useful for training purposes, but was also used widely at the front as a scouting and reconnaissance machine. A final version, the BIII, with further minor modifications, was designed in 1917 in order to allow the type to continue in military service as an effective training aircraft.

LVG CI & CII

The LVG CI was the first operational two-seater in the German air service to be equipped with defensive armament – a ring-mounted machine-gun in the rear cockpit. Based on the LVG BI, the new armed reconnaissance biplane, which was powered by the 150hp Benz Bz III engine, was introduced in response to the armed Allied aircraft that made their first appearance on the Western Front in 1915. It was quickly superseded by the CII, a development of the **LVG BII**, which appeared in 1915 and was produced in much larger numbers. Apart from its 160hp Mercedes D II engine, it was almost identical in appearance to the BII. Armed initially with only the observer's **Parabellum machine-gun**, later production models were equipped with a forward-firing Spandau gun.

The CII was used widely for reconnaissance work (both visual and photographic) and occasionally for light bombing duties (carrying a bomb load of no more than 22lb). It was in fact responsible for the first aircraft attack on London, on 28 November 1916, when a single machine bombed Victoria station.

About 250 CIs and CIIs were produced by the LVG firm and two sub-contractors; they remained in service until 1917.

LVG CV

A large two-seater that was used for reconnaissance and light bombing. The observer's ring-mounted Parabellum machine-gun is clearly visible in the rear cockpit

Widely used on reconnaissance and artillery observation duties from mid-1917 until the Armistice, the CV was one of the most successful aircraft of its type to appear in the latter part of the war. One of the largest German two-seaters, with a wingspan of 45 feet, it represented a considerable improvement over its predecessor, the **CII**. It was powered by the 200hp Benz Bz IV engine, which gave a maximum speed of 103m.p.h. and an endurance of $3\frac{1}{2}$ hours. The CV was neat and streamlined in appearance, with unstaggered two-bay wings of unequal span, dragonfly-shaped lower wings, and an oval tailplane. Armament was in standard C-type form: a **Parabellum machine-gun** in the rear cockpit and a single fixed Spandau gun at the front.

Like the similar DFW CV, the LVG CV was used successfully on the Western Front and in Palestine on a wide range of front line duties, including light bombing and ground attack as well as artillery observation and reconnaissance. It could carry up to 250lb of bombs on external racks under the wings. The CV normally operated with an escort as its defensive capabilities were no more than adequate when flying alone. Its main weakness was, however, the poor forward view from the front cockpit, attributable to the design of the wings.

LVG CVI

The German CVI, which appeared early in 1918, was a slightly modified version of the **LVG CV** two-seater biplane. Changes in the wings and fuselage were made to improve the crew's view and the observer's field of fire, while simplifying their construction at the same time. The same 200hp Benz Bz IV was used but there was an improvement in performance because the CVI weighed slightly less. Armament was identical to the CV and it carried out similar duties – reconnaissance and artillery observation – on the Western Front. Some 1,000 examples had been produced by the end of the war, with about 500 CV and CVI machines on active service at the front in August 1918.

LYAUTEY, MARSHAL HERBERT, 1854–1934

Prior to his appointment as War Minister in the **Briand** cabinet in December 1916, Lyautey was Resident General of Morocco. He worked to restore the authority of the ministry which had been reduced during **Joffre**'s term as commander-in-chief. However, he had only limited success and in spite of strong efforts he was unable to prevent **Nivelle**, the new commander-in-chief, from proceeding with his ill-fated plan for an offensive in the spring of 1917. Lyautey resigned in March 1917 as a consequence of his refusal to disclose aviation secrets to the Chamber of Deputies; the whole Briand government fell over the issue two days later.

LYS OFFENSIVE, 9–29 April 1918

Following the end of the **Somme offensive, Ludendorff** turned to the British front in Flanders for his second major assault of 1918. It was only thinly defended by the First and Second Armies, which were separated by the River Lys. His immediate objective was the rail centre of Hazebrouck, with the possibility of advancing to the coast if good progress were made. The attack, which was preceded by an intensive artillery bombardment lasting 36 hours, began early in the morning of 9 April. The Sixth Army (General Ferdinand von Quast) moved west from Neuve Chapelle along a 12-mile front from the La Bassée canal to Armentières. This area was held by the left wing of the First Army, with two Portuguese divisions receiving the opening blows; they were pushed back nearly four miles. The next day the battle was extended northwards as four divisions of the German Fourth Army attacked beyond Armentières to the Ypres–Comines Canal. **Plumer**'s Second Army was thrown back, eventually beyond Messines and Wytschaete, which the British had taken the year before.

By 12 April the Germans, who had created a breach 30 miles wide, were only five miles from Hazebrouck, their immediate objective. It was clear that the British, who had no reserves, were facing a serious crisis. **Haig**, who demanded immediate French reinforcements, issued his famous order of the day: 'There must be no retirement. With our backs to the wall and believing in the justice of our cause each one must fight on to the end.'

Plumer was put in charge of the whole of the threatened front and one of his early actions was to withdraw troops to more defensible positions in front of Ypres. By 18 April, the German advance had been halted at Meteren and in front of Kemmel Hill. This was partly because Ludendorff's control was 'weak and hesitating'. The operation was much bigger than he had orginally intended and he was too restrictive in his deployment of additional troops, although in the end 44 German divisions were involved.

A Vickers gun, operated by men of the Machine-Gun Corps, attacks a German aircraft during the Lys offensive

Ludendorff then turned his attention further north, attacking the Belgians beyond Ypres on 17

April without success, with further abortive assaults being mounted along the whole line on the following day. During a lull in the fighting French reinforcements arrived at the front in large numbers. Preceded by a diversionary attack at Villers-Bretonneux near Amiens, the German offensive was resumed with a major assault on Mount Kemmel, which was lost by the new French troops on 25 April. Further operations were abandoned on 29 April, when Luden-

dorff's attempt to seize the rest of the Flanders heights ended in failure.

The second German offensive of 1918 had resulted in an advance of up to 10 miles and an awkward salient to defend. None of their strategic objectives had been achieved, and the Channel ports remained safe in Allied hands. The Germans had lost some 350,000 men, the Allies about 305,000, the great majority of whom were British, since the beginning of Ludendorff's offensive on 21 March 1918.

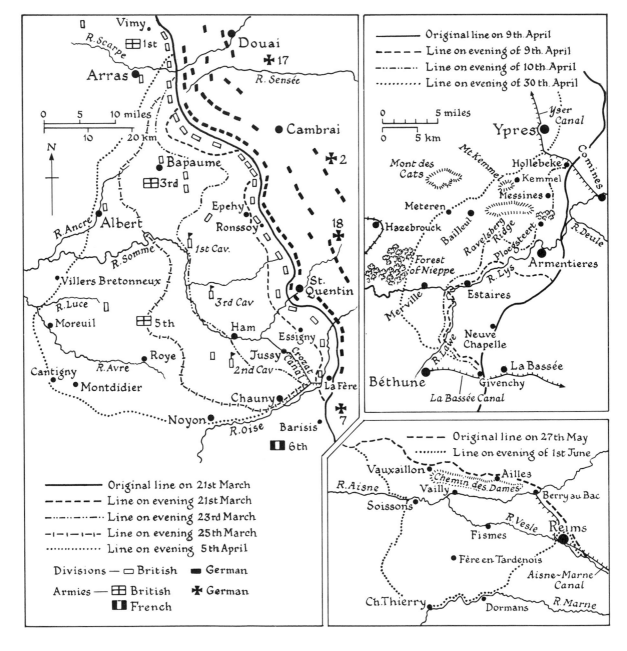

MACCHI M-TYPES

The first flying boats to be designed and produced in Italy were the Macchi L1 and L2, which gave reliable service in the first part of the war. They were closely modelled on a **Lohner** flying boat that had been captured by the Italians in May 1915.

The M3, which appeared in 1916, was Macchi's first original flying boat design, although it was a logical development of the earlier Lohner-based models. Some 200 examples of this two/three-seat general purpose machine were acquired by the Italian navy and they served in the Adriatic until the Armistice, being engaged mainly on reconnaissance and bombing duties. The aircraft carried four 110kg bombs and one or two machine-guns. A 160hp Isotta-Fraschini engine provided the M3 with sufficient power to match its Austrian adversaries, at least in the first part of its operational career, and in fact in 1916 an M3 established a flying boat altitude record of 5,400m. An enlarged version of the M3 – the two-seater M8 – appeared late in 1917. Designed for coastal patrol duties, it was equipped with a radio and photographic equipment as well as the standard defensive armament.

Macchi responded to the appearance of the **Brandenburg KDW** flying boat in 1916–17 with a single-seat fighter of its own. Mostly powered by the same 160hp engine as the M3, the Macchi M5 had a maximum speed of 118m.p.h., an excellent rate of climb and good manoeuvrability. Armed with twin 6.5mm **Fiat-Revelli** machine-guns, it was employed on escort and defence duties with five *squadriglie* of the Italian navy. An improved version of this fighter, the M7, appeared towards the end of the war but only a few had been produced by November 1918. Powered by the 250hp Isotta-Fraschini V6 engine (as were some later M5s), it had a maximum speed of 130m.p.h. and was capable of at least matching the performance of any of its adversaries. Further flying boat designs were being produced as the war drew to a close but none had appeared in sufficient numbers before the Armistice to make any operational impact.

McCUDDEN, JAMES, 1895–1918

Britain's fourth ranking air ace gained his wings in May 1916, originally joining the RFC as a mechanic before the war. After a brief period flying two-seaters, he transferred to a fighter squadron (No 29) in August 1916. It was equipped with **Airco DH2s** and within a month McCudden had achieved his first victory. His score gradually increased over the next few months and he was rewarded with a commission and the Military Cross.

His most successful period was as commander of B Flight, No 56 Squadron, where he served from August 1917 until the following April, flying **SE5s**. At that point his personal score had risen to 57 (of which the majority were two-seaters). The total score of his flight during this period was almost as impressive: 70 German planes had been destroyed for the loss of only four. A notable instance was his fight with the German ace, **Werner Voss**, who was killed by one of his colleagues after a 10-minute engagement.

McCudden's success as a fighter pilot and patrol was partly attributable to his fine marksmanship (particularly over long distances) and detailed study of tactics. His mechanical knowledge was excellent, as might have been expected, and he often examined his own machine and its armament before going on patrol. Although he was a remote figure to his colleagues, he was acknowledged as a fine and courageous leader.

On leaving No 56 Squadron, in April 1918, Major McCudden's achievements were recognised with the award of a Victoria Cross, but in a little over three months he was to be tragically killed. On 9 July 1918, while on his way to take up the command of No 60 Squadron, his engine failed on take off and, unable to control it, his aircraft crashed to the ground.

MACKENSEN, FIELD MARSHAL AUGUST VON, 1849–1944

A volunteer in the Franco-Prussian War, Mackensen was a Prussian cavalry officer whose name was 'specially associated with enterprises demanding surprise and speed'. Promoted to field marshal during the war, Mackensen had the 'secret of inspiring his troops to their highest achievements'. The highlights of his first few months of campaigning as commander of the Ninth Army on the Eastern Front were his successful attack on **Rennenkampf's** army in the **First Battle of the Masurian Lakes** in September 1914 and the seizure of **Lodz** on 6 December 1914. His major opportunity came in the spring of 1915 when, as commander of a new Eleventh Army, he drove the Russians out of **Galicia**, achieving the breakthrough at **Gorlice-Tarnow** on 2 May. Ably supported by **Seeckt**, his chief of staff and 'guiding brain', he successfully pursued the enemy during the summer as the Russian retreat continued as far as Brest-Litovsk and the Pripet Marshes.

With his military reputation standing high, Mackensen was placed in command of the invasion of Serbia, which he overran with the German, Austrian and Bulgarian troops at his disposal. In 1916, he made a major contribution to the invasion of Rumania, first in his seizure of the Dobruja and later in his involvement in the thrust towards Bucharest, which fell early in December. Mackensen remained in Rumania as head of the army of the occupation until the end of the war. He was then interned in France and did not return to Germany until 1919.

One of Mackensen's greatest wartime achievements: German troops enter Bucharest, December 1916, marking the virtual collapse of Rumanian resistance

MADDEN, ADMIRAL SIR CHARLES, 1862–1935

Although much of his career was spent at the Admiralty, during the war years Madden served at sea with the **Grand Fleet**. From 1914, he was chief of staff to **Jellicoe**, his brother-in-law, who valued his tactical skills and organisational ability. When **Sir David Beatty** succeeded Jellicoe as commander-in-chief of the Grand Fleet in 1916, Madden became second-in-command, with direct responsibility for the 1st Battle Squadron. In 1919 he was promoted full admiral and given command of the new Atlantic Fleet.

MADSEN MACHINE-GUN

One of the world's first light machine-guns, this Danish-produced weapon, which dated from 1904, was widely used during the First World War, although it was not officially adopted by any of the armies of the major powers. Difficult and expensive to produce, it had a highly complex recoil-operated mechanism, which used the Peabody-Martini hinged breech block action. Little heavier than a typical service rifle, it was equipped with a 20-round overhead box magazine, the first of its kind, and in standard form accepted 8mm ammunition. This water-cooled weapon could fire 450 rounds per minute and was normally used with a tripod mounting.

With its excellent reputation for reliability and its availability in a variety of calibres, the Madsen was tested by several armies and air services. The British and German armies used it for experimental purposes, but it was only accepted for operational use by some Central European forces, which ordered it in small numbers. The gun was also employed by the Russians on their giant Sikorsky **Ilya Mourometz** bombers, but most air forces preferred to use other light machine guns as their standard aircraft armament. The weapon was also in evidence during the Second World War and remained in production for almost 50 years.

MAISTRE, GENERAL PAUL, 1858–1922

French general who commanded XXI Corps on the Western Front for much of the war. In May 1917, he was appointed to the command of the Sixth Army, which had been virtually destroyed during the ill-fated **Nivelle** offensive. Within a few months Maistre had achieved his objective of restoring its fighting effectiveness. After a brief interlude in Italy, he returned to France in the spring of 1918 and, as an army group commander, was involved in all the major operations of the last few months of the war.

MAJESTIC

The largest class of battleships ever to be constructed, *Majestic* and her eight sisters were completed in 1895–98.

Similar in appearance to the Royal Sovereigns, the Majestics carried four 12-inch main guns that were more than equal to the earlier 13.5-inch weapons because of design improvements; secondary armament was increased to twelve 6-inch guns. Greater protection was provided because of the availability of lighter armour; they had a displacement of just under 15,000 tons and a maximum speed of 18 knots. In 1905–06, *Mars* became the first battleship equipped to burn oil fuel and all but two of the class followed.

Some of the Majestics – *Mars*, *Hannibal* and *Victorious* – were used in supporting roles only but the others were more actively employed by the Royal Navy. *Majestic* and *Prince George* were both sent to the **Dardanelles**, the former being torpedoed by a German submarine in May 1915; *Prince George* was severely damaged there but survived the war.

MANGIN, GENERAL CHARLES, 1866–1925

French general who played a key part in the counter-offensives at **Verdun** from October 1916, retaking Fort Douaumont and capturing nearly 7,000 prisoners. Before the end of the year he was appointed to the command of the Sixth Army, which was to play a key role in **Nivelle**'s plans for a spring offensive. A protégé of General Nivelle, Mangin was one of the few senior officers at the front who supported the action in April 1917. As the offensive ended in failure, the Fifth Army dissolved in mutiny and Mangin's loyalty to his chief received no recognition: he was, in fact, quickly relieved of his command, sacrificed by Nivelle as his scapegoat. Restored to the army in 1918, Mangin headed the Tenth Army in the first Allied counter-offensives of the year. During the **Second Battle of the Marne** in July 1918, he attacked the west flank of the salient, adding to his reputation as 'a most vehement warrior'. He was nicknamed 'the Butcher' because he was allegedly 'careless of human life'.

MANNERHEIM, GENERAL CARL, BARON, 1867–1948

Finnish general who served in the Russian army from 1899, distinguishing himself during the Russo-Japanese War and the First World War. He returned to his native country after the **Russian Revolution**, when Finland proclaimed its independence. Helsinki was occupied by Finnish communists early in 1918 and in the ensuing civil war Mannerheim led the 'Whites'. With German help he defeated the communists, although he was to be concerned with Finland's defences against the Soviet Union for the rest of his public life. He was President of Finland, 1944–46.

MANNLICHER RIFLE

The standard rifle of the Austro-Hungarian army during the First World War, the Mannlicher Modell 1895 was preceded by several other straight-pull bolt-action weapons designed by Ferdinand von Mannlicher. These earlier patterns were consigned to the reserves as production centred on the M1895, which was also known as the 8mm Repetier-Gewehr Modell 1895. It was manufactured in large quantities at Budapest as well as Steyr.

Conventional in appearance, the weapon had a long barrel (765mm) and was strong and reliable. It fired 8mm round-nosed cartridges (held in a five-round clip-loaded magazine) at a muzzle velocity of 2,000 feet per second. Two carbine variants of the basic design, which were also produced in very large numbers, appeared in the same year, 1895: the cavalry carbine and, for troops such as artillerymen, engineers and signallers, the 8mm Repetier-Stützen-Gewehr Modell 1895.

The Modell 1895 was also adopted by Bulgaria in 1897 and was later used by several other armies; after the war large quantities were transferred to the Italian army as reparations. These were still in use in the Second World War, as were various Mannlicher adaptations, of which the Italian Mannlicher-Carcano rifle was the most important.

MANNOCK, EDWARD, 1887–1918

Britain's ace of aces, Edward 'Mick' Mannock, who concealed a sight defect in order to join the RFC, did not begin operational flying until April 1917. Although he was relatively unknown outside the service during and after the war, he was highly regarded by his colleagues as an outstanding fighter pilot, patrol leader and tactician. His career began with No 40 Squadron, flying a **Nieuport Scout** during 'Bloody April', when air combat was particularly intensive. His first hit – a balloon – was achieved on 7 May and he shot down his first aircraft a month later.

His score grew over the next two months and he was awarded the Military Cross, as well as being promoted to captain and appointed a flight commander. By the time he left No 40 Squadron early in

1918, his score had risen to 23. He returned to France in March 1918 with No 74 Squadron, which had been equipped with **SE5a**s. Motivated by a real and growing hatred of his opponents, Mannock was determined to increase his score: in three months with the squadron he added 39 German aircraft to his total, of which 24 were brought down in a single month. He also shot down three aircraft in a single dogfight during this period.

Mannock sought to reduce the risks of combat as much as possible by careful preparation and a detailed study of tactics, which convinced him of the need for formation flying. Never reckless he always tried to ensure that he was in the best possible position before attacking. He was also an outstanding leader, giving priority to training inexperienced pilots and giving them full support on their initial missions. Promoted major, he was appointed in July 1918 to the command of No 85 Squadron in succession to **W. A. Bishop**. In a short time Mannock had increased his score to 73, gaining his last victory shortly before he was shot down by German ground troops on 26 July 1918. He was awarded the Victoria Cross posthumously about a year after his death.

MARCH, GENERAL PEYTON, 1864–1955

After a period of service in France in charge of the AEF's artillery forces, March was appointed chief of staff of the United States army early in 1918. During his tenure in Washington, he presided over the rapid expansion of the army and was responsible for its reform and reorganisation. His quest for improvement under wartime conditions inevitably resulted in an increase in the powers of his office, a fact resented by some of his colleagues. March remained chief of staff until 1921.

MARLIN MACHINE-GUN

The Marlin, which first appeared in 1916, was a development of the .30-inch **Colt-Browning**, a light machine-gun that was used by the Allies in the first part of the war and was nicknamed the 'Potato Digger'. Modified for aircraft use, this air-cooled gun was lighter than the original and had a gas-operated piston instead of a pendant lever below the barrel. It had a belt-feed system, with a capacity of 250 rounds, and used the same calibre ammunition as the Colt. The firing mechanism was subsequently redesigned to enable the weapon to be used with mechanical synchronising gear.

Produced in quantity for the United States Army Air Service, by the end of the war it had been fitted to some of the aircraft in use with 22 AEF squadrons. It was more reliable than most of its counterparts and could fire at the rate of 600 rounds per minute. A much smaller number of tank machine-guns, incorporating minor changes, were also made.

MARNE, FIRST BATTLE OF THE, 5–9 September 1914

Following the Allied defeats in the **Battle of the Frontiers**, 14–25 August 1914, the five German armies at the centre and right continued their advance, entering France on a line from Amiens to Verdun. They were led, on the German right, by the First Army (**Kluck**) which moved forward rapidly.

The opposing French Sixth Army (**Maunoury**) was unable to check Kluck's advance and by the end of August the Germans were within 30 miles of Paris. On Maunoury's right was the BEF, which, following its defeats at Mons, and **Le Cateau**, retreated rapidly, exposing the flanks of the French Fifth Army (commanded by **Franchet d'Espérey**, who replaced **Lanrezac** during the battle) as well as those of the Sixth. The British crossed the Marne on 3 September, turning eastwards. By this time the Sixth Army had been ordered to reinforce the Paris garrison which seemed increasingly vulnerable to enemy attack. Further east the situation appeared to be less dangerous, with the French Fifth, Ninth (**Foch**), Fourth (**Langle de Cary**) and Third (**Sarrail**) Armies yielding ground more slowly. In the face of continued German pressure in the critical Paris area, **Joffre** ordered the French retreat to continue to a line south of the Somme.

Kluck responded to this apparently favourable situation by changing the direction of his advance, making a fateful modification to the **Schlieffen Plan**. The latter had called for the invading German forces to move west of Paris, encircling the French from the south. However, Kluck now believed that the Allies were virtually beaten and he swung east of the capital with the aim of rolling up the left of the French line quickly. The Germans moved south-east across the Marne on 4 September, only a day behind the Allies; on the fifth Kluck was directly east of Paris moving towards the Seine.

This change of plan, which had exposed his right flank, was quickly discovered by Allied air reconnaissance. **Galliéni**, military governor of Paris, urged Joffre to launch a counter-attack on this vulnerable wing. The commander-in-chief did not make an immediate decision but eventually agreed to do so. Orders were issued to Maunoury's Sixth Army during the evening of 4 September, but the other commanders did not receive Joffre's instructions for a counter-attack until the early hours of the fifth; both d'Espérey and French felt that it was too late to put the order into effect on that day as their troops had already begun to march southwards.

Realising the dangers of the situation, **Moltke** ordered the First and Second Armies on the right

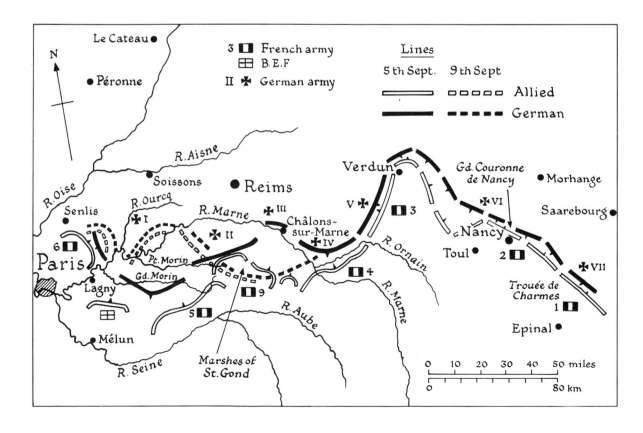

wing to face the east side of Paris in order to cover the rest of his armies against attacks from that direction. The other German armies were to continue to advance, but the Third was to halt at the Seine. Maunoury's counter-offensive began on 6 September, with 150,000 men striking the German IV Reserve Corps along the Ourcq River.

British troops crossing the Marne, September 1914

As the bulk of Kluck's First Army fell back to deal with the attack, a 30-mile gap opened up between him and Bülow's army. The Allies advanced into this thinly defended area, with the right wing of the French Fifth army turning on the German Second. The left attacked the remaining two corps of Kluck's army. The British, moving forward cautiously 'found no enemy: only a hole'. They did not realise how favourable their position was and failed to capitalise on it. To the right, the Ninth Army struck at the junction between the German Second and Third Armies and only held its position with difficulty during fierce counter-attacks. In fact, Foch was forced to call on Franchet d'Espérey for assistance, reducing the amount of support he could give to the British.

Further east, a vital contribution was made by the French First (**Dubail**) and Second (**Castelnau**) Armies, which held the fortress towns – Epinal, Charmes, Nancy, Toul – along the Moselle River. For 18 days the right wing fought off constant attacks by the German Sixth (**Rupprecht**) and Seventh Armies. Between the two fronts, from Verdun to the Upper Marne, the French Third and Fourth Armies successfully contained attacks by the German Fifth and Fourth Armies.

On the main front the battle raged for three days – 6–8 September – over a distance of 100 miles from Verdun to Compiègne. The French Sixth Army only held its ground with considerable difficulty and 600 taxis were used to bring vital reinforcements from Paris. However, at German headquarters, which was dominated by fear of a breakthrough and rumours of a Russian landing on the Belgian coast, there was considerable pessimism about the outcome of the battle. Communications with the front were poor and the information received by Moltke was often inaccurate.

Colonel Hentsch was sent by Moltke on a fact-finding tour of the front on 8 September with powers to order a withdrawal if necessary. His controversial mission was soon overtaken by events: Kluck was forced to order, on 9 September, the first stage of a withdrawal northwards to protect his left against the British who were now recrossing the Marne. On the same day the whole attack was called off and the entire German line began a fighting retreat of 40 miles back to the River Aisne.

German dead (men and horses) on the Marne, the battle that stopped the enemy thrust into France

The Battle of the Marne, one of the decisive engagements of history, ended all hopes of a quick German victory. The Schlieffen Plan lay in ruins. The Germans, hindered by poor leadership, had failed to reach Paris or destroy the Allied armies. It was an Allied strategic victory, which cost both sides heavy casualties – a quarter of those involved – and ensured that the war would be a long one.

MARNE, SECOND BATTLE OF THE, 15 July–5 August 1918

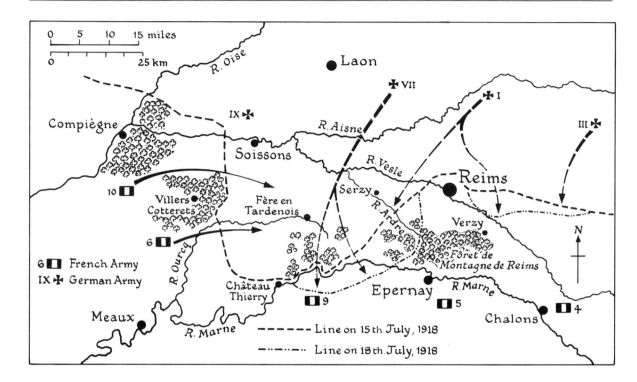

British soldiers man a machine-gun post during the Second Battle of the Marne, 1918

Ludendorff's last all-out offensive of the war began as yet another diversionary attack designed to draw Allied reserves from Flanders, where a new German assault was imminent. The immediate aim of the action was the crossing of the River Marne, to the east of Paris. Three and a half German armies were to make converging attacks from both sides of Reims: two – the First (Mudra) and the Third (Einem) – were positioned to the east. Their assault on the French First Army (**Gouraud**) on 15 July made little progress, and was halted at 11.00 a.m. on the first day. Heavy artillery fire and an elastic defence in depth along Gouraud's 26-mile front had helped the French to hold the line. The attack was not renewed here.

On the other front, south-west of the city, the German Seventh Army (Boehn), supported by a new Ninth Army (Eben) was, initially, more successful. Attacking on a 22-mile front, it smashed through the French Sixth Army (Degoutte) and crossed the Marne at Dormans, between Rueil and Château-Thierry.

With six divisions, Boehn created a bridgehead nine miles long and four miles deep before being halted by the French Ninth Army (De Mitry), supported by British, American and Italian units, on 17 July. Thirty-six Allied divisions had brought an offensive by 52 German divisions to an end.

On 18 July, the Allies launched a major counter-offensive against the Marne salient, which ended with its elimination. The main attack was led by the French Tenth Army (**Mangin**) and the Sixth Army (Degoutte) in the east and south. Supported by 14 Allied divisions and 350 tanks, they advanced up to five miles on the first day. Secondary assaults were made by the French Fifth Army (**Berthelot**) and the Ninth from the west.

The continuing Allied advance into the salient soon threatened German communications between Châ-teau-Thierry and Soissons and they began to withdraw from the Marne. Soissons was freed on 2 August and by the next day the Germans had fallen back to a line along the Vesle and Aisne Rivers at the base of the old salient. The Allied counter-offensive was brought to an end on 6 August, when no more progress could be made against the enemy, which was now much more firmly entrenched.

A German offensive had been turned into an Allied victory; it marked the beginning of the enemy retreat that ended only with the Armistice. Of more immediate importance, it had caused the proposed German offensive in Flanders to be postponed and then abandoned completely. French losses amounted to 95,165 men, while German casualties were about 168,000, including nearly 30,000 prisoners.

MARSHALL, GENERAL SIR WILLIAM, 1865–1939

Appointed commander of British forces in Mesopotamia on the death of **Sir Frederick Maude** in November 1917, Marshall, a veteran of the Western Front and **Gallipoli**, had already served in this theatre for over a year. Once he had organised Baghdad's defences against a Turkish counter-attack, he turned his attention to the Iraqi oilfields. In spite of the transfer of the 7th Division to Palestine, Marshall's forces defeated the Turks at **Sharqat** on 29 October 1918, thus ending the war in Mesopotamia.

MARTINSYDE F4

The F4 Buzzard was a single-seat biplane that appeared too late for operational use, although some had been delivered to the RAF before the Armistice. Powered by a 300hp Hispano-Suiza engine, it had maximum speed of almost 130m.p.h. at 10,000 feet and was one of the fastest and most effective British fighters of the time. Armament consisted of two fixed, synchronised .303 **Vickers machine-guns**. A slightly earlier variant, the F3, was powered by a smaller 275hp Rolls Royce Falcon III engine. It was produced in very small numbers and four were allocated to home defence duties in 1918.

MARTINSYDE G100 & G102

The G100 was a single-seat tractor biplane that was designed as a long-range escort fighter. Nicknamed the 'Elephant', its distinguishing features included a large wing area and a relatively powerful engine – a 120hp Beardmore. Armament normally consisted of one forward-firing .303 **Lewis machine-gun** mounted on the upper wing, although some Elephants were equipped with a second Lewis gun mounted on the cockpit. There were, however, considerable difficulties in operating the second gun successfully.

The G100 served with the RFC from early in 1916: on the Western Front they were allocated in small numbers to two-seater squadrons and only one squadron (No 27) was exclusively equipped with the type. They were used for photographic reconnaissance and as fighters. In aerial combat the Elephant soon revealed serious limitations: its weight and size meant that it was not nearly as manoeuvrable as other fighters then in service and the pilot's view was restricted. It did, however, have good load-carrying capabilities and in mid-1916 it was decided to use the G100 primarily as a bomber. It could deliver a maximum of 220lb of bombs.

A later version, the G102, which was equipped with the larger 160hp Beardmore engine, had a slightly increased load of 260lb. It had a top speed of 104m.p.h. and an endurance of $4\frac{1}{2}$ hours. In total, 270 Elephants of both types were produced, remaining in service with No 27 Squadron until November 1917, when they were replaced by the **Airco DH4**. Elephants were also present, in smaller numbers, in Palestine and Mesopotamia until the end of the war.

MARTINSYDE SI

The SI was a small tractor biplane that was developed by Martin and Handasyde in the summer of 1914 as a sporting single-seater. Adopted for military purposes by the RFC on the outbreak of war, it was armed with a single .303 **Lewis machine-gun** above the centre section. It was powered by an 80hp Gnome engine, giving a maximum speed of 87m.p.h. at sea level, and early examples had an unusual four-wheel undercarriage.

In 1915, the SI served in small numbers on the Western Front, where it made little impact, and in Mesopotamia, where it played a useful reconnaissance role during the British occupation of **Kut** in September 1915. Some SIs remained in England where they were used for training purposes or, more rarely, in an anti-Zeppelin role.

MARWITZ, GENERAL GEORG VON DER, 1856–1929

Commander of a cavalry corps on the outbreak of war, Marwitz participated in the invasion of Belgium and in the 'Race to the Sea'. Varied service as head of VI Army Corps, including periods on both fronts, preceded his appointment to the command of the Second Army in December 1916. He held the Cambrai sector and, on 20 November 1917, opposed the major British assault led by a mass formation of tanks operating independently for the first time. His successful counter-attack forced the enemy to withdraw and brought the **Battle of Cambrai** to an end. On the 'black day of the German army', 8 August 1918, Marwitz again faced a mass tank attack, but this time his units suffered badly. For the remainder of the war he commanded the Fifth Army in Champagne.

MASARYK, THOMAS, 1850–1937

Co-founder and first president of Czechoslovakia, Masaryk escaped from Vienna in December 1914. During his wartime exile he campaigned for an independent Czechoslovakia and founded, with Eduard Beneš, the Czech National Council. In June 1918, he secured the support of the United States and other Allied powers for the creation of a Czech republic, an aspiration which became a reality as the Austrian empire disintegrated at the end of the war. Masaryk was elected president in November 1918 and remained in office until 1935.

MASCHINENGEWEHR 08

The standard machine-gun of the German army during the First World War, the Maschinengewehr 08 (MG08) was an almost unchanged Maxim derivative. Using the standard recoil-operated mechanism, it fired a 7.92mm rifle cartridge at a cyclic rate of 300 rounds per minute (450rpm with a muzzle booster). Cartridges were fed into the weapon from a fabric belt which held 250 rounds. This water-cooled weapon was reliable and solidly constructed, weighing about 62kg (including two spare barrels and a sledge mounting). Alternative mountings included a stretcher carried by two men and a tripod. The MG08 was produced at the government factory at Spandau and by Deutsche Waffen und Munitions-fabriken.

At the beginning of the war the German army, unlike its main adversaries, had fully appreciated the tactical importance of the heavy machine-gun. A total of 12,500 MG08s had already been delivered, six to each regiment. In the hands of specially trained German troops on the Western Front the MG08, with its capacity for prolonged fire, was used with devastating effect against Allied infantry. Continuing in German army service until well into the 1930s, it also provided the basis for the **Maschinengewehr 08/15**, a lightened wartime version.

MASCHINENGEWEHR 08/15

A lightened version of the **Maschinengewehr 08**, the 7.92mm MG08/15 used the same **Maxim** operating system and was also water-cooled. It had a pistol grip and butt, a bipod and other minor changes. The fabric ammunition belt held 50, 100 or 250 cartridges and the weapon had a cyclic rate of 450 rounds per minute. Weighing 18kg, it was never a true light machine-gun and was not always easy to deploy in battle. The MG08/15 was, however, widely used to great effect in the closing stages of war, helping to cover the withdrawal of the German army. At this critical period, a new air-cooled version – the MG08/18 – had appeared but few reached the front line before the Armistice. Although the water jacket had been removed there was only a very small reduction in weight and serious overheating problems could arise.

A further development of the MG08/15 – the LMG08/15 aircraft gun – was much more successful. Known as the Spandau (from its place of manufacture) it was a lightened, air cooled version, the water jacket (now slotted) being retained to support the recoil of the barrel. Ammunition was fed from a drum magazine that held 47 rounds. The LMG08/15 supplemented the standard **Parabellum** aircraft machine gun, which was in short supply; it was widely used as a pilot's gun, having been modified to work with a synchronising mechanism.

MASURIAN LAKES, FIRST BATTLE OF THE, 9–14 September 1914

After their great victory over **Samsonov** at the **Battle of Tannenberg** (26–31 August 1914), the Germans turned north-east to attack the other arm of the Russian pincer movement that had sought to envelop them in East Prussia. The Russian First Army (**Rennenkampf**), which had remained well away from the Tannenberg battlefield, was moving slowly forward through the Insterburg Gap between Königsberg and the Masurian Lakes. When informed of Samsonov's defeat, Rennenkampf fell back to a securer position extending from the Baltic Sea (Labiau) south-east to Angerburg.

The German Eighth Army (**Hindenburg/Ludendorff**), which had been reinforced by two corps from France, began the assault on 7 September, with the aim of driving the enemy up towards the coast.

During the following two days Rennenkampf came under particularly heavy pressure on the left flank from General Hermann von François' I Corps and, fearing that he would be outflanked, ordered his troops to begin withdrawing on 9 September. A counter-attack by two Russian divisions against the German centre held up their advance for 48 hours and allowed many more Russian troops to escape capture. By 13 September, East Prussia had been cleared of the Russian army, at a cost of 10,000 German casualties; it was another major German victory even though there had been no envelopment. The Russians lost 125,000 men, 150 guns and a considerable amount of transport. **Zhilinsky**, the army group commander who was the architect of the Russian invasion, was dismissed for incompetence.

MASURIAN LAKES, SECOND BATTLE OF THE, 7–21 February 1915

The Winter Battle of Masuria was part of **Hindenburg**'s plan for a decisive assault on the Eastern Front that would force Russia out of the war. In East Prussia two German armies were to attack the Russian Tenth Army (General Sievers) – consisting of four corps – which was positioned north of the Masurian Lakes.

The battle began on 7 February 1915 in a heavy snowstorm, when the German Eighth Army (**Below**) advanced eastwards against the Russian left flank in a surprise attack. As the Russians began to fall back, the German Tenth Army (**Eichhorn**) advanced from the north against the enemy's right on the second day. Strong resistance from the Russian XX Corps in the Forest of Augustow held up the German advance and allowed the other three corps to escape. XX Corps surrendered on 21 February, bringing the battle to a

conclusion and increasing the number of Russian prisoners to 100,000. The Russians also suffered 100,000 casualties, but German losses during the battle were relatively small. Many German troops did, however, suffer from exposure in the extreme cold.

Further German progress eastwards was halted when the Russian Twelfth Army (**Plehve**) attacked the German right flank on 22 February. Although Hindenburg had managed to advance 70 miles during the Winter Battle of Masuria, his victory had little strategic value. To the south he had even less success: the main thrust was provided by the Austro-German South Army, which advanced through the Carpathians in February and March, but was soon halted and pushed back.

MAUDE, GENERAL SIR FREDERICK STANLEY, 1864–1917

A veteran of the Western Front and **Gallipoli**, Sir Stanley Maude, 'a truly great soldier', was sent with his troops to Mesopotamia after being evacuated from the Dardanelles in January 1916. The reinforced Mesopotamian army, with Maude providing full support, was unable to raise the siege of **Kut**, and **Sir Charles Townshend** capitulated in April 1916, after nearly four months. Although he was a relatively junior major-general, Maude was appointed commander of all British forces in Mesopotamia in August 1916. He spent the next three months carefully preparing for a major counter-offensive against the Turks, which began on 12 December 1916. Outnumbering the enemy by a significant margin, Maude recaptured Kut in February 1916 and seized **Baghdad** during the following month. Maude defeated the Turks again at **Ramadi** in September, consolidating the British position in Mesopotamia. He did not, however, live long to enjoy the fruits of his victories – promotion to lieutenant-general – because in November 1917 he died of cholera in Baghdad after drinking contaminated milk.

MAUNOURY, MARSHAL MICHEL, 1847–1923

French artilleryman who was recalled from retirement on the outbreak of the First World War. At first he commanded the hastily organised Army of Lorraine, but his appointment only lasted a few days: on 26 August 1914 he was asked to head a newly constituted Sixth Army north-east of Paris, under the overall command of **General Galliéni**, military governor of the capital. On 5 September, he executed Galliéni's plan for a counter-strike against the enemy as it wheeled east of Paris. Advancing eastwards towards the Ourcq River, he attacked the right flank of the German First Army (**Kluck**). Maunoury was forced on to the defensive after Kluck brought up reinforcements and two days' intense fighting followed. With the First Army pinned down and with reports of a British advance, the enemy's progress was brought to an end, enabling the French to regain the initiative as the battle spread along the whole front west of Verdun. He was severely wounded early in 1915, bringing his front line service to an end. Maunoury was posthumously created Marshal of France for his critical role in determining the outcome of the **Battle of the Marne**.

MAUSER ANTI-TANK RIFLE

In 1918 Mauser responded to the appearance of the British **Tank Mark IV** by developing the world's first anti-tank rifle. This single-shot weapon, which had a long barrel fitted to an enlarged **Mauser rifle** mechanism, was carried and operated by one man. Employed by the German army in the closing stages of the war, the Tank Gewehr's 13mm armour-piercing ammunition was capable of penetrating the structure of every Allied tank, although a hit did not always mean that it would be immobilised. The new weapon prompted other manufacturers to produce similar designs in the post-war period.

MAUSER AUTOMATIC PISTOL

The Mauser military automatic pistol (C96) was the most powerful weapon of its kind in use during the First World War. Invented in 1894, this locked-breech weapon fired a 7.63mm Mauser round at about 1,425 feet per second. It had a box magazine – holding six, 10 or 20 rounds – in front of the trigger, a long tapering barrel and a large hammer. The weapon could be fitted with a wooden shoulder stock and holster, turning it into a short carbine. In its original form the Mauser pistol was not adopted by the German army, which preferred the **Luger**, or any other major army. Some were, however, supplied to the Italian navy and to Russia and Turkey.

Wartime supply difficulties forced the German military authorities to reconsider their position and in 1915 it was ordered in large quantities. Based on the 1912 variant, in which the operation of the safety catch was considerably modified, it was rechambered for the 9mm Parabellum cartridge (and had the figure '9' stamped on the butt grips), but was otherwise unchanged. After the end of the war the Luger remained the standard German army pistol and the Mauser disappeared from official service use.

MAUSER RIFLE

One of the most successful and widely copied rifles ever produced, the German Mauser Gewehr 98 was well constructed and had a strong bolt action. The bolt, which used a rather clumsy straight pull arrangment, had three locking lugs for additional safety. The rifle used the regular 7.92mm cartridges, which were held in an integral box magazine, containing five rounds, and were loaded from a charger clip. It had a long barrel (29.15 inches) and an elaborate backsight. Although it was not capable of rapid fire, it was always reliable and accurate.

Adopted by the German army in 1898, the original model was widely used until 1945, even though a later carbine version became its standard weapon during the First World War. The Karabiner Modell 98, which appeared in a revised form in 1908, was 43.3 inches long and had a 23.6-inch barrel; the bolt was turned down to make it easier to hold. In other respects it was identical to the Gewehr 98. There was also a sniper's version, equipped with an optical sight, that was used extensively in the trenches of the Western Front. Every Mauser model served the German front line solider well during the First World War and required relatively little maintenance.

MAX OF BADEN, PRINCE, 1867–1929

The last Chancellor of the German Empire, Max's appointment in October 1918 followed the decision to seek an immediate armistice. Max agreed that Germany should negotiate with the Allies from a position of relative strength and secured **Ludendorff**'s dismissal to facilitate the process. He was, however, unable himself to persuade the Kaiser to abdicate, an essential step in view of the internal political turmoil and the need to convince the Allies of

a move towards liberal democracy. Max's eventual announcement of the Kaiser's departure on 9 November and the establishment of a regency led to his immediate fall from office. The Social Democrats, who withdrew from the Cabinet, proclaimed the birth of the German republic, a change much more in line with popular aspirations, and Ebert became chancellor.

MAXIM MACHINE-GUN

The world's first automatic machine-gun, the creation of the American inventor Hiram Maxim, appeared in 1884. It used the power of recoil forces, generated by the powder charge, to operate the whole mechanism continuously at a cyclic rate of up to 600 rounds per minute. This revolutionary new weapon, which was water-cooled and belt-fed, was soon demonstrated to all the major armies of Europe, but it was only slowly adopted because of military conservatism.

Although Britain was in fact the first country to use the Maxim, Germany was to show a much greater appreciation of its potential. The German army adopted the **Maschinengewehr 08**, a virtually unmodified Maxim that was produced in 7.92mm calibre at the government factory at Spandau. Some 12,500 examples were available to the army on the outbreak of war. The Russians also produced their own version of the Maxim – the **Pulemyot Maxima**

1910 – which was more extensively modified, with its own special mounting, although the basic operating mechanism was unchanged. **Vickers**, the British company which produced most of the early Maxim guns, designed its own lightened version of the original. The Vickers became the standard medium machine-gun of the British army during the First World War. Production gradually increased during the war, with a peak being reached in November 1918, when some 5,000 guns a month were being made.

Until the arrival of the tank and the return of mobile warfare, the defensive firepower of the Vickers and other Maxim derivatives dominated the battlefields of the Western Front. The Maxim was largely superseded by technologically more advanced weapons during the inter-war years although the Russian variant was still in use during the Second World War.

M-CLASS SUBMARINE

Armed with a 12-inch gun (from a pre-dreadnought battleship), the British M-class submarine was intended to reinforce a torpedo attack with its stock of 50 shells. The gun could be fired within seconds of the boat reaching the surface, but it was never tested

in action. Only one M-class submarine was in fact made before the Armistice, production being halted because of fears that Germany would be encouraged to produce a similar weapon.

MEDIUM TANK MARK A

With the appearance of the British **Tank Mark I**, attention was focused on the need for a lighter and faster machine capable of co-operating with the cavalry. Its main function would be to advance rapidly once the enemy's defences had been breached by heavy tanks. Development work was carried out by Sir William Tritton, who also produced the Mark I, and the result was the 'Tritton Chaser' or Medium Tank Mark A, as it was officially designated.

The need to restrict weight was an important

factor and the 14mm armoured hull consisted of no more than a simple box shape crew compartment at the rear and a long, low bonnet covering the two 45hp Taylor engines located towards the front. Mounted side by side, each power unit drove one track and gave the machine a relatively high speed of 8m.p.h., although this maximum was often difficult to attain in a vehicle with unsprung suspension. It had a good range of 80 miles but its trench-crossing ability was very poor, being limited to gaps of no more than seven feet. Unlike the Mark I the new machine was designed to be driven by one man but even the most experienced drivers had difficulty in coordinating the two engines, particularly when varying the individual throttle openings in order to steer it. Operated by a crew of four, the Medium Tank was equipped with three fixed **Hotchkiss machine-guns**, the single **Lewis gun** mounted in a revolving turret being found only in the prototype.

Some 200 Medium Tanks, or 'Whippets' as they were universally known, were produced in Mark A form and served with the Tank Corps in France from early in 1918 until the Armistice. They were first used in action during the German offensive in March and were much in evidence during the **Battle of Amiens** and other major engagements in the final period before the Armistice. It was, in fact, involved in the last tank action of the war on 5 November 1918. Although there were problems in liaising with the cavalry on the battlefield, the Whippet's experiences confirmed the value of the medium tank. An improved version, the Mark B, was ordered in larger quantities, but production models did not reach the front before the end of the war.

MEGIDDO, BATTLE OF, 19–21 September 1918

Defeated Turkish troops on the march after the decisive British victory at the Battle of Megiddo

After the **fall of Jerusalem** in December 1917, **General Allenby**'s plans to renew the Allied offensive were delayed by the massive German attacks on the Western Front in March 1918. Many of his troops were recalled to Europe and for the next few months he was confined to small operations east of the Jordan, in co-operation with Arab forces under **Feisal** and **T. E. Lawrence**. It was not until the summer that reinforcements started to arrive and Allenby could plan the final destruction of the Turkish army in Palestine.

For this purpose his forces were concentrated on the Mediterranean shore above Jaffa, opposite part of a thinly defended Turkish line that ran east to the Jordan Valley. Along it were positioned, from left to right, the Turkish Eighth, Seventh and Fourth Armies, under the command of **General Liman von Sanders**. He had 44,000 troops at his disposal, the British 69,000. Following earlier British activity in the area as many as a third of the enemy troops were concentrated east of the River Jordan on the Turkish left, where the main assault was expected. The British attack was, in fact, to be made on the Turkish right, but the secrecy of the preparations and the formation of dummy camps misled the enemy.

The Battle of Megiddo opened on 19 September at 4.30 a.m. with an artillery bombardment along a 65-mile front; an infantry attack followed and within three hours the line held by the demoralised Turkish Eighth Army had been broken. The Desert Mounted Corps rode fast northwards, with the aim of crossing the hill chain which ends in Mount Carmel and then descending into the Plain of Esdraelon. They would then move eastwards to the Jordan at Beisan, completely cutting off the northern retreat of the Turkish Seventh and Eighth Armies. Their supply lines had already been disrupted by Lawrence of Arabia's attacks on the Hejaz Railway and the RAF cut their communications with headquarters, helping to delay attempts to halt the cavalry wheel until it was too late. The mounted corps had in fact covered over 70 miles in 36 hours, reaching Beisan according to plan.

The Seventh and Eighth Armies were forced to move eastwards across the Jordan, having lost 25,000 men as British prisoners. By 21 September, they had been destroyed as fighting forces. On the Turkish left, the Fourth Army was also compelled to retreat towards Damascus; it came under attack from Arab forces and was cut to pieces. Meanwhile to the north, Nazareth was seized and Liman von Sanders narrowly missed capture. Allenby had routed the Turks in one of the war's most decisive battles and there was nothing to stop him advancing further north, with **Damascus** as the immediate prize.

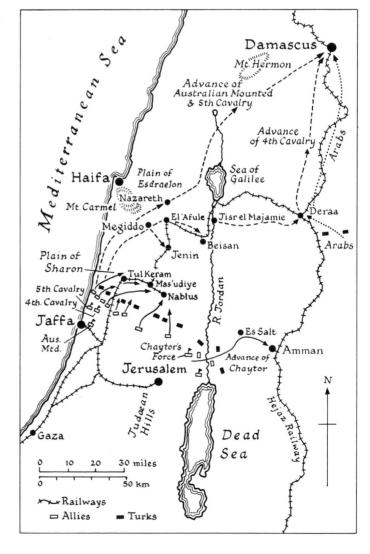

MESOPOTAMIAN FRONT, CHRONOLOGICAL LIST OF EVENTS

MESSINES, BATTLE OF, 7–14 June 1917

In order to relieve German pressure on the French army, which had been seriously weakened by the failure of the **Nivelle** offensive and the mutinies that followed, **Haig** planned a major new offensive for the summer of 1917. He wanted to break out of the Ypres salient, between the North Sea and the Lys River. However, before he could do so the German positions to the right, on the dominating Wytschaete–Messines ridge, had to be taken. Preparations for such an attack had been underway for as long as 18 months: under the direction of the methodical commander of the British Second Army (**General Plumer**), a million

pounds of high explosive had been placed under the German front line. Tunnelling companies had dug tunnels from 200 to 2,000 feet in length in order to lay 19 mines at depths of up to 100 feet.

The preliminary artillery bombardment began on 21 May and by the time the main attack was launched on 7 June some 3.5 million shells had been fired. When the mines were detonated, the sound could be heard clearly in London, 130 miles away; over 10,000 Germans were killed. To complete the destruction of the enemy trenches, gas containers and cans of boiling oil were propelled into them.

The Second Army (nine divisions), advanced quickly and seized the ridge, taking 7,000 prisoners, while the British Fifth Army (**Gough**) and the French First Army (**Anthoine**) advanced through the gap. On 14 June, the battle came to an end as enemy resistance stiffened, but the rest of the salient had been taken. It was 'one of the most complete local victories of the war' and for the first time German losses (25,000) exceeded those of the British (17,000). There was no reason now to delay the main Flanders campaign of 1917.

Minelaying at Messines, 1917: British sappers tunnel under the ridge

METAXAS, COLONEL JOHN, 1871–1941

A future dictator of Greece (1936–41), Metaxas was chief of staff of the Greek army for much of the war period. He was **King Constantine**'s closest military adviser and was influential in maintaining Greece's neutral stance, although he himself was strongly pro-German. When Constantine was deposed in June 1917, **Venizelos** returned to power, and Metaxas was forced to follow the king into exile.

MEUSE-ARGONNE OFFENSIVE, 26 September–11 November 1918

The final Allied offensive on the Western Front was designed to force the Germans to retreat from the Hindenburg Line, to damage their lateral rail communications and ultimately to bring about their final surrender. **Foch** planned four major attacks, which were to be launched at about the same time. In

Flanders, the Belgian army was to attack at Ypres, while Anglo-French forces were to launch a massive assault along the **Cambrai–St Quentin** line. In the Argonne and Meuse area, the French and Americans were to trap the Germans in the southern arm of the pincer movement. If the Allies could reach Mézières and Sedan, up to 30 miles away, they would be in a position to threaten the main German armies to the north.

Commanded by **General Pershing**, the American front ran for 17 miles, from Forges on the Meuse to the middle of the Argonne Forest. His three corps (III, V and I), which had just arrived from the St Mihiel operation and had very little time to prepare for the new offensive, opposed **Gallwitz**'s Army Group. To Pershing's left was the French Fourth Army (**Gouraud**) whose line extended to Auberive on the Suippe: it faced **Crown Prince Frederick William**'s Army Group. In total, 37 Allied divisions opposed 24 German.

The attack on the German defences, which consisted of three heavily fortified lines, began on 26 September. Supported by 189 tanks, the Allies advanced rapidly at first: the Americans covered nine miles during the first five days, although the French made less dramatic progress in the Argonne Forest,

where the difficult conditions worked in the enemy's favour. The advance slowed as the Germans brought in reinforcements, although the first two defensive lines had been penetrated by the time fighting died down on 5 October.

On 12 October, the American forces were reconstituted as two separate armies, with Pershing, who had been criticised for the relative lack of progress of the southern pincer, appointed as a group army commander. The Second Army (**Bullard**), on the right, was to move north-east between the Meuse and the Moselle in a diversionary attack, while the First (**Liggett**) was to renew its advance northwards. Operations began once more on 14 October, but little progress was made because the troops were exhausted and communications were disrupted. As a result, heavy losses were sustained and the fighting died out again.

On 1 November, offensive operations were resumed along the whole front and the First Army, reorganised and replenished with rested troops, attacked northwards again. On this occasion considerable progress was made almost at once as the German front to the north was broken. At the same time the enemy was expelled from the dominating heights east of the Meuse. The Americans now moved quickly up the Meuse Valley as German resistance weakened, arriving before Sedan on 6 November. The French, who had finally cleared the Argonne, also advanced rapidly, capturing Mézières and Charleville. They had lost the race to Sedan, but the American commander, Liggett, permitted them to enter the city first.

As the war came to an end, plans for an advance on Metz were abandoned. The final Allied offensive of the First World War forced an enemy retreat along the whole line and convinced the German government of the need to arrange an Armistice. American successes in the first phase of the Meuse–Argonne offensive had been limited, but the final attack established that 'the American army could produce leadership and staff work worthy of the gallant sacrifice of the fighting troops'. That sacrifice had been heavy, with the loss of 117,000 Americans since 26 September.

MICHELER, GENERAL ALFRED, 1861–1931

Commander of the French Tenth Army at the **Somme** in 1916, Micheler later headed 'the Group of Armies of Reserve', the force which attempted, without success, to penetrate German lines during the **Nivelle** offensive in April 1917. He had actively opposed the whole plan but did not openly break with Nivelle until after it had failed, when the latter dismissed some of his closest colleagues in an attempt to preserve his own position. This episode did not end Micheler's wartime career, but following later disagreements with **Pétain** he was dismissed in the summer of 1918.

MILITARY MUTINIES

The six-day rebellion at Etaples – a base to the rear of the lines in Flanders – in September 1917 and a few other isolated acts away from the front were the extent of the British army's experience of mutiny during the First World War. Patriotism and harsh discipline, which included execution for desertion and cowardice, meant that most British troops accepted the horrors of **trench warfare** and remained obedient to military authority.

The long war of attrition on the Western Front had a very different impact on the French army, which was almost destroyed by the mutinies of May–June 1917. Over a million men and 54 divisions were affected by the revolt, which involved 'deserting, refusing duty, waving red flags, calling for peace and threatening to march on Paris'. The intolerable strain of **Verdun**, which had cost the French army over 500,000 casualties, and the failure of the **Nivelle** offensive (April 1917), which had promised a breakthrough, created the conditions for a mutiny, which was also fostered by the activities of 'home front traitors'. The outbreak may also have been influenced by the March revolution in Russia.

Pétain, who succeeded Nivelle as commander-in-chief, was responsible for restoring order and settling the army's immediate grievances. Some 23,000 mutineers were convicted and 432 received the death penalty; only 55 were actually shot. The fighting effectiveness of the French army was restored more slowly but it was in good shape by the time the Germans began their offensive in the spring of 1918.

For the rest of 1917 the British army was forced to assume the primary role on the Western Front and it was fortunate that the Germans did not discover the extent of the collapse until it was too late.

Other examples of mutiny during the First World War include the breakdown of discipline among front line Italian troops when facing defeat by Austria in October 1917 and the disorders within the German army during the closing stages of the war. Disaffected troops also played an important role in the events leading up to the Bolshevik revolution in November 1918.

Mutiny was not confined to land forces during 1914–18, and several navies, including the Russian navy at Kronstadt and Austrian navy at Cattaro, were affected by revolts. The German **High Seas Fleet** was the most seriously undermined by mutiny, with major outbreaks occurring in both 1917 and 1918. Plans to mount a final 'death ride' against the **Grand Fleet** were the immediate cause of the mutiny which began on the ships based at Kiel on 29 October 1918. The mutineers, some 40,000 strong, soon moved ashore and their seizure of Kiel itself on 4 November marked the beginnings of the German revolution. As a result, the German government resolved to end the war as quickly as possible to avert a revolutionary takeover. The ending of the war did not bring mutinous activity immediately to an end as there were major protests in Britain and France about the authorities' failure to demobilise troops quickly enough.

MILLERAND, ALEXANDRE, 1859–1943

French Minister of War during the first year of the Great War, Millerand established good working relations with **General Joffre**, who was given a free hand in the development of military strategy. Miller-and, who helped to solve the French shell crisis in 1914, lost his post when the **Viviani** government fell in October 1915.

MILLS BOMB

The British army's standard hand grenade during the First World War, the first Mills design was officially adopted early in 1915 and production began in June. By 1917, to meet the needs of **trench warfare** on the Western Front, a million Mills bombs were being produced every week. Five variants appeared during the war, but the basic design remained the same. It was a fragmentation grenade and had a cast iron body, serrated to allow a better grip, with a finger lever that was held in place by a ringed split pin. As it was prepared for use the lever was gripped and the safety pin was withdrawn. The pressure of the striker spring overcame the lever which flew off. The spring forced the striker down on the cap, which in turn ignited the fuse. Five seconds later the fuse fired the detonator and the grenade exploded. Most Mills bombs were hand thrown, although some had a threaded hole in the base into which a rifle rod could be inserted.

MILNE, ADMIRAL SIR ARCHIBALD BERKELEY, 1855–1938

Appointed commander-in-chief of Britain's Mediterranean fleet in 1912, Milne owed his position to royal influence rather than professional ability. His lack of judgement and initiative were in fact clearly revealed almost as soon as the war began. In a very confused political and military situation in the Mediterranean area, the forces under his command failed to intercept the German warships *Goeben* and *Breslau* as they escaped through the eastern Mediterranean to Turkey.

Returning home soon afterwards, Milne blamed equally **Sir Ernest Troubridge** for failing to engage the ships with his cruiser squadron and the Admiralty for its unclear and incomplete orders. In particular, the Admiralty never gave any indication that neutral Turkey rather than the Atlantic might be their intended destination. Although Milne escaped official censure while Troubridge was court-martialled, it was clear that the navy's most senior officers held him directly responsible for failing to stop the German ships. **Fisher**, in fact, referred to him contemptuously as 'Sir Berkeley Goeben' and he was never again employed by the Royal Navy.

MILNE, FIELD MARSHAL GEORGE, BARON, 1866–1948

A future Chief of the Imperial General Staff (1926–33), Milne was commander of British forces at **Salonika** from 1916 until the end of the war. He had arrived there at the beginning of 1916 as head of XVI

Corps, after a period on the staff of the Second Army in France. Considerable difficulties – including disease, relationships with the Allies, and troop shortages – faced Milne in Salonika, but he was generally successful in maintaining good working links with successive Allied field commanders in Greece. Milne was also constrained by the British government's reluctance to authorise offensive operations in Macedonia, and it was not until April 1917 that an attack occurred.

A British diversionary action near Lake Doiran was part of a larger Allied offensive against the Bulgars, which failed with heavy losses. Renewed on a larger scale in September 1918, Milne's forces again played the same role, in order to prevent the enemy from striking against the flank of the advancing French and Serbian troops. More successful on this occasion, the Allies, including the British, moved forward to seize key points in Bulgaria and concluded an armistice with the government. After hostilities with Turkey had ended, Milne and some of his troops occupied Constantinople, remaining in command there for two years.

MILNER, ALFRED, VISCOUNT, 1854–1925

An experienced colonial governor, Viscount Milner became a member of **Lloyd George**'s War Cabinet on its formation in December 1916. He was one of its key members, providing a link with Britain's colonial empire, and had a considerable influence on the prime minister. Establishing closer co-operation with the country's wartime allies was an important feature of his work: he was involved in the creation of the Supreme War Council and in February 1917 he headed a military mission to Russia. He also fostered closer Anglo-French military relations, particularly in facilitating the appointment of **Marshal Foch** as supreme commander of the Allied armies on the Western Front. In April 1918, he left the War Cabinet to become Secretary of State for War, a post he held until the General Election of 1918.

MINELAYER

It was not until the First World War that **mines** were used in sufficient quantities to require the use of warships specially designed or adapted for laying these weapons. Most ships used for this purpose were passenger liners or **destroyers** that had been converted to enable mines to be launched over the stern. Minelaying **submarines**, which could carry out their work with relatively little risk of detection, were also produced during the war. The German ocean-going **UC-series** boats are a notable example of this type.

MINERVA ARMOURED CAR

When Belgium was invaded in August 1914 unmodified private cars were used in the initial raids against the advancing German forces. Improvised protection was soon added but by the end of August the first armoured cars were being produced by the Minerva factory in Antwerp.

Using 5mm plate, an armoured hull was added to the chassis of a Minerva touring car. It had an enclosed bonnet and driver's cab, but the crew's compartment was open, consisting of vertical sides and a rounded rear section. It was powered by a Minerva four-cylinder sleeve valve engine, the only significant modification to the chassis being the fitting of dual rear wheels to compensate for the extra weight. Armament normally consisted of an 8mm **Hotchkiss machine-gun**, although the autocannon version was fitted with a 37mm Puteaux cannon instead.

The Minerva, which established a standard pattern for armoured-car design, was in use throughout the war on the Western Front and in aid of the Russians. The Belgian army continued to operate them until well into the 1930s.

MINES

Laid extensively by the principal naval powers during the First World War, mines were subject to rapid technical development as the war progressed. A naval mine was an explosive device, moored to the sea bed, that was designed to sink a ship on detonation. There were two main types available at the beginning of the war, of which the contact mine was the most widely used. It was activated when a ship's bottom hit one of the several soft detonator 'horns' that protruded from the casing. Controlled mines, which were fired by observers on the shore, were used for defensive purposes, including the protection of harbours. By 1918, the British had added a third type – the magnetic mine – which was detonated by the magnetic field of a ship as it passed over the mine.

The British had lagged far behind Germany in mine technology and reliability during the early stages of the war, ethical objections to their use being one of the reasons for the delay in development. Germany also made more progress in developing minelaying techniques, pioneering the use of the submarine for this purpose.

Minesweeping normally involved towing a serrated wire sweep, stretched between two minesweepers. Inserted in the sweep were cutters designed to sever the wire of the mine, which caused it to rise to the surface where it could be destroyed. Mines exacted a deadly toll during the war and their place in modern warfare was assured. The first Royal Navy ship to be sunk by a German mine was the *Amphion* on 6 August 1914. By the end of the war subsequent British losses included four battleships, three cruisers, 214 minesweepers and 259 merchant ships.

British minesweeper A88 on patrol

MIŠIĆ, FIELD MARSHAL ZIVOJIN, 1855–1921

The Balkan wars of 1912–13 established Mišić's military reputation and at the beginning of the First World War he was appointed deputy chief of staff of the Serbian army under **Radomir Putnik**. During the Austrian offensive in November 1914, he commanded the First Army, contributing to the successful Serbian counter-attack. Austria had been expelled by mid-December 1914 and Mišić became a field marshal. When the enemy returned in greater strength in the autumn of 1915 Serbia was doomed, although Mišić objected to the inevitable policy of withdrawal.

When the reconstituted Serbian army joined the **Salonika front** in 1916, Mišić continued to lead the First Army during a frustrating period of stalemate. Early in 1918, he was appointed chief of staff and effective commander-in-chief of the Serbian army. He developed a plan to break the deadlock on the Serbian front, convincing **Franchet d'Espérey**, who turned it into a major offensive. Mišić's optimism was justified and by 1 November the chief of staff and his army had returned to Belgrade.

MITCHELL, WILLIAM, 1879–1936

Mitchell's professional life was dominated by his vigorous advocacy of air power and the need for an independent United States air force, a campaign that led to a court-martial and his resignation in 1926. His views had been shaped by his experiences during the First World War, when he played an important role in the fledgling American air service. An adviser to **General Pershing** on American aviation requirements in France, Billy Mitchell was given command of the first operational units to arrive there.

In August 1918 he was appointed commander of the Air Service, 1st Army, with 49 squadrons at his disposal, and was promoted to the rank of brigadier-general. During the autumn offensive around **St Mihiel** he deployed some 1,500 machines, the largest force yet assembled in one place. In October, during the **Meuse–Argonne offensive**, Mitchell organised intensive attacks on enemy troops, while bombing targets in German territory in even greater numbers. Mitchell's plans for the concentrated bombing of strategic sites in Germany on a much larger scale were halted by the Armistice. Mitchell himself flew on some operational missions and was awarded the Distinguished Flying Cross.

MOEWE

Germany's most successful **commerce raider**, *Moewe* was formerly a banana carrier of 4,788 tons, launched in 1914. During her first voyage of just over two months, mainly in the Atlantic, she sank 15 ships, returning home in March 1916. On *Moewe*'s second four-month sortie, which began late in November 1916, her activities resulted in the destruction of 27 ships and the disruption of Allied ship movements over a wide area. Returning home unscathed she was employed as an auxiliary minelayer for the remainder of the war.

MOLTKE

Although this German battlecruiser did not make the impact of her identical sister ship *Goeben*, she also had an eventful war, serving with the Scouting Group of the **High Seas Fleet** throughout. She was present at the **Battle of the Dogger Bank** and at **Jutland** was hit by four shells. Torpedoed by British submarines in 1915 and again in 1918, after she had stripped one of her turbines, *Moltke* survived the war. She surrendered to the Allies and was scuttled at **Scapa Flow** in June 1919.

MOLTKE, GENERAL HELMUTH VON, THE YOUNGER, 1848–1916

The nephew of Field Marshal Helmuth von Moltke, architect of German victory in the Franco-Prussian War (1870–71), Moltke the younger succeeded Schlieffen as Chief of the General Staff in January 1906. Although Moltke rightly had doubts about his own suitability, **Kaiser Wilhelm II** had appointed him in the hope that he would display some of his uncle's genius. Moltke, who viewed a European war as inevitable, retained the **Schlieffen Plan** but unwisely made several major changes to it. To avoid violating Dutch neutrality by passing through Maastricht, two of his five armies would need to be forced through the Liège bottleneck. He also further weakened the all-important right wing of his armies in order to strengthen the German position in Alsace-Lorraine, where the main French attack was expected.

During the first critical weeks of the war, Moltke was based far from the front line and he overestimated the extent of his initial successes. As a result the German thrust through Belgium was further blunted by detaching troops to deal with the surviving enemy fortresses, including Antwerp, and by dispatching several divisions to the Eastern Front. Problems with Moltke's strategic plan came to a head during the critical **Battle of the Marne**, when he also faced a complete breakdown of communications with his field commanders. A worried Moltke sent **Colonel Hentsch** to the front and the offensive was quickly abandoned. Following this strategic defeat, Moltke was removed on 14 September, but was appointed deputy chief of staff at the end of the year. In 1915 he attempted, unsuccessfully, to regain his office, now held by **Falkenhayn**.

Moltke unwisely modified the Schlieffen Plan and contributed to the German reverse at the Marne

MONASH, GENERAL SIR JOHN, 1865–1931

'The only general of creative originality produced by the First World War', Sir John Monash succeeded Sir William Birdwood as commander of the Australian Army Corps on the Western Front from May 1918. A reserve soldier before the war, he commanded an infantry brigade that was sent to Egypt in February 1915 as part of the Australian–New Zealand Army Corps (**ANZAC**). He served throughout the **Gallipoli** campaign and gained a reputation for excellent leadership, organisation, and planning.

Late in 1916, Monash arrived in France as a major-general in command of the Third Division, which was to play an important part at **Messines** and **Passchendaele** in 1917. Monash's reputation grew as he responded effectively during the German offensives of 1918, with the battle of Hamel (4 July) and the

Australian advance on 8 August ('the black day of the German army') being notable examples. The remarkable capture of Mont St Quentin (1 September) and the Australian role in the autumn offensive against the Hindenburg Line were further testimonies to his generalship.

Monash was noted for his thorough preparation for battle, his emphasis on effective coordination, and the need to conserve life. His objective was 'to advance under the maximum possible protection of the maximum possible array of mechanical resources'. Standard tank tactics were also modified by arranging that tanks should advance with the infantry rather than ahead of them, an innovation adopted by the British army after a successful trial during the Battle of Hamel.

MONRO, GENERAL SIR CHARLES, 1860–1929

Rising to prominence as **Sir Ian Hamilton**'s successor at **Gallipoli**, Monro recommended the immediate evacuation of the expeditionary force as soon as he arrived there in October 1915. He had previously served with distinction on the Western Front and at the end of 1914 had replaced Haig as commander of I Corps; when his Mediterranean command came to an end in January 1916, he returned there as head of the First Army. In the autumn of 1916, he was appointed commander-in-chief in India, where he was responsible for ensuring an increasing flow of Indian troops to the battlefields of Europe. He remained in India until 1920.

MORANE SAULNIER AI

The AI fighter was a single-seat parasol monoplane which entered operational service with the French Aviation Militaire in January 1918, but was withdrawn only four months later. Powered by the 150hp

Gnome Monosoupape engine, it had swept-back wings with a large cut-out in the trailing edge. A complex arrangement of struts connected the wings to the circular section fuselage, which tapered to a point at the rear. Armament consisted of one or two forward-firing .303 **Vickers machine-guns**. Although 1,200 AIs were built, few were used for their original purpose. Possible structural problems, an unreliable power plant and the existence of better alternative machines all contributed to its early demise as a fighter. It did, however, continue to perform a useful function as an advanced trainer with the French, Belgian and American air services until the end of the war and beyond.

MORANE SAULNIER BB

Strongly resembling the **Morane Saulnier Type N** monoplane fighter, this two-seat biplane first appeared in 1915. It was armed with one or two .303 **Lewis machine-guns** and was powered by a 110hp Le Rhône engine, which gave reasonable perfor-mance. The French showed no interest in it, but it was used by the RFC and RNAS in limited quantities for reconnaissance duties. The BB was withdrawn from service early in 1917 after an undistinguished career, but was retained for training purposes.

MORANE SAULNIER TYPES L & LA

The Type L was the first of a series of two-seater parasol monoplanes produced by the French Morane Saulnier Company. Generally known as the Morane Parasol, it was frail in appearance and gained a reputation for being difficult to handle. The fabric-covered wooden wing was raised well above the box-like fuselage, providing excellent visibility. It was powered by a Gnome or Le Rhône 80hp engine and wing warping was used to provide lateral control. Initially there was no fixed armament and crews often carried a cavalry carbine.

The Parasol served in large numbers with the French Aviation Militaire in 1914–15 and in more limited quantities with the RFC, RNAS and Russian air service. About 600 were produced in France and a large number of copies were built by the Germans. The Parasol was used extensively for reconnaissance work on the Western Front and also for agent dropping. It was faster and more manoeuvrable than the German two-seaters then in service and French crews were successful in bringing a number of them down with hand-held weapons. One of the RFC's earliest combat victories – in February 1915 against an **Aviatik** – was in fact won on this aircraft.

In March 1915, the Parasol was equipped with the first forward-firing machine-gun (an 8mm **Hotch-kiss**) in a tractor-engined aircraft; the airscrew was protected from stray bullets by steel bullet deflectors fitted to it by **Roland Garros**, the pioneer French pilot. Garros scored three hits with his unique weapon before being shot down on 19 April 1915. Its discovery prompted the Germans to develop an effective interrupter gear, which appeared on **Fokker E-types** later that year. The Parasol was also used for light bombing, with improvised racks that could carry up to six 20lb bombs. In a Parasol so equipped F/Sub Lt Warneford, RNAS, destroyed Zeppelin LZ 37 over Bruges on 7 June 1915, the first time an airship of this type had been successfully attacked in the air.

A development of the Parasol – the LA – appeared in 1915. It had a rounded fuselage, ailerons instead of wing warping, and an airscrew spinner. It was in service from 1915 to 1917, but was not adopted on a large scale by either the French or British.

MORANE SAULNIER TYPE N

The Type N monoplane first appeared a few months before the war as a racing aircraft but it was quickly adapted as one of the first single-seat fighters to enter service. Constructed of wood, its circular section fuselage and its large airscrew spinner, which fully covered the engine and was nicknamed 'the Kettle', gave it a streamlined appearance. The Type N was fitted with an 80hp Le Rhône engine which produced a maximum speed of 90m.p.h. at sea level and a good rate of climb. As few as 40 Type Ns were built; they served briefly with the French Aviation Militaire, the RFC and the Russian air service. Fitted with deflector plates, the French version was normally equipped with a single fixed .303 **Vickers machine-gun**, while the RFC model had a .303 **Lewis gun**.

The Aviation Militaire made little use of the aircraft and it had been replaced by the **Nieuport** fighters even before the first deliveries had been made to the RFC in March 1916. Unofficially named 'the Bullet' by the British, the Type N saw much action during the difficult summer of 1916 and scored several hits. However, the Bullet's high landing speed and the sensitivity of its elevator controls made it difficult to fly and operational use ceased in the autumn. Two developments of the Type N – Types I and V, with a 110hp engine – saw only limited service with French and British forces in 1916. A larger number were sent to Russia and were still flying in 1917.

MORANE SAULNIER TYPE P

This two-seater parasol monoplane was similar in appearance to the Morane Saulnier Type LA, but was designed on a larger scale. More bracing struts were provided and it normally had a large airscrew spinner. A more powerful engine – the 110hp Le Rhône – was normally fitted, giving a maximum speed of 100m.p.h. at 2,000m, with an endurance of $2\frac{1}{2}$ hours. However, some examples were equipped with the 80hp Le Rhône engine because of supply difficulties with the larger power unit. At first the Type P was armed with a **Lewis** or **Vickers machine-gun**

firing forwards over the wing and a spigot-mounted Lewis gun in the rear cockpit. Later examples were fitted with a synchronised Vickers gun and a ring-mounted machine-gun for the observer.

This aircraft undertook reconnaissance duties on the Western Front in 1916–17, with the French Aviation Militaire and with No 1 and No 43 Squadrons, RFC. It was withdrawn as **Nieuport Scouts** and **Sopwith Camels** came into service, after a total of 565 examples had been built.

MORS ARMOURED CAR

Using the chassis of one of the Mors touring cars, these French-produced armoured vehicles were used by the Belgian army from 1914 to 1917. Powered by a Belgian Minerva engine, the Mors had a tall, boxed-shaped hull encased in 5mm armour plate, with only the driver's compartment enclosed. The rear section was completely open and had no doors, with the crew entering the vehicle by climbing over the top. It carried a single, pivot-mounted 37mm Puteaux

cannon, with provision for a **Hotchkiss machine-gun** immediately above it. Both weapons were protected by a large three-sided shield.

The Mors supplemented the **Minerva armoured car** in the early period of mobile warfare, but was more extensively used by a Belgian armoured-car unit supporting Russian forces on the Eastern Front until August 1917.

MOSIN-NAGANT RIFLE

Replacing the obsolete single-shot Berdan rifle, the Mosin-Nagant was the standard Russian service rifle of the First World War.

First entering service in 1891, it was an amalgam of two separate rifles. The bolt action, a relatively complicated design that was similar to some French patterns, was based on the work of Sergei Mosin, a Tsarist army officer. Emil Nagant, a Belgian, contributed a five-cartridge box, with a control latch that freed the top round from magazine spring pressure during the loading process. A long spike bayonet, with the socket method of attachment, was normally a permanent fixture during the war and the sights were adjusted to compensate for the additional weight. A variant for the dragoons also appeared in 1891, but it was little smaller than the standard rifle; it was not in fact until 1910 that a proper carbine appeared.

Officially known as the Russian 3-line rifle model 1891 – the line being an old Russian linear measurement – indicating that its calibre was 7.62mm, it proved to be a sound and reliable service weapon. In a modified form it was still in service with the Soviet army during the Second World War.

MOTORCYCLES

During the First World War the military role of the motorcycle was rapidly developed. As well as being widely used for the delivery of despatches and the rapid movement of key personnel, it had a direct operational role as a machine-gun carrier. In 1915, for example, the Machine-Gun Corps had selected the Vickers-Clyno motorcycle combination as the most suitable machine for this purpose. Powered by a 5/ 6hp V-twin engine, it had a **Vickers machine-gun**, which was often protected by an armoured shield, mounted on the sidecar chassis, which also accommodated the gunner on a low seat. It was used in conjunction with unarmed combinations which carried supplies of ammunition and spares. The Clyno was successfully employed on the Western Front in

A convoy of heavily armed motorcycle despatch riders

support of infantry, enabling the gunner and his weapon to reach the required position as soon as possible. Motorcycle units also used other makes for mobile attack duties, including the BSA, which could be fitted with an armoured sidecar equipped with a **Lewis machine-gun**.

MOUNTBATTEN, PRINCE LOUIS OF BATTENBERG, 1854–1921

Appointed First Sea Lord in 1912, Prince Louis' tenure at the Admiralty did not long survive the outbreak of war. Following attacks on his German origins, he resigned his office in October 1914 and was succeeded by **Admiral Fisher**. Just prior to the declaration of war Prince Louis had made the critically important decision to keep the reserve fleet in commission rather than disperse it after completion of the general test mobilisation in July.

MULHOUSE, BATTLE OF, 7–10 August 1914

Held by the Germans since 1871, Alsace was the subject of the first significant French action of the war, even though initially it was a reconnaissance in force rather than a real invasion. As the German army attacked France through Belgium, **Joffre**, the French commander-in-chief, struck in the north-east, sending General Bonneau's VII Corps over the Vosges Mountains on 7 August. It advanced to Altkirch, losing 100 men as the enemy was engaged, but entered Mulhouse unopposed the following day. In the early hours of 9 August, the Germans counter-attacked, having quickly moved up reinforcements from the Seventh Army (General von Heeringen) in Strasbourg. After 24 hours the French, who feared envelopment, withdrew south-west towards Belfort, finally stopping some ten miles away.

Joffre responded decisively to this unsatisfactory turn of events: Bonneau was charged with a lack of aggressiveness and was removed from his command, while a new Army of Alsace, under **General Pau**, was organised on the right flank. He renewed the attack on 19 August and actually managed to reach the Rhine before being forced to abandon it because of the urgent need for reinforcements in the west. However, the eastern foothills of the Vosges, which had been lost to the Germans in 1871, were recovered and Pau was in fact the only French general to capture any enemy territory in the first year of the war.

MÜLLER, GEORG VON, 1854–1940

Chief of the German Navy Cabinet, 1908–18, Müller remained at the centre of naval policy-making throughout the war. His close working relationship with the Kaiser and his role in trying to reconcile the views of political and naval leaders on key issues often brought him into conflict with his professional colleagues. His opposition to an all-out attack on the **Grand Fleet** and, during the first half of the war, to unrestricted submarine warfare also caused friction within the navy. Although he was a late convert to the benefits of a new U-boat compaign, he never regained the confidence of his naval critics. In fact, when **Scheer** assumed the supreme command in August 1918, plans were made to remove Müller from office, but the war ended before they could be implemented.

MURRAY, GENERAL SIR ARCHIBALD, 1860–1945

An experienced professional soldier whose reputation was established during the South African War, Murray went to France in August 1914 as chief of staff to the British Expeditionary Force under **Sir John French**. The traumatic early days of the war took their toll on Murray, who returned home in poor health early in 1915. A period as deputy chief of the Imperial General Staff followed before his appointment as commander of British forces in Egypt at the end of the year.

Under his command the defence of the Suez Canal took a more active form and his troops gradually moved across the Sinai to establish a new defensive line 100 miles to the east. It was not until he tried to advance into southern Palestine that he ran into serious difficulties. The first attack on **Gaza** in March 1917 almost succeeded, but a second unsuccessful assault against strengthened Turkish defences only a month later was very difficult to justify. The defeat ended Murray's career at the front; he was replaced by **Allenby** in the hope that a more effective offensive strategy would emerge.

NAGANT REVOLVER

Adopted by the Russian army in 1895, the Nagant revolver was in operational use throughout the First World War. Conventional in appearance, it had a seven-round cylinder and an overall length of 229mm. An unusual feature was its gas seal mechanism which sought to maximise performance by reducing the leak of propelling gas between the barrel and the cylinder. The Nagant revolver was manufactured in Belgium as well as in Russia, in both single- and double-action forms.

NAMUR, SIEGE OF, 20–25 August 1914

As the German First, Second and Third Armies wheeled through Belgium towards the French frontier, the Belgian army offered little resistance, except at the supposedly impregnable fortress of Namur. **Bülow**'s Second Army reached it on 20 August and left six divisions to besiege it, while the main force moved forward to engage the French Fifth Army, under **General Lanrezac**, on the Sambre. Opposing 100,000 German troops and 500 guns was a Belgian garrison of only 37,000 men of the 14th Division, commanded by General Michel. Although the defenders had been depleted because of the withdrawal of the main Belgian army to Antwerp, the city had been expected to hold out for weeks or even months as it was ringed with ten forts and well protected by minefields and trenches.

Events rapidly proved otherwise: on the first day, five forts were lost and the Belgians were pushed back during a fierce battle. Heavy casualties were sustained during a continuous bombardment by heavy artillery, including the siege mortars used at **Liège**, and the surviving forts were forced to surrender on 25 August. As many as 50,000 prisoners were taken 'as the great cornerstone of the frontier' passed into German hands. Lanrezac had already been defeated two days earlier and the fall of Namur meant that the Allies were unable to make a defensive stand against the massive German onslaught until they reached the **Marne**.

NAROCH LAKE, BATTLE OF, 18 March 1916

As soon as the German offensive at **Verdun** began on 21 February 1916, **Joffre** sent an urgent appeal to the Russians to mount a diversionary attack. The Tsar, commander-in-chief of the Russian army since September 1915, responded positively without fully considering whether his troops were prepared for action. It was to be the first of three Allied requests received by the Russians during 1916. The offensive, which started as early as 18 March, was aimed at the German lines in the Lake Naroch-Vilna area in White Russia (Byelorussia), north of the Pripet Marshes. It was mounted by the inner flanks of the two northerly Russian army groups, commanded by **Kuropatkin** and **Evert** respectively, on a 90-mile front either side of the lake.

After a two-day artillery bombardment, the longest yet on the Eastern Front, the Russian Tenth Army attempted to move forward but was cut down by the well-organised and well-fortified German defenders with heavy losses. At no point on the front did the Russians manage to penetrate more than a few hundred yards, even though they outnumbered the enemy by five to two. Supported by heavy artillery bombardments, the Germans soon recovered all the ground they had lost. Within a month the fighting, which the Russians had prolonged unnecessarily, had died out. A smaller operation near Riga, which had begun on 21 March, suffered the same fate. The Russians lost about 110,000 men, the Germans 20,000, with the severe winter weather conditions adding to the casualties on both sides. The failed offensive damaged Russian morale and did nothing to stop the war of attrition at **Verdun**. Stavka now resumed its preparations for the main summer (**Brusilov**) offensive.

NASSAU

Germany's first dreadnoughts, the Nassau class battleships were ordered in 1907 and produced quickly in response to the British lead in this new type. An enlarged version of the pre-dreadnought **Deutschland**s, Nassau had a displacement of 18,570 tons and a maximum speed of 18 knots. Main armament consisted of twelve 11.1-inch guns – there were twin turrets fore and aft on the centre line and two on each beam; it was well equipped with secondary armament. The relatively light main guns enabled additional armour protection to be fitted and in this respect they were superior to contemporary Allied ships.

Completed in 1909–10, *Nassau*, *Posen*, *Rhineland* and *Westfalen* all served with Battle Squadron I of the **High Seas Fleet** from 1914 and all were present at **Jutland**. Only *Posen* was undamaged. *Rhineland*, which ran aground in April 1918, was the sole ship of this class not in service at the end of the war.

NAVAL WAR, CHRONOLOGICAL LIST OF EVENTS

Heligoland Bight, Battle of, 1914
Coronel, Battle of, 1914
Falkland Islands , Battle of the, 1914
Dogger Bank, Battle of the, 1915

Atlantic, Battle of the, 1915–17
Dardanelles operation, 1915
Jutland, Battle of, 1916

NEPTUNE

This dreadnought battleship served with the British **Grand Fleet** throughout the First World War, and was in action at the **Battle of Jutland**, which it survived without damage or casualties. *Neptune*, which was completed in 1911, had been produced in response to a need to increase the guns that could be fired on the broadside, in line with naval develop-ments in other countries. Its predecessor, *St Vincent*, had eight such guns but on the new ship there were ten, because its midships turrets had been staggered to provide cross-deck firing for the first time. To avoid increasing *Neptune*'s overall length as a result of this change, the two aft guns were mounted on top of each other.

NEUILLY, TREATY OF, 27 November 1919

Bulgaria was reduced in size and made liable for reparations by the terms of the Treaty of Neuilly, the post-First World War peace settlement that was signed with the Allies on 27 November 1919. Greece and Rumania were the beneficiaries of this relatively modest redistribution of territory. Bulgaria's army was not to exceed 20,000 men.

NEUVE-CHAPELLE, BATTLE OF, 10–13 March 1915

A German artillery barrage tries to stop the British bringing up reinforcements to the front line during the Battle of Neuve-Chapelle

Joffre's plans for a renewed Allied offensive in Artois in March 1915 depended on the British relieving two French corps in the Ypres salient. Delays in releasing these troops occurred because of the demands of the **Gallipoli campaign** and the slow arrival of British reinforcements. As a result the French, who were heavily committed in **Champagne**, decided not to proceed with the action at that time. However, the British had been inactive since December 1914 and **Sir John French** decided to go ahead with his share of the original plan alone, partly in order to counteract the low opinion which many French officers had of BEF's offensive capability.

The British attack began opposite the village of Neuve-Chapelle, with the intention of seizing the Aubers ridge and threatening Lille. It was an excellent choice because the area was held by only one German division. **Sir Douglas Haig**, commander of the First Army, moved up four divisions in secret and on 10 March, after an intensive artillery bombardment, launched the well-prepared attack on a two-mile front. At first all went according to plan. The village was captured and the German positions were overrun, but the British failed to exploit the initial victory effectively. Many of the problems that were to be evident in every trench attack were soon revealed, including difficulties in coordinating the advance. Delays resulted and the Germans, who rushed up 16,000 reinforcements, counter-attacked. Although the fighting continued until 13 March, the British took no more ground, with all their gains having been secured in the first few hours.

A dent in the German line no more than $1\frac{1}{4}$ miles wide and 1,000 yards deep had been made at a cost of about 13,000 casualties on each side; the British retained the village and captured 1,600 prisoners. Neuve-Chapelle had been a costly gamble, and over 15 per cent of BEF's entire supply of ammunition was consumed. Arrangements were now made to resume the French plan for a combined offensive, but they were forestalled by the German attack against **Ypres** on 22 April.

NEVADA

The first American super-dreadnoughts, the Nevadas, which were completed in 1916, were the only First World War warships to be armoured on the 'all-or-nothing' system. The key areas of the hull were enclosed with heavy armour, while the remainder was unprotected because lighter plate was of no value against large-calibre armour-piercing shells. Equipped with ten 14-inch guns, *Nevada* and *Oklahoma* were the first American warships to adopt triple turrets. They were easily recognisable as, unlike earlier US dreadnoughts, they only had a single funnel. Both ships served with the 6th Battle Squadron, British **Grand Fleet**, from August 1918.

NEW YORK

The first American battleships to be fitted with 14-inch armament, *New York* and her sister ship *Texas* were similar in appearance to the **Wyoming**s. The 10 heavy guns were mounted in twin turrets: two superfiring fore and aft and one in the centre. Some of the twenty-one 5-inch secondary guns were poorly positioned and unusable in bad weather; five were removed during the war. Completed in 1914, these ships had a maximum speed of 21 knots, a displacement of 27,000 tons and a complement of 864 men. *New York* served as flagship, 6th Battle Squadron, **Grand Fleet** from December 1917 and *Texas* also joined the same unit slightly later. Both were present at the surrender of the German **High Seas Fleet** in November 1918. By this time *Texas* may have been fitted with flying-off platforms for aircraft, but her first aircraft did not take off until March 1919; she was the first American battleship to be so converted.

NICHOLAS, KING OF MONTENEGRO, 1841–1921

The last king of Montenegro, Nicholas ruled from 1910 during a period when the country was undergoing economic and social modernisation. Intervention in the Balkan Wars, 1912–13, produced territorial gains, but revealed weaknesses in the performance of the armed forces. Montenegro entered the First World War alongside Serbia in opposition to Austro-Hungary, but her military role was very small. Late in 1915, after the fall of Serbia, Montenegro was overrun by the Austrians and Nicholas went into exile. His hopes of a return to power were destroyed in 1918 when a political assembly criticised his weak response to the Austrian invasion and decided to depose him. The dynasty was brought to an end and union with Serbia was agreed.

NICHOLAS II, TSAR, 1868–1918

The last Tsar, 1894–1917, Nicholas presided over the disintegration of Russian government and society under the impact of the First World War, a conflict he had entered with great reluctance. Military defeat is only part of the explanation for the **Russian Revolution** as Nicholas himself contributed directly to his own downfall.

His personal inflexibility and implacable opposition to moderate political reform, the excessive influence wielded by Rasputin and his strong preference for reactionary politicians who upheld the traditional authority of the Tsar, were all important contributory factors. His distaste for more liberal politicians was increased by their opposition to his decision to remove **Grand Duke Nicholas** as commander-in-chief and to assume command on the Eastern Front himself in September 1915. It was a post for which Nicholas had no qualifications: he was, in fact 'incapable of command, yet would delegate it to no one else. Henceforward the Russian army drifted without a leader or a strategy, offering the Germans only the shadow of a threat.'

Bread riots in Petrograd in March 1917 marked the beginning of the revolution that led to the loss of military support at all levels for the Tsar and, within a few days, to his abdication and arrest at Pskov, the headquarters of the Northern Front. Imprisoned by the Provisional Government, the Tsar, his wife and their three children were eventually executed by the Bolsheviks in July 1918.

Military defeat led the Tsar himself (right) to take command, with disastrous results

NICHOLAS NICHOLAIEVICH, GRAND DUKE, 1856–1929

Uncle of Tsar **Nicholas II**, Grand Duke Nicholas was an experienced and popular professional soldier who had been involved in the modernisation of the Russian army after the Russo-Japanese War. At the beginning of the First World War he was unexpectedly appointed commander-in-chief rather than the lesser posting to the command of the Sixth Army that had been expected. One possible explanation is that the Tsar had intended to assume the supreme command himself but had changed his mind at the last moment. In any event it was **General Danilov**, the quarter-master-general, who was the effective wartime direc-tor of military strategy and the Grand Duke was perhaps little more than a figurehead. His position was further weakened by the fact that the effective control of operations was in the hands of the commanders of the fronts – the North-Western and the South-Western – facing Germany and Austria respectively.

Whatever the reality of power within Stavka

(General Headquarters), the Grand Duke's position was undermined by the **Central Powers**' offensive in 1915, which pushed back the Russian army by up to 300 miles and resulted in the loss of Poland. He was criticised for his poor coordination of subordinate commanders and in September the Tsar assumed command of the Russian army. The Grand Duke was sent to the Caucasus as governor-general and here he supported **General Yudenich** in his successful operations against the Turks. As the March Revolu-tion began the Tsar sought to reappoint him as commander in chief but the move was quickly cancelled by the new Provisional Government and the Grand Duke retired.

NIEUPORT 10

The French Nieuport 10 was a two-seat tractor biplane, based on earlier Nieuport biplanes, that first appeared in 1914. It had wings of unequal length and V-strut bracing, standard features of a long series of Nieuport designs, including the famous Nieuport 17 Scout. By the end of the war about 7,000 Nieuport machines had been produced in total. Two versions of the 10, with alternative seating arrangements, were manufactured, placing the observer either behind or in front of the pilot; both were powered by an 80hp Gnome or Le Rhône engine.

The 10 served with the French Aviation Militaire in 1915 as a reconnaissance aircraft, although no *escadrille* was completely equipped with it. The French need for fighters at this time was, however, so great that many 10s were soon converted. They were flown as single-seaters to compensate for the addition of a **Lewis machine-gun** mounted above the top wing. The Nieuport 10 was also used by the RNAS and by Italy, where some were built by Macchi under licence for the Italian air force. In France, the 10 was gradually replaced by the **Nieuport 12**.

NIEUPORT 11

The 11 was a single-seat biplane, based on a pre-war racing design and the operational experience of the **Nieuport 10**, which first appeared in 1915. Nick-named Bébé (Baby), because of its small size, this fighting scout was powered by an 80hp Gnome or Le Rhône rotary engine, giving a maximum speed of 97m.p.h. at sea level, an endurance of $2\frac{1}{2}$ hours, and a good rate of climb. It retained the sesquiplane layout of the Nieuport 10 and was armed with a .303 fixed **Lewis gun** which fired over the top wing.

Examples were delivered to the air forces of Britain, Belgium, Russia and Italy (where 646 were

made under licence), as well as to the French Aviation Militaire. The 11, which was flown by several famous fighter pilots, made an important contribution to winning the battle against Fokker monoplanes at **Verdun** and elsewhere on the Western Front in 1916. It was also operational in other theatres, including the **Dardanelles**, where it was used by the RNAS. In 1917, the Nieuport 11 was withdrawn from service: it was obsolete and several had been lost because of failures in the lower wing structure. Some 11s were replaced by the more powerful **Nieuport 16** and a number were converted to training aircraft.

NIEUPORT 12

Generally known as the Nieuport two-seater, this fighting, reconnaissance and light bombing aircraft appeared in 1915. The 12 was a slightly larger version of the **Nieuport 10** biplane and was normally powered by a 110hp or 130hp Clerget rotary engine, producing a maximum speed of 78m.p.h. at 5,000 feet. Standard armament was a single **Lewis machine-gun** in the rear cockpit for the observer, although when the 12 was used as a single-seater a forward firing gun of the same type was mounted over the upper wing. Later examples were equipped with a synchronised **Vickers gun**.

The Nieuport 12 served with the French Aviation Militaire, the RFC and the RNAS, primarily on the Western Front. They were also active as single-seat fighters with the RNAS (No 3 Wing) in the **Dardanelles**. Although the 12's performance and manoeuvrability were relatively poor, some examples were still serving with the RFC in 1917. In France they had been withdrawn from the front the year before, although a number were retained for training purposes.

NIEUPORT 16

The Nieuport 16 single-seat fighting scout was a larger and more powerful version of the **Nieuport 11**, which served in limited numbers with the French Aviation Militaire and RFC in 1916–17. It was powered by the 110hp Le Rhône, enclosed in a redesigned cowling, giving a maximum speed of 102m.p.h. at sea level and the ability to reach 3,000m in just over 10 minutes. Unlike its predecessor, standard armament was a synchronised **Vickers machine-gun**, although some 16s in RFC service were fitted with a movable **Lewis gun** on a Foster mounting. Several examples were additionally equipped with eight electrically fired Le Prieur rockets, which were used in attacks on **Zeppelins** and enemy **observation balloons**.

Like the Nieuport 11, the 16 was active on the Western Front in 1916 in the struggle against the **Fokker monoplanes**. It was also used on reconnaissance missions and after its retirement from the front was employed briefly as a training aircraft.

NIEUPORT 17

A development of the **Nieuport 11 and 16**, the 17 was one of the most successful fighters of the war, with a longer operational career than most of its contemporaries.

It retained the familiar V-strut sesquiplane formula, although the wing area was increased and the airframe modified. The lower wing was strengthened as structural failure had been a problem on the earlier Nieuports, although this modification did not prove to be a complete cure. It used the same engine – 110hp Le Rhône – as the Nieuport 16, giving a maximum speed of 102m.p.h. at sea level, an endurance of up to two hours, and the ability to climb to 2,000m in just under seven minutes. In a later variant (Nieuport 17bis) this engine was replaced by the 130hp Clerget. Armament originally consisted of a **Lewis machine-gun** mounted above the top wing; later a synchronised **Vickers** was used. Like the 16, Le Prieur rockets were sometimes fitted to the 17 when it was used for balloon bursting.

Known as the Superbébé, the Nieuport 17 first appeared on the Western Front in May 1916, where it served with the French Aviation Militaire, the RFC and the RNAS. It had excellent manoeuvrability and

The most notable of the Nieuport fighters, the 17 had a fine combat record in 1916–17

good pilot visibility, as well as rapid forward and climb speeds – qualities that were quickly revealed in combat with the **Fokker monoplanes** during the **Battle of the Somme**. As a result it was popular with several of the leading aces, **Ball**, **Baracca**, **Bishop**, **Fonck**, **Guynemer**, Navarre and **Nungesser** being among those who flew it regularly. Bishop in fact scored 36 of his confirmed hits in this aircraft.

In Italy the 17 was produced under licence and became an important component of the Italian fighter force. It was also used by Belgium and Russia; 75 were supplied to the AEF in France for use as pursuit trainers. The Nieuport 17 was produced in large quantities and as late as August 1917 more than 300 examples remained in operational service with the French. However, it was by now under-armed and outclassed by the faster **Spad VII** and other aircraft, and was rapidly withdrawn from the front.

A two-seater trainer conversion of the 17 was designated the Nieuport 21. Equipped with an 80hp Le Rhône engine, it was used by France and Russia; the United States acquired nearly 200 Nieuport 21s powered by the larger 110hp Le Rhône engine.

NIEUPORT 23

Almost identical to the **Nieuport 17**, the 23 was a single-seat fighter that was in operational use on the Western Front in 1917–18. It had improved streamlining, a 120hp Le Rhône engine and was marginally heavier. A different type of synchronising mechanism was used, with the result that the **Vickers machine-gun** was slightly offset to starboard. The Nieuport 23 served with the air forces of France, Britain, Russia and the United States.

NIEUPORT 24 & 27

Encouraged by the outstanding success of the **Nieuport 17**, a further development of the well-tried V-strut sesquiplane design – the Nieuport 24 – emerged from the production lines in 1917. Variations on the earlier model included a circular section fuselage, a curved tailplane, a fixed vertical fin, and a 130hp Le Rhône engine. A version with a Nieuport 17-type tail unit and differences of detail was known as the 24bis. In British service the more streamlined 24 was armed with a **Lewis gun** which fired over the top wing; otherwise it was fitted with one or two forward-firing synchronised machine-guns. The Nieuport 24/24bis were operational in 1917–18 with the air forces of France, Britain (RFC and RNAS) and Italy, and the AEF also acquired over 250 machines for training purposes.

The final version of the Nieuport V-strut series was the 27, which was generally similar to its immediate predecessor. It had further streamlining, an oval-shaped fin and modified undercarriage. It was delivered to the French, British, American and Italian air forces late in 1917. By this time the basic Nieuport fighter design was already obsolete and had been outclassed on the Western Front by the later **Spads**. The 27 did, however, continue in use as a trainer after its withdrawal from the front early in 1918.

NIEUPORT 28

A radical departure from the earlier series of V-strut sesquiplanes, the Nieuport 28 was a single-seat biplane fighter that appeared in 1917. It was the first completely new Nieuport design since the **11** and its parallel struts, untapered wings with curved tips and circular section fuselage all contributed to its elegant appearance. Twin synchronised **Vickers** or **Marlin** guns were fitted as standard and the aircraft was normally powered by a single 160hp Gnome Mono-soupape engine. The plane was fast – it had a maximum speed of 122m.p.h. at 6,560 feet – and manoeuvrable, but the standard engine was unreliable and the fabric covering of the upper wing often became detached in action.

It was fortunate that when the 28 appeared the AEF was seeking an aircraft to equip its first fighter squadrons: the Nieuport was readily available and 297 examples were acquired for American use in France. They served at the front until they were phased out in favour of the **Spad XIII** during the summer of 1918. In spite of its weaknesses, the Nieuport 28 was used successfully for several months and was flown by some of America's leading aces, including **Ricken-backer** and **Lufbery**.

NIVELLE, GENERAL ROBERT, 1856–1924

Destined for rapid promotion and an even more sudden downfall, Colonel Nivelle, a French artillery-man, was a regimental commander at the outbreak of war. His leadership and initiative in battle had brought him to the command of III Corps by the end of 1915 and to the head of the Second Army in April 1916. The second phase of the **Battle of Verdun**, when he was in direct charge, established him as a national military figure: during the autumn of 1916 he applied successfully new artillery tactics – 'the creeping barrage' – in which the infantry and the artillery made a combined advance. They were used to their greatest effect in the recapture of Fort Douaumont on 24 October; its loss in the opening phase of the battle of Verdun had been a great blow to French prestige and its recovery did much for Nivelle's career.

Less than two months later he was in fact selected to succeed **Joffre** as commander-in-chief of the French army, mainly because he held out the prospect of an early end to the war of attrition on the Western Front. He planned a major spring offensive which aimed to destroy the enemy's forces in battle by an 'act of brute force'. The decisive attack would be on the **Aisne** front, where Nivelle's artillery techniques and massed reserves would ensure a breakthrough. Approval for the operation was secured, although at one point it was necessary for him to threaten to resign in the face of opposition from some of his senior colleagues.

The sceptics were soon proved to be correct: the main assault, which was launched on the Chemin des Dames ridge above the River Aisne on 16 April 1917, was a costly failure, and did not penetrate beyond the German first line. Large casualties, far higher than predicted, were sustained and a battle of attrition developed. The disaster precipitated widespread mutinies in the French army and within a month Nivelle had been replaced by **Pétain**. He spent the rest of the war in North Africa, his military career and reputation in ruins.

NIXON, GENERAL SIR JOHN, 1857–1921

Appointed commander of the British forces in Meso-potamia in April 1915, Nixon was charged with preparing a plan for an advance from Basra north-wards, with the aim of securing the area already under

Allied control. In June, Anglo-Indian troops under **Major-General Sir Charles Townshend** captured Amara on the Tigris and then routed the Turks at **Kut**, 300 miles inland, in September. Nixon's over-optimistic assessment of the prospects for further success, which was not shared by Townshend, led to the decision to move on Baghdad, without waiting for the reinforcements that had been promised by the War Office. The advance was checked by a larger Turkish force at **Ctesiphon** on 22 November 1915, and the remnants of Townshend's division were forced back to Kut, where they were besieged. By the time the garrison had surrendered in April 1916, Nixon had resigned his command on health grounds. An inquiry in London criticised his precipitate decision to advance beyond Kut and although no further action was taken against him, his army career was brought to a close.

NJEGOVAN, ADMIRAL MAXIMILIAN, 1858–1930

Njegovan succeeded Anton von Haus as fleet commander of the Austro-Hungarian navy in February 1917 and was subsequently appointed commander-in-chief. His term of office coincided with the growth of national and political tensions within the navy and following the serious mutiny at Cattaro Bay in February 1918 he was quickly replaced. Rear Admiral Horthy became fleet commander and Vice Admiral Franz von Holub was appointed as head of the naval section of the War Ministry.

NORMAN THOMPSON NT2B

The NT2B was a two-seat flying boat that was widely used by the RNAS for basic training from 1917 until the end of the war. Known as 'Ruptured Duck' by those who flew her, the NT2B was a biplane with dual controls, no armament and a single engine. A variety of different power plants was used, including the 160hp Beardmore, the 200hp Sunbeam, and the 150 or 200hp Hispano-Suiza. About 150 examples were manufactured, although a lesser number was actually used by the RNAS.

NORMAN THOMPSON NT4 & NT4A

The NT4 was a four-seat anti-submarine biplane, powered by two 150hp Hispano-Suiza pusher engines, which first appeared in 1915. Armament consisted of light bombs and a forward-firing .303 **Lewis machine-gun**, mounted above the roof of the enclosed cockpit. A slightly modified version, designated the NT4A, was fitted with twin 200hp engines of the same type, which gave a maximum speed of 95m.p.h. Built in small quantities, the NT4 and NT4A carried out patrol duties from seven air stations around the coast of Britain. They were later used by the RNAS for training purposes but had been withdrawn from service by the Armistice.

NORTH SEA CLASS AIRSHIP

The largest of the 'Blimps' (the nickname for all non-rigid British airships) to appear during the First World War, the North Sea or NS class entered service with the Royal Navy early in 1917. Unlike its predecessors, which included the **Coastal Class** and the **Sea Scout**, the NS type had separate control and engine gondolas, suspended from the large envelope (with a volume of 10,194m³). The crew of ten, housed in the enclosed control gondola, operated the twin 260hp Fiat A12 engines, with a cruising speed of 43m.p.h. and a maximum endurance of 24 hours. Armament consisted of three .303 **Lewis machine-guns** and a bomb load of up to 800lb.

The navy successfully operated just over 100 NS-class airships, primarily on convoy protection duties and in conjunction with surface ships.

NOYON-MONTDIDIER OFFENSIVE, 9–13 June 1918

As the **Third Battle of the Aisne River** drew to an end, **Ludendorff** decided to maintain the pressure on the Allies by launching his fourth offensive in 1918, to the north in the Oise Valley. If successful it would join the Amiens salient with the Aisne-Marne salient and the German army would then be in a position to threaten Paris. The attack began on 9 June when the Eighteenth Army (**Hutier**) advancing south by the River Matz, a tributary of the Oise. The French Third Army (Humbert) had been warned of the impending attack by German deserters and had launched an artillery bombardment before it began. In spite of this advantage and the fact that there was no great difference in the size of the opposing forces, the Germans advanced by as much as six miles on the first day.

The French fought badly at first, but they soon recovered the position and future German progress was much slower. Hutier had been aiming for Compiègne, where he was due to link up the Seventh Army (**Boehn**). The latter had moved west from Soissons on 10 June, but made little progress. Meanwhile on 11 June, **General Mangin** 'organised with extraordinary speed the first deliberate counter-attack of the year.' A force of five divisions (two of which were American), supported by tanks, attacked the German Eighteenth Army and forced it on to the defensive. On 13 June, Ludendorff abandoned the whole costly operation; the French had suffered 35,000 casualties, the Germans rather more.

NUNGESSER, CHARLES, 1892–1927

The third-ranking French fighter ace, Charles Nungesser was a popular hero, known as 'the indestructible', who continued to fly throughout the war in spite of several serious accidents. Originally a cavalryman, he demonstrated his courage, determination and initiative during the opening stages of the war when he seized a German staff car behind enemy lines. He drove it across to his own side, under fire from Allied troops. Like many of his colleagues, Nungesser exchanged life in the trenches for that in the air, joining the Aviation Militaire in January 1915. While serving in *Escadrille VB106* on reconnaissance and bombing duties, he shot down his first enemy aircraft.

Eager for more action, in November 1915 he transferred to *Escadrille N65*, a fighter unit using **Nieuport 11**s. He celebrated the move by flying low

over Nancy, a feat that almost resulted in his imprisonment. He decorated his machine with a morbid emblem − the skull and crossbones and a coffin − of the violent death that he himself only narrowly avoided.

The first such incident occurred in January 1916 when he was seriously injured testing a new aircraft. Back in action two months later, he acquired further wounds during the **Battle of Verdun**. Commissioned in April 1916, his score gradually increased, reaching 17 hits by September and 21 by December. He was then absent until the spring of 1917, while his old wounds received further medical attention.

Nungesser's return was marked by an invitation from the Germans, who challenged him to a single combat over Douai. Not unexpectedly, when he arrived there were six enemy aircraft waiting for him, and in revenge he shot two of them down and scattered the rest. Further hits followed during the summer, but his physical condition was so poor that he had to be carried to his machine. Given a respite from the front line, his return was delayed as a result of a serious car crash. During 1918, his career was further disrupted for medical reasons, but he managed to raise his score to 45, his last victory being in August. Nungesser continued to search for adventure after the war and disappeared without trace while attempting to fly across the Atlantic.

OBSERVATION BALLOONS

At the end of the 19th century the standard spherical balloon, which had been used, with little success, as a tethered military observation post, was replaced by the kite balloon. Created by the Germans specially for this purpose, the *Drachenballon* adopted features of the kite and the balloon to provide a stable platform that was held facing the wind.

It consisted of a large oblong envelope (70 x 20 feet), with fins on each side; a large air bag and a long kite-like tail provided further stabilisation. Raised and lowered by means of a motor winch, the kite balloon could operate at altitudes of up to 2,000m, in winds not exceeding 40m.p.h. The observer, who was accommodated in a small wicker basket suspended below the envelope, had a parachute available in case of an enemy air attack. Nicknamed 'sausages' by the Allies, these balloons were used by the Germans in large numbers as the war of movement in France ended late in 1914. The French responded by developing the Caquot balloon, which was based on

the German design, but offered even greater stability.

The kite balloon was to see extensive service on all fronts during the First World War. They were also employed at sea to direct gunfire and as a protection against submarine attacks. In clear weather the observer would have a superb view extending over many square miles. Using a radio, he was responsible for directing artillery on the enemy's positions and for reporting its effects; he also monitored the enemy's movements.

Balloons were formidable targets: they were heavily protected by anti-aircraft guns, machine-guns, and other weapons, and they could be reeled in fairly quickly. Not a single balloon was shot down by artillery during the war, but some fighter pilots specialised in 'balloon bursting'. Each service produced its own balloon ace and they included the American **Frank Luke**, **Willy Coppens** (Belgium), and the German ace, Hendrick Gontermann.

OLIVER, ADMIRAL SIR HENRY, 1865–1965

Following **Lord Fisher**'s return to the Admiralty in October 1914, Sir Henry Oliver, who had previously been Director of Naval Intelligence, was appointed Chief of the Naval War Staff. Dedicated to work and unable to delegate, he played a key role in shaping

British naval policy for most of the war period. During the last few months before the Armistice, he returned to sea in command of the 1st Battle Cruiser Squadron of the **Grand Fleet**.

ORION

This class of larger British battleships or 'super-dreadnoughts' was constructed as part of the Royal Navy's 1909 building programme. *Orion* had a displacement of over 25,000 tons and was armed with 13.5-inch guns, which had greater hitting power and a better range than the normal 12-inch. All armament was mounted on the centreline and for the first time it had superimposed turrets both forward and aft; side

armour was extended to upper deck level. It was a powerful, elegant ship with low lines and it provided the basis for a further five classes, its only weakness being the location of the tripod mast between the funnels. *Orion* and her sister ships – *Conqueror*, *Monarch* and *Thunderer* – served with the **Grand Fleet** during the war and all survived the **Battle of Jutland** without damage.

ORLANDO, VITTORIO, 1860–1952

Vittorio Orlando succeeded **Paolo Boselli** as Prime Minister of Italy at the end of October 1917 in the aftermath of the **Caporetto** disaster. Securing Allied military support to reinforce the Piave front, he worked energetically to restore public morale. **Cadorna**, the failed chief of staff, was replaced by **General Diaz**, who communicated more effectively with the rank and file but was more cautious than his predecessor. It was not in fact until political pressure was applied by Orlando that Diaz launched the final Italian offensive towards **Vittorio Veneto** in October 1918. Orlando led the Italian delegation to the **Paris Peace Conference**, but in the face of opposition from **Woodrow Wilson** he was unsuccessful in securing Italy's more ambitious territorial objectives.

OSTERKAMP, THOMAS, 1892–1975

The German navy's highest scoring fighter pilot of the Great War, Thomas Osterkamp achieved the remarkable success of being an ace in both world wars. In the First World War he scored all his 32 victories while serving with the navy's fighter wing based in Flanders. (Gotthard Sachsenberg, commander of the wing, was the second ranking naval ace with 31 victories.) Osterkamp subsequently fought against the Bolsheviks and in the Second World War was on active service again during the Battle of Britain.

PACKARD-Le PÈRE LUSAC-II

This fast and manoeuvrable American escort and patrol fighter, which first appeared in September 1918, was designed by Captain Le Père of the French aviation mission to the United States. Armed with two .30 **Marlin** machine-guns and powered by a supercharged 425hp Liberty engine, it might have made a considerable impact if the war had continued into 1919. However, plans for large-scale production were cut short by the Armistice.

PAINLEVÉ, PAUL, 1863–1933

Head of a short-lived coalition government (September–November 1917), Painlevé had first been brought into the French cabinet by **Briand** in October 1915 as Minister of Public Instruction. During his term as Minister of War (from March 1917), he helped to ease **General Nivelle** from his command and actively supported his ally, **Pétain**, in his efforts to restore the fighting effectiveness of the French army during the summer of that year. His premiership brought few positive results beyond the creation of the Supreme War Council, the response to his call for the increased integration of Allied strategy on the Western Front. After his fall from power in November 1917, he played no further part in the direction of the war effort.

PARABELLUM MACHINE-GUN

The German Parabellum machine-gun, which first appeared in 1911, was a much lightened development of the **Maxim**, suitable for use in the air. Designed and produced by the Deutsche Waffen und Munitions-fabriken, this 7.92mm gun had a cyclic rate of up to 750 rounds per minute; it weighed 9.80kg and was 1,223mm in length. The gun was drum fed and the barrel casing was slotted to facilitate air cooling. It had a pistol grip and a wooden stock; sometimes the weapon was fitted with optical sights.

The Parabellum was widely employed by the German air service as the standard observer's weapon, and was in operational use from 1915 until the end of the war. Used singly or in pairs, they proved to be reliable and effective in combat and were amongst the best weapons of their type. A heavier, water-cooled version, the MG14, was used as a **Zeppelin** gun.

PARIS GUN

The giant of the artillery war, the Paris gun could make little impact on the French capital

One of the most unusual weapons of the First World War, the long range 21cm Paris gun began its bombardment of the French capital on 23 March 1918. Initially it was positioned in the Forest of Crépy, some 80 miles from Paris, but was later moved further west. It fired a total of 367 shells, the last falling on 9 August, when it was withdrawn in the face of the Allied advance. As a result, 256 Parisians were killed and 620 wounded, but it made no impact on the course of the war: the effects of the bombardment, which were timed to coincide with the German Spring offensives, were too localised to disrupt the life of the capital.

The Paris gun, which weighed 142 tonnes, was based on a 38cm naval gun body, into which was inserted a gun liner; in total, the barrel was 43 yards long and to prevent it sagging wire bracing was incorporated. A small shell was fired into the upper atmosphere where air resistance is low, enabling it to travel a long distance. The barrel had a high rate of wear, which required it to be changed after a few days. The bore in fact increased in size with every shot and to compensate each shell had a slightly different calibre. Seven barrels and three mountings may have been built, but definite information is unavailable because no trace of the weapon has ever been found.

PARIS PEACE CONFERENCE, 18 January 1919 – 20 January 1920

Held in Paris, this congress of Allied powers reached agreement on the content of the First World War peace settlement. During the first six months the proceedings were dominated by the leaders of the four principal Allied powers – **Wilson, Lloyd George**, **Clemenceau** and **Orlando**. Remaining items were then delegated to Foreign Ministers and finally to a Council of Ambassadors. The conference

Presenting the Terms of Peace to Germany, 1919. In addition to the representatives of Germany and the major allies, the following countries were also represented: Canada, New Zealand, Italy, Portugal, China, Guatemala, Japan, Haiti, Siam, South Africa, India and Serbia

was prolonged by disagreements among the major powers over, for example, the role of the planned League of Nations and the proposed settlement in the Adriatic. Domestic pressures also complicated matters: there were demands for harsher peace terms from groups in Britain and France, while a growing isolationism in the United States undermined the undertakings given by Woodrow Wilson. A further difficulty was that in some areas nationalists had already seized territory whose future was still under discussion. The conference did, however, fulfil one of the key aims of the **Fourteen Points** – increasing national self-determination – and the agreements reached there were embodied in a series of treaties: **Versailles**, **St Germain**, **Neuilly**, **Trianon**, and **Sèvres**.

PAŠIĆ, NIKOLA, 1845–1926

The dominant figure in Serbian politics during the war, Pašić was Prime Minister from 1910. He was too moderate and cautious to have supported the Sarajevo assassins, although he did little to try to stop their activities. Serbia's carefully drafted reply to the Austrian ultimatum was personally delivered by Pašić, who had no real doubts about the outcome. It was not, however, until October 1915 that a successful enemy invasion was launched and Pašić and his government were forced into exile.

From his base on Corfu, Pašić pursued his aim of securing the expansion of an independent post-war Serbia, but in 1917 he was compelled to sign the Pact of Corfu, which provided for the formation of a united South Slav state. It is not surprising, therefore, that he was excluded from the discussions in November 1918 that led to the creation of Yugoslavia. Pašić was then sent to the **Paris Peace Conference**, where his conflict with his old political enemy Ante Trumbic, now Foreign Minister of Yugoslavia, did little to help the development of the new state.

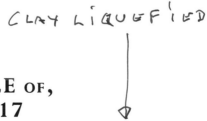

CLAY LIQUEFIED

PASSCHENDAELE, BATTLE OF, 12 October–10 November 1917

The final stages of **Third Ypres**, which had begun on 31 July, were known as the Battle of Passchendaele. After more than two months' hard fighting, Britain and her allies had progressed no further than the foot of the Passchendaele ridge, some four miles from their starting point. In the hope that the Allies would be in a better position to launch a new offensive in the following spring, **Haig** wanted to drive the enemy from the higher ground around Passchendaele village before winter closed in. **Plumer** and **Gough**, the British commanders, did not, however, share Haig's enthusiasm for continuing the offensive, but they did not actively oppose his plans.

The first attack towards the village of Passchendaele – about a mile away on the ridge – was launched on 12 October. Australian and New Zealand troops engaged the Germans but little progress was made. Torrential rain and continuous shelling had reduced the ridge to a sea of mud and water. Many soliders drowned in the water and tanks sank into the mud.

The offensive was not renewed until 26 October, when there was a slight improvement in the weather but not in the ground conditions. The Canadian Corps, which had been brought up specially for the purpose of capturing Passchendaele, led the attack, supported by four divisions of the British Fifth Army on their right. Advancing slowly along two narrow causeways, they were surrounded by bogs and were battered by shells, mustard gas (used by the Germans for the first time) and air attacks. They eventually reached the crest of the ridge on 30 October.

The attack was resumed on 6 November, when the Canadian First and Fourth Divisions made their final advance into the village of Passchendaele, which had already been reduced to rubble by Allied artillery. Further ground on the ridge was won before operations finally ended on 10 November.

Limited tactical gains – a vulnerable salient of five miles – had been achieved during the final phase of the battle at an enormous cost (250,000 Allied casualties overall), although the original aim of Third Ypres – to break out of the salient – had been abandoned long before.

Often incorrectly applied to the Third Battle of Ypres as a whole, the name Passchendaele soon came to represent 'the blindest slaughter of a blind war'. The Germans regained all the ground they had lost during **Ludendorff**'s offensive in the spring of 1918.

Passchendaele: battered by German artillery fire, the ground is churned into a sea of mud and boulders

PAU, GENERAL PAUL, 1848–1932

A veteran of the Franco-Prussian War, General Pau was recalled from retirement on 10 August 1914. **Joffre** appointed him to the command of the newly formed Army of Alsace, on the extreme right of the French line. His offensive against Alsace, which had been lost to the Germans in 1871, was launched on 19 August and actually reached the Rhine before being abandoned because of the need for reinforcements further west. Some of the province recovered by Pau was retained and he had the distinction of being the only French commander to seize territory from the Germans in the first year of the war.

PENNSYLVANIA

A development of the **Nevadas**, *Pennsylvania* and her sister ship *Arizona*, which were completed in 1916, had improved main armament: twelve 14-inch guns in four triple turrets. She also had twenty-two 5-inch guns (one more than the Nevada class) but armour was the same as her predecessors. *Pennsylvania* served as flagship of the US Atlantic Fleet from 1916, while *Arizona* joined the 6th Battle Squadron, British **Grand Fleet**, just after the end of hostilities.

PERSHING, GENERAL JOHN, 1860–1948

Commander of the **American Expeditionary Force** in Europe, 'Black Jack' Pershing was an experienced soldier whose active service dated back to the Cuban campaign in 1898. His performance during the pursuit of Pancho Villa, the anti-American bandit, in Mexico in 1916–17, even though the operation was unsuccessful, suggested that he was the only serious candidate for the European command. He arrived in France in mid-1917 and soon alarmed the US War Department with his rapidly escalating estimates of the number of troops – from less than one million to over three million – that would be required. 'A dour, immovable man', Pershing was unwilling to commit his forces before they were fully trained and present in sufficient numbers to intervene decisively. He was also adamant in his refusal to amalgamate his forces with those of the Allies, partly because of his doubts about the quality of British and French forces. It was also important that the American contribution to the war should be readily in evidence.

After **Ludendorff**'s March 1918 offensive began, Pershing changed his position on the use of American troops: 'Everything that we have is at your disposal to use as you like – we are here to be killed,' he wrote to **Foch**. In practice, however, Pershing maintained close control over his troops and they were only permitted to hold sections of the front as complete divisions. It was on this basis that the AEF fought creditably at **Cantigny**, Château-Thierry and **Belleau Wood**.

It was not in fact until September that Pershing was able to mount his own independent operation, when his troops successfully reduced the **St Mihiel** salient. He immediately transferred his troops to the Argonne Forest, where they launched the final offensive jointly with the French on 26 September. Progress was slow and there was little evidence of tactical flair or innovation, although the Germans were forced to draw in reserves from elsewhere; as a result, **Clemenceau** called unsuccessfully for Pershing's removal. In October, Pershing reorganised his forces (and his commanders) and when the second phase of the offensive began on 1 November much more was achieved.

'Black Jack' Pershing, AEF commander, 1917–19

During the autumn, Pershing argued that the Allies should seek the military defeat of Germany and her unconditional surrender, but the French and British were war weary and in no mood to listen. He returned to the United States in September 1919 and was advanced to the unique rank of 'general of the armies' in recognition of his wartime services.

PÉTAIN, MARSHAL HENRI, 1856–1951

Marshal of France and head of the Vichy regime, Pétain was a colonel, aged 58, when the war began. His slow career progress was explained by his lack of combat experience, the absence of patrons and his lone opposition to the French doctrine of *attaque à outrance*. He believed that a major offensive could only succeed after the defence had been decisively weakened by an overwhelming concentration of artillery firepower. In August 1914 Pétain was given command of a brigade in the Fifth Army, although he remained a colonel until the end of the month. He fought his first offensive action at the Battle of Guise, the day after his promotion to brigadier.

Following **Joffre**'s wholesale dismissal of incompetent generals, Pétain was appointed to the command of the Sixth Division, where he raised morale by his leadership and strict discipline; it played an important part at the **Marne**. Pétain was promoted again in October, being given command of XXXIII Corps. In May 1915, Pétain's corps broke through at

Arras, reaching the crest of Vimy Ridge, but he was unable to exploit the success.

In July 1915, he was moved to the command of the Second Army, which was preparing for a new offensive in **Champagne**. He was rightly sceptical about the value of an all-out attack of this kind, favouring more limited operations that would conserve scarce manpower.

In February 1916, the Germans launched a massive attack on **Verdun** with the aim of 'bleeding France white'. At the moment of crisis, when the fall of the fortress itself seemed imminent, Pétain was summoned to direct the defence of the salient. Ordered to hold it at all costs, he took immediate steps to contain the Germans: the artillery was reorganised and placed under his personal command; the army's massive supply requirements were organised effectively; and

Pétain, who rebuilt the French army after the mutinies of 1917, meets King George V

troops served at Verdun on a rotating basis to avoid too long a period in the terrible conditions there. Retaining responsibility for Verdun on assuming the command of the Centre Army Group in May, Pétain had maintained the army's will to resist and his success made him a national hero.

It was not, however, sufficient to secure him the job of commander-in-chief, which went to **General Nivelle**, who was associated with the successful autumn counter-strokes at Verdun. However, when Nivelle's plans to end the war in one great blow ended in failure and mutiny in April–May 1917, Pétain replaced him, his main task being to rebuild the army. The leading mutineers were executed and defeatist propaganda suppressed. His understanding of the needs of the common soldier led to improvements in his living conditions; he made regular visits to the front, assuring the troops that there would be no more wasteful offensives.

To help build up the army's morale, he embarked on a series of limited attacks in the autumn of 1917 at Verdun and Malmaison and by 1918 it was in a much better position to face the German spring offensives. However, his own views on how the Allies should respond to the expected attack – by an elastic defence in depth – found little support. To improve coordination of the Allied armies, **Foch** was appointed generalissimo on the Western Front, with Pétain losing his seniority on the French side and having a reduced role in the final stages of the war. After the Armistice Pétain was created Marshal of France and enjoyed great national prestige, having made his greatest contribution after the breakdown of the army in 1917.

PETER, KING OF SERBIA, 1844–1921

Just before the war Peter Karadjordjevic, King of Serbia, 1903–14, stepped down in favour of his son Crown Prince Alexander, who became prince regent. Although he was in poor health his wartime appearances at the front and at army parades helped to maintain Serb morale. With the enemy invasion in October 1915, Peter left for exile and retirement in Greece. He was crowned ruler of the new kingdom of Yugoslavia late in 1918 but immediately passed the throne to Alexander.

King Peter escapes through the mountains of Albania after the defeat of the Serbian army

PEUGEOT ARMOURED CAR

Peugeot started manufacturing armoured cars at the beginning of the war, although its early products were little more than standard touring cars with limited armour and a machine-gun. In 1916, a more advanced model appeared. It was based on the standard 18hp Peugeot chassis, but had double rear wheels to compensate for the additional weight of the fully armoured, box-shaped body. It was produced in automitrailleuse and autocanon forms, with an 8mm **Hotchkiss machine-gun** or a 37mm Puteaux cannon respectively. The Peugeot continued in French service until the end of the war, although by that time few examples were still operational.

PFALZ DIII

The Pfalz single-seat biplane fighter served with the German air service from August 1917 until the end of the war. Pfalz's first original D-class design was heavily influenced by the Roland fighters that the company had previously built under licence. Its streamlined fuselage, with a pointed nose, was even more shark-like in profile than the **LFG Roland DI** and **DII**, which had been nicknamed 'Haifisch' or 'Shark'. The design of the single bay, unequal chord wings facilitated an excellent forward and downward view from the pilot's cockpit. Powered by the 160hp Mercedes D III engine, it had a maximum speed of 102m.p.h. at 9,840 feet and a ceiling of 17,000 feet. It was armed with twin fixed, forward-firing Spandau machine-guns, which were almost totally concealed inside the fuselage. When the Pfalz DIIIa appeared early in 1918, the machine-guns were placed in a more conventional position on top of the fuselage to allow easier access for maintenance purposes. This variant also had a more powerful 180hp Mercedes D IIIa engine and more rounded wing tips.

Some 600 DIII/DIIIas were produced in total fully equipping twelve *Jastas*, with another 34 having some on strength. Numbers serving on the Western Front reached their peak in the first few months of 1918 and the aircraft made a useful contribution to the

The sturdy Pfalz fighter of 1917–18

German successes of that period. With excellent diving capabilities, the DIII was widely used in attacks on balloons and airships.

In other respects it had a mixed reputation as a fighter, comparing unfavourably in terms of manoeuvrability and speed with contemporary German designs like the **Albatros DVa** and the **Fokker DVII** and with the new Allied fighters that reached the front in the last few months of the war. In the absence of suitable alternatives, however, as many as 300 DIII/DIIIas were still in front line use in August 1918.

PFALZ DXII

The DXII followed the **DIII** as the next Pfalz fighter to be produced in quantity, entering service on the Western Front from August 1918. It was introduced to supplement the **Fokker DVII**, which was not available in sufficient numbers to meet the growing losses at the front. The design of this single-seat, two-bay biplane was in fact generally influenced by the excellent Fokker machine, although the fuselage profile owed much to the Pfalz DIII. Power was provided by a 180hp Mercedes D IIIa engine which gave a maximum speed of 106m.p.h. and a ceiling of 18,500 feet. Armament consisted of the standard twin fixed, forward-firing Spandau machine-guns mounted in front of the cockpit.

About 180 DXIIs were delivered to ten *Jastas* on the Western Front in the last three months of the war. Some were also allocated to home defence fighter units. The DXII was received without enthusiasm by those fighter pilots who had expected to fly the much-favoured Fokker DVII rather than an unknown machine of uncertain performance. The DXII did, in fact, have a good maximum speed and, because of its strong construction, a better diving capacity than the Fokker, although the latter was more manoeuvrable and could climb faster. The Pfalz fighter was able to engage its British opponents effectively and would almost certainly have made a greater impact had the war lasted longer.

PFALZ EI & EII

A single-seater fighter scout, the EI mid-wing monoplane was used by the German air service from 1914. Basically a **Morane Saulnier Type H** built under licence, it was powered by an 80hp Oberursel rotary engine in a horseshoe cowling. It had a maximum speed of just over 90m.p.h. and could climb to 2,000m in 12 minutes. A variant with a 100hp Oberursel but otherwise little changed was designated the EII. A single forward-firing Spandau machine-gun was operated with Fokker-type interrupter gear, although some of the earliest examples were unarmed. The EI and EII were the main production aircraft, although not many more than a hundred were built, and later Pfalz E-types made little impact.

Used initially on unarmed scouting duties, their main role in 1915–16 was to protect slower two-seaters and they were allocated in small numbers to reconnaissance units. The EI and EII were very similar in appearance to the Fokker monoplanes and Allied pilots found it almost impossible to distinguish between them. By mid-1916, like the **Fokker E-types**, they had been outclassed by more powerful and manoeuvrable biplanes, although they had a longer operational life on the Eastern Front and were retained as training aircraft.

PFLANZER-BALTIN, GENERAL KARL, BARON von, 1855–1925

Brought back from retirement in 1914, Pflanzer-Baltin served as commander of Austria's Seventh Army in **Galicia** for the first two years of the war. He was a 'master of improvisation' who 'conducted an unorthodox campaign for much of the war in the Carpathian Mountains'. From July 1918 until the end of the war Pflanzer-Baltin commanded Austrian forces in Albania. Communications there were poor and at first he refused to believe that the war was over when he heard the news. It was not in fact until 18 November that Pflanzer-Baltin left the country, ending his command of the last unit of the Austro-Hungarian army still in existence.

PHÖNIX CI

Like the **Ufag CI**, the Phönix CI two-seater, which appeared in 1918, was a development of the **Brandenburg CII** 'star-strutter'. It had unequal span wings, braced by parallel pairs of V-struts, a deep fuselage and a horn-balanced rudder. Power was provided by a single 230hp Hiero engine which gave a maximum speed of 110m.p.h. at sea level. The observer was armed with a ring-mounted **Schwarzlose machine-gun**, while the pilot used a weapon of the same type mounted under the engine cowling and synchronised by Zapanka mechanical gear; some CIs also carried a small bomb load in external racks. Both descendants of the Brandenburg were in fact accepted for military use after competitive testing as there was little difference between them. The Phönix had greater stability, a shorter take-off run, and a higher ceiling than the Ufag CI, which had a faster maximum speed. About 110 Phönix CIs were built and they were used by the Austrian air service for photo-reconnaissance duties until the end of the war.

PHÖNIX DI, DII & DIII

The Austrian Phönix DII reconnaissance aircraft

The Phönix DI single-seat fighter served with Austrian forces in the final year of the war. A development of the **Brandenburg DI**, which Phönix had produced under licence, it was designed to take the more powerful engines that had recently become available. This single-bay biplane was powered by the 200hp Hiero engine, which gave a maximum speed of 112m.p.h. at sea level. It was armed with twin forward-firing 8mm **Schwarzlose machine-guns** which were enclosed in the fuselage and were therefore inaccessible in flight. The DII had balanced elevators and other minor changes, but retained the same engine as the DI, while the DIIa had the larger 230hp Hiero and ailerons on both wings. The DIII was an improved version of the DIIa, with the guns directly accessible to the pilot.

The main weaknesses of the D-type designs were their relatively slow rate of climb and poor manoeuvrability, the structural problems evident in early production machines having been quickly resolved. Phönix D-types were used widely by the Austrian air service on escort and photographic reconnaissance duties, while others were allocated to fighter units. The Austrian navy also employed a number of these machines to good effect over the Adriatic in the closing stages of the war.

PIAVE RIVER, BATTLE OF THE, 15–22 June 1918

With Russia out of the war, Austria came under pressure from her German ally during the spring of 1918 to launch a major new attack on the Italian Front. Reinforced to 58 divisions (compared to their opponent's 57), the Austrians decided to make a final effort, without German help, to bring about Italy's defeat. A great pincer movement was planned, but personal rivalries meant that the two front commanders were given forces of equal strength, ensuring that neither was able to achieve a decisive breakthrough.

Conrad, the former Chief of Staff who was now based in the Trentino, was alloted the main task of reaching Verona, while to the left **Boroevic von Bojna** on the Piave was to cross the river and aim for Padua and the Adige. After some diversionary attacks, the main Austrian assault was launched on 15 June. On the right in the mountains the limited advance made by Conrad's Tenth and Eleventh Armies was checked on the second day. The Italian Fourth and Sixth Armies, which included Anglo-French troops, launched a strong counter-attack and the Austrians were unable even to hold on to their limited gains; 40,000 men were lost.

More progress was made on the lower Piave, where Boroevic attacked between the Montello and the sea. His Fifth and Sixth Armies crossed the river and advanced three miles on a 15-mile front before meeting the Italian Third and Eighth Armies. A desperate battle ensued over the next eight days, with the Austrians advancing further before a strong counter-attack on 18 June forced them to pull back. A lack of reinforcements and restrictions on the movement of supplies (all but four of the bridges thrown across the Piave by the Austrians had been destroyed by air raids and heavy rain) had severely weakened Boroevic's position, and by 21 June his flank had been turned. The next day they were forced back across the Piave, suffering heavy losses – there were 150,000 Austrian casualties in total, including 24,000 taken prisoner. **General Diaz**, the over-cautious Italian commander, did not pursue the enemy across the Piave and the unsuccessful Austrian offensive was brought to a close. Conrad was replaced by **Archduke Joseph** and the Austrian army was permanently paralysed. Morale declined rapidly and desertion became commonplace as many soldiers from the subject nations realised that they had little to gain by fighting for Austria.

PILSUDSKI, JOSEPH, 1867–1935

Polish nationalist and soldier who led the struggle to liberate Russian Poland, Pilsudski was the first head of the independent state that was created in November 1918. Before 1914 he had formed several Polish military units on Austrian territory and during the war they fought against Russia alongside the forces of the Habsburg Empire. After the fall of the Tsar and the formation of a satellite Polish state in 1917, under the domination of the Central Powers, conflicts developed between Germany and Polish nationalists. In July, Pilsudski and some of his men were arrested and imprisoned by the Germans until the autumn of 1918. As the war ended Pilsudski was proclaimed head of the new Polish state.

PLAN XVII

Produced by **Joffre** in April 1913, Plan XVII was the French strategic plan for an opening offensive in the event of a German declaration of war. The French main effort would be on her eastern frontier – an immediate dual offensive into Alsace-Lorraine, where it was believed, quite incorrectly, the main German offensive would come. They would advance north and south of the Thionville–Metz area in order to recover the provinces lost in the Franco-Prussian War (1870–71). In addition, two French armies in the north would move if the Germans violated Belgian territory west of the Meuse.

Joffre's assumption, which was not universally shared by his colleagues, that the German front line army would not be strong enough to make a major thrust further west proved to be a disastrous miscalculation. Schlieffen had correctly anticipated the French scheme when he prepared his own plans: German forces would wheel through the heart of Belgium and, with the use of reserves, would have a significant margin over their French opponents. Joffre also placed too much reliance on the ability of a small British expeditionary force to reinforce the French left and on the Russians to engage a substantial proportion of the German army on the Eastern Front.

PLEHVE, GENERAL WENZEL von, 1850–1916

Commander of the Fifth Army on the Eastern Front at the beginning of the war, the elderly Plehve was one of Russia's more able generals. He was a 'little wizened man, broken in health but full of moral and intellectual energy'. Sustaining heavy losses during the Austrian offensive in **Galicia** in August 1914, Plehve withdrew at the correct moment rather than risk encirclement and defeat on the battlefield. In November, he intervened effectively during the Battle of **Lodz** to assist the endangered Russian Second Army. Before Plehve's departure from active service, his forces played an important part in halting the German advance eastwards in September 1915.

PLUMER, FIELD MARSHAL HERBERT, FIRST VISCOUNT, 1857–1932

One of Britain's most able First World War generals, Plumer had established his reputation during the South African War and subsequently served as quartermaster-general. In December 1914, he was appointed to the command of II Corps, and succeeded **Smith-Dorrien** as head of the Second Army in April 1915. After organising the retreat of British troops at the close of the **Second Battle of Ypres**, he held the salient for two quiet years, as major British offensives were launched elsewhere.

Plumer's opportunity came in 1917, when the British agreed to launch a major attack following the failure of the **Nivelle** offensive. **Haig** turned his attention to Flanders and as a preliminary to an offensive at Ypres, Plumer was ordered to seize the high ground around **Messines**. 'Cautious, methodical and imperturbable', he 'never moved without careful preparation' and this operation was no exception. The explosion of 19 enormous mines and a massive artillery bombardment preceded the advance by 12 infantry divisions on 7 June 1917. A 'siege war masterpiece', it was a complete success, with relatively few British casualties; it was Plumer's finest achievement. The main attack at Ypres, mounted by **General Gough**, was, however, a complete failure and, on 25 August, command of the operation passed to Plumer. Such limited gains as were made during the **Third Battle of Ypres**, albeit at a terrible cost, were attributable to the work of the Second Army.

Plumer spent the next few months in Italy, commanding the Allied force sent there to support the Italian army after the **Caporetto** disaster. Returning to France early in 1918, he held the Ypres salient in the face of **Ludendorff**'s attack on 21 March. He participated in the final offensive against the Germans in October and after the Armistice was appointed commander of occupied German territory. In 1919, he was raised to the peerage for his wartime services.

Plumer: the victor of Messines, an achievement that owed much to his careful, methodical approach

POINCARÉ, RAYMOND, 1860–1934

French lawyer and politician who was president of the Third Republic throughout the war. An active and influential head of state, Poincaré was not constrained by the largely ceremonial nature of his office. He selected premiers, influenced the composition of cabinets and was involved in discussions on military strategy. At a time of crisis in November 1917, he reluctantly called on **Clemenceau** to form a government and soon discovered that France's principal wartime prime minister had no place for an active president. The two men also clashed during the **Paris Peace Conference** when Poincaré's demands for more severe terms were rejected by Clemenceau. He remained President until early in 1920.

POLIVANOV, GENERAL ALEKSEI, 1855–1920

'The only efficient Minister of War Russia had during the whole war', General Polivanov succeeded **Sukhomlinov**, whose position he had helped to undermine, in June 1915. He gave priority to improving the supply of weapons and equipment to the Russian army, but his work was cut short by his dismissal in March 1916. His political liberalism and his close connections with Duma leaders were anathema to reactionary elements in the government.

POMILIO P-TYPES

This series of two-seater armed reconnaissance biplanes served with the Italian air force from March 1917 until the end of the war. The first version, the PC, was powered by a 260hp Fiat A-12 engine, partially enclosed in a pointed metal cowling. A **Fiat-Revelli machine-gun** was mounted above the upper wing and fired over the propeller; the observer used a second Revelli in the rear cockpit. With a maximum speed of 112m.p.h. at sea level, it was faster than most fighters of the time and was able to dispense with an escort. It was, however, quickly superseded by the PD because of serious problems of instability, which caused several fatal crashes. This interim design incorporated a fin fitted beneath the fuselage and other changes in order to give it greater stability.

The PE, which appeared in February 1918, was more substantially redesigned, with a bigger tailplane and an enlarged upper fin. Fitted with the more powerful 300hp Fiat A-12bis engine, it had a synchronised forward-firing machine-gun in the front cockpit and one or two machine-guns on a Scarff ring-mounting in the rear. With no stability problems, the PE was the most successful of the Pomilio series and came into general use as an artillery and reconnaissance aircraft. At the **Battle of Vittorio Veneto** (October 1918), for example, 112 PEs were operational, more than half the total aircraft present. The P-types were in fact the most widely produced Italian machines of the war: at one point 1,616 examples were in service with as many as 30 squadrons of the Italian air force.

POTEMKIN

Completed in 1904, this famous pre-dreadnought battleship became flagship of the Russian Black Sea Fleet. It was relatively slow (16 knots), had limited armour protection, and was fitted with four 12-inch guns in fore and aft twin turrets. However, the performance of *Potemkin* (or *Panteleimon* as it was renamed after the crew's mutiny in June 1905) compared favourably with that of Turkish warships of the period. Like other old Russian battleships, she was used principally for shore bombardment, although in April 1915 she scored two hits on *Goeben*. Named *Potemkin* again by the Provisional Government of March 1917 and then *Fighter for Liberty*, she was abandoned by her crew after the Russo-German armistice of December 1917. Later captured by the Germans, she was surrendered to the Allies in November 1918; her engines were subsequently immobilised to prevent her operational use by the Bolsheviks during the civil war.

POTIOREK, FIELD MARSHAL OSKAR, 1853–1933

An experienced professional soldier, Potiorek had been in charge of security arrangements in Serbia when **Franz Ferdinand** was assassinated. His wartime service as supreme commander of Austrian forces on the Serbian front did nothing to improve his reputation. He launched three unsuccessful offensives against Serbian troops led by **Marshal Radomir Putnik**, which ended in Austria's ignominious defeat, with heavy losses, in December 1914. Potiorek was removed from his command and replaced by **Archduke Eugen**; it was not until October 1915 that Serbia was successfully invaded.

PREZAN, LIEUTENANT-GENERAL CONSTANTINE, 1861–1943

On Rumania's entry into the war in August 1916, Prezan commanded the Fourth Army, taking part in the invasion of Transylvania. When it failed Prezan was switched to the command of a new army group which moved against the German armies – headed by **Falkenhayn** and **Mackensen** – that were converging on Bucharest. Although Prezan was an able commander, the Rumanians were defeated in the Battle of the Arges River (1–4 December) and the army's remnants were forced northwards. He was appointed chief of staff late in 1916, with responsibility for the reconstruction of the shattered Rumanian army, retaining his position after the failed offensive of July 1917. The army was partially demobilised after a peace treaty had been concluded with the Germans in May 1918 but Prezan remained at its head.

PRINCIP, GAVRILO, 1894–1918

Princip was the young Bosnian terrorist who assassinated the heir to the Austro-Hungarian throne, **Franz Ferdinand**, and his wife, Countess Sophie Chotek, as they drove through the streets of Sarajevo on 28 June 1914, setting in train the events that were to lead to the outbreak of the First World War. Motivated by the aim of securing political and economic reform for Bosnia, Princip was provided with arms by the secret Serbian organisation known as the 'Black Hand'. He was captured and sent to prison for 20 years, but died there in 1918.

PRITTWITZ, GENERAL MAXIMILIAN von, 1848–1929

Commander of the German Eighth Army on the outbreak of war, Prittwitz was charged with the defence of East Prussia against Russian attack. He first engaged the advancing Russian forces under **Ren-**

nenkampf near **Gumbinnen** on 20 August 1914, but withdrew after two of his divisions had fled from the battle. With the news that **Samsonov**, to the south, was moving westwards more quickly than had been expected, Prittwitz decided to retreat more than 100 miles to the Vistula. Although he reversed this precipitate decision the next day after talking to his staff, it was too late: **Moltke** had already decided to replace him with **Hindenburg** and **Ludendorff**. The long military career of the 'panic-striken' Prittwitz, who had a fear of taking calculated risks, was over.

PROPAGANDA

The Great War was the first time that modern propaganda methods were widely used. They involved the 'direction and control of public opinion for certain ends', including the encouragement of recruiting and ensuring that public support for the war remained high. The morale of the home front was of critical importance in determining the outcome of this conflict – the first total war – which demanded the full use of each belligerent's entire physical and human resources. Information was censored, simplified and moulded to meet government objectives. In England, for example, an image of the German as 'the Evil Hun' was created, built on a negative picture that had already been developed as pre-war tensions had mounted; people were encouraged to hate the enemy by the spread of atrocity stories.

Horatio Bottomley persuades men to join up at a recruiting meeting in Trafalgar Square

Externally, propaganda was directed against the enemy with the aim of reducing its ability to wage war. The institutions of government were likely to be undermined by lowering the morale of troops at the front and the civilian population. In Austro-Hungary, for example, Allied propaganda encouraged the development and expression of nationalism among the subject peoples of the Empire. An Allied campaign against the morale of enemy troops on the Western Front during the final few months of the war had the effect of 'eating away German confidence like some corrosive acid'. Neutrals and allies were also the target of wartime propaganda activity. For instance, skilful British propaganda may have helped to bring America into the war in 1917.

In Britain, the popular press, which was more influential than ever before, was the main method of conveying propaganda to the home front, although the new medium of film became increasingly important as its potential was more widely appreciated. Other means used to communicate with the civilian population included public meetings, popular literature and war art. The activities of innumerable relief organisations and charities also helped to shape public attitudes to the war.

Britain used the press in neutral countries by providing it with material that presented the Allied cause in a favourable light. Propaganda newspapers were also produced and circulated in these areas. The enemy's front and rear areas could be communicated with directly by means of subversive pamphlets dropped from aircraft and balloons.

For most of the war, propaganda activities in Britain were not centrally organised or coordinated, with the press, a variety of government departments and patriotic organisations mounting their own separate campaigns. It was not until 1917 that a national organisation was created to manage propaganda at home, in response to increasing evidence of war weariness and the need to counteract the activities of pacifist groups.

The priority given to propaganda in Britain at that time was reflected in the creation of a Ministry of Information, under Lord Beaverbrook, early in 1918. Lord Northcliffe was appointed as the new Director of Propaganda to enemy countries. Germany was much slower in recognising the importance of propaganda in modern warfare and she never matched the British effort in terms of volume, quality or impact. It was a mistake that Germany did not repeat in the Second World War.

PULEMYOT MAXIMA 1910

The PM 1910 was the second Russian-produced version of the **Maxim machine-gun**, the first having appeared in 1905. It was very similar to the original Maxim guns supplied to Russia by Vickers, although some variants had two modifications: a fluted jacket and a large filling cap, designed to improve cooling. This strongly constructed weapon, which weighed over 52lb, proved to be extremely reliable in the poor conditions of the Eastern Front, even with minimal maintenance. It had a cyclic rate of fire of 520–600 rounds per minute and the 7.62mm ammunition was loaded from a 250-round belt. The gun was normally transported on a carriage, known as a Solokov mounting, which had a pair of wheels and a turntable. An alternative sledge mounting was often used in the winter. The Pulemyot Maxima model 1910 continued in production after the war, remaining in service with the Soviet army until 1943.

PUTNIK, FIELD MARSHAL RADOMIR, 1847–1917

An experienced professional soldier who led the Serbian army during the Balkan wars (1912–13), Putnik had been chief of staff and, on three occasions, war minister before the First World War. He had been particularly active in improving the equipment and training of the armed forces, which had urgently needed modernisation. When the war began Putnik was chief of staff and he repelled two Austrian invasion attempts in the first few months: they were defeated at the **Battle of the Jadar** in August and again in December 1916 at the **Battle of Kolubra**, the enemy being expelled from the country on both occasions.

In October 1915, the attack was renewed in considerable strength, with Austrian, German and Bulgarian troops launching coordinated attacks. Putnik was soon forced to retreat in the face of overwhelming enemy numbers. With a victory for the Central Powers in sight, Putnik skilfully avoided a major engagement but planned and successfully carried out the evacuation of the Serbian army. It escaped over the Albanian mountains to the Adriatic and a temporary base on Corfu. Putnik, who had become a popular hero, survived the difficult journey but the whole struggle had undermined his health and he took no further part in the war.

Q-SHIPS

The Q-ship Hyderabad *was, unusually, a specially constructed decoy vessel rather than a conversion*

The most notable decoy ships of the First World War, Q-ships were used by the Royal Navy in an attempt to combat the U-boat threat. They were apparently genuine merchant ships that were equipped with concealed guns and torpedoes, and sometimes with false colours. Many different types of vessel were converted, from small sailing ships to 40,000-ton tramp steamers, and there were also a small number of purpose-built versions. Q-ships operated on the assumption that U-boats would not normally use a torpedo to sink a small vessel of this kind, but would surface and destroy it more economically by gunfire. As the German submarine appeared, the Q-ship would uncover its weapons and open fire.

The first decoy vessels appeared in November 1914, but the first successful use of a Q-ship operating alone did not occur until July 1915, when the collier *Prince Charles* sank U36 off the Orkneys. A month earlier the armed trawler *Taranaki* had been involved in the destruction of U40 off the coast of Aberdeen: it towed the British submarine C24, which was directed on to its target by a telephone link.

Although these 'mystery ships' may have had some romantic appeal, in practice they were not a great success. At the beginning of the war they were not available in sufficient numbers to make an impact, but as the Q-ship fleet expanded the Germans became aware of their activities and adjusted their tactics accordingly. Merchant ships were now much more likely to be torpedoed by submerged U-boats without warning. Almost 200 Q-ships were produced and 31 were sunk; they were responsible for the destruction of 11 U-boats, their last victim sinking in the autumn of 1917, when they were finally withdrawn.

QUEEN ELIZABETH

The Queen Elizabeth-class battleships, which gave outstanding service with the Royal Navy in both world wars, represented a considerable advance in design when they appeared in 1915–16.

All oil-fired, these super-dreadnoughts were equipped with additional boilers to produce an increased maximum speed (compared to the **Iron Dukes**) of 24–25 knots. They were intended to form a 'fast squadron' which would perform a similar role to that originally allocated to the much less well protected battlecruisers. In particular, they would improve tactical flexibility and help to frustrate the withdrawal of the enemy. Additional space for the extra propulsion machinery was found by removing Q-turret and the associated shell rooms from the original design. New 15-inch guns, which could fire a 1,920lb shell over 35,000 yards, were fitted, eight of them providing a greater weight of broadside than ten 13.5-inch guns. Secondary armament was similar to that of the Iron Dukes but armour was further improved.

Queen Elizabeth and the other ships of the class – *Warspite*, *Valiant*, *Barham*, *Malaysia* – formed the 5th Battle Squadron of the **Grand Fleet**. All except *Queen Elizabeth* were present at **Jutland**, where they played a valuable role and only one – *Valiant* – was undamaged. Queen Elizabeth was involved in the **Dardanelles operation** in 1915, and in 1917–18 was the flagship of **Admiral Beatty**. She was also the ship in which the formal instrument of internment of the **High Seas Fleet** was signed in November 1918.

QUEEN MARY

Similar in appearance to *Lion*, the *Queen Mary*, which was completed in 1913, was improved in several respects. She was not in fact one of the Lion-class battlecruisers, although she was often referred to as such. The main differences included round funnels, increased power, larger shells for the 13.5-inch guns and modified side armour. *Queen Mary* served in the 1st Battle Cruiser Squadron of the **Grand Fleet** and participated in the action at **Heligoland Bight**. At the **Battle of Jutland** she was engaged by *Derfflinger* and *Seydlitz* at just under 15,000 yards, and scored four hits on the latter. Return fire damaged one of her guns and almost immediately further hits caused two turret magazines to explode, indicating the ship's vulnerability to plunging fire and the absence of flashtight doors. She rolled over and sank rapidly, with the loss of 1,266 lives.

RADETZKY

Designed in 1905, these Austro-Hungarian pre-dreadnought battleships were not completed until 1910–11. They followed the Erzherzog Karl-class and had much improved main armament – four 12-inch guns in twin turrets fore and aft on the centre line. Secondary armament – eight 9.45-inch guns – was mounted in four-wing twin turrets. Armour protection was also excellent, although these ships were relatively slow, with a maximum speed of 20.5 knots.

Radetzky and her sister ships – *Erzherzog Franz Ferdinand* and *Zrinyi* – constituted the 2nd Division of the 1st Battle Squadron of the Austro-Hungarian navy. They were used to bombard shore positions in Italy and Montenegro in the first months of the war but from May 1915 saw no further operational service.

RADOSLAVOV, VASIL, 1854–1929

Pro-German wartime premier of Bulgaria who concluded a treaty of alliance with the **Central Powers** in September 1915. In return for military support, an enlarged Bulgaria would become the dominant power in the Balkans after the war; it was an offer unmatched by the Allies who had also sought her support. Early successes in Serbia and Macedonia temporarily silenced Radoslavov's opponents, but soon there were objections to the increasing German demands on Bulgaria. She was put under considerable pressure to join the invasion of Rumania and her limited food reserves were depleted for the benefit of the civilian population of Germany. Radoslavov's government fell in June 1918 when it became clear that Bulgaria would not receive the promised territorial gains for participating in the operations against Rumania.

RAFA, BATTLE OF, 9 January 1917

After the fall of El Arish in December 1916, the last remaining Turkish force in Egypt was the garrison at Rafa, 25 miles away. A small force of mounted troops, mainly Australians and New Zealanders, under the command of Major-General Sir Philip Chetwode, attacked the strong Turkish positions on 9 January 1917. After a 'brilliant little fight', the defences were stormed and the garrison surrendered. About 200 Turks were killed and over 1,600 taken prisoner; the British lost only 71 men. With the fall of Rafa, the way was open for a British advance on **Gaza**, the entrance to Palestine.

RAMADI, BATTLE OF, 28–29 September 1917

After the fall of **Baghdad** on 11 March 1917 and the seizure of the surrounding areas, **Sir Stanley** **Maude**, the British commander-in-chief, postponed further offensive action against the surviving Turkish forces in central Mesopotamia until cooler weather arrived in the autumn. In September, his troops marched sixty miles north-west to Ramadi, on the right bank of the Euphrates, where there was a large Turkish garrison. On 28–29 September, the British attacked, overwhelming the Turks, who offered no real resistance, and captured the majority of them. Further actions were fought at Daur and Tikrit on 1–4 November. Plans to capture the oilfields were suspended following Maude's death in November, but were reactivated in 1918 under his successor, **General Marshall**.

RAPALLO CONFERENCE, 5 November 1917

As the **Battle of Caporetto** drew to a close early in November 1917, the Allies met at Rapallo in order to consider ways of helping the defeated Italians. The discussion soon encompassed much wider issues affecting the conduct of war than immediate support for Italy. At **Lloyd George**'s suggestion it was agreed to establish a Supreme War Council with the aim of remedying one of the weaknesses – lack of coordination – of the Allied war effort. Meeting regularly at Versailles, it would consist of the Prime Ministers of France, Britain and Italy and the President of the United States, or their representatives. The delegates at Rapallo agreed that it should discuss military policy and the distribution of troops between different theatres, including the vulnerable Italian front. Although it had little immediate impact on the course of the war, the Supreme War Council provided Lloyd George with a source of military advice independent of his own generals. More importantly, the Council could be regarded as the 'forerunner of true unity of command' as it developed on the Western Front in 1918.

RAWLINSON, GENERAL HENRY, 1st BARON, 1864–1925

Appointed to the command of the newly formed British Fourth Army late in 1915, Rawlinson, formerly head of IV Corps, proved to be one of the most able British army commanders of the First World War. His first major task in his new command – leading the attack during the **First Battle of the Somme** – did not, however, add much to his reputation. There were disagreements with **Haig** about how the attack should be conducted, and the tactics Rawlinson eventually adopted 'effectively destroyed any existing possibility of success'. At the end of the first day (1 July 1916) 57,000 men had been lost; nothing had been gained and the long battle of attrition began. He commanded the British left during the closing stages of the **Third Battle of Ypres** in November 1917 and headed the Second Army while **Plumer** was absent during the winter of 1917–18.

As the commander of a reconstituted Fourth Army he planned the Allied victory at **Amiens** on 8 August 1918; the 'black day of the German army' was perhaps Rawlinson's greatest achievement. His highly experienced force, accompanied by 500 tanks, had broken the German lines in this totally unexpected assault, which had been prepared in great secrecy. During the subsequent Allied offensive Rawlinson's army, located in the centre, was highly successful. It advanced a further 60 miles and was positioned south-east of Maubeuge when the Armistice was announced, having fought four more major battles and 18 smaller engagements.

R-CLASS SUBMARINE

The first class designed specifically to kill enemy submarines, the British Rs were faster submerged (14 knots) than they were on the surface (9 knots), enabling them to locate and overtake their targets. Positioned in the bows were six 18-inch torpedo tubes and five hydrophones, which were intended to facilitate the underwater firing of torpedoes. Only ten R-class boats had been completed by the end of the war and they were soon decommissioned; it was not until the latter part of the next war that priority was again accorded to submarines of this kind.

REGINA MARGHERITA

Launched in 1901, the Italian battleships *Regina Margherita* and *Benedetto Brin* were designed to match the firepower and speed of their foreign contemporaries, but not their armour protection. With a displacement of 13,215 tons, they had four 12-inch, four 8-inch and twelve 6-inch guns and could reach a maximum speed of 20 knots. There was a crew of 812. *Regina Margherita* sank in December 1916 after hitting two mines laid by a German U-boat; *Benedetto Brin* was sunk in Brindisi harbour in September 1915 as a result of Austrian sabotage.

RENAULT ARMOURED CAR

The improvised armoured cars made by the large Renault company in the early days of the war were soon superseded by a standard production model. It had a simple, open-topped armoured hull resting on a

Renault lorry chassis which was fitted with a 4,600cc four-cylinder engine and dual rear wheels. Operated by a crew of three or four it appeared in automitrailleuse or autocanon forms and was equipped with either an 8mm **Hotchkiss machine-gun** or a 37mm Puteaux cannon respectively. The Renault armoured car was produced (with minor design modifications) in significant numbers during the war, although losses were high and few were still operational by the Armistice.

RENAULT FT-17 TANK

In the latter stages of the war the Renault FT-17 was the principal French armoured fighting vehicle, a light tank specialising in infantry support. Equipped with a radio, it was also employed as a command vehicle, operating with the French army's heavy **Schneider** and **Saint Chamond tanks**. Design and production were personally supervised by Louis Renault, the energetic head of the car manufacturer that was awarded the original order in 1916. As military demand for the tank increased, other companies produced the machine.

front and the gunner in between; it had a maximum speed of almost 5m.p.h. and a range of 22 miles. A fully revolving turret was another novel feature in a mass production tank, although initially it caused manufacturing problems. At first its only offensive armament was a single air-cooled 8mm **Hotchkiss machine-gun**, although an alternative model equipped with the 37mm Puteaux light cannon, appeared later. A self-propelled gun version, with a 75mm field gun mounted on a flat platform, was also produced in 1918.

The Renault FT-17 was the principal French contribution to wartime tank design

The new model used for the first time a layout that formed the basis for tank design in the future. It consisted of a small and narrow armoured box, without a chassis. The engine, lifted from an 18hp Renault car, was at the rear, with the driver at the

Although the first FT-17 tanks were delivered late in 1917, it was not until 31 May 1918 that they were used in action on the Western Front, helping to halt the last German offensive. They quickly demonstrated their manoeuvrability, but were not present in sufficient numbers to make much of an impact. Used more widely in the later Allied advances of 1918, the Renault was used by the AEF as well as by the French army, and by the Armistice over 2,000 had been commissioned. It was exported to several countries between the wars and was still in French service during the Second World War, a tribute to the quality of its design and construction.

RENNENKAMPF, GENERAL PAUL von, 1853–1918

Russian general appointed at the beginning of the war to the command of the First Army, which faced East Prussia on the North-Western Front. The first Russian offensive of the war began on 17 August 1914 when Rennenkampf's army and the Second Army (**Samsonov**) crossed the border. The Germans launched unsuccessful attacks against the enemy at Stallupönen and **Gumbinnen** before producing an effective response: their forces were to be concentrated against the Second Army, while delaying Rennenkampf with no more than a cavalry division. With no orders from his army group commander, **Zhilinsky**, and preoccupied with supply problems, the slow and cautious Rennenkampf failed to act until it was too late. He may also have been greatly influenced by his strong personal emnity towards Samsonov.

After the **Battle of Tannenberg** the Germans turned their attention to Rennenkampf. The opponents met at the **First Battle of the Masurian Lakes** (9–14 September, 1914), where the Russian commander suffered heavy losses before disengaging. Although he was blamed by some for not helping Samsonov and for running away in September, Rennenkampf survived in command in the short term. **Lodz** (18–25 November 1914) was to be his last battle; his failure to act decisively enabled the German XXV Reserve Corps, which had almost been encircled, to escape and cost him his military career. He was shot by the Bolsheviks for refusing to accept a command in the Red Army.

RENOWN

Completed in 1916, the battlecruisers *Renown* and *Repulse* were authorised by the British government in response to a request from **Lord Fisher**. Support for his enthusiasm for fast, lightly armoured warships of this kind had been provided by the success of *Inflexible* and *Invincible* in pursuing the enemy during the **Battle of the Falkland Islands**.

These long, elegant ships had a displacement of 26,500 tons and a maximum speed of 32 knots. Their draught was limited because they had been designed with Fisher's projected amphibious landings on the northern coast of Germany in mind. Only six 15-inch guns (instead of Fisher's planned twelve) could be provided for each ship within the limited construction period available; secondary armament consisted of seventeen 4-inch guns in five triple mountings and two singles. *Renown* and *Repulse* were the first ships to have anti-torpedo bulge protection designed as an integral part of the hull. Armour was, however, very limited for ships of this size and by the time they were commissioned the fatal weakness of battlecruiser design – inadequate armour protection – had been dramatically revealed at the **Battle of Jutland**. As an interim measure, at **Jellicoe**'s request, further armour was added to the decks of both ships during 1916–17.

Renown and *Repulse* joined the 1st Battle Cruiser Squadron, Grand Fleet, in the summer of 1916 and they served with it for the remainder of the war. *Repulse* was in action against German light cruisers on 17 November 1917 in the Heligoland Bight but otherwise they saw no combat. Both ships were further modified between the wars and served in the Second World War.

REPARATIONS

After the First World War the Allies imposed payments on Germany, Austria and Hungary in partial compensation for the costs they had incurred in defeating them. German reparations, which were not fixed until April 1923, amounted to £6,600 million (plus interest), with lesser sums for her former allies. After the first instalment of £50 million had been paid, Germany suspended payments as the effects of inflation began to have an impact. The Allied occupation of the Ruhr followed as a result.

The level of repayments was substantially reduced by the Dawes and Young plans, but in 1932 reparations were abandoned altogether in the wake of the Depression. No more than a small fraction of the total had in fact been paid. The wisdom of imposing reparations had been questioned by several participants at the **Paris Peace Conference** in 1919, including **Keynes** and other economists, and their existence was an important influence on the domestic politics of the Weimar Republic.

RÉPUBLIQUE

The French République-class battleships represented a significant improvement over their predecessors in terms of displacement (14,605 tons), increased armament (four 12-inch guns and eighteen 6.4-inch), and better armour protection. Secondary guns as well as

the main armament were mounted in turrets. Completed in 1906, *République* and *Patrie* were key units of the French battle fleet and they served in the Mediterranean throughout the First World War.

REUTER, ADMIRAL LUDWIG von, 1869–1943

Appointed commander of the scouting forces of the **High Seas Fleet** in August 1918, Admiral Reuter had been captain of *Derfflinger* at the beginning of the war and was present at the **Battle of the Dogger Bank**. At the **Battle of Jutland** he commanded the Fourth Scouting Group of light cruisers. On the conclusion of the war, he was charged with the task of bringing to England the German ships to be interned at **Scapa Flow** under the terms of the Armistice.

There they were to remain, under Reuter's command, until peace terms (which would involve their surrender) had been agreed. When, in mid-1919, it became clear that a treaty was to be signed, he ordered all his ships to be scuttled. Reuter said later that 'it was unthinkable to surrender defenceless ships to the enemy'. Scuttling took place on 21 June 1919 and Reuter, along with his colleagues, was held as a prisoner of war until January 1920.

REVENGE

The last British battleships to be laid down before the war, the Revenge class was originally intended to consist of seven ships, but two – *Repulse* and *Renown* – were redesigned as battlecruisers.

Although the new class was generally similar to the **Queen Elizabeths**, one important difference was its reduced power, even though oil-fired boilers rather than coal burners were installed during the course of construction. With a maximum speed of 23 knots, they had a displacement of 27,500 tons and a complement of 950 men. There was some improvement in the deck armour and two ships of the class – *Ramillies* and *Resolution* – were fitted with hull bulges which enhanced anti-torpedo protection and only slightly reduced speed. Armament was very similar to the Queen Elizabeths', with eight 15-inch and fourteen 6-inch guns. The arrangement of the secondary armament was improved by moving the 6-inch guns further aft to reduced the possibility of flooding.

These five ships were completed in 1916–17, but only *Revenge* herself and *Royal Oak* were commissioned in time to serve at the **Battle of Jutland**, where they were both undamaged. *Royal Sovereign*, *Resolution* and *Ramillies* also served with the 1st Battle Squadron, Grand Fleet, until the end of the war. Modified during the inter-war years, the Revenge class was widely used during the Second World War.

RIBOT, ALEXANDRE, 1842–1923

A former French foreign minister, Ribot was a political moderate who had played an important role in securing France's military alliance with Russia in 1892. He was responsible for the country's finances during the first two years of the war, before his brief term as premier (March–September 1917). He auth-orised the ill-fated **Nivelle offensive** even though he had doubts about it, but was 'wiser in the aftermath', allowing the professional authorities 'the latitude to restore the army by internal reforms and by the abandonment of large scale offensives.'

RICHTHOFEN, MANFRED von, 1892–1918

The Red Baron: the war's greatest fighter pilot

The 'ace of aces' of the First World War, the German fighter pilot Manfred von Richthofen had scored 80 victories by the time of his death in April 1918. A member of the Prussian nobility, Richthofen had been commissioned into an élite cavalry regiment in 1912, but as the war began it became clear that the era of the cavalryman was over. He eventually transferred to the air service in May 1915, serving as an observer, first on the Eastern Front and then, from August 1915, with the Ostend Carrier Pigeon Unit, a secret group established to pioneer long-range bombing tactics. By the end of the year he had qualified as a pilot and spent the first few months of 1916 flying two-seaters. At Verdun, his initial posting, Richthofen scored his first unconfirmed hit, but his real chance came in August 1916 when **Oswald Boelcke** selected him to join *Jagdstaffel 2*.

Boelcke's new fighter squadron was intended to help restore Germany's ascendancy in the air over the Western Front. Its first offensive patrol was made on 17 September 1916 and on the following day Richthofen, flying an **Albatros DII**, scored his first officially confirmed victory – an **FE2b**. He then achieved an average of one hit a week for the rest of the year, his most notable adversary being **Lanoe Hawker**, the English ace, whom he shot down on 23 November 1916. After this victory he always tried to bring back a trophy from his victims' aircraft.

By January 1917 his score had risen to 15 and he received his first command, *Jasta II*. With Boelcke now dead, Richthofen replaced him as Germany's leading ace and fighter commander. A fine marksman and tactician, with well-developed hunting instincts, he was cold-blooded, ruthless and aloof, showing his victims no mercy. To emphasise his special status Richthofen's aircraft were always painted red, a practice followed by his colleagues in *Jasta II*. His new unit, which included some of Germany's finest pilots,

was equipped with powerful Albatros fighters and inflicted heavy casualties on the RFC, particularly during 'Bloody April' 1917. By this time his score had risen to 52.

In June he was promoted to the command of *Jagdgeschwader 1*, a new fighter wing consisting of four *Jastas*, which the RFC had dubbed the 'flying circus'. The unit was soon equipped with the **Fokker DrI** triplane, a highly manoeuvrable fighter ideally suited to Richthofen's aggressive tactics. By the end of 1917 the Red Baron's score had risen to 63. Germany's unchallenged ace had been a national figure for some time but he had long ago exceeded the average life of a fighter pilot on the Western Front. The end came on 21 April 1918, after 17 further victories: he was killed by a single bullet during a dogfight with **Sopwith Camel**s over the Somme.

OR BY GROUND FIRE?

RICKENBACKER, EDWARD, 1890–1973

The highest scoring American ace of the war, Edward Rickenbacker had already made a name for himself in American motor racing before the war. He first went to France as **General Pershing**'s driver, but soon transferred to the aviation section as an engineering instructor. Learning to fly in his own time, it was not until March 1918 that he obtained a transfer to the 94th Aero Squadron, United States Army Air Service, whose 'Hat in the Ring' insignia was soon to become famous. Rickenbacker was present on 19 March when an American patrol, led by **Raoul Lufbery**, the *Escadrille Lafayette* ace, flew over German lines for the first time.

On 29 March Rickenbacker scored his first hit and within a month had gained four more, thereby qualifying as an ace after a very brief period of service. Ill health then grounded him until September, but shortly after his return he was appointed commander of the 94th. Flying the **Spad XIII**, Captain Rickenbacker's score rapidly increased until the Armistice; at that time he had 26 confirmed victories (of which four were balloons), although his actual score was probably much higher. He became a successful businessman after the war but it was not until 1930 that he was awarded the Congressional Medal of Honour in recognition of his wartime services.

RIFLE PATTERN 1914

This **Mauser**-based rifle, which appeared in prototype form in 1913, had been produced by the War Office in response to criticisms of the Short Magazine **Lee Enfield** (SMLE). The project was, however, temporarily shelved as several design problems with the 7mm-calibre weapon were in evidence. Relatively easy to mass produce, the weapon, known as the

Pattern 1914, was ordered in large quantities from American manufacturers such as Remington and Winchester on the outbreak of war. It was rechambered for the standard 7.7mm (.303-inch) cartridge and had a five-round magazine concealed in the body.

In service the Pattern 1914 rifle (officially known as Rifle No 3, Mk I) proved to be unpopular: it was long, difficult to handle and badly balanced. It was, however, reliable and extremely accurate over long distances, being widely used as a sniper's rifle. Although it was gradually replaced in British service by the SMLE, the Pattern 1914 was not finally withdrawn until 1919. It was still in production when the Americans entered the war and their forces adopted it as an interim weapon until supplies of standard arms increased. Rechambered for the American 7.62mm rimless cartridge, it was known as the M1917 or Enfield.

RIGA OFFENSIVE, 1 September 1917

After the failure of the **Kerensky offensive** in July 1917 and the rapid disintegration of the Russian army, **Ludendorff** proposed an attack which he hoped might produce the fall of the Provisional Government and bring the war on the Eastern Front to an end. The Russian bridgehead over the Dvina at Riga – long viewed by the Germans as a threat to their security – was the target. It was thought to be sufficiently close to Petrograd (300 miles) for a German victory to have an immediate impact.

The operation was launched by the Eighth Army (**Hutier**) on 1 September, using the shock tactics that its commander had developed and which were to be widely applied in the future. Riga was threatened with a holding attack, which began without warning with a massive artillery bombardment – Colonel Georg von Bruchmüller, an outstanding artilleryman, having assembled some 575 guns on a 4,600-yard front. The main assault was carried out by three divisions that crossed the river to the south by rafts and pontoon bridges.

Very little resistance was encountered as the Russian Twelfth Army (**Kornilov**), which was unwilling to fight, had already begun to evacuate the bridgehead and completed it during the first night. Only about 9,000 Russian prisoners were taken and neither side sustained many casualties. It was notable as the last battle fought between the armies of the Russian and German governments during the First World War.

German plans to march on Petrograd soon proved to be unnecessary. The defeated Russian commander, Kornilov, led an unsuccessful coup a few days after the Battle of Riga, which had the effect of further weakening the Kerensky regime and bringing the Bolshevik revolution a step nearer. Following **Lenin**'s seizure of power an armistice agreement with Germany was signed (15 December 1917), bringing hostilities on the Eastern Front to an end.

ROBERTSON, GENERAL SIR WILLIAM, 1860–1933

Chief of the Imperial General Staff from 1915 until his abrupt departure early in 1918, 'Wully' Robertson was the first ranker to gain admission to the Staff College. His great energy and ability helped him to rise rapidly up the military hierarchy: in August 1914, he was quartermaster-general of the BEF, under **Sir John French**. He succeeded in keeping the army properly supplied as it retreated through France. Although relations between the two men were never good, Robertson remained in France until December 1915, having succeeded **Murray** as BEF chief of staff earlier in the same year.

On leaving his post at the front, Robertson was appointed Chief of the Imperial General Staff and the Cabinet's principal adviser on strategy, **Kitchener**'s powers at the War Office having been trimmed. His views on grand strategy remained unchanged throughout the war: he was a diehard 'Westerner' who believed in concentrating all available effort in France, the only front where the decisive breakthrough could be made. It was not surprising, therefore, that the final decision to end the **Gallipoli expedition** was made soon after his arrival.

Conflicts over strategy led to Robertson's eventual dismissal as chief of staff

He worked closely and harmoniously with **General Haig**, commander of BEF, 1915–18, and consistently supported his costly war of attrition. Not surprisingly, he came into conflict with **Lloyd George** who, as Secretary of State for War and Prime Minister, was a leading 'Easterner'. Apart from disagreements over strategy, there were major conflicts over command arrangements during the **Nivelle offensive** and about the establishment of a Supreme War Council, which tended to weaken Robertson's powers. The failure of the **Third Battle of Ypres** completed the prime minister's disillusionment with Robertson and in February 1918 he was replaced by the more pliant **Sir Henry Wilson**.

Robertson was then given an appointment at home – the Eastern Command: 'the advocate of the Western Front received the command in eastern England – a good joke at his expense, possibly deliberate.' In June 1918, he became Commander-in-Chief, Home Forces, and from April 1919 he headed the British army of occupation on the Rhine.

ROCQUES, GENERAL PIERRE, 1856–1920

Long periods of colonial military service did little to prepare General Rocques for the mass combat of the Western Front, where his leadership of the French First Army was undistinguished and lacked initiative. The army's need for a pliant figure in the War Ministry explains his unexpected appointment as Minister of War in March 1916, although in practice he was often to come into conflict with **Joffre**. His relations with **Briand**, the premier, also proved to be difficult and in December 1916 he was dismissed by him, following disagreements about the future of **General Sarrail**, the French commander in the Balkans.

ROLLS ROYCE ARMOURED CAR

The Rolls Royce, the most successful armoured car of the First World War, began life in an improvised form as part of **Commander Samson**'s force at Dunkirk. Locally modified touring vehicles, which were in action from the beginning of the conflict, were soon superseded by the first Admiralty pattern Rolls Royce armoured car, which arrived in Belgium from September 1914 onwards. It was based on the 40/50hp Silver Cloud chassis (with double rear wheels) and provided only limited protection for the occupants. The engine was fully enclosed but the crew's compartment was open, with no more than the sides and rear being fully armoured. Above the driver's head, which was afforded some cover, was a single machine-gun.

The need for an improved hull was quickly recognised and a fully enclosed turreted armoured car was soon being designed to Admiralty specifications.

A 1914 pattern Rolls Royce armoured car at Arras, 1917

The Silver Cloud chassis, which had acquired an excellent reputation for reliability and ruggedness, again formed the basis of the new vehicle, although its suspension and axle casings were strengthened. Its 7,428cc engine produced a maximum speed of 50m.p.h. and a range of 150 miles. The hull was constructed of 9mm armour and the engine, driver's cab and fighting compartment were completely covered; there was an open platform at the rear. A revolving turret was located above the crew's accommodation; in it was mounted a **Vickers machine-gun** operated by two of the three men normally present.

By the beginning of 1915, sufficient turreted Rolls Royces had been built to equip six RNAS squadrons and they became the most extensively used armoured car of the war, serving in widely scattered locations – France, Egypt, Gallipoli, South West Africa and East Africa. With the disbandment of the RNAS Armoured Car Division later in 1915, some were transferred to the army and remained on active service, primarily in Egypt, Palestine and Russia. Operated successfully even under very unfavourable conditions, the Rolls Royce became the standard British type: those surviving at the end of the war continued in military service throughout the inter-war years, being supplemented in 1920 by a new version that was very similar to the original.

ROMANI, BATTLE OF, 3 August 1916

Early in 1916, the British began moving slowly from the Suez Canal towards Palestine, with the aim of establishing a new defensive line 100 miles away. **Sir Archibald Murray** had some excellent Australian and New Zealand troops under his command but progress was slow because a pipeline and road and rail link were being constructed as they moved forward.

At the same time the Turkish army was planning a second thrust towards the canal, with the objective of establishing a position within artillery range that could disrupt shipping. Under the command of the able German soldier, Baron Kress von Kressenstein, 15,000 Turkish troops, supported by German artillery and machine-gun units, attacked Romani, a railhead 20 miles east of the canal. Initially, they were opposed by a similar number of British troops but reinforcements soon arrived. With the British left on the shore and unapproachable, the Turks predictably tried to turn the British right. Progress through the soft sand was difficult and slow, with Murray's preparations – a false flank and a mounted reserve – enabling a successful attack to be made on the Turkish flank. However, the principal counter-attack was delayed and the main Turkish force managed to withdraw. Retreating with great skill, Kress fought successful

rearguard actions for two days after the main engagement. Altogether the Turks had lost some 6,000 men, with British casualties amounting to 1,100.

Murray's forces resumed their slow march eastwards reaching their objective, El Arish, near the Palestine border, in December 1916. With its fall on 21 December, the whole of the Sinai Peninsula had been cleared.

RONARC'H, VICE-ADMIRAL PIERRE, 1865–1940

Rear Admiral Ronarc'h's first wartime experiences were land based, leading a force of marines during the **Battle of the Marne** and on the northern sector of the Western Front. Returning to the sea as vice-admiral in 1915, he was placed in charge of French anti-submarine warfare before assuming responsibi-

lity for the defence of the French side of the English Channel. From May 1916 until the end of the war, he successfully carried out the unexciting but critically important task of ensuring the safe passage of millions of combat troops between England and France.

ROSS RIFLE

The standard service rifle of the Canadian army during the First World War, the Ross proved to be a failure in the appalling conditions of the Western Front. It first appeared in 1896 and was adopted by the Canadian army in 1905, the principal service model being the Mark 3, one of a large number of variants produced. It had a straight pull bolt system, inspired in part by the Austrian **Mannlicher** rifle, and a box magazine containing five .303 cartridges. A high degree of accuracy was an essential feature of the design and was reflected in the rifle's long barrel and the attention given to sighting systems. Over 342,000 Ross rifles were produced for the Canadian army and some 67,000 were delivered to Britain.

The British army, which had only accepted the weapon under wartime pressures, had previously rejected it as unsuitable for active service. Its concerns were soon justified when the design of the bolt action was found to have serious weaknesses: dirt caused the bolt to jam, it was difficult to maintain, and sometimes it would spring back and hit the soldier firing it. As a result it was replaced in 1915 with the British Rifle No 3 Mk 1 (also known as **Rifle Pattern 1914**), being used for training purposes for some time. However, with its great accuracy it was more successfully employed as a sniper's rifle (fitted with a telescopic sight) and was retained on the Western Front after the standard model had been withdrawn.

ROSTISLAV

The world's first oil-fired battleship, *Rostislav* served with the Russian Black Sea Fleet during the First

World War. Launched in 1896, she had a displacement of 8,880 tons and four 10-inch and eight 6-inch guns (with the secondary armament, unusually, being in four twin turrets). Used extensively in operations against Turkey, she was operated by the independent Ukraine from April 1918 and then passed through German and British hands. *Rostislav* was scuttled in 1920 to prevent her seizure by the Bolsheviks.

ROYAL AIR FORCE

In August 1914, the Royal Flying Corps, recently divorced from the **Royal Naval Air Service**, had 179 aircraft under its control, although only a small proportion was operational. Every serviceable machine was sent across the Channel and, by mid-August, the RFC was operating with the British Expeditionary Force in northern France. Under the control of army headquarters, it was commanded by Brigadier-General Sir David Henderson. Its main initial task was to provide the army with information about enemy dispositions during the war of movement. Despite earlier scepticism about the value of aerial reconnaissance, the BEF regarded the RFC's reports as being of 'incalculable value in the conduct of operations'. The RFC was also heavily involved in artillery spotting from the beginning, its effectiveness increasing as radio sets were introduced. Towards the end of the year, wings, consisting of between two to four squadrons, were created and allocated to corps headquarters. This reflected the fact that much of its work was carried out for the latter rather than GHQ.

The RFC's inadequate organisation was stretched to the limit during this initial period. **Trenchard**, who was to command the RFC in France from August 1915, remained at home with the task of creating a wartime air force and the infrastructure associated with it. One of his functions was the formation of new squadrons for service in France: there were just eight there early in 1915, but plans were agreed for 100 squadrons, reflecting the need to support the growing British military presence at the front. Actual expansion was in fact slow – reaching only 12 squadrons by October 1915 – and reflected in part the inadequate supply of aircraft. The early RFC machines – the **BE2** being a major type – were not equipped to respond to the air fighting that was developing over the Western Front. The **Fokker** monoplane reigned supreme in 1915–16 until the Allies introduced new machines that checked and eventually overcame this early fighter. To meet these new challenges, RFC expansion continued during 1916, reaching 27 squadrons by July.

At the beginning of the year the RFC had been reorganised: each army was provided with two wings, organised into brigades. The Corps Wing had responsibility for short-range reconnaissance, artillery spotting, and ground attack duties, while the Army Wing was concerned with longer-range strategic tasks. In accordance with Trenchard's strategic ideas, the latter took the air war into Germany, seeking out the enemy over his own territory regardless of cost. During the **Battle of the Somme**, Trenchard achieved British mastery in the air by these methods.

At this time the Germans had some 50 fewer machines than the RFC, but the new D-type aircraft, which first appeared in October 1916, soon changed the balance again. The British response was to expand the RFC further. Early in 1917, an increase of 106 active and 97 reserve squadrons was authorised. However, numbers alone were not sufficient to cope with these machines and 'Bloody April' 1917 was its worst period of the war. For example, an RFC pilot could not expect to survive for more than three months in the first part of 1917. With the appearance of the **Sopwith Camel** and other new machines by the end of September the RFC was once more in the ascendant.

Apart from operations in overseas theatres, another major RFC responsibility was home defence, which had been taken over from the RNAS in February 1916. The first daylight raid on London, 13 June 1917, produced something of a crisis, and led to immediate plans to expand the RFC to 200 squadrons as well as to an inquiry into air defence and air organisation. The Smuts Committee recommended the creation of an independent air force which should incorporate the RFC and RNAS under a unified command. This was accepted and the Royal Air Force was created on 1 April 1918.

One of the major new tasks of the RAF was the development of strategic bombing against Germany, following the successful experiments that predated the formation of the new air force. As a result, the Independent Force, under Trenchard, was created and more than 500 raids were carried out. During the last months of the war the RAF achieved complete command of the air over France as the final land battles were fought. Aircraft production in Britain expanded rapidly during 1918 and by the Armistice the RAF had a strength of 22,677 machines organised in 188 squadrons.

ROYAL AIRCRAFT FACTORY BE2, BE2a & BE2b

This two-seat tractor biplane was a standard type in service with the RFC on the outbreak of war. A development of the BE1 prototype, the BE2, which first appeared in 1912, was designed by Geoffrey de Havilland and built initially by the Royal Aircraft Factory. With equal span, unstaggered wings, it was normally powered by a 70hp V8 Renault engine, which gave a maximum speed of 70m.p.h. and a ceiling of 10,000 feet. The aircraft was unarmed and the pilot was positioned in the rear cockpit. Most of the early production aircraft, which served in the RFC (Military Wing) from 1913, were in fact BE2as, which had a new tailplane and unequal span wings. The BE2b, which was developed in 1914, incorporated several further changes, including modified flying controls and increased protection for the front cockpit.

During the first year of the war, the BE2 series served mainly on the Western Front as a reconnaissance aircraft and occasional bomber. The first British aircraft to land in France after the outbreak of war was in fact a BE2a, flown by Lieutenant H. D. Harvey-Kelly, No 2 Squadron. When they went across the Channel to war on 13 August 1914, No 2 Squadron took 12 BE2as and No 4 eleven. The aircraft also served with five other RFC squadrons and with Dunkirk Squadron, RNAS.

Like the earliest production machines, the wartime BE2as and BE2bs had no fixed armament, but the observer was often armed with a rifle, and a small bomb load of 100lb (or its equivalent) could be carried. A raid near Courtrai station on 26 April 1915, when a 100lb bomb was dropped from a BE2b, resulted in Lieutenant W. B. Rhodes Moorhouse being awarded the first Victoria Cross for an aerial action.

By the autumn of 1915 few examples of this early BE series remained in France. It had given good, reliable service but with no defensive armament it had rapidly become obsolete. At least 164 machines were produced by as many as nine different manufacturers.

ROYAL AIRCRAFT FACTORY BE2c & BE2d

The BE2c, which first appeared in June 1914, was a development of the Factory's BE2b. This two-seat, two-bay biplane had ailerons added to all four wing sections, increased rudder area, wings with greater stagger and a new undercarriage. These modifications had the effect of increasing the BE2c's stability – officially regarded as a critical feature at a time when reconnaissance rather than combat was envisaged as aviation's main role in war. The BE2c was normally powered by the 90hp RAF 1a engine, which gave a top speed of 72m.p.h. at 6,500 feet, and could climb to 10,000 feet in 20 minutes. The observer occupied the front seat and at first his only armament was a single rifle or carbine. It could normally accommodate ten 20lb or two 112lb bombs although this load might be slightly increased when the aircraft was flown solo.

The BE2c was used on the Western Front for reconnaissance, artillery spotting and bombing duties, from January 1915. Its main weaknesses – a lack of manoeuvrability (because of its inherent stability), low maximum speed and poor rate of climb – soon became apparent with the development of large scale air fighting. Although defensive armament was greatly enhanced with the addition of one or more **Lewis machine-guns**, the BE2c developed a reputation as 'Fokker fodder', with losses rapidly mounting towards the end of 1915. The RFC did, however, retain it for operational use on the Western Front until 1917, although other aircraft were used in the offensive against the **Fokker monoplanes**.

The BE2c rendered more valuable service on home defence duties where its stability was a positive advantage in attacking **Zeppelins** on night raids over Britain. Flown solo from the rear cockpit, with an upward firing Lewis machine-gun, BE2cs destroyed five German airships. The aircraft was also operated by the RNAS from several coastal air stations, where it was widely used on anti-submarine patrols. The BE2c saw active service on almost all the other war fronts and both the RFC and RNAS employed it extensively as a trainer until the Armistice.

The operational effectiveness of the design was enhanced in a modified version, the BE2d, which appeared in the spring of 1916. The observer was now placed in the rear cockpit with a Lewis machine-gun and a large fuel tank was fitted under the upper wing, increasing the aircraft's range significantly. About 1,300 examples of both types were manufactured for the British air service.

ROYAL AIRCRAFT FACTORY BE2e

The BE2e, the final variant of this Royal Aircraft Factory series, served with the RFC from July 1916 until the Armistice. A development of the **BE2c**, this tractor biplane had lighter controls, single bay wings of unequal span, and a larger fin. Unlike the **BE2d**, the observer occupied the front cockpit, reducing the effectiveness of the single **Lewis machine-gun**; bombs were also carried when the aircraft was flown solo. It was normally powered by the same 90hp RAF 1a engine as its predecessor, but was marginally faster, with a maximum speed of 90mph at sea level. This may explain why it was manufactured in larger numbers than any other BE-type, with about 1,800 examples being produced. However, its rate of climb, taking almost 24 minutes to reach 6,500 feet, was less good than the BE2c.

The BE2e served with 18 RFC squadrons on the Western Front, although it was no more popular with aircrews than the earlier BE2 models. In its reconnaissance, artillery spotting and bombing duties, the BE2e, with its unsatisfactory defensive armament was no match for the new **Albatros** and **Halberstadt** fighters, and it suffered badly during 'Bloody April' 1917. It was also used widely on other fronts (including the Middle East, Africa and Aden) and for home defence, when some were equipped with Le Prieur rockets. In the latter stages of the war, large numbers were used by the RFC and RNAS as training aircraft.

ROYAL AIRCRAFT FACTORY BE8

This two-seat tractor biplane, which first appeared late in 1912, served with the RFC from April 1914. Known as the 'Bloater', the BE8 was powered by an 80hp Gnome rotary engine, which gave a maximum speed of 70m.p.h. at sea level. It had twin-bay equal- span wings, which had marked stagger, with lateral control being provided by wing warping. It could carry a 100lb bomb or an observer armed with a rifle.

The BE8 served with five RFC squadrons on the Western Front from August 1914 as a reconnaissance aircraft and light bomber. However, it had little operational use and following its withdrawal from active service in 1915, it was employed as a trainer. A revised version, the BE8a, with shorter span wings, a modified tailplane and an improved fuselage, was used by the RFC as a trainer from 1916, but never reached the front. About 60 of both types were produced in total.

ROYAL AIRCRAFT FACTORY BE12

An improvised fighter and light bomber, the BE12 was produced in response to the serious threat posed by the **Fokker** monoplanes in 1915. It was based closely on the Factory's **BE2c**, which had already proved to be of limited value against the new German fighters. The main differences were a more powerful engine (150hp RAF 4), a single seat, and modified tail surfaces. Maximum speed was 99m.p.h. at 3,100 feet, with a ceiling of 12,500 feet. Standard armament consisted of a synchronised **Vickers machine-gun**, but other arrangements, including upward-firing guns, were not uncommon.

The BE12 arrived on the Western Front in June 1915 but only three months later **Major-General Trenchard** concluded that the 'BE12 aeroplane is not a fighting machine in any way'. The main problems were its slow speed and inherent stability. However, in the absence of a suitable alternative, the BE12 was retained in France for use as a light bomber, carrying a load of up to 336lb. It also served in the Middle East and on home defence duties, where a lack of manoeuvrability was less important and it achieved more. Two variants – the BE12a and BE12d – with minor design changes also appeared and total production for the whole series was about 600 aircraft.

ROYAL AIRCRAFT FACTORY FE2b & FE2d

Following the standard pusher layout, with a wooden nacelle and tailbooms, the FE2b and its successor were two-seater biplanes which served with the RFC in a variety of roles for nearly three years. The FE2b, which first appeared in the autumn of 1915, originated with the FE2 of 1912 and the subsequent FE2a (1914–15), which was produced in very small numbers. Designed as a fighter-reconnaissance aircraft from the beginning, it had a .303-inch **Lewis machine-gun** mounted on a bracket in front of the observer's forward cockpit. A second Lewis, which fired rearwards over the top wing was also operated by the observer in a standing position, at some risk to his own personal safety. At first the FE2b was fitted with a 120hp Beardmore engine, but was later replaced by a 160hp version; it was capable of 92m.p.h. at ground level.

The 'Fee', as it was known, arrived in France early in 1916. Although it was relatively slow and difficult to manoeuvre, it was able to match the enemy's **Fokker** monoplanes. On one notable occasion, in June 1916, a FE2b crew shot down **Max Immelmann**, the famous Fokker ace. At about the same time an improved 'Fee' – the FE2d – appeared at the front; it had a 250hp Rolls Royce engine, which improved the maximum speed slightly.

It soon became clear, however, that both versions were outclassed by the new German fighters arriving at the front, and from the autumn of 1916 they were gradually converted to a night bombing role. Sixteen squadrons and one flight were so equipped, with some 'Fees' remaining in France until the end of the war. It was able to carry up to three 112lb bombs or their equivalent.

The FE2b were also employed on home defence duties, sometimes in single seat form, but its poor rate of climb (almost 10 minutes to 3,000 feet) and low ceiling (9,000 feet) were severe limitations. A few examples were also modified for ground strafing. Total production of the FE2b amounted to 1,484, compared with 385 for the improved version.

ROYAL AIRCRAFT FACTORY FE8

The last pusher-type fighter in RFC service, the FE8 arrived on the Western Front in August 1916. It had not been possible to adopt a tractor arrangement when design work started in the spring of 1915 because no synchronising mechanism was then available. There were long delays before the production model appeared, with the result that it was already obsolete when operational use began. The FE8 retained the standard nacelle and tailbooms configuration of the pusher aircraft, with two bay wings of narrow chord and conventional construction. Powered by a single 100hp Gnome Monosoupape rotary engine, which proved to be unreliable in service, it had a maximum speed of no more than 94m.p.h. It was armed with a single .303 **Lewis machine-gun** mounted in front of the cockpit.

On arriving in France, the FE8, which served with four RFC squadrons, was quickly engaged in an unequal struggle with the much faster and more modern **Albatros** fighters, which were armed with twin machine-guns. Dramatic confirmation of the aircraft's weaknesses came on 9 March 1917, when a formation of Albatros DIIIs, led by **von Richthofen**, engaged nine FE8s, destroying four and damaging a similar number. FE8s remaining in service were withdrawn over the next few months as replacements (in the form of **Nieuport 17**s and **Airco DH5**s) became available. A total of 300 examples were produced by two contractors.

ROYAL AIRCRAFT FACTORY RE5

This two-seat reconnaissance aircraft and bomber served with the RFC from 1914. A pre-war design, it was the first of the series of Reconnaissance Experimental (RE) aircraft, designed by the Royal Aircraft Factory, to enter production. The RE5 was a large two-bay biplane which had equal span wings, a deep fuselage, and a tail unit with a triangular fin. Both wings had ailerons for lateral control. It was powered by a 120hp Austro-Daimler engine, which gave a maximum speed of 78m.p.h. at sea level. Like the earlier RE prototypes, the RE5 was highly stable in the air, a characteristic that proved to be a serious operational weakness. The observer, who was unarmed except for a rifle, sat in the spacious front

cockpit. A small bomb load of 60lb could also be carried.

The RE5 served with five RFC squadrons on the Western Front, but only 24 were produced. One of the few notable episodes associated with the aircraft was the award of a Victoria Cross to Captain J. A. Liddell, No 7 Squadron, who brought back his badly damaged RE5 after being severely injured in a battle near Bruges in July 1915.

Most RE5s had been withdrawn from active service by the end of 1915 as their weaknesses became increasingly evident; some were more successfully used for experimental purposes.

ROYAL AIRCRAFT FACTORY RE7

The RE7 was a two-seat day bomber designed by the Royal Aircraft Factory specifically to carry its new 336lb bomb (or its equivalent). A development of the **RE5**, it appeared in 1915 with enlarged two-bay

wings and a rectangular tailplane of increased dimensions. The standard power plant was the 150hp RAF 4a, although some earlier models were fitted with alternative engines because of supply difficulties. The

Factory engine was notoriously unreliable and was underpowered for an aircraft of this size: maximum speed at sea level was only 85m.p.h. and a climb to 10,000 feet took over half an hour. Defensive armament was also inadequate: a single **Lewis machine-gun**, secured by various improvised mountings, was operated by the observer in the front cockpit, which had a restricted field of fire.

The RE7 served on the Western Front from the end of 1915 for a very limited period, with no more than 224 machines being delivered to the RFC. Only one unit serving in France – No 21 Squadron – was solely equipped with this aircraft, the remaining RE7s being allocated to individual squadrons in small numbers. At first it was used on reconnaissance and escort duties, but without great success because of its performance limitations. It achieved better results as a bomber, striking behind enemy lines from the **Battle of the Somme** onwards. Within a few months, however, the RE7 was being gradually withdrawn in favour of another machine from the same manufacturer, the superior **Royal Aircraft Factory BE12**. The RFC retained it in service as a training aircraft and for target towing purposes.

ROYAL AIRCRAFT FACTORY RE8

Produced as a more heavily armed replacement for the ageing **Royal Aircraft Factory BE2** series, the RE8 two-seater biplane was an artillery spotter, reconnaissance and bomber aircraft which entered service late in 1916. Widely known as the 'Harry Tate' (after a famous music hall entertainer of the day), it was unattractive in appearance and proved to have serious operational weaknesses. The RE8 had unstaggered single-bay wings, a fuselage angled upwards towards the tail and a very small fin. Powered by a 150hp RAF 4a engine, which was unreliable at first, it had a maximum speed of no more than 98m.p.h. at 6,500 feet. Armament consisted of a single forward-firing **Vickers machine-gun** and one or two Lewis guns in the rear cockpit; up to 260lb of bombs could also be carried.

The 'Harry Tate', a standard RFC/RAF reconnaissance and light bomber aircraft

Design problems emerged almost as soon as the RE8 arrived in France. Apart from teething troubles with the power plant, the RE8 had a pronounced tendency to spin, although the problem was soon solved by adding a large lower fin. It also had weak upper wing extensions and manoeuvrability was poor because it was excessively stable. The aircraft also often caught fire when making a crash landing because of the close proximity of the engine and the fuel tank. As a result of these difficulties No 52 Squadron – the first RFC squadron to be fully equipped with RE8s – exchanged them for the BE2s of No 34 Squadron early in 1917. However, modifica-tions were made and eventually the RE8 served with 19 RFC squadrons and almost 4,100 machines were built.

The RE8 was, in fact, the most widely used British two-seater on the Western Front and made a major contribution to photo-reconnaissance, ground attack and artillery observation in the last 18 months of the war. The underlying weaknesses of the design did, however, remain and its vulnerability to enemy attack meant that it had a high casualty rate. It also served in Italy, Palestine and Mesopotamia, and some were operated by the Belgian Aviation Militaire.

ROYAL AIRCRAFT FACTORY SE5 & SE5a

One of Britain's most successful First World War fighters, the SE5 single-seater was designed by the Royal Aircraft Factory around the new 150hp His-pano-Suiza engine in the summer of 1916. A single-bay biplane, it had a wooden box girder fuselage and a tailplane that could be adjusted in flight. A **Vickers machine-gun**, mounted on the port side of the fuselage, was synchronised to fire through the air-screw. There was also a **Lewis gun**, mounted on the upper wing, which proved to be very difficult to reload in flight, and some machines carried four 25lb Cooper bombs under the fuselage.

After the Sopwith Camel, the strong and manoeuvrable SE5 was Britain's finest fighter aircraft

The SE5 arrived in France in April 1917 with No 56 Squadron RFC, but a modified version, the SE5a, with significantly improved performance, soon appeared. Powered by the 200hp Hispano-Suiza, it had a modified nose and different exhaust pipes. The larger power plant caused considerable problems, both in terms of reliability and availability in sufficient numbers, and eventually it was replaced by the 200hp Wolseley W.4a Viper engine.

As a result, it was not until early in 1918 that the SE5a appeared at the front in large numbers, but by the Armistice some 2,700 SE5/SE5as had been delivered to the RAF. The SE5a was regarded as an excellent fighting machine by most British pilots: it was fast (maximum speed 126m.p.h.), easy to fly, performed well at combat height and was a stable but manoeuvrable gun platform. It was also soundly constructed, although some early examples suffered structural failure. Several British aces, including **Mannock**, **Bishop**, Beauchamp-Proctor and **McCudden**, flew the type with considerable success, and, in partnership with the **Sopwith Camel**, it restored Allied air superiority on the Western Front in 1917–18. It was retained in front line use until the end of the war although it quickly disappeared from the peacetime RAF.

ROYAL NAVAL AIR SERVICE

Naval aviation in Britain dates back to 1908, when the Royal Navy became involved in the development of rigid airships. Experiments with heavier-than-air machines followed and in 1912 the Royal Flying Corps, with separate naval and military wings, was created. With a proper organisational basis for the first time, British naval aviation began to develop more rapidly and by the summer of 1914 it had 31 seaplanes, seven airships, and 40 land planes, including **Farmans**, **BE2s**, and **Sopwiths**. Its progress was

Campania, a converted seaplane carrier, was fitted with a 120-foot flight deck in 1915

acknowledged in July 1914 when it was reconstituted as an independent force – the Royal Naval Air Service – under the Admiralty.

At the beginning of the war it was primarily concerned with patrolling the North Sea, but its duties were soon expanded. The Eastchurch Wing (**Samson**) was sent to Ostend at the end of August, with the aim of establishing control over a wide area of Belgium and Northern France and preventing airship raids on Britain. It was this group that made the first British raid on German territory, when the Zeppelin sheds at Düsseldorf were attacked on 22 September 1914. The RNAS was in fact the true pioneer of strategic bombing and the techniques associated with it; it also promoted the development of specialist bomber aircraft. Its achievements included the first ever night bombing raid in December 1914 and the work of No 3 Wing, based at Luxeuil, which operated against armaments factories in Germany in 1916–17, using the **Sopwith 1½-Strutter**. Bombing operations, as well as reconnaissance, also formed part of its work in the **Dardanelles**.

One of the principal responsibilities of the RNAS squadrons at home was the air defence of Great Britain, a task which the RFC was unable to take over until March 1916. Anti-submarine and anti-Zeppelin patrols over home waters were another major func-tion mainly carried out by aircraft operating from coastal air stations. These operations were expanded as U-boat activity increased and long-range flying boats – the **Curtiss** and **Felixstowe** types – became available.

During the second half of the war the North Sea was patrolled systematically using the spider's web search pattern, which enabled a check to be kept on an area of 4,000 square miles. In 1917, for example, there were 175 sightings of enemy submarines and 107 attacks. The RNAS was also engaged in some notable dogfights with enemy seaplanes over the North Sea.

Naval aircraft operated from ships as well as from coastal air stations, but on a much smaller scale. The **aircraft carrier**, equipped with special decks, appeared in 1917–18, but had very limited operational use during the First World War. Taking-off platforms were fitted to some warships or towed by them, and in the closing stages of the war more than 100 aircraft were being carried by the **Grand Fleet**.

The separate existence of the RNAS came to an end in April 1918, when the two air services were brought together once more as the **Royal Air Force**. With 2,900 aircraft, 103 airships, 126 air stations, and 55,000 officers and men, British naval aviation early in 1918 bore little resemblance to the embryonic force with which the country had entered the war.

ROYAL NAVY

The largest navy in the world in 1914, the Royal Navy had, under **Lord Fisher**'s direction, maintained its superiority over its German rival during the pre-war arms race. The introduction of the 'all-big gun' battleship – the revolutionary **Dreadnought** – in 1906 had, however, made it more difficult for Britain to maintain this lead. The new warship had rendered all existing battleships obsolete. As a result, the famous 'Two Power' standard, by which the Royal Navy was numerically equal to any two foreign navies, could no longer be preserved.

On the outbreak of war, the British had 29 dreadnoughts compared to Germany's 13, as well as another 17 under construction. Germany had seven in the pipeline. The Royal Navy's superiority in pre-dreadnoughts, which still had an important wartime role, was even more marked: 40 compared to Germany's 22. Britain's other major contribution to warship design was the battlecruiser, where speed and firepower were given priority over armament. Here, too, Britain led Germany by eight ships to five. This design was a major influence on other British warships of the period and, as a result, armour protection was often less than adequate. There were also weaknesses in gunnery and in tactics, where there was little innovation.

In August 1914, the **Grand Fleet**, the navy's principal battle fleet, consisted of four battle squadrons, a battlecruiser squadron, two cruiser squadrons, and a light cruiser squadron. A new Channel Fleet, consisting of four squadrons of pre-dreadnoughts, including some brought from the reserves, was also formed. It provided protection for the troop transports that ferried nine million soldiers across the Channel without a single loss.

From its bases at **Scapa Flow** and Rosyth, the Grand Fleet, under **Jellicoe**'s command, operated a policy of containing the German **High Seas Fleet** in the North Sea by means of a distant blockade. A close blockade of the German coast was ruled out because it would have resulted in unacceptable losses from German U-boats and mines. Each navy had to try to bring the other to action, but the expected decisive fleet action in the North Sea did not materialise: caution on both sides in the use of their forces led to long periods of inactivity. Inconclusive engagements at **Heligoland Bight** and the **Dogger Bank** were followed by the **Battle of Jutland** (1916), the only occasion when the main battle fleets fought each other. Although the Royal Navy was unable to achieve anything more than a draw at Jutland, the Germans realised that the High Seas Fleet would never be able to defeat its stronger opponent. They were now even more unwilling to risk their battle fleet, which remained in port for most of the rest of the war.

Under its new commander, **Beatty**, the Grand Fleet was reorganised after Jutland: improved protection to magazines, new shells and new methods of coordinated fire control were provided as the lessons of the battle were absorbed.

A more serious threat replaced the High Seas Fleet in British home waters as the Germans turned to the U-boat for salvation. Unrestricted submarine warfare caused heavy Allied losses in the first part of 1917 but the Royal Navy's response was slow and inadequate. It was not until political pressure overcame naval conservatism that the **convoy system** – the single most important measure in defeating the U-boat – was introduced in May 1917.

Containing the German fleet in the North Sea represented only a part of the Royal Navy's wartime role across the globe. The threat posed by German cruisers soon disappeared as they were sunk or captured in the first few months of the war. The **Battle of the Falkland Islands** (December 1914) was a notable British victory, wiping out a serious threat to Allied shipping. With Britain quickly establishing domination of the seas, German merchant ships were forced to seek refuge in neutral ports contributing eventually to severe shortages in supplies of food and raw materials.

The Navy's activities in the Mediterranean were less successful. The failure to intercept the *Goeben* and *Breslau* at the beginning of the war had far-reaching political consequences. The naval assault on the **Dardanelles** was badly planned, led to the loss of two pre-dreadnoughts, and failed to secure its objectives. These shortcomings do not, however, affect the navy's achievement in ensuring that the Allies never lost control of the seas during the war, although they came close to it in 1917. The Royal Navy sustained heavy losses in capital ships but its operational effectiveness was little affected.

RUMANIA, INVASION OF, 1916–17

After two years' political debate, Rumania belatedly joined the war on the Allied side on 27 August 1916. Motivated by the prospect of territorial gains – she had reached a specific agreement with the **Entente Powers** – the early success of the **Brusilov offensive** had encouraged her to take action. The day after her declaration of war the Rumanian First, Second and Fourth Armies moved northwards on a 200-mile front into the Hungarian province of Transylvania – one of her principal territorial objectives. To the south, the Rumanian Third Army was to defend the line of the Danube against an expected attack from Bulgaria. The Central Powers had in fact already worked out a plan of action, which involved the invasion of Rumania from the north (under **Falkenhayn**) and from the south (under **Mackensen**).

Field Marshal von Mackensen moved first, crossing into the Dobrudja on 2 September with a mixed force of Bulgars, Germans and Turks. Pressing forwards between the Danube and the Black Sea, the enemy captured Tatrakan, a fortress on the Danube, on 6 September. In spite of Russian assistance, the Rumanians were forced to retreat and by 23 October, Constanza, the country's only Black Sea port, had been taken, ending any hope of direct Allied assistance. Part of Mackensen's force moved towards the mouth of the Danube while the rest were sent westwards in preparation for an attack on Bucharest.

Rumanian reinforcements had already been dispatched to the Dobrudja from the Transylvania front, where the advance still continued. They had moved over 40 miles against the Austrian First Army (**Arz von Straussenburg**) in 14 days, but were soon to be checked. Opposing the Rumanian army, to the left, was the German Ninth Army, commanded by the former German chief of staff, General von Falkenhayn, who started to counter-attack on 18 September. He won a decisive victory at Hermannstadt (27–29 September), forcing back the Rumanian First and Second Armies into the mountains. To the left the Austrian First Army drove back the Rumanian Fourth Army into the Carpathians.

Early in November, after he had been reinforced, Falkenhayn made a passage through the Transylvanian Alps, and soon all the Rumanian defensive positions had been abandoned. He then pushed on into the Rumanian plain, gradually wheeling to the left, and was joined by the five German divisions, under Mackensen, which had been transferred from the

Dobrudja. They crossed the Danube above Sistova on 23 November, and moved eastwards in line with their countrymen.

The Rumanians now made a final effort to avert disaster. **General Averescu**, the Rumanian commander-in-chief, struck at the gap between the German armies, but he was decisively defeated at the Arges River, west of Bucharest, on 1–4 December. The capital fell two days later without further fighting and the Germans soon reached the oilfields to the north. The Rumanians fled north-east pursued by the Germans and with Russian support they made a stand near the Sereth River on 22–30 December. Retreating behind this natural barrier, the Rumanian army, which now amounted to only 150,000 men (compared to 500,000 originally), retained a small foothold in its own country.

The Germans lost some 60,000 men during the campaign, but they had gained substantial supplies of grain and oil, although many installations had already been put out of action by British agents. Rumanian losses – about 400,000 men and three-quarters of their territory – were much heavier. The front saw no more action until the second Brusilov offensive in July 1917; a truce was eventually agreed in December 1917 and a peace treaty was signed on 7 May 1918.

RUMPLER 6B

This single-seat seaplane served with the German navy from July 1916 until the Armistice. It was developed from the two-seater **Rumpler CI** in order to meet the urgent need for fighters to defend the main German seaplane bases; the better-known **Albatros W4** and the **Brandenburg KDW** were also produced for the same reason. Modifications included the creation of a single cockpit, redesigned wings with forward stagger, a large rudder, and twin step floats. The 160hp Mercedes D III engine, which gave a maximum speed of 95m.p.h. at sea level, was retained and standard armament consisted of a single forward-firing Spandau machine-gun.

The 6B-1, as it was designated, operated from the seaplane bases of Ostend and Zeebrugge, and over the Black Sea, where it destroyed several Russian flying boats. The 6B-2, which first appeared in October 1917, was based on the **Rumpler CIV**, but used the same power plant and armament as the earlier version. Although their performance was not as good, 50 Rumpler 6B-2s were built, compared with only 38 6B-1s.

RUMPLER BI

This two-seat, two-bay biplane was a pre-war design widely used for reconnaissance purposes on the Western and Eastern Fronts in the first year of the war. Nearly 200 examples were built by Rumpler and Pfalz for the German air service. Powered by the 100hp Mercedes D I tractor engine, it was unarmed except for the observer's rifle or carbine. When the BI was superseded by armed C-types in 1915, it was retained for some time as a training aircraft.

RUMPLER CI

This armed two-seater biplane, which appeared early in 1915, was one of the first German C-types to be produced and one of the most successful; it was also amongst the longest serving. Powered by the 160hp Mercedes D I engine, which gave a maximum speed of 95m.p.h., it had swept back wings and a triangular tailplane. The observer was equipped with a **Parabellum machine-gun** on a Schneider ring mounting; the pilot, who sat under the top wing, was unarmed at first, but later examples were fitted with a synchronised, forward-firing Spandau machine-gun. Up to 220lb of bombs could also be carried. A later version, the CIa, was identical to the CI except that it was fitted with the 180hp Argus As III engine.

The Rumpler CI/CIa were widely used for reconnaissance and light bombing duties on all fronts, and by October 1916 the number in operational use had reached a peak of 250. When these machines became obsolete on the Western Front they were transferred in significant numbers to the Middle East, where they were intensively used in 1917. After their withdrawal from operational service early in 1918, the CI/CIa were retained by the German air service for training purposes until the end of the war.

RUMPLER CIV & CVII

The Rumpler CIV, a powerful reconnaissance aircraft with a distinctive vertical exhaust, was one of the best German aircraft of its kind

The CIV, one of the best German aircraft of its kind, followed the **CI** as the next Rumpler C-type to be produced in quantity (the CIII having been withdrawn after no more than two months' service).

The new design was based on the powerful 260hp Mercedes D IVa engine, which produced a maximum speed of 106m.p.h. at 1,640 feet. It also had an excellent rate of climb, a ceiling of 21,000 feet, and an endurance of up to four hours. Its elegant appearance was a product of the clean lines of its fuselage, the staggered swept back wings, and the novel dragonfly profile of the lower wings. The tailplane had the distinctive curved wingnut shape associated with Rumpler designs. As in the CI, armament consisted of a forward-firing Spandau machine-gun and a **Parabellum gun** in the rear cockpit for the observer; a bomb load of no more than 220lb could also be carried.

The CIV served widely on the Western Front and also in Italy and Palestine from 1917 until the end of the war. It was employed extensively on long-range reconnaissance missions for which its excellent performance at high altitudes made it well suited.

Superior to most Allied fighters at these levels, it had a reputation of being difficult to shoot down.

First produced towards the end of 1917, the next production machine in the series, the Rumpler CVII, was powered by a high compression 240hp Maybach engine which produced even better results. In other respects, however, the CVII was little different to its predecessor, retaining the wing design that had contributed significantly to its success. In its standard form, this long-range reconnaissance aircraft had the normal C-type armament and a radio. A photo-reconnaissance version, the CVII (Rubild), was fitted with additional specialist cameras, with as much other equipment as possible being removed. As a result this variant had an increased ceiling of 24,000 feet, well above the limit of other aircraft then in service on the Western Front. Even at lower levels, the CVII's opponents had considerable difficulties in engaging it effectively: at 20,000 feet, for example, it was capable of reaching 100m.p.h., a figure only the best Allied fighters could match. Not surprisingly the CVII was retained in service until the end of the war.

RUMPLER CVIII

This two-seat biplane was one of the few aircraft that was designed during the war specifically for training purposes. Based on the earlier C-types, with the same method of construction, it had wings similar to those of the **CI**, while the tail surfaces were identical to those of the **CIV** and **CVII**. With the 180hp Argus As III engine fitted, it gave good performance not far removed from that of the two-seaters in operational use in the last year of the war. This realism was enhanced by the two machine-guns (a Spandau and a **Parabellum**) that were fitted.

The CVIII entered service late in 1917 with the flying training units of the German air service; training focused on the role of the observer and the aircraft was fully equipped for instruction in reconnaissance, gunnery, photography and the use of radio. By improving the training of two-seater crews it was hoped that their effectiveness in the planned offensives on the Western Front in the spring of 1918 would be increased.

RUPPRECHT, CROWN PRINCE OF BAVARIA, 1869–1955

At the beginning of the war Rupprecht commanded the German Sixth Army, which comprised the three corps of the semi-autonomous Bavarian Army. Positioned in Lorraine, it defeated the French at Morhange (20 August) and advanced through the Vosges. His unwise attempt to seize Nancy was defeated after a costly battle that was only abandoned after the chief of staff intervened. During the Race to the Sea, Rupprecht was appointed to a new Sixth Army in Flanders and he remained on this part of the front, opposite the British, for the remainder of the war. His success as a front line commander led to his promotion to a new Army Group Crown Prince Rupprecht in August 1916.

Noted both for his courage and his pessimism, Rupprecht successfully urged a German withdrawal to the Hindenburg Line early in 1917. As the war of attrition continued and Germany's position weakened, he recognised the need to bring the conflict to a close many months before the high command came to the same conclusion. In fact, during the autumn of 1918, as his armies engaged the Allies by the Scheldt and Lys rivers, Rupprecht still had every expectation that 'the Prussians will fight on to the last Bavarian'.

RUSSIAN AIR SERVICE

At the beginning of the First World War the Russian air service had more military aircraft at its disposal than any of the other combatants. Many of the 263 machines were, however, unfit for active service and the force expanded relatively slowly from a limited base: by February 1917, for example, it had just over 1,000 aircraft. Other problems further reduced its operational impact, including the wide variation in aircraft types, which caused supply problems; insufficient numbers of trained pilots; and the slow growth of specialist groups. It was not until 1916 that squadrons were reorganised into separate reconnaissance, fighter and bomber units, with the result that their impact was increased.

The bomber element, equipped with the outstanding four-engine **Sikorsky Ilya Mourometz** machine rather than the normal French import, was particularly successful. The small 'Squadron of Flying Ships' carried out over 400 raids on the Eastern Front between February 1915 and October 1917, dropping 2,000 bombs and destroying nearly 40 enemy aircraft. In general, however, the impact of the Russian air service on the course of the war on the Eastern Front was negligible. Air operations were limited in scale and encounters with enemy fighters were rare, certainly in the first part of the war. Germany and Austria were able to maintain a dominant position in the face of relative Russian weakness in the air, using no more than a fraction of the resources that were required on the Western Front.

RUSSIAN ARMY

The Russian imperial army of 1914 was a numerically strong conscript force, consisting of eight armies (14 divisions each), which had to defend vast land frontiers. It derived much of its power from the fighting qualities of its soldiers, who were noted for their 'courage, tenacity, ingenuity and self sacrifice'. In other respects, however, it suffered severe weaknesses, including the mediocrity of much of its high command and of many of its senior field commanders. (**Grand Duke Nicholas**, the commander-in-chief, an able and experienced officer, was an exception to the general rule.)

There were severe shortages of weapons and equipment, with insufficient machine-guns and artillery being a major weakness; the Germans had twice as many heavy guns in the field as the Russians. At the end of 1914, only one in ten infantry recruits could be equipped with the standard Russian rifle, the 7.92mm **Mosin-Nagant**. These supply shortcomings were a consequence of Russia's limited industrial base and the fact that national resources had not been properly mobilised for war. She was also isolated from her Allies.

On the outbreak of the First World War, the Russian army was forced to launch immediate offensives against Germany and Austria, well before the slow process of mobilisation had been completed. Six armies were positioned at the Front: two against Germany and four against Austria. Its twin offensives in East Prussia and **Galicia** helped to relieve pressure on the French, but the cost to Russia was high. The **Battle of Tannenberg** (August 1914) was a disastrous defeat from which the army never fully recovered; its partial success in Galicia reflected an even worse performance by the Austrian army. In total, some 1,200,000 Russian troops were killed or wounded in the first five months of the war.

Even heavier manpower losses were sustained in 1915 during **Hindenburg**'s major offensive on the Eastern Front. Decisive defeat was avoided but the poorly equipped Russians were forced to abandon their gains in Galicia as well as Poland, White Russia and the Baltic provinces. In the aftermath of this major setback, **Nicholas II** assumed command of the army, Grand Duke Nicholas being sent to the Caucasus front (where operations had started in November 1914). The supply of weapons and equipment improved during 1916 as war production increased, with the army being better placed to execute the plans that were being developed for a major new attack.

The **Brusilov offensive**, which made considerable gains at Austria's expense, was the most successful Russian operation of the war even though other, less dynamic commanders failed to capitalise on its success. As a diversionary action it helped to relieve enemy pressure at **Verdun** and on the Italian front. However, it had cost a million Russian casualties and may have helped to bring the Revolution nearer, although war weariness and food shortages on the home front were the immediate causes.

Some army units supported the insurgents in March 1917 and the High Command helped to persuade the Tsar to abdicate. During this period, army discipline inevitably suffered and some soldiers drifted away from the front. However, the front was held even though revolutionary agitation continued to weaken the army. A major new offensive was launched by Brusilov in July with some of the units that still remained operational; ending in defeat, it accelerated the disintegration of the Russian military. In the final engagement of the pre-revolutionary army, on 1 September, **Riga** was lost to the Germans. Having failed to defeat the enemy, **Kornilov**, the commander-in-chief, tried to mount a counter-revolution in September, but most of his force quickly deserted him. In fact, when the Bolsheviks seized power in November no troops could be found to rally to the defence of the old order. **Lenin** and **Trotsky** secured an armistice on 15 December 1917 and the remnants of the Russian army finally left the war.

RUSSIAN NAVY

Following Russia's disastrous defeat in the war against Japan in 1904–05, the long process of reconstructing her naval forces began. Major ship-building programmes were authorised, with further funds being committed as international tension increased in the period before the First World War. It was the sixth largest fleet in the world and was divided between the Baltic, Black Sea, White Sea and the Pacific. On the outbreak of war, with the rearmament programmes not due to be completed until 1917, the Russian navy adopted a defensive strategy. The Baltic fleet was to defend Petrograd, the capital, and protect the right flank of the army front. The defence of its Sebastopol base and the laying of mines were the principal tasks of the Black Sea Fleet. Both fleets were of more or less equal strength.

In the face of intensive German submarine activity, the Baltic Fleet acted with great caution: for example, the dreadnoughts were kept in harbour, with convoy duties being carried out by older battleships. However, German offensive plans were similarly curtailed by the minelaying activities of their opponents. One spectacular success of the Baltic Fleet was the recovery of the German navy's secret codebook from the cruiser *Magdeburg*, which was sunk in August 1914. As a result the British Admiralty's intelligence organisation (Room 40) was able to read German codes for the rest of the war, as the enemy was unaware of its loss until the summer of 1918.

The Black Sea Fleet, which was superior to its Turkish opponents, operated more vigorously and only the *Goeben* represented a serious threat to its operations. Even so, no Russian ships were lost in the Black Sea as a result of enemy action. The Black Sea fleet provided escorts for Russian troopships on their way to the Caucasus and attacked Turkish shipping with submarines and mines. The operational effec-

tiveness of the Russian navy was much affected by discontent during the war, and there were mutinies in the Baltic fleet from as early as 1915. In November 1917, the support of the sailors of the Baltic Fleet helped to ensure the success of the Bolshevik Revolution. Much of the Baltic Fleet was seized by the Germans in 1918, with the remainder being damaged during the civil war.

RUSSIAN REVOLUTION

Rebel soldiers and students fire on police in Petrograd during the March Revolution

The failure of government to respond effectively to the pressures and consequences of the First World War was one of the main causes of the Russian Revolution. Severe food shortages in the winter of 1916–17 led to riots in Petrograd (St Petersburg) in March 1917, the country already feeling demoralised

by military setbacks, enormous casualties and political instability. The Tsar's authority disintegrated as troops from the Petrograd garrison joined the rioters instead of suppressing them and on 11 March a Provisional Government, under Prince Lvov, was appointed by the Duma. The Army High Command, which believed that only a democratic republic could now win the war, helped to persuade **Nicholas II** to abdicate.

The liberal Provisional Government soon encountered severe internal difficulties in pursuing the war against Germany. The powerful Soviet of Workers', Peasants' and Soldiers' Deputies constantly challenged its authority, particularly after **Lenin**'s return from exile in Zurich in April 1917. **Ludendorff**, who was anxious to undermine the Russian war effort whenever the opportunity arose, had permitted the Bolshevik leader to travel home through Germany, in a sealed train provided by the General Staff. The Bolsheviks, who believed that the war had already been lost, aimed to transform society by world revolution: 'if revolutionary Russia withdrew from the war, the people in every other belligerent country would follow her example. There would be universal revolution, followed by universal peace.' Their propaganda activities were certain to undermine further the discipline of the Russian army, which had already suffered from mass desertions from the front.

In these difficult circumstances, **Kerensky**, the Minister of War, gathered together the remaining operational forces for a final offensive, which began on 1 July and ended in complete failure. A Bolshevik uprising on 16–17 July collapsed and there was a clampdown on its leaders, but this proved to be only a temporary setback. The Provisional Government, with Kerensky now prime minister, was further weakened by the loss of **Riga** on 1 September and by an abortive coup. This attempted counter-revolution, organised by **Kornilov**, the commander-in-chief, had been defeated by Bolshevik Red Guards, who proved to be the only effective force left in Petrograd.

Lenin's seizure of power on 7 November was triggered by Kerensky's heavy-handed attempts to suppress the opposition press. In a virtually bloodless coup, the Bolsheviks occupied the key buildings in Petrograd, including the Winter Palace, where members of the government were arrested. Without military or popular support, the Provisional Government was powerless to act and it fell.

The implementation of Lenin's reform programme depended on ending Russian involvement in the war and he soon made a call for a general armistice and a peace based on idealistic principles. It was rejected by the Allies and Russia began separate discussions with the Germans. A ceasefire was arranged by the Soviet Government on 15 December and was followed by negotiations which led to the imposed **Treaty of Brest-Litovsk** on 3 March 1918.

The Bolshevik revolution was opposed by a variety of internal and external forces and soon led to a costly civil war that lasted until 1921. The Allies, who were dismayed at Russia's withdrawal from the war and its conversion to socialism, sent troops to Russia in 1918, but their intervention was ultimately ineffective in the face of a united Red Army under **Trotsky**'s command.

RUZSKI, GENERAL NIKOLAI, 1854–1918

Russian general who commanded the Third Army during the **Galician campaign** (August–September 1914), where he was noted for his excessive caution. This did not, however, prevent his appointment as commander of the North-Western front in September 1914, where the tactical victory at **Lodz** (November) was his greatest achievement. For a few months before the March Revolution Ruzski commanded the Northern Front, but the Provisional Government had reservations about his political reliability and he was removed.

SABLATNIG FLOATPLANES

During the war Sablatnig Flugzeugbau produced eight different floatplane types, of which only three went into production for the German navy. The SF2 was a two-seat, twin-float biplane, with a long, elegant fuselage and a 160hp Mercedes D III engine. No more than 26 examples were built in the year to May 1917, and they were allocated to seaplane bases in small numbers, mainly for training purposes. A high performance version of the SF2, designated SF5, appeared in 1917 and was powered by a 150hp Benz Bz III engine. It had a maximum speed of 85m.p.h. at sea level and an endurance of $4\frac{1}{2}$ hours.

Some were used for training purposes, but the remainder, equipped with an observer's gun and a radio, operated from air stations on the North Sea and Baltic as reconnaissance and coastal patrol aircraft. The SF5 was not used very intensively because of its poor performance and vulnerability to enemy fighters, particularly the Russian **Nieuports**. A total of 91 SFs were built by Sablatnig and two sub-contractors. The final design to go into production was the SF8, which appeared in the spring of 1918. This unarmed trainer was powered by the same engine as the SF5, but was produced in smaller quantities.

SAINT CHAMOND TANK

The development of the Saint Chamond, which was similar in many respects to the **Schneider heavy tank**, was authorised largely because of bureaucratic rivalries – normal departmental channels within the French government had been by-passed when the earlier machine was approved. Both tanks were based on the American-produced Holt chassis, although the

tracks of the Saint Chamond were significantly longer; it had a larger box-type hull with a pitched top and a considerable amount of overhang at the front and rear. Operated by a crew of nine, the tank was powered by a 90hp four-cylinder Panhard engine, which was used to drive an unusual electric transmission. It had a maximum speed of about 5m.p.h.

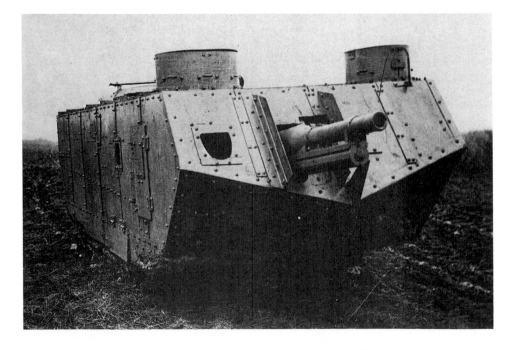

This French heavy tank, the Saint Chamond, suffered from several design weaknesses

and a range of 37 miles. The arrangement of the armament was an improvement on the Schneider and consisted of four **Hotchkiss machine-guns** and a 75mm gun (Model 1897) mounted in the centre at the front.

The Saint Chamond proved to be no more successful than its rival and when it was used in action for the first time, on 5 May 1917, several faults were uncovered. These included the hull, which was much too long for the chassis, resulting in poor climbing ability and instability in certain conditions; the unreliable electric transmission; and the tracks, which were too narrow. Although the tank was modified as a result, there was little enthusiasm for it and official attention focused on the combat potential of the **Renault light tank**. However, the original order of 400 machines was completed in full early in 1918 and they were used intensively during the final months of the war, although relatively few were still operational at the time of the Armistice. Like the Schneider, some Saint Chamonds were produced as unarmed supply carriers.

St-ETIENNE MACHINE-GUN

Named after the government arsenal where it was designed and produced, the St-Etienne machine-gun or Mitrailleuse Modèle 1907 was the second attempt to improve upon the **Hotchkiss gun** (Model 1897) used by the French army. The first was the unsuccessful Puteaux machine-gun, which appeared in 1905 and was withdrawn two years later. Like the Hotchkiss, it was a gas-operated weapon but the piston movement was reversed, making the mechanism more complicated. Overheating problems meant that the return spring could not be enclosed, with the result that dirt could easily enter the system causing the mechanism to jam. The St-Etienne also used one of the least satisfactory features of the Hotchkiss – the metal strip ammunition feed holding 24 or 30 rounds. The gun had a cyclic rate of fire of 400–500 rounds per minute and weighed about 56lb. With insufficient automatic weapons available in 1914, the French army was compelled to use this unreliable weapon. Modifications were made in 1916, but the basic faults remained and the St-Etienne was withdrawn from front line service soon afterwards.

St-ETIENNE SEMI-AUTOMATIC RIFLE

Officially designated the RSC Modèle 1917 (after the designers Ribeyrolle, Sutter and Chauchat), this semi-automatic, gas-operated rifle had a clip-feed magazine holding five rounds. It was selected from several competing designs mainly because it was the only one that used the standard 8mm Lebel cartridge, which was then being produced in vast quantities. The weapon was far from ideal as it was large (52 inches) and heavy (11lb 9oz) and used a non-standard cartridge clip. The St-Etienne rifle was used by the French army in limited numbers in the last year of the war; an improved version – the Modèle 1918 – did not materialise until after the Armistice.

St GERMAIN, TREATY OF, 10 September 1919

The post-First World War treaty between the Allies and the new republic of Austria was signed on 10 September 1919. It deprived Austria of a significant part of the German-speaking population and reduced her overall population from nearly thirty million people to eight million. Italy, Czechoslovakia, Yugoslavia and Rumania were the beneficiaries of this radical redistribution of territory. The Treaty of St Germain also confirmed Austria's total loss of all the non-German areas of the former Habsburg empire. Her army was to be limited to only 30,000 men, reparations were to be paid, and *Anschluss* (union with Germany) was forbidden.

St JEAN de MAURIENNE, TREATY of, April 1917

Italy was promised a segment of Turkish territory around Smyrna as a result of this secret agreement signed by Britain, France, Russia and Italy in April 1917. Never implemented because of Greek counter-claims and the growth of Turkish nationalism, the Treaty of St Jean de Maurienne compensated Italy for the fact that the other Allied powers had already decided on the distribution of the remainder of the Ottoman empire after Turkey's defeat.

St MIHIEL OFFENSIVE, 12–16 September 1918

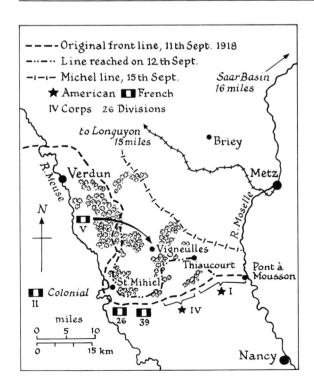

After a long debate **Marshal Foch** reluctantly agreed, in August 1918, to accede to **Pershing's** demand for a separate American front on which a US army, under its own independent command, would operate. As a result, the American First Army took over the St Mihiel sector on 30 August; it was to reduce the salient, which reached as far as the River Meuse south-east of Verdun. It had been held by the Germans since 1914 and had represented a continuing threat to Allied forces in Champagne. **Ludendorff** was well aware of the danger which the arrival of the Americans represented and on 8 September the evacuation of the salient began. However, he did not act quickly enough and the American assault began on 12 September before the evacuation could be completed.

The First Army (16 divisions) struck in dense fog on both sides of the salient: the main assault was alloted to I and IV Corps on the south face, while V Corps was positioned on the east. The French II Colonial Corps, which was located at the apex of the salient, was engaged in a holding action. Strong air cover was provided by a mixed Allied force of 600 planes, under the command of **Colonel William Mitchell**. French tanks and artillery also provided support. The Allies were opposed by nine German divisions, with five nearby in reserve. The action was a total success and by the end of the first day the converging attacks had met at Hattonchâtel; by 16 September, the Germans had been swept from the entire salient.

Pershing suffered about 7,000 casualties in what had been the largest American battle since the Civil War; as many as 15,000 German prisoners were taken and 250 guns captured. The American action, which demonstrated the quality of the US army, could have been continued but Pershing had already agreed immediately to transfer his army westwards to the Argonne Forest. American and French forces would launch a major offensive there on 26 September.

St VINCENT

Very similar to the **Bellerophons**, this class of three dreadnought battleships was completed in 1910. *St Vincent* did in fact differ from its predecessors in several minor ways: it was slightly longer, used 50-calibre rather than 45-calibre 12-inch guns and had modified armour. *St Vincent*, *Collingwood* and *Van-*guard joined the British **Grand Fleet** in August 1914 and they all saw action at the **Battle of Jutland**. *Vanguard* was destroyed by an explosion of faulty ammunition at **Scapa Flow** on 9 July 1917, with the loss of 804 men, but her sister ships continued to serve until the end of the war.

SALANDRA, ANTONIO, 1853–1931

Prime Minister of Italy when war broke out, Antonio Salandra secured popular support for his policy of refusing to meet the country's treaty obligations to Germany and Austro-Hungary. He was, however, aware of the risks of staying neutral for too long and entered negotiations with both sides. Only the **Entente Powers** were willing to recognise various Italian territorial claims (**Treaty of London**, April 1915) and Salandra's government decided to join them. However, before war was declared the parlia-mentary majority in favour of Italy's continued neutrality forced Salandra's resignation. Popular support ensured his return and hostilities against Austria began on 24 May. Instead of the short campaign that had been expected, however, there was a long stalemate on the **Isonzo** front, punctuated by a series of costly but unproductive offensives. This war of attrition undermined support for Salandra's government and it finally collapsed in June 1916.

SALMSON 2

The Salmson 2 was a well-constructed two-seat, two-bay reconnaissance biplane, which appeared in prototype form early in 1917. The main activity of the Société des Moteurs Salmson had been the production of aeroplane engines, including the water-cooled 260hp Canton-Unné radial engine, which powered the Salmson 2. This gave a maximum speed of 115m.p.h. at 6,500 feet and the ability to reach 5,000m in just under 28 minutes. It had equal span wings and a rounded fuselage, but no fixed fin or tailplane. The aircraft's only significant defect was in the crew's seating arrangements: the observer was positioned behind the wings and communication with the pilot was very difficult. Given the military designation 2A.2, it was well armed, with twin ring-mounted **Lewis machine-guns** for the observer and a forward-firing synchronised **Vickers**.

The 2A.2 entered service with the French Aviation Militaire early in 1918 and with American forces from the following April. It became the standard American reconnaissance aircraft and 705 machines were deli-vered to the AEF. Some of these were fitted with a **Marlin** machine-gun in place of the standard Vickers. It was used primarily on the Western Front in a reconnaissance role, but was also employed for ground attack and bombing purposes; it also served with two French squadrons in Italy. A total of 3,200 Salmson 2A.2s had been built by the end of the war.

Salmson 2: a standard French reconnaissance aircraft of conventional design

SALONIKA FRONT,
3 October 1915–30 September 1918

In September 1915, Bulgarian mobilisation alerted the Allies to enemy plans for another assault on Serbia. In response, two divisions, one British and one French, under the command of **General Sarrail**, were sent to the Greek port of Salonika as Serbia itself had no direct access to the sea. They arrived in neutral Greece on 5 October, shortly after **Venizelos**, the pro-Allied prime minister had resigned; his agreement to their movement through the country was cancelled but no resistance was offered when they landed. It marked the beginning of the Allies' long and costly involvement in Greece. Its value was intensively debated by 'Easterners' and 'Westerners', the latter arguing that it was a wasteful diversion of manpower from the critical theatre – the Western Front.

On 12 October, Sarrail pushed north up the Vardar valley and, supported by two more French divisions, entered Serbia. At Krivolak, 40 miles from the border, their progress was blocked by a much larger Bulgarian force, ending the possibility of linking up with the retreating Serbian army. The British division (Mahon) went no further than the frontier because the British government, which was unenthusiastic about the whole operation, wanted to minimise its involvement. The French retreated with considerable skill as the Bulgarians pushed forward, but fortunately they did not, for political reasons, cross the border into Greece.

Allied forces remained in Salonika, partly because of the dangers of re-embarkation, although conditions on shore were far from ideal. The troops, who were enclosed in a massive barbed-wire 'cage', lived in an unhealthy climate where malaria and other diseases were rife. In response to **Joffre**'s pressure for diversionary action to relieve the pressure on **Verdun**, Britain relaxed her opposition to a further offensive on the Salonika front. Sarrail's force had been increased to five British and six French divisions, and was reinforced by Serbian troops arriving from Corfu. The first stage of the operation, which began in April 1916, was to move out of the barbed-wire enclosure and up to the frontier. This was accomplished successfully, with the Greek army offering no opposition. In response, the Bulgarians, with the endorsement of the Greek government, occupied Fort Rupel in the Struma Valley, seven miles inside the Greek border.

Plans were now made for an Allied offensive, probably beginning on 20 August; the main attack would be made due north, to the west of the Vardar. After breaking through they would turn east, clear the Vardar Valley and assist Rumania if she entered the war.

However, the Bulgarians, who were fully aware of the Allied plans, attacked first, on 17 August, at both ends of the Allied line. The Bulgarian east wing advanced south from Rupel and the French were forced to retreat, but the British, now under the command of **General Milne**, held them at the Struma. To the west, the Serbs were thrown back and the front was not stabilised until 27 August.

The long postponed Allied attack, which was now a counter-offensive, eventually took place on 12 September. The two Serbian armies and three and a half French divisions made slow progress, having advanced some 30 miles through mountainous country in little over a month. Monastir was taken on 19 November, but in view of the desperate situation in Rumania, Sarrail was ordered to halt and consolidate his line. The British had extended their line westwards in support of the French, but their position on the Struma seemed uncertain for a period as the Greeks surrendered Kavalla to the Bulgarians. This episode increased pressure, internal and external, on the Greek monarchy to abandon its sympathetic attitude towards the Central Powers. By the beginning of 1917 there were 600,000 troops at Salonika, but only 100,000 were effective.

The Allied governments eventually authorised a further offensive in Macedonia. The main attack

Sandbag billets being constructed by British troops near Salonika in 1917

began on 9 May 1917 with the Serbians and French planning to break through and swing west across the Vardar; the British were to make a strong diversionary attack west of Lake Doiran. The offensive quickly failed and was abandoned on 23 May, with the loss of 14,000 men. The front now remained quiet until late in 1918, although there were important political developments during the previous year. **King Constantine** abdicated and Greece entered the war on the Allied side; Sarrail was replaced by **Guillaumat** towards the end of the year. However, the new Allied commander was himself recalled to the Western Front in July 1918 and it was his successor, **Franchet d'Espérey**, who led the final campaign on this front.

The enemy line had been weakened by the withdrawal of German troops and resistance quickly collapsed when the main Allied assault was launched on 15 September 1918. Some 200,000 Serb, French, British and Greek troops opposed a larger Bulgarian force. The First and Second Serbian Armies were positioned at the centre of the front, with the French on their left and right. Within two days the Serbs had pushed the demoralised enemy back some 20 miles, forcing a general retreat across the whole front. By 25 September, they had reached the Vardar and split the Bulgarian front. To the east, the British diversionary attack had reached Strumitza by 26 September, while the French took Skoplje on the 29th. As the Allied advance continued, the Bulgarians, by now facing total defeat, were compelled to sign an Armistice on 29 September. The Allies occupied the country as a base for future operations against Hungary and Turkey. By the end of the war, Franchet d'Espérey had completed the liberation of the Balkans and had planned to march on Budapest, following his crossing of the Danube on 10 November.

British casualties in this final operation were relatively small, but the Allies presence at Salonika had been costly: 481,000 casualties from malaria as against 18,000 from combat.

SAML 1 & 2

The SAML 2: an Italian development of the German Aviatik two-seater reconnaissance aircraft

The SAML 1 was a two-seat, three-bay reconnaissance biplane that served with the Italian air force from early in 1917 until the end of the war. It was essentially an enlarged version of the German **Aviatik BI**, which was built under licence in Italy in large numbers. The SAML 1 was well constructed and had the same good flying qualities as the Aviatik. Powered by a 260hp Fiat A-12 engine, it was armed with a single tripod mounted **Fiat-Revelli** machine-gun in the rear cockpit; a quantity of bombs could also be carried. The SAML 2 had two bay wings, a reduced span, and a second machine-gun mounted over the top wing. The same engine as the SAML 1 was used at first, but later examples were powered by the 700hp A-12bis engine.

The two variants served with 16 reconnaissance squadrons in Italy, Albania and Macedonia, and were used for artillery spotting and light bombing as well as for visual and photographic reconnaissance. A total of 657 machines had been produced by the end of the war.

SAMSON, COMMANDER CHARLES, 1883–1931

Charles Samson was one of Britain's pioneering naval aviators, learning to fly in 1911 and commanding the first naval air unit at Eastchurch. Involved in many of the navy's peacetime experiments with aircraft, he had a varied and eventful war.

On the outbreak of hostilities Samson and his No 1 Wing, RNAS, were ordered to Belgium, where they were to operate against **Zeppelin** airship bases. His ageing collection of pre-war aircraft generally proved to be of limited value even for reconnaissance purposes, although some bombing raids were carried out on targets in Germany. Eager to make a contribution to the quickly developing war of movement, he supplemented them with an improvised force of armoured cars. Equipped with **Maxim machine-guns** and rifles, these locally converted vehicles were used to attack German troops as they advanced towards the Channel, with notable engagements at Douai, Cassel and elsewhere.

Recalled early in 1915 and decorated for his services, Samson served in the **Gallipoli** campaign, commanding No 3 Squadron (as the Eastchurch unit was now designated). Used extensively for reconnaissance and bombing duties, it was soon expanded as No 3 Wing RNAS. In 1916–17, he commanded a seaplane carrier, Ben-my-Chree, in the eastern Mediterranean, operating against Turkish troops and communications in Palestine.

Samson's distinguished wartime service was concluded with the command of Great Yarmouth Air Station. Here he made the first experimental flight of a **Sopwith Camel** from a lighter (which in operational use would be towed by a warship). This arrangement was intended to meet the growing menace of German seaplane fighters in the last few months of the war.

SAMSONOV, GENERAL ALEXANDER, 1859–1914

A veteran of the Russo-Japanese War and a former military governor of Turkestan, Samsonov commanded the Russian Second Army, which advanced into East Prussia from the south on 20 August 1914. Driven westwards by **Zhilinsky**, commander of the North-West Front, Samsonov's doubts about the wisdom of an offensive were soon justified: separated from **Rennenkampf**'s First Army by the Masurian

Lakes he was surrounded and spectacularly defeated by the Russians at **Tannenberg** on 29 August. Some 100,000 Russian prisoners were taken. Samsonov disappeared into the woods and killed himself. Limited co-operation between Samsonov and Rennenkampf, who were enemies, lack of secrecy, and incompetent leadership all contributed to Samsonov's defeat.

SARIKAMISH, BATTLE OF,
29 December 1914–3 January 1915

Turkey entered the war on 29 October 1914 when, without warning, her fleet bombarded the Russian Black Sea ports of Odessa, Sevastopol and Theodosia. Russia responded by declaring war on Turkey on 2 November. Fighting between the two countries on land was largely confined to the remote and moun-

tainous Caucasus front, where the oil fields of Baku were the ultimate Turkish objective, although **Enver Pasha**, the war minister, had more grandiose political aims. Operations began in November when a Turkish army of 95,000 men, under Enver's command, sought to draw the Russian army from its bases at Kars and

Ardahan and then defeat it. In response the Russians (60,000 strong) left Kars and advanced into Asia Minor, the two armies meeting at Sarikamish on 29 December. It was half-way between Kars and Erzerum, some 30 miles inside the Turkish border.

After five days' fighting in very poor weather conditions, General Vorontsov defeated the larger Turkish force, which lost as many as 30,000 men. In the disorder that followed the battle, the Turks lost more men and their army had been reduced to 18,000 by the time it had reached Erzerum two weeks later.

The outcome of the campaign was a disaster for Turkey and had long-term effects on her fighting strength. There was relatively little action on this front for the remainder of 1915, as both sides were preoccupied elsewhere. However, under General **Yudenich**, the able new commander, the Russians advanced as far as Lake Van (19 May) on the Turkish right flank, but were forced to retreat a few weeks later. Further operations were suspended while the Russians made preparations for a large-scale offensive to be launched early in 1916.

SARRAIL, GENERAL MAURICE, 1856–1929

'The only Republican general', Sarrail was a radical and an anti-cleric in a conservative and Catholic French army. His rapid promotion was assisted by his political connections, and by 1911 he was a *général de division*. On 2 September 1914, he replaced Ruffey as commander of the Third Army, then positioned near Verdun. Sarrail fortunately disregarded his orders to abandon the fortress and withdraw to the south. His bold initiative worked: after intense fighting the Third Army held on to its positions and the progress of the German Fifth Army (**Crown Prince Wilhelm**) was brought to a halt, thereby disrupting an important element of the **Schlieffen Plan**.

After the **Battle of the Marne**, this part of the battle front – the Argonne sector – stabilised quickly and was relatively quiet until the enemy's surprise offensive in June 1915. The Third Army suffered heavy losses and **Joffre**, whose relationship with Sarrail was poor, used the opportunity to remove him. However, political support for Sarrail in the National Assembly meant that he soon had to be found an alternative post: he was appointed to the command of an army of the east that had not yet been constituted and it was not until September that

agreement was reached to send an Allied force to **Salonika**.

Sarrail arrived there on 12 October and his troops immediately advanced up the Vadar Valley in support of Serbia. They were too late to provide any assistance and retreated before they could be engaged by the Bulgarians.

Apart from the capture of Monastir in November 1916 and an abortive attack in April 1917, no serious offensive was launched during Sarrail's period in command. Inaction was partly explained by Allied disagreements over strategy but also by the personality of the unpopular Sarrail, whose 'conduct and reputation for political intrigues failed to command the confidence and co-operation essential if such a mixed force was to "pull its weight"'. The operations that Sarrail did mount added little to his military reputation and he was only retained in command for so long because of his political links. However, in December 1917, soon after **Clemenceau** became prime minister, he was replaced by **General Guillaumat**, whose military reputation was high. Sarrail's wartime career was at an end.

SAVA ARMOURED CAR

The large pre-war SAVA touring car provided the basis for an armoured vehicle, which the Antwerp-based motor manufacturer designed and produced with great speed in the autumn of 1914. To the SAVA chassis was added a fully enclosed armoured body, with a dome-shaped turret towards the rear; armament consisted of a single 8mm **Hotchkiss machine-gun**. An important feature of this advanced design was the sloping of the frontal armour to give maximum protection to the driver. With the arrival of trench warfare, this armoured car disappeared permanently from the battlefield.

SAZONOV, SERGEI, 1860–1927

Russian Minister of Foreign Affairs, 1910–16, Sazonov was an effective diplomat who enjoyed the confidence of his Allied counterparts during the war. He recognised that the regime could not survive without moderate internal reform and the satisfaction of national aspirations in Poland and elsewhere in Eastern Europe. Inevitably he became the target of reactionary elements and was dismissed in July 1916. Boris Stürmer, the premier, took over responsibility for foreign affairs.

SCAPA FLOW

A large area of enclosed water in the Orkney Islands, ringed by off-lying islands, that was an important anchorage for the British **Grand Fleet** during the First World War. It was from here, for example, that the fleet left for **Jutland** in May 1916. At the end of the war, the German **High Seas Fleet**, under the command of **Admiral von Reuter**, was interned at Scapa Flow, pending the negotiation of a peace treaty. When their surrender to the British was imminent, the ships were successfully scuttled on 21 June 1919: they were later raised and towed away for breaking.

SCHARNHORST

Scharnhorst: *the German armoured cruiser that was sunk off the Falkland Islands*

Like other German armoured cruisers of the period, *Scharnhorst* and her sister ship *Gneisenau* were designed to act as station ships in the colonies rather than serve with the battle fleet. Both ships were in fact stationed at Tsingtao, the German colony in China, on the outbreak of war and were the principal units of **Vice-Admiral Graf von Spee**'s East Asiatic Squadron. Launched in 1906, these ships had a displacement of over 12,000 tons and 17cm main armament.

In August 1914 Spee's force started to move across the Pacific with the objective of disrupting British trade with South America before aiming for home.

Scharnhorst and *Gneisenau* and three light cruisers successfully engaged a force under the command of **Rear-Admiral Sir Christopher Cradock** at the **Battle of Coronel**, off the coast of Chile, on 1 November 1914. The British suffered a severe defeat but an opportunity for revenge soon appeared. Spee's force entered the South Atlantic but soon encountered **Sturdee**'s much more powerful force in the Falkland Islands on 8 December. *Scharnhorst* and *Gneisenau* were both sunk after a long pursuit, both ships maintaining a determined resistance to the end. *Scharnhorst* went down taking everyone with her, but some 200 of *Gneisenau*'s crew were saved.

SCHEER, ADMIRAL RHEINHARD, 1863–1928

Commander-in-chief of the German **High Seas Fleet** at the **Battle of Jutland**, Scheer was commander of the Second Battle Squadron, which was composed of pre-dreadnought battleships, at the beginning of the war. He moved to the command of the Third Battle Squadron, which operated dreadnoughts, in December 1914. When Hugo von Pohl left the command of the High Seas Fleet because of ill health, Scheer was appointed in his place in January 1916, raising his flag in the battleship *Friedrich der Grosse*. He proved to be an outstanding fleet commander who recognised the importance of training and of maintaining the morale of his officers and men.

Scheer planned a more active role for the main battle fleet than his predecessor, with the aim of turning the balance of naval power in Germany's favour. U-boats would play an important part in this new offensive, but the surface fleet, assisted by aerial reconnaissance, would seek out isolated British squadrons.

At the Battle of Jutland, he used **Hipper**'s scouting force to entice **Beatty**'s Battle Cruiser Force from its base and to draw it towards the main German fleet. During the course of the battle Scheer was himself lured towards the **Grand Fleet**, unaware of its presence in the area. Cut off by **Jellicoe** from his base, Scheer tried twice to find a way round the British fleet. Pounded by superior forces, he extricated himself with great skill on both occasions, with the help of poor visibility. During the night he finally

managed to pass behind the Grand Fleet, which was hindered by a lack of information, and made for home. On his return to Germany Scheer presented Jutland as a victory but although his forces had sunk more ships than the Grand Fleet, his claim was an empty one. Strategically Jutland was a British victory, Germany being compelled to return to unrestricted submarine warfare to strike effectively at England.

Apart from an abortive sortie in April 1918, Scheer kept the High Seas Fleet in port for the rest of the war. In August 1918 the German naval high command was reorganised and Scheer was appointed to the head of a new Supreme Command. Beyond authorising a massive new submarine construction programme, there was little he could do to influence the course of events; he retired from the navy soon after the Armistice.

SCHLANKE EMMA

Produced in three versions, the Austrian-made Skoda 30.5cm howitzer was used by the German army in the reduction of the Belgian forts in August 1914. Transported in three sections, it was assembled on site and weighed 28 tons. A rotating base supported the massive barrel, which was mounted in a cradle; the latter was moved by means of an elevating wheel and rack. The gun, which could fire a 633lb shell over a distance of almost seven miles, was nicknamed 'Slender Emma' in reply to '**Big Bertha**', a German heavy howitzer also present in Belgium. The Austrian howitzers returned home as the first phase of the war came to an end.

SCHLIEFFEN PLAN

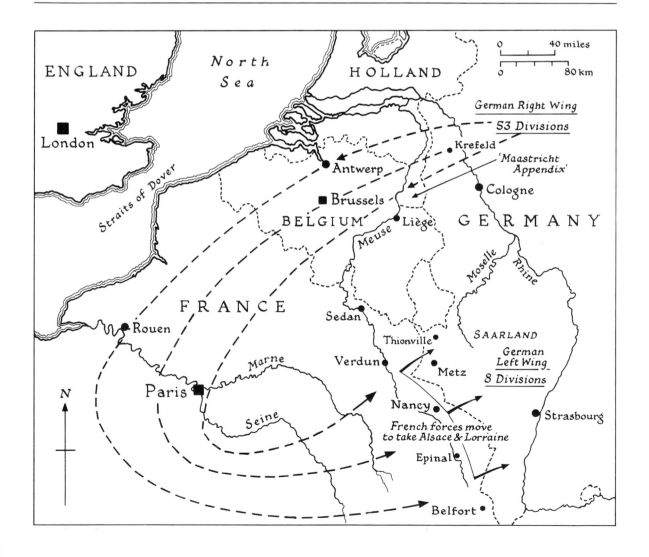

The German operational plan for use in the event of a war with France was prepared by General Count Alfred von Schlieffen shortly before his retirement as Chief of the General Staff in December 1905. It was based on the assumption that a future war would be fought simultaneously against France and Russia, with Britain supporting them. The Russians, who were expected to mobilise slowly, were to be held in the east with a relatively small force. The German army would be concentrated against France, its more dangerous opponent, which was likely to attack as soon as war was declared.

Schlieffen predicted that the French would move between Belfort and Sedan, with the aim of securing the return of Alsace-Lorraine; they would be given additional encouragement to attack there by a German feint and withdrawal. Accepting that the fortified frontier facing Germany could not be crossed, Schlieffen's main thrust against France, which would be made in overwhelming strength, would push through the Netherlands and Belgium in a wide arc, the right wing passing to the west of Paris. The principal French force between Verdun and Belfort would be attacked in the rear from the left and right and would face almost certain destruction.

Following success in the west, the Germans would be quickly transported by rail to the Eastern Front, where a short campaign was expected to end in a Russian defeat.

Although it may be questioned whether the plan, even in its original form, would have ensured a German victory, modifications by Schlieffen's successor, **Moltke**, certainly severely weakened it. His unwillingness to violate Dutch territory meant that the German army would be forced through the narrow strip of Belgian territory by Liège. More important, the proportion of troops allocated to the critical right wing was reduced by a third (to about 1,500,000 men). The released men were redirected to the Eastern Front and to Alsace-Lorraine because Moltke was unwilling to contemplate the surrender of any German territory, even for tactical reasons. The modified Schlieffen Plan determined the course of the war during its first few weeks although it was subject to further major revision: **Kluck**'s First Army on the extreme right had moved eastwards by the end of August, crossing to the left of Paris. The **Battle of the Marne** marked the final failure of the Schlieffen Plan, which had been undermined by ill-judged modifications and faulty implementation in the field.

SCHNEIDER TANK

French efforts to produce an armoured vehicle to overcome the machine-gun and barbed wire of the Western Front began in 1914 but, like the British, did not produce results for almost two years. The first French tank, the Char Schneider, which appeared in prototype form early in 1916, was based on experiments with the American-produced Holt tractor. A long armoured box, with a pointed front and wire-cutting device, was mounted on a chassis and suspension that were based on the Holt design, but with extended tracks. It was powered by a 70hp four-cylinder engine, which gave a maximum speed of 5m.p.h. and a range of 30 miles; the unsatisfactory clutch-and-brake method was used to steer it. Armament consisted of two **Hotchkiss machine-guns** (one on each side) and a 75mm short calibre gun mounted in a sponson on the right hand-side towards the front. The crew of six, commanded by an officer who drove the vehicle, entered by means of double doors at the rear of the hull.

The Schneider: another unsuccessful French heavy tank

Production problems and training needs delayed the tank's appearance on the battlefield. Not until 16 April 1917, when a force of 132 Schneiders was assembled, were they first used in action, months after the independently produced British tank had fought its first engagement. They were not a success: over half the force was immobilised, indicating serious design faults – vulnerability of the internal petrol tanks to a bullet in the side, poor ventilation and limited crew visibility – that were never fully rectified.

Extra armour was added to some Schneiders, but production was slowed down and the original order of 400 tanks was not completed until August 1918. As a result, a quantity of Mark V tanks was acquired from the British to supplement the inadequate supply of heavy tanks available to the French army. The Schneider company also produced an unarmed version for use as a supply tank and a less successful self-propelled gun – a 220mm Longue Modèle 1917 – mounted on the Holt track unit.

SCHÜTTE-LANZ AIRSHIP

Used on a limited scale by the German army and navy during the First World War, the Schütte-Lanz airship was the **Zeppelin**'s only serious competitor. It was a rigid airship, with a framework of laminated plywood, and incorporated a number of novel features: a streamlined hull; a separate, enclosed control car; and direct connection of the propellers to the engines. These fragile machines, whose wooden structure absorbed much moisture as they travelled over the North Sea, were never popular with the German navy, which only acquired eight examples.

The navy's first Schütte-Lanz airship, the SL3, was powered by four 210hp Maybach engines. It could carry a load of 30,865lb at a maximum speed of 53m.p.h. The German army also operated a small number, again with limited success, on the Eastern Front, where conditions were not particularly favourable to airship operation. The Schütte-Lanz, did, however, make an important contribution to German airship design and many of its innovations were adopted by the Zeppelin Company.

SCHWARZLOSE MACHINE-GUN

The standard machine-gun of the Austro-Hungarian army during the First World War, the Schwarzlose was a heavy, water-cooled weapon. A simple, well-constructed gun, which was operated by the unusual delayed blowback method, it proved to be very reliable on the battlefield and had a range of about 1,500 yards. It used the standard 8mm Austrian service cartridge, which was loaded from a 250-round fabric belt, and had a relatively low cyclic rate of fire of 400 rounds per minute. One of the gun's distinctive features was the long cone-shaped flash eliminator; this concealed the muzzle flash that was produced because the barrel was too short for the 8mm cartridge.

The standard weapon was the Model 1912, the earlier MO7 and MO8 subsequently being brought up to the standard of the later gun. Wartime use was confined to the Austro-Hungarians and their Italian enemy: the latter had captured large quantities and their own front line troops used them extensively. A lightened, air-cooled version of the Schwarzlose – the Maschinengewehr 07/16 – was developed for use by the Austrian air service. Although its low rate of fire and short barrel reduced its effectiveness, it was widely used as an aircraft gun.

SEABROOK ARMOURED CAR

Based on the American-produced Seabrook 5-ton lorry chassis, this heavily armoured vehicle served on the Western Front in 1914–15. It carried a 3-pdr naval gun mounted on a turntable over the rear wheels and its armoured sides could be let down to form a firing platform. Originally three Seabrooks were allocated to each RNAS armoured car squadron, with the aim of providing support to the standard vehicles – the **Rolls Royce** and **Lanchester** – then in service. However, their weight and lack of manoeuvrability limited their speed and effectiveness in this role and as a result in May 1915 they were grouped together in heavy squadrons of their own, with six vehicles in each, for the remainder of the year.

SEA SCOUT AIRSHIP

Introduced in 1915, this small non-rigid airship was used by the Royal Navy for anti-submarine patrols and convoy protection. Sea Scout-class airships, popularly known as 'Blimps', which soon became the nickname for all airships of this type, were produced in three different forms. The SSZ was the only type built in quantity, with nearly 70 being delivered to the navy.

The balloon envelope was constructed of fabric and rubber and its shape was maintained under pressure; a gondola held the crew of three (pilot, radio operator and mechanic) and its armament – a **Lewis machine-gun** and up to 100lb of bombs. With a single 75hp Rolls-Royce engine, the SSZ could cruise at 35m.p.h. and had a normal endurance of seven hours, although this could be extended considerably.

Sea Scouts were used intensively in 1917–18 in the struggle against German submarines in the English Channel and elsewhere, spotting a significant number and destroying or disabling some. They were also widely used as convoy escorts, releasing naval vessels that would otherwise have been used. Cheap and quick to produce, the Sea Scout proved to be an excellent investment.

SEEADLER

The only square-rigged ship to be used as a **commerce raider** during World War I, *Seeadler* was the former merchant vessel *Pass of Balmaha*; she had a displacement of 1,571 tons and an auxiliary diesel engine. This American-owned ship was seized by a German U-boat in the North Sea in July 1915 while it was in British custody. The German Admiralty was persuaded to use her as a commerce raider and she left home on 21 December 1916, under the command of Count Felix von Luckner. The idea proved to be sound: cruising the Atlantic and Pacific she was responsible for the destruction of as many as 16 Allied merchant vessels. Her career came to an abrupt end on 2 August 1917, when she was wrecked in the Society Islands.

SEECKT, GENERAL HANS VON, 1866–1936

Responsible for rebuilding the German army after the war, Seeckt made his reputation as a brilliant staff officer in the first year of the conflict. His opportunity came in March 1915 when he was appointed chief of staff of the newly formed Eleventh Army, under **von Mackensen**, in Galicia. Seeckt was his commander's 'guiding brain', planning and organising the offensive against the Russians, which led to the breakthrough at **Gorlice-Tarnow** (May 1915) and the German advance of 300 miles. His other major achievement while serving with Mackensen was the successful invasion of **Serbia** in October 1915. Seeckt was subsequently given other staff appointments on the Eastern Front before his departure to Constanti-nople late in 1917 as chief of staff to the Turkish Army Command. It was not, however, until he was appointed to the head of the post-war army that his wartime services were fully recognised by his own country.

SERBIA, INVASION OF, 1915

After the failure of its successive attempts to occupy Serbia in 1914, Austria, which did not find it 'pleasant to swallow such military rebuffs', was determined to strike again as soon as possible. However, no further action was considered until Bulgaria was persuaded to enter the war in September 1915. This time, Germany, which wanted to establish a direct railway link with Constantinople, was also to be actively involved. Some 300,000 German, Austrian and Bulgarian troops, under the command of **Field Marshal von Mackensen**, and a vast array of artillery were assembled along the Serbian border, to try to ensure that the fourth invasion was successful. The Serbs had only five small armies (200,000 men) under the command of **Radomir Putnik**.

The invasion began in the north on 6 October 1915, when the Austrian Third Army (**General von Kövess**), positioned opposite and west of Belgrade, crossed the Save River. To the east of the capital, the German Eleventh Army (**General von Gallwitz**) moved across the Danube. On 9 October, Belgrade, which had come under pressure from both armies, was forced to surrender. In spite of their determined resistance, the Serb First and Third Armies were now compelled to pull back into the centre of the country. They came under further pressure from a major Bulgarian flank attack. In the north-east the Bulgarian First Army crossed the frontier on 11 October and attacked in the direction of Nish. The Bulgarian Second Army (**General Zhekov**), which was posit-ioned in the south-west, advanced on Uskub, where the two railway lines from the north met on the Upper Vardar. By 23 October, the Salonika–Belgrade railway had been cut. The Serbs were denied any assistance from the small Allied force of three divisions (**General Sarrail**) that was advancing from Greece up the Vadar River. It was no match for the Bulgarians and retreated before their left wing could engage it.

During more than a month of fierce fighting the Serbs had twice avoided encirclement − in the Morava Valley (1 November) and at Pristina (10 November) − as they retreated south-westwards. Instead of surrendering they decided to retreat through the mountains of neutral Albania. Some 100,000 Serbian soldiers (and 25,000 Austrian pri-soners) survived this epic march to reach the Adriatic; in January 1916, they were transported to the Greek island of Corfu, which had been seized by the **Entente Powers** for the purpose of accommodating them. Mackensen's advance had already been brought to a halt on 4 December at the Greek and Albanian frontiers. This successful operation removed Serbia from the war, although part of its army had survived to fight on the **Salonika front**, where it arrived in the spring of 1916. The main German objective − clearing the railway from Berlin to Constantinople − had also been achieved.

In a final phase of the campaign, Montenegro was invaded by the Austrians under Kövess and its army surrendered on 25 January 1916. He advanced into Albania, seizing a number of ports on the Adriatic coast.

SÈVRES, TREATY OF, 10 August 1920

The post-First World War peace settlement embodied in the Treaty of Sèvres, 10 August 1920, was agreed by the Allies and Ottoman Turkey, but was never ratified. By its severe terms, Greece gained Thrace and the Turkish Aegean Islands, while Italy retained the Dodecanese and Rhodes; the League of Nations was to administer the Dardanelles and the Bosphorus. Arabia, Armenia, Mesopotamia and Syria were all to gain their independence. The effect of the treaty was to reduce Turkey to a relatively small area in Europe and Asia Minor and its terms were completely unacceptable to **Kemal Atatürk** and the republican movement. As a result Turkey successfully negotiated a more favourable agreement – the Treaty of Lausanne – with the Allies on 24 July 1923.

SEYDLITZ

Flagship of the scouting force of the German **High Seas Fleet**, *Seydlitz* sustained serious damage at **Dogger Bank** and **Jutland**. This battlecruiser was hit as many as 25 times on the second occasion and was badly flooded, being the most severely damaged German ship to survive the battle.

Based on *Moltke*, *Seydlitz*, which was completed in 1913, had an additional weather deck and a longer hull. Armament and armour remained unchanged but she had an increased maximum speed of 26.5 knots. She was interned at **Scapa Flow** at the end of the war and was scuttled there on 21 June 1919.

SHARQAT, BATTLE OF, 29–30 October 1918

Late in the war, **Sir William Marshall**, the British commander in Mesopotamia, resumed the offensive north of Baghdad, with the aim of capturing the Mosul oilfields. The British government had decided, following the successes in Palestine, to try to eliminate all Turkish influence from the area prior to the expected surrender.

An Anglo-Indian force, commanded by General Sir Alexander Cobbe, left Baghdad on 23 October 1918, reaching the Little Zab River, 77 miles away, in only 39 hours. The Turkish Sixth Army, under General Ismael Hakki, had planned to engage the enemy at this point but was forced to withdraw when the British threatened its rear.

The Turks withdrew to Sharqat, 60 miles distant, pursued by the British. Cobbe attacked on 29 October and after a day's fighting Hakki surrendered, even though his lines had not been breached. Over 18,000 Turks were taken prisoner, with the British losing 1,886 men. This action brought the war in Mesopotamia to an end; Mosul itself was occupied without incident by an Indian cavalry division on 14 November.

SHCHERBACHEV, GENERAL DMITRY, 1857–1932

Russian infantry general who applied French methods of intensive artillery bombardment of a narrow sector to the very different conditions of the Eastern Front.

He employed such tactics in the Strypa offensive in November 1915 with disastrous results. It was only when very different methods were used by **General**

Brusilov in his major offensive in 1916 that Shcherbachev operated successfully, destroying an entire corps of the Austrian South Army. From April 1917 until the end of the war he commanded Russian forces on the Rumanian front.

SHORT 184

The first torpedo-carrying seaplane to be designed specifically for the purpose, the Short 184 represented an important stage in the development of naval aviation. It was produced with strong encouragement from the RNAS, following the first successful launching of a torpedo from a British aircraft on 28 July 1914. The new type was a two-seat tractor biplane, with three bays and folding wings, and an undercarriage of three pontoon floats, supplemented by air bags at the wing tips. Originally powered by a 225hp Sunbeam Mowhawk, a variety of other standard engines (up to 275hp) was used to improve performance. The 260hp Sunbeam, for example, gave the 184 a maximum speed of 84m.p.h. and an endurance of 2 hours 45 minutes.

Its single 14-inch torpedo was carried between the twin floats and a bomb load of 400lb was held in a rack at the front of the fuselage. It was armed with a single ring-mounted .303 **Lewis machine-gun**, operated by the observer from the rear cockpit. As a torpedo carrier the 184's greatest moment was on 12 August 1915 in the **Dardanelles**, when it became the first aircraft to sink an enemy ship by means of an air-launched torpedo. Two further Turkish ships were destroyed soon afterwards, but these early successes were not to be repeated, partly because of operating problems. When armed with a torpedo the aircraft was difficult to take off and manoeuvre, even in favourable conditions, and its torpedo role was, therefore, gradually reduced.

The 184 was employed widely on reconnaissance, anti-submarine and, to a lesser extent, bombing duties, operating from virtually every coastal air station in Great Britain and from several bases in the Mediterranean and Middle East. Seaplane carriers also provided a mobile base for some 184s, including the single aircraft that provided the only aerial reconnaissance during the **Battle of Jutland**.

In the course of its long operational career, the 184 was gradually modified and improved, and several different variants were produced. Type D, for example, was a conversion to a single-seater, with an additional bomb load of nine 65lb bombs being carried in place of the observer. As a standard patrol aircraft, the 184 was manufactured in quantity, and over 650 had been commissioned by the RNAS before the war ended.

SHORT 320

The 320 was a two-seat patrol seaplane, the last of several Short seaplane designs to enter service during the war. Designed to carry the new Mk IX 18-inch 1,000lb torpedo over long distances, this two-bay biplane was powered by a single 310hp or 320hp Sunbeam Cossack engine. It had a maximum speed of 79m.p.h. at 2,000 feet and an endurance of six hours. Defensive armament consisted of a single .303 **Lewis machine-gun** mounted on the front cockpit; the pilot was seated at the rear.

Twelve 320s were allocated to No 6 Squadron RNAS at Otranto, where they were used in September 1917 in an unsuccessful torpedo attack on Austro-Hungarian submarines at Cattaro on the Adriatic. The aircraft was, for unknown reasons, never again used as a torpedo carrier and it was equipped to carry two 230lb bombs instead. A total of 127 machines were manufactured and they were widely used on anti-submarine patrols in British waters and in the Mediterranean. Some 50 aircraft were still in use at the end of the war.

SHORT 827/830

The 827/830 was a two-seat reconnaissance and bombing seaplane, resembling the Short 166, which served with the RNAS from 1915 until the Armistice. This two-bay biplane was armed with a single, free-mounted .303 **Lewis machine-gun** and a small bomb load carried in racks beneath the fuselage. The aircraft had two alternative engines: the 827 had a 150hp Sunbeam Nubran, giving a maximum speed of 61m.p.h., while the 830 had a 140hp Salmson water-cooled power plant. More than 100 Short 827s were constructed, compared with only about twenty 830s.

The aircraft were operated from seaplane carriers and were used in anti-submarine and anti-Zeppelin patrols from several RNAS coastal air stations. They were also usefully employed in the East African campaign and in Mesopotamia.

SHORT BOMBER

The Bomber was a land plane version of the successful **Short 184** seaplane, which appeared in 1915 in response to an RNAS competition for a long-range bomber. The Short design was officially accepted and 83 examples were eventually built. Modifications included extended three-bay wings, a four-wheel undercarriage, and, on later production aircraft, a lengthened fuselage. It was normally powered by a 250hp Rolls Royce engine, which gave a maximum speed of 77m.p.h. at 6,500 feet and an endurance of six hours. Crew seating and defensive armament were unchanged from the original 184, but the maximum bomb load (carried on racks beneath the wings) was significantly increased to over 900lb.

Its first operational use was with No 7 Squadron RNAS at Coudekerque, where it was employed from November 1916 in raids on enemy naval installations. Early in 1916, No 3 Wing – the new RNAS strategic bombing unit – had also been due to use the Bomber against German industrial targets, but operations were delayed until the autumn: 15 examples were transferred to the RFC, where they were urgently needed in preparation for the **Battle of the Somme**. The last Bombers were withdrawn from service by April 1917, having been gradually replaced by the more advanced **Handley Page 0/100**.

SIA 7 & 9

An armed two-seat reconnaissance and bomber aircraft, the SIA 7B1 first appeared in 1917. Produced by Savoia and Verduzio, who also designed the **Ansaldo Scouts**, this two-bay biplane was powered by a 260hp Fiat A-12 engine. A **Fiat-Revelli** machine-gun was mounted over the top wing and there was another Revelli on a hinged mounting in the rear cockpit; a small bomb load could also be carried under the lower wings. The aircraft had many positive features – it was manoeuvrable and fast, with a good rate of climb and excellent range – but these were soon overshadowed by a series of failures in the wing structure.

A strengthened version – the 7B2 – appeared in May 1918. It was powered by a 300hp Fiat A-12bis engine, and the crew's view was improved by raising the cockpits to the level of the engine. However, the new model was quickly discovered to have the same structural weakness as the old, and in mid-1918 both types were withdrawn from service. As many as 501 SIA 7B1s were built, but only 71 modified 7B2s were produced before production was halted.

The SIA 9B, a substantially larger development, emerged in February 1918. It was fitted with a 700hp Fiat A-14 engine, the most powerful used by any Allied aircraft during the war. This two-seater, which could carry a bomb load of 770lb, had a range of 370 miles. Like the 7B1 and 7B2, it suffered from structural problems and was not accepted by the army, although 62 examples served with three squadrons of the Italian navy. When SIA became Fiat Aviazion later in 1918, the plane was substantially redesigned: in its new form (the Fiat R2) structural problems were eliminated, but few saw operational use before the Armistice.

SIEMENS-SCHUCKERT DI

This single-seat German fighter was a copy of the outstanding **Nieuport 17**, an aircraft that made an important contribution to Allied air superiority in the summer of 1916. When it appeared in the autumn of 1916, the DI was virtually indistinguishable from the original, except for the 110hp Siemens-Halske Sh I rotary engine and the single or twin Spandau machine-guns. Only 95 machines were produced – a fraction of the original order – because of the appearance of the superior **Albatros D-types** in the spring of 1917. The DI was mainly used in the less demanding combat conditions of the Russian Front, although it did appear in small quantities on the Western Front and was also used for training purposes.

SIEMENS-SCHUCKERT DIII & DIV

Although it languished in relative obscurity, the Siemens-Schuckert fighter was one of the best aircraft of its type to appear during the First World War.

Designed to accommodate the new 160hp Siemens-Halske Sh III rotary engine, it was a single-seat, one-bay biplane with a short, round fuselage of complicated construction and a balanced rudder and elevator. It had a four-bladed airscrew with a large spinner and armament consisted of twin Spandau machine-guns. The DIII entered service with *Jagdgeschwader II* in April 1918, but it eventually had to be temporarily withdrawn while a new engine – the 200hp Sh IIIa – was fitted because of severe difficulties with the original power unit. It was also criticised for its relatively low speed in level flight (113m.p.h.), although it had an outstanding rate of climb (5,000m in 13 minutes) and was highly manoeuvrable. No more than 80 DIIIs were produced because of these design problems.

Several modifications, including the redesign of the top wing, were made in order to improve performance, and the new model, which first appeared in prototype form early in 1918, was designated the DIV. With an increased top speed of 119m.p.h. and an even faster climb rate, it was ordered in some quantity. It did not, however, become operational until August 1918 and, because of production difficulties, only 119 machines had been delivered by the Armistice. The DIII/IV never reached German front line units in sufficient numbers to make a significant impact, although some were usefully employed in a home defence role as interceptors.

SIEMENS-SCHUCKERT R-TYPES

Seven aircraft in the *Riesenflugzeug* (giant aeroplane) category were produced by Siemens-Schuckert during the period 1915–17. Numbered RI to RVII, these heavy bombers all followed a similar pattern, varying mainly in their dimensions and engines, although 260hp Mercedes motors were often used. All were powered by three engines mounted in the fuselage and accessible from the enclosed cabin, with an indirect drive to two tractor airscrews. The massive unequal span wings were swept back and the fuselage consisted of two triangular-shaped booms, one mounted above the other, to which were attached a triangular tailplane and twin rudders.

RIV to RVII saw limited service on the Eastern Front early in 1917, possibly in response to the threat posed by the Russian **Sikorsky Ilya Mourometz** bombers. The first three R-types were used exclusively as trainers, as were two of the later examples after their withdrawal from operational service.

SIKORSKY ILYA MOUROMETZ

The world's first four-engined aircraft, designed by Igor Sikorsy in 1913, provided the basis for the series of giant bombers that served exclusively with the Russian Imperial Air Service during the First World War. Known collectively as the Ilya Mourometz (after a hero in Russian mythology), the aircraft was produced in five different forms and 80 examples appeared in total before the Revolution.

Basically it was a greatly enlarged version of a typical biplane of the day, but with a spacious, enclosed cabin, double rudders and a stabilising fin. The different models conformed to this basic layout but had varied dimensions, engine sizes and types, armament and bomb loads. With a wingspan of 35m, type G, for example, had four engines, producing 580–760hp, depending on the type fitted, a maximum speed of 78m.p.h. and a range of 400 miles. It could carry a bomb load of 450–700kg and was normally armed with three or four machine-guns, although more were sometimes carried. A crew of up to seven was needed to fly and maintain the aircraft – routine engine servicing could be carried out while it was in the air – and operate the armament.

Initially, the Ilya Mourometz ran into difficulties when the first two production aircraft failed as they entered service, but fortunately it won a reprieve after an intervention by the Russian manufacturers. A new unit, the Squadron of Flying Ships (the EVK), was formed and equipped with the new aircraft and pilots were given special training before flying them. The squadron began bombing operations in February 1915, attacking targets in Germany, Lithuania and Austria, from its base near Warsaw. Between 1915 and 1917 they dropped about 65 tonnes of bombs during more than 400 raids and by the closing months of the war there were five operational wings of Ilya Mourometz aircraft.

Only three machines were lost during the war, two which were attributable to mechanical causes and sabotage. The Germans lost many planes in their attacks on this giant bomber but were unable to shoot more than one of them down, a tribute to the efficiency of its defensive armament. This distinguished Russian aircraft continued in service during the Civil War, when it was used by both the Bolsheviks and the White Russians.

SIMS, ADMIRAL WILLIAM, 1858–1936

A noted Anglophile, Admiral Sims was sent to London in April 1917 to coordinate British and American naval efforts. Often in conflict with the cautious US Chief of Naval operations, **Admiral Benson**, he was successful in securing the assistance of additional American forces to meet the U-boat threat in European waters.

In June 1917, he was appointed to the command of these European-based forces, a post he held for the rest of the war. When hostilities ended Sims accused Admiral Benson and **Josephus Daniels**, the Secretary of the Navy, with failing to respond with sufficient energy to the challenge of war in 1917.

SLAVA

Slava was the only Borodino-class battleship in Russian service during the First World War, the others having been destroyed or surrendered during the Russo-Japanese war at the Battle of Tsushima in May 1905. With a displacement of 10,140 tons, Slava was larger than her predecessor, *Tsessarevitch*, but had less power and severe weaknesses in the armour protection. Armament consisted of four 12-inch and twelve 6-inch guns, the secondary armament being in six twin turrets. *Slava* served with the Baltic Fleet during the war and was so badly damaged by the German dreadnought *König* in October 1917 that she was scuttled.

SMITH & WESSON REVOLVER

One of several military handguns produced by Smith & Wesson, this .45-inch revolver was acquired in large quantities when the United States entered the First World War. A total of 153,000 examples were in fact delivered to the American army before the Armistice. It was one of the main available alternatives to the **Colt automatic pistol**, the standard US army weapon, which could not be supplied in large enough numbers to meet wartime demand. Modified to accept the .45 automatic cartridge, of which there was a steady supply, the Smith & Wesson .45 revolver proved to be a reliable service weapon and it was retained in military use until after the Second World War.

SMITH-DORRIEN, GENERAL SIR HORACE, 1858–1930

Appointed to the command of II Corps in August 1914, Smith-Dorrien was an experienced soldier who had served extensively in Britain's colonial wars. His brief wartime career with the BEF in France was blighted by disagreements with its commander, **Sir John French**, and eventually led to his premature departure.

After their defeat at Mons, where Smith-Dorrien's troops were the most heavily involved, the two British corps were ordered to withdraw to the south-west. Separated from **Haig**'s corps by the forest of Mormal, he decided, contrary to French's orders, to fight a delaying action at **Le Cateau** on 26 August because of the condition of his own troops and the proximity of the enemy. Although British losses were heavy, the Germans also sustained large casualties and attempted no immediate pursuit. French at first commended Smith-Dorrien for his brave stand but later condemned it, referring to the 'shattered condition of the Second Corps'.

Early in 1915, he was appointed to the command of the Second Army, which in April was holding part of the Ypres salient. The success of the German army in reducing the size of this salient, following its surprise gas attack on 22 April, led Smith-Dorrien to conclude that his position was indefensible and that a withdrawal towards Ypres should be made. In response to this proposal, French reacted angrily, sending him home at short notice and replacing him with **Sir Herbert Plumer**. Even though British troops were soon drawn back by the new commander, exactly as Smith-Dorrien had recommended, his abrupt removal effectively ended his distinguished military career.

SMUTS, GENERAL JAN CHRISTIAN, 1870–1950

Smuts: active service in Africa was followed by the Imperial War Cabinet in London

A minister in **Louis Botha**'s Cabinet and a future Prime Minister of the Union of South Africa (1919–24), Jan Smuts made a significant contribution to the military struggle against the Germans in Africa and in Europe. A veteran of the South African War, he supported Botha in the conquest of **South-West Africa** in 1915. Early in 1915, he was given command of the British and colonial forces in East Africa, with the rank of lieutenant-general in the British army. Smuts had some limited success against the smaller German forces under the determined and skilful leadership of **Lettow-Vorbeck**: he advanced southwards, capturing the greater part of the country but was unable to defeat his elusive opponent before being recalled in January 1917.

He was sent to London as a representative on the Imperial War Cabinet, but he was soon appointed to the British War Cabinet itself as minister without portfolio. **Lloyd George** employed him on several sensitive missions and he played an important role in the creation of an independent **Royal Air Force**. He served as a South African delegate to the **Paris Peace Conference** and expressed considerable disquiet about the crippling reparations and other provisions that were likely to undermine peace.

SOMME, FIRST BATTLE OF THE, 1 July–18 November 1916

Joffre's original plans for a French offensive on the Somme were disrupted by **Verdun**, but the serious crisis there made a diversionary attack by the Allies even more necessary. The British would now make the main attack on a front of 18 miles, which stretched from Maricourt, north of the River Somme, to Gommecourt. The Fourth Army (**Rawlinson**) was to take charge of the attack; on its left was the right-hand corps of the Third Army (**Allenby**). Facing the 19 British divisions was the German Second Army (**Below**), occupying strong positions on the crests of hills. They were well protected in deep dugouts. South of the Somme was the French Sixth Army (**Fayolle**), consisting of eight divisions positioned on a 10-mile front opposite Péronne.

A massive preliminary bombardment, which began on 24 June, continued for eight days. The assault began at 7.30 a.m. on 1 July, when over half a million troops advanced across no man's land. The French achieved the greatest success in their secondary sector, their heavy artillery having prepared the ground more effectively than the British, who had insufficient heavy guns. On most of the British front, with one exception, virtually no progress was made in the face of fierce German resistance, particularly from a relatively small number of machine-gunners. By the end of the day the British had suffered 58,000 casualties (19,000 were killed), the largest loss ever sustained by the British army in a single day. The only real success came at the southern end of the British front, where an advance of one mile was achieved and the villages of Montauban and Mametz were taken.

Further small gains were made in this area in a series of limited, local engagements, but it was not until 13/14 July that any real progress was made. A surprise night attack by four divisions, under Rawlinson's command, broke through the German line, advancing 6,000 yards. The initial objective – Bazentin Ridge – was achieved before German reinforcements closed the gap.

The hopes of a further advance which this success encouraged were soon dashed. Another attack by Rawlinson on 23 July on the ridge by Pozières ended in failure, although Pozières itself was captured by two Australian divisions. In response to British progress on 14 July, the command of the rapidly expanding German forces on the Somme was reorganised. The front was split between Below, who retained responsibility for the northern sector, and Gallwitz, who held the front south of the Somme and was in overall command as head of the army group defending this sector.

A costly war of attrition, in which the British infantry was assisted by Allied air superiority, followed during August as **Haig** prepared for a major new assault. Early in September, the front was extended by some 12 miles south of the Somme as the French Tenth Army (**Micheler**) entered the battle.

The new British attack (the Battle of Flers-Courcelette) began on 15 September on a 12-mile front south-west of Bapaume. Twelve divisions, supported by 36 tanks secretly shipped to the front, faced six and a half German divisions. The value of the tank, used in battle for the first time, was immediately evident, but they were not available in sufficient numbers or reliable enough to produce a decisive breakthrough. Haig was, in fact, severely criticised by some tank experts for what they regarded as the premature use of the weapon in insufficient numbers. Substantial gains were made in the centre of the line, with an average advance of one and a half miles along the whole front.

The offensive was slowed by poor weather and the arrival of more German reinforcements. Further British gains were made on 25/27 September at the actions of Morval and Thiepval Ridge. In October the weather worsened and the Somme became a 'wilderness of mud'. Haig pressed on in a series of limited attacks, beginning with the Battle of Transloy Ridges (1–20 October). On Joffre's instruction the battle continued into November with Beaumont Hamel, a field fortress, and Beaumont itself falling before

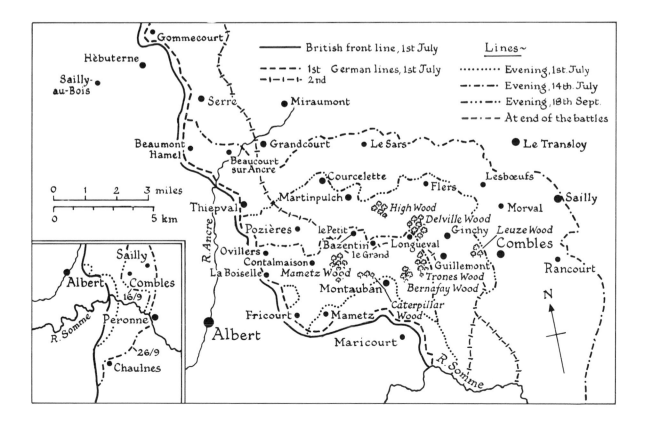

winter snow brought the Battle of the Somme to an end after five months.

The British had gained a crescent-shaped area about six miles across at its widest point, but there had been no breakthrough and losses had been enormous. Their casualties amounted to almost 419,000 men, with the French losing 194,451 and the Germans 650,000. The 'flower of Britain', the volunteers of Kitchener's Army, had been sacrificed for what appeared to be very little. However, as a diversionary attack it had achieved its objective and it had also inflicted permanent damage on the German army.

British artillery bombardment of the enemy trenches on the first day of the Somme

SOMME OFFENSIVE, 21 March – 5 April 1918

After the ending of hostilities on the Eastern Front, **Ludendorff** planned a major new offensive in France in the spring of 1918. Transferring as many troops as possible from the east, he sought to achieve a conclusive victory on the Western Front before the Americans could build up sufficient strength to intervene decisively. He selected the British-held line from Arras to St Quentin and La Fère for the initial attack, since much of it was lightly defended. The German aim was both to drive the British back against the Channel coast and to separate them from their French allies to the south. It was to be the first of five German offensives during 1918 and was for the Allies one of the most serious crises of the war; for a time a German victory seemed possible.

The front south of Arras, which extended for 50 miles to La Fère, was held by the Third Army (**Byng**) on the left and the Fifth Army (**Gough**) to the right, a total of 26 divisions initially. British strength was distributed unevenly: Gough's army, which held much of the line, had only 12 divisions, while Byng had 14. Opposing them from left to right were the German Seventeenth (**Below**), Second (**Marwitz**) and Eighteenth Armies (**Hutier**), a total of 63 divisions.

The offensive, which began in heavy fog on 21 March, was preceded by a massive 6,000-gun bombardment and a gas attack. The Germans advanced along the entire front, progress being most rapid in the south. In fact, in response to the events of the first day, Gough withdrew his army behind the Crozat Canal. The right of Byng's army was also forced to move back in order to remain in contact. Soon Gough was compelled to order a general retreat behind the Somme as Hutier continued to apply considerable pressure. Further north, on 25 March, the Second Army forced a gap between the two British armies and for a while it seemed as if the whole front was about to collapse. Exploiting this apparently favourable situation, Ludendorff widened his objectives, ordering the Second Army to aim for Amiens and Hutier to move towards Paris. As originally planned, Below was expected to push the British towards the Channel coast.

The Allies responded to this crisis by appointing **Foch** to coordinate the efforts of the Allied armies on the Western Front. French reinforcements, which had been slow in arriving at the front, now began to appear in greater numbers and **General Fayolle** was placed in command of the mixed forces south of the Somme. On 26 March, the Third Army, with strong air support, halted the enemy advance north of the Somme. Two days later the Germans launched 'operation Mars' which failed to capture Arras, in spite of a major commitment of troops. The offensive in the north was now at an end.

Further south, however, the Germans continued to make considerable progress. Montdidier, 40 miles from the starting line, fell on 27 March, threatening Amiens, an important railway junction. However, strong Allied resistance halted the Germans at Villers-Bretonneux, 10 miles away. Ludendorff's troops were now exhausted and on 5 April he abandoned the whole operation.

Ludendorff's first and biggest offensive of 1918 had resulted in the greatest advance since the first months of the war, but it had failed to achieve any

decisive results. He had made the error of concentrating his efforts on the strongest sector – that held by the British Third Army – until it was too late. The operation was also affected by severe transport problems and the low morale of undernourished troops. Casualties on both sides were enormous: 240,000 Allied losses were slightly less than those sustained by the Germans. Unable to make any further progress here he turned to Flanders, where he launched the **Lys offensive** on 9 April.

A rifle pit on the Somme, March 1918, hastily prepared as German pressure intensified

SOPWITH 1½-STRUTTER

Entering service with the Royal Naval Air Service early in 1916, the Sopwith Strutter was Britain's first two-seater fighter. Both the pilot and the observer were armed with .303-inch machine-guns (a **Vickers** and **Lewis** respectively), and for the first time the forward-firing weapon was synchronised with the airscrew. This small, single-bay tractor biplane with equal span wings had three other unusual features: air brakes, a tailplane adjustable in flight, and short centre section struts, from which its popular name was derived. Power was provided by a not particularly reliable 110hp Clerget engine; later models had a

130hp version, which gave a maximum speed of 102m.p.h. at 6,500 feet.

In RNAS service the aircraft partially equipped No 5 Wing at Coudekerque, where it was used as an escort on long-range bombing raids. It also carried out bombing duties itself with No 5 Wing, attacking important naval targets. Its bombing role was expanded with the formation of No 3 Wing, RNAS, and a single-seat version, carrying four 65lb bombs in place of the observer, was brought into service at Luxeuil. Here the Strutter became the first British aircraft to undertake strategic bombing raids, when

German industrial targets were attacked from the autumn of 1916.

This versatile aircraft was also used by the RNAS on anti-submarine patrols for the rest of the war, and among its achievements was the sinking of a U-boat in the Mediterranean in September 1917. A small number of 'Ship's Strutters' were specially equipped to operate from naval vessels, and in April 1918 it became the first two-seater to take off from a British warship.

The Strutter was also adopted by the RFC, serving with No 43, 45 and 70 Squadrons on the Western Front from April 1916; they were outclassed there as a fighting aircraft during 1917 and were phased out as the **Sopwith Camel** came into use. In total, some 1,500 examples were built for the British service. It was also widely employed by other Allied powers, including the United States, Russia and Belgium. The main foreign user was France, where 4,500 were constructed for the Aviation Militaire.

SOPWITH BABY

This single-seat seaplane, widely used by the Royal Naval Air Service in 1916–18, was a development of the Sopwith Schneider, itself virtually identical to the **Sopwith Tabloid**, apart from its floats. Widely used during the first part of the war, the Schneider was powered by the 100hp Gnome Monosoupape engine, enclosed in a distinctive bull-nosed cowling. They were armed with a **Lewis machine-gun**, inclined upwards through the top wing, and could carry a single 65lb bomb below the fuselage. They were operated from naval air stations around the coast of Britain and on seaplane carriers in the North Sea and Mediterranean. The Schneider had a variety of roles – reconnaissance, bombing, and fighter

patrols – and was heavily involved in operations against **Zeppelins** and enemy submarines.

The Baby, which first appeared in the autumn of 1915, was fitted with the more powerful 110hp Clerget engine – subsequently the 130hp version, with the larger power plant giving a maximum speed of 100m.p.h. and an endurance of two hours. Some examples were fitted with a forward-firing synchronised Lewis gun or with Ranken anti-Zeppelin darts; they could now carry two 65lb bombs. Otherwise the Baby differed little from its precedessor, and was employed on much the same operational duties as the Schneider until the end of the war. A total of 457 examples of the Baby were built.

SOPWITH CAMEL

The most famous British fighter of the war, the Sopwith Camel was produced in response to the appearance of the twin-gun **Albatros D-types** on the Western Front in the autumn of 1916. A development of the **Sopwith Pup**, this small single-bay biplane was more successful in combat than any other wartime aircraft, shooting down 1,294 enemy machines.

Conventional in appearance, with clean, simple lines, it had a short, wooden box-girder fuselage with rounded top decking. Officially named the F1, it was universally known as the Camel from the hump-shaped cover which enclosed the breeches of the

synchronised twin **Vickers machine-guns**. The Camel was, in fact, the first British fighter to be so armed. A variety of rotary engines was used; powered by the 130hp Clerget, for example, it had a maximum speed of 115m.p.h., and ability to climb to 15,000 feet in 20 minutes 40 seconds, and an endurance of 2½ hours. It was, however, the Camel's legendary manoeuvrability and agility that gave it a decisive edge over all its rivals, except perhaps the **Fokker DrI**. These characteristics were the result of the aircraft's forward centre of gravity (the engine, armament and cockpit were all contained within the first seven feet of the fuselage) and the torque from the powerful rotary engine. It was particularly noted for its ability to make extremely tight turns, although it was inherently unstable and had a marked tendency to spin unless corrective action was taken immediately. Its accident rate was high and it had a bad reputation in training squadrons where it was widely employed.

The Camel entered service on the Western Front with the RNAS early in May 1917 and first went into action on 4 July, destroying at least one enemy aircraft. During the same month the first deliveries were made to the RFC and it was ultimately used by 11 squadrons in France. The Camel was also used by the Belgian, Greek and American air services during the war. It quickly established itself as an outstanding combat aircraft and was flown by some of Britain's leading aces, including **Collishaw** and **Barker**. Its most notable unconfirmed victory is the destruction of **von Richthofen**'s Fokker DrI on 21 April 1918, although no firm evidence is ever likely to be found as to whether it was a Camel or ground fire that was responsible for his death.

The Camel was also used, unmodified, as a ground attack aircraft, normally carrying four 20lb Cooper bombs. Without armour protection, the Camel had a very high casualty rate, and an armoured version, the Sopwith TF1, appeared in prototype form. Although it did not enter production, it led to the development of the **Sopwith Salamander**. Camels served in most theatres of the war, including England, where they were allocated to home defence units; in this role a night fighter variant, with a pair of **Lewis machine-guns** above the top wing centre section, was developed.

As well as employing the standard machine, the RNAS also used a variant known as the Sopwith 2F1 or Ship's Camel. With a detachable rear fuselage, a reduced wingspan and landing gear that could be jettisoned, this shipboard aircraft was flown from aircraft carriers as well as from a variety of warships; it could also take off from lighters towed by destroyers. Used primarily on anti-Zeppelin patrols over the North Sea, the 2F1 also attacked the airship sheds themselves. A raid on Tondern in July 1918 destroyed two Zeppelins and was the first time a land target had been successfully attacked by carrier-borne machines.

A total of 5,410 Camels were produced, of which 129 were Ship's Camels. By the end of the war over 2,500 were in service on the Western Front, constituting about 40 per cent of Britain's fighter strength there. Several air forces continued to use the Camel after the war, although it was quickly superseded in Britain.

The Sopwith Camel: Britain's finest and most successful fighter aircraft

SOPWITH CUCKOO

The first landplane torpedo carrier that could operate directly from a carrier, the Cuckoo represented an important step in the development of naval aviation, but saw no combat service during the war.

Designed in 1917 in response to an Admiralty requirement and manufactured from May 1918, this three-bay biplane had folding wings and a single 200hp Sunbeam Arab tractor engine. The Cuckoo carried an 18-inch Mk IX torpedo below the fuselage, between the legs of its wide track undercarriage, performing with much greater ease and effectiveness than earlier seaplanes which had used the weapon. The Cuckoo was ordered in quantity by the RAF, although only 90 examples had been delivered by the Armistice. One Cuckoo-equipped unit served on HMS *Argus* during the last few weeks of the war, but hostilities ended before the enemy could be engaged. The Cuckoo remained in RAF service until 1923.

SOPWITH DOLPHIN

This single-seat fighter biplane entered service with the RFC towards the end of 1917. It was powered by a 200hp Hispano-Suiza engine, which proved to be unreliable but gave excellent performance, particularly at high altitudes. An unusual feature was its 'backward stagger wings', which were intended to give an improved upward view, but exposed the pilot to the risk of serious injury in the event of the aircraft overturning on landing. In other respects, however, visibility was relatively poor. Of the normal wood-, frame- and wire-braced construction, the aircraft was well armed, being designed to carry four machine-guns. There were twin fixed **Vickers guns** mounted above the engine and a pair of **Lewis guns** on the centre section of the upper wing, although in practice the latter tended to be removed on operations.

A total of 1,532 Dolphins were constructed before the Armistice and they served with four RFC squadrons – No 19, 23, 79 and 83 – throughout 1918. Although the aircraft was initially unpopular with pilots, it had a good operational record. They were used widely on escort duties, participating in attacks on German airfields and other installations. In a ground attack role the Dolphin could carry four 25lb Cooper bombs. As a result of the aircraft's successes in the summer and autumn of 1918, it has been suggested that it was the best operational fighter of the period.

SOPWITH PUP

Widely regarded as 'the perfect flying machine', the Pup was a single-seat fighting scout. Its unofficial name, which was universally used in spite of Admiralty opposition, was given because it looked like a smaller version of its immediate predecessor, the **Sopwith 1½-Strutter**. The construction of this compact and lightweight tractor biplane was simple but strong. It had a standard box-girder fuselage and a single-bay wing cellule. The standard Pup engine was the 80hp Le Rhône rotary engine, which gave a maximum speed of 112m.p.h. at sea level and a ceiling of 17,500 feet. Other units used included the 80hp Clerget or 80hp Gnome; some Pups employed on home defence duties were powered by the 100hp Monosoupape.

The Pup was normally armed with a single forward-firing .303-inch **Vickers machine-gun**, synchronised for operation through the airscrew; as an alternative, some were fitted with eight Le Prieur rockets. Pups built for use at sea were equipped with a **Lewis gun**, which fired upwards through a centre section cut-out.

The first Pups were delivered to No 1 Wing, RNAS, on the Western Front in September 1916. No 8 Squadron, equipped with Pups, shot down 20 enemy aircraft in the last two months of 1916, as it operated at the front in support of the RFC. The Pup soon demonstrated that it could hold its height better than the enemy and that it was fully manoeuvrable at altitudes of up to 15,000 feet. The RNAS also used the aircraft on shipboard duties, including regular anti-Zeppelin patrols. It was heavily involved in take-offs from naval vessels and other experimental flying at sea and was, in fact, the first aircraft to land successfully on a ship's deck.

The first RFC unit to be equipped with the new aircraft was No 54 Squadron, which arrived on the Western Front at the end of 1916. Only two other front line RFC squadrons received the Pup, which remained in France until the end of 1917, proving to be more than a match for the German **Albatros** fighters. The RFC subsequently used it extensively for home defence and training duties until the end of the war. In total, the RNAS operated about 170 Pups, while the RFC had as many as 1,670.

The Pup: another notable Sopwith fighter, operated at sea as well as on land

SOPWITH SALAMANDER

The TF2 Salamander was the first British production aircraft to be specifically designed for ground attack duty. The need was urgent because since 1917 the British had been using unmodified fighters for this purpose and unacceptably large losses had resulted. Initially, the **Camel** had been modified as the Sopwith TF1 (Trench Fighter), but had not entered production.

The second attempt was the Salamander, a variant of the **Snipe** with the same 230hp Bentley BR 2 engine, but with a modified fuselage – the whole front end was constructed of heavy armour plate, giving good protection from German bullets. The extra weight meant that the machine had a reduced top speed (117m.p.h. at 10,000 feet) and a slower climb rate than the Snipe, but performance was still satisfactory for its intended duties. Armament consisted of two synchronised **Vickers machine-guns** and four 25lb Cooper bombs.

Only ordered into production in the summer of 1918, very few examples had reached the RAF by the Armistice and only two went to France. There is no doubt that the Salamander would have proved to be an effective trench fighter had the war continued.

SOPWITH SNIPE

A standard RAF fighter of the post-war period, the 7F1 Snipe first appeared in mid-1917 but only saw limited operational use in the last few months of the war. Production was delayed until the spring of 1918 because of the need for a protracted period of development. Designed as a replacement for the **Camel**, this single-bay biplane had a more powerful 230hp Bentley BR 2 engine – a development of the 150hp BR1 used in the earlier machine. In appearance it was very similar to its predecessor, but had a deeper fuselage to house the larger engine. It was armed with two **Vickers machine-guns** and could reach 121m.p.h. at 10,000 feet.

Delivered from the summer of 1918, it was generally used for escort work and equipped three units – No 43 and No 208 Squadron RAF and No 4 Squadron Australian Flying Corps. No more than 497 machines had been delivered by the end of 1918, although if the war had continued the original production order of 1,700 Snipes would probably have been fulfilled. The Snipe is best remembered as the aircraft flown by the Canadian ace, **Major W. G. Barker**, who won the Victoria Cross for his epic struggle against a formation of 60 **Fokker DVII**s on 27 October 1918. The Snipe was retained in RAF service until 1927.

SOPWITH TABLOID

The development of this small tractor biplane marked the beginning of the famous series of Sopwith single-seaters that served with distinction during the war. Based on a two-seater racing machine of 1913, the Tabloid's performance was unmatched in the period immediately before the outbreak of war: its 80hp Gnome engine produced a top speed of 92m.p.h. and an initial climb rate of 1,200 feet a minute. It had a square fuselage and single-bay, staggered wings.

Available only in small numbers in August 1914, the Tabloid was soon sent across the Channel and used by the RFC and RNAS for scouting and light bombing duties (carrying a bomb load of no more than 20lb). At first unarmed, the pilot later carried a rifle or was equipped with a .303 **Lewis machine-gun** that fired over the top of the wing. These arrangements were, however, never very satisfactory and the RFC disposed of its Tabloids at the earliest possible moment. The aircraft was used more extensively by the RNAS, both in Belgium and the **Dardanelles**, but its only noteworthy achievement was an attack on the airship sheds at Düsseldorf on 7 October 1914. As a result, a **Zeppelin** was destroyed, the first to be lost at the hands of a British aircraft. Production of the Tabloid ended in June 1915, with no more than 39 machines having been produced.

SOPWITH TRIPLANE

One of the finest British fighters of the war, the Triplane or 'Tripehound' was the first production aircraft of its type, having appeared in prototype form in May 1916. This single-seater fighting scout was developed from the basic **Pup** design, with a similar box-girder fuselage and tailplane, but had three narrow chord wings of reduced span. The purpose of this unique arrangement was to enhance its fighting effectiveness by improving its manoeuvrability and rate of climb, while increasing the pilot's view all round. The new design achieved all of these objectives, with its climb rate being particularly outstanding – 12,000 feet in 13 minutes. The Triplane was normally powered by the 130hp Clerget, although some had the 110hp version; armament consisted of a single .303 **Vickers machine-gun**.

Entering service in February 1917, the aircraft's operational service was very brief as all the existing machines had been replaced by the **Sopwith Camel** before the end of the year. Although it had originally been destined for the RFC, British use was in fact confined to the RNAS – Squadrons No 1, 8, 9, 10, 11, 12 employing it to great effect on the Western Front, where it outclassed all of its opponents. No 10 Squadron (B Flight) in particular destroyed as many as 87 German aircraft between May and July 1917, with the flight leader, **Raymond Collishaw**, being personally responsible for 16 of them. The Triplane prompted the Germans and the Austrians to produce their own triplane designs, but the Sopwith model had not been matched by the time it was rather abruptly withdrawn from service. The aircraft's considerable reputation rested on no more than 147 machines – the total number delivered to the RNAS.

The appearance of the Sopwith Triplane, a highly manoeuvrable fighter prompted the enemy to produce its own triplane

SOUCHON, VICE-ADMIRAL WILHELM, 1864–1946

On the outbreak of war the German navy's Mediterranean Squadron was commanded by Rear-Admiral Wilhelm Souchon, an experienced naval officer with a high professional reputation. Confirmation of his skills was soon provided when the ships under his command – the battlecruiser *Goeben* and the light cruiser *Breslau* – made their dramatic escape to Constantinople in August 1914. Both were transferred to the Turkish navy and Souchon himself became its supreme commander. Under German influence Turkey joined the war and Souchon was involved in operations against the Russian fleet in the Black Sea. By the time he returned to Germany in September 1917, Souchon was a vice-admiral and had been awarded the Pour Le Mérite. He commanded the Fourth Squadron of the **High Seas Fleet** for much of the remainder of the war.

SOUTH CAROLINA

The first American 'all-big-gun' battleship, *South Carolina* was in fact designed before *Dreadnought*, although her period of construction was longer and she did not appear until 1908. Eight 12-inch guns were mounted on the centre line, with twin superfiring turrets mounted fore and aft, an arrangement that was influenced by the need to limit, for financial reasons, her displacement to 16,000 tons. With a maximum speed of no more than 18 knots, *South Carolina* and her sister ship *Michigan* could not be used operationally with subsequent dreadnought designs, and in 1917–18 they were employed as convoy escorts.

SOUTH-WEST AFRICA, OPERATIONS IN, 1914–15

The German colony of South-West Africa, was a considerable territory, mainly semi-desert, which extended from the Orange River as far as Portuguese Angola, 800 miles to the north. It remained out of reach of Allied forces during the first few months of the war because of an anti-British rebellion in South Africa, which occupied a large number of troops. Once it had been suppressed, the Prime Minister, **Louis Botha**, turned his attention to South-West Africa; he assumed command of operations and planned converging advances from the west and south. The British enclave at Walvis Bay, which had been seized by the Germans at the beginning of the war, was retaken on 25 December 1914.

From this coastal base a force of 20,000 men moved eastwards following the lines of the railway (necessary because of the need to carry water). Karibib was captured on 5 May 1915 after intensive fighting, enabling Botha to advance on the primary objective, Windhoek, the capital and centre of radio communications, 170 miles inland. Some 6,000 German troops, under the command of Major Francke, were unable to save the town, which fell on 12 May. The survivors fled north-east towards Otavi. Continuing his advance in the same direction, Botha used his cavalry strength to cut off the German escape route into Angola and on 9 July they were forced to capitulate.

Far to the south, a separate campaign was being waged simultaneously by three South African forces with a total strength of 35,000 men. They advanced from Luderitz Bay, the Orange River and Kimberley, defeating the Germans at Keetmanshoop and at Gibeon on 17 April. In total more than 5,000 German troops surrendered or were captured during the campaign; casualties were relatively light, with the Germans losing 1,274 men and the South Africans 593. German South-West Africa subsequently became a South African protectorate.

SPAD VII

One of the outstanding fighter aircraft of the war, the Spad VII saw service with almost all the Allied air forces, first entering service with the French Aviation Militaire in the autumn of 1916.

It was designed to make use of the new 150hp Hispano-Suiza V8 engine, although production models could easily be adapted to accommodate more powerful units of up to 200hp. The 180hp engine produced an excellent maximum speed of 132m.p.h. and a good rate of climb, reaching 4,000m in just over eight minutes, although the aircraft was not as manoeuvrable as some of its contemporaries. This strong, compact machine had two bay wings of unequal span and a flat-sided fuselage with streamlined top and bottom decking. Standard armament consisted of a single .303 **Vickers machine-gun**, slightly offset of starboard, with some Spad VIIs carrying two small bombs on external racks.

As many as 5,600 examples of the Spad VII were produced by eight different companies, an indication of its success. Widely used by many *escadrilles* of the French air service at the front, including the notable Les Cigognes, it is particularly associated with the exploits of **René Fonck** and **Georges Guynemer**, who demonstrated its great effectiveness against the German fighters of the day.

However, by mid-1917, the Spad VII began to be phased out in favour of the **Spad XIII**. The British also had an urgent need for modern fighters to replace their ageing designs and the Spad VII served with three squadrons on the Western Front. Some of the machines were acquired direct from France, but a larger number was manufactured under licence in England. It was, perhaps, not quite so enthusiastically received by some RFC pilots as it had been in France, some comparing it unfavourably with the **Royal Aircraft Factory SE5a**. Other air forces using the Spad included the Italian (where it served with 91a Squadriglia, the Squadron of Aces), the Russian (where it was equipped with Le Prieur rockets), and the AEF, which acquired it in significant numbers.

This French fighter, the Spad VII, was widely deployed and proved to be popular with the leading aces

SPAD XI

This two-seat French reconnaissance aircraft, which first appeared in September 1916, was similar in appearance to the highly successful **Spad VII** single-seat fighter. Major differences included a longer fuselage and swept-back wings with positive stagger. Armament consisted of one or two .303 **Lewis machine-guns** on a ring mounting for the observer and a synchronised **Vickers** at the front; a small bomb load could also be carried under the lower wings. Problems with the power unit – a 235hp Hispano-Suiza – delayed production for some time and it did not enter service with the French Aviation Militaire until the summer of 1917.

In service on the Western Front its several weaknesses soon became apparent: it was difficult to control, it stalled easily, and had a poor rate of climb. Viewed as a stop-gap until sufficient **Breguets** and **Salmsons** became available, it was eventually withdrawn by the French in July 1918. The Spad XI was also used by the Belgian Aviation Militaire (three *escadrilles*) and the AEF (two squadrons), remaining in service until the Armistice. A new version, the Spad XVI, with a more powerful engine, appeared at the beginning of 1918, but it was no more successful than its predecessor.

NO U.S. PLANES ARRIVED IN FRANCE UNTIL 1919 - A YEAR AFTER WWI ENDED.

SPAD XIII

The standard French fighter of the last year of the war, the Spad XIII was produced in larger numbers than any other Allied scout.

A development of the **Spad VII**, it was a single-seater biplane which first appeared in prototype form in April 1917. It was larger than its predecessor, had a more powerful 200 or 235hp Hispano-Suiza engine, and was armed with twin .303 **Vickers machine-guns**. The first production machines were delivered as early as May, but large scale manufacture was delayed until the spring of 1918 because of problems with the power plant. With a maximum speed of 134m.p.h., when equipped with the 200hp engine, performance was impressive and it was in fact one of the fastest fighters then in service. Noted for its rugged construction, it had outstanding diving capabilities, but was not as manoeuvrable as some of its adversaries. It was also difficult to handle at low speeds and the pilot's field of view was not perfect. However, its positive features far outweighed any possible limitations and as many as 8,472 Spad XIIIs had been built by the Armistice.

Flown by the leading French aces of the day, they equipped more than 80 *escadrilles* of the Aviation Militaire, replacing the outdated Spad VII and **Nieuport** scouts. The French retained it in service until 1923. The Spad also enjoyed an excellent reputation among American pilots and almost 900 machines were acquired, equipping 16 pursuit squadrons of the AEF, including its élite units. The type was also used by most other Allied air forces, but in smaller numbers.

The final Spad to appear during the war was the XVII, a development of the XIII. Only 20 were produced and they were allocated to Les Cigognes in the summer of 1918.

Spad XIII: a twin-gun fighter that was based on the Spad VII

SPAD A2

Early in the war when no interrupter gear existed, various methods were used – including, for example, the pusher engine – to provide aircraft with forward-firing guns. One of the strangest solutions, entering service in 1915, was the French Spad A2, a two-seater tractor biplane with a separate cockpit for the observer in front of the propeller. When access to the 110hp Le Rhône 9J engine was required, the observer's nacelle could be moved forward: it was attached to the top plane by steel tubing and to the undercarriage by wooden struts, being pivoted at a point in front of the axle. The observer was armed with a .303 **Lewis machine-gun** on a mounting that provided very limited movement.

Although there was an excellent view from the forward position, the A2 had few other advantages. Structurally it was not strong, limiting its manoeuvrability, and was unpopular with observers, who were very exposed and very likely to be crushed by the engine in the event of a crash. They were, however, protected from the airscrew immediately behind them by a wire screen. The efficiency of the propeller was impaired by the front nacelle and the pilot's view was obstructed by the observer.

Not surprisingly, the A2's operational life in the French Aviation Militaire was very limited and only 42 were delivered. Russia received a slightly larger number (57) and retained it for longer because of the difficulty in obtaining replacements. The Spad A4, a development of the earlier machine which appeared early in 1916, enjoyed no greater popularity.

SPEE, MAXIMILIAN, GRAF, von, 1861–1914

At the beginning of the war Vice-Admiral von Spee was commander of the German East Asiatic Squadron, which consisted of two armoured cruisers, *Scharnhorst* and *Gneisenau*, and three light cruisers, *Emden*, *Leipzig* and *Nürnberg*. As a result of Japan's entry into the war, he was unable to remain in the China Seas, where he had planned to attack British merchant shipping, and moved to the west coast of South America. When he arrived off Chile, near the port of **Coronel**, on 1 November 1914, he met and decisively defeated a British squadron under the command of **Sir Christopher Cradock**.

Spee then decided to make for Germany, with the aim of attacking Port Stanley in the Falkland Islands on the way. However, as the squadron approached the colony it was sighted and a powerful British squadron, assembled there specially for the purpose, gave chase. Four of the five German ships were sunk on 8 December and von Spee, along with 2,000 of his officers and men, was lost. Spee enjoyed a high professional reputation in the German navy and on his return home he was to have been appointed commander-in-chief of the **High Seas Fleet**.

SPRINGFIELD RIFLE

The standard rifle of the United States army during the First World War, the Springfield was adopted in 1903 as a replacement for the obsolete Krag-Jorgensen gun. A modified **Mauser**, it was built under licence at the Springfield Arsenal and elsewhere. Originally designed around a blunt-nosed cartridge, it was modified to accept the pointed bullet first adopted by the German army before production began. The integral box magazine held five .30 rounds and the weapon had a muzzle velocity of 853m per second. The designers avoided the need to develop a carbine version by producing a short (24-inch) barrel rifle that could be used by both infantry and cavalry. A well constructed and accurate weapon, it remained in American service until the Korean War. The original M1903 was the Springfield used most widely by the AEF in France, although a later variant (the Mark I), a conversion to an automatic rifle, was widely available.

STANDARD EI

This American single-seater was originally designed as a fighter but its performance proved to be inadequate for a combat role. It was, however, accepted as an advanced trainer by the United States air service and the first batches were in use in the closing months of the war. A two-bay biplane, it was unarmed and powered by a single 100hp Gnome or Le Rhône rotary engine. The Gnome-powered EI had a maximum speed of 120m.p.h. at sea level.

STANLEY, EDWARD, EARL OF DERBY, 1865–1948

A former Conservative Member of Parliament before his succession to the earldom in 1908, Lord Derby first came to national prominence during the war when he was appointed director of recruiting in 1915. An advocate of compulsory service, Derby first launched a system of voluntary recruitment, which involved enrolling all eligible single men between the ages of 18 and 41 for possible enlistment. The 'Derby scheme' soon proved to be a failure and early in 1916 **conscription** was introduced. Towards the end of the year, Lord Derby became Secretary of State for War, in recognition of the assistance he had given in helping **Lloyd George** to power, although he was excluded from the inner decision-making bodies of the government. Enjoying good relations with his senior military colleagues, Derby came into conflict with the prime minister on several occasions, threatening to resign on two. Both moments of crisis concerned Lloyd George's plans to relinquish control of British forces in France for particular operations. Derby left the War Office in April 1918 and ended the war as British Ambassador to France.

STEYR AUTOMATIC PISTOL

The standard pistol of the Austro-Hungarian army during the First World War, the recoil-operated Steyr Model 1912 replaced the 8mm Repetierpistole M07 or Roth-Steyr, although the earlier type was still used by the cavalry during the war. The M12, which was also adopted by the Rumanian army in 1913, was the locked-breech type. It fired its own unique 9mm cartridge, which was specifically designed for this particular gun; it was held in an eight-round magazine that was an integral part of the butt. The Steyr pistol was strongly constructed and acquired an excellent reputation for accuracy and power. It was still in service during the Second World War, having been modified for use by the German army.

STOKES MORTAR

'The outstanding and ubiquitous' British trench weapon of the First World War, the Stokes four-inch mortar reached the Western Front late in 1915. Its development had been delayed by official opposition, but **Lloyd George**'s support ensured that it eventually emerged. A quick-firing, light mortar, the basic design was used by many armies. It was operated by a team of three: one carried the barrel; another the base plate and sight; while the third was responsible for the bipod. It used a simple, unstabilised cylindrical projectile, which could be propelled with reasonable accuracy over a range of up to 1,500 yards. Drop-fired, it was originally exploded by a time fuse (after 25 seconds), although later an impact fuse was developed. The term Stokes bomb was soon used loosely to describe any British mortar bomb.

An Australian soldier operates the Stokes mortar on the Western Front

STURDEE, ADMIRAL SIR FREDERICK DOVETON, 1859–1925

Sturdee gained distinction early in the war as commander of the British force of two battlecruisers that destroyed **Vice-Admiral von Spee**'s flotilla at the **Falklands** in December 1914. In recognition of his great victory, Sturdee, who had served as Chief of the Naval War Staff during the first few months of the war, was given command of the First Battle Squadron of the **Grand Fleet**, where he remained until 1918. Although he failed to secure command of the fleet on **Jellicoe**'s departure, he was promoted admiral in 1917 and ended his naval career as commander-in-chief at the Nore, 1918–21.

SUBMARINE

At the beginning of the war, Britain and France possessed about half of the 400 submarines then in existence. The submarine arm of the German navy had only 20 operational boats available, but an urgent construction programme was introduced as soon as war was declared. These mobilisation or Ms-type ocean-going boats were supplemented by smaller, mass-produced coastal submarines. The Germans took the lead in the development of more specialist types, including minelayers and large submarine cruisers, the latter having displacements of up to 3,200 tons. Production priorities were varied as German naval strategy changed: for example, after the first period of unrestricted warfare ended, **U-cruisers**, which could operate according to the prize laws, were ordered. The number of operational U-boats reached its peak in October 1917 when 140 units were in service.

British submarines had a different parentage – the American Holland design – from their main opponent, and were largely small coastal types, reflecting

an early Admiralty view that they were mainly useful for harbour defence. Dimensions and performance gradually expanded in the **D-** and **E-class** units as official views of their wartime role became more realistic. The L-class replaced the E-class as the standard British submarine in the latter part of the war. Some of the other British wartime designs were more unusual and less successful: the steam-driven **K-class** boats, for example, which were intended to operate with the fleet, had many advanced features, but were incapable of performing the tactical role assigned to them. With a displacement of 1,700 tons they were the largest British submarine of the war and had a maximum speed of 24 knots.

U-boats played the dominant part in German naval strategy, particularly in the period after the **Battle of Jutland** (May 1916), when her dreadnoughts were virtually confined to port. Operating on the surface and below and equipped with both guns and torpedoes, German submarines sank over 11 million tons of Allied shipping during the war, of which the great

British submarine with light cruiser Lowestoft *in the background*

proportion (almost eight million tons) was British. As many as 2,600 Allied ships of all kinds were sunk, the heaviest losses being sustained during the **Battle of the Atlantic** (1915–17).

During the first few months of 1917, Britain was brought close to defeat as Germany's second period of unrestricted submarine warfare exacted a heavy toll. However, the long overdue introduction of the **convoy system,** assisted by new techniques of anti-submarine warfare, transformed the situation. German U-boat losses began to rise and by the end of the war 178 had been sunk by the British. Submarine technology had progressed so rapidly during the war that its basic design had changed little by the time the Second World War began.

SUETER, SIR MURRAY, 1872–1960

The first director of the Air Department of the Admiralty (1912–15), Sir Murray Sueter was largely responsible for the creation of the Royal Naval Air Service, which broke away from the RFC in 1914. In his earlier naval career he had been associated with the development of radio telegraphy and with the introduction of submarines, and he was to be an innovative head of the RNAS. He presided over the rapid expansion of the service on the outbreak of war and was an important influence on the adoption of the seaplane for naval use. Sueter was also among the first to see the potential of torpedo-carrying aircraft.

His interests extended well beyond naval aircraft

and he encouraged the development of non-rigid airships or 'Blimps', which were used successfully in significant numbers over the North Sea. (However, his earlier experiences with rigid airships, as Inspecting Captain of Airships, 1908–11, had been much less happy.) A further example of his creativity was the service's pioneering use of **armoured cars** during the early war of movement on the Western Front. In 1915–17, he was responsible for naval aircraft construction, followed by a period in command of RNAS units in southern Italy in 1917–18. As a result of differences with the Admiralty, Sueter was unemployed for the last few months of the war.

SUEZ CANAL, DEFENCE OF, 1914–16

During the first few months of the war urgent preparations were made for the defence of Egypt, which was made a British protectorate, from Turkish attack. British troops had been withdrawn from the Sinai Peninsula behind the Suez Canal, 'the jugular vein of the British empire', which provided the basis for the successful defence of Egypt. The British commander, General Sir John Maxwell, had available

some 30,000 troops, mainly from India, to meet the Turkish threat, which materialised early in 1915.

Organised at the prompting of Baron Kress von Kressenstein, an able German staff officer attached to the Turkish army, a force of 20,000 men, led by **Djemal Pasha**, moved secretly across the Sinai desert. This difficult and dangerous journey completed, the Turkish assault began on 3 February 1915:

three boats actually crossed the canal but all their occupants were killed or captured. The main force came under heavy fire from ships' guns at some distance from the canal and with losses mounting Djemal soon withdrew to his rear base at Beersheba. He had lost about 2,000 men, while British casualties amounted to only 150. Adherence to a defensive strategy as well as the absence of sufficient desert transport meant that Sir John Maxwell was unable to pursue his enemies across Sinai.

Exaggerated fears of a further major Turkish attack led to an increase in the number of British troops stationed in Egypt and to the construction of an elaborate system of defences to the east of the canal in 1915–16. Under the command of Maxwell's successor, **General Sir Archibald Murray**, British forces pushed out into Sinai early in 1916. The aim was to secure a line between El Arish and Kossaima, 100 miles distant, as the most suitable position to defend the canal.

SUFFREN

Launched in 1899, this French battleship had turreted secondary guns, an arrangement that was not to be introduced by other navies for some time. *Suffren* also had main armament of four 12-inch guns, a maximum speed of almost 18 knots and a complement of 714.

She sustained some damage during the **Dardanelles operation**, but in November 1916 she was torpedoed by the German submarine U52 while travelling unescorted off Lisbon. She sank with the loss of all her crew.

SUKHOMLINOV, GENERAL VLADIMIR, 1848–1926

Russian Minister of War from 1909 to 1915, Sukhomlinov was associated with the modernisation of the army before the war. However, his reforms aroused the opposition of traditional elements within the military and he was eventually denounced for alleged corruption and incompetence. Beyond a four-year plan for the expansion of the army, the main changes he introduced were a review of mobilisation procedures, the reorganisation of reserve forces and an increase in heavy field artillery.

Sukhomlinov's position was weakened when it

became clear that the war would not be over quickly: Stavka emerged as an alternative source of power and undermined his ability to manipulate the promotion system. The shell shortage issue in 1915 provided the opportunity for his critics in the army and Duma to demand his resignation. He was dismissed in June and arrested on suspicion of corruption; his management of the War Ministry was to be investigated and he remained in captivity until released by the Bolsheviks in May 1918.

SWIFTSURE

Originally built for the Chilean navy, *Swiftsure* and her sister ship *Triumph* were acquired by the British government in 1903 and both played a useful role in the first half of the war. *Triumph* was involved in the

operations against **Tsingtao**, in co-operation with the Japanese navy, before being recalled to participate in the **Dardanelles** expedition. She was torpedoed by a German submarine off the peninsula in May

1915. *Swiftsure*, which had been on patrol in the Red Sea, was also ordered there, returning home after the evacuation.

These ships differed considerably from the standard British warships of the day. Lightly built with longer and narrower hulls, they had a displacement of 11,800 tons and were the first battleships capable of exceeding 20 knots. They were, however, less well protected and their armament was unusual: four 10-inch and fourteen 7.5-inch guns.

SYKES–PICOT AGREEMENT, May 1916

The partition of the Ottoman empire was the subject of this secret Franco-British agreement of May 1916. Designed to meet French fears that Britain was 'planning to run off with all Turkey-in-Asia', it divided the region into spheres of influence. France was allocated Syria, Lebanon and Cilicia, while the British would be dominant in Palestine, Basra and Baghdad; Jerusalem would fall within an international zone. This agreement, which was not fully implemented in the Paris peace settlement, was inconsistent with British pledges to the leaders of the **Arab revolt** that a united Arab state should be created and it caused considerable difficulties when it became public knowledge.

TANK MARK I

Protracted British efforts to produce a 'landship' capable of overcoming the trenches, barbed wire and machine-guns of the Western Front eventually resulted in the development of 'Mother'. This prototype tank, which was successfully demonstrated in January 1916, had the distinctive lozenge-shaped hull and all-round tracks that were to be common to all British heavy tanks of the First World War. Both features helped to maximise the tank's trench crossing ability.

Following this trial an order for 100 tanks (later increased to 150) was placed. Designated the Mark I, the new model, which was almost identical to 'Mother', was described as a tank rather than a landship for security reasons in an attempt to disguise its true identity. The hull was a simple steel box consisting of armour plate varying in thickness from 6 to 12mm. A 105hp Daimler engine, which dominated the single internal compartment, produced a maximum speed of 3.7m.p.h. and a range of 22 miles. Steering was provided by a two-wheeled trailed unit but this was soon discarded because it was vulnerable to enemy attack and was less effective on uneven ground. The clutch and brake method was used instead but four men were required to operate it.

Half of the Mark Is ordered were armed with a 6-pounder naval gun on each side and were known as 'males'. The weapons were mounted in sponsons or half turrets, which gave a wide field of fire; a top turret was rejected to avoid a high centre of gravity. The 'females' were armed with four side-mounted **Vickers machine-guns** and were intended to operate against infantry formations. Both types were also equipped with a single **Hotchkiss machine-gun**.

The world's first operational tank went into action on 15 September 1916, during the **First Battle of the Somme**. Thirty-seven tanks, manned by the new Heavy Section, Machine-Gun Corps, were involved. Although the engagement was unsuccessful in achieving a breakthrough, partly because of unsuitable ground, insufficient tank, and mechanical problems, there were many indications of the potential of the new machine. Confirmation of its likely future value was provided in **Sir Douglas Haig**'s order for 1,000 tanks a few days later, although there was still some scepticism amongst the more conservative senior officers about its value.

TANKS, MARKS II & III

Almost identical to the **Mark I Tank** in appearance and performance, these interim models were produced early in 1917 pending the development of a new British tank that was to be produced in large numbers. Like their predecessor they were both produced in 'male' and 'female' forms with modifications being confined to points of detail. The Mark II, for example, had wider track plates fitted at every sixth link, while the Mark III also had improved armour. Fifty examples of each were made and they served with the surviving Mark Is on the Western Front until the autumn of 1917, when they were superseded by the **Mark IV**. After their front line use had ended a number were converted into supply tanks and other specialist vehicles.

TANK MARK IV

The British Mark IV tank was similar in size and appearance to its predecessors but incorporated a variety of improvements derived from the operational use of the **Mark I**s. Some of these changes had already been incorporated in the Marks II and III, interim designs produced in small quantities in 1916.

The main visible modification was the Mark IV's smaller sponsons, which unlike those of the Marks I–III were swung inwards rather than removed before the tank was transported by rail. The new male version also now used the short 6-pounder rather than the longer 40-calibre guns that proved not to be sturdy enough for land use. Secondary armament consisted of four .303 **Lewis machine-gun**s, replacing the **Vickers** and **Hotchkiss** weapons used previously; the female version was also equipped with six of these weapons. The air-cooled Lewis did not, however, prove to be very satisfactory as a tank weapon and in later models was replaced by the Hotchkiss.

The improved British Mark IV Tank, highly prized by the Germans as well as by its country of origin

In order to give greater protection against German armour-piercing bullets, 12mm armour was used much more extensively in the new tank. Other changes included an improved petrol feed system, a silenced exhaust system and more efficient ventilation. Ditching had been a problem with the Mark I tank and in order to overcome it each Mark IV was equipped with a large wooden beam which could be attached to the tracks by a chain; the tracks pulled the beam under the tank enabling it to free itself. From the time of the **Battle of Cambrai** the Mk IV also carried fascines, bound bundles of brushwood that were dropped into wide trenches as an aid in crossing them.

The Mark IV was produced in larger quantities than any other British tank during the First World War: a total of 1,015 were made, of which 595 were Females and 420 Males. It also equipped four German tank companies, the Beute Panzerwagen IV (Captured Armoured Vehicle), outnumbering the A7V, the only German-produced tank of the war. Appearing in France in April 1917, it was first used in action during the **Battle of Messines** in June, although it made its greatest impact in the Battle of Cambrai in September 1917. As many as 450 Mark IVs took part in the operation and although the offensive was ultimately unsuccessful it fully demonstrated the tank's future potential. The Mark IV, which also featured in the first tank versus tank engagement in April 1918, remained in use until the end of the war. The most important variant to appear was the unarmed tank tender, powered by an up-rated 125hp Daimler engine, which transported tank supplies across the battlefield.

TANK MARK V

Similar in appearance to its lozenge-shape predecessors, the Mark V tank incorporated several important mechanical changes. It was equipped with a new transmission – the Wilson epicyclic gearbox – which meant that the tank could be driven by one man for the first time. The standard Daimler power unit was replaced by the more powerful 150hp Ricardo engine, which was specially designed for this purpose, and produced a higher maximum speed of 4.6m.p.h. Armament and visibility were also improved, but the Mark V was not as well ventilated as its predecessors.

The new machine first arrived in France in May 1918 and by the Armistice some 400 had been built, equally divided between male and female variants. Armament was identical to previous models, except that all the machine-guns fitted to the Mark Vs were of the **Hotchkiss** type. First used operationally in July, a force of 324 Mark Vs was in action at the beginning of the **Amiens offensive** in August; in September they led the way through the Hindenburg Line, using 'cribs' – a cylindrical frame that was placed in the trenches – to help them across.

Work had in fact already begun on improving the Mark Vs trench-crossing ability. The 'tadpole tail' extension – an early contender – proved to be unsatisfactory and was discarded in favour of a more radical modification which involved cutting the Mark V in half and inserting extra side panels. The length of the Mark V*, as it was designated, was increased by six feet and it was now able to cross a trench up to 14 feet wide without any difficulty. Some 600 Mark V*s (of which the majority were females) were produced and they served alongside the standard version in France in the final months of the war.

British Mark V Tanks in action during the Battle of Amiens

TANKS

The tank emerged as a direct response to the static **trench warfare** of the Western Front and the need to achieve a breakthrough. The possible means to overcome the enemy's barbed wire and machine-guns and cross his trenches was suggested to the War Office as early as October 1914. As a result, an armoured vehicle mounted on a Holt caterpillar tractor was produced in prototype form, but the project was abandoned by a sceptical War Office after trials early in 1915. It was the Admiralty, under **Winston Churchill**, that now pursued the idea but the initial plans of the Admiralty Landships Committee were, as its title indicates, over-ambitious and led nowhere.

An initiative by Ernest Swinton, a Royal Engineers officer who played a key role in the emergence of the tank, led to the development of two more practical prototypes: 'Little Willie' and 'Big Willie', and a larger version better known as 'Mother'. The latter, which could more easily meet the War Office's crossing and climbing requirements, passed its trials in February 1916.

An order for 100 machines, produced as the **Mark I**, was then placed. Operated by a crew of eight, it was armed with five machine-guns ('female') or two 6-pounder guns ('male'); maximum speed was less than 3.7m.p.h. At the same time the French had been developing their own designs independently and two

machines – the **Schneider** and the **Saint Chamond** – both using the Holt caterpillar chassis, appeared in 1916. Neither of these heavy tanks could match the performance of their British counterparts, although the later **Renault FT-17** was a highly successful light tank that appeared at the front in large numbers.

Tanks were first used at the **Somme** on 15 September 1916, when 37 tanks attacked the German lines. The machine's potential was demonstrated even though there were too few available to make an impact; **Haig** suggested that 1,000 tanks should be ordered and the first tank corps was soon formed.

During 1917, tanks were used in small numbers at **Arras**, **Messines** and **Ypres**, but it was not until November that they were employed *en masse*. The initial attack at **Cambrai** was made by 378 tanks which successfully broke through the German lines; the exploitation was left to the cavalry and it quickly ran into difficulties. It was clear that faster tanks would be needed to follow up a breakthrough and a medium tank – the Whippet – suitable for the purpose was ordered; it appeared in March 1918.

The Germans, who at first failed to appreciate the significance of the tank, produced their first machines in time for the March 1918 offensive. The **A7V Sturmpanzerwagon**, as it was designated, had some major design weaknesses, performing badly during the first battle between opposing tank forces

The British Medium A (Whippet) Tank

at Villers-Bretonneux on 24 April. The reputation of the tank was overshadowed by the German gains in 1918 and it was not until the Battle of Hamel in July that its position was restored.

On 8 August, the Allies launched the greatest tank attack of the war at **Amiens**, employing over 600 machines in total. On 'the black day of the German army' some 324 heavy tanks broke through the German lines, and Whippets were moved up to exploit the gap. As the Allied advance continued during the autumn, its progress was influenced by the level of tank support available. The tank had made an important contribution as a supporting weapon during 1914–18, but it was not until the Second World War that its full potential was realised.

TANK PRODUCTION, 1916–18

	Heavy	Medium	Light
Great Britain	2,617	281	———
France	———	800	3,500
Germany	20	———	———

TANNENBERG, BATTLE OF, 26–30 August 1914

After the success at the **Battle of Gumbinnen** (20 August 1914), the Russian First Army (**Rennenkampf**) failed to push forward quickly, giving the Germans the opportunity to reorganise following the dismissal of **General von Prittwitz**. The new commander of the Eighth Army, **General von Hindenburg** and his chief of staff, **Ludendorff**, arrived in East Prussia on 23 August, with a new plan to halt the Russian offensive which was, in fact, similar to the action already proposed by **Max Hoffman**, chief of operations under Prittwitz.

A single cavalry division would delay Rennenkampf while the remainder of the German forces would move south-east to the region around Tannenberg. There they would attack the Second Army (**Samsonov**), then moving up from the south, taking advantage of the emnity between the two Russian commanders, which made it unlikely that Rennenkampf would provide any real assistance. Samsonov's five corps had crossed the frontier on 22 August, on a front of almost 60 miles, and had engaged the German XX Corps (Scholtz), which withdrew to Tannenberg after a day's heavy fighting. Under Ludendorff's plan, XVII Corps (**Mackensen**) and I Reserve Corps (**Below**) would attack the Russian right flank while I Corps (**François**) would move on their left; the centre would be hit by XX Corps.

The Germans, who launched their large double envelopment on 26 August, benefitted from the interception of uncoded Russian radio messages, which provided invaluable information about troop strengths and locations. Unaware of the German forces ranged against them, the Russians renewed their advance on the same day, along the whole front.

The battle began on Samsonov's right flank when the detached VI Corps ran into Mackensen's XVII Corps; with the help of Below's force the Russians were pushed back. Samsonov attacked again on the following day, but soon came under heavy pressure on his left, near Usdau. François attacked there and, with the support of an artillery bombardment, forced the enemy to retreat. On 28 August, the Russian left flank retired across the border and François moved eastwards, while on the right the Germans attacked towards Allenstein; in the centre the situation was less certain for the Germans, but Samsonov was unable to follow up some initial successes. In fact, after a tour of the front which had been designed to encourage stronger resistance, he decided that the position could not be saved and ordered a general retreat.

Moving eastwards through a narrow strip of densely wooded land between the marshes, the two centre corps, which had advanced further west, were the most vulnerable and were soon forced to surrender. On 29 August, the encirclement of the Russians was complete as François moved across their rear as far as Willenburg; the destruction of the enemy followed immediately.

The Russian Second Army lost 125,000 men and 500 guns; the Germans no more than 15,000 men. General Samsonov killed himself on 29 August as the scale of the Russian disaster became clear to him. It was a major boost to the Germans and undermined Allied confidence in the Russians. Ludendorff now turned towards Rennenkampf, who had failed to come to Samsonov's assistance even when ordered to; his army was defeated at the **First Battle of the Masurian Lakes** (September 1914). This success cleared the Russians from East Prussia. German territory was never again to be invaded by the Russians during the First World War. The victory of Tannenberg 'remains a great achievement, as it was a unique one in the history of the war', resulting in the encirclement of an army and the destruction of two and a half army corps.

THAON DI REVEL, ADMIRAL PAOLO, 1859–1948

Admiral di Revel was appointed Chief of Staff of the Italian navy in 1913 and held the post throughout the war. In February 1917, following the retirement of the **Duca di Abruzzi**, he also became naval commander-in-chief. Di Revel, who made a substantial contribution to the modernisation of the navy before the outbreak of war, was particularly concerned to preserve its operational independence from Allied control from 1915 onwards.

THOMAS MORSE S-4

Widely used by the United States Air Service from November 1917 until the Armistice, the S-4 was an advanced trainer with good flying qualities. Like the **Standard EI**, this American aircraft had been conceived as a single-seat fighter but had been rejected in favour of superior European designs. Two variants of the S-4 appeared, representing minor differences in the wings and control areas, and in total nearly 600 examples had been delivered by the end of the war.

The original power plant was the unreliable 100hp Gnome Monosoupape, which was eventually replaced by the 80hp Le Rhône. The S-4 could be fitted with a .30-inch **Marlin** machine-gun or a camera gun.

TIGER

An improved version of the *Queen Mary*, *Tiger* was the battlecruiser equivalent of the Iron Dukes. Elegant in appearance, she was the fastest capital ship of her time, with a maximum speed of 29 knots; she was also the largest, with a displacement of 28,430 tons, because of the large space needed for the operating machinery. The last coal-burning capital ship built for the Royal Navy, *Tiger* was armed with eight 13.5-inch guns; secondary armament consisted of twelve 6-inch guns, six to each side, and two 3-inch anti-aircraft guns.

Completed in October 1914, *Tiger* joined the **Grand Fleet** and was soon in action at the **Battle of the Dogger Bank** with the 1st Battlecruiser Squadron. At **Jutland** she sustained 15 hits, and it was a tribute to the quality of her construction and her more extensive armour protection that repairs took no more than a month to complete.

TIRPITZ, GRAND ADMIRAL ALFRED von, 1849–1930

German grand admiral who, as Secretary of State of the Ministry of Marine, 1897–1916, played a key role in the dramatic growth of the navy in the pre-war period. Indeed, he was given the title of 'Father of the German navy'. The naval race between Germany and Britain intensified after the appearance of the *Dreadnought* but by 1914 Tirpitz's navy had almost as many battleships and battlecruisers as her principal maritime opponent. As State Secretary, Tirpitz's powers were confined to administration, but on the outbreak of war he argued for his own appointment as naval commander-in-chief, to resolve the problem of divided responsibilities in wartime.

The proposal was rejected and Tirpitz found increasingly that he was excluded from discussions on wartime strategy. His own views were in any case often widely at variance with the official position. For example, he was bitterly disappointed that his own major creation – the battle fleet – was to have a passive role and was not to be risked at sea. He wrote subsequently that 'it only needed the right command to bring out all its qualities and lead the fleet to victory'. As an alternative, Tirpitz was a strong advocate of unrestricted submarine warfare on Allied shipping. Not unexpectedly, he objected strongly to the constraints associated with the re-introduction of U-boat warfare early in 1916. Frustrated by his inability to influence the direction of policy, Tirpitz resigned in March 1916 from the post he had held for almost 19 years.

Tirpitz: creator of the modern German navy

TOGOLAND

Togoland, the small German territory in West Africa, fell to the Allies unexpectedly quickly during the first month of the war. Small British and French invasion forces from the Gold Coast and Dahomey marched across the frontiers of Togoland at the earliest opportunity. On 27 August 1914, after only three weeks' fighting, the small enemy garrison had surrendered. As a result of this defeat Togoland ceased to be the centre of German radio communications in Africa.

TORPEDO

The most destructive naval weapon of the First World War – it sank far more vessels than mines or gunfire – the torpedo was a self-propelled missile launched from a ship, submarine or aircraft. It moved through the sea just below the water and detonated against the side of an enemy ship. The Whitehead 'fish-type' torpedo, which had first been adopted by the Royal Navy in the 1870s, was used by Britain and several other countries during the war. It was propelled by a compressed air engine and was equipped with mechanisms to control its direction, depth and balance in the water. Normally $17\frac{1}{2}$ or 22 feet in length and 18 or 21 inches in diameter, it had a range of 3,750 yards at 44 knots or 10,000 yards at 28 knots.

Torpedoes were carried by destroyers and coastal motor boats, but it was the submarine that used the weapon to its greatest effect. The first successful launching of a torpedo from a British aircraft occurred on 28 July 1914. This led to the development of the **Short 184**, the first torpedo-carrying seaplane to be designed specially for the purpose. Operating difficulties did not prevent the Short from becoming the first aircraft to sink an enemy ship by means of an air-launched torpedo, on 12 August 1915.

British Torpedo Boat 110 on patrol

TOWNSHEND, GENERAL SIR CHARLES, 1861–1924

An experienced soldier of the empire, Townshend was appointed to the command of the Sixth (Indian) Division in Mesopotamia in April 1915. In order to secure the Basra area, **Sir John Nixon**, the British commander ordered an advance northwards up the Tigris and Euphrates rivers. Townshend's division began its notable 'regatta' up the Tigris in May, capturing Amara and then moving on to **Kut**, which was taken on 29 September after a skilfully conducted operation.

Although he was sceptical about the prospects for further success, Townshend was ordered by Nixon to advance on Baghdad, without waiting for the reinforcements promised by the War Office. The British were halted at **Ctesiphon** where they encountered a much larger Turkish force firmly entrenched on the banks of the Tigris. Their assault soon failed and after repelling heavy counter-attacks they were forced to retreat to Kut, which was reached on 3 December. Surviving three initial Turkish assaults, the British were besieged from 6 December 1915 until 29 April 1916. A relief force was unable to break through and, near starvation, Townshend was compelled to negotiate the surrender of his men.

Unlike his troops, Townshend was imprisoned in relative comfort near Constantinople until the last days of the war. He was then released so that he could act as an intermediary for the Turks in seeking the best possible terms for their surrender. Townshend returned home after the Armistice had been signed, on 30 October 1918.

TRENCH WARFARE

The failure of the Allies or the Germans to outflank the other during the 'Race to the Sea' (15 September– 24 November) marked the end of the war of movement on the Western Front. Separated by a narrow strip of land, the opposing armies created a line of static trenches that ran from the Belgian coast to the Swiss border, passing across northern France. A strange episode in the history of trench warfare was the Christmas truce of 1914 during which British and German troops left their positions and fraternised for several days. During the first winter both sides consolidated their initial positions by joining unconnected trenches together. The trench system typically consisted of three lines – front, support and reserve trenches – in close proximity; they were linked by communication trenches to the rear areas. Normally about seven feet in depth, the trenches had a parapet of earth or sand bags to protect the defending troops from the enemy's small arms fire.

Accommodation for the rank and file was very primitive at first and often consisted of no more than a hole in the trench wall. Protection was gradually improved but it was not until 1916 that the Allies provided a shell-proof cover, although the Germans had introduced a concrete dug-out during the previous year. Troops normally spent eight days at a time in accommodation of this kind, with a similar period in reserve before moving into rest camp.

At the front they were in constant danger from artillery shells, mortars and snipers' bullets. They also faced aerial attack as the war progressed. Food was very restricted because of supply problems and disease was rife in the damp, rat-infested conditions. Many troops suffered from 'trench foot', a painful swelling of the feet.

At the heart of this defensive system was the heavy machine-gun, which dominated the battlefield with its continuous fire. The Germans, who pursued a largely defensive strategy until 1918, were the acknowledged masters of machine-gun tactics. Heavy howitzers firing high explosive shells also had an important defensive role, but the principal task of artillery was to prepare the ground for major infantry assaults. Another essential feature of the trench system was the barbed wire that both sides laid in no man's land, separating the opposing armies which were normally no more than 250 yards apart. With troops protected from direct attack from small arms fire, a number of specialist weapons quickly appeared, including hand grenades and mortars.

From 1915 the British and French launched a series of offensives designed to recover the territory lost in 1914. Each attack followed a similar pattern. An artillery bombardment marked the beginning of an offensive. Once it had softened up the enemy's front line, troops cut gaps in the barbed wire, and the infantry moved forward across no man's land. Before 1918 they were rarely able to do more than breach the first defensive line before the momentum of the offensive had been lost. Artillery could not completely obliterate the enemy's forward positions and the superiority of the surviving defensive weapons, when combined with a ready supply of reserves, ensured that the attacking infantry was pushed back with heavy losses. As a result, the temporary trenches of 1914–15 became permanent and a breakthrough did not materialise until 1918.

In the absence of an alternative strategy, the war of attrition continued, with losses mounting rapidly as various methods of overcoming the deadlock were sought. Gas was used by both sides but soon lost its impact with the development of counter-measures. Tunnelling was an important feature of trench warfare but it was a slow and costly method of gaining ground. The most notable example of the use of tunnelling was the **Messines** ridge operation (June 1917) when nearly a million pounds of high explosive were detonated.

Artillery bombardments assumed massive proportions as German defences were strengthened, while gunnery techniques were gradually improved. Important use was made of the rolling barrage and aerial reconnaissance. However, defensive measures were also evolving during the war, the most important innovation being the German system of defence in depth. The Hindenburg Line, which was constructed in 1917, replaced the earlier linear trench lines. Consisting of three defensive areas several miles in depth, it constituted a formidable barrier to an attacking force. It did not seek to defend every inch of

A British communications trench during the Battle of Messines

The bombardment of Messines, 6 June 1917: a view from the trenches

ground but tried to prevent the enemy advancing through the zones. One of its main features was the removal of the majority of the defending troops out of enemy artillery range.

The Allied equivalent to this flexible system was still under construction when the Germans launched their offensive against the Allied trenches in the spring of 1918. Using new techniques to overcome the power of the defence, including a surprise artillery bombardment, storm troops and highly flexible tactics, the Germans at first seemed to have achieved a breakthrough. However, the effective Allied deployment of reserves and German logistical problems – transport and supply – meant that the Allied line still remained unbroken. The counter-offensive that followed the last German assault in July finally broke the trench barrier. The combined effect of the tank, which presented 'an offensive antidote to defensive strength' and overwhelming Allied numerical superiority together restored the war of movement on the Western Front.

TRENCHARD, HUGH, VISCOUNT, 1873–1956

A stagnant army career, spent mainly in the colonies, persuaded Major Trenchard to learn to fly in 1912. Successfully completing the course, although he was never an outstanding pilot, Trenchard transferred permanently to the new Royal Flying Corps. He was appointed adjutant of its Central Flying School, which had recently opened, and was involved in devising a programme of instruction for aspiring pilots. On the outbreak of war he remained at home, organising and training new squadrons at Farnborough for the RFC in France.

His disappointment was, however, short-lived because in November 1914 he moved to France as commander of 1st Wing. He developed its military potential by securing more radio and photographic equipment and by experimenting with tactical bombing. During this period he developed the close working relationship with **Douglas Haig**, then commander of the First Army, that was to last throughout the war. His organisational and leadership abilities were further recognised in August 1915 when he succeeded Sir David Henderson as commander of the RFC in France.

Although Trenchard was not universally popular – he was given the nickname 'Boom' – he successfully developed and preserved the morale of his aircrews during the difficult period of the **Fokker** ascendancy in 1915. As British strength built up and new machines arrived he was able to put his tactical ideas – particularly the importance of the aircraft as a weapon of attack – into practice. His insistence on offensive action as the key to air mastery had gradually swung the air battle on the Western Front in the RFC's

Trenchard and Queen Mary inspecting British fighters

favour by the summer of 1916, although the costs were high. During the **First Battle of the Somme**, for example, he lost 500 airmen and in Bloody April 1917, when the Germans again had superior aircraft, there was an even higher rate of loss.

Trenchard's reputation grew during 1917 and as Britain's most experienced air commander he was the obvious choice as chief of staff of the new Royal Air Force; he was appointed in January 1918. Lacking the necessary political skills for operating in Whitehall, he soon quarrelled with the first Air Minister, Lord Rothermere, about the tasks to which the RAF should give priority. He resigned in April 1918 shortly before the new force officially came into existence.

After a brief period of unemployment, he returned to France to lead the Independent Force, Britain's strategic bombing group. Operating with only nine squadrons, the force carried out raids on civilian and military targets in Germany until the end of the war. Known as the 'Father of the Royal Air Force', Trenchard played a fundamental role in developing the wartime air force as a separate military force and in establishing the principles of its use. From 1919 until his retirement in 1929, he served as Chief of the Air Staff for the second time, and in 1927 was created the first Marshal of the Royal Air Force.

TRIANON, TREATY OF, 4 June 1920

The peace treaty between Hungary and the Allies after the First World War, which reduced the country to a fraction of its former size. As a result, her population in the 1920s was less than eight million people, compared with 21 million in 1914. Rumania gained most territory, but Czechoslovakia, Poland, Yugoslavia, Italy and the new Austrian republic were also beneficiaries. In addition, Hungary was liable for **reparations** and her army could not exceed 35,000 men. During the inter-war years the Hungarian government sought to change the terms of the treaty, which were strongly opposed by the whole country.

TROTHA, ADMIRAL ADOLF von, 1868–1940

Commander of the dreadnought *Kaiser* until the beginning of 1916, Trotha was then appointed chief of staff to **Vice-Admiral Scheer**, head of the **High Seas Fleet**. Trotha, who was awarded the Pour Le Mérite for his service at **Jutland**, remained in post after the appointment of **Admiral von Hipper** as Scheer's successor in August 1918. Together they devised the abortive Plan 19, by which the High Seas Fleet was to launch an all-out attack on the British on 30 October 1918, in order to salvage the German Navy's honour. Trotha's naval career continued after the war when he became deeply embroiled in right-wing politics.

TROTSKY, LEON, 1879–1940

Russian revolutionary whose role in the Marxist-inspired opposition to the Tsar culminated in his appointment as Commissar for Foreign Affairs when the Bolsheviks seized power in November 1917. Unable to make progress in bringing all the combatant nations to the conference table, Trotsky was forced to sign an armistice with the Germans on 15 December 1917.

This was followed by a peace conference with the **Central Powers** at Brest-Litovsk in eastern Poland. In the vain hope that workers' unrest in Germany and Austro-Hungary would lead to revolution, Trotsky sought to delay signing the dictated treaty as long as possible. On 10 February 1918, he made his famous declaration of 'no war, no peace': Russia would neither accept peace nor pursue the war. Trotsky's delaying tactics were unsuccessful as the German armies renewed their advance eastwards and, following his resignation, the Bolsheviks were forced to accept the **Treaty of Brest-Litovsk** (3 March 1918).

During the Civil War Trotsky was Commissar of War and he proved to be an outstanding military organiser. He created the Red Army and played a leading role in securing the Bolshevik victory.

TROUBRIDGE, ADMIRAL SIR ERNEST, 1862–1926

The subject of a famous court-martial during the opening stages of the war, Admiral Troubridge's naval career dated back to 1875. Much of his career had been spent on shore and included periods as naval attaché in Tokyo and chief of the naval war staff. In August 1914, he was in command of the cruiser squadron of the British Mediterranean fleet, whose commander-in-chief was **Sir Archibald Milne**. Almost immediately after war had been declared, Troubridge was involved in the pursuit of the German warships *Goeben* and *Breslau*, which he failed to engage south of Greece. Their arrival in the Dardanelles facilitated Turkey's entry into the war, with disastrous long-term consequences for the Allies.

A court of inquiry described Troubridge's action as 'deplorable and contrary to the traditions of the British navy' although there was no suggestion of cowardice. In the court-martial which followed, in November 1914, his successful defence to the charge of negligence was that the Admiralty had specifically ordered him not to engage a superior force. Following his acquittal Troubridge never again served at sea, but unlike Milne continued to be employed for the rest of the war – first as head of a naval mission to Serbia and then on the Prince of Serbia's personal staff.

TSESSAREVITCH

Laid down in 1899, this Russian battleship was built in France and French influences were much in evidence in its design. It had a displacement of 12,915 tons, four 12-inch guns and a maximum speed of 18.5 knots. In action during the Russo-Japanese War she was hit several times, but her career in the First World War as a unit of the Baltic Fleet was much less eventful. *Tsessarevitch* was slightly damaged in October 1917 while fighting German dreadnoughts off Moon Island, her only major engagement of the war.

TSINGTAO

Germany's only possession in China, Tsingtao was seized by Japanese and British forces in November 1914. It was a fortified naval base at the end of the Shantung peninsula and its capture was one of Japan's principal war aims. Some 23,000 Japanese troops, under the command of **General Kamio**, were involved in the operation, which began with landings some distance north of the fortress. They were joined by a token force of 1,500 British soldiers sent by a government that feared Japanese expansionism. Bombarded by land artillery and by Japanese and British warships, the small garrison of 4,000 men surrendered on 7 November, just before a general assault was to be launched. The Germans suffered 700 casualties, while Japanese losses amounted to 1,800. It was not until the Washington Conference in 1922 that the Japanese agreed to evacuate Tsingtao.

TURKISH ARMY

In August 1914, the Turkish empire was defended by a total of 36 army divisions, some 150,000 combat troops, which were organised into 13 corps and three armies. The First Army was based in Constantinople, while the Second was responsible for the defence of the coast of Asia Minor and the Third was to be deployed in the Caucasus. The Yemen, Mesopotamia and the Hejaz were each garrisoned by two divisions. Turkey mobilised in September 1914, a month before her entry into the war. During 1914–18, some 2,850,000 men served in the Turkish army and a further seventy divisions and four army groups were formed. Total casualties amounted to 325,000 men killed and 400,000 injured.

The process of modernising the Turkish army had begun after the Balkan Wars, with a German mission, headed by **General Liman von Sanders**, making a major contribution. It was, however, a process that was far from complete by October 1914, particularly among the units remote from the capital. Long lines of communication were in fact one of the army's greatest weaknesses, with the movement of troops to the Caucasus and Mesopotamia being particularly difficult. There were also shortages of equipment, including artillery, which had been lost in the Balkan Wars but not yet replaced. A shortage of qualified Turkish officers meant that some 800 Germans were drafted in to serve in senior staff positions. Finally, the army included a large number of Arab troops whose unreliability was soon to be revealed. Desertion was to be a serious problem for the whole army, with as many as 400,000 troops absent from the front at one point.

The basis of the Turkish army's strength was 'the fighting qualities of the Anatolian peasant, disciplined, frugal, hardy and brave, normally quiet and good-tempered, but savage when his blood was up'. The Turks made a considerable contribution to the military effort of the Central Powers, fighting on four main fronts – Mesopotamia, the Caucasus, Egypt/ Palestine, and Gallipoli – as well as sending some of its best troops to Europe. However, the army's major organisational limitations and its disastrous defeats in the Caucasus in 1914–15, which permanently affected its fighting strength, ensured its eventual defeat by the Allies in October 1918.

TYRWHITT, ADMIRAL SIR REGINALD, 1870–1951

Commander of the Royal Navy's Harwich Force throughout the war, Commodore Tyrwhitt was an outstanding naval leader who displayed great initiative and courage. His force of light cruisers and destroyers, which was very intensively used and suffered heavy losses, was first in action at the **Battle of Heligoland Bight**, in an operation he had planned jointly with **Commodore Roger Keyes**. Tyrwhitt was present at the **Battle of the Dogger Bank** but, much to his regret, the Harwich Force missed **Jutland** because of Admiralty orders.

An important function of Tyrwhitt's force was to counter the regular bombardments of the east coast by German battlecruisers: on 25 April 1916, for example, a powerful enemy force was turned back off Lowestoft. Tyrwhitt was a powerful advocate of naval aviation and many seaplane raids against German land targets were launched from his ships. His successful wartime career concluded with the surrender of German U-boats to the Harwich Force after the Armistice.

U9

One of the 20 German U-boats in service in August 1914, U9 was responsible for the first major wartime success gained by a submarine. She sank three British heavy cruisers, *Aboukir*, *Hogue* and *Cressy* on 22 September 1914, graphically demonstrating the weapon's military potential. Like other early German submarines, U9 had a potentially dangerous kerosene engine. She had a displacement of 493 tons and a range of 1,800 nautical miles. Her armament consisted of four torpedo tubes (two bow, two stern) and she carried six torpedoes.

U31

The German Mittel-U type was a medium-sized submarine, beginning with batch U19–22, which first appeared before the war. Produced in small batches, between 1913 and 1917, they were subject to continuous design improvements. The U31 class (U31–41), ordered pre-1914, was representative of this type. Armed with four torpedo tubes and one 4.1-inch gun, it was powered by two 925hp diesel engines (or by two 600hp electric motors when submerged) and had a maximum surface speed of almost 17 knots. Operated by a crew of up to 39, it had a surface displacement of 685 tons. One of the boats of this series, U35, was in fact the most successful submarine of the First World War, sinking 224 ships of 535,900 gross tons. On the outbreak of war, further U-boats constructed in this series were known as Mobilisation (or Ms) boats, the first batch being designated U51–56. Relatively few of these boats were built, partly because priority was often given to the construction of more specialist submarines.

UB-CLASS SUBMARINE

The UB I (UB 1–17) was a small coastal submarine that first appeared early in 1915. Used by Austria and Bulgaria as well as Germany, it was slow and had a short range; its service was confined to the coastal waters of the North Sea, the Mediterranean and the Baltic. It had a surface displacement of 127 tons, a 60hp propulsion unit (driving a single screw) and two torpedoes. The German navy soon acquired a more powerful twin screw version in the UB II (UB 18–47), which had a displacement of 263 tons. It had more powerful twin engines (142hp each), much increased range (6,650 nautical miles) and larger torpedo tubes.

Despite these changes, the UB IIs lacked the range and speed for the operations around Britain and the Mediterranean that were necessary when, early in 1917, Germany reintroduced unrestricted submarine warfare. With Mobilisation (Ms) boats in short supply, the UB III (UB 48–155) was introduced as an alternative. Using the **UC II** minelayer as the prototype, this new torpedo U-boat had a double hull, a surface displacement of over 500 tons, twin 550hp engines, and a range of up to 9,000 nautical miles. It had five 500mm torpedo tubes and carried 10 torpedoes. This successful submarine, which was, in effect, a reduced version of the Ms boat, was to be the model for the type VII, which was developed when Germany began to build U-boats again under the Nazis.

U-BOAT

German submarine or *Unterseeboot*. See **Submarine**.

UC-CLASS SUBMARINE

The world's first submarine minelayers, the German UC I-class (UC 1–15) appeared early in 1915. Of simple, single-hull construction, these coastal ships had a displacement of 168 tons, a 90hp heavy oil engine (which gave a maximum surface speed of six knots), and a range of 750 nautical miles. Twelve mines were carried in six almost vertical flooded tubes; there was no other armament. The enlarged UC II series (UC 16–79), which emerged in 1916, were double-hulled boats, with a displacement of at least 417 tons. They had more powerful engines and an increased range of at least 7,300 nautical miles. The new version carried more mines (18), as well as seven torpedoes and a 8.8cm U-boat gun. The final series of coastal minelayers – the UC III (UC 90–114) – were slightly larger (displacement: 491 tons), but their performance and armament were similar.

German minelaying submarine UC5. The UC-class appeared early in 1915

U-CRUISER

By 1915, the British naval blockade of Germany had produced severe shortages of raw materials and in response the idea of an unarmed, cargo-carrying U-boat was developed. The largest submarine yet produced by Germany, *Deutschland* appeared in the spring of 1916. It made two successful journeys to the United States, although *Bremen*, which appeared soon afterwards, was lost on its maiden voyage. Along with other cargo U-boats under construction, *Deutschland* was subsequently converted as a U-cruiser, armed with heavy artillery and designated U151–157. Taken over by the navy early in 1917 they were equipped with two 15cm guns and two bow torpedo tubes; they had a surface displacement of 1,500 tons and a low maximum speed of 11 knots.

The operation of cargo U-boats provided valuable experience for the construction of specially designed U-cruisers, which were first ordered in August 1916. They were required as **commerce raiders** operating according to Prize Laws, after the abandonment of the first period of unrestricted U-boat warfare. Although the building of these large, powerful and well-armed boats was given priority, the first batch (U135–138) did not appear until early in 1918. The specification of a later batch, U139–141, included twin 1,750hp engines, a range of 12,000 nautical miles, a surface speed of 10 knots and the following weapons: two 15cm guns and six torpedo tubes. The delayed introduction of these boats and the small numbers involved reduced their impact considerably, although in other circumstances they might have posed a significant threat to Allied shipping.

UDET, ERNST, 1896–1941

Credited with 62 victories, Udet was the highest scoring German ace to survive the war, his total being second only to that of **Manfred von Richthofen**. He served with the early fighter units and brought down his first enemy aircraft in March 1916. By the end of 1917 his score had risen slowly to 15 officially confirmed hits, although the real figure was said to be considerably higher.

It was, in fact, only after he joined von Richthofen's *Jagdgeschwader I* in March 1918 that his reputation as an exceptional fighter pilot developed and, flying a **Fokker DVII**, many of his victories were gained during the intensive fighting of the summer

months. Oberleutnant Udet had several narrow escapes during more than three years' service on the Western Front; on one notable occasion early on, his gun jammed when engaged in combat with **Guynemer**. Fortunately for Udet, the French ace decided to withdraw rather than to press home his advantage. Udet returned to military aviation in the 1930s when the Nazis formed the Luftwaffe and by 1939 he was its Director-General of Equipment.

In spite of his achievements, Udet considered himself to have been a failure and he committed suicide in 1941.

UE-CLASS SUBMARINE

The first submarine minelayers – the German **UC-class** boats – had a limited range, were small and had other operational limitations. The UE class of ocean-going minelayers, which entered service in 1915, greatly enhanced Germany's capacity to strike at Allied naval and commercial shipping. The UE I series (U 71–80) could carry 34 mines, which were expelled through two tubes; four torpedoes were also carried. With a displacement of 755 tons, the twin 450hp diesel engines were not really sufficiently powerful but they were the only type available in sufficient

quantities. It had a range of some 8,000 nautical miles. One of the mines sown by this class may have been responsible for the destruction of the British cruiser *Hampshire*, which was lost on 5 June 1916 with **Lord Kitchener** on board. A much enlarged UE II series (U117–121, 122–126) appeared in 1918. With a displacement of 1,164 tons and twin 1,200hp engines, it could carry 42 mines (and a further 30 in deck containers) over an increased range of 9,400 nautical miles.

UFAG CI

The Ufag CI, like the **Phönix CI**, was a development of the **Brandenburg CI** 'star-strutter', which had been produced in experimental form only. Similar in many respects to the rival Phönix machine, this two-seater biplane had the same 230hp Hiero engine and identical forward and rear armament. Differences included the Ufag's parallel interplane struts, its equal span, slightly staggered wings, and the shape of its tail surfaces. After testing, both descendants of the Brandenburg were accepted by the Austrian air

service, as the performance differences between them were small. With a maximum speed of 118m.p.h. the Ufag was faster and more manoeuvrable, but it had a lower ceiling than the Phönix.

In operational use from the spring of 1918, the Ufag CI was widely employed on reconnaissance and artillery-spotting duties in the last few months of the war. It is uncertain how many were manufactured but it is likely that it was built in larger numbers than the Phönix CI, of which 110 were made.

UNITED STATES AIR SERVICE

Although the first American squadron had arrived in France by September 1917, it was not until the following spring that combat missions began, a year after her entry into the war. On 3 April 1918 the 94th Aero Squadron, United States Army Air Service engaged the enemy over the Western Front. The first combat victories soon followed, on 14 April, when two German aircraft were shot down. American day bombing raids date from June 1918 when the 96th Aero Squadron began operations.

When America declared war, its air service had about 260 aircraft, but none of these was suitable for combat use. Under Allied pressure, plans for a massive expansion of the American air effort and of aircraft production were drawn up. There were to be 263 operational US squadrons in France by the end of 1918 and thousands of aircraft were to be built in American factories. These over-ambitious plans were never realised: there were only 45 US squadrons on the Western Front at the time of the Armistice and there was a heavy dependence on foreign aircraft, particularly French models. Overall American strength in November 1918 was 740 aircraft and 800 pilots, and control was exercised by the commander of AEF, **General John Pershing**.

The American air service made its major contribution to the war effort in the autumn of 1918. It had been reorganised as a result of the formation of the American First Army and three wings (49 squadrons, some of them French) had been brought together under the command of **William Mitchell**. Large groups of aircraft were deployed during the **St Mihiel offensive** and in subsequent operations, forcing the Germans on to the defensive in the closing stages of the war.

UNITED STATES NAVY

The growth of the modern American navy, which dated back to the 1890s, was given a new impetus by the First World War. To meet potential threats in both the Atlantic and Pacific Oceans, demands for parity with Britain, the largest foreign navy, were finally accepted in 1916, and a major shipbuilding programme was authorised. At this point Germany was viewed as the most likely opponent and the American fleet was concentrated in the Atlantic.

When the United States entered the war in April 1917 destroyers and submarines were sent to European waters to join the battle against the U-boat and production of anti-submarine vessels was dramatically increased. A further major American contribution to the submarine war was the North Sea mine barrage. Stretching from Scotland to Norway, it was laid by the United States during 1918 and accounted for at least five enemy submarines.

When America first entered the war, its main battle fleet had remained in home waters, but in November 1917 the Fourth Squadron was sent to reinforce the **Grand Fleet**; it became the Sixth Battle Squadron and was integrated into the British service. Additional American warships were subsequently dispatched to Ireland, and from this base they were to repel any sorties by German battlecruisers into the Atlantic. In spite of its active naval role in 1917–18, American losses were relatively low at 389,000 tons. This included an armoured cruiser, two destroyers and two submarines.

VENIZELOS, ELEUTHERIOS, 1864–1936

Greek statesman who first became Prime Minister in 1910 and led Greece during the Balkan Wars. During the First World War Venizelos' pro-Allied policy was strongly opposed by **King Constantine**, whose refusal to authorise Greek military aid to the Allies led to the Prime Minister's resignation in March 1915. Soon restored to office, he was ousted by the King in October after accepting the obligations of Greece's defensive treaty with Serbia and giving permission for an Anglo-French landing at Salonika.

Events came to a head in the summer of 1916 when supporters of Venizelos staged a military uprising in response to the passivity of the Greek army in the face of Bulgarian attacks. Venizelos established a rebel government on Crete, which later moved to Salonika; war was declared on Germany and Bulgaria. Anglo-French military intervention in Athens in December 1916 eventually led to the dethronement of Constantine and Venizelos' triumphant return as the legitimate Prime Minister. War was, at long last, officially declared against the **Central Powers**. Venizelos remained in power after the war and was a participant at the **Paris Peace Conference**.

VERDUN, BATTLE OF, 21 February–18 December 1916

A TOTAL WASTE OF BOTH ARMIES

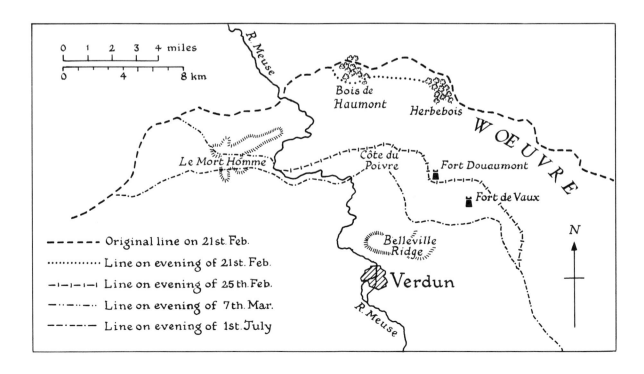

German stormtroopers move forward during the Battle of Verdun, 1916. The longest battle of the war, it was also the most costly in terms of casualties

Planned as a battle of attrition that would 'bleed France white', the Germans had assumed correctly that the ancient fortress of Verdun would, for reasons of national pride, be defended until the end. Verdun lay in the middle of the base of a north-east-facing salient, with the front line running some three miles beyond the outer forts. It was defended by the French Second Army. The opening bombardment, which lasted for 21 hours, began on 21 February 1916, with the German Fifth Army (**Crown Prince Wilhelm**) advancing on the east bank of the Meuse on an eight-mile front; by the third day this force of one million men had gained up to three and a half miles. As German pressure increased, the Woevre plain, on the east side of the salient, was abandoned, even though it had not been attacked. The loss of Fort Douaumont, which the French had failed to secure as they retreated south, was a great blow to the army's prestige.

In these unpromising circumstances, when the battle seemed almost lost, **Joffre**, who had decided to hold Verdun at all costs, placed **Pétain** in command of the front. The new commander moved quickly to organise Verdun's only link with the French rear areas – a secondary road to Bar le Duc, some 40 miles away. An effective supply system was established along the Sacred Way, as it came to be called, with lorries passing through every few seconds; they were barely affected by continuous German shelling. French artillery was expanded and reorganised, with flanking fire from the west bank to the Meuse helping to bring the first major attack to a halt on 28 February.

In order to silence these guns, **Falkenhayn**, the German chief of staff, extended the attack to the west of the Meuse on 6 March. They advanced two and a half miles but were at first unable to secure Le Morte Homme (Hill 295), the dominating hill held with great determination by their opponents. The Germans also failed to stop the flanking fire from this part of the front, which continued undiminished. They had, however, managed to advance to within three miles of Verdun by the end of March.

The French army's ability to resist was increased by the frequent rotation of units, a practice introduced by Pétain, and by the removal of ineffective commanders. Pétain himself was promoted in April, but remained ultimately responsible for the defence of Verdun as army group commander. **Robert Nivelle**, who succeeded him as head of the Second Army, established a national reputation as a result of his successful direction of the second phase of the battle in the autumn.

The third German assault began on 9 April, with heavy attacks being launched south of Douaumont. German progress was slower now and the fighting increasingly took the familiar form of trench warfare. It continued until 29 May when Le Mort Homme was finally taken. Little further German progress was made on the west bank and the critical battles were subsequently fought to the east. The action there was renewed early in June and Fort Vaux surrendered on the 7th after a bitter struggle.

The final French crisis began on 21 June. The Germans launched a major assault with the aim of capturing the forts of Souville and Tavannes, on the heights of the River Meuse. With these positions in enemy hands, Verdun itself would have been vulnerable and the French might have been forced to abandon it. Pétain had, in fact, already prepared a plan for a voluntary withdrawal, but Joffre informed him

that the west bank was to be held at all costs. The Germans used phosphene gas for the first time in this part of the battle and although casualties were massive they were unable to break the defences. With the failure of the final assault on 11 July, Verdun was secure. The fighting had resulted in 315,000 French casualties, but German losses (280,000) were also unacceptably high. Falkenhayn lost his job as a result and was replaced by the **Hindenburg/Ludendorff** team.

After a three months' lull in the battle, the French, who had been reinforced during the summer, went over to the offensive. **Charles Mangin** attacked on 24 October, recapturing the forts of Douaumont and Vaux; the Germans suffered heavy losses of men and equipment. German strength at Verdun was also affected by their manpower needs at the **Battle of the Somme** and other operations during this period. After a gap of several weeks because of ammunition shortages, the French Second Army, under Mangin, attacked again on 15 December on a wider front with even greater success. They advanced by up to two and a half miles and took 11,000 prisoners.

This action brought Verdun, the longest battle of the war, to an end. It was also the costliest: the Germans lost 434,000 men, the French 542,000. The impact of the 'hell of Verdun' on the French soldier was graphically described by Pétain: 'in their unsteady look one sensed visions of horror, while their step and bearing revealed utter despondency. They were crushed by horrifying memories.'

VÉRITÉ

Similar to the preceding *République* class, except for their more powerful secondary armament, these French pre-dreadnought battleships were completed in 1907–08. They had a displacement of 14,900 tons, a complement of 742 and their armament consisted of four 305mm and ten 194mm guns. *Vérité*, *Démocratie* and *Justice* served in the Mediterranean throughout the war, a fourth ship of the class, *Liberté*, having blown up in 1911. During the Russian Civil War *Justice* went to the Crimea with other French warships in support of White land forces in the area.

VERSAILLES, TREATY OF, 1919

The treaty between the Allies and Germany, determined at the **Paris Peace Conference**, that ended the First World War. Germany, which had not been a participant at the conference, eventually signed the treaty under protest, but the United States Congress refused to ratify it. Although one of its major objectives was to prevent Germany re-emerging as a major military power, it was widely viewed in Allied countries as not being harsh enough. The treaty was, however, an important influence on the resurgence of German nationalism and the rise of the Nazi Party. Hitler repudiated the treaty in 1935.

Its principal terms were:

- return of Alsace-Lorraine to France; Malmédy and Eupen to Belgium; Memel to Lithuania; and North Schleswig to Denmark, subject to a plebiscite. Danzig was to be a free city under the League of Nations;
- the Rhineland to be demilitarised and occupied by the Allies for 15 years; the Saar to be placed under the League of Nations, with French control of the coal mines;
- payment of reparations: 'Germany accepts the responsibility of Germany and her allies for causing all the loss and damage to which the Allied and associated governments and their nationals have been subject as a consequence of the war';
- Germany's army to be limited to 100,000 men, with no conscription, tanks or poison gas. No air force to be permitted and the Germany navy to be confined to surface ships under 10,000 tons;
- all German colonies to become League of Nations mandates;
- no union (*Anschluss*) between Germany and Austria;
- the inclusion of the covenant of the League of Nations;
- provision for the trial of the former Kaiser and other German war leaders.

Chiefs of the inter-Allied missions at Versailles, 1919

VICKERS FB5

Known unofficially as the 'Gunbus', the Vickers FB5 was a two-seat fighter/reconnaissance biplane which was in service with the RFC for about 18 months. Based on a series of pre-war prototypes, the FB5 was one of the first fighters designed for the purpose and was an early indication of the combat potential of aircraft. It followed the standard pusher configuration and was powered by the 100hp Gnome Monosoupape engine which provided relatively poor performance: a maximum speed of 70m.p.h. at 5,000 feet, a ceiling of 9,000 feet and an endurance of 4½ hours. The observer in the front cockpit was normally armed with a single .303 **Lewis machine-gun**, although some machines were subsequently fitted with a second gun of the same type. A more common supplement to the standard armament was the **Lee-Enfield rifle** carried by many observers.

The Gunbus served with seven RFC squadrons on the Western Front. Arriving there in July 1915, the FB5 was used for aerial combat and for light bombing and at first it performed these roles effectively. Better German aircraft soon appeared and the outclassed aircraft, whose slow speed was its decisive weakness, was officially declared obsolete early in 1916. By the middle of the year surviving machines had been returned to England where they were used by training squadrons. Well over 100 examples were produced altogether.

An early purpose-built British fighter, the Vickers FB5 did not survive for long on the Western Front

VICKERS FB9

An improved version of the **FB5**, the Vickers FB9, which appeared in December 1915, was known unofficially as the 'Streamline Gunbus'. It had modified wings and tailplane, a streamlined nacelle and a new V-strut undercarriage. It retained the armament and 100hp Gnome Monosoupape pusher engine of its predecessor, but had a slightly higher maximum speed and better flying qualities. It did not, however, perform well enough to outclass its opponents and never became the replacement for the FB5 that it was intended to be. Produced in small numbers, it was used only very briefly on the Western Front, appearing during the opening stages of the **Battle of the Somme**. Withdrawn in July 1916, it was, like the FB5, used by RFC training squadrons.

VICKERS FB19

The FB19 fighting scout was a small single-seat tractor biplane that first appeared in RFC service in the autumn of 1916, after a year of development. The initial batch was armed with a single .303 **Lewis machine-gun** mounted in front of the cockpit, slightly offset to port, and the 110hp Le Rhône engine was normally fitted. Several were delivered to the Russian air service but no more than four were acquired by the RFC. In a Mk II version, the wings were given forward stagger to improve the pilot's view and the 110hp Clerget became the standard engine, giving a maximum speed of 98m.p.h. at 10,000 feet and an endurance of three hours. The machine-gun was now mounted in a recess and, using Vickers-Challenger interrupter gear, fired through a hole in the cowling.

The aircraft did not meet combat requirements in France, but twelve Mk IIs served with the RFC in the Middle East from mid-1917 until about the end of the year. Seriously underpowered when compared with their opponents, the record of the Vickers' scout in Palestine and Macedonia was uninspiring.

VICKERS MACHINE-GUN

The standard machine-gun of the British army during the First World War, the Vickers was a modified version of the original **Maxim**. It was reduced in weight (to 40lb) and had an improved mechanism, but in other respects this recoil-operated machine-gun differed little from its parent. The Vickers was water-cooled, with the barrel enclosed in a jacket containing seven pints and a condenser system to reduce water consumption. Standard .303 ammunition was fed from a fabric belt holding 250 cartridges and the weapon had a slightly low cyclic rate of fire of 450 rounds per minute. The barrel was worn out after 10,000 rounds or an hour's continuous firing and needed to be changed, a relatively simple task for trained personnel. It was normally mounted on a heavy tripod when used by the infantry.

The Vickers was officially adopted by the British army in November 1912 and, with very minor modifications, remained in service for over 50 years; it was also accepted by the United States army and by a number of other countries. Although Britain had been the first to use the Maxim, it had not, unlike Germany, fully recognised the tactical significance of the machine-gun. Available only in limited numbers in 1914, no more than two were allocated to each infantry battalion. It soon became obvious that to employ the Vickers to its greatest effect specialist troops would be needed and, in October 1915, the Machine-Gun Corps was founded; as a result, British expertise in its maintenance, resupply and operational use developed rapidly.

Although the Vickers did jam occasionally, it was generally a very reliable weapon and there are many examples of its continuous employment over long periods. One of the most notable and well known is the attack on High Wood on 24 August 1916, during the **Battle of the Somme**, when 10 Vickers guns fired almost a million rounds over a 12-hour period. Impressive achievements of this kind meant that the weapon was still very much in evidence in the Second World War.

During the Great War the Vickers was also widely fitted to tanks and armoured cars and was used at sea and in the air. An air-cooled version appeared in 1916 and was first fitted to the **Sopwith 1½-Strutter** using synchronising gear. To facilitate the circulation of air the barrel jacket of this much lighter gun was louvred. Some of these aircraft weapons were modified to increase the rate of fire to nearly 1,000 rounds per minute.

VILLAR PEROSA SUB-MACHINE-GUN

The appearance of the world's first sub-machine-gun, in 1915, was an important step in the development of modern weaponry. Known also as the Revelli, after its designer, or the Fiat, one of its manufacturers, the Villar Perosa incorporated many of the features to be found in later automatic weapons. Its twin barrels were, however, unique; they could be fired separately or together and each had detachable box magazines holding twenty-five 9mm Parabellum cartridges. Operated by a retarded blowback action it had a very high cyclic rate of fire – 1,200 rounds per minute – from each barrel. There was a safety lever between the two rear spade grips.

When it entered the war, the Italian army had very few light machine-guns and at first the Villar Perosa was used as a substitute. However, its pistol type ammunition had limited range and striking power and it could never perform this tactical role effectively. Eventually it was properly used by the infantry as a sub-machine-gun, and training was given in its use as a short-range assault weapon. In fixed positions it could be used with a shield and bipod. Many Villar Perosa guns were converted before the end of the war to provide a more conventional automatic weapon – the **Beretta sub-machine-gun** – and relatively few examples survived in their original form.

VIRGINIA

Completed in 1906–07, the Virginia class of pre-dreadnoughts was obsolete by the time America entered the war and they were excluded from front line duties. They had a displacement of 15,000 tons, a maximum speed of 19 knots and a crew of 812. Well protected, they had twin 12-inch turrets fore and aft, above which were located four of her eight 8-inch guns. This arrangement had the effect of making the Virginias top heavy and they had a pronounced tendency to roll. *Georgia* and *Virginia* served with the 3rd Division, Battleship Force, US Atlantic Fleet, from April 1917. *Nebraska*, *New Jersey* and *Rhode Island* were involved in training and convoy duties in 1917–18.

VIRIBUS UNITIS

Austro-Hungary's first dreadnought battleships, the Viribus Unitis class was ordered in 1910 in response to Italy's programme of naval construction. Based on the pre-dreadnought **Radetzky** class, these compact ships had a displacement of just over 20,000 tons and a maximum speed of 20 knots. Armament was much improved with twelve 12-inch guns mounted in triple turrets on the centre line, producing a weight of broadside of 11,904 lb. Armour was less satisfactory, underwater protection being particularly poor.

Completed between 1912–15, *Viribus Unitis*, *Tegetthoff*, *Prinz Eugen* and *Szent István* formed the 1st Division of the 1st Battle Squadron of the Austro-Hungarian navy. *Szent István* was torpedoed by the Italians in June 1918 while serving with a force sent to attack the Otranto barrage; *Viribus Unitis*, the fleet flagship, was sunk by an Italian manned torpedo on 1 November 1918, shortly after it had been handed over to Yugoslavia. *Tegetthoff* and *Prinz Eugen* survived the war unscathed.

VITTORIO VENETO, BATTLE OF, 23 October – 3 November 1918

Following the Austrian defeat at the **Piave** in June 1918, **General Diaz**, the Italian chief of staff, had been unwilling to exploit his success. Uncertain of further victories he had limited himself to local operations. However, as the fortunes of war on the Western Front changed during the summer, ruling out further German intervention in Italy, he modified his position. He now planned a double offensive. The main assault would be mounted on the Piave with the aim of advancing as far as Vittorio Veneto. This would separate the Austrians in the Adriatic plain from those in the mountains, enabling the latter to be rolled up.

At Monte Grappa to the west, the front was to be penetrated by the Italian Fourth Army. This was the pivot of the two Austrian army groups – Archduke Joseph's in the Trentino and Boroevic von Bojna's to the east, running along the Piave. Opposite the Austrians on the river, extending from the sea, were the Italian Third, Tenth, Eighth and Twelfth Armies. In total the Italians and their Allies amassed 57 divisions, of which three were British and two were French. In addition a token American regiment was present. The Austrians, who had 52 divisions, also possessed fewer guns: 6,030 compared to the Allies' 7,700.

Operations began on 23 October 1918 with the secondary thrust in the mountains. Resistance was much stronger than had been expected and the Italians were unable to make any appreciable gains. The Austrians were, however, forced to bring up reserves from the Lower Piave, where the main attack began at the same time. The Tenth Army (Lord Cavan) secured Papadopoli Island on 25 October; two days later, having been delayed because the river was in flood, it was the first to secure a bridgehead on the far bank. It met only light Austrian resistance. Fifteen miles to the north, General Graziani's Twelfth Army was also soon across. The Eighth Army secured the third bridgehead on Graziani's right, but failed to make progress on the British left. Cavan sent out two detachments to mop up remaining Austrian resistance on the river and the bridgeheads were soon joined.

Meanwhile, on 27 October, Cavan's main force pushed forward, throwing back part of the Austrian Fifth Army. By 30 October, the Tenth and Third Armies had reached the River Livenza with little difficulty. On the same day the Eighth Army took Vittorio Veneto and the Austrian armies were split. The advance had now reached a depth of 15 miles from a starting line 35 miles in length.

Weakened by defeat and the political disintegration of Austro-Hungary, the Austrian army quickly disappeared as an effective fighting force. The Italians pursued their defeated opponents as far as the Tagliamento (2 November) before a truce was agreed. On the mountain front to the west, British and French troops drove through to Trent and arranged the surrender of the local commander. A general armistice was signed at Padua on 3 November and hostilities were concluded on the following day. Some 300,000 Austrian prisoners were taken, along with large quantities of equipment. This final campaign had cost the Italians 38,000 casualties.

VIVIANI, RENÉ, 1862–1925

Appointed Premier of France by **President Raymond Poincaré** just before the war, Viviani, a moderate socialist, remained in office until October 1915. 'Indecisive and overly reliant on others', his influence on the direction of the war was limited by **Joffre**'s assumption of wide ranging powers on military matters. By the autumn of 1915, Viviani had lost support in the National Assembly, with the fall of **Serbia** and the failure of the **Champagne offensive** both contributing to the demise of his government.

VOISIN 1 to 10

This highly successful series of French two-seater pusher biplanes, which were among the most widely used aircraft of the First World War, served at the front throughout the conflict. By the outbreak of war, Types 1, 2 and 3 had already appeared. The Voisin 1 was powered by a 70hp Gnome and Type 2 by an 80hp Le Rhône engine, but otherwise they were little different, sharing a steel frame, equal span wings and a four-wheeled undercarriage. In service with the French Aviation Militaire in the early days of the war, they were used for reconnaissance and light bombing duties, carrying a small bomb load vertically on the sides of the nacelle.

The third pre-war design – the Type 3 – had unequal span wings and a more powerful 120hp Salmson Canton-Unné engine. Unlike its predecessors, it was armed – with a single flexibly mounted **Hotchkiss machine-gun** – and it was in fact a Voisin that scored France's first confirmed air victory of the war in October 1914. Equipping the first *Groupes des Bombardement*, the Type 3 was used for both day and night bombing, its most notable

achievement being an attack on the poison gas factory at Ludwigshafen in May 1915. This model served with most of the Allied air services, with over 800 being built for the French Aviation Militaire alone.

The next variant in the series, the Type 4, was designed specifically for ground attack and escort duties and was equipped with a 37mm or 47mm cannon, a weapon of little use in aerial combat. It also featured staggered wings and other more minor design changes. Types 5 and 6, with 150 and 155hp Salmson engines respectively, were more powerful versions of the Type 3 and were introduced towards the end of 1915. A total of 350 Type 5s were manufactured. With a maximum speed of no more than 65m.p.h. at sea level and a limited bomb-carrying capacity, modifications were needed if the Voisin's effectiveness was to be preserved and its operational life extended.

The Type 8, which appeared late in 1916, sought to bring the design up to date with a 220hp Peugeot engine, which gave a maximum speed of 82m.p.h., and a much increased bomb-carrying capacity of

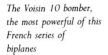

The Voisin 10 bomber, the most powerful of this French series of biplanes

396lb. Some 1,100 examples of this type were built and it served almost exclusively as a night bomber with the French Aviation Militaire, with a few still in front line use at the end of the war.

Early in 1918 appeared a replacement for the Type 8 – the Voisin 10 – powered by a more reliable 300hp Renault engine. With a further increase in bomb load to 600lb, it was usefully employed in attacking German industrial targets in the closing stages of the war. Some 900 examples of the Type 10, the last of the acclaimed Voisin bombers, had been produced by the time of the Armistice.

VON der TANN

The first German battlecruiser, *Von der Tann*, graphically demonstrated the superiority of her design over British types at the **Battle of Jutland**. In the opening minutes of the engagement she sank *Indefatigable* after hitting her fore and aft magazines. *Von der Tann* herself was hit more than 50 times but she survived, a tribute to the quality of her design and construction. The German ship's armour provided much better protection than its English equivalent and its lower superstructure meant that it was a less easily identifiable target. Her armament consisted of eight 11-inch guns in four twin turrets: two on the centre line fore and aft and two in wing positions, with sufficiently wide arcs to provide an eight-gun broadside. She had a displacement of 19,064 tons and a maximum speed of 24.75 knots. *Von der Tann* served with the **High Seas Fleet** throughout the war and was interned at **Scapa Flow**; she was scuttled there on 21 June 1919.

VOSS, WERNER, 1897–1917

German fighter ace whose reputation as a pilot was second only to **von Richthofen**'s. Joining the air service in August 1915, Voss initially flew as an observer during the **Battle of the Somme**, but he soon successfully applied for pilot training. His first operational posting was to *Jasta* 2 in November 1916, and within six days he had brought down a **BE2c**, the first tangible evidence of his skill as a fighter pilot. During the following weeks his score steadily mounted and by February 1917 it had reached 22, only six less than von Richthofen's at this point.

Moved south during the **Nivelle** offensive, he returned to the British sector in July 1917, as commander of *Jasta* 10. Like the other German aces he soon acquired the new **Fokker DrI**, a highly manoeuvrable triplane that caught the Allies off guard. Voss's score steadily increased but his good fortune ran out on 23 September 1917, when he came across British ace **James McCudden** leading a group of five **SE5**s from No 56 Squadron. The ensuing dog fight lasted 10 minutes but the odds were too great and Voss was brought down.

Werner Voss had scored 48 victories in less than a year at the front, with the last being gained during the first patrol of the day on which he died. McCudden himself acknowledged his adversary's outstanding qualities: 'I shall never forget my admiration for that German pilot . . . His flying was wonderful, his courage magnificent, and in my opinion he is the bravest German airman whom it has been my privilege to see fight.'

WAR IN THE AIR

Military aviation was still in its infancy when the First World War began, only 11 years after the Wright brothers' flight. Its role was expected to be limited to reconnaissance activities in support of ground forces and the number of operational aircraft available to the air forces of the major powers was small. During the initial war of movement on the Western Front, they quickly demonstrated their value in providing ground forces with regular information about enemy troop dispositions. As **trench warfare** developed towards the end of 1914, the cavalry was unable to carry out its traditional reconnaissance role and aircraft provided the only reliable source of information about the enemy's activities.

Once aerial photography was introduced it was possible to build up a more systematic picture of the enemy's trench system than had been possible by direct personal observation. As heavy artillery became increasingly important in the trenches, the role of the air services was expanded to include the spotting of enemy batteries and the ranging of guns on to targets.

With aircraft demonstrating their value over the trenches of the Western Front, each side sought to protect its own machines and destroy the opposition. The typical two-seater tractor biplane of the period was not designed for air combat and initially fighting in the air was sporadic. Hand-held weapons were widely used at first, although observers were soon equipped with machine-guns. However, real air combat could not begin until specially designed fighter aircraft had been developed. These needed to be equipped with forward-firing machine-guns synchronised to fire through the airscrew. The French had fitted a crude device to the **Morane Saulnier L** in the spring of 1915, but it was the Germans who produced the first effective synchronising mechanism. It was first used on the **Fokker EI** monoplane and quickly transformed Germany's position in the air.

The RFC's reconnaissance machines were not equipped to deal with this challenge and their opponents had established air superiority towards the end of 1915. The first German fighter aces, notably **Boelcke** and **Immelmann**, developed the tactics that were to provide the basis of aerial combat for the remainder of the war. Changes in organisation soon followed as the first specialist fighter units appeared and formation flying was developed. The primary tactical unit was to be the flight of six aircraft.

The British and French responded by developing their own new machines, including the notable **Nieuport Scout**, and by continuing offensive action over German territory even in the most unfavourable circumstances. As a result, the Germans lost their early dominance and suffered badly at **Verdun** and during the **Battle of the Somme**, and Allied reconnaissance machines were able to operate with little risk of interception. In response the German air force was reorganised and re-equipped with fast and manoeuvrable D-type fighters, which were produced in much larger quantities. By the end of 1916 the Allies had again lost the initiative and suffered heavily as a result. 'Bloody April' 1917 was the lowest point in the fortunes of the RFC.

The arrival of the **Sopwith Camel**, the **SE5** and other machines gradually redressed the balance. In the final phase of the war both sides massed large numbers of aircraft together in an attempt to achieve dominance over the battlefields. Despite the introduction of new machines, including the fine **Fokker DVII**, the Germans were unable to match the Allies' supply of manpower and material in the closing months of the war and they lost control of the skies permanently. In these favourable circumstances, the use of machine-guns and bombs against enemy troops became increasingly important in the Allied offensives of 1918.

The development of strategic bombing was another major feature of the air war. Both Britain and Germany launched air strikes against their opponents' territory during the first few months of the war, although it was not until 1915 that regular sorties by **Zeppelins** began. There were 51 airship raids on England during the period 1915–18, causing over 550 civilian deaths. When the airship became vulnerable to attack because of improvements in aircraft performance the Germans switched to the new heavy bomber – the **Gotha IV** – that had been developed. Raids on England began in May 1917 and continued for a year, although improved British air defences forced the enemy to abandon daylight bombing after a few months. The RFC responded with its own strategic bombing programme but the scale of its operations never matched expectations.

Neither side secured any real gains from these campaigns although the future potential of striking directly at an enemy's human and industrial resources had been established. Innovation was also a feature of naval aviation during the war. The British service pioneered strategic bombing and demonstrated the potential of anti-submarine patrols. There were also numerous experiments in operating aircraft from ships, although their immediate operational impact was limited.

During the course of the First World War the role of the air services of the major powers had been transformed: by the end of the war they were separate services operating independently in a variety of roles rather than as the reconnaissance branches of their respective armies. The creation of the Royal Air Force in April 1918 as an independent service in its own right was a recognition of this change. A measure of their impact was the fact that, by 1918, armies could no longer 'operate successfully without air superiority having first been achieved over the battlefield'.

WARNEFORD, REGINALD, 1891–1915

Flight Sub-Lieutenant Reginald Warneford, flying a **Morane Saulnier L**, was responsible for the first successful attack on an airship from the air. Operating above Zeppelin LZ37 near Ostend on 7 June 1915, Warneford released his entire supply of Hales bombs, causing the airship to explode and crash to the ground. Shortly afterwards, Warneford himself was to make a forced landing in enemy territory in order to carry out emergency repairs. Fortunately he managed to take off undetected and was acclaimed a hero on his return. On 11 June 1915, he became the first member of the RNAS to receive the Victoria Cross, but died in an air crash only a few days later.

WARSAW OFFENSIVE, 28 September–31 October 1914

Once East Prussia had been secured, following the Russian defeats at **Tannenberg** and the **First Battle of the Masurian Lakes**, in the second month of the war, the Germans turned their attention to the enemy positions in Poland. On the southern front the Austrians, who had been forced back through Lemberg after some initial successes in Poland, were in a critical situation. To assist their Austrian ally and to prevent the invasion of Silesia, four corps of the German Eighth Army (**Hindenburg**) were transferred from Prussia to Western Poland. Some 750 trains were used in this massive operation, which placed the four corps – now constituted as a new Ninth Army under Hindenburg – in the vicinity of the

Austrian left flank near Cracow in the last week of September. Hindenburg's advance on Warsaw began on 28 September, when he moved forward on a broad front between Cracow and Czenstochowa. On the German right the Austrians renewed their offensive in occupied Galicia. They progressed as far as Przemysl, which was relieved on 9 October, but made no further progress. The Russian left was therefore secure.

Grand Duke Nicholas responded to the main German threat by drawing 12 corps from his army in Galicia and moving them behind the Vistula. Conducted with great speed and efficiency, this huge transfer would allow the Russian forces assembled between Warsaw and Novo-Georgievsk to envelop Hindenburg's left in a decisive action. The full array of Russian forces comprised the Fifth, Fourth and Ninth Armies on the Vistula; the Third and Eighth on the right, behind the San; with the Second and First guarding the left. In addition, the Russian Tenth Army had invaded part of East Prussia and was engaging the few German troops who remained to defend it.

Information about Russian troop dispositions was available to Hindenburg through intercepted radio messages. It revealed the danger to the German left, where units under **Mackensen**'s command had arrived within seven miles of Warsaw by 12 October. Further south the Germans had arrived at the Vistula, repelling, in fierce fighting, the Russians who had tried to cross the river. Another corps advanced on Ivangorod, but Austrian troops soon took over the positions there. The German forces thus relieved

were sent to reinforce Mackensen's troops, which had been ordered, on 12 October, to halt and dig in. However, Mackensen was only able to hold on for a few days as the Russians began a slow advance towards Silesia. In the south, the Russians had crossed the San and were advancing into Galicia again.

There was now a danger that Mackensen might be cut off from the German frontier and on 27 October a general retreat was ordered. The Germans destroyed communications as they moved back and hindered the Russian pursuit as much as possible. By the end of the month they had reached their starting line, having sustained about 40,000 casualties. The planned Russian attack on Silesia had been delayed by the German offensive but it was to be resumed as soon as the railway network had been reconstructed. To meet this threat, the German Ninth Army was moved north-west to the Posen-Thorn area where Hindenburg was planning an attack against the Russian right.

WEBLEY REVOLVER MARK VI

Dating back in its original form to 1887, the .455 Webley Mark VI was the standard British service revolver of the First World War. Noted for its strength and reliability, this model was adopted by the army in 1915 and more than 300,000 examples were produced over the next three years. A six-chambered

revolver with automatic extraction, it could be reloaded quickly using a device for inserting all six cartridges at once. A detachable stock was available to increase the weapon's effective range and a seven-inch bayonet could also be fitted.

WEBLEY SELF-LOADING PISTOL

This recoil-operated automatic pistol was adopted by the Royal Navy in 1913 and was widely used during the First World War. Solid but unattractive in appearance, its complicated locked breech design had a tendency to jam when dirty although it was generally reliable. The magazine, which was accommodated in the long butt, held seven .455-calibre

rounds. A modified version with a shoulder stock, a special backsight and a manual safety catch, was issued to the RFC from 1915. The weapon did not compare favourably with other automatic pistols then available, such as the **Luger**, and it was rejected for British army use.

WEMYSS, ROSSLYN, BARON WESTER WEMYSS, 1864–1933

First Sea Lord in the last year of the war, Wemyss was a rear admiral in command of the Royal Navy's 12th Cruiser Squadron in August 1914. The dull routine of escort duties in the Atlantic and the Channel was succeeded by his appointment, in February 1915, as governor of Lemnos Island, which served as the base for the **Gallipoli operation**. When **Admiral Sackville Carden** became ill after the failure of the naval assault in the **Dardanelles**, Wemyss was appointed second-in-command to **Vice-Admiral De Robeck**, the new commander-in-chief. He took an active part in the landing operations in April 1915, commanding the First Naval Squadron. After the evacuation from Gallipoli, Wemyss was appointed commander-in-chief of the East Indies and Egypt station. During his tenure there he attempted unsuccessfully to save the garrison at **Kut**.

Returning to England in mid-1917, he was appointed Deputy Sea Lord, responsible for expanding the naval war staff. On **Jellicoe**'s dismissal in December 1917 he became First Sea Lord and worked closely with **Sir Eric Geddes**, the political head of the navy. He was fully involved in planning the **Zeebrugge raid** and helped to deal with the U-boat threat. He represented the interests of the Allied naval powers at the final Armistice negotiations with the Germans at Compiègne and played a major role in drafting the naval clauses of the **Treaty of Versailles**.

WESTERN FRONT, CHRONOLOGICAL LIST OF EVENTS

Liège, Battle of, 1914
Mulhouse, Battle of, 1914
Namur, Siege of, 1914
Frontiers of France, Battles of, 1914
Le Cateau, Battle of, 1914
Marne, Battle of the, 1914
Aisne River, First Battle of the, 1914
Antwerp, Siege of, 1914
Ypres, First Battle of, 1914
Champagne, First Battle of, 1914–15
Neuve-Chapelle, Battle of, 1915
Ypres, Second Battle of, 1915
Artois, Battle of, 1915
Champagne, Second Battle of, 1915
Artois-Loos, Battle of, 1915
Verdun, Battle of, 1916
Somme, Battle of the, 1916

Arras, Battle of, 1917
Aisne River, Second Battle of the, 1917
Messines, Battle of, 1917
Ypres, Third Battle of, 1917
Cambrai, Battle of, 1917
Somme Offensive, 1918
Lys Offensive, 1918
Aisne River, Third Battle of the, 1918
Cantigny, Battle of, 1918
Belleau Wood, Battle of, 1918
Noyon-Montdidier Offensive, 1918
Marne, Second Battle of the, 1918
Amiens Offensive, 1918
St-Mihiel Offensive, 1918
Meuse-Argonne Offensive, 1918
Cambrai-Saint Quentin Offensive, 1918

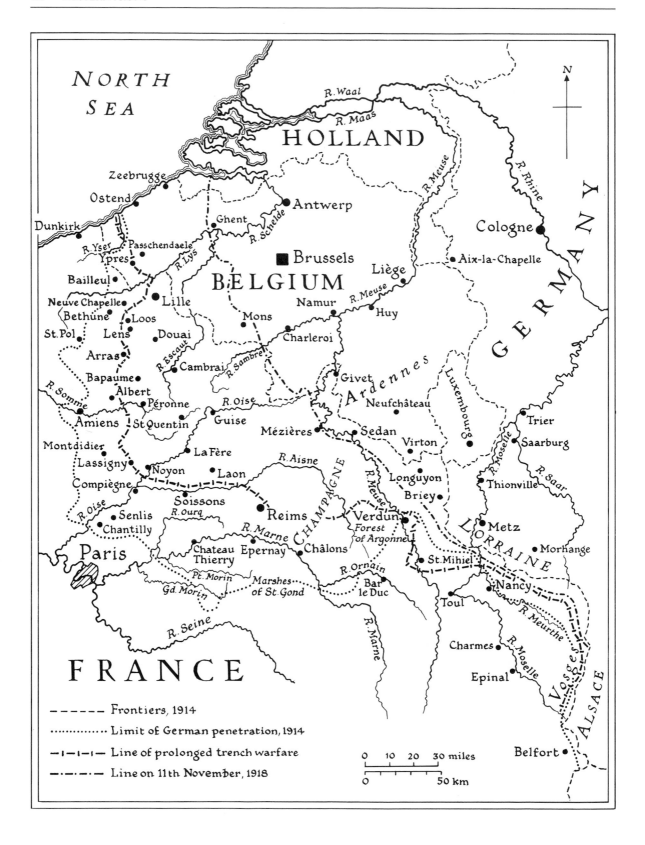

NORTH SEA

R. Waal

R. Maas

HOLLAND

R. Meuse

R. Rhine

Zeebrugge

Ostend

Antwerp

Cologne

Dunkirk

Ghent

Aix-la-Chapelle

GERMANY

R. Yser

Passchendaele

R. Schelde

Ypres

Brussels

Liège

Bailleul

BELGIUM

R. Meuse

Neuve Chapelle

Lille

Namur

Huy

Bethúne

Loos

Mons

St. Pol

Lens

Douai

Charleroi

Arras

R. Escaut

R. Sambre

Bapaume

Cambrai

Givet

Ardennes

Luxembourg

Trier

Albert

Péronne

R. Oise

Neufchâteau

R. Somme

St Quentin

Guise

Mézières

Sedan

Virton

Saarburg

Amiens

Montdidier

La Fère

R. Aisne

Longuyon

R. Moselle

Thionville

R. Saar

Lassigny

Noyon

Laon

CHAMPAGNE

R. Meuse

Briey

Compiègne

R. Oise

Soissons

R. Ourq

Reims

Verdun

Forest of Argonne

LORRAINE

Metz

Senlis

Chantilly

R. Marne

Châlons

Morhange

Paris

Chateau Thierry

Epernay

R. Ornain

St. Mihiel

Pt. Morin

Marshes of St. Gond

Bar le Duc

Nancy

Gd. Morin

Toul

R. Meurthe

R. Seine

R. Marne

Charmes

R. Moselle

FRANCE

Epinal

Vosges

ALSACE

Belfort

N

– – – – Frontiers, 1914

· · · · · · · · · · Limit of German penetration, 1914

–ı–ı–ı– Line of prolonged trench warfare

–·–·–·– Line on 11th November, 1918

0   10   20   30 miles

0   50 km

WEYGAND, GENERAL MAXIME, 1867–1965

Serving as commander of the French 5th Hussars at the beginning of the war, Weygand was picked from relative obscurity by **Joffre** to be chief of staff of the Ninth Army, which was then being formed under **Foch**. He remained with Foch throughout the war, being promoted major-general in 1916. The two men worked closely and effectively together and in 1917,

for example, he substituted for Foch as French military representative on the Supreme War Council. In April 1918, Weygand returned to his more familiar role as chief of staff when Foch was appointed Supreme Allied Commander. He held a succession of senior military posts before his retirement in 1935 and was recalled to service during the Second World War.

WHITE ARMOURED CAR

Based on the White truck chassis, imported from the United States, this French-produced armoured car first appeared in 1915. It was the most successful vehicle of its kind in French army service and over 200 examples, many more than any other car, were in operational use at the Armistice. Some modified versions were still employed at the beginning of the Second World War.

The hull consisted of 5mm armour, the box-shaped

front protecting the 35hp four-cylinder engine and the driver and co-driver. To the rear was an enclosed turret, which was well supplied with observation ports; on opposite sides were mounted either a 37mm cannon and an 8mm machine-gun or two machine-guns. Operated by a crew of four, this heavy vehicle, which weighed 6,000kg, had a maximum speed of no more than 28m.p.h. and a range of about 150 miles.

WIGHT 'CONVERTED' SEAPLANE

The Wight 'Converted' Seaplane was a two-seat, three-bay biplane, based on a prototype Wight bomber of 1916 that never entered production. Most examples were powered by a single 275hp Rolls Royce Eagle engine, although later batches had the 265hp Sunbeam Maori. The Eagle gave a maximum speed of almost 85m.p.h. at 2,000 feet, with an endurance of $3\frac{1}{2}$ hours. Armament consisted of a .303 **Lewis machine-gun** on a Scarff ring-mounting in the rear cockpit and there was provision for up to 500lb of bombs under the fuselage.

No more than 37 of these planes served with the RNAS, because of the adoption of the **Short 184** as a standard type, and they did not long survive the war. They were, however, widely used on anti-submarine patrols and performed effectively. One was responsible, on 18 August 1917, for the first sinking of a U-boat in the English Channel as a result of an attack from a British aircraft.

WILHELM, GERMAN CROWN PRINCE, 1882–1951

With little military experience – he had commanded a Guards' regiment for a brief period before the war –

the German Crown Prince was placed at the head of the Fifth Army in August 1914. His army was positioned at Metz, the pivot of the German wheel as it moved through Belgium; ignoring orders to remain stationary, Wilhelm advanced as far as Verdun before being brought to a halt. After the **Battle of the Marne** and the German withdrawal behind the Aisne, this part of the front quickly stabilised. It was not in fact until the **Battle of Verdun**, when Wilhelm was formally in command of the German offensive, that a major engagement occurred. He retained responsibility for this sector after his promotion, in September 1916, to a new Army Group Crown Prince Wilhelm, which also held the Aisne–Champagne front. His forces played an important role in the offensives of 1918 and he recognised earlier than his military chiefs that the war was lost. Wilhelm resigned his army commission at the end of the war and followed his father into exile in the Netherlands.

WILHELM II, KAISER, 1859–1941

The son of Frederick III and the eldest daughter of Queen Victoria, Wilhelm III acceded to the throne as German Emperor and King of Prussia in 1888. He dismissed Chancellor Bismarck in 1890 and during the remaining years of peace was closely associated with Germany's rapid growth as a leading naval and military power. Wilhelm's aspirations for Germany as a major world force and his many ill-judged statements on international issues brought him into conflict with Britain, France and Russia. Personal tensions between Wilhelm and his uncle, Edward VII, made his relationship with Britain particularly difficult.

Although his pre-war role may have been a minor contributory factor in the events leading to the war, the widely held contemporary view of the Kaiser as a warmonger is exaggerated. When the famous blank cheque was issued to Austria on 6 July, he accepted the need for a possible brief war, but had no conception of the nature of the European conflict that was about to take place. For much of the war he played the part of war leader, but lacked the strategic insights and other attributes that were needed. The real centre of power lay elsewhere, particularly after **Hindenburg** and **Ludendorff** assumed effective control in 1917 and the Kaiser's influence on the course of events was often negligible.

Internal revolt and the Allies' demand for progress towards democracy as a precondition for peace undermined his position as the war drew to a close. On the clear advice of the army high command, the Kaiser abdicated on 9 November 1918, two days before the Armistice and fled to the neutral Netherlands. He was safe here from the requests that were made at the **Paris Peace Conference** that he should be handed over to the Allies and tried as a war criminal. More urgent business ensured that this item was eventually pursued no further and Wilhelm lived in Holland for the rest of his life.

The Kaiser (centre) discusses strategy with Hindenburg and Ludendorff

WILSON, FIELD MARSHAL SIR HENRY, 1864–1922

British field marshal who was Chief of the Imperial General Staff from February 1918. Before the war he had, as a senior staff officer, prepared plans for the deployment of the British army in France in the event of a European war. On the outbreak of the First World War he became deputy chief of staff of the BEF under **French** and **Murray**. Questions were raised about his reliability and judgement as the British retreated from Mons and he was passed over when Murray's successor as chief of staff was appointed in January 1915. An ardent Francophile, he was moved to French headquarters as chief liaison officer, a post he held throughout 1915 and again in 1917; for most of 1916 he spent an uneventful period as commander of IV Army Corps.

Returning home in May 1917, Wilson established close links with **Lloyd George** and supported him in his campaign against **Haig**. He was appointed British military representative on the Supreme War Council and early in 1918 became chief of staff in place of **Robertson**. He concurred enthusiastically in the plan to appoint **Marshal Foch** as Allied military commander in response to the new German offensives of 1918, even though it meant that his own role in the strategic direction of the war would be considerably reduced. Sir Henry Wilson could never be regarded as a 'great captain, much less a great field commander. Instead his love of intrigue turned him into a politician rather than a soldier.'

Wilson: a more pliant chief of staff than his predecessor, Sir William Robertson

WILSON, WOODROW, 1856–1924

Twenty-eighth President of the United States, Woodrow Wilson adopted a policy of strict neutrality on the outbreak of war in Europe in 1914. By February 1915, however, he had announced that America would hold Germany 'to a strict accountability' for

the destruction of any of her ships. Wilson expressed himself in stronger terms after the sinking of the *Lusitania* and he subsequently threatened to end diplomatic relations with Germany, prior to her suspension of submarine warfare in the spring of

1916. His efforts, in 1915–16, to act as a mediator in Europe were rebuffed by both sides and his threats to back them up by the use of force were soon found to be empty.

Wilson fought the presidential election of 1916 around the slogan 'He has kept us out of the war', and he retained office by a narrow margin. American intervention in Europe came a step nearer when Germany decided, early in 1917, to resume unrestricted submarine warfare. Following the interception of the **Zimmermann telegram** and the destruction of four American ships on 22 March, the president asked Congress for a declaration of war. He declared that 'the world must be made safe for democracy'.

America entered the war on 6 April 1917 and Wilson selected **General Pershing** as commander of the **American Expeditionary Force** that was sent to Europe. Wilson took a close interest in the running of the war, particularly in ensuring that there were sufficient supplies of men and material. America had joined the war as an associated rather than an Allied power, Wilson having been careful to avoid entering into any diplomatic agreements that might restrict his role when the peace settlement came to be agreed.

In January 1918, he announced his own peace programme, the **Fourteen Points**, that provided the basis for the Armistice and the **Paris Peace Conference**. Wilson himself headed the American delegation to Paris, primarily because he wanted to ensure that the Conference accepted the covenant of the League of Nations. He was, however, forced to compromise on other issues, even though the 'most essential part' of the peace settlement was secured. In the United States the plan received a less enthusiastic reception and the Senate refused to ratify the **Treaty of Versailles**, which included the League covenant. A nationwide tour to appeal to the people ended in his physical collapse; he remained an invalid for the rest of his life.

WINCHESTER RIFLE

Associated with the early days of the American West, the lever-action Winchester was widely used by the Russian army during the First World War. Russian domestic industry was unable to produce the **Mosin-Nagant rifle** in sufficient quantity during the war and alternatives were sought overseas, some 294,000 examples of the Winchester Model 1895 being acquired. A direct descendant of the famous Model 1873, this military version was more solidly constructed and was rechambered for the 7.62mm Russian cartridge. The lever action loaded ammunition from a five-round tubular magazine that was concealed under the barrel. A major military drawback of this obsolete weapon was the difficulty of operating the lever action in the prone position without becoming exposed to enemy fire. However, the Winchester proved to be reliable enough in action and was still much in evidence during the Russian civil war and after.

WOLF

The former merchant ship *Wachtfels* of 5,890 tons, *Wolf* was commissioned as a German **commerce raider** in May 1916. Leaving Germany in November 1916, her primary task was to lay mines in Allied shipping lanes, the first batch being positioned off Cape Town. After her supply of mines had been exhausted she moved through the Pacific searching for Allied merchant ships and sank a total of 12. *Wolf* also captured a British vessel which she used to mine Aden until it was intercepted and scuttled. In spite of intensive efforts by British warships, *Wolf* evaded capture and returned to Germany unscathed in February 1918.

WYOMING

The first American dreadnoughts equipped with twelve 12-inch guns (of a new, longer pattern), the Wyomings were enlarged versions of the **Delaware** and **Florida** classes. The two additional heavy guns were mounted in an aft superfiring turret. Completed in 1912, they had increased secondary armament (twenty-one 5-inch guns), a maximum speed of 20.5 knots and a displacement of 26,000 tons. Both *Wyoming* and *Arkansas* joined the 6th Battle Squadron, **Grand Fleet**, in the last year of the war and were present at the surrender of the German **High Seas Fleet** in November 1918.

YANUSHKEVICH, GENERAL NIKOLAI, 1868–1918

Without obvious qualifications for the post but with powerful political connections, Yanushkevich was appointed chief of staff of the Russian army early in 1914. When the supreme command (Stavka) was formed on the outbreak of war he was appointed chief of staff to **Grand Duke Nicholas**, the new commander-in-chief. Yanushkevish was, however, little more than a figurehead, selected to prevent anyone more dangerous from taking on the post, with **General Danilov** in effective control of operations. In the wake of the Russian retreat during the summer of 1915, Yanushkevich was replaced by **Alekseev** as the **Tsar** took over the supreme command.

YPRES, FIRST BATTLE OF, 30 October–24 November 1914

As the 'Race to the Sea' drew to a close, the British made one last attempt to turn the Germans' northern flank. An advance between La Bassée and Armentières on 12 October made good progress initially but was soon opposed by eight newly formed infantry divisions (the Fourth Army, under **Duke Albrecht of Württemberg**). The British fell back to prepared positions and their accurate firepower brought the enemy action to an end. By the time the Battle of Ypres began a few days later the formation of a line running from Switzerland to the Channel had been completed. The subsequent autumn fighting in Flanders extended from the sea at Nieuport to the La Bassée Canal, almost 45 miles away in a direct line.

The first phase of the fighting began on 20 October with an attack by the German Sixth Army (**Crown Prince Rupprecht**) and the Fourth Army along the whole front. The Fourth Army was to break through on the Yser between Ypres and Nieuport, and envelop the Allies' northern flank. Held by the Belgian army, which had not yet recovered from the retreat from Antwerp, this part of the front witnessed the most intensive fighting of the first phase of the battle. The Belgians put up much stronger resistance than had been expected but could not hold their position. They fell back to the Dixmunde–Nieuport railway line as the Germans crossed the Yser on 24 October. Further progress was brought to a halt when, five days later, the Belgians opened the sluices at Nieuport and let in the sea in front of them. Elsewhere on the line to La Bassée the British and French maintained their positions.

The German action was renewed on 30 October on a smaller scale on the front from Gheluvelt, five miles to the east of Ypres, to the Messines Ridge. To the north of this line, where I Corps (**Haig**) was positioned, the situation was very uncertain for a time and at Gheluvelt itself the Germans broke through, although they were soon driven out again. The regular waves of enemy attacks proved very costly to both sides, the Germans themselves referring to 'the murder of the children of Ypres'. To the south the British Cavalry Corps (**Allenby**) was driven from Messines Ridge. Allied reinforcements were moved to the front around Ypres to stabilise the Allied position and to prepare for the next attack.

The third major assault, which began on 11 November, covered an even narrower area. The centre of the attack was astride the Menin Road, with Ypres itself being the principal objective. South of the road the British successfully withstood the continuous German attacks, but to the north they broke through. Fortunately the enemy hesitated at this critical point even though there was nothing in front of them apart from a line of British guns. A counter-attack by an improvised force, which included cooks and batmen, was a success and Ypres, a symbol of Allied resistance, was saved.

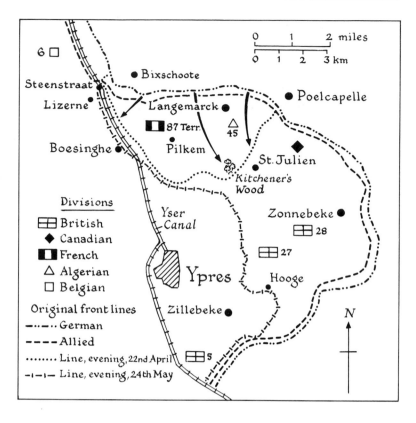

Although the crisis was over, fighting continued until 24 November, the last day of the Battle of Ypres. Casualties were severe on both sides with the loss of irreplaceable professional manpower. The British suffered losses of 50,000 men killed or wounded; the French and German casualties were much higher. As the fighting subsided, open combat was replaced by the trench, which dominated the Western Front until 1918.

YPRES, SECOND BATTLE OF, 22 April–25 May 1915

Allied preparations for another combined offensive in the spring of 1915 were interrupted by a surprise German attack on the Ypres salient on 22 April. A short bombardment by 17-inch howitzers was followed by the appearance of greenish yellow clouds of poisonous chlorine gas (in use for the first time on the Western Front), which drifted towards the left of the salient. The French Algerian and territorial divisions holding this area fled in terror towards Ypres and the canal running north from it. The German Fourth Army advanced two miles but then halted early the next day: no plans had been made to progress further and the troops would have run into their own gas.

The British Second Army (**Smith-Dorrien**), which moved to the left to fill the four-mile gap created by the French, launched several small counter-attacks which prevented the Germans from moving forward immediately. However, on 24 April a further gas attack was launched at the apex of the salient, and the Canadians, who held this position, were forced to give some ground.

Under constant attack from three sides, the salient had been considerably reduced in size: the highest ground had been lost and it was no more than three miles across, although it was still five miles deep. **Foch**'s assurances of a counter-offensive came to nothing, even though two French divisions had been brought in as reinforcements. In these unpromising circumstances, Smith-Dorrien proposed a withdrawal of $2\frac{1}{2}$ miles to a more defensible position covering Ypres. In his view, nothing less than a well-planned offensive, with large reinforcements, was likely to push the enemy back. **Sir John French**'s outraged response to the suggested move was to send him home, but when his successor, **Sir Herbert Plumer**, advocated the same course of action, it was agreed. After several postponements the move was successfully completed on 1–3 May.

The Germans, who still aimed to eliminate the Ypres salient, renewed their attack on 8 May. Known as the battle of Frezenberg Ridge, this fierce struggle lasted for six days. Losing valuable ground on the ridge, the British were forced back a further three-quarters of a mile in the centre but otherwise held their ground. Further losses resulted when the assault was renewed on 24–25 May, opening with a heavy gas attack.

This action brought the long battle to an end. In

Stretcher-bearers taking a wounded soldier for treatment

reducing the Ypres salient to a flat curve just east of the city, the Germans had achieved their greatest success of the year, although shortages of troops and ammunition had prevented them from making the major breakthrough that could have been achieved. In terms of casualties the five-week battle of Ypres was relatively costly, with the heavier British losses (59,000) compared to the German (35,000) being explained by the use of poison gas. The French suffered 10,000 casualties.

YPRES, THIRD BATTLE OF, 31 July–10 November 1917

Haig's plan to break the deadlock on the Western Front by a major campaign in Flanders in the summer of 1917 had been under consideration for 18 months. Apart from diverting pressure from the French army, which had been seriously weakened by mutiny in April–May 1917, the operation would aim to recapture the Flemish ports. The British Second and Fifth Armies would break out of the Ypres salient, which was surrounded by the German army, occupy the

high ground to the east, advance several miles and then attack Ostend and Zeebrugge from the rear. Once this objective had been gained, the two armies would push the Germans out of Belgium.

As a prelude to the campaign, **Plumer**'s Second Army captured, on 7 June 1917, **Messines Ridge**, which guarded the southern flank of Ypres Ridge. This operation put the German Fourth Army (Sixt von Armin), which held this front, on the alert and it soon became obvious, from their position overlooking the front, that a new attack was being prepared. The Germans had spent the previous year turning their line into a fortress, defended by numerous machine-gun positions protected by concrete pillboxes.

Delays occurred and it was not until 11 July that an air offensive began, followed by a massive artillery bombardment, which started on the 18th. The attack itself began on 31 July, when the British Fifth Army (**Gough**), consisting of nine divisions, attacked north-east from the Ypres salient. The French First Army (**Anthoine**) was on his left and Plumer was on his right. Initially, good progress was made, but after strong counter-attacks Gough had advanced no more than two miles. Heavy rain fell on the first night, flooding the swampy ground, whose drainage system had been destroyed by the 10-day bombardment, the heaviest of the war. As a result, the whole operation was held up.

The next significant operation, the Battle of Langemarck, which did not begin until 16 August, was also a failure, with only the centre group of the Fifth Army moving forward a few hundred yards. During this period successful diversionary attacks were mounted by the Canadians at Lens (15–25 August) and by the French at Verdun (20 August).

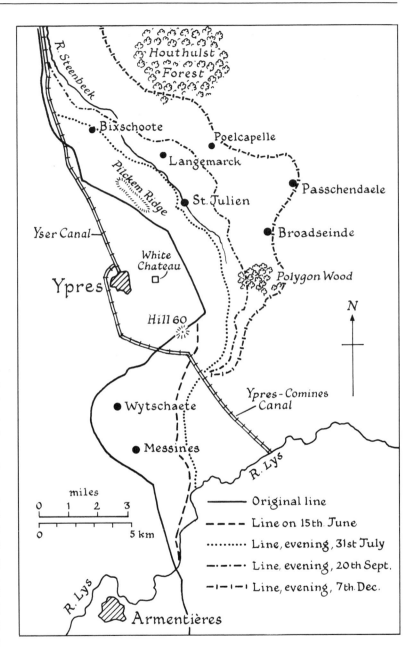

At this point Haig decided to hand over the direction of the main advance to Plumer in the south, extending the front of the Second Army northwards to include the Menin Road sector. He planned to secure the ridge east of Ypres by three battles, each with limited objectives. The advancing troops were to be protected by powerful barrages, with the main assault being made on a narrow front. Aided by the drying out of the ground, the operation opened with the Battle of the Menin Road Ridge (20–25 September), and continued at Polygon Wood (26 September) and at Broodseinde (4 October). As a result the Second Army was now on the crest of the Ypres Ridge and although the weather had now deteriorated, Haig decided to press on, in spite of advice to the contrary from his subordinate commanders.

The poor state of the ground contributed to the lack of British progress at the Battle of Poelcappe, where the Australians made the main assault. After the first **Battle of Passchendaele**, 12 October, which ended in failure, Haig abandoned his strategic aims, but was still determined to secure the ridge before winter. The Canadian Corps was brought up and the attack was renewed on 26 October: progress was inevitably slow in the appalling ground conditions and the enemy's increasing use of mustard gas. On 6 November, the village of Passchendaele was entered and the whole campaign was concluded a few days later when more of the ridge had been taken.

The Third Battle of Ypres cost the British nearly 310,000 casualties (the Germans slightly less) and had consumed all of the available reserves, but it achieved none of its strategic objectives. However, the Germans could no longer look down on the Ypres salient, which had been deepened by about five miles, and they had been prevented from attacking the French. Haig himself was widely criticised for prolonging the operation at an unnecessarily heavy cost in British lives and it further strained his relations with **Lloyd George**.

Australian troops on the Menin Road, Ypres, September 1917

YUDENICH, GENERAL NIKOLAI, 1862–1933

Serving on the Caucasus front throughout the First World War, Yudenich was a fine military leader and organiser, one of the few successful Russian generals of the period. He played an important role in defeating the Turkish invasion under **Enver Pasha** in 1914–15 and as commander of the Caucasus army he planned and led the Russian offensive of 1916. A series of victories culminated in the defeat of the Turkish Third Army at **Erzincan** in July 1916, a major Russian success that stabilised the front until after the **Revolution**.

ZAYONCHKOVSKY, GENERAL ANDREI, 1862–1926

General Zayonchkovsky commanded the small Russian force of three divisions that was sent to the Rumanian border area of Dobruja in August 1916. The presence of these troops, however, was no deterrent to the Bulgarians, who invaded early in September and had soon captured the whole province. Zayonchkovsky, who had a very negative view of the Rumanian army's capabilities and had pleaded unsuccessfully with Stavka for reinforcements, was removed from his command.

ZEEBRUGGE RAID, 23 April 1918

Although German U-boat operations had been contained by 1918, they remained a serious threat to Allied shipping, particularly in the English Channel. Many of the enemy submarines operating in this area were based at the Belgian seaports of Zeebrugge and Ostend, which were both connected by canal to the inland port of Bruges, where further U-boats and destroyers were accommodated. The possibility of neutralising these bases had often been considered by the Admiralty but action was not authorised until **Vice-Admiral Sir Roger Keyes**, commander of the Dover Patrol, developed a plan for a blocking operation. Some 75 ships, under Keyes' command, took part in the raid, which began in the early hours of 23 April 1918.

A diversionary attack was mounted against the mile-long Zeebrugge mole, with some 200 marines being landed from the old cruiser *Vindictive*. They were to destroy German gun positions and blow up installations, but immediately came under heavy fire and were unable to achieve all of their objectives. The bridge connecting the mole to the shore was destroyed by an old submarine that had been packed with high explosive.

At the same time three obsolete cruisers filled with concrete – *Thetis*, *Intrepid* and *Iphigenia* – were moved into the inner harbour under heavy German fire. *Thetis* did not reach the canal entrance – she had to be scuttled prematurely after hitting an obstruction – but the other two were sunk at its narrowest point. However, they were not positioned correctly and failed to block the channel completely. As a result, it could still be used by U-boats and small destroyers.

Vindictive and the other ships then withdrew, bringing the 'courageous and thrilling exploit' to a close. There were nearly 200 British dead and a larger number wounded. The operation is noted for its examples of individual heroism, with as many as eight VCs being awarded. It provided a much needed boost to British morale even if at best it had been no more than a partial success.

The raid on Ostend, which was mounted at the same time, was a complete failure, with the two blockships being unable to reach the harbour entrance. Another attempt to close the canal at Ostend was made on 9 May. It was also unsuccessful, with the blockship being grounded in thick fog.

ZEPPELIN AIRSHIP

The German army and navy used Count Zeppelin's rigid airship during the First World War, principally for strategic bombing and reconnaissance duties. On the outbreak of war the navy had only one Zeppelin in its possession – L3 – which was in fact the first airship to raid Britain, on 19–20 January 1915. (The first Zeppelin bombing raid of the war had been on Antwerp on 25 August 1914.) The L3 was typical of

German naval
Zeppelin L12

the small Zeppelins used by both services in the first part of the war. Powered by three 200hp Maybach engines, it was metal framed, had a volume of 793,518 cubic feet and a cruising range of 683 miles. Operated by 16 men, it was 518 feet long and had a diameter of over 48 feet. An emergency programme in 1914–15 soon put the navy on an equal footing with the army, which had 12 Zeppelins at the beginning of the war.

Larger wartime designs, with improved altitude and bomb-carrying capacity, started to appear in 1915. The P-type, for example, could carry two 100kg and twenty 50kg high explosive bombs and 90 incendiary bombs, and was more suitable for the planned raids against civilian targets in Britain, France and even Russia. The first Zeppelin to appear over London was the military airship LZ38, which reached the north-east of the capital on 31 May 1915. She dropped her bomb load without interference from Allied aircraft, which were unable to operate at the required altitudes. Other targets during 53 airship raids on Britain, 1915–18, included the Midlands, Tyneside and Humberside. Some 5,751 bombs were dropped and 556 civilians were killed. The peak year for Zeppelin activity against Britain was 1916, when 22 raids were mounted, including the largest single attack involving 16 airships on 2–3 September. On this occasion a British aircraft brought down an airship (a Shütte-Lanz) over British skies for the first time.

A new series of super-Zeppelins, which provided the basis for the company's designs for the remainder of the war, appeared in 1916. Even with their much improved ceiling they were soon vulnerable to attack from the more powerful aircraft that were beginning to appear, and as a result the number of raids was reduced considerably. In fact, during the last airship raid on Britain, on 5 August 1918, the latest Zeppelin (the X-type), with a volume of 2,196,573 cubic feet and a ceiling of 22,970 feet was shot down by a British aircraft.

The later Zeppelins are also associated with the plan to send supplies to **Lettow-Vorbeck**'s forces in East Africa, some 3,600 miles from the nearest airship base. On 23 November 1917, as it passed west of Khartoum, L59 was recalled by radio because the defeat of German forces in the colony seemed imminent.

Reconnaissance missions over the North Sea and Baltic comprised the more routine duties of the Zeppelin, with over 1,000 being undertaken. They were also present at more than one naval engagement, including the **Battle of Jutland**, where unfavourable weather conditions hindered them.

ZEPPELIN AIRSHIPS, 1914–18

In service	115	Wrecked on landing	19
Scrapped	22	Destroyed in sheds	8
Transferred to Allies	9	Destroyed accidently	26
Damaged	7	Landed in enemy territory	7
Destroyed in air	17		

ZEPPELIN STAAKEN RVI

The Zeppelin Staaken RVI was perhaps the most notable of the *Riesenflugzeug* (R) class giant aircraft that were produced by several German manufacturers during the First World War.

With the appearance of the Russian **Sikorsky Ilya Mourometz**, Count von Zeppelin initiated work on a German multi-engined bomber in November 1914. The VGO1, as it was designated, was a giant biplane with a wingspan of 140 feet and three 240hp engines. Although this first machine established the viability and potential of the design and resolved some of the technical problems associated with its great size, it was found to be seriously underpowered. As a result, later designs, including seaplane variants, used between three and six engines in a variety of different arrangements. Most of these prototypes were used operationally, with the Eastern Front being given priority.

The RVI was the only design to enter production, with 18 being made by four companies. Retaining the basic structure and dimensions of its predecessors, this reliable and well-defended aircraft had an 18-wheel undercarriage and a huge biplane tail unit, itself the size of a typical fighter of the period. Power was provided by four 260hp Mercedes D IVa or 245hp Maybach engines in tandem pairs, each driving one tractor and one pusher propeller. It had a maximum speed of 85m.p.h., a ceiling of just over 14,000 feet and a duration of 7–10 hours. Depending on the length of the mission, as much as 2,000kg of bombs could be carried, varying in size from 100 to 1,000kg. The 1,000kg was in fact the largest aerial bomb then in use, and one of the RVIs dropped the only three bombs of that size to fall on Britain during the war.

The RVI, which had an enclosed cabin with the latest instruments, was operated by a crew of seven, including gunners to fire its five machine-guns, a radio operator and a mechanic, who serviced the engines while the aircraft was airborne.

Entering service from June 1917 with *Riesenflugzeug-abteilungen* (Rfa) 500 and 501, which were based near Ghent, they carried out night raids on Britain, often accompanied by **Gotha** bombers, and were used against strategic and tactical targets on French territory. For example, in the five months from mid-December 1917, 11 attacks were made on southern England by the RVIs of Rfa 501, and over 27,000kg of bombs were dropped with no losses. More R-type designs, with further variations in engine numbers and size, appeared before the end of the war, but none was produced in quantity.

ZHEKOV, GENERAL NIKOLA, 1864–1949

On Bulgaria's entry into the war in October 1915, General Nikola Zhekov, a former war minister, was appointed chief of staff. Under his leadership Bulgarian forces helped to bring about the fall of Serbia and capture the extensive Macedonian front, which was shortened as a result of their successful offensive in August–September 1916. Zhekov was, however, concerned about the role of the German High Command in determining Bulgaria's military policy and the burdens their demand for manpower placed on the Bulgarian army. The failure of the Bulgarian government to supply its army in Macedonia properly led to political conflict and in the spring of 1918 he was involved in attempts to overthrow the pro-German premier, **Vasil Radoslavov**.

Zhekov was absent in Germany for medical treatment during the final critical phase of the war, when the Allies broke through the Bulgarian lines and forced an Armistice on the Sofia government. Criticisms were made of Zhekov's disposition of troops at the front and on his return he was imprisoned for his wartime conduct.

ZHILINSKY, GENERAL YAKOV, 1853–1918

Commander of Russia's North-Western Front against Germany at the beginning of the war, Zhilinsky had been involved in pre-war planning with France. Charged with coordinating the invasion of East Prussia, his faulty plan and incompetent leadership contributed significantly to the disastrous defeat of **Samsonov**'s Second Army at **Tannenberg** and to the withdrawal of **Rennenkampf**'s army during the **First Battle of the Masurian Lakes**. He was dismissed in September 1914 but his excellent political connections ensured his reappearance during the following year as Russian representative to the French High Command.

ZIMMERMANN TELEGRAM

An enciphered diplomatic telegram that helped to bring the United States into the First World War. Sent by Arthur Zimmermann, German Foreign Secretary, to Count von Bernstorff, the German Ambassador in Washington, on 19 January 1917, it announced the beginning of unrestricted submarine warfare on 1 February 1917. In the expectation that this would soon bring the Americans into the war, the telegram also enclosed proposals for a German–Mexican alliance. Mexico would, with German support, declare war on the United States, with the aim of reconquering Texas, New Mexico and Arizona. Japan would also be invited to join the alliance.

The telegram was intercepted both by the British and the Americans and it caused much public anger when it was published on 1 March. Zimmermann himself actually confirmed the authenticity of the telegram and its contents inevitably created a climate in which the United States could contemplate the possibility of war. Washington declared war on Germany on 6 April 1917.

CHRONOLOGY

1914

JUNE 28	Archduke Franz Ferdinand of Austro-Hungary assassinated at Sarajevo
JULY 6	Kaiser promises German support for Austro-Hungary against Serbia
23	Austro-Hungary sends Serbian government a ten-point ultimatum
25	Serbia replies to Austro-Hungary
28	Austro-Hungary declares war on Serbia The First World War Begins
30	Russia begins general mobilisation
31	Germany demands that Russia ceases mobilisation
AUGUST 1	Germany declares war on Russia Germany mobilises France mobilises Italy declares her neutrality German–Turkish treaty signed
2	Germany invades Luxembourg British fleet mobilises
3	Germany declares war on France Germany invades Belgium British ultimatum to Germany
4	Britain declares war on Germany Germany declares war on Belgium
5	Turkey closes the Dardanelles
6	Austro-Hungary declares war on Russia Serbia declares war on Germany
7	British troops arrive in France Montenegro declares war on Austro-Hungary
10	France declares war on Austro-Hungary *Goeben* and *Breslau* enter Dardenelles
11	Montenegro declares war on Germany
12–21	Austrian invasion of Serbia halted at the Battle of the Jadar
12	Britain declares war on Austro-Hungary
14–25	Battle of the Frontiers
14–22	Battle of Lorraine
16	Liège surrenders
17	Russians invade East Prussia Battle of Stallupönen
20–25	Battle of the Ardennes
20	Battle of Gumbinnen Germans occupy Brussels

22–23	Battle of the Sambre
23	Germans invade France
	Battle of Mons
	Namur captured
	Austro-Hungary invades Russian Poland
	Japan declares war on Germany
23–24	Battle of Krasnik
25–27	Battle of Le Cateau
25	Austro-Hungary and Japan at war
26–31	Russians defeated at the Battle of Tannenberg
27	Austro-Hungary declares war on Belgium
28	Battle of Heligoland Bight
29	Battle of Guise
September 3–11	Austrians defeated at the Battle of Rava Russka
5–10	Battle of the Marne
8–17	Austria's second invasion of Serbia halted
9–14	First Battle of the Masurian Lakes; Russian retreat from East Prussia
14	Falkenhayn replaces Moltke as German chief of staff
15–18	First Battle of the Aisne
15	Australians seize New Guinea
October 9	Germans capture Antwerp
9–19	Battle of Warsaw
October 18–November 30	Battle of the Yser
October 29	Turkey enters war on the German side
	Trench warfare begins on the Western Front
30	First Battle of Ypres begins; fighting ends 24 November
November 1	Battle of Coronel
	Hindenburg assumes command on the Eastern Front
2	Britain begins blockade of Germany
3	Montenegro declares war on Turkey
November 5–December 15	Serbia repels third Austrian invasion
November 6	France declares war on Turkey
	Britain declares war on Turkey
	Japanese attack Tsingtao
9	*Emden* destroyed
11–25	Battle of Lodz
December 3–9	Battle of Kolubra River
8	Battle of the Falkland Islands
16	German fleet shells Scarborough and Hartlepool
20	First Battle of Champagne begins; concluded 10 March 1915
29	Battle of Sarikamish; continued 1–3 January 1915

1915

JANUARY 19	First Zeppelin raid on Britain
23	German and Austrian offensive in the Carpathians
24	Battle of the Dogger Bank
FEBRUARY 4	German submarine warfare against merchant vessels begins
7–21	Winter Battle of the Masurian Lakes
19	Britain bombards Turkish forts in the Dardanelles
MARCH 10–14	Battle of Neuve Chapelle
22	Przemysl surrenders to Russians
APRIL 22–MAY 25	Second Battle of Ypres
APRIL 25	Allies land in Gallipoli
	Treaty of London
MAY 2–JUNE 27	German breakthrough at Gorlice-Tarnow
MAY 7	*Lusitania* sunk by German U-boat
MAY 9–JUNE 30	Second Battle of Artois
MAY 23	Italy enters war on Allied side
JUNE 22	Lemberg recaptured by the Central Powers
23	Italy begins operations on the Isonzo front
JULY 9	German forces in South-West Africa surrender
AUGUST 5	Germans capture Warsaw from the Russians
6–21	Second Allied landings on Gallipoli fail
21	Italy declares war on Turkey
25	Germans capture Brest-Litovsk
SEPTEMBER 1	Germany ends unlimited submarine warfare
SEPTEMBER 25–NOVEMBER 6	Allied offensives at Loos and in Champagne
SEPTEMBER 28	Allied troops enter Kut
OCTOBER 6	Serbia invaded by Germany, Austria and Bulgaria
9	Allied troops arrive at Salonika
15	Britain declares war on Bulgaria
22	Battle of Ctesiphon
23	Allied evacuation of Gallipoli approved
NOVEMBER 27	Serbian army collapses and is evacuated to Corfu
DECEMBER 3	Joffre becomes French commander-in-chief
7	Siege of Kut begins
17	Haig replaces French as British commander-in-chief in France

1916

January 8	Austro-Hungarian offensive against Montenegro; capitulates 16 January
11	Corfu occupied by Allies as a base for the Serbian army
	Russian offensive in the Caucasus begins
24	Scheer appointed commander of the High Seas Fleet
27	Military Service Act introduces conscription in Britain
February 21–December 18	Battle of Verdun
February 28	German Cameroons surrenders
March 1	German submarine warfare extended; abandoned 10 May
9	Germany declares war on Portugal
18	Battle of Lake Naroch
April 23	Easter Rising against British in Ireland
29	British troops at Kut surrender to Turks
May 10	Austrian offensive in the Trentino begins; ends 9 July
May 31–June 1	Battle of Jutland
June 4–September 20	Russian (Brusilov) offensive
June 5	Arab revolt in the Hejaz begins
	Hampshire sunk off Orkneys; death of Lord Kitchener
June 24–November 13	Battle of the Somme
July 25	Battle of Erzincan
August 3	Battle of Romani
27	Rumania enters war and invades Transylvania
	Italy declares war on Germany
29	Hindenburg becomes Chief of the German General Staff; Ludendorff appointed his deputy
30	Turkey declares war against Rumania
September 1	Bulgaria declares war against Rumania
6	Central Powers create unified command
September 10–November 19	Allies launch offensive on Salonika front
September 15	British use tanks for the first time (at Somme)
October 15	Germany renews U-boat war according to prize rules
24	Fort Douaumont, Verdun, recaptured by the French
November 1	Allied forces capture Monastir
25	Beatty replaces Jellicoe as commander of the Grand Fleet; Jellicoe appointed First Sea Lord
December 3	Nivelle succeeds Joffre as French commander-in-chief
6	Bucharest captured
7	Lloyd George becomes British Prime Minister
13	British begin offensive in Mesopotamia
	Nivelle replaces Joffre as French commander-in-chief

1917

JANUARY 31	Germans resume unrestricted U-boat campaign
FEBRUARY 23–APRIL 5	Germans withdraw to the Hindenburg Line
FEBRUARY 22–25	British recapture Kut
MARCH 1	Zimmermann telegram
11	British enter Baghdad
12	First Russian Revolution
15	Tsar Nicholas II abdicates
APRIL 6	USA declares war on Germany
	Nivelle offensive on Western Front begins
9–16	British offensive at Arras
16–20	Nivelle offensive unsuccessful
APRIL 29–MAY 20	Mutinies in the French army
MAY 5–15	Allied offensive on Salonika front
10	Britain introduces convoy system
12	Tenth Battle of the Isonzo begins
15	Pétain becomes French commander-in-chief
JUNE 4	Brusilov replaces Alekseev as Russian commander-in-chief
7–8	British capture Messines Ridge
12	King Constantine of Greece abdicates
25	American troops land in France
JULY 1	Second Brusilov offensive
20	Pact of Corfu
22	Battle of Marasti
31	Third Battle of Ypres begins; ends 10 November
AUGUST 2	Kornilov replaces Brusilov as Russian commander-in-chief
6–20	Battle of Marasesti
19	Eleventh Battle of the Isonzo
SEPTEMBER 1	Riga offensive
8	Kornilov coup attempt fails
27–28	Battle of Ramadi
OCTOBER 24	Italians defeated at Caporetto
NOVEMBER 4	British forces arrive in Italy
5	Allies agree to establish a Supreme War Council at Versailles
7	Bolsheviks seize power in Russia
	British seize Gaza
19	Clemenceau becomes French premier
20	British tanks gain victory at Cambrai
DECEMBER 2	Fighting ends on the Eastern Front

7	USA declares war on Austro-Hungary
9	British capture Jerusalem from the Turks
	Rumania signs armistice
15	Armistice signed between Germany and Russia
22	Russia and the Central Powers start peace talks at Brest-Litovsk

1918

JANUARY 8	President Wilson outlines his Fourteen Points
FEBRUARY 18	Fighting between Russia and Germany resumes
21	British capture Jericho
MARCH 3	Treaty of Brest-Litovsk signed by Russia and Germany
21	German breakthrough on the Somme
23	Artillery bombardment of Paris begins; ends 7 August 1918
29	Foch becomes supreme Allied commander on the Western Front
APRIL 9	Germans Lys offensive in Flanders
23	Zeebrugge/Ostend raid
MAY 7	Treaty of Bucharest concluded by Rumania and the Central Powers
MAY 27–JUNE 6	German Aisne offensive
MAY 28	Battle of Cantigny
JUNE 9–13	Germans launch Noyon-Montdidier offensive
15–22	Italians repulse Austrian attack across the Piave
JULY 13	Turkish army launches final offensive in Palestine
15–18	Second Battle of the Marne
	German retreat begins
JULY 18–AUGUST 5	Allied Aisne-Marne offensive
AUGUST 8	Allied Amiens offensive on Western Front successful: 'black day of the German army'
SEPTEMBER 12–16	American offensive at St Mihiel
15–29	Allied offensive against Bulgarians
19–21	Battle of Megiddo
25	Bulgaria seeks armistice
26	Foch begins final offensive on Western Front
29	Bulgaria concludes armistice
OCTOBER 1	British forces enter Damascus
5	British troops breach the Hindenburg Line
6	Germany requests armistice
9	Allies seize Cambrai
20	Germany abandons submarine warfare
26	Groener replaces Ludendorff

29	German High Seas Fleet mutinies
	Battle of Vittorio Veneto; ends 4 November
30	Turkey makes peace
NOVEMBER 3	Austro-Hungary makes peace
4	Armistice concluded on the Italian front
9	Kaiser Wilhelm II abdicates
	German Republic proclaimed
10	Emperor Charles of Austria abdicates
11	Germany signs armistice
	Fighting ends
12	Austria proclaimed a republic
13	Hungary signs armistice
14	Czechoslovakia proclaimed a republic
	Lettow-Vorbeck surrenders in Rhodesia
	German U-boats interned
21	German High Seas Fleet surrenders to Britain
27	Germans evacuate Belgium
DECEMBER 1	Yugoslavia proclaimed an independent state

1919

JANUARY 4	Peace conference convenes in Paris
JUNE 21	German fleet scuttled at Scapa Flow
28	Treaty of Versailles
JULY 9	Germany ratifies Treaty of Versailles
21	Britain ratifies Treaty of Versailles
SEPTEMBER 10	Treaty of St Germain signed by Austria and Allies
NOVEMBER 19	US Senate refuses to ratify the Treaty of Versailles
27	Treaty of Neuilly signed by Bulgaria and the Allies

GUIDE TO FURTHER READING

GENERAL

Barnett, C., *The swordbearers: Studies in Supreme Command in the Great War*, London, Eyre & Spottiswoode, 1963

Cruttwell, C. R. M. F., *A History of the Great War, 1914–1918*, Oxford, Clarendon, 1934

Edmonds, J. E., *A Short History of World War I*, London, OUP, 1951

Falls, C., *The First World War*, London, Longmans, 1960

Ferro, M., *The Great War, 1914–1918*, London, Routledge, 1973

Gilbert, M., *First World War Atlas*, London, Weidenfeld and Nicolson, 1970

Liddell Hart, H. B., *History of the World War, 1914–1918*, London, Faber, 1934

Pitt, B., *1918: The Last Act*, New York, Norton, 1964

Robbins, K., *The First World War*, Oxford, OUP, 1984

Taylor, A. J. P., *The First World War: An Illustrated History*, London, Hamilton, 1963; *War by Timetable: How the First World War Began*, London, Macdonald, 1969

Terraine, J., *The Great War, 1914–1918: A Pictorial History*, London, Hutchinson, 1965

Williams, J., *The Home Fronts: Britain, France and Germany, 1914–1918*, London, Constable, 1972

Wilson T., *The Myriad Faces of War: Britain and the Great War, 1914–1918*, London, Polity Press, 1986

Woodward, L., *Great Britain and the War of 1914–1918*, London, Methuen, 1967

Wren, J., *The Great Battles of World War I*, London, Hamlyn, 1972

WESTERN FRONT

Cooper, B., *The Ironclads of Cambrai*, London, Souvenir, 1967

Ellis, J., *Eye-deep in Hell: Life in the Trenches, 1914–1918*, London, Fontana, 1977

Farrar-Hockley, A., *Death of an Army*, London, Barker, 1967; *The Somme*, London, Batsford, 1964

Horne, A., *The Price of Glory: Verdun, 1916*, London, Macmillan, 1962

Macdonald, L., *Somme*, London, Michael Joseph, 1983; *They Called It Passchendaele: The Story of the Third Battle of Ypres, and the Men who Fought it*, London, Michael Joseph, 1978

Macksey, K., *The Shadow of Vimy Ridge*, London, Kimber, 1965

EASTERN FRONT

Jukes, G., *Carpathian Disaster: Death of an Army*, New York, Ballantine, 1971

Stone, N., *The Eastern Front, 1914–1917*, London, Hodder & Stoughton, 1975

OTHER THEATRES

Barker, A. J., *The Neglected War: Mesopotamia, 1914–1918*, London, Faber, 1967

Falls C., *Armageddon 1918*, London, Weidenfeld, 1964; *Caporetto, 1917*, London, Weidenfeld, 1966

Farwell, Byron, *The Great War in Africa 1914–1918*, London, Viking, 1987

Gardner, B., *German East Africa: The Story of the First World War in East Africa*, London, Cassell, 1963

James, R. R., *Gallipoli*, London, Batsford, 1965

Palmer, A. W., *The Gardeners of Salonika*, London, Deutsch, 1965

NAVAL WARFARE

Bennett, G., *Naval Battles of the First World War*, London, Batsford, 1968

Hough, R., *The Great War at Sea, 1914–1918*, Oxford, OUP, 1983

Liddle, P., *The Sailor's War, 1914–1918*, Poole, Blandford, 1985

MacIntyre, D., *Jutland*, London, Evans, 1957

Marder, A., *From the Dreadnought to Scapa Flow: the Royal Navy in the Fisher Era, 1904–1919*, 5 vols, London, OUP, 1964–70

Preston, A., *Battleships of World War I: An Illustrated Encyclopaedia of the Battleships of All Nations, 1914–1918*, London, Arms & Armour Press, 1972

Van der Vat, Dan, *The Grand Scuttle. The Sinking of the German Fleet at Scapa Flow in 1919*, London, Waterfront, 1986

Warner, P., *The Zeebrugge Raid*, London, Kimber, 1978

AIR WARFARE

Bruce, J. M. *The Aeroplanes of the Royal Flying Corps (Military Wing)*, London, Putnam, 1982

Clark, A., *Aces High: the War in the Air over the Western Front*, London, Weidenfeld and Nicolson, 1973

Jones, H. A. & Sir W. Raleigh, *The Official History of the War in the Air*, 6 vols, Oxford, Clarendon, 1922–28

Lewis, C. D., *Sagittarius Rising*, London, Davies, 1936

Liddle, P., *Airman's War, 1914–1918*, Poole, Blandford, 1987

Munson, K., *Aircraft of World War I*, London, Ian Allen, 1967

Simkins, P., *Air Fighting, 1914–18. The Struggle for Air Superiority over the Western Front*, London, Imperial War Museum, 1978

Smith, Myron J. jr., *World War I in the Air: A Bibliography and a Chronology*, New York, Scarecrow Press, 1977

WEAPONS

Brooks, S., *Armoured Warfare. The Development and Role of Armoured Fighting Vehicles*, London, Imperial War Museum, 1980

Ellis, J., *The Social History of the Machine-Gun*, London, Croom Helm, 1975

Fitzsimons, B. ed., *Tanks and Weapons of World War I*, London, Phoebus, 1973

Funcken, L. & F. Funcken, *The First World War: Arms and Uniforms*, 2 vols, London, Ward Lock, 1974

Hogg, I. V., *The Guns, 1914–18*, New York, Ballantine, 1971

Hogg, J. V. & J. Weeks, *Military Small Arms of the Twentieth Century*, London, Arms and Armour Press, 1974

Terraine, J., *White Heat. The New Warfare 1914–18*, London, Sidgwick and Jackson, 1982

Acknowledgements

The publishers are grateful to the following for permission to reproduce the illustrations included in this volume:

Imperial War Museum: pp, v, vi, 10, 13, 17, 18, 20, 26, 28, 29, 32, 33 (*top and bottom*), 30, 40, 42, 44, 45, 46 (*top and bottom*), 51, 54, 57, 59, 58 (*top and bottom*), 61, 62, 64, 67, 68, 69, 71 (*bottom*), 73, 77, 79, 84, 87, 91, 92 (*top and bottom*), 93, 100, 101, 102, 104, 111, 114, 121, 124, 128, 130, 131, 134, 136, 138, 144, 150, 153, 154, 163, 165, 170, 171, 173, 176, 177, 178, 182, 183, 185, 186, 187, 189, 196, 198, 202, 204, 207, 290 (*top*), 216, 220, 221, 227, 233, 234, 235, 238, 243 (*top*), 244, 255, 263, 270, 275, 282, 285, 287, 288, 289, 291, 294, 299, 302, 304, 307, 310, 318, 320, 324, 330, 334, 336, 342, 352, 354, 355, 357, 359, 361, 363, 364, 367, 368, 371, 372, 373, 377, 379 (*left and right*), 380, 385, 391, 392, 396, 405, 409, 411, 413;

Topham Picture Library: pp. i, ii, v, 21, 27, 71, 82, 96, 116, 120, 126, 135, 145, 147, 148, 156, 158, 160, 162, 166, 168, 175, 181, 191, 192, 243 (*bottom*), 252, 260, 266, 272, 279 (*left and right*), 286, 297, 311, 335, 376, 380, 404;

Camera Press: pp. 53, 107, 200 (*bottom*), 205, 219, 231, 262, 340;

MARS: pp. 283, 319, 339;

John Massey Stewart: p. 328.

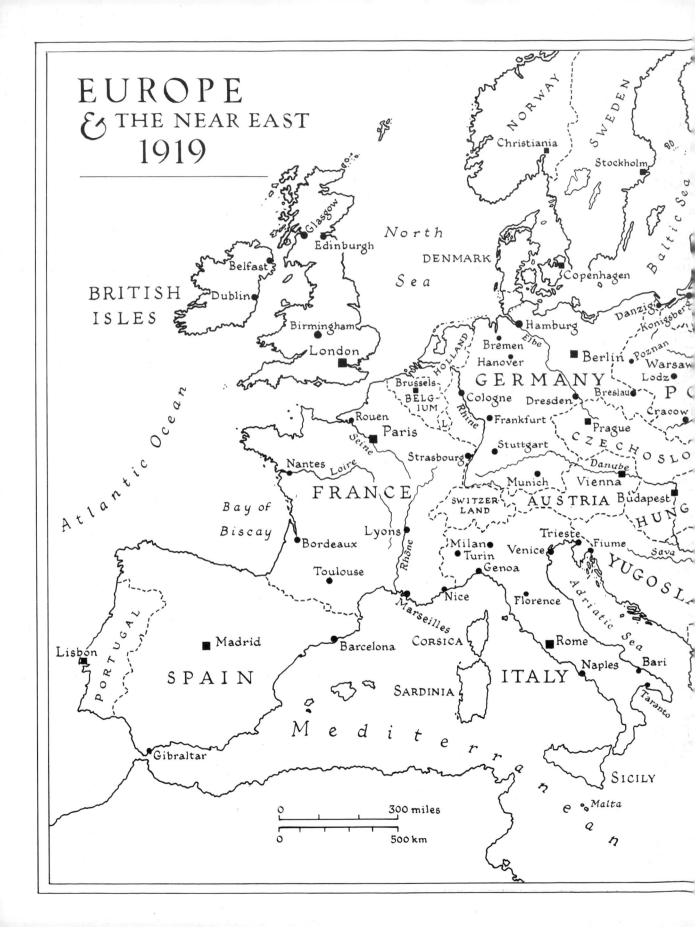

EUROPE
& THE NEAR EAST
1919

NORWAY

SWEDEN

Christiania

Stockholm

North
Sea

DENMARK

BRITISH
ISLES

Glasgow

Edinburgh

Belfast

Dublin

Birmingham

London

Baltic Sea

Copenhagen

Danzig

Königsberg

Hamburg

Elbe

Bremen

Hanover

Berlin

Poznan

Warsaw

GERMANY

Lodz

PO

Brussels

HOLLAND

Cologne

Dresden

Breslau

BELG-
IUM

L.

Rhine

Frankfurt

Prague

Cracow

Rouen

Paris

Seine

Strasbourg

Stuttgart

CZECHOSLO

Atlantic Ocean

Nantes

Loire

FRANCE

Munich

Danube

Vienna

SWITZER-
LAND

AUSTRIA

Budapest

Bay of
Biscay

Lyons

Rhône

Milan

Turin

Trieste

Venice

Fiume

Sava

HUNG

YUGOSL

Bordeaux

Genoa

Toulouse

Nice

Florence

Adriatic Sea

Marseilles

CORSICA

Rome

PORTUGAL

Lisbon

Madrid

Barcelona

SPAIN

SARDINIA

ITALY

Naples

Bari

Taranto

M e d i t e r r

Gibraltar

SICILY

e

Malta

a

n

0   300 miles

0   500 km